Praise for

EDWARD RUTHERFURD

New York Times bestselling author

"Edward Rutherfurd has written about Dublin with love.
[A]n expertly researched . . . and highly readable account of a
place he has grown to know well . . . a giant, sprawling, easy-
to-read story told in James Michener fashion."
—MAEVE BINCHY, on *The Princes of Ireland*

"Leaps through the centuries . . . a sweeping, carefully
reconstructed portrait of a nation."
—*The New York Times*

"Spellbinding . . . [a] page-turning Dublin saga . . .
Rutherfurd does a magnificent job of packaging a crackling
good yarn within the digestible overview of complex historical
circumstances and events. . . . Ambitious in scope, teeming
with a huge cast of finely drawn and realized characters, and
dripping with authentic historical detail, [this] eminently
readable narrative will satisfy the appetites of discerning historical fiction aficionados."
—*Booklist*

"The closest thing we've got to a James Michener successor."
—*The Seattle Times*

ALSO BY EDWARD RUTHERFURD

Sarum

Russka

London

The Forest

The Princes of Ireland

THE REBELS
OF IRELAND

⊰ THE DUBLIN SAGA ⊱

EDWARD
RUTHERFURD

SEAL BOOKS

Seal Books and colophon are trademarks of Random House of Canada Limited.

THE REBELS OF IRELAND
Seal Books/published by arrangement with Doubleday Canada
Doubleday Canada edition published 2006
Anchor Canada edition published 2007
Seal Books edition published March 2008

ISBN 978-0-7704-2967-6

The Rebels of Ireland is a work of fiction. Though some characters, incidents, and dialogues are based on the historical record, the work as a whole is a product of the author's imagination.

Text design by Caroline Cunningham

Seal Books are published by Random House of Canada Limited. "Seal Books" and the portrayal of a seal are the property of Random House of Canada Limited.

Visit Random House of Canada Limited's website:
www.randomhouse.ca

PRINTED AND BOUND IN THE USA

OPM 10 9 8 7 6 5 4 3 2 1

To the memory
of
Margaret Mary Motley
de Renéville
born
Sheridan

acknowledgments

I AM GRATEFUL to the following, whose kind coopera-
tion and professionalism were at all times of the greatest
assistance: the director and staff of the National Library of
Ireland; the director and curatorial staff of the National
Museum of Ireland; the librarian and staff of Trinity College
Library; the management and staff of the Office of Public
Works at Dublin Castle.

I gratefully acknowledge permission to quote the Orange
Toast from *Personal Sketches and Recollections*, published by
Ashfield Press.

Special thanks are due to Sarah Gearty, of the Royal Irish
Academy, for kindly preparing maps, and to Mrs. Heidi
Boshoff, without whose astounding proficiency in the typing
of the manuscript this book could not have been completed.

I owe a large debt of gratitude to the following, whose help,
guidance, and technical advice were invaluable during this project: Joseph Byrne, author of *War and Peace, the Survival of the
Talbots of Malahide*; Dr. Declan Downey, lecturer at the School
of History, University College, Dublin; Professor Colm
Lennon, Department of Modern History, National University
of Ireland, Maynooth; James McGuire, editor of the Royal Irish

Academy's *Dictionary of Irish Biography.* I am grateful for having a chance to read in its entirety the unpublished thesis of Maighread M. B. Ni Mhurchadha, *Contending Neighbours: Society in Fingal 1603–60.*

But above all, I am indebted to three scholars without whose guidance, patience, and encouragement this project could not have been completed. Between them they have read and helped me revise this manuscript. Any errors that remain are mine alone. I thank Dr. Raymond Gillespie, senior lecturer in the Department of Modern History, National University of Ireland, Maynooth; Dr. James Kelly, of St. Patrick's College, Drumcondra; and Dr. T. P. O'Neill of University College, Dublin.

Finally, as always, I thank my agent, Gill Coleridge, without whom I should be entirely lost, and I thank my wonderful editors, Oliver Johnson at Century and William Thomas at Doubleday, whose exemplary thoroughness and creative responses to problems have so hugely improved this manuscript.

CONTENTS

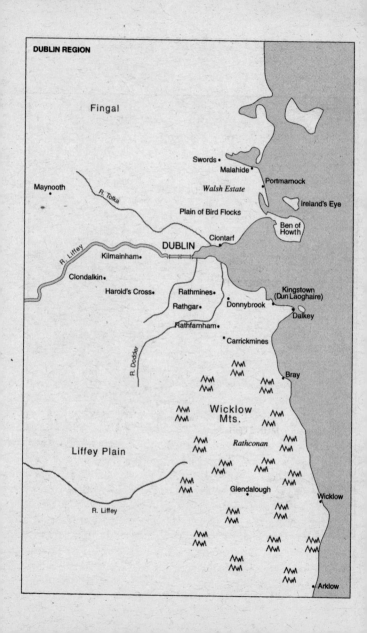

DUBLIN REGION

Fingal

Maynooth

R. Tolka

Swords
Malahide
Portmarnock

Walsh Estate

Ireland's Eye

Plain of Bird Flocks

R. Liffey

DUBLIN

Clontarf

Ben of
Howth

Kilmainham

Clondalkin

Harold's Cross

Rathmines

Rathgar

Kingstown
(Dun Laoghaire)

Donnybrook

Dalkey

Rathfarnham

R. Dodder

Carrickmines

Bray

Wicklow
Mts.

Liffey Plain

Rathconan

R. Liffey

Glendalough

Wicklow

Arklow

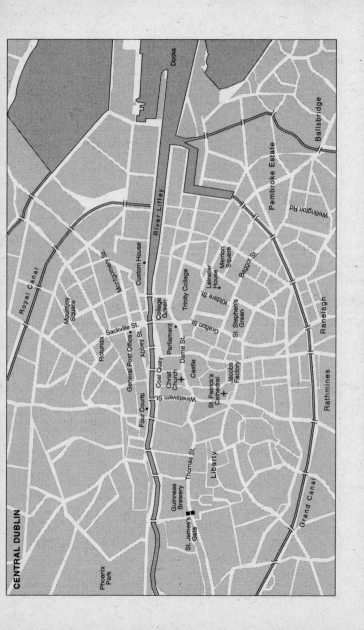

CENTRAL DUBLIN

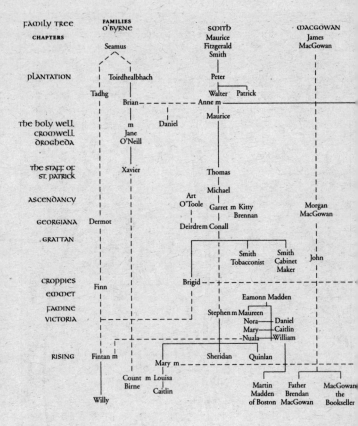

FAMILY TREE

CHAPTERS

FAMILIES
O'BYRNE

SMITH
Maurice
Fitzgerald
Smith

MACGOWAN
James
MacGowan

Seamus

PLANTATION — Toirdhealbhach — Peter

Tadhg

Walter — Patrick

Brian — — — — Anne m

THE HOLY WELL.
CROMWELL.
DROGHEDA

m
Jane
O'Neill

Daniel

Maurice

THE STAFF OF
ST. PATRICK

Xavier

Thomas

ASCENDANCY

Michael

Art
O'Toole

Garret m Kitty
Brennan

Morgan
MacGowan

GEORGIANA

Dermot

Deirdrem Conall

GRATTAN

Smith
Tobacconist

Smith
Cabinet
Maker

John

CROPPIES

Finn

Brigid

EMMET

Eamonn Madden

FAMINE

Stephen m Maureen

VICTORIA

Nora —— Daniel
Mary —— Caitlin
Nuala —— William

RISING

Fintan m

Mary m

Sheridan

Quinlan

Count m Louisa
Birne

Caitlin

Martin
Madden
of Boston

Father
Brendan
MacGowan

MacGowan
the
Bookseller

Willy

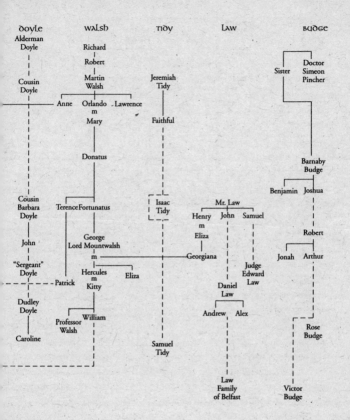

DOYLE
Alderman Doyle

Cousin Doyle

Cousin Barbara Doyle

John

"Sergeant" Doyle

Dudley Doyle

Caroline

WALSH
Richard

Robert

Martin Walsh

Anne — Orlando — Lawrence
m
Mary

Donatus

Terence Fortunatus

George Lord Mountwalsh
m

Hercules — Eliza
m
Kitty

Patrick

Professor Walsh   William

TIDY
Jeremiah Tidy

Faithful

Isaac Tidy

Samuel Tidy

LAW
Mr. Law

Henry   John   Samuel
m
Eliza

Georgiana

Judge Edward Law

Daniel Law

Andrew   Alex

Law Family of Belfast

BUDGE
Sister   Doctor Simeon Pincher

Barnaby Budge

Benjamin   Joshua

Robert

Jonah   Arthur

Rose Budge

Victor Budge

INTRODUCTION

T HE PRINCES OF IRELAND follows the destinies of
six fictional Irish families:

The O'Byrnes, who spring from the union of Conall,
descendant of a High King of Ireland, and Deirdre, daughter
of a local chieftain at the time of Saint Patrick.

The MacGowans, pre-Celtic craftsmen and merchants.

The Harolds and the Doyles, both Viking families who
become farmers and merchants.

The Walshes, Flemish knights originally, who settle in
Wales before crossing to Ireland at the time of Strongbow's
Anglo-Norman invasion in the twelfth century.

And the Tidy family, craftsmen and small local officials,
who arrive to try their luck in medieval Ireland.

The Princes of Ireland, the first book in Edward Rutherfurd's
magnificent Dublin Saga, swept the reader through more than
a thousand years of Irish history, telling Ireland's story through
the adventures and fates of several Irish families, whose stories
continue in this volume.

The Saga opens in A.D. 430, with the stirring and tragic
tale of Conall, nephew of the High King at Tara, and his fierce
love for the beautiful Deirdre. When the High King chooses

Deirdre as a second wife, the lovers flee. They live a blissful year in hiding, but there comes an inevitable reckoning. Conall frees Deirdre from her obligation to the High King, but at the cost of his life: in an ancient druidic ritual, he agrees to sacrifice himself to save his love and heal the land from strife. Here we see pagan Ireland in all its mythic glory, a land of warriors and ecstatic festivals, where clan warfare is kept in check by the wiles of the High King while druids augur the fate of the people.

Twenty years later Deirdre is living in the small settlement of Dubh Linn with her son, Morna. He bears a striking resemblance to Conall, his father. A group of horsemen arrive, led by a greying man whom Deirdre recognizes as one of the druids who presided over Conall's sacrifice. But the druid has changed—he is now a follower of Patrick, a man who preaches a strange new religion that honors only one god and rejects the practice of human sacrifice. In the person of Saint Patrick, Rutherfurd shows how the saint's genius and humanity converted the people of Ireland to the Christian religion.

The cataclysm that transformed Celtic Ireland came in the ninth century, with the Viking invasions. Arriving in fearsome longboats, the Vikings were famous as plunderers of monasteries. But many of these invaders chose to stay in Ireland, setting up fertile farmsteads and burgeoning ports. They also created an enduring place name for the land: by converting the island's Celtic name (Eriu) into their own tongue, the Nordic name Ireland was born. The Vikings also transformed Dubh Linn's name into Dyflin, which became the richest port in all of Ireland. This merging of Scandinavian and Celtic cultures is brought to life in *The Princes of Ireland* through the story of Harold and Caoilinn. He is a Dyflin shipbuilder who follows ancient Norse gods, and whose ancestors were among the bravest Norwegian warriors. She is a beautiful and spirited descendant of Conall, and she cannot imagine marrying a man who is not a Christian.

They live during a time when the High Kingship of Ireland is in dispute. In 999, the great King Brian Boru launched a military campaign to unite Ireland under his command. In the novel, he gains a loyal follower in Harold. Yet Brian's kingship of Ireland is opposed: many of his fellow Irishmen are against him. Caoilinn hates him.

Fourteen years after Brian Boru's rise to power, the recently widowed Harold and Caoilinn begin a tender courtship, but it falls apart when she learns of Harold's allegiance to King Brian. The reign of Brian ends when he is slain by Viking invaders during the historic Battle of Clontarf. Though Brian Boru decisively won the battle, staving off further Viking raids, his death made it a Pyrrhic victory for the Irish. In the ensuing peace, Harold the Norseman and Caoilinn the Celt put their differences aside and wed happily.

In 1167, a century after the Norman conquest of England, King Henry II sets the stage for the annexation of Ireland by England. King Henry himself belongs to the Plantagenet dynasty from Anjou, in France. Henry allows one of his magnates—the clever, calculating Strongbow—to carve out English settlements in Ireland. Rutherfurd captures this turbulent transition by introducing a young Welsh soldier of Flemish descent named Peter FitzDavid, who sails to Ireland with Strongbow.

Peter befriends a Dublin family descended from Caoilinn. The patriarch is a married priest with children (practices not uncommon for a priest in the Celtic Irish Church). Peter is intrigued by Conn's attractive daughter, Fionnuala. She doesn't hesitate in sparking a brief affair with the well-mannered soldier from England. Their trysts end after Strongbow asks Peter to recruit her as a spy and Fionnuala unwittingly provides information leading to a humiliating defeat for the High King, one of many blows lying in store for the Irish at the hands of a powerful new master.

In 1171, King Henry travels to Ireland personally, accompanied by 4,500 troops, for the purpose of reminding Strongbow that no matter how many victories he scores, he must always submit to the king. After the English victories in

Ireland, the Pope sends a letter of congratulation to King Henry, commending him for his military triumphs in subduing the Irish. The Pope makes it clear to Irish clergymen that their kinsmen have won no favor with Rome. In the ensuing years, the king rewards his English invaders with copious amounts of Irish property. Peter is eventually granted ownership of Fionnuala's family estate in reward for two decades of loyal service to the crown. In a scene depicting the anguish of these transactions, Fionnuala demands that Peter allow her brother to continue living on the land that has been in their family for hundreds of years. Peter is unmoved, and agrees to let her brother remain only if he pays timely rent. Now married to an O'Byrne, she warns Peter that her children may one day come down from the hills and seize the land that is rightfully theirs.

By 1370, the English in the Dublin region are living in a state of constant friction with the Irish in the hinterland. Rutherfurd illustrates this in a suspenseful vignette involving the tiny but strategically located fishing village of Dalkey. Nearby, the Justiciar in Dublin has installed John Walsh's family at the ancient castle of Carrickmines to create another English stronghold against Irish resistance. Rumor spreads that the O'Byrnes are planning a raid on Carrickmines. The warning travels to the Justiciar, who convenes a group of advisors that includes Walsh as well as Doyle of Dublin, who made a fortune in the wine trade. Doyle proposes that Carrickmines be fortified with troops, including the only squadron stationed at Dalkey, to set a trap for the O'Byrnes. In reality, Doyle has secretly plotted to create this diversion. While a staged, minor scuffle ensues at Carrickmines, Dalkey is left unattended. This gives Doyle, the descendant of Danish pirates, a tantalizing opportunity for smuggling; colluding with other residents of Dalkey, he unloads the valuable cargo of three ships under the cover of night, thereby avoiding massive tariffs.

The fifteenth century in England is marked by the Wars of the Roses, bloody feuds between rival branches of the Plantagenet royal House. Though the wars culminate in 1485 with mortal defeat for Richard III and victory for Henry Tudor, an Anglo-Irish faction continues to back the Yorkist cause. They crown a young pretender, who claims to be the Earl of Warwick, as the new King of England and set sail for England, plotting to topple King Henry. The disastrous results only lead to further subjection in Ireland, which is divided between those living within the Pale (Dublin's surrounding counties, dominated by the English) and the more Irish world, beyond the Pale. Through interlocking plots we follow the lives of four sixteenth-century families: the Tidys, the Walshes, the Doyles, and the O'Byrnes.

For those within the Pale, scrupulous English appearance was essential. These codes are vividly portrayed when Henry Tidy's fiancée, Cecily, is arrested for wearing a scarf that signals her alliance with the Irish. Henry was hoping to apply for a franchise soon, to become a freeman of Dublin. Alderman Doyle helps get the charges dropped, but he warns Henry to be careful; the revelation that his fiancée is Irish might ruin his chances. This seemingly minor incident bodes the schisms that will divide Dublin society in decades to come.

This precarious political climate is felt in the Walsh household as well. William Walsh tells his wife, Margaret, that his work as an attorney is going to take him into the far south of Ireland. He warns her to keep his trip confidential; though his assignment there is legitimate, plots are brewing against King Henry VIII, and spies might think he is visiting rural Munster for more sinister reasons. But Margaret reveals the Munster secret to Joan Doyle, wife of the alderman. William is subsequently denied a chance to run for Parliament, though John Doyle does gain a seat. Margaret's distrust for Joan—compounded by long-standing rumors that the Doyles cheated Joan's family out of land—cause her to hate the other woman.

But it is King Henry VIII's momentous decision to annul his marriage to his Spanish wife, Catherine of Aragon, that will change Ireland's history. The Pope has granted annulments before, but Catherine's nephew has just become Holy Roman

Emperor. The Pope dare not offend the Hapsburg monarch in favor of an upstart Tudor king. Henry VIII breaks with the Pope and the Reformation in England—and Ireland—has begun.

The spurning of the Pope also piques the cultural differences between Henry and Cecily Tidy. At an elaborate Corpus Christi Day pageant, Cecily blurts out that the new queen is a heretic; she then says the king will burn in hell. Henry Tidy is aghast, and as fate would have it, she has made these proclamations before a figure who will soon rouse the Irish into taking up arms against the king. He is Lord Thomas Fitzgerald, an influential member of the aristocracy who wears the finest silk tunics available and is hence called Silken Thomas.

Soon after the Corpus Christi incident, Silken Thomas withdraws his English loyalty and in essence proclaims himself the new protector of Ireland. Like many of his countrymen who envision a glorious renewal of Gaelic dominance in Ireland, Sean O'Byrne is thrilled by this turn of events and even pays a call to the Walshes, asking William to swear his loyalty to Silken Thomas.

Cecily Tidy joins in the fervor as well, calling out to Thomas from a high window and shouting a string of pledges that echo in the street. Her public oaths to the Fitzgeralds horrify her husband. He knows that she has now ruined any chance he might have had in rising through the ranks of English power brokers.

The Doyles continue to oppose the Fitzgeralds in favor of the pro-Tudor Butlers.

Concerned about the looming battles, Alderman Doyle decides Joan would be safer in Dalkey and makes plans for her to be escorted there. He doesn't realize that Margaret has crafted a vengeful plan of her own, arranging for Sean O'Byrne to kidnap Joan on the road and hold her for a ransom to be shared equally between Margaret and the O'Byrnes. But the raid does not go as planned. Joan is unharmed, but one of Sean's sons is killed. When William Walsh hears the news, he reveals to his wife that Joan has recently shown incredible generosity toward him, offering a loan to help with his dire financial circumstances. Margaret feels ashamed when she realizes she has misinterpreted all of Joan's seemingly cruel actions and spurned a woman whose intentions were actually never anything but kind.

For the O'Byrnes, however, more strife is in store. Sean and Eva have been raising a foster child named Maurice, who was born into the powerful Fitzgerald family. When Maurice is no longer a child, Lady Fitzgerald announces that Sean O'Byrne is his father; this is why she put the child in Sean's care. In the wake of Eva's fury and humiliation, Maurice flees to Dublin. There in the heart of the English Pale, a family friend advises him to erase all Irish traces of his name. Thus Maurice Fitzgerald, whose lineage includes princely O'Byrnes, noble Walshes, courageous Conall, and centuries of chieftains, becomes Maurice Smith.

It becomes clear that the romantic revolution of Silken Thomas's dreams are receiving no support from the continent; Henry VIII sends in troops, and in 1536 the Irish Parliament passes measures renouncing the Pope and swearing allegiance to the Tudor king. Seventy-five of the men who had acted with Silken Thomas are sentenced to execution. The fall of the Fitzgeralds signals an irrevocable defeat for all of Ireland.

The Princes of Ireland closes with the image of Cecily Tidy gazing in horror as a fire blazes in front of Christ Church Cathedral. Icons are being publicly burned in an attempt to purge Ireland of Catholicism, a practice that would herald new battles for the very soul of the island as politics and religion begin their fiery mingling. Rutherfurd paints an ominous concluding scene in which ornate relics are added to the pyre, and the Bachall Iosa—the jewel-encrusted reliquary of the Staff of Saint Patrick himself, one of the holiest and most awesome relics in Ireland—disappears forever. It is a haunting moment, destined to transform the descendants of princes into rebels.

The Rebels of Ireland continues the story of these families and of the additional fictional families of Smith, Pincher, Budge, Law, Madden, and others.

THE REBELS

OF IRELAND

pLANTATION

⊰ 1597 ⊱

Octor Simeon Pincher knew all about
Ireland.

Doctor Simeon Pincher was a tall, thin, balding man, still
in his twenties, with a sallow complexion and stern black eyes
that belonged in a pulpit. He was a learned man, a graduate
and fellow of Emmanuel College, at Cambridge University.
When he had been offered a position at the new foundation
of Trinity College in Dublin, however, he had come thither
with such alacrity that his new hosts were quite surprised.

"I shall come at once," he had written to them, "to do
God's work." With which reply, no one could argue.

Not only did he come with the stated zeal of a missionary.
Even before his arrival in Ireland, Doctor Pincher had
informed himself thoroughly about its inhabitants. He knew,
for instance, that the mere Irish, as the original native Irish
were now termed in England, were worse than animals, and
that, as Catholics, they could not be trusted.

But the special gift that Doctor Pincher brought to Ireland
was his belief that the mere Irish were not only an inferior

people, but that God had deliberately marked them out—along with others, too, of course—since the beginning of time, to be cast into eternal hellfire. For Doctor Simeon Pincher was a follower of Calvin.

To understand Doctor Pincher's version of the subtle teachings of the great Protestant reformer, it was only necessary to listen to one of his sermons—for he was already accounted a fine preacher, greatly praised for his clarity.

"The logic of the Lord," he would declare, "like His love, is perfect. And since we are endowed with the faculty of reason, with which God in His infinite goodness has bestowed upon us, we may see His purpose as it is." Leaning forward slightly towards his audience to ensure their concentration, Doctor Pincher would then explain.

"Consider. It is undeniable that God, the fount of all knowledge—to whom all ages are but as the blinking of an eye—must in His infinite wisdom know all things, past, present, and to come. And therefore it must be that even now, He knows full well who upon the Day of Judgement is to be saved, and who shall be cast down into the pit of Hell. He has established all things from the beginning. It cannot be otherwise. Even though, in His mercy, He has left us ignorant of our fate, some have already been chosen for Heaven and others for Hell. The divine logic is absolute, and all who believe must tremble before it. Those who are chosen, those who shall be saved, we call the Elect. All other, damned from the first, shall perish. And so," he would fix his audience with a terrible stare, "well may you ask: 'Which am I?'"

The grim logic of John Calvin's doctrine of predestination was hard to refute. That Calvin was a deeply religious and well-meaning man could not be doubted. His followers strove to follow the loving teachings of the gospels, and to live lives that were honest, hardworking, and charitable. But for some critics, his form of religion ran a risk: its practice could become unduly harsh. Moving from France to Switzerland, Calvin had set up his church in Geneva. The rules governing his community were sterner than those of the Lutheran Protestants, and he believed that the state should enforce them by law. Following their strict moral regime—and reporting their neighbours to the authorities for any failure to live according to God's law—his congregation did not only seek to earn a place in Heaven, but also to prove to themselves and to the world that they were indeed the predestined Elect who had already been chosen to go there.

Soon Calvinist communities had sprung up in other parts of Europe. If the Scottish Presbyterians were known for their somewhat dour adherence to the doctrines of predestination, the Church of England and its sister Church of Ireland had nowadays a Calvinistic air. "Only the Godly are part of the Church," its congregations would declare.

But could it be that certain among the community might in fact not be chosen to go to Heaven at all? Most certainly, the Calvinists would concede. Any moral backsliding might be an indication of it. And even then, as Doctor Pincher put it in one of his finest sermons, there remained a great uncertainty.

"No man knows his fate. We are like men walking across a frozen river, foolishly unmindful that, at any time, the ice may crack, and buckle, and drop us down into the frozen waters—below which, hidden deeper yet, burn the fiery furnaces of Hell. Be not puffed up with pride, therefore, as you follow the law of the scriptures, but remember that we are all miserable sinners and be humble. For this is the divine trap, and from it there is no escape. All is foretold, and the mind of God, being perfect, will not be changed." Then, looking round at his disconsolate congregation, Doctor Pincher would cry out: "And even though, if God has so ordained, you may be doomed, yet I beseech you, be of good cheer. For remember, no matter how hard the way, we are commanded, always, to hope."

Might there, perhaps, be hope for some of those not in the Calvinist congregation? Perhaps. No man could know the mind of God. But it seemed doubtful. In particular, for those in the Catholic Church, the future looked bleak. Did they not indulge in popish superstitions and worship the saints as idols—things specifically prohibited in the scriptures? Hadn't they had opportunity to turn away from their errors? To Doctor Pincher it seemed that all followers of the Pope in Rome must surely be on their way to perdition, and that the natives of Ireland, whose bad character was so well-known, were probably in the devil's clutch already. And might they not yet be saved if they converted? Could not their case be remedied? No. Their sin, to Doctor Pincher, was a clear sign that they had been selected to be damned from the first. They belonged, like the pagan spirits that infested the place, deep underground. Such were the thoughts that had strengthened the keen resolve of Doctor Pincher as he crossed the sea to Dublin.

Yet what of his own fate? Was Simeon Pincher sure, in the secret places of his heart, that he himself was one of the Elect? He had to hope so. If there had been certain sins, indiscretions at least, in his own life, might they be signs that his own nature was corrupt? He turned his face from the thought. To sin, of course, was the lot of every man. Those who repented might indeed be saved. If sins there had been in his life, therefore, he repented most earnestly. And his daily conduct, and his zeal for the Lord, proved, he hoped and believed, that he was, indeed, not the least amongst God's chosen.

‡

It was a quiet day, with a light breeze, when he arrived at Dublin. His ship had anchored out in the Liffey. A waterman rowed him to the Wood Quay.

And he had just clambered onto the terra firma of Ireland represented by the old quay when, quite suddenly, something happened and the world turned upside down.

The next thing he remembered, he was lying facedown, conscious of a great roar, and that something had given him a huge blow in the stomach so that he could hardly breathe. He looked up, blinked, and saw the face of a man, a gentleman by his clothes, dusting himself off and gazing down at him with concern.

"You are not hurt?"

"I do not think so," Pincher answered. "What has happened?"

"An explosion." The stranger pointed, and, twisting round, Pincher saw that, in the middle of the quays, where he had noticed a tall building with a crane standing before, there was now a broken stone stump, while the houses in the street opposite were blackened ruins.

Pincher took the stranger's proffered arm gratefully as he stumbled to his feet. His leg hurt.

"You are just arrived?"

"Yes. For the first time."

"Come, then, Sir. My name, by the way, is Martin Walsh. There's an inn close by. Let me help you there."

Having left Pincher at the inn, the obliging gentleman went off to inspect the damage. He returned an hour later to report.

"The strangest business. An accident without a doubt." It seemed that a spark from a horse's shoe upon a cobble had ignited a keg of gunpowder, which had set off a large gunpowder store by the big central crane. "The lower part of Winetavern Street is destroyed. Even the fabric of Christ Church Cathedral up the hill has been shaken." He smiled wryly. "I have heard of strangers bringing bad weather, Sir, but an explosion is something new. I hope you do not mean the Irish any further harm."

It was gentle banter, kindly meant. Pincher understood this very well. But he had never been very good at this sort of thing himself.

"Not," he said with grim satisfaction, "unless they are papists."

"Ah." The gentleman smiled sadly. "You will find many of those, Sir, in Dublin."

It was not until after this Good Samaritan had conducted him up to Trinity College and seen him safely into the care of the porter there that Doctor Pincher discovered that Mr. Walsh himself was of the Roman faith. It was an embarrassing moment, it couldn't be denied. Yet how could he have guessed that the kindly stranger, so obviously English, so clearly a gentleman, could be a papist? Indeed, as Walsh had warned him, he was soon shocked to discover that many of the gentlefolk and better sort in Dublin were.

But this very discovery only showed, he was also to understand, how much work there was to be done.

<h2 style="text-align:center">⊰ 1607 ⊱</h2>

A midsummer evening. Martin Walsh stood with his three children on the Ben of Howth and stared across the sea. His cautious, lawyer's mind was engaged in its own careful calculations.

Martin had always been a thoughtful soul—old for his years, people used to say. His own mother had died when he was three, his father Robert Walsh a year after. His grandfather, old Richard, and his grandmother had brought him up and, used to the company of older people all the time, he had unconsciously taken on many of their attitudes. One of these had been caution.

He gazed fondly at his daughter. Anne was only fifteen. It was hard to believe that he must already make such decisions about her. His fingers clasped the letter in the hidden pocket in his breeches, and he wondered, as he had been wondering for hours: should he tell her about it?

The marriage of a daughter should be a private family affair. But it wasn't. Not nowadays. He wished his wife were still alive. She would have known how to deal with this. Young Smith might possess a good character or a bad one. Walsh hoped that it was good. Yet something more would be necessary. Principles, certainly. Strength, without a doubt. But also that indefinable and all-important quality—a talent for survival.

For people like himself—for the loyal Old English—life in Ireland had never been more dangerous.

✦

It was four and a half centuries since the Norman-French king Henry Plantagenet of England had invaded and, taking the place of the old High Kings of Ireland, bullied the Irish princes into accepting him as their nominal lord. Apart from the Pale area around Dublin, of course, it had still been Irish princes and Plantagenet magnates like the Fitzgeralds—who were soon not much different from the Irish—that had ruled the island in practice ever since. Until seventy years ago, when King Henry VIII of England had smashed the Fitzgeralds and made plain, once and for all, England's intention to rule the western island directly. He'd even taken the title King of Ireland.

A few years later, the disease-ridden English monarch with the six wives had been dead. For half a dozen years his son Edward, a sickly boy, had ruled; his daughter Mary for another five. But then it had been Elizabeth, the virgin queen, who for nearly half a century had remained on England's throne. They had all tried to rule Ireland, but they hadn't found it easy.

Governors were sent over, some wise, some not. English aristocrats, almost always, with resonant names or titles: Saint Leger, Sussex, Sidney, Essex, Grey. And always they encountered the same, traditional Irish problems: Old English magnates—Fitzgeralds and Butlers—still jealous of each other; Irish princes impatient of royal control—up in Ulster, the mighty O'Neills had still not forgotten they had once been High Kings of Ireland. And everyone—yes, including the loyal Old English gentry like the Walshes—only too glad to send deputations to the monarch to undermine the governor's authority wherever the governor did something they didn't like. If they came to turn Ireland into a second England, this was not only supposed to be for the benefit of the Irish. With them came a collection of fortune hunters—the New English, they were called—hungry for land. Some of these rogues even tried to claim they were descended from long-forgotten Plantagenet settlers and that they had ancient title to Irish property.

So was it surprising that the English governors found that Ireland resisted change, or new taxes, or English adventurers trying to steal their land? Was it surprising that during Martin Walsh's childhood there had been more than one local rising, especially down in the south, where the Fitzgeralds of Munster felt threatened? There was more than a suspicion, however, that some of the English officials were deliberately trying to stir up trouble. "If they can provoke us into rebellion," some Irish landowners concluded, "then our estates are confiscated and they can get their own hands on them. That's the game." But it was at the end of Elizabeth's long reign that the big rebellion had come.

Of all the provinces of Ireland, Ulster had the reputation as the wildest and the most backward. Ulster chiefs had watched the progress of the English officials in the other provinces with disgust and increasing restlessness. The greatest of them all, O'Neill—who had been educated in England and held the English title Earl of Tyrone—had usually managed to keep the peace up there. Yet in the end it had been Tyrone who led the revolt.

What did he want? To rule all Ireland as his ancestors had done? Perhaps. Or just to frighten the English so much that they'd leave him to rule Ulster as his own? Also possible. Like Silken Thomas Fitzgerald, sixty years earlier, he had appealed to Catholic loyalties against the heretic English and sent messages to the Catholic king of Spain asking for troops. And this time, Catholic troops—four and a half thousand of them—had actually come. Tyrone was quite a skilful soldier, too. He'd destroyed the first English force sent against him up in Ulster, at the Battle of the Yellow Ford, and people had rallied to his cause from all over the island. That had only been a decade ago, and no one in Dublin had known what was going to happen; but in due course Mountjoy, the tough and able English commander, had broken Tyrone and his Spanish allies down in Munster. There was nothing Tyrone could do after that. At the very moment that old Queen Elizabeth had been on her deathbed in London, Tyrone, last of the princes of Ireland, had capitulated. The English had been surprisingly lenient; he was allowed to keep some of the old O'Neill lands.

There was a new king, Elizabeth's cousin James, on the throne now. Tyrone's game was over, and he knew it. Yet was Ireland any safer?

⁜

He glanced out to sea. To his right lay the broad sweep of Dublin Bay, curving out to the southern headland and the harbour of Dalkey. Turning left, he looked down to the strange little island with the cleft in its cliff—Ireland's Eye, people sometimes called that island now—and northward across the waters to where, in the distance, the blue-grey mountains of Ulster rose up steeply. If he was going to broach the subject, he thought, now was the time. They'd be gone in the morning.

Martin Walsh's character could be guessed from his appearance. There were a few splashes of dried mud and plenty of dust on his soft leather boots, because, having ridden past the castle of his friend Lord Howth at the base of the headland, he had chosen to walk up to the summit. But his breeches and doublet, which had been carefully brushed that morning, were still spotlessly clean. As the day was warm, he had ridden out without a cloak or even a hat, and his hair, still mostly brown, hung loose to his shoulders. He had a small pointed beard, which was grey. Careful, clean, calm, not proud, a family man.

The only other thing a new acquaintance need observe was the silver crucifix upon a chain beside his heart.

The letter had been brought to him by a messenger that morning; and having read it and digested its surprising contents, he could only conclude that the author had sent it in a hurry upon learning that Lawrence and Anne were about to depart.

"I have received a letter from Peter Smith," he said quietly. "About his son Patrick. Do you know him?"

His other two children said nothing, though Lawrence looked at Anne sharply, then glanced enquiringly at his father.

"I met him once or twice, Father," she answered. "When I was in Dublin with Mother."

"You spoke with him?"

"A little."

"What opinion had you of him—of his character, I mean?"

"That he is honest and pious."

"He pleased you?"

"I think so."

Martin Walsh considered. He knew the family slightly. Smith was a respectable Dublin merchant and a Catholic. That much was certain. But beyond that? Though Smith lived in Dublin, he had twenty years ago lent money to a landowner south of the city on the collateral of the landowner's estate; after which, as was the custom with Irish mortgages, he had enjoyed the use of the estate himself until he was repaid. Smith was, in Walsh's view, at least half a gentleman. And he had a strangely aristocratic air about him. There had always been a little doubt about the family's origins—Walsh didn't like that. Peter Smith hadn't discouraged the rumour that his own father Maurice had been born a Fitzgerald. The MacGowans said he'd been the natural son of O'Byrne of Rathconan up in the Wicklow Mountains. Take your pick. Noble, you might say, either way. But the truth was that he hardly knew the family. He'd heard there were several children, though he wouldn't have recognised them. He would have to find out more. His cousin Doyle, no doubt, would know something.

As for Peter Smith's letter, he found no fault with it. After some pleasant compliments about his daughter, and her reputation, it had asked whether he would discuss the possibility, nothing more, of bestowing this jewel upon his son, who was so greatly struck by her beauty and her good character. It would be discourteous if he didn't at least speak to the Dublin merchant.

"The letter speaks of a betrothal. It seems strange that he should ask for you upon so small acquaintance," he remarked. Princes might marry with nothing more than an ambassador's report and a miniature portrait, but the gentry around Dublin usually were well acquainted before they married.

"I should wish to know him better, Father, if his interest in me is serious."

"Of course, my child." He nodded, and let his eyes turn again towards the sea.

So he did not notice the look that Orlando gave his sister, or the warning glare she gave him in return.

‡

Orlando was so excited. And he felt so pleased with himself. Because he had guessed.

The first time had been the previous summer, while Anne was home from France. They had gone for a walk together and were about a mile away from home when they encountered the young man. Anne and the man had seemed to recognise each other, but Orlando had not learned the stranger's name. They had strolled together a little way to some trees and, finding a large log, Anne and the man had sat on it to talk, while Orlando had explored the wood. For some reason, Anne had made him promise to keep the meeting a secret; and it had made him feel very proud that his big sister would trust him like this.

Although she was six years older, Anne had always been a presence in his life. His older brother Lawrence was always kind, and was Orlando's hero; but he had already been abroad at his studies ever since Orlando could remember, and so he was at best an occasional presence in the house. Until two years ago, Anne had still been doing her lessons with Father Benedict in the chamber they called the schoolroom beside the hall. It was she who, before it was his turn to begin with Father Benedict, had taught him his alphabet, and she who, in the summer evenings, would sit and read to him, with her brown hair falling thickly down one side so that he could lean his head on her shoulder and bury his face in the soft scent of her hair as he listened. Or often she would tell him stories about silly people she had invented and make him laugh. She was a wonderful older sister.

Then their father had sent her away to a French family in Bordeaux. "I don't want my daughter growing up like some provincial English girl," he'd said. But if, after her first year away, she had become rather serious, she was always kind, and the funny Anne he loved would sometimes break through. When she told him to keep a secret, he'd rather have died than give her away.

In the weeks that followed, they had ridden out several times to meet the young man. Twice these encounters had taken place on the long, sandy beach opposite the little island with the cleft in the cliff, and Anne and the man had ridden off along the strand while Orlando played in the dunes. Each time she had sworn him to secrecy, telling her parents, "I took Orlando riding along the beach," and no one had been any the wiser.

On her return home this summer, the meetings had resumed. He had also taken letters from her and delivered them to the young man, who was waiting in the nearby wood. Yet still he had not known the young man's name, or the nature of their relationship. And when, once or twice, he had dared to ask, his sister's answers had only confused him.

"He gives me messages for another girl at the seminary in France. He talks to me about her. That's all."

"Is he going to see her?"

"One day, I expect."

"Is he going to marry her?"

"That's a secret."

"What's her name? And what's his name? And why does he have to give messages to you? And why can't we tell anyone?"

"Those are all secrets. You're too young to understand. If you ask any more questions, you silly boy, I won't take you out with me anymore." He wasn't sure what it all meant, but he didn't want to risk being left behind, so Orlando asked no more. Only yesterday morning, she had taken him aside and earnestly made him promise never, at any time, to tell what he had seen; and he had sworn on his life he would not. But he had wondered why.

And now he had guessed. The young man must be Peter Smith's son. And it was Anne herself he'd been courting. And nobody knew except him. His eyes were shining at the thought that he had taken part in such an adventure. And if Anne, for whatever reason, had felt she must deceive their father, he scarcely gave it a thought.

✛

Lawrence cleared his throat. He was looking serious. If there had been friction between Martin Walsh and his eldest son, they were both careful to hide it from Anne and Orlando, especially since their mother had died. Respectfully, therefore, he indicated that he would like to speak with his father apart.

"Are we sure," he quietly asked, "of the family's religion?"

For that was where the danger lay.

If the Reformation, like a series of earthquakes, had opened great chasms across Europe, the tremors in Ireland, at first, had been minor. King Henry had closed some monasteries and disposed of their land; there had been outrages, like the burning of holy relics in Dublin and the loss of Saint Patrick's Staff. But the reign of the boy-king Edward—in which there had been a Protestant revolution in England—had been so short that the Protestants hadn't had time to make much headway across the water in Ireland, before Queen Mary had brought her father's kingdom back to Rome. Bloody Mary, they called her in England, yet you had to feel sorry for her. Proud and royal, she had seen her poor mother rejected and humiliated. No wonder she was so fiercely loyal to her Catholic heritage. Had she even understood the disgust of her English subjects, who valued their island independence, when she married her cousin Philip II of Spain? Childless, deserted by Philip, she had soon died and the English had told her Spanish husband not to show his face there again. In Ireland, however, the reign of Mary had been quiet enough. The lands of the monasteries Henry had dissolved were not given back to the Church—Catholic Irish gentlemen were not so pious that they wanted to part with this welcome windfall. But in things spiritual, Mary's reign had been a return to normality.

No, it was in Elizabeth's long reign that Ireland's religious troubles had really begun. Yet for all this, you could scarcely blame the queen.

The watchword of Queen Bess had always been compromise. There must be a national Church, it was argued, or there would be disorder. But the English Church that Elizabeth designed was such a clever amalgam that, it was hoped, moderate Catholics or Protestants could find it acceptable. The message to her subjects was clear. "If you will outwardly conform, you may in private believe what you like."

But history was against her. The whole of Europe was separating into armed religious camps. The Catholic powers were determined to fight back against the Protestant heretics. King Philip of Spain, having failed with her half sister Mary, even offered to marry Elizabeth to secure England for his family and the Catholic faith. But Elizabeth's subjects were becoming more Protestant, even Puritan, and when in 1572 the French royal family organised a great massacre of Protestants on Saint Bartholomew's Day, in which thousands of innocent women and children were killed, the Catholic cause in England was hugely damaged. But the greatest blow to Elizabeth's hopes of compromise had come from Rome itself.

"The Pope has excommunicated the queen." His grandfather Richard had come home with the news one day. It was one of the earliest events in his childhood that Martin Walsh remembered. "And I could wish," his grandfather would always say afterwards, "that he had not done it." Catholics no longer owed the queen any allegiance. Soon the Council in England, afraid that Catholics might be traitors, clamped down on them. Priests arriving from the continent were arrested as spies and insurgents. A number were executed. And when, at last, Philip of Spain had sent his mighty Armada across the seas to conquer the heretic island—and might have succeeded if a great storm hadn't blown his galleons round the coast—the minds of most Englishmen became set in a simple prejudice: the Catholics were the enemy.

Except, perhaps, in Ireland. "In the time of my father," Queen Elizabeth could remember, "when the Jesuits went to the O'Neills advocating treason, the O'Neills sent them away." Even as late as the Armada, when a Spanish galleon had been shipwrecked on his coast, Tyrone had massacred the unlucky crew, just to show the English queen that her native Irish lords could be trusted. The English Council did understand that their Catholic faith, as such, would not necessarily lead the Irish princes into conflict with the crown. As for the Old English, proud of their loyalty, where nearly all the gentry and most of the merchants were quietly Catholic, the queen and her Council had tried to maintain the compromise. If Richard Walsh was unwilling to renounce the Pope for Elizabeth's Church—"the Church of Ireland, as she is pleased to call it," he would say with a wry smile—he did admit, after attending a service once: "They follow the proper forms so closely, you'd almost think you were in a Catholic church." If you didn't attend, you had to pay a fine; but these weren't always collected. Even Catholic priests, so long as they gave no trouble, were usually left alone. More serious, and more insulting, was the rule that Catholics could not hold public office. "But they can't apply it, you know," Richard liked to point out. "Often as not, the only local gentleman fit to be a magistrate is a Catholic." The rule would then be ignored. In such an environment, men like Richard Walsh could manage their dual loyalties.

But as the years went by, it had become harder. The New English arrived and took up position. Little by little, the Old English Catholics were being squeezed out of the business of government. The rules against their religion were tightened. "We're treated like strangers in our own country," the Old English began to complain.

With the death of Queen Elizabeth, the throne had passed to her cousin James Stuart, King of Scotland. His tempestuous mother, Mary Queen of Scots, had been a Catholic whose plots against the heretic Queen Elizabeth had finally cost Mary her head. Her son James had been brought up a Protestant by the Scottish lords. But might the new king show more sympathy towards the loyal Catholic gentry of Ireland? There had been hints that he might. Until last year.

November 5, 1605: the date that shook all England. A group of Catholic conspirators, led by one Guy Fawkes, attempted to blow up the Houses of Parliament, Lords, Commons, and King James as well—only to be discovered by the royal network of spies. For centuries to come, the outrage would be rehearsed in popular rhyme.

> *Remember, remember*
> *The fifth of November,*
> *Gunpowder, treason and plot.*
>
> *I see no reason*
> *Why gunpowder treason*
> *Should ever be forgot.*

For the Puritans of England, and the English Parliament, there could be no trusting of Catholics after that.

So where did that leave the Walshes? In difficulty. Perhaps, one day, in danger. That was how Martin Walsh saw it. And so what sort of son-in-law did he need? A Catholic, of course. He had no wish to have Protestant grandchildren. A man like himself: loyal, but intelligent and courteous. A man who did not allow his head to be ruled by his heart. A man ready to compromise. Was young Smith such a man? He didn't know.

All this time, he realised, his elder son had been watching him intently. Martin smiled.

"Do not fear, Lawrence, I shall make diligent enquiries, you may be sure."

But Lawrence did not return his smile. Indeed, it seemed to Martin that the glance he now received from his son was suspicious and cold. Then Lawrence spoke.

And, as he winced, Martin gazed at him sadly. It was not easy for a father to be despised by his son.

‡

Lawrence almost wished he hadn't spoken. He hated to hurt his kindly father. If only this great chasm didn't lie between them—yet he hardly knew what could be done about it. The chasm had opened because of education.

Martin had bought a pleasant estate in Fingal, on the edge of the ancient Plain of Bird Flocks, the heart of the Old English Pale. Though his friend the lord of Howth had joined Elizabeth's Church of Ireland, most of the local gentry, like the nearby Talbots of Malahide, were loyal Catholics who would employ Catholic tutors to teach their children. Yet deep compromises, you couldn't deny it, were built deep into the system. The very money for their own house, for instance, derived from an estate that old Richard's wife, a Doyle, had bought cheap when the monasteries were dissolved. Their Doyle cousins—purely for worldly advantage—had gone across to the Church of Ireland Protestants ten years ago. Lawrence had been disgusted, but his father, good Catholic though he was, had taken it philosophically and was still on friendly terms with his Protestant cousins. Only when it came to his own education had such compromise been impossible.

"The English aren't only Protestant. They're turning Puritan," Martin had declared. "You couldn't possibly be educated there." But what were the alternatives? Ireland had always lacked a university of its own; but recently a new place of learning, called Trinity College, had been set up in Dublin to supply that lack. It had soon become clear, however, that Trinity was intended for the New English Protestants, and so the Catholics naturally shunned it. That left only the seminaries and colleges of continental Europe. And so, like many other gentlemen of his kind, Martin Walsh had sent his son to a continental college: that of Salamanca, in Spain. And there, thanks be to God, thought Lawrence, he had encountered a different world.

When the mighty Catholic Church had been confronted by the Protestant Reformation, some within it had reacted with outrage; but often brave and pious Catholics took a different view.

"The Protestants are right," they agreed, "when they say that corruption and superstition can be found in the Church. But that is no reason to destroy a thousand years of spiritual tradition. We must purify and renew Holy Church; when that is done, the faith will shine out with a new and intense light. And that sacred flame must then be protected. We must be prepared to fight to defend the Church against its enemies." Thus was born the movement known as the Counter-Reformation. The Catholic faith—pure, incorruptible, simple but strong—was going to fight back. Its best men and women were to prepare for battle. And where would the Church find recruits for the great cause? Why, in the places where the best young men were educated, of course. The seminaries.

Lawrence had loved Salamanca. He had lived at the Irish college and attended the University, where the curriculum had been rich and varied.

It was at the start of his third year that the principal had summoned him and quietly asked if he had a vocation for the religious life. "Both I and all your teachers agree that you should continue, and undertake a study of divinity. Indeed, we think you have the makings of a Jesuit."

To join the Jesuit order—this was an honour indeed. Founded only seven decades before by Ignatius Loyola, the Jesuits were some of the Church's intellectual elite. Teachers, missionaries, administrators, their task was not to withdraw from but to interact with the world. As the Counter-Reformation assembled the army of soldiers of Christ, the Jesuits were in the vanguard. Intellect, worldly skill, strength of character: all were required. Since the days when the family first came to strengthen the faith in Ireland four centuries ago, all his heritage, it seemed to Lawrence, had prepared him for such a role. "It may be," the principal told him, "that we are destined to light in Ireland a brighter and a purer fire than has ever flamed there before."

It had rather surprised Lawrence that his father had not been pleased.

"I'd hoped for sons from you," Martin complained. Though he understood this well enough, such considerations seemed to Lawrence to be unworthy. "You're still a dear fellow," his father had once remarked to him sadly one day, "but something's come between us. I can sense it."

"I hardly know what," Lawrence had answered in genuine surprise.

"It's a glint in your eye. You're no longer one of us anymore. You might be French or Spanish."

"We are all members of a universal Church," Lawrence reminded him.

"I know." Martin Walsh had smiled sadly. "But it's a hard thing for a father to be judged by his son and found wanting."

There was some truth in this complaint. Lawrence couldn't deny it. Nor was the problem confined to his own family. He knew of several other young men who had returned from the seminaries to find the easygoing religion of their families lacking in urgency and correctness. He understood his father and sympathised. But there was nothing he could do.

So this business of the Smiths and his sister, it seemed to Lawrence, was a potentially serious matter. What influence might such an alliance have upon the family? He tried to remember anything he had heard about them. There were two sons, he believed. Hadn't one of them failed to complete his schooling?

Even more important was the question of their faith. Were they sound? Were they compromisers? If only he could feel confident in his father's rigour on such matters; but he wasn't sure he could.

Even so, it was a little tactless of him now to say to his father: "I hope there is no chance that Smith could turn into a heretic like your cousin Doyle."

He realised as soon as he said it that he should have phrased it differently. It had sounded faintly accusing, as though Doyle were his father's relation, for whom Martin was somehow responsible, and nothing to do with himself. He saw his father wince.

"I have already told you, Lawrence, that I shall attend to this matter. Go to Spain, Sir, and attend to your studies."

Nor was it forgivable that in an instant of anger he had replied:

"And you may be sure, Father, that I shall cause enquiries to be made, too." It was said quietly, so that Orlando and Anne should not hear. But the message was clear: his father was no longer to be trusted. His authority was questioned.

⁘

What were they saying? Anne listened, but she couldn't hear. They seemed angry. Did they know she had deceived them?

She hadn't meant to deceive them. Not at all. But she had fallen in love. She hadn't meant to do that, either. But then it had been too late.

Her mother had still been alive the first time she had seen him. Two years ago. They had gone out to a festival at the Curragh. It had been a big affair; English and Irish had come there from far and wide. She had paused for a while to listen to some pipes, while her parents had wandered off to watch a horse race. After listening to the pipers, she had begun to walk across the big open space when she had noticed, a little way off, that some of the young Wicklow men had started a hurling match and that, although this was an Irish game, some of the English youth of Dublin had gone out to challenge them. It was a spirited game, which the Wicklow men were winning easily; but just before the end, a pair of Dubliners in a daring move had broken through and the younger of them had scored dramatically. Moments later, the game had ended, and she had just begun to move away when she saw the two young Dublin men coming in her direction. Hardly realising she was doing so, she waited for them to come near. She could see they had noticed her. They were grinning like a pair of boys after their game.

"Did you enjoy watching?" The elder of the two was a dark-haired young man with firm, regular features and a pleasant smile. "I am Walter Smith and this is my brother Patrick." He laughed. "As you see, we did not win our battle." He gave her a discreet, searching look, but she did not see it, for her eyes were already upon Patrick.

He was taller than his brother. Slim and athletic. Yet there was something gentle in his manner. His face was oval and wore a couple of days' stubble—obviously, his beard grew thickly. His brown hair was close-cropped, and she noticed that over his brow it was already thinning. His eyes, also brown, were soft, and they rested upon her.

"Did you see me score?"

"I did." She laughed. He's pleased with himself, she thought.

"I did well at the end," he said.

"They let us through once," his brother remarked amiably, "out of charity."

"No so." He looked disappointed. "Do not listen to this fellow." The soft brown eyes were looking into hers now, and to her surprise, she felt herself blush. "What is your name?" he asked.

She hardly knew whether to expect to meet Patrick Smith or his brother again. So she had experienced a little stab of excitement a few days later when, coming into Dublin with her mother, she had caught sight of him beside Christ Church. He had come over at once, introduced himself to her mother politely, and chatted easily enough to discover that it was often her habit to ride over on a Thursday to Malahide to visit an old priest who lived there. The following week, he had been waiting by the path to Malahide, and rode with her for a mile along the way.

Soon after this, she had gone away to France, and during that year her mother had died. Only days after the news had come, she received a letter from him, sending his sympathy and saying that he was thinking of her. In the long months that followed, when she experienced great loneliness, she thought of him quite often. And, though she loved her brother, and knew that her father loved her perfectly, there was nonetheless an aching emptiness in her life where her mother's love and presence had always been.

He came to meet her within days of her return. It had been Anne's idea to take Orlando with them. After all, a girl like herself could hardly disappear alone day after day without exciting comment. As for walking out alone with a young man, and without her father's permission, it was unthinkable. So she had practised the subterfuge.

She didn't enjoy it. She was a normal girl, but she was also serious. She believed in the true faith of her ancestors. She loved her family and trusted them. Each night, she said prayers for her mother's soul and asked the Blessed Virgin to intercede for her. She hated deceiving her father; she knew it was a sin. If her mother had still been there, she supposed, she would have talked to her about Patrick Smith; but a father was different. Even so, she longed to ask his advice. And she would have done, except that one thing held her back. Fear. Fear that her father might refuse to let her see him anymore.

She needed him. When they went along the pathways together, she felt an ease and happiness unlike any other she had known before. When he stood close to her, she sometimes almost trembled. When his soft eyes looked down into hers, she felt as if they were melting. The excitement of their meetings, and the growing sense of being loved, filled the void her mother's death had left. By that summer, it had seemed to her she could not do without him.

And what would her father have said if he knew? He'd certainly have intervened. As for her brother Lawrence, she didn't like to think what he'd have said. No, there would be an end to her meetings with Patrick Smith if her family discovered them.

It was a week ago that Patrick had asked her to marry him. They knew that the thing must be done carefully and in the proper manner. His father would approach hers. The two families would consider each other—they'd be bound to do that anyway. And whether or not Patrick's father had any previous knowledge of his younger son's courtship, they both agreed that Martin Walsh must be kept in ignorance. "I daren't tell him now," Anne said, "for if he supposed we had deceived him, it would only hurt him and perhaps set him against us."

For an awful moment, she had been afraid that Orlando might blurt something out; but he had remembered his promise and kept quiet. She resolved to have one more talk with him—a very firm one—before she left in the morning.

With luck, by the time she returned from France, she and Patrick would be betrothed. And her dear father would think he'd arranged it all.

‡

Martin Walsh had turned his face from Lawrence and gazed thoughtfully back at Anne. She was already a handsome young woman now, and she reminded him of his dear wife. Yet she was also still a girl. Innocent. To be protected. Well, he'd talk to his cousin Doyle about the Smith family. But on one matter he was quite determined: he would consider Anne's happiness above everything. That must be his guide.

Behind her in the water below, the little island with its cleft rock seemed to be bathed in a dying orange flame. Across the landscape, far away to the north-west, lay the hump of the Hill of Tara. The sun, bloodred now, was dropping behind it. Martin turned round once more, to gaze southward across Dublin Bay. It was darkening. On the far side of the bay, the little borough of Dalkey, too, was darkening. And farther to the south, where the distant volcanic hills had been caught by the evening sunlight, the entire coastline was sinking to a monotone beside the iron-grey, sullen sea.

They came down from the Ben of Howth and began riding westwards across the old Plain of Bird Flocks towards their home. The sun was sinking behind faraway Tara, but the sky overhead was still pale and a great gleam was coming from behind the horizon in the north so that you could see the landscape clearly. They were still some way from home when, about half a mile in front of them, they saw two figures riding down the road from the north towards Dublin. The shapeless form behind, who led a packhorse, was no doubt a servant; but the man who led the way was a striking figure. At that distance, and in the fading light, his tall, thin body, leaning slightly forward, seemed like a stick or, as he moved continually forward, like a single black pen, drawing an inky line across the land.

So absorbed was Orlando in watching this strange sight that he hardly heard his father's murmured curse, or realised that he was supposed to stop, until he felt Lawrence's restraining hand upon his arm.

"Who is that?" he asked.

"A man you do not wish to meet." His father's voice was very quiet.

"A Protestant." From his tone, Lawrence might have said, "The devil himself."

They watched in silence as the sticklike figure crossed the empty plain, seemingly unaware of their presence.

"That," his father said at last, "is Doctor Pincher."

✛

It had been that morning when Doctor Pincher came round the side of the mound on the slope above the River Boyne. Like so many others who had come that way, he had gazed down to where the swans glided in their stately fashion upon the Boyne's waters, and noted the quiet peace of the place. Like others, he had stared at the huge grass-covered mounds that stood like silent giants along the little ridge and wondered what the devil they were and how they came to be there. Had anyone been able to tell him—which they couldn't—that the ancient mounds had once been tombs constructed according to precise astronomical calculation, he would have been astonished. Had any Irish-speaking local informed him—which they didn't, because he spoke no Irish and wouldn't have asked them anyway—that under those mounds lay the bright halls of the legendary Tuatha De Danaan, the genius warriors and craftsmen who had ruled the land before the Celtic tribes had come, he would have snorted with disgust. But he did notice that, in front of the largest of the mounds, there seemed to be a broad scattering of white quartz stones. He wondered if, perhaps, they had any value.

As Doctor Pincher crossed the Boyne below the ancient tombs and made his way southwards that morning, his mind had been busily occupied. For he had just spent several days up in Ulster, and they had been interesting. Very interesting. So much so that, during all that morning and afternoon, he had not spoken a single word to his servant, not even when they stopped to eat.

He had been ten years in Ireland now, and his views on the Irish had not changed. King James himself had it correctly: he referred to the native Irish Catholics as wild beasts.

Some might have thought—given that the king's own mother, Mary Queen of Scots, had been a notable Catholic, and that the rulers of Scotland descended from Irish tribes— that these opinions seemed strange. But since the new Stuart monarch was divinely anointed, and a scholar besides, the correctness of his judgement could not be doubted. As for their governance, the repeated Irish attempts to evade British rule proved that they were incapable of governing themselves.

As he came to the Plain of Bird Flocks, Doctor Pincher saw the Walshes. He ignored them.

Whatever his views about the Irish, his teaching position at the new foundation had given Pincher some cause for satisfaction. Trinity College was resolutely Protestant, and he was not the only teacher there with Calvinist learning. Hardly surprisingly, therefore, the Catholics avoided Trinity, while the government servants and other new arrivals from England gave it their enthusiastic support. Pincher's successful lectures on the classics, philosophy, and theology soon ensured that he was asked to preach at Christ Church Cathedral itself, where he earned a good reputation with his listeners. His stipends from teaching and preaching allowed him to live well.

Especially as, so far, he had not married. He had it in mind to do so, but although he had met young women, from time to time, to whom he was attracted, sooner or later they had always said or done something that indicated to Pincher that they were unworthy, and so he had never brought the business to any conclusion. He had other family, however. A sister who after a somewhat prolonged spinsterhood had married a worthy man called Budge. And not six months ago, a letter had come with the announcement that she had borne her husband a son and that his name was Barnaby. Barnaby Budge. It was a solid, godly sounding name. And until such time as he should marry and produce children himself, Pincher considered this infant child his heir.

"I mean to do something for him." So he had written to his sister. And though he wrote it out of natural family affection, he had a further reason, too. For, if truth were told, in years past, his sister had sometimes shown a slight lack of respect in her manner towards him. The fault was his own. He couldn't deny it: certain features of his youth; that foolish business that had caused his rapid departure from Cambridge—she had known about that too, alas. These remembrances gave Pincher some pain. His exemplary career in Dublin had put to rest any question about his character long ago. His reputation was solid. He'd worked hard and he'd earned it. For years he had saved. He had been prudent. But he still lacked the tangible proof of his position: property; best of all, some land. And now, it seemed, the means were at hand.

Ulster. It was God's reward.

Several times as he rode southwards that day, he had found fragments of the Twenty-third Psalm coming into his head with wonderful appropriateness. *The Lord is my shepherd, I shall not want.* He had been a faithful servant, God knew. He should have faith now that the Lord would provide. *Thou preparest a table before me in the presence of mine enemies . . . my cup runneth over.* Yes, the chosen congregation would be fed, feasted even, in the midst of the Irish. *Thou makest me to lie down in green pastures. . . .* Ah, those he had seen, this very week. The green pastures of Ulster. The reward of the Lord. Very soon, the sower should sow his seed upon the good ground there.

It had been a friend, a godly man, who had told him of a farm up there. The leaseholder was planning to give it up in a year or so, and the place could probably be bought at a good price. The land was excellent. If he went up there now, he might secure a promise that it would be offered to him first.

So he had visited Ulster and been much impressed. The place was wild, of course, but fertile. In particular, he had been glad to find, along the coast, that communities of Scots, staunch Calvinists like himself, had already crossed the sea and set up little farming and fishing colonies of their own. As for the property in question, he had inspected it, and there had been a meeting of minds. The place, if he wished it, could be his. But more inspiring even than this prospect, for a godly man, had been another thought that the sight of the land, and the good people he found there, had put into his mind.

Just think, he had said to himself, if this land could be planted.

Plantation. It was actually the Catholic queen, Mary Tudor, who had begun the process of plantation. Despite the fact that the Irish were Catholic, she distrusted them; and so she had set up two areas on the edge of South Leinster, which were called Kings Country and Queens Country, in which colonies of English settlers were established to act as a sort of military garrison for the area. The process was known as plantation. Other plantations had also been tried, especially down in Munster, where tracts of land had been seized by the government after the big rebellion in Queen Elizabeth's reign, in the hope that the settlers might teach the Irish how to live as sturdy English yeomen. Although these plantations had not always been successful, the English royal council was still enthusiastic for them. As for Pincher, it seemed to him that the plantations were a wonderful opportunity to do God's work. Weren't they exactly the same as the new colonies—Virginia and others—in the New World? Armed communities of godly pilgrims amongst native heathens who, in due course, would either be converted or pushed back into the wilderness, and probable extinction?

The procedure of plantation was straightforward enough. A huge area would be set aside for subdivision into parcels of land of various sizes. English and Scottish investors—they were called undertakers—would be invited to underwrite the venture, and they in turn were to manage their land grant, supply sturdy tenants from England—yeomen, craftsmen, and the like, of good Protestant persuasion—and enjoy the eventual profits of their enterprise. Thus, they would become landowners of an ideal community. And for a modest investor like himself, there should be excellent opportunities to acquire leases from the undertakers, which could be sublet for a handsome profit.

No wonder then that his heart rose in exaltation as he considered the idea: a huge tract of Ulster, rid of its papists.

Would it ever come to pass? Who knew? In God's good time, he had to believe that it would. Meanwhile, he would begin, if all went well, with a little foothold in the place.

So he was in a cheerful mood as, coming to the Plain of Bird Flocks, he caught sight of the Catholic Walshes away to his left. He did not let their presence trouble him.

Since that embarrassing first meeting, he had only encountered the Catholic lawyer occasionally. He suspected that Martin Walsh did not like him, though Walsh was far too much of a gentleman ever to show it. For Walsh's Jesuitical son, he had only loathing. Of his two other children he knew nothing. But he bore families like the Walshes no special ill will. The fact was—you couldn't escape it—that Walsh was a gentleman even if he was a papist. So long as he was loyal to the English crown—and Martin Walsh was certainly that—there was no need to dispossess them as if they were mere Irish. Pincher wasn't quite certain what the fate of families like the Walshes should be. They'd be pushed quietly out of power, of course. Some, like the Jesuit Lawrence, would be dealt with in due course. Others would gradually be worn down. They were not the first priority.

And then a happy thought struck him. By the time his nephew Barnaby Budge was a man of his own age, would Walsh's younger son still be a papist, enjoying all the fruits of the Walsh family estate? No, he did not think so. Indeed, Pincher cheerfully considered, he could practically guarantee it. By then, to be sure, the Walshes and their kind would be finished.

+‡+

It was early in August when Orlando was told by his father: "You're going to meet young Smith. The man your sister is to marry."

Orlando knew that his father had been busy with the matter ever since Anne and Lawrence had left for the continent. There had been discussions with his cousin Doyle, long talks with certain Dublin priests, and meetings with the Smiths themselves. After each of these negotiations, his father would return from Dublin looking preoccupied, but as to the substance of the discussions, his father had never divulged anything. So when his father told him that the young man was to come out to their house alone on a Saturday afternoon, spend the night there, and then go to Mass with them the following morning, he was highly excited, as well as full of joy for his sister.

"I think you'll like him," his father said kindly.

"Oh, I'm sure I shall," Orlando replied.

And how carefully he had prepared himself. He had not forgotten his promise to his sister. No one should ever know about the clandestine meetings of the lovers. Neither by word nor by sign would he give anything away. When he met young Smith, he would look as if he had never seen him before in his life. Again and again, he went over it in his mind. He thought of every foolish slip he could make and prepared for them all. As the day approached, he felt nervous and excited; but he was sure of himself also. He would not let them down.

He spent the morning with one of the farmhands. He was unloading a cartload of turves, brought down from a bog to the north, when he saw the figure in the distance, riding towards the house. His father was inside, and for a moment he wondered whether he should run out to meet young Smith, to let him know that his secret was safe and that he wouldn't be giving him away. But after a moment's hesitation, he decided that this might make Fintan suspicious and that it would be better to leave everything exactly as he'd planned it. So he turned round instead and went into the house, and found his father and told him that a stranger was approaching.

It was his father, therefore, who went out through the door to greet the young man and call to the groom to take his horse, while Orlando, pretending to be shy, remained inside in the shadows of the hallway.

From where he stood, it seemed to Orlando as if he were gazing along a tunnel towards the great gash of bright sunlight of the open doorway. He heard the voices outside, saw shadows move briefly before the entrance, then saw two figures, his father leading, blocking out the sunlight. They were inside, moving towards him. This was his moment.

"Well," he heard his father say, "here he is."

And then, blinking slightly as the sunlight came pouring in again though the doorway behind them, he found himself staring with horror and evident astonishment at the face of young Smith.

For it wasn't young Smith at all. It was somebody else entirely.

✣

It had been Doyle who began the business. When Martin Walsh had gone to see him about the letter from Peter Smith, he had answered without hesitation.

"The Smiths are of good reputation, Cousin Martin. The father is a worthy man, and a man of substance. And a good Catholic, too, you'll wish to know, although others can inform you of that better than I. He has two sons, however. For which of them does he ask your daughter?"

"The name he gives is Patrick."

"Ah." Doyle shook his head. "That won't do. It's Walter you want: the older one. He isn't betrothed, so far as I have heard."

"The objection to Patrick?"

Doyle drew a long breath and let the air out slowly between his teeth.

"No crime, Cousin. No great wickedness. The younger son, of course. But his character . . ." He paused. "He was sent to a seminary, you know. But he never completed his studies. He never completes anything. A lack of steadfastness. A weakness, I'd say, which he masks with his gallant manners."

"Gallant?"

"Oh yes." The merchant grinned as he launched into a little parody of the courtly style. "He is a very paragon of all the noble virtues. He rides, and shoots an arrow, runs like a deer. He writes a verse and sings in tune, and dances. They say that women melt before his eyes."

"I see," said Martin grimly.

"Patrick is Smith's first offer, Cousin. But Walter is your man. He is capable and industrious, and a very pleasant fellow. Smith will be only too glad to contract a marriage with the Walsh family, so you may dictate the terms."

Doyle was able to give Martin Walsh a good deal of other useful information, and Walsh had parted from him with his last words singing in his ears.

"Remember, Cousin Walsh, don't let him fob you off with Patrick."

When Walsh had called upon Smith, he had asked to see both his sons and had quickly decided for himself that Doyle's assessment had been right. Patrick, he considered, was ambitious, but ingratiating and soft. Walter, who, though polite, made fewer efforts to please, was clearly his own man. When he informed Smith that he preferred Walter, a look of fleeting concern had crossed the merchant's face.

"Yet she and Patrick so delight in each other," he protested, "they are like two turtle doves."

"She scarcely knows him," Walsh replied firmly.

"Ah." Smith had looked a little strange, but quickly recovered himself. "That must be considered further," he had said.

There had been some negotiations over the next two weeks, but it had seemed to Martin Walsh that his cousin Doyle's assessment had been correct and that Smith would yield his better son rather than lose the chance of the connection with the Doyles. Meanwhile, he had several conversations with young Walter and found him admirable in every respect. In due course, the betrothal had been arranged to everyone's satisfaction—or so he had thought.

÷

Orlando hardly knew what to say or think. All that day and the next, he said very little. Indoors and at meals, he sat on his three-legged stool and stared at Walter Smith like an idiot. Fortunately, his father took this for childish shyness and thought nothing of it. But all the time Orlando was wondering: Did Anne know about this? Shouldn't he tell her, and if so, how? On the Sunday evening, after Walter Smith had departed, he went to his father.

"I should like to write to Anne, Father."

"A letter to your sister. I am glad to hear of it," Walsh kindly replied. "You may add your word to the letter I am already writing."

This was not what Orlando had in mind, but there was nothing he could do about it. And so, below his father's neatly organised script, the following message appeared in Orlando's childish hand:

"Father says I may rejoice with you, since you are betrothed to Walter Smith. He seems a fine gentleman, but I had never seen him before." He had done his best to use more ink on the last few words, so that they would stand out more boldly. His father glanced at it, briefly remarked upon his poor penmanship, but made no other comment.

After that, there was nothing more Orlando could do. He did his lessons with the old priest as usual. The house was quiet.

✥

The sudden arrival of Anne ten days later took everyone by surprise. After receiving the letter from her father and Orlando, she had left Bordeaux, without permission or anyone's knowledge, the very same day. Pawning a gold crucifix and chain her father had given her, she had used the money to travel to the coast, where she had found a ship bound for Dublin. Her father hardly knew whether to be impressed by her courage or furious at her disobedience.

Then she told him she was in love with Patrick. And so shaken was he by her vehemence that he even wrote to Lawrence to ask his advice. He was even more distressed because, until that moment, he had not known she had any strong feelings about the young man at all; and even his natural anger and hurt at her deception had been overwhelmed by the sight of her tears. "I was thinking only of your happiness, my child," he assured her. And yet, whatever pain she was suffering now, he knew that in fact his decision was correct. She might be in love with Patrick, but in the long run, he wouldn't make her happy. Walter would. Gently and earnestly, he tried to make this clear to her. "There are times when it is not wise, Anne, to let your head be ruled by your heart," he urged her. But she was not really listening to him. "At least meet Walter and come to know him," he suggested. But she only wanted to see Patrick, her own true love, and poor Martin Walsh, wishing more than ever that his dear wife was still alive, was not sure whether to allow this or not. A week went by. She moped about the house. They had several unsatisfactory conversations. He wondered whether to send her back to the seminary. He also considered whether he should summon Walter Smith to visit so that she could see for herself what a good fellow he was; but he feared that she might reject him so firmly that the young man wouldn't want her anymore. Should he change his own mind about Patrick? He knew that would be a mistake, but it was terrible for him to see his daughter in such pain and to feel that he was failing her. The second week, she became pale and listless, and he was about to send for a physician.

Then Lawrence arrived.

He had come with remarkable speed. To his own surprise, Martin was actually glad to see him. Lawrence did remark that he assumed his sister had been soundly whipped; but when his father had been shocked, he had said no more on the subject. And indeed, from that moment, his presence had been a blessing.

He had been quiet and very calm. With his sister, he had been gentle, offering no reproofs, but asking only that, each day, they might pray together. He kept a friendly eye on young Orlando, took him for one or two long walks, and even went out hunting rabbits with him.

❖

For Orlando, the arrival of Anne had come as a relief. Within hours, he had been closeted with her and told her all he knew about Walter Smith.

"I didn't tell about your meetings," he assured her.

"I know. And I shan't tell anyone how you helped, either. Though as to my seeing Patrick," she shook her head, "it hardly seems to matter now anyway."

Although he knew all about her conversations with his father, and saw her tears, Orlando learned little more from his sister for several days. It was clear that she did not want to discuss it with him. Then one afternoon she called him to her and quietly told him: "There is something, little brother, you can do."

The next morning, he rode out alone. He had no lessons that day, and his father was too preoccupied to take much notice. He rode his pony down the road across the Plain of Bird Flocks, and by midmorning he was in sight of the city. Crossing the Liffey by the old bridge, he entered the gate and made his

way across Winetavern Street, where the house of the Smiths
was. At the entrance to the yard at the back, he found a servant
boy and asked him if Patrick Smith was there. Learning that he
was, he asked the boy to tell him that a friend of his was waiting outside. A few minutes later, the young man appeared.

When Orlando saw him, he almost cried out for pleasure.
Patrick Smith looked so exactly as he remembered him, not
changed at all. Handsome, smiling, his soft brown eyes registering their pleasure at seeing Orlando.

"You have probably heard, Orlando, that my brother and
not I is to be betrothed to your sister," he said gently.

"She is back. She is at the house."

"She is here?" He looked astonished. "Come, let's walk
down onto the quay. Tell me everything."

So Orlando told him about his sister's tears, and her arguments with her father.

"She wants to marry you," he blurted out. It was hard to
tell whether Patrick looked more shaken or pleased by this
news. "She wants to see you, but my father does not give his
permission. You must meet her in secret."

"I see. You must understand, Orlando, that my father has
also forbidden me to see your sister."

Orlando gazed at him in astonishment.

"But you'll come?" He could not imagine that the handsome young hero would allow such a small thing to stand in
his way. "You want to see her?"

"Oh, I do. You may be sure."

"I shall tell her you will come, then?" And he explained
how the meeting could be arranged.

"I shall need to ride out without my father's knowledge. Or
my brother's." He paused a moment, glancing along the quay.
"I shall come as soon as I can get away. Tomorrow, perhaps. Or
the day or two after. Very soon."

"I'll wait for you there," said Orlando.

And wait he did. The place was well-chosen—a disused
chapel, seldom visited, by the edge of the Walsh estate. Rather

than have Anne wait out there each day, which might have seemed suspicious, Orlando would wait. As soon as Patrick Smith arrived, Orlando would run back to the house, which wasn't far, to fetch her, and then keep watch outside while they met.

The next day, he waited three hours until dusk. The day after it was raining, but he waited all the same and walked home soaked. The third day, the weather was fine but there was no sign of Patrick Smith. The next day, the same.

"Why doesn't he come?" Anne cried. "Doesn't he care for me?"

"He'll come. He said he would," Orlando cried. And the next day, he waited once more. "Perhaps I should ride into Dublin again," he said that evening.

"No, he is not coming," Anne said quietly. "Wait no more." And soon after that, he heard her weeping. But though she became sad and listless, he did wait at the chapel several more days. But from then until Lawrence arrived and upset the routine, there was no sign of Patrick Smith, nor any word from him.

The first day that Lawrence took him for a walk, he had been anxious to get back so that he could run out to the meeting place again; but Lawrence kept him too long. He also asked Orlando several questions.

They were all very friendly, about his studies and trivial things, to put him at his ease. At one point he told Orlando: "I am worried about Anne. It grieves me to see her in such pain. Do you think she truly cares for this Patrick?"

"I think she does," said Orlando.

"And Walter Smith—what did you think of him?"

Orlando gave him the best account he could of the young man, from what he had seen during his visit. "I think he is a good enough man," he admitted, and Lawrence nodded approvingly.

"How does he compare with Patrick, though?" he enquired.

"Oh, well . . ." He was just about to answer when he spotted the cunning trap, and inwardly cursed his elder brother. "I can't really tell. Anne says that Patrick is taller."

"You have not seen him yourself?" The dark eyes were piercing. Lawrence seemed to see every guilty secret in his mind.

"She was with our mother when they met, but I was not there," Orlando answered with a shake of the head. A clever answer, which was even true. "Hmm," said Lawrence.

He did not bring up the subject again. Not long after that, he had gone into Dublin for the day. It was the following morning that Orlando overheard his father in conversation with him.

"You tell her yourself," he heard his father say irritably.

"It is for the best, I assure you," Lawrence's voice replied. "I shall be kind."

And so, it seemed, he was.

"I was sitting on the bench in front of the house, just sitting there in the sun," Anne told Orlando afterwards, "when he came and sat beside me. He was kind. He talked of love."

"Lawrence talked of love?"

"Yes. It seems he was once in love. Think of that!" She smiled, then frowned. "I believe he was speaking the truth."

"He is on your side against Father?"

"Oh no. He spoke of Patrick. He said that first love is strong, but that we may not come to see whether a lover's character will truly suit us until we have known them for a long time. 'Then how are those to find happiness who are betrothed to a person they scarcely know?' I asked him."

"He had no answer for that?"

"He did. 'Their parents are better judges than themselves—or hope they are,' he said. Then he laughed. I was quite surprised. 'And Father thinks that Walter would suit me better?' I said. 'There is no question of family fortune here,' he says. 'They are brothers, after all. It's a question of character. You love Patrick at present, but in years to come, I promise you,' and he gave me one of his earnest looks, 'it is Walter who will be a good husband and bring you a far greater happiness than you imagine.' That's what he told me."

"What did you say?"

"I asked him if Father would compel me to marry Walter. 'No,' he cries, 'not at all. He will not. Ask him yourself. He wishes you to return to France until the spring. When you return, you shall meet Walter and come to know him. But if then he is not to your liking, if you do not think I mean that you could love and honour him, then the betrothal shall be undone.'"

"He said nothing else?"

"Yes. After I had been silent a little while, he took my arm and smiled and said to me: 'Remember, Anne, this little rhyme, for there's much wisdom in it.

> Head over heart,
> The better part.
> Heart over head,
> Better dead.

I assure you I know it to be true.'"

"That was all?"

"No. There was one thing more. I shan't be seeing Patrick again."

"He forbade you? I'll go to Dublin and bring him here if you like," Orlando cried.

"You don't understand." She grimaced. "He's gone. He's not here anymore. He's left on a ship."

"Where to?"

"Who knows? England, France, Spain—America, for all I know. He's been sent away and won't be back until I've married someone else—I can promise you that."

"Is it Peter Smith's doing? Surely Patrick himself didn't just . . ."

"No. Don't you see? It was Lawrence. Behind my back he'd already arranged it all. Oh, I could see it. I could see it all. I hate him," she suddenly screamed. Then she burst into tears.

But three days later, quietly enough, she left with Lawrence to return to France. There was, after all, nothing else that she could do.

✦

With Anne and Lawrence gone again, the house reverted to its habitual peace in the great quiet of Fingal. Orlando resumed his studies. Martin Walsh went into Dublin once or twice a week. On Sundays, they went across to Malahide Castle, where the priest said mass or conducted a service discreetly within the old stone house. September was warm. The weather was fine. Martin Walsh, enjoying the genial calm of his estate, had not gone into Dublin for some days, when one afternoon, just as he was about to go into the house after a walk, Orlando saw the figure of their cousin Doyle riding towards him. The big man dismounted quickly and gave Orlando a friendly nod.

"Is your father here? Ah. Here he is," he continued as Martin Walsh appeared at the door. "I've news for you, Cousin—unless you've already heard?"

"I've heard nothing." He glanced at Orlando and gave Doyle a questioning look.

"The boy may hear it. All the world will know soon enough. It's the news from Ulster." He took a long breath. "The Earl of Tyrone has gone."

"Died?"

"No. Taken a ship and sailed away. O'Donnell, Earl of Tyrconnell, has gone with him, and others besides. The earls have flown, Cousin Walsh, they've turned their backs upon Ireland, and they won't return."

Walsh stared. For a moment or two, he didn't speak. Then he shook his head in amazement and asked a single question.

"Why?"

The Earl of Tyrone. Orlando had never seen him, of course, but he had been there, a tall, dark figure in his imagination, heroic, almost godlike, the last great prince of ancient Ireland, heir to the O'Neill High Kings, dwelling up in Ulster. Orlando had an idea that Tyrone might still return and drive the English officials out of Dublin one day; then no doubt he'd resume the kingship of his ancestors at royal Tara. And Old English though he was, Orlando had found this vision of an ancient Irish ascendancy more exciting than frightening. As for O'Donnell, he was the greatest Irish prince in Donegal. The north and north-west, the remains of the ancient tribal lands; Tyrone and Tyrconnell, last of the ruling princes of Ireland: fled.

"Why?" Doyle shrugged. "The word in Dublin is that O'Donnell's been plotting with the King of Spain, just as Tyrone did before, and he discovered that the government had got wind of it. So he ran while he could."

"But Tyrone? The man was well set. They left him a free land in his own territory. He had no good reason to flee."

"I would agree. But he saw it otherwise. The English officials are starting to buzz around Ulster. And no one will believe he wasn't involved somehow with O'Donnell and the King of Spain." He sighed. "Besides, an Irish prince like that is not bred for times like these. He'll never be a royal servant."

"To be Earl of Tyrone is hardly to be a servant."

"But to him it is. The Irish are free, Martin. They have their clans, their ancient tribes, their hereditary family positions, but their spirits are free. As for their princes, they answer to themselves. Tyrone will never do the bidding of some puffed-up little English official with nothing but his temporary office behind him—and whom Tyrone regards as a heretic anyway. It's not in the man's nature."

"So he's flown."

"Like a bird. Like an eagle, I should say."

"What will he do?"

"Wander Europe. Find a Catholic prince he may serve without dishonour to his name or his religion. Command his armies. Remember, he knows those Catholic kings and their armies already. They will honour him."

"That is true." Walsh nodded and sighed. "You'll eat with us, and drink with me tonight?"

Doyle smiled.

"It was my intention."

They ate early in the evening in the house's spacious hall, and Orlando was able to observe the two men as they talked—his father, with his quiet, stately manner, and Doyle, dark, somewhat shorter, more intense. Through the meal, the talk was naturally about the politics of Tyrone's departure and what it would mean.

"Undoubtedly the government will confiscate all the earl's land," Walsh remarked. "The legal means can be found to do it."

"I suspect they will end by making a plantation up there. All the men who want land on easy terms will be rejoicing tonight," Doyle said. But the thought did not seem to give him much pleasure personally.

When the meal was ended, the two men continued to sit at the table, drinking quietly together; and though Orlando knew that his participation was not required, he was able to sit quietly at the end of the hall by the big open fireplace, where the two men seemed to forget his presence. For even if they said little, or he failed to understand what they said, he wanted nonetheless to be in the company of his father and his cousin upon such an important occasion. He observed them both closely, therefore. And, young though he was, he sensed their mood and imbibed it, and for the rest of his life it would become a part of him.

This much was certain: for both these men, the evening was full of melancholy and a sense of loss. Doyle, descendant of Vikings and generations of Dublin merchants, a Protestant in name—or Church of Ireland, anyway—and Walsh, his cousin, a Catholic gentleman whose family had been a mainstay of the Old English gentry in Ireland for nearly five hundred years; two men at the heart of the English Pale, yet two Irishmen, too: for both of them, the departure of Tyrone and

Tyrconnell was a personal blow. They clearly felt emotionally closer to the native Irish prince than to any Englishman sent out from London.

"The Flight of the Earls," Doyle mused. "It's the end of an age."

"May God bring them better fortune." Walsh raised his wine goblet.

"I'll drink to that," said Doyle.

And young Orlando, silently watching, understood that, in ways not yet clear, the world in which he lived had just changed forever.

It was the following morning, after Doyle's departure, that his father called Orlando. "You're coming with me," he told him; and when Orlando asked where they were going: "Portmarnock."

The little seaside hamlet of Portmarnock lay by the road strand of sand dune and beach that stretched southwards for several miles along the edge of the ancient Plain of Bird Flocks. Orlando supposed he would be required to saddle up his pony, but his father told him: "No, we shall walk."

There was a light breeze. Clouds drifted across the sky, which changed accordingly from blue to grey. Orlando contentedly went along, side by side with his father, speaking a little from time to time, eastwards towards Portmarnock. As they left their own land, they passed the little deserted chapel where he had waited for Patrick Smith. "It's shameful that our own government forbids us to use it," his father remarked.

As they walked, evidence of the Old English medieval occupation was all around: fields of wheat and barley; high, dark hedgerows; stone walls; here and there a stone church or a small fortified house. But soon they came to a somewhat less tidy terrain where the cattle grazed—the open seaward sweep down towards the coastline, which still possessed the echoing bareness of the days long ago when Doyle's ancestor, Harold the Viking, and others like him had laid out their Nordic farmsteads on the plain of Fingal.

Their destination, however, which they reached in less than an hour, was older by far than any of these. It stood alone, just apart from the hamlet of fishermen's cabins.

"Your brother does not approve of this place," Walsh remarked with a small grimace, "or of my coming here." It was the first time Orlando had ever heard his father say anything that hinted at the friction between himself and Lawrence. "But I come here by myself from time to time."

It was nothing much to look at. Orlando had often passed within a quarter mile of it on his way to the beach. An old well, surrounded by a little stone wall. At some time a conical stone roof had been built over it, though this had now fallen into disrepair. The well was quite deep, but leaning over the parapet, Orlando could see the faint, soft gleam of the water far below. The well at his own house was nearly as deep but had never seemed especially interesting; this well, however, was different. He didn't know why—perhaps the relative isolation of that lonely place—but there was something strange and mysterious about that water down below. What was it? Was it a glimmering entrance to another world?

"The well is sacred to Saint Marnock," his father's voice spoke quietly behind him. "Your brother Lawrence says it was a pagan well long ago. Before Saint Patrick came, no doubt. He says such things are superstition, unworthy of the faith." He sighed. "He may be right. But I like the old ways, Orlando. I come here like the simple folk to pray to Saint Marnock when I am troubled."

Saint Marnock: one of scores of local saints, their identities half forgotten except in their own localities, but often as not with a saint's day, and a well or sacred place where they might be remembered. "I like the old ways, too," said Orlando. He was sure he did, because it made him feel close to his father.

"Then you can say a prayer for your sister, and ask the saint to give her guidance." And moving round to the other side of the well, Walsh himself went down on his knees and fell into his own silent prayers for a short while. Orlando, having knelt also, did not like to get up until his father did; but once Walsh had done so, Orlando went round to his side, where, to his surprise, his father put his arm around his shoulders.

"Orlando," he said gently, "will you promise me something?"

"Yes, Father."

"Promise me that you will marry one day, and have children—that you will give me grandchildren."

"Yes, Father, I promise. If it is God's will."

"Let us hope that it is, my son." He paused. "Swear it to me, here by this well, upon Saint Marnock."

"I swear, Father. Upon Saint Marnock."

"Good." Martin Walsh nodded quietly to himself, then, glancing down at his son, gave him the sweetest smile. "It is good that you have sworn. I should like you always to remember this day, when your father took you to the Holy Well of Saint Marnock. Will you remember this day, Orlando?"

"Yes, Father."

"All your life. Come." And, still with his arm round his son, Walsh led him along the path through the dunes and out onto the broad, sandy beach. It was low tide and the beach extended far out into the sea, which was glittering softly in the sun.

To their right, the strand stretched away in a pale swath towards the Ben of Howth, whose hump rose high out of the waters. In front of it, the little island of Ireland's Eye rested like a ship at anchor. Far away in the other direction, hazily visible in the northern horizon, the blue Mountains of Morne, guardians of Ulster, seemed asleep.

Orlando glanced up at his father. Martin Walsh was staring out to sea, apparently lost in thought. Orlando looked down at the litter of broken seashells at his feet. A cloud gently cut out the sun, and the sparkle left the sea.

"The end of an age, Orlando." His father's voice was no more than a murmur. Then he felt his father's hand gently squeeze his shoulder. "Remember your promise."

᛭

It was a wet, wintry day in Bordeaux, early the following year, when Anne Walsh received the letter from her father.

> My dearest Daughter,
>
> You must prepare yourself, for I have news of great sadness to impart. Two weeks ago, Patrick Smith embarked from the port of Cork on a merchant ship, on which he had arrived the week before. The morning they left, the weather was calm. But that same day, towards evening, a great storm arose, and having swept the ship back towards the Irish coast, overwhelmed it and dashed it against the rocks. In this wreck, it is my grief to tell you, all that were aboard were lost.
>
> I know, my dearest Anne, how sorrowful these tidings must be to you, and can do no more than mourn with you and tell you that you are never out of my thoughts.
>
> Your loving Father.

It was over, then. Her love had departed and was lost forever, without hope of recall. She burst into tears and wept, without ceasing, for over an hour.

After the first spasm of grief, however, came rage. Not at her father—he had not done this—but at Lawrence. It was he, she thought bitterly—Lawrence with his interference and his conniving, self-righteous Lawrence with his sneaking ways—who had killed Patrick. Had it not been for Lawrence, he'd never have gone away, never have been in Cork, not have been drowned. And leaving off her tears, in a paroxysm of hurt and fury, she cursed her brother and wished him dead in Patrick's place.

Then she gazed out, as the rain outside pattered and ran down the windowpanes, pointlessly, and stared at the greyness,

and felt a great desolation. She scarcely cared what happened
to her now.

≈ 1614 ≈

Tadhg O'Byrne was ahead of them all. He knew because he
had been watching. "There's been drinking at this wake," he
told his wife, "But I'm ahead of them. I am at the front. I have
such a head on me—like a rock."

"You have," she said. "So."

"I am a mountain," he proclaimed, although in stature, and
in strength of body, he was somewhat less than most other
men.

Tadhg, or Tadc as it was often written: a common name.
The English often made it Teague, although it was usually pronounced like the first syllable of Tiger. "There have been some
great Tadhg O'Byrnes," he would say, "powerful chiefs." And
indeed there had. The problem for Tadhg was that he himself
was not. And, in his eyes at least, he should have been.

And not Brian O'Byrne.

Sixty years had passed since Sean O'Byrne of Rathconan
had died and been succeeded by his son Seamus. When it had
come to choosing a successor to Seamus, however, his eldest
son, by the universal agreement of his own family and every
significant person in the area, was deemed worthless. The
choice of the clan had fallen upon the third of Seamus's four
sons, a splendid fellow, who under Irish law and custom had
therefore come into Rathconan and the somewhat shadowy
chieftainship which it represented. Brian O'Byrne was the
grandson of the splendid fellow. Tadhg O'Byrne was the grandson of the worthless one.

The wake was for Brian's father. People had come from all
over that part of Wicklow and beyond: O'Tooles and O'Mores,

MacMurroughs and O'Kellys. And, of course, O'Byrnes: O'Byrnes of the Downes, O'Byrnes of Kiltimon, O'Byrnes of Ballinacor and of Knockrath; O'Byrnes from all over the Wicklow Mountains. All had come to pay their last respects to Toirdhealbhach O'Byrne of Rathconan and to welcome his handsome young son Brian into his inheritance. And scarcely one of them had taken the least notice of Tadhg O'Byrne, who was, by universal acknowledgement, of no account.

"Look at that." Tadhg was staring so bitterly at young Brian O'Byrne that he didn't even know if his wife was still listening. He didn't care anyway. "There's a boy," he sneered, "that sleeps in a feather bed."

If Brian O'Byrne was twenty years old, a good height, fair-haired and handsome, Tadhg was even prouder of his own appearance. He was thirty-four now. His hair was dark and fell in thick ringlets to below his shoulders in the traditional Irish manner. For the occasion, he had changed his usual saffron-coloured linen shirt for a white one, belted at the waist; and he wore a light woollen mantle over his shoulders. Many of the other men wore dark jackets, out of respect for the occasion, but Tadhg would never bother with a jacket. Most of the men wore trews or woollen stockings, but as the day was warm, he had left his legs bare. His feet were stuffed into heavy brogues. He might have been a shepherd or a workman.

And there was his young cousin, the young chief, heir to Rathconan, which should have been his: young Brian with his fair hair cut short, his black embroidered doublet and breeches, his silken stockings and his fine leather shoes. He even wore a golden ring. All of which caused his kinsman Tadhg to spit and mutter:

"Englishman," and "Traitor."

This was somewhat inaccurate. The clothes, as such, would have been worn by a gentleman in many parts of Europe, including every native Irishman's hope, the most Catholic kingdom of Spain. And several of the richer and more impor-tant Irish gentlemen at the wake were similarly dressed.

Whether they usually dressed this way out of a general sense of what was fashionable in England, France, or Spain, or whether to make themselves more acceptable to the English administrators in Dublin would have been hard to say. Certainly, the English administrators themselves would not have assumed that the adoption of English manners was any guarantee of friendliness towards the English crown. "Several of those infernal Irish rebels in the time of Queen Elizabeth had even been to Oxford!" they remembered with disgust. But such subtleties were lost upon Tadhg. "Englishman," he hissed. And in his heart was only a single thought: one day I'll pull him down.

✢

It was a notable gathering. Young Brian felt a justifiable pride—not just that so many great men had come from far and wide to pay their last respects to his father, but that they had come with such obvious affection; and he, in turn, felt full of love for them all.

Above all, he loved Rathconan. It was always the same, unaltered since the days of his great-grandfather Sean, a century ago: a modest fortified house with a square stone tower, not in the best of repair, that looked down from the slopes of the Wicklow Mountains towards the distant blue haze of the sea. The untidy cluster of farm buildings nearby was the same; so was the little chapel where, in Sean O'Byrne's day, Father Donal had celebrated Mass. Even the descendants of Father Donal were still there. One was a priest himself, though unlike Father Donal, he had no wife and children, for few priests lived in that old Irish way now. His brother, on the other hand, a scholar and a poet, hired himself out very successfully as a teacher to families in the area, which profession allowed him to keep body and soul together—and also to father children whose number was not precisely known. Priest and scholar, cattlemen and shepherds, Rathconan families and their neighbours, this was the little world that Brian O'Byrne, educated by the priest and his brother, clothed by a Dublin tailor, and guided by a wise and loving father, had come to inherit and to take pride in.

He was proud of being an O'Byrne, too. Though, with the O'Tooles, they were the most famous of the old Wicklow Mountain ruling families, you couldn't exactly point to any of them and say: "There's an O'Byrne for you." Some were dark, some fair, some tall, some short. Six hundred years of breeding, even in a single region, will usually provide a variety of types. Nor could you be sure of their political allegiance. Generally, by the end of Queen Elizabeth's long reign, the O'Byrnes in the northern section of Wicklow, nearer to Dublin, had come to cooperate with the English government, like it or not; though none of them had gone so far as to turn Protestant. Down in the southern mountain passes, however, the powerful O'Byrne chiefs had kept a magnificent independence. When Tyrone struck against the English crown, it was the chief of the southern O'Byrnes who was his most important ally. "It was O'Byrne that was his link to the King of Spain. It was he who made it a great campaign for the Catholic cause," Brian's father had told him proudly. "Yet you were not in favour of Tyrone's actions," Brian had reminded him. The O'Byrnes of Rathconan, with the northern O'Byrnes, had stayed out of the conflict.

"That is true," his father had said, with some regret. "But it was a fine thing all the same."

His father had given moral leadership in the area during two very difficult decades. Tall, brave, handsome, an ancient Irish prince to his fingertips, no one had any doubt where his heart lay. But he was cautious and wise. When Tyrone's great adventure had failed, he had been sorrowful but not surprised. In 1606, a year before the Flight of the Earls, the great, wild mountain country of Wicklow had finally been designated an English shire—the last part of Ireland, despite its closeness to Dublin, to be brought under English administration. Not that you'd have seen much difference up in the high and empty passes. But all the same, in theory at least, the Irish independence of the region was over. Yet on this subject, too, his father had been philosophical.

"In generations past, we raided the English farms down on the plain. And they sent soldiers up into the hills, and sometimes they were ambushed and killed, and at other times they beat us. Those days, however, are over. There are other and better ways to live." So he would counsel his neighbours. And to Brian he would always say: "If you want to preserve Rathconan and all the things you love, then you must be wise. Play the English at their own game. Learn to change."

"But what sort of change, Father? How will I have to change?"

"I don't know," his father had answered frankly. "You will have to be wise in your own generation. That is all I can advise."

And now, all too soon, his own time had begun. His father had not been so old, but he had been stricken by sickness for more than a year, sunken by the end, ready to go.

The wake had begun some time ago. The body had been handsomely laid out. There had been keening. But most of the visitors had come to pay their quiet respects. The food and drink provided had been liberal. A piper was playing a quiet lament; before long some more cheerful music would begin. He had already received the condolences of each of the guests; now he was making the rounds himself, to make sure that all the courtesy and hospitality the occasion demanded was fulfilled. He had just noticed Tadhg O'Byrne scowling at him and muttering something. He would rather have avoided the fellow, but supposed he ought to go over to him. And he was just bracing himself to do so when, staring down the slope, his eye was caught by a strange figure he had never seen before, riding slowly up the track towards the house.

He was a tall, thin man. His doublet, cape, and breeches were all an inky black. He wore a high black hat with no feather. Behind him rode a servant dressed in grey. Though the track was sunlit, it was as though a small cloud of gloom had dropped its shadow into the mountain passes.

Brian wondered who the man was.

✛

Doctor Simeon Pincher had been in a bad temper when he met Doyle. But that wasn't surprising. Doctor Pincher had been in a bad temper for over a year.

In Ireland, as in England, the Irish Parliament was not in regular session, but met from time to time when there was specific business to transact. Last year, however, a Parliament had been called to assemble in Dublin, and a very impressive gathering it was proving to be. If the old parliaments in Tudor and Plantagenet times had mostly consisted of gentlemen from the English Pale around Dublin, this one had drawn men from every part of the island.

There had been some trouble at first. The Old English, mostly Catholic, had threatened not to take part; but they had finally settled down to business and proceeded, it had seemed to Pincher, in the right direction. The Oath of Supremacy had been affirmed as compulsory for all government officials. They must swear to recognise the king's spiritual authority over the Pope's, or lose their jobs. A move had been made to insist that every lawyer must swear, too. That would have ended the legal practice of loyal Catholics like Martin Walsh, and the idea was dropped. Recusant Catholics who refused to drop the old faith were to pay fines, although the Parliament, sadly, wasn't yet ready to compel them to attend the Church of Ireland. "I'd compel them," Pincher had firmly declared. And proclamations against foreign education and against the regular priests were also being issued. Despite its faults, however, the Parliament was moving in the right general direction. And the chief reason lay in its composition.

For the Protestants outnumbered the Catholics. A hundred and thirty-two to a hundred. A few of the Catholics were native Irish lords, but most were Old English. So who were all these Protestants? Were they the old guard who had chosen the Church of Ireland, men like the lord of Howth, or Doyle of Dublin? Some, to be sure. But the men who had swelled the Protestant numbers, the men who would make the difference in the long run, were the new arrivals: they were the men from the plantations. And that, strangely enough, was the thing that angered Pincher. Not that he was angry with the plantation men: far from it. He was angry with himself.

"It was lack of faith," he had confessed to his sister in a letter. "Want of courage." He had failed to invest.

The trouble had been the scale of the thing. When he had made his visit to Ulster seven years ago, he had seen the opportunities for a successful plantation. So when, after the Flight of the Earls and the confiscation of the Tyrone and Tyrconnell territories, there had been talk of an Ulster plantation, he had not taken up the farm he could have had, in the hope of something better. But such huge tracts of Ulster and Connacht had become available that the entire scale of operations had changed. The Undertakers were operating on a vast scale. The city of London had taken over the whole area of Derry and changed its name to Londonderry. Where it had been supposed that men would take on a thousand acres or two, developers were snapping up thousands, even tens of thousands, of acres.

The outside world was changing. The Dublin familiar to Walsh, Doyle, or even Pincher was that of the late Elizabethan age. But the last decade in London had seen a transformation. It was the age of the daring merchant-adventurer. King James, freed from his dour youth in Scotland, was indulging his taste for luxury. The English court was corrupt; greed and excess were the watchwords. Daring, grasping men looking for quick returns were encouraged. Such was the spirit of the men who undertook the plantation of Ulster.

And seeing such great fellows moving upon Ulster, Pincher had held back. His time was limited, he told himself:

he had to teach and preach. His capital was modest. The business was too big for him. This was an alien world of which—he had the honesty to admit it—he was a little afraid. And so he had hung back.

So now, seeing all these new gentlemen from the plantations coming into Dublin, he was overwhelmed by a sense of failure. Like one of the foolish virgins in the Gospel parable, he had been unprepared; when the moment came, he had been found wanting. Only the day before, one of the young scholars at Trinity College had come upon the good doctor sitting under a tree, lost in thought. As he was coming from behind, the doctor had not been aware of his approach, and the young scholar, drawing close, had heard Pincher murmur to himself, quite distinctly: "Predestined profit; justified returns." Then the doctor had sadly shaken his head; and the young scholar, puzzled by the words but feeling he should not be there, had tiptoed away.

Simeon Pincher, therefore, confessing his fault, was determined to remedy it; and until he had found a means of doing so, he lived every day of his life in a state of suppressed irritation.

The morning he spoke with Doyle, however, he had been preparing for a venture which, from everything he had heard, seemed likely to bring him, safely and securely, the profits which were surely by now his due. And he had been wondering how best to plan the journey he must make when, entering the precincts of Christ Church, he had caught sight of a small group of familiar figures; it occurred to him that one of them might be useful to him.

Doyle was the first one he acknowledged, with a polite inclination of the head. A man of substance, a pillar of the Church of Ireland, a member of the Trinity Guild. He owed Doyle a favour, too. The previous Sunday, he'd been due to preach in Christ Church, and as well as the usual collection of government officials from Dublin Castle, he'd known the congregation would be swelled by a number of Protestant

Members of Parliament. It was an opportunity for him to make a good impression. There was only one problem.

The aldermen of Dublin were supposed to accompany the mayor to the cathedral on Sundays. But since many of them were papists, they would often attend Mass themselves beforehand, bring the mayor ceremonially to the cathedral, deposit him in his seat, and then calmly leave for a local inn, where they'd have a few drinks, returning only after the sermon to escort the mayor out again. Not only was this the sort of casual Irish behaviour that appalled Pincher, but he dreaded it happening on the day he preached. It would look to the visitors as if the aldermen couldn't be bothered to hear him preach. So he had spoken to Doyle.

Sometimes in the past, Pincher had suspected that Doyle might not like him. But he had certainly stood by him last Sunday. No fewer than ten aldermen had turned up. When three of them had seemed about to leave, Doyle had given them such a look they had reluctantly sat down again. They had even stayed awake while he preached. He owed a debt of gratitude to Doyle for that. No question.

Beside Doyle stood young Walter Smith. A serious young man. A pity he was a papist. For that reason, normally, Pincher would have taken as little notice of him as possible. But he remembered that Walter Smith was married to Walsh the lawyer's girl, and he knew that Walsh and Doyle were cousins. Out of courtesy to Doyle, therefore, he nodded politely to Walter Smith as well.

The third man was Jeremiah Tidy. And now Doctor Pincher smiled.

"Good day, Master Tidy."

"Good day to Your Honour."

Thank God for Tidy. A reliable man. Three generations of service to Christ Church and the Church of Ireland. Jeremiah had been born and bred to it, knew every inch of the building from the extensive crypt to the top of the tower. He'd been only twenty years old when he'd been appointed sexton, on account of his long family connection, and he was still only twenty-five now. But with his slightly hunched shoulders and his little pointed beard, he had already achieved an agelessness that was pleasing to his employers.

It was Tidy who watched over the graves and tombs; Tidy who, with the verger, arranged the services and rang the great bell which regulated the life of the cathedral and city alike; Tidy who for a modest fee was always happy to take on extra jobs to oblige you. Reliable. Respectful. He had a great reverence for Trinity College, also. "It was my mother's family, the MacGowans, who supplied all the doors and windows in the college, Your Honour," he would remind Doctor Pincher. "And a fine place it is, I'm sure you will agree, Sir."

"It is indeed," Pincher would agree.

"A place well-suited, Your Honour, to a fine Cambridge scholar such as yourself." What was it in the sexton's soft voice that he found disconcerting? It was so polite, so respectful, so gently insinuating. Was it almost too respectful? He glanced at the sexton with a slight frown of uncertainty.

A Cambridge man like him: what did Tidy mean by it? Pincher used to wonder. If he meant anything at all. Was it possible, the learned doctor would ask himself, that the sexton had somehow come to hear about that foolish business at Cambridge? He couldn't imagine how. But why should he mention Cambridge in that way, whenever they met? Surely not, he told himself. It could not be. The business had been in another country, long ago. And besides . . .

It was Tidy, in fact, who had mentioned to him that the cathedral clerk had heard of an excellent living with some promising land becoming available shortly. And it was thanks to that timely information, and an immediate visit to the chapter clerk, that Pincher was now about to set off on another journey, southwards this time, that might bring him some of the profits which, surely by now, he deserved.

And it was when he had told the three men of the route he proposed to take, and asked for their advice about where to break his journey, that after thinking for a moment or two, Doyle had suggested:

"You could rest with the O'Byrnes at Rathconan, I should say."

On hearing the name, Pincher had blanched. A papist? A native Irish chief? Despite the diverse allegiances of the various O'Byrnes, despite the tradition of Irish hospitality to travellers that went back to the dawn of time, despite even the fact that Wicklow was now an English shire, Doctor Pincher had heard too many stories of the wild O'Byrnes in the past not to feel nervous at the prospect of such an encounter. But he saw young Walter Smith nod in agreement, and even Tidy looked perfectly calm at the prospect. Doyle, guessing his thoughts, smiled.

"You'll receive a good welcome there," he assured him. "The O'Byrnes of Rathconan are quite English in their ways."

And, no doubt to put him at his ease, Tidy chimed in:

"They'd have great respect, Your Honour, for a Cambridge scholar such as yourself."

✛

So here he was, approaching the house at Rathconan, and a scene that filled him with horror.

An Irish wake. Obviously, Doyle had not been aware of any death in the O'Byrne family when he had suggested the visit, and Pincher wondered what to do. Should he try to find another house? Some distance to the south lay the ruins of the ancient monastery of Glendalough. He could reach it by dusk, he supposed. Was there any sort of house there? He wasn't sure. He certainly had no wish to sleep in some peasant's hut, or out in the open in the wilds of the Wicklow Mountains. Should he turn away now, or ask for directions to another place? He was still hesitating when he saw a handsome, fair-haired young man, dressed in English style, coming towards him.

"I am Brian O'Byrne," he introduced himself politely, and gazed at him, Pincher noticed, with a pair of the most unusual green eyes.

Explaining his business, and that Doyle had sent him, Pincher apologised for his intrusion. "Doyle would not have known of my father's death when he sent you," the young man replied. "I am sorry for your trouble," Pincher answered. Could O'Byrne suggest another house in the area where he might find shelter? But young Brian wouldn't hear of it. "There's a chamber on the upper floor where you can rest the night comfortably enough—even if I cannot promise you silence." And so, uncertain where else to go, and not wishing to offend the young chief, Pincher rather unwillingly allowed himself to be escorted towards the old stone tower.

There was a great crowd of people outside, several hundred of them. Tables had been set up, well stocked with food and sweetmeats. Some of the guests were drinking wine, but most appeared to be imbibing ale or whiskey. Leaving his servant to see to the horses, and hoping the fellow would not be drunk when he needed him, he accompanied young Brian O'Byrne inside. He knew enough to be prepared for what must follow, as his host led him toward the room at the back of the tower. There, laid out on a large table covered with white sheets, was the body of Toirdhealbhach O'Byrne, washed and shaven, a fine-looking man, it had to be said, even when sunken in death with a crucifix in his folded hands. There were no others in the room, the company having all come to pay their respects long since, except for a middle-aged woman, a cousin of the deceased, who sat on a stool in a corner so that the dead man should not be left alone. The room was well lit by the small plantation of candles on a narrow table by the wall, whose waxy smoke gave the room a churchlike atmosphere.

Trying to avert his eyes from the cursed rosary, Pincher murmured, as he knew he must, that the former chief had been most handsomely laid out, and not knowing the gentleman himself, could only add, once again, that he was sorry for their

trouble. After that, he politely withdrew and followed his
young host up a spiral stair to a spacious chamber containing
a wooden bed, no worse than his own in Dublin. A short while
later, Brian O'Byrne reappeared bearing food and wine himself, which, with all the business of his father's wake going on,
was exceedingly civil of him, Pincher had to acknowledge. His
host also made clear to him that, should he at any time wish to
join the company below, he would be more than welcome. An
offer well-understood as kindly intended; though noncommittally, gratefully it was declined. And so for the rest of the
evening Doctor Pincher, being predestined for higher things
than the company of the Irish, kept to his chamber.

If only it weren't for the noise. The customary wailing of
the women, the wild songs of lament and the cries of grief, he
had always found disgusting. "In their grief," he had once written to his sister, "they are like savages." That, mercifully, had
been over before he arrived. But worse was to come.

Some aspects of the wake he could understand. The coming together of friends and neighbours, the sharing of bereave-
ment, the kind words, even the gentle telling of stories about
the departed one: all this, it seemed to him, was proper. He did
not even mind the food and drink, so long as everyone maintained sobriety. And indeed, when a child had died, or a parent been snatched away from the young family who needed
them, these wakes were sad and solemn affairs, when neighbours gave support and charity. He certainly saw no harm in
that. But when a man had lived a long life and death was
expected, when as well as telling kindly stories, the guests
started asking riddles, or playing games—even involving the
corpse himself—then it seemed to Pincher that the fundamen-
tal lack of seriousness, of decency—indeed, the pagan nature
and immorality—of the native Irish lay exposed. It was
hideous to him.

That in this ancient process there might be great wisdom;
that after the catharsis of grief fully expressed, there might be
closure; and in the affectionate games and humour—this sharing

of life with the dead—there might be a healing and a coming to terms with the awfulness of death: such notions had no place in his own, monotone picture of the universe. He had no idea why they did it.

The sun was setting when he heard the women singing— a slow, eerie, nasal chant that he knew was called a *cronan*— not unpleasing to the ear. These went on for some time as the dusk fell; and since he heard no other sounds, he assumed they were being listened to in silence. Looking out of his window as the last of the *cronans* ended, he could see that the first stars had appeared in the gloaming. And then, after only the shortest pause, the gentle drone of a single bagpipe started to rise into the air. And now even Doctor Pincher sat down on the bed to listen.

A piper's lament. The haunting strain echoed around the hillside, mournful yet strangely comforting. And despite himself, Pincher experienced that special sensation, the melancholy yet thrilling warmth about the heart that only the sound of the pipes can bring. He listened, and wished it might go on forever. But after a time it ended.

Then there was a little pause, followed soon after by a lilting tune, half soulful perhaps, but in which the more cheerful sound of a fiddle joined beside the piper like a good companion. The melody was pleasant, Pincher supposed; but it seemed to him that there had been enough music, and that it would be more fitting if, having paid their respects, the guests were now to take their leave. He was glad when the music stopped.

He lay down on the bed and closed his eyes. From below, he could hear the faint sounds of conversation, even of laughter. It had been a long day. He hoped that he might fall asleep. In the morning, he thought, he would leave at the earliest opportunity. If he could just shut out the voices and lie very still, he could begin to drift into sleep. He breathed slowly, kept his eyes shut. He felt himself drifting.

And then the fiddles began. Loudly. Several of them, accompanied by a whistle. A merry sound. There were shouts, laughter. By all that was unholy: they were playing a jig. He started in fury from his bed and rushed to the window. Torches were being lighted outside. He could see the company all round the tower. They were dancing. It was like a pagan orgy or a scene from the infernal regions. They were dancing a jig.

He gazed in horror. Not only were they merrily dancing, but the jig went on and on, as if to see who could dance the longest without dropping.

And now—he had known it from the beginning, of course—but now, having heard, having seen with his own eyes, having looked down upon this dreadful jig, it seemed to Doctor Pincher that he understood with a new and ghastly clarity that, even if they smiled at you or put on English clothes, these Irish papists were, indeed, lower than the beasts. They were all, all destined for eternal damnation. There could be no possible doubt of it. With a cry of anguish, he turned round, threw himself facedown upon the bed, and tried to stop his ears.

But the dancing and the music went on. Some of the dances were jigs; others he did not recognise. He had heard that the Irish performed a sword dance. For all he knew, they might be doing that. What he knew for certain was that he could get no rest.

Perhaps, if he could distract his mind from the sounds below, he could get to sleep. He tried thinking about the journey he was to make the following day. That prospect, at least, brought him some comfort.

Both Trinity College and Christ Church Cathedral were endowed with many lands—on which, from time to time, good leases might be obtained; and he had long been hoping to obtain one of these. But the opportunity that had now presented itself was even better.

For of all the Protestant landlords in Ireland, none was richer, or more godly, than Richard Boyle, the great Protestant settler. Having acquired, from the reign of Queen Elizabeth, vast tracts of land in Munster, he was the patron of numerous livings, from which a good Protestant preacher might derive an income. "I've just heard there's a living coming free any day in north Munster. And you're just the kind of godly man that Boyle would approve of," the Chapter Clerk had told him. "It's a little wild there, however. The land will have to be cleared before you can grow anything. Would you mind that?"

"Oh no," said Pincher. "I shouldn't mind at all."

Woodlands. For centuries, the vast forests that had once covered most of the island had been a valuable source of timber. Mostly, it had been exported. Some of the greatest English cathedrals had roof beams of Irish oak. And during the huge building of Tudor England, timber had been increasingly in demand. Gradually, therefore, the forests of Ireland had yielded to the axe. Most of the best oak trees in the Dublin region had already gone, but farther south there were still plenty of fine old forests waiting to be cut down. And the harvesting of woodlands provided an instant, one-time cash crop that could make a new lease highly profitable for an investor. Sometimes entire hillsides would be stripped in a matter of months.

"I shall let in light," Pincher had declared with feeling, "where before there was darkness."

The track across the hills, he had been told, led past some of the finest views in all Ireland. In a couple of days, it was to be hoped, he would reach his destination spiritually refreshed. He closed his eyes and tried to imagine the journey. And although he was conscious of the music outside, he might have slipped into unconsciousness once or twice before, at about midnight, he became aware that the music had finally stopped and he felt ready to sink, at last, into a deep sleep.

Indeed, for a moment he almost supposed he was dreaming when a sudden creak made him sit up with a start, to see that the heavy oak door of the chamber was slowly opening.

There were so many sleeping in the rooms below and the hall that they had left candles flickering all over the house so that people would not fall over each other if they moved about in the night. It was by the light of several candles, therefore, that Pincher could now see, framed in the doorway, the terrible figure who was about to enter his room. A wild Irishman's dress, bare legs, a pale face with staring eyes, and a great, ugly mass of hair falling in ringlets to below his shoulders—faced with such an apparition, it was no surprise that Doctor Pincher should have convulsively clutched at the bedclothes and opened his mouth, ready to cry out "Help" or "Murder" if the creature took another step.

But Tadhg O'Byrne did not enter yet. He stood at the door, preferring to sway a little, cautiously, before committing himself to a further step into the unknown. He was not drunk. He might have been a little while ago, but he was rather in a state where his thoughts and actions, though carefully considered, were somewhat slow. He had tried to sleep on the floor beside the bench in the main hall upon which his wife already lay deeply unconscious. But he could not seem to get comfortable. He had considered going outside. The night was not cold, and a good Irishman like himself, as he was proud to say, would be as happy sleeping on the ground like a cattleman, or a hero from olden times, as lying about in a house. But on balance he had decided to rest inside and, walking carefully over several bodies he had managed, taking his time, to negotiate his way to this place where he had encountered a door. Unable to see the quaking preacher in the darkness, he now very reasonably enquired:

"Is there room for a body to sleep in there?"

The question, being asked in Irish, was not understood by Pincher, but clearly some response was required.

"Go away," the philosopher cried.

The reply, in English, surprised Tadhg O'Byrne, but was perfectly understood. He studied it. The first thing about the answer, apart from the language, was that it came only from a single source. He listened for the sounds of others breathing but heard none. Framing his next question in English therefore:

"Is it a woman you have with you?" he obligingly asked.

"Certainly not!" hissed Doctor Pincher.

Though he was not trained in philosophy, it was clear to Tadhg, after only another moment or two, that the figure in the dark had, willfully or not, been guilty of a non sequitur. For if there were no others in the room, and the stranger was not engaged with a woman, then, *ipso facto*, there was no need for him to go away. Not wishing to offend, he went over this in his mind again to make sure it was correct; but he could find no weakness in his reasoning. And he had just come to this definite conclusion when Doctor Pincher made a great mistake. Speaking very slowly and clearly, on the assumption that the figure before him must, by its every appearance, be both drunk and stupid, he carefully enunciated:

"This . . . is . . . my . . . bed."

"Bed?" This was a new consideration. "Is it a bed you have there?" Tadhg might despise the presumed decadence of his kinsman Brian when it came to feather beds, but at this moment, the prospect of sharing a comfortable bed rather than the hard floor seemed to him a good one. Entering now, and closing the door behind him, he made his way with surprising accuracy to the bed and stretched out his hand to where, shrinking in disgust and some terror from him, Doctor Pincher had inadvertently supplied the very space he was seeking. "There now," he said companionably, "there's room enough for the two of us."

And he would have fallen asleep at once beside the startled preacher if a sudden curiosity had not seized him. Who might this English stranger be who was given a chamber to himself at the wake of O'Byrne of Rathconan?

"A fine man," he opined into the inky darkness. "There's no question, Toirdhealbhach O'Byrne was a fine man." He paused, expecting some response, but the stranger beside him was as silent as the corpse below. "Had you known him long?" he enquired.

"I did not know him at all," said Pincher's voice, coldly.

It was clear to Pincher that his life was not in any immediate danger from this loathsome figure. The main question in his mind was whether to get off the bed and sleep on the hard floor himself, or to remain where he was and endure the closeness, and the smell, of his presence.

"But you came to his wake from respect, no doubt," said Tadhg. English or not, one couldn't deny that this was a proper if unusual thing to do. "Would you mind if I ask your name? Myself being Tadhg O'Byrne," he obligingly supplied.

Why was it, Pincher wondered, that these Irish must have such barbarous names? The sound of them—Tighe O'Byrne beside him, Turlock O'Byrne the corpse below—was bad enough; their spellings, Tadhg and Toirdhealbhach, defied all reason. He placed a silent curse upon them all. He certainly had no wish to engage in conversation with Tadhg; on the other hand, if he refused to reply, it might make the creature angry.

"I am Doctor Simeon Pincher, of Trinity College, Dublin," he said reluctantly.

"Of Trinity College?" An Englishman and a heretic, therefore. But a scholar, perhaps, all the same. "You'd be learned, I dare say," he ventured, "in Latin and Greek?"

"I lecture in Greek," Pincher said firmly, "in logic and in theology. I preach at Christ Church. I am a fellow of Emmanuel College, Cambridge." He hoped this impressive list might reduce his unwelcome companion to silence.

Tadhg might have little use for Englishmen and heretics, but he was impressed. This was a gentleman and a scholar, a learned man who had come all the way from Dublin to pay his respects to a leading O'Byrne. Courtesy was due. He lay there in silence, wondering what he should say to such a distinguished person. And as he did so, a further thought occurred to him. Here was an important man of learning sharing a bed with him, and no doubt imagining that he, Tadhg O'Byrne, was a poor sort of fellow. He owed it to himself to let the stranger know that he, too, was a person of some account. Not his equal in learning, to be sure, but a gentleman like himself at least.

"And you wouldn't know, I don't suppose, who I might be?" he suggested.

"I suppose not," sighed Doctor Pincher.

"Yet it's myself," Tadhg announced proudly, "that is the rightful heir to Rathconan."

The effect of this statement was highly satisfactory. He felt the doctor's body give a small start in the bed.

"But I understood that Brian . . ."

"Ah." Now Tadhg bent to his theme. "He has it. That he has. But has he the right to it?" He paused to let the question establish itself in the surrounding dark. "He has not. It's myself that is in the senior line, you see. His family took it, but they've no right to it. Their claim is false," he ended triumphantly.

The fact that under the very law, that ancient Irish law and custom, which he so ardently defended, Brian's ancestors had been rightfully chosen and his own rejected, the fact that as a good Irishman he had no claim to Brian's position whatever and that any good Irishman would have told him so in no uncertain terms, and the even more astounding fact that it was only under the English law, not the Irish, that the claim of the eldest son had any particular significance—all these facts had miraculously been dissolved in the blackness of the night, or rather, they had been hastily buried underground by Tadhg, like a criminal burying a body.

"So you mean," Pincher sought to clarify, "that Brian O'Byrne does not in fact possess a clear title to this property?"

"He does not. Under English law." He did not like to say it, but he knew that this would be the way to impress a Trinity College man. "Under the king's law, he's no right to it at all. It's myself who is the rightful heir."

"That," said Doctor Pincher, "is very interesting. I think," he added after a short pause, "that I should like to go to sleep."

And Tadhg O'Byrne, having made his point to his own satisfaction, was contented enough to fall into unconsciousness, which he did immediately. But Pincher did not sleep. He had no wish to sleep just yet. Instead, he lay there thinking. The information he had just received, if correct, was highly significant. Not, of course, that the disgusting wretch lying beside him would ever derive any benefit from it. God forbid. But if the kindly young man who had welcomed him to his house had any sort of defective title to the property, there were legal ways in which he might be dispossessed. Pincher wondered if anyone else in Dublin knew about this. Possibly not. The value of an estate like Rathconan would be many times greater than the profits he had in prospect down in Munster, no matter how closely the oak trees grew.

He wondered how he might turn this unexpected news to his advantage.

⁜

For some time now, it had seemed to Orlando that his father was out of sorts. He was conscious of these small changes of mood because he saw his father almost every day.

Though he was sixteen, Orlando was still at home. Martin Walsh had quietly resisted the several attempts of Lawrence to have Orlando sent to Salamanca. "No, I'd rather have him with me," he would say. "He can get a fair education from the teachers we have here. I shall teach him the law myself." Once, overhearing an argument between his brother and his father, Orlando had heard his father declare: "Have a care, Lawrence. The government men in Dublin Castle are suspicious of foreign colleges. My loyalty is not in question, but remember that there are men in the Castle who would like to forbid Catholic lawyers to practice. They already know very well that you're a Jesuit. As it's Orlando who will inherit this estate after I am gone, it may be wiser that they don't see him going off to a seminary. It's better they see him safely at my side." Orlando heard Lawrence murmur something in reply, but could not make out the words. He did hear his father answer, very firmly: "I think not. Speak of it no more."

Martin Walsh usually went into Dublin to transact business a day or two each week. Quite often, he would take Orlando with him, and it was easy to see, wherever he went, how much his honest, cautious father was liked and respected.

"A lawyer," Martin would tell him, "comes to know a great many men's secrets. But men must know they can trust him with their confidences. A lawyer knows everything, Orlando, but tells nothing. Remember that."

Sometimes, he would genially point to a pretty girl and ask Orlando if he'd like to marry her. This had fallen into a comfortable routine. Orlando would always say that she wasn't pretty enough and tell his father he'd have to do better. Then his father would ask him how many children he wanted. "Six boys and six girls: a round dozen," he'd say. And Martin would look pleased.

Often as not, they would call in on his sister. Anne had three girls already, and they still hoped for a boy, whom they would call Maurice. She had filled out a little since her marriage, and she was always busy with her household and her children, but in other ways it seemed to Orlando that she was still the same. Her husband Walter had proved to be a great success. The older Orlando grew, the more he liked him. A kindly, manly fellow, he was obviously devoted to Anne. Though it was certain that he would one day inherit a large fortune from his father, old Peter Smith would proudly say: "He's no need of me, though. He's already a man of substance on his own account." Old Peter Smith preferred to spend his time out at the estate he held in Fingal, but Walter and Anne spent most of the time in the city with their children. They had a handsome, gabled house on Saint Nicholas Street near the old Tholsel town hall. The only subject that was never mentioned was the drowning of Patrick Smith. But Orlando felt sure that his sister must be happy with her life now, even so.

It would be at the end of the day, sometimes, after they had ridden back to the house in Fingal, that Orlando would notice his father looking a little tired and depressed. He supposed it might just be fatigue after the long hours of business. Martin's hair was mostly grey now. When he sat in his chair in the evening and gazed down thoughtfully at the floor, it couldn't be denied that his face looked somewhat haggard and older. Occasionally, Orlando would observe him suddenly wince and shake his head. But then, when he rose from this chair, Orlando would see him straighten his back, take a deep breath, push out his chest, and give himself a little nod of approval. And then he would reassure himself that his father was still strong and would be with him for many a year.

It was unusual for his father to conduct Dublin business out at the house, so Orlando was surprised one evening, as they were riding home, when his father remarked: "I have received a message from Doctor Pincher. He wishes to call upon me tomorrow morning. On a private matter, he says." Though he had only occasionally caught sight of the tall, thin doctor of Trinity College, the black image of Pincher crossing the Plain of Bird Flocks the evening before Anne departed for the seminary was still indelibly imprinted on his mind. "What did he want?" he asked his father. "I have no idea," Walsh replied.

It was with great curiosity, therefore, that, just before eleven o'clock the next day, Orlando watched as the single horseman, thin as a quill and dressed in black, drew up the sunlit path to the house. There he was greeted by his father, who took him inside. He wished he could have gone in with them to listen.

⁘

The two men sat opposite each other across a table. Walsh, comfortably dressed in a spruce-green doublet, looked exactly the member of the gentry that he was. Doctor Pincher was all in black, except for a narrow white collar with the thinnest possible embroidery of lace.

"I came to ask if you would act for me," he began, "in a matter that I wish to be secret."

"Such requests are not unusual," Walsh answered easily. "But we have never had dealings before."

"You are surprised, perhaps, that I should entrust such a matter to . . ." He hesitated.

"A Catholic?"

"Indeed." Pincher inclined his head politely. For though he had no doubt that his Protestant faith made him, in God's eyes, the superior of the papist, Pincher could not help being uncomfortably aware that Walsh was by birth the lauded gentleman which he was not.

"I am glad to entrust myself to a Catholic lawyer, Sir," he allowed himself a smile, "though I might hesitate to go to a Catholic surgeon." It was not often that Doctor Pincher made a joke; but this was one of them.

Walsh did his best to smile.

"Please proceed," he said.

"It is a question of title," Pincher began.

His journey down into Munster had been a great success. The living with its small church and smaller house was perfect. He could preach there now and then, and put a poor curate in to take care of the daily ministry. But the land was excellent. He had found agents who would cut the trees and carry the timber down to the coast for shipment. The prices offered were excellent. It was clear to him that shipping even half the woodland would yield him a handsome profit. Nor had he had any difficulty in recommending himself to Boyle, who had already been assured by the doctor's obliging friends at Christ Church and Trinity that Pincher was, indeed, just the sort of godly man to be encouraged. He had secured the living at once. But the prospect of this God-given increase in his wealth, the new and brighter light it shed upon his life, had strengthened his faith and given him courage to aim at even higher things.

Having gone down to the port of Waterford to make his enquiries about the shipping, he had decided to return to Dublin in a coastal vessel that had just been leaving. It had been an easy and pleasant voyage. And as he had watched the coastline slip by, he had found his mind repeatedly going back to that strange night he had spent at Rathconan. Whether it was blind luck or the unseen hand of the deity, there seemed no doubt that a potentially important piece of information had been placed before him.

As he explained to Walsh what he wanted, the lawyer's face remained impassive, though once or twice, a slight twitch might have betrayed some emotion.

"So," he summarised, "you believe that under English law, Brian O'Byrne may not have a valid title to the Rathconan estate. You wish me in the first place to investigate this matter. If the information proves to be correct, you may wish to retain me as counsel should you, alone or with others, wish to make application to obtain that estate."

"Correct."

There had already been active voices from government officials and other greedy people urging a thorough investigation of defective land titles, in precisely the hope of finding native Irish estates that could be legally taken away from their customary owners, so that the English crown could either take them or release them to its friends or onto the market.

"So that, should there be any fault with the title, you will have this information before any of the others, who will doubtless be eager to seize Brian O'Byrne's inheritance from him."

"Precisely," said Doctor Pincher.

"Should young O'Byrne's title be found defective, is there any other claimant?"

"Perhaps. A mere Irishman of no account who, I am sure, has no document of title of any kind."

"Might I ask," Walsh inquired, "why you have done me the honour to come to me, and not to another?"

"I am generally informed, Sir, that you are more fully acquainted with the landholdings of this part of Ireland than any man living."

This, as it happened, was probably correct. For five generations, since long before the monasteries were dissolved by

King Henry VIII, even since Plantagenet times, Martin Walsh's ancestors had been involved in the legal affairs of the church and lay estates all down the eastern side of Ireland. There was hardly an estate in Leinster or Meath that the family didn't know well, and many in Ulster and Munster, too. The knowledge had been passed down the generations. Martin had already, in his gentle way, been feeding it to young Orlando for some years. If Pincher wanted discreet investigations made about Rathconan, he couldn't have come to a better place.

Walsh nodded. Then he leant forward slightly.

"I am but a lawyer, Sir, and you are a philosopher. May I put to you one other question which I myself am not learned enough to answer?"

"I am at your service," said Doctor Pincher.

"Well, then," said the lawyer softly, "it is this, and pertains to philosophy rather than to law. Even if, in strict law, we find that Brian O'Byrne has no sound English title to Rathconan, should we be troubled in our conscience, would you judge, by the young man's loss of it?"

"I should say no."

"How so?"

"Because he holds it, if not by law, then by a barbarous custom, and not honestly."

"By the custom of the mere Irish." He nodded. "That would be so, no doubt. And Irish custom, being barbarous, has no moral claim to our consideration. It is, so to speak, unnatural."

"You have it," said Doctor Pincher, pleased that they had understood each other.

Martin Walsh gazed at him without expression. It would have amused him to ask the philosopher whether, in his personal view, avarice should still be accounted a deadly sin; but he forbore to do so. Instead, he quietly observed:

"I should tell you now that there are some, even in Dublin Castle, who wish to proceed with caution. If, as may be supposed, young O'Byrne of Rathconan is well-affected, those persons will think it wiser not to dispossess him of lands that many will believe he holds rightly. There has been no rebellion here. Nor has he abandoned his lands like Tyrone. Whatever the law, such people would say, such dispossession would be unwise and only stir up further trouble." It was, indeed, exactly the counsel he would have given the English government himself.

"You and I," Pincher said, "would think otherwise, I hope."

Was it possible, Walsh wondered, that this interview was a trap of some kind? Might Pincher have been sent by either the government or, more likely, some faction to test his views and the extent of his loyalty? It was possible, but unlikely. His views were the same as most of the Old English he knew, and would have been expected in Dublin Castle. But his loyalty wasn't in question.

No, his judgement was that Pincher was playing exactly the game he said he was. Even after living seventeen years in Ireland, the Trinity man was so blinkered by his own prejudices that he imagined that he, Martin Walsh, because he was Old English, would happily aid in the dispossessing of this coreligionist O'Byrne because O'Byrne was Irish. Did Pincher have any idea of the curious mutual respect that had arisen as the Walshes of Carrickmines beat off the raids of the O'Byrnes down the centuries? Had he any notion that there was at least a trace of Walsh blood in the veins of young Brian O'Byrne, let alone that Walsh's own daughter Anne was married to a man who, although his name was Walter Smith, was almost certainly an O'Byrne by natural descent? Such deep and tangled roots would have been quite unknown to Pincher.

"I will make enquiries," he replied. "But I should counsel you now that I do not know whether this business can be brought to a successful conclusion."

Soon after this, Doctor Pincher left, with the promise that Walsh would write to him when he had any news.

It was early afternoon when he called Orlando to walk out with him.

"Where are we going, Father?" he asked.

"Portmarnock."

There was a light breeze, agreeably cool. It gave him pleasure that Orlando enjoyed keeping him company. The boy himself could not possibly imagine the comfort that this presence brought to his father, nor would Martin have burdened him by letting him guess. So they walked together, for the most part, in silence. No doubt his son was curious about the visit of Doctor Pincher, but there might be reasons why it was better he should know nothing; and in the meantime, there were a few, more important things he wished to say.

They had just started down the long slope that led across the coastal open ground when he glanced at his son and quietly asked:

"Tell me, Orlando, would you ever break the law?"

"No, Father."

"So I should hope." He walked on in silence for a few moments. "I have often spoken to you of the confidence and trust that must be the rule between a client and his lawyer. That trust is sacred. To break it is like breaking the law. It is against everything I stand for. It is a treason."

"I know, Father."

"You do." Martin Walsh drew a deep breath and nodded to himself thoughtfully. "And yet, my son," he continued quietly, "there may be a time in your life when you have to consider doing such a thing. It is possible that there may be larger matters that you must consider."

There was no need to say more. He knew that Orlando would remember what he had said. He turned his mind back to his own immediate problem. The course of action he was considering would certainly be a betrayal. Yet was it the right thing to do? Perhaps. If it were ever discovered, it might make him powerful enemies; but when he considered all the circumstances, he was inclined to take the chance and to act now. He had a feeling that there was not much time.

As they came in sight of Portmarnock, he turned to Orlando again.

"When I'm uncertain what to do, I always pray," he remarked. "How do you pray, Orlando?"

"I say the prayers I know, Father."

"Good. But they are only the means, you know. The words of the prayers are a way of leading us to empty our minds of all other considerations until we are ready to hear the voice of God."

"Do you ever hear a voice, Father?"

"Like a human voice, Orlando? No, though some have done so. God's voice is usually silent, best heard in silence."

When they reached the holy well, Walsh knelt down and prayed quietly for some time while Orlando, not wishing to interrupt him, knelt at a short distance and tried to do the same. When Walsh had finished, he gazed thoughtfully at the well for a few moments, and then, motioning to Orlando to join him, began to slowly walk home. They hardly spoke, because Walsh wanted to remain in his silent, rather abstracted state; but when they were halfway home, he put out his hand and allowed it to rest upon the boy's shoulder for a little while.

When they entered the house again, he told Orlando to prepare himself for a long journey the following day. Then he retired to his chamber and, selecting a large sheet of paper, he spread it on a table and sat down to write. He wrote carefully, taking several hours over the task, and carefully folding and sealing the letter with wax when he had done. Having finished, he felt so tired that he did not bother to eat but went straight to his rest.

The next morning, however, he was up at first light, feeling refreshed.

✢

When Orlando received his instructions from his father, he was greatly astonished. He had never been asked to do such a thing before.

"You are to go into Dublin to your cousin Doyle. Tell him that I shall come to him myself by noon. Meanwhile, here is a note from me to him, asking that he supply you with anything you ask. You will ask for a fresh, strong horse and a change of clothes. Then I wish you to leave Dublin without being recognised, and to ride south." Now he produced the sealed letter he had written the evening before. "You are to keep this with you at all times. On no account must it fall into other hands. You will reach your destination tonight, and remain there until morning. Then you can return the way you came."

"Where am I going?" asked Orlando.

"Rathconan," answered his father. Then he gave him the rest of his instructions.

⁘

The day was fine, the sky clear, and Orlando's heart was singing as he set out on his task. The contents of his father's letter were unknown to him, but to be sent out on a mission like this, with the injunction that he was never in his life to tell a soul what he had done, was a thrilling prospect. The secret errands he had performed for his sister when he was a little boy had been a fine adventure; but for his father, whom he so revered, to entrust him with such an important affair—it made him swell with pride and happiness.

He accomplished the change in Dublin easily enough, and with his face half hidden by a battered, wide-brimmed hat, he set out from Dublin's gates, through Donnybrook, towards the Wicklow Mountains. No one from Dublin watched him as he cleared the southern orchards; no one could possibly have guessed where he was headed. Sometimes cantering easily, sometimes at a walk, he crossed the plain and made his way up into the hills. At noon, he rested for an hour; and by late afternoon he was at Rathconan.

Following his father's instructions, he did not give his name, but when Brian O'Byrne came out to see what he wanted, he gave him the letter and explained that he was ordered to watch O'Byrne read it. Slightly surprised, Brian led him inside, where they went up to the hall.

He was quite surprised to find O'Byrne such a young-looking man, only a few years older than himself; with his tousel of fair hair he seemed almost boyish. But there was a quiet look of authority in his strange green eyes that impressed Orlando. Sitting at an oak table, O'Byrne read slowly and carefully, his face once or twice registering some surprise. Then he got up, fetched paper, pen, and ink, and wrote down a few words. When this was done, he glanced at Orlando.

"You are his son?"

"Yes."

"Do you know what is in this letter?"

"My father said it was better I should not know."

"He is right." Brian O'Byrne nodded.

The contents of the letter had considerably shaken him. It told him in the briefest terms that his inheritance might be at risk, and counselled him to take immediate action. Martin Walsh had been appalled not so much at the naked avarice of Pincher—God knows the lawyer was hardly a stranger to avarice in all conditions of men—but at the absolute political folly of the legalised theft of land from a well-disposed Irishman like Brian O'Byrne. It was precisely the sort of stupidity on the part of the New English which could still, one day, make the island ungovernable. And it was this higher sense of duty which, after his prayers, had decided him to break his duty of confidence and intervene.

It was quite often the case that the English government had regularised the land titles of men like Brian O'Byrne. He knew one or two officials in Dublin Castle who had similar views to his own, and whose names he had given young O'Byrne in his letter. A discreet word with Doyle might also bring some other Protestant gentlemen in to help. But with the Parliament and their friends, let alone Doctor Pincher looking for such opportunities, he advised O'Byrne to go down to Dublin quietly and without delay, "before the hounds pick up your scent." For reasons he could not give, however, his own part in this affair must never be known. "I have broken a lawyer's oath to tell you this," he wrote frankly.

"Tell your father, Orlando Walsh, that the O'Byrnes of Rathconan are forever in his debt," Brian said with feeling.

"I am to watch you burn the letter," said Orlando.

"You shall." O'Byrne led him to the fire, and together they watched until the incriminating letter was harmless ashes.

"You must eat with me," said Brian.

"I'm to sleep in the stable and not give my name," said Orlando.

"Ah yes, of course." O'Byrne smiled. "But I promise you this, Orlando Walsh, I shall know you as a friend another time."

⚜

Orlando set out at dawn the next day. The sky over the Wicklow Mountains was clear. A soft breeze was coming from the sea. He was feeling so proud of himself, having accomplished his mission to the letter, and he could not wait to let his father know.

In the middle of the morning, the wind changed and began to come form the north, a little colder. And as he reached the high slope from which the whole panorama of Dublin Bay spread out, he saw that a long, greyish bank of cloud had moved down from Ulster and was already casting a dull shadow over Fingal in the distance. He had made good progress, however, and it was not even noon when he entered the city and rode into the courtyard of his cousin Doyle's house.

Doyle and his wife were not at home, but a servant told him: "He says you're to ride on as soon as you arrive." As

Orlando had planned to do exactly that, he quickly changed to his own horse and set off at once.

The shadow of the cloud bank passed over him just after he crossed the Liffey. As he rode on, the greyness of the day became more encompassing and oppressive, although once or twice, away to his right, he saw the sun's light harshly cut through the cloud in a silvery gash over the sea. His heart was full of happiness as he rode across the familiar plain. He smiled as a flock of pale seagulls suddenly rose from the field in front of him and wheeled loudly in the iron-grey sky. And he felt a surge of warmth as, passing through a familiar little wood, he came in sight of the house.

He was surprised to see his sister at the door.

"Hello, Anne," he said.

"Thank God you've come. He's been waiting for you."

"I know." He smiled. But she gave him a strange look.

"You don't know, Orlando." He was starting into the house, but she put a restraining hand on his arm. "You can't see him for a few minutes yet. Lawrence is with him." She took a deep breath. "Your father's been taken very poorly, Orlando. He's not well at all."

Orlando felt himself go pale.

"When?"

"Early this morning. They sent word to us in Dublin and we came at once. Nobody knew where you were."

"I was doing something for Father."

"He said as much. He said you'd be coming by our cousin Doyle's, so we sent a message there to tell you to come home at once. What in the world were you doing?" And seeing him shake his head: "It doesn't matter anyway. He can still talk, at least. Stay downstairs. I'm going to tell them you're here." And she left him.

He waited alone. The house seemed strangely quiet. Some time passed. Then Lawrence came down the stairs.

His brother was dressed in a black soutane. He was looking grave. When he saw Orlando, he did not smile, but he came to him and took his arm gently, in a kindly gesture.

"You must prepare yourself. Our father has suffered a crisis. It was an apoplexy, and you will find him greatly altered since yesterday. Are you ready for this?" Orlando nodded dumbly. "Good. I have been praying with him. But your presence will bring him great comfort." He paused and glanced at Orlando curiously. "Where were you, by the way?"

"I cannot tell you, Lawrence. I was doing something for Father."

"You can surely give me some account of your absence?" The question was not unkind, but there was the faintest hint of disapproval in it.

"I promised Father."

"I see." A small frown crossed his face, but the Jesuit smoothed it away. He glanced up the stairs to where Anne had now appeared. "He is ready?"

"Yes." Anne gave Orlando an encouraging smile.

"Is he dying?" asked Orlando.

Nobody replied.

He went up the heavy wooden staircase, and went to the door of his father's chamber. It was ajar. He pushed it open.

His father was alone. He was propped up in a half-sitting position on the carved oak bed. His face was strangely sallow, his eyes sunken, but he gazed at Orlando fondly and did his best to smile.

"I am sorry you should see me like this, Orlando."

For a moment, Orlando was unable to speak.

"I am sorry, too." It was not what he wanted to say at all, but he could not think of the right words.

"Come." His father motioned him to approach. "Did you do as I asked?"

"Yes, Father. Everything."

"That is good. I am proud of you. Did he say anything?"

"That he was forever in your debt."

"He burned the letter?"

"Yes. I watched."

"Not that its discovery would matter much now." His

father spoke the words more to himself than to Orlando. He sighed. The sigh had a faint rasp. Then he smiled at Orlando. "You did well. Very well."

Orlando wanted so much to say something, to tell his father how much he loved him. But he did not know how. He stood there helplessly. His father was silent for a few moments, his eyes closed. He seemed to be gathering his strength. Then he opened them and looked into Orlando's eyes. It seemed to Orlando that he saw a trace of urgency and fear in his father's gaze.

"Do you remember your promise to me, Orlando? About your marriage?"

"Yes, Father. Of course I do."

"You promise me to have children."

"I did."

"You will?"

"Yes, Father. A dozen at least. I promise."

"That is good. Thank you. Take my hand." Orlando took his father's hand. It felt rather cold. His father gently squeezed his hand. "No father, Orlando, could have a better son." He smiled, then closed his eyes.

A little while passed in silence except for his father's breathing, in which there was faint, wheezing sound. Orlando stood there, still holding his father's cold hand.

Then, without opening his eyes, his father called out quietly: "Anne."

And from outside the door, his sister quickly appeared.

"God be with you, my son," his father said. Then Anne took him out.

She told him to go downstairs. A few moments later, he saw Lawrence going back up. Then he waited, miserably. About half an hour later, Anne came down and told him that his father was gone.

✦

Early the next morning, Orlando walked out alone. The sky was still grey. He walked at a quiet, steady pace along the path past the deserted chapel and was soon on the long slope that led towards the sea. He hadn't encountered a soul when he reached the holy well at Portmarnock.

He knelt down beside the well and started to pray. But though the words came, he could not seem to concentrate as his father had told him he should.

He stood up. He walked three times round the well, saying the paternoster four times. He knew that such little ceremonies could be effective. Then he knelt again. Still he could not find the quietness he sought. He tried to think of the old saint, whose gentle presence blessed the waters of the well. But still nothing came. Then he thought of his father and whispered:

"I promise, Father. I promise. A dozen at least." Then he burst into tears.

It was more than an hour before he got back to the house. He found Lawrence, looking for him outside.

"Where were you, Orlando?" he asked.

"At the well at Portmarnock," answered Orlando truthfully.

"Ah." Lawrence looked thoughtful. "I think it is time," he said, not unkindly, "that you went to Salamanca."

⇥ 1626 ⇤

At the age of thirty-four, Anne Smith had every reason to be grateful. She had known sadness: she had suffered a couple of miscarriages and lost two children, both boys, in infancy. But most of the mothers she knew had experienced similar misfortunes: these were wounds that healed. She was still blessed with four healthy children, three girls and a boy; and there might be more in the future.

And then there was her brother Orlando. She had half expected him to marry as soon as he returned from Salamanca. She knew about the promise he had made to their father and his intense desire not to let his father down. Once, when she had remarked with a laugh that he might have to be content with less than a dozen children, he had replied: "At least I can try." He had spoken the words with such earnestness that she had hardly liked to say anything more. Certainly, there was no shortage of families glad to marry their daughters to young Orlando Walsh. But he had taken a few years, trained to be a lawyer like his father, and then settled down with a pleasant girl from one of the Catholic gentry families of the old English Pale. He was managing the estate well. Many of his father's clients had come to him. Anne had not heard that his wife Mary was pregnant yet; but they'd only been married a year. On Orlando's account, therefore, it seemed to her that there was every reason to be optimistic.

But in the wider context of the world also, there were reasons why a good Catholic family like the Walshes might feel a modest sense of hope.

England had a new king. If old King James had been the son of that ardent Catholic Mary Queen of Scots, the Presbyterian lords of his native Scotland had seen to it that James himself, though reluctant to persecute Catholics, remained firmly Protestant. But now the old king had died, and a year ago his son King Charles—a serious young man— had shocked his Protestant subjects by marrying the sister of the most Catholic king of France. Where Charles's own religious sympathies might lie was not yet clear. "But it must surely be a cause for rejoicing," Anne had remarked to her brother Lawrence, "that the king has chosen one of the true faith to be his bride." And though Lawrence was always cautious, even he had answered, "It is to be hoped," and given her an encouraging smile.

Ireland was a strange place. The Earls had fled; Munster and Ulster were being planted; Protestants had the upper hand in Parliament. Yet in the almost two decades since her marriage, it seemed to Anne that the everyday life of most ordinary Catholics had changed surprisingly little. The Protestants might pass legislation against them, but the laws were still only fitfully applied. Even here in Dublin, the very centre of English rule, life was full of curious anomalies. Christ Church Cathedral, that great medieval monument to Irish Catholic tradition, was now the home of the so-called Church of Ireland—which of course was Protestant and English. The government men from Dublin Castle and the Protestants of Trinity College went there. But almost every parish church in the city was serving a community of merchants and craftsmen who were still mostly Catholic. By law, Catholic priests were forbidden. "But we don't let that worry us," her kindly husband Walter would cheerfully remark. In their own parish church, Smith and his fellow merchants supported no fewer than six Catholic priests; but if any official should ask who they were, he'd be told: "They are singing men." Of course, everyone knew they were priests. Even Doctor Pincher probably realised. But the men in Dublin Castle had no wish to offend the rich and useful merchants of Dublin, and the six priests were left to go about their business discreetly. "Just so long," Walter drily put it, "as nobody asks them to sing."

Surely, therefore, it was not too much to hope that men like her brother Orlando and her husband Walter—men of substance and good character, loyal to the English crown— might be able to persuade the new king to restore to the Catholic community the rights it deserved.

Nobody could fail to trust her solid, dependable, loving husband. You only had to look at him. Walter had not grown heavy with the years, but his body had thickened. His hair was iron grey. He had attained authority and respect. The important religious Guild of Saint Anne had their chantry in Saint Audoen's church; but all the guild's records were kept in an iron-bound chest which was lodged in Walter Smith's house. He always wore his authority lightly, however. Quiet and cheerful, invariably kind, you would say upon meeting him that he was first and foremost a stout, middle-aged, Catholic family man—and you would be right. He had given Anne a wonderful family. The eldest girl looked like her. Everyone said so. She'd no doubt be marrying soon. The second looked more like Walter; the third reminded her of an aunt she had known as a child. But young Maurice was the one that people remarked upon. He had been named after Walter's grandfather. His physique reminded her of Walter's brother Patrick, and so did his face. That alone would have made him a handsome young fellow. What really struck everyone, however, were his eyes, which were an extraordinary green. He was eight years old now, with a bright intelligence. "It only remains to be seen whether he will turn into a humble merchant like me," his father would say with amusement, "or a clever lawyer like his uncle Orlando. It gives me such pleasure," he would gently add to Anne, "that when I look at my son I also see the face of my dear brother Patrick again."

They did not often speak of Patrick; but it was typical of Walter's kindness and delicacy that he should say such a thing to her, knowing that it was Patrick she had first loved. And she, for her part, would gently touch his arm and reply: "We both miss him, but you do more than I. I was lucky that I married you." God knows, it was the truth.

>*Head over heart,*
>*The better part.*

Her brother Lawrence's advice had not been wrong. I am lucky, she thought, and I know it. The whole of Dublin would say so. The whole of Ireland would agree. I am truly blessed. And she scarcely knew why she needed to remind herself of the fact.

The priest who had married them had been a wise man. An old friend of her father's, a man in his fifties, with an ample girth and a comfortable manner. He'd been a parish priest for thirty years, and there wasn't much he hadn't seen. Before the wedding, he had called Walter and her together and given them some simple and sage advice. No matter what they did, he told them, every day of their married life in the future, they should always consider, before they said or did anything, how that would seem to the other. Was it kind and respectful of their feelings? "From a lifetime of observation and experience I can say," he told them, "that if you just do this I can—almost—guarantee that you will have a happy marriage." She had always done so faithfully, and so had Walter. She knew that what the priest said was true. It was nearly ten years now since he had passed on to a better world, but his words still echoed in her mind as if he had spoken them only the day before. "I can guarantee that you will have a happy marriage." A joyful message. With that one little caveat. "Almost."

He knew what he was saying, that kindly priest. But why—why couldn't such things be guaranteed? Why should it be, why would God so ordain it that two good people, who loved each other, might not be happy?

Walter did not often laugh out loud, but sitting at home in the evening, if one of the children amused him, he would give a quiet chuckle. There was nothing wrong with his chuckle, she supposed. Yet for some reason it irritated her. She had often told herself not to be foolish. The thing was trivial and she should ignore it; but somehow she could not. Once or twice, she had gently asked him why he did it, why he didn't just smile, or laugh out loud. "I don't know," he had said amiably. "It's the way I've always been. Why?" And she had almost blurted out, "Because it irritates me." But the fear that this would hurt him, and place a barrier between them, made her hold back. "Nothing. I only wondered," she had said.

In any case, the chuckle itself was not really the issue. The problem was the mind that lay behind it—that and his happy assumption that whatever was in his mind at that moment was something that she equally shared.

Walter Smith was a devout man, but also wise and worldly. He looked after his family. She had no doubt that if he had to, he would gladly lay down his life for them. Above all, he enjoyed domestic order. "Thank you," he would say to her with such feeling, "for my home." And though he was too wise to express the knowledge, because this was her domain, she knew very well that he was aware of the exact location of every pot, pan, and ball of thread in the house. Always calm, always fair, he encouraged his children to lead ordered lives in their turn; and, of course, she supported him in this. You had to admire him. But did he never desire something more?

She always remembered how one day they had been standing together on the old city wall as a great cloud formation, dark and magnificent, had come rolling down from the Wicklow Mountains. She had watched, enraptured, as the grumbles of thunder grew louder and the flashes of lightning drew menacingly towards the city. "Isn't it splendid?" she had cried excitedly. "Oh, Walter, isn't it magnificent?"

"We'd best get home, or we shall get very wet," he remarked.

"I don't care," she laughed. "I shall be soaked, then." And she had turned. "Don't you ever want to let the storm engulf you?"

"Come, Anne," he had said quietly. And though she had not wanted to, she had gone home with him.

Would his brother Patrick have made her go indoors? Surely not. He might have made a terrible husband. Almost certainly, in fact. But he would have stayed with her to enjoy the wild exultation of that thunderstorm.

That night, when Walter had made love to her in his usual, unvarying fashion, she had had to disguise the fact that her body felt heavy, wooden, and unresponsive. It was not the first time she had done so, and not the last. He, of course, had no idea of her small deception, nor did she ever intend that he should.

But whenever her dear husband gave his happy little chuckle, which assumed that all his family shared his contentment at their comfortable, ordered life, she would experience that same, sickening little sinking of the heart. Then, seeing her children look at them both with such trust and happiness in their faces, she would smile and tell them: "Children, you are lucky to have such a good father." And she would kiss him. And no one would ever guess that she wanted to scream.

⁜

Jeremiah Tidy did not often make his son come with him when he went about his work in the cathedral. "The boy has other things to do," he told his wife. But today he had ordered the seven-year-old boy to accompany him, and so young Faithful Tidy was standing obediently by his side. There were reasons why Tidy wished this to be so.

Accordingly, as the two men came into the cathedral and moved towards them, the boy watched carefully. When his father made a humble bow to the two men, he waited just a moment and then, when he saw the taller of them glance at him, he too made a low bow.

"Ah, yes." Doctor Pincher's smile was somewhat thin, but it was a smile of recognition nonetheless. "Faithful Tidy. A worthy name." He turned to Doyle. "Shall we conduct our business?"

No one knew when it had first begun, but at some time in the four and a half centuries that the English had been in Ireland, the custom had grown up that bargains should be sealed upon the tomb of Strongbow, the mighty lord who had brought the first great retinue of Anglo-Norman knights into the land. And so it was today that Doyle the merchant and Doctor Pincher of Trinity College stood by the big stone tomb in the cavernous space of the cathedral and struck their bargain on the stone. No pen and ink were necessary. Tidy stood as witness. As far as anyone in Dublin was concerned, the deal was as formalised as if it had been written in the Book of Life itself.

It had been Tidy, hearing that Doyle was making an investment in a new venture, who had spoken privately with the merchant and then suggested to Pincher that he might be interested in taking a share. This was part of Tidy's strategy of making himself useful to the doctor whenever he could, and the reason why he was standing as witness to the bargain. He had known that the business would especially appeal to Pincher, not only for its potential rewards but because it also promoted the Protestant faith.

Ever since the terrible massacre of the Huguenots in France five decades before, a steady stream of these harmless and worthy French Protestants had left their native country for other, more tolerant lands. Merchants and craftsmen mostly, these hardworking tradespeople had already formed small communities in London and Bristol, and recently a few had started appearing in Ireland, too. Their religion was usually a moderate sort of Calvinism; and having suffered persecution themselves in Catholic France, they desired only to live at peace with their neighbours. "Some communities of quiet, hardworking Huguenots might set a good example to the Irish," the English authorities judged. A Huguenot glassworks was already being set up in the southern town of Birr, and men like Doyle were glad to use their skills in other modest ventures. The present business, in which Pincher had just taken a share, was a small ironworks.

Having completed the transaction, Doyle turned to Pincher and remarked that he looked unwell. It was true that Pincher was pale and had sneezed twice during the brief proceedings.

"It is nothing," Pincher said weakly. "Or nothing," he added to Tidy, "that could not be cured by a bowl of your wife's excellent broth."

Mistress Tidy was a kindly woman whose protective instincts caused her to take a motherly interest in everyone with whom she came in contact in the cathedral precincts. She had a great reverence for Doctor Pincher's learning, but considered that he needed a wife to look after him, and would often bring him cakes and sweetmeats, and make sure that his linen was in good order—which ministrations Pincher was grateful to receive.

"I shall send her to you," the sexton assured him as Pincher departed.

Doyle remained, to speak to Tidy.

If there was one thing you could say about Jeremiah Tidy, it was that he was competent. Some years ago when the post of verger had fallen vacant, it had been given to the sexton, so that Tidy now held both positions together, at the combined salary of five pounds eight shillings a year. If the Chapter Clerk kept the records of the cathedral's administrative meetings, its great roll of property and land, its rents and leases, and the precentor took charge of the cathedral's choir and music, it was Jeremiah Tidy who was now the effective guardian of all the other day-to-day arrangements within the precincts.

The matter to be discussed was a solemn one. The merchant's mother-in-law had died the day before and the funeral had to be arranged. Indeed, Doyle had almost postponed his meeting with Pincher on account of it. But this was not a native Irish affair; there was no wake, but only a quiet period of Protestant mourning; and he had needed to come into Christ Church to talk to Tidy anyway.

Doyle had married wisely. His mother-in-law had belonged to the powerful network of Old English families who had joined the Church of Ireland. Ussher, Ball, and a dozen others—these were the names which were constantly to be found holding important positions in the Irish Church and state. The funeral would be a grand affair, therefore, attended by these families, as well as members of Dublin's Catholic community who would come out of friendship and respect.

For some time the two men went over the arrangements for the service. With Tidy in charge, Doyle would know that nothing would be left to chance, no detail overlooked. The verger's five-shilling fee for this service would be well earned. As an extra kindness, Tidy had offered to speak to the precentor himself about the musical arrangements. When he and

Doyle were both satisfied that the service itself had been fully covered, Tidy introduced the final subject.

"You'll be wanting the bell to be rung?"

"Of course," Doyle replied.

The great bell of Christ Church not only rang to announce the cathedral services. Every morning at six and every evening at nine, it rang out over Dublin to signal the start and end of the working day. There were numerous other reasons for the bell to be rung. It would toll mournfully to mark the passing into eternity of a gentleman, or ring out gladly to give the happy news of an important birth. Tidy was in charge of the bell, and for each of these bellringings he was paid. His salary covered the regular ringing; the Dublin corporation paid him a further, handsome stipend of twenty pounds a year for the morning and evening bells; and for each special occasion, a further fee was negotiated.

"I could give her the same peal as I did for the lady Loftus," Tidy suggested. This had been the widow of a prominent citizen who had died the year before.

"How much did that cost?" the merchant inquired.

"Twelve shillings and sixpence," said Tidy.

"That seems a lot." Rich though he was, even Doyle was a little taken aback by the amount.

"She was a very pious lady, Sir," the sexton replied.

"Ah." Doyle sighed. "Very well, then." And having set the time for the service the following day, he departed.

During all this conversation, young Faithful Tidy had stood nearby, quietly watching. Now his father called him to his side.

"Well, Faithful," he enquired, "what did you think of that?"

"Is the twelve shillings for the bell in addition to the five shillings verger's fee?" asked the boy.

"It is," said Tidy.

Faithful looked impressed.

"Doyle is rich," he remarked.

"True. But the man for you to mark, Faithful, is not Doyle, but Doctor Pincher," his father explained.

"Old Inky?" It was a disrespectful term the children of the precinct sometimes applied to the black-robed lecturer.

"You're to treat him with respect," his father said sharply. "That man, Faithful," he quietly added, "will one day set you upon the road to fortune."

Orlando had already sent word that he would go with them, and Anne would have been going to the funeral herself—after all, Doyle was a cousin—but her second daughter was in bed with a fever that day and she had preferred to stay at home with her while Walter and her eldest girl went to Christ Church to represent the family. They were about to leave, when her brother arrived at the door.

To her surprise, she saw that he was accompanied by another man, whom she had never seen before—a handsome, fair-haired man, a few years younger than herself, she guessed, who stood just behind Orlando in the entrance.

"This is Brian O'Byrne of Rathconan," Orlando announced. "He's coming out to Fingal with me, but as he never knew Doyle's mother-in-law, I thought he might wait for me here at the house until the funeral is over."

"By all means," said Walter easily. "Anne is remaining anyway, and so he can keep her company." He came forward to greet the visitor, who bowed politely in Anne's direction. Anne naturally knew of the O'Byrnes of Rathconan, but had never met any of them that she could remember, so she simply smiled and bade him welcome. It was young Maurice, who was standing closer to the door, and who had been gazing into the visitor's face with fascination, who now cried out:

"Look, he has green eyes just like me."

O'Byrne took a step forward to look at the boy's eyes for himself.

"What is your name?" he asked.

"Maurice, Sir."

"Well, Mwirish," he pronounced the name in the Irish

fashion, "you certainly have green eyes." He laughed softly. It was nearly ninety years since Maurice Fitzgerald, natural son of Sean O'Byrne, had come down to Dublin and taken the English name of Smith. Brian assumed his host was aware of the fact that they were therefore distant cousins, but he spoke with caution all the same.

"In the O'Byrne family," he remarked casually, "the green eyes do not appear in every generation, but they always seem to return sooner or later." He gave Walter a questioning glance, and Walter nodded to show that he understood. "Does the boy know?" he murmured softly, so that Maurice should not hear. Walter shook his head. "He won't hear it from me, then," O'Byrne said softly; and then to the boy: "So it may be the same in your family, too, young Mwirish."

At that moment, the great bell of Christ Church began to toll, and a few moments later, Walter and Orlando left.

The next hour passed very pleasantly for Anne. While she occupied herself with the household and kept an eye on her sick daughter, Brian O'Byrne sat down in the parlour with Maurice, who was clearly fascinated by him. Walter Smith had a chess set and had taught his son to play—an accomplishment of which Maurice was proud—and he had soon asked the Irishman if he knew how to play. It was funny to see the two figures, both with their emerald eyes, sitting opposite each other engrossed in the game. Anne was also amused to observe that O'Byrne, with a kindly deviousness, was letting Maurice win. "Checkmate," she heard her son happily exclaim, in due course; followed by O'Byrne's own, pleasant voice, mournfully agreeing: "You are right, Mwirish. I am destroyed."

She had some conversation with him also, learned about Rathconan, that he had married a few years ago and that he had two children. He also explained, with feeling, his debt to her father. It was because of it, he told her, that when he had recently needed to transact some legal business, he had gone straight to her brother Orlando. Her brother, it seemed, had taken a liking to the handsome Irish gentleman, and she could quite see why. Indeed, she found herself hoping she might meet him again.

It was well into the second hour when, Anne's daughter needing her attention, Brian O'Byrne suggested that he and Maurice should go out to meet the others on their return.

He and the boy walked towards the old Tholsell and the cathedral crypt in which, after the funeral service, the burial was taking place. They stood together across the street, at a little distance, quietly talking until, after a little time, the crowd of mourners began to emerge. Some of these began to move in the direction of Doyle's house, where refreshments would be served; others stood around in groups, chatting together. After a few minutes, they saw Walter Smith and Orlando coming out. O'Byrne remained where he was, but Maurice went over and guided them towards his new friend, where they all paused for a few moments to watch the rest of the congregation flowing out into the broad street.

"I have already spoken to Cousin Doyle and his family," Orlando explained to O'Byrne. "So you and I should ride out to Fingal now." O'Byrne thanked Walter Smith for his hospitality, therefore, and bidding goodbye to young Maurice, prepared to take his leave. As he and Orlando turned, they noticed Doctor Pincher across the street. He was looking pale, as if unwell. But neither of them thought much about it.

✣

Although the paleness of Doctor Simeon Pincher was partly due to the head cold which not even the healing broth of Mistress Tidy could entirely allay, the more immediate reason—the sudden blow which had just caused the blood to drain from his face—was the little scene he had just witnessed.

It was a decade since he had given up his attempt to attack the O'Byrnes' legal title to Rathconan. After the sudden death of Martin Walsh, he had allowed two months to pass before finding another lawyer, and been dismayed to discover that a new title had been mysteriously granted to young O'Byrne in the interval. Was it coincidence, or had there been some double-dealing? It was hard to imagine a man like Martin Walsh violating the confidentiality of his profession; nor was Pincher aware of any particular connection between the respectable Fingal lawyer and the Irishman in the Wicklow Mountains. The thing was suspicious, but a mystery; and though he had made some enquiries at Dublin Castle, he could learn only that Brian O'Byrne had sought to regularise his position and that a number of Protestant gentlemen close to the government had urged that it would be wise to grant the harmless young man what he asked. There had been little point in pursuing the matter, therefore, and Pincher had reluctantly let it drop. But the sense that, in some way he could not fathom, he had been cheated remained with him.

And now what had he just seen? Right across the street from him, Orlando Walsh, Walter Smith the merchant, and Brian O'Byrne all standing together, with every appearance of being close friends; and then Walsh and O'Byrne moving off in each other's company, glancing across the street to where he stood, meanwhile, as if he were of no account at all. What did it mean? A terrible sensation, that he was looking at some sort of conspiracy, assailed him. These people were hand-in-glove in some way that he did not fully understand. He was aware, of course, that Orlando's sister had married Smith; but where did O'Byrne the Irishman fit in? He had no idea, but as he gazed across the street, he had an overpowering, sickening feeling that he had been duped.

The next day he questioned Tidy closely, but the sexton had explained that as a good Church of Ireland man himself, he had little knowledge of these Catholic families. "The Doyles I would know about, your Honour, and the Walshes perhaps, being English. But the O'Byrnes . . ." He had spread his hands. "I'm surprised you would ask me that, Sir."

"No, no. Of course not," Pincher had said, not wishing to offend him. But he had set further enquiries in motion. And two weeks later, one of the clerks in Dublin Castle had informed him: "It seems there was a rumour that Smith's grandfather was born an O'Byrne."

That was it, then. Now Pincher understood. He had gone to Martin Walsh in all good faith, because Catholic or not, Walsh was still an English gentleman. Meanwhile Smith, masquerading as an English merchant, was nothing more than a foul Irishman from the Wicklow wilderness—whom Walsh, who must have known it, had allowed to marry his daughter. And having received his confidence, Walsh had then broken his professional oath and tipped off O'Byrne. It explained everything. There wasn't a doubt of it.

He'd been hoodwinked. Left stranded in an Irish bog. They'd made a fool of him, these cursed Catholics, with their lies and double-dealing. They were all laughing at him behind his back, and they had been for years. He felt a surge of fury. But if he had been made a fool of, what did that make them? Traitors. Traitors pure and simple. Old Martin Walsh might have seemed a gentleman. But I should have known from the first, Pincher told himself, that a man with a Jesuit for a son could only be a traitor. Old English or native Irish from the hills and bogs, they were all the same. They were Catholics, and that was all that mattered. From that day forward, in the mind of Doctor Pincher, one thing was clear. The baseness, the contemptible nature which, until now, he had ascribed to the mere Irish, should instead be applied to all who held the Catholic faith. It was their religion which not only condemned them to perdition, but turned them into villains even before they got there. And from that day forward he kept a promise to himself, like a knife sheathed in his heart, that when the hour came, he personally would strike, with righteousness, at Smith, Walsh, and O'Byrne, who had dared to mock him.

As for Rathconan—the estate he had hoped with no good reason, and with inadequate means, to steal from the O'Byrnes—it now seemed to him to be a rightful inheritance that had been stolen from him. And this knowledge, too, he kept locked in his heart like treasure in a chest.

In this unfortunate state of mind, the Doctor of Divinity passed many months.

✣

The letter which whipped Doctor Pincher into a frenzy came in the spring of 1627. It came from his sister. It concerned Barnaby.

Perhaps Mrs. Tidy was right in thinking that Doctor Pincher needed a wife. But having lived his life on his own narrow terms for so long, it would have been hard for Pincher to change his habits to suit another. As for the things of the body, as a young man he had put them aside, like a soldier on campaign, because he was afraid to compromise his moral reputation. And with the passing of time those needs had so dwindled that now, as an older man, his fears were more comprehensive, and his hesitancy had become a vocation.

But if Simeon Pincher was a confirmed bachelor, his ambition for his family had never lessened; indeed, with the years it had rather increased. He might not yet have achieved the landed estate that he craved, but he was a man of some substance, and a significant figure in Dublin. Some years ago, he had suggested to his sister that his nephew Barnaby might care to come to Dublin and study at Trinity College, where Pincher would have seen to it that his nephew received nothing but the best. His sister had written back, however, that Barnaby, though a youth of unimpeachable godliness, was not of a scholarly turn of mind, and that he had been apprenticed to a notable draper instead. The draper, she assured her brother, was a man of considerable learning and had promised that under his care, Barnaby would read all the books that were good for him.

Thwarted in this hope, Pincher had bided his time; but now that Barnaby had reached the age of twenty, he had written again suggesting that his nephew might pay a visit to Dublin where he should meet none but the best society. It would enable him to get to know the young man, who would after all be his heir, he pointed out; and though he did not say so, it would also allow Barnaby to discover what an important man his uncle was in Dublin. It was his sister's reply to this amiable suggestion that had wrought such fury in the doctor's soul.

Her letter started well enough, with proper thanks to him for remembering his nephew. It then reminded him that if he wanted to renew his acquaintance with his family, and see his own sister as well as her good husband, as well as his nephew, he had only to come to England, where he could be assured of a family welcome. If this was a gentle rebuke, the doctor had to admit that it was merited. Why was it that he had never troubled, in all these years, to make the journey to see his sister in her home? Partly it was pride—or rather, vanity. Pincher admitted this honestly to himself. He had wanted to return in triumph, with an estate to his name. This did not show true affection on his part, and Pincher rightly censured himself. Why was he so anxious to cut a fine figure? Because his sister had always indicated, in her quiet way, that she did not have a very high opinion of him. And even now, after thirty years, he lacked the humility to accept the justice of her view and to admit his shortcomings. At this, also, the reverent doctor bowed his head in shame.

And if his sister's letter had ended there, he might have gathered up his humility like a cloak about him and returned, as a humble Christian should, to the somewhat chilly bosom of his family. But it didn't.

She was unwilling, she said, that her son should visit Ireland. Barnaby, she explained, had grown from a godly boy to a young man with the sternest imaginable faith. Indeed, he had even considered leaving England's shores. Her brother must know that some of the English Puritans were hoping to set up a colony of the saints in America, and Barnaby had already spoken earnestly of leaving hearth and home to join such a venture when the opportunity arose. And who could blame him when the true Protestant religion was under threat from every side, and King Charles and his papist queen were so clearly not to be trusted? "We tremble for Barnaby's safety," she wrote, "but never for his soul."

Why then, she asked, would it be of benefit to Barnaby to visit Ireland, where by all accounts popish idolatry, far from being expunged, was actually thriving? The plantation of Ulster had been undertaken to turn that land into a great Protestant colony; yet all reports were that the new English landlords were letting the land back to the very same Catholic Irish beasts who had occupied it before. Down in Munster, English gentlemen, yeomen of substance, and honest craftsmen had been offered land. "Yet it is said that none but villains and adventurers who have a past to hide do live in those parts." As for Dublin itself: "It seems, Brother, that you gladly suffer the papists to use the churches, and to sit in the city council, and for all I know to eat at your table."

He gazed at the letter, stunned. Part of what made it so distressing was that some of her allegations were true. There were good English settlers down in Munster, of course, but many of the sturdy English yeomen, merchants and craftsmen who were the backbone of England, had no reason to leave their solid positions to cross the Irish Sea, and many who had come to Ireland had since returned. A good many of the fellows who had taken up Munster lands were men of dubious reputation who had hoped, on the cheap, to pass for gentlemen in Ireland. As for Ulster, her charges could not be denied. The new plantations were not turning out properly at all. The English and Scottish undertakers had been quite unable to find enough good Protestant tenants for their huge landholdings. So they had frequently let the native Irish back onto the land—which the Irish regarded as their own anyway—on short-term leases at the most exorbitant rents they could get away with. Instead of a quiet pattern of yeomen farmlands and market towns, Ulster was turning into a patchwork of embattled townships and rack-rented fields. In the capital, meanwhile, the good Protestant men at Trinity and in Dublin Castle might feel the same as he did, but although they all wanted in theory to see the end of Catholicism, their actions in practice were feeble. It was the same even in Christ Church: the cathedral community was an enclave, living proudly apart in a sea of unregenerate Roman superstition; yet to his knowledge, Christ Church lands were still being subleased by Catholic gentlemen who even used those very lands to support their own private priests.

But she saved her unkindest cut for the end. She had hoped years ago when he had left Cambridge—"in a manner I choose to forget," she reminded him—that he had reformed his life. But from what she heard about Ireland, she wrote, that issue must be in doubt. She did not care, therefore, to send Barnaby to him.

+

Would she never forget? Would she never forgive that business at Cambridge? Was it his crime, he wondered, or the false allegation that stirred her fury the most?

Strangely, it had begun in church. He had been asked to preach in a village not far from Cambridge. Sir Bertram Fielding and his lady had been in the congregation. He had been invited to dine with them the following week. All this was usual enough. It was the way a young man made friends and obtained preferment.

Lady Fielding was a fine, big-busted woman—about thirty-five, he'd guessed. He'd noticed her large brown eyes light up when he entered her husband's house. She had signalled that she liked him, squeezed his hand, too, when he departed. But he had given it no further thought.

Was it by chance, three days later, that she should have met him when he was taking his usual afternoon walk down to the river? No. He had innocently mentioned this regular habit when he had dined in her house. Was it by design that she persuaded him to show her the college? Undoubtedly. Was it with intention that she asked to see his rooms? It was. Oh, indeed it was.

He had been innocent until then. It was unusual, but certainly not unknown. He had kept himself pure, in the service of the Lord. Perhaps, he supposed, that was what had attracted her. She was quite determined not to leave him as innocent as she had found him. And she had known how to set about the task of seducing him. With little murmurs of delight she had undressed him, discovering his pale body, and taught him how to discover hers. Even now, his shame was tinged with delight and pride—alas, pride—at the memory of those things they had done together.

They had met many times. It had not been difficult. Her husband had several times been in London. Often she had come to his rooms in college. It had not been during the university term, so the undergraduates were not in the college and there were relatively few people about. For a period of nearly six weeks he had fallen into the sins of lust and, worse, adultery.

He had never discovered how Sir Bertram had come to know of their affair. But obviously, his suspicions must have been aroused. Perhaps he'd had his wife followed.

For then had come that terrible evening when, at dusk, and alone with Lady Fielding in his rooms, he had been disturbed by such a hammering at the door that he had supposed the college must be on fire. Pulling on a nightshirt, he had opened the door.

The next few minutes were ones that he wished he could forget. Sir Bertram was not quite as tall as he, but he was burly. And he was wearing his sword. It was the flash of the drawn blade in the candlelight that had caused Simeon Pincher to flee. What else could he do? He was still in the doorway when Sir Bertram had seized the back of his nightshirt. At the top of the staircase, it had ripped. By the time he had struggled and tumbled downstairs, and rushed out into the court, he realised to his horror that his tattered nightshirt was in Sir Bertram's hand, and that he himself was entirely naked.

But Sir Bertram was still behind him. As he started to run, he felt a hot, searing flash of pain across his shoulders. Fielding had hit him with the flat of his sword. He fled, but though he was nimble, his assailant was surprisingly fast. Again Sir Bertram slashed at him, and this time, as Pincher almost got away, the point of the sword ripped across his back, tearing the flesh.

Round the court they ran, Pincher naked, the priest behind him. Thank God it was not broad daylight; but all the same, there was enough light to see his shame. He would have run out past the porter's lodge into the street, but without any clothes on, he could not do that. As it was, with Fielding showing no sign of giving up, he was forced to cry out for help as he ran. One or two windows started to open round the court; and he scarcely knew what might have happened if the porter had not rescued him, rushing him into the lodge and slamming the door in Sir Bertram's furious face. Ten minutes later, Sir Bertram and his lady left the college; and Simeon Pincher, wrapped in a blanket the porter had lent him, returned, shivering with shock, to his rooms. Only when he got back and removed the blanket did he discover how much he had bled. He would bear the scar across his back for the rest of his days.

He knew very well that the porter had a shrewd idea what had been passing between him and the lady. But fortunately, he had kept his wits about him while he waited in the lodge. When the porter had asked whether he should summon the proctor, he had shaken his head.

"The fellow is a madman," he had replied. The lady had come to him for spiritual counsel. Her husband, who always imagined she was being unfaithful with every man she spoke to, had come to his rooms, stripped him, and chased him out. "I shall consider legal action later," he said. He was not sure that the porter believed this tale. Probably not. But he judged it best to stick to the story, and later that evening he repeated it to the Master of the college.

"The indecency is to be regretted," the Master said grimly.

"By me most of all," Pincher agreed. "For I was the victim."

"It is fortunate that there were not many people to see. Do you mean to take legal action?"

"I am hesitant. The man is to be pitied. But my real concern," Pincher said cleverly, "is that if I take action, it would bring the college's name into court. For the sake of the college, I wonder if it would be best to do nothing."

"Ah," said the Master. "Quite so."

Within the hour, the porter and all fellows resident had received firm instructions not to speak of the incident to anyone. In all likelihood, Pincher had supposed, the Fieldings would have no reason to make the matter public, either.

But no matter how stoutly its walls enclosed Emmanuel's reputation, such a story was sure to seep out. Within days it had spread to other colleges. It the process, it soon began to change shape. There was talk of orgies, even of pagan ceremonies, though naked men and women were always involved. Soon Pincher became aware that people were looking at him curiously in the street. His reputation was tarnished. Once, he saw a passing lady draw away from him. The next day, he did not go for his usual walk, but stayed in his rooms.

Yet the real blow, when it came, was not at all what he had imagined. A lawyer came to his rooms—a small, narrow-faced man who reminded the young man of a ferret. He came from Sir Bertram Fielding.

"Sir Bertram is about to institute proceedings against you," the lawyer informed him. "His wife is ready to testify."

"To what?"

"Rape."

Pincher gazed at him in utter astonishment.

"Rape? By whom?"

"By you, of course. You assaulted her."

"I did no such thing."

"Her word against yours. People saw you running naked." The lawyer shook his head. "Bad business. You'll be destroyed anyway. Not the sort of thing the college likes. End of your hopes, I should say." He paused, watching the look of horror on Pincher's face. "You might avoid it though, I think."

"How?"

"Leave the college."

"Leave?"

"Leave Cambridge. Go elsewhere. If you did that, I think, the matter might be dropped. Nothing more said. Business closed. You could do that, I think."

Pincher was silent. He thought of the letter he had received a little while before from Dublin, a letter which so far he had not troubled to answer.

"I shall need a little time to consider," he replied slowly. "But if this comes to court, I shall deny the charge and take the lady's reputation down with mine."

"Fair enough," said the lawyer. "You have a month. How's that?"

Pincher had written to Trinity College that very day.

But he had made one, sad mistake. Going to see his sister before his departure from England, he had told her the story, expecting her sympathy. It had not been given. No word of pity, charity, or affection had ever come. Not then, not since, not now, even after all these years.

And what of his life since? What would he have had to show his nephew if he had come to Dublin? His modest fortune? His position at Trinity? His profession of the Protestant faith, in a world of unworthy compromises? Where was God's holy fire? Would the righteous young man be impressed or disgusted by his uncle? Dear God, Simeon Pincher realised, the latter probably. His sister was in the right. He had forgotten how his life would look to an English Puritan; he had been in Ireland too long.

All afternoon he sat there, staring in front of him. Early in the evening, Tidy's wife arrived with a beef pie. He thanked her, absently, but did not move. At last he got up, held a taper to the small coal fire in the grate, and lit a candle, which he placed on the table before him.

And it was only some time later, after he had gazed sadly at its flame and thought about Walsh and O'Byrne, his sister and his pious nephew Barnaby, that Doctor Pincher came to the decision that was to change the rest of his life. He knew now what he had to do. But he would have to prepare carefully, and in secret.

+‡+

It was two months later that Orlando Walsh called a family conference in Fingal.

His brother Lawrence and Walter Smith were asked to come; also Doyle, who, though he nominally belonged to the Church of Ireland, had no strong religious feelings, and had always been a loyal cousin. More surprising to the others, Orlando had also asked his friend O'Byrne to attend. "I want," he explained to Lawrence, "the view of an Irish gentleman as well. And O'Byrne can be trusted." For there were important matters to discuss.

It was a conference of men. Orlando's wife Mary was away visiting her mother just then; O'Byrne and Lawrence came alone. Anne arrived with Walter Smith because she loved to visit her childhood home. "But I shall be glad to leave you men to talk," she told her brother cheerfully.

The weather was pleasant. It was the eve of May Day, as it happened.

As they assembled in the parlour, around the oak table, Orlando looked at his companions with satisfaction. Walter Smith, Doyle, and O'Byrne were dressed like Dublin gentlemen in breeches and stockings; he himself wore trews. It was common in the countryside, even in English Fingal, for gentlemen to wear a mixture of English and Irish dress, and he had already remarked with a smile to O'Byrne: "I look more Irish than you do." Lawrence was dressed sombrely in his usual soutane, his greying hair adding to his appearance of severe distinction.

In the years since their father's death, Orlando had come to understand his brother better, and to respect him accordingly. When he decided to take up his father's profession of law, he had studied with a lawyer in Dublin, where he had advanced rapidly; and while there he had often spent his evenings with Lawrence at the Jesuit lodging house. And so the two brothers had grown together like two sides of the same family coin—the one in holy orders, the other a landowner and professional man whose religious life would always remain as intense as it was private.

There was only one difference between them. Lawrence still remained the more coldly intellectual of the two. His rigorous distaste for dubious relics, sacred wells, and all the latent paganism of the island's traditional Catholicism would have done credit to a Puritan. But partly out of affection for his father's memory, and partly because of his own temperament, Orlando continued to hold some of these in reverence. Only that winter, on a visit to O'Byrne at Rathconan, he had ridden with his friend over to Glendalough and spent all day at the ancient monastic site and its two mountain lakes, praying for nearly an hour at the little hermit's retreat of Saint Kevin. And every month, without fail, he would make the little pilgrimage on foot to the well at Portmarnock. If Lawrence was determined to purify and strengthen Holy Church, Orlando, more emotional, in ways he could not quite put into words, had a desire to restore that which was lost.

And it was the life of the Catholic community in Ireland that he wanted now to discuss.

If the recent marriage of King Charles of England to a French princess had seemed a hopeful sign to Catholics in Ireland, the last weeks had brought even more encouraging news. Opening the discussion, Orlando put the position succinctly.

"We all know that King Charles needs loyal Catholic subjects in Ireland. Ever since his marriage, we have hoped that he might do more to show himself our friend. And now it seems that he may be taking the first step."

Even in the latter part of the previous year, there had been hints from royal courtiers to Irish friends. A few letters between prominent men in Ireland and the court had nurtured these first seeds; and in the last few weeks, the business had begun to take shape. "If we submit proposals for improving the position of the loyal Catholic gentry of Ireland, the king has indicated privately that he will look kindly upon them. That is my understanding." He glanced around them for comments.

"That's the word in Dublin," Doyle agreed. "We're all hearing it now, Catholic and Church of Ireland men alike. What is also certain is that this is coming from London direct. The government men in Dublin Castle have no part in it. They have heard the news, but they hate the idea. They'd sooner see the Catholics suppressed, not encouraged."

"They'll have to follow the royal will, however," Orlando pointed out. "They have no choice. The news is very good," he smiled at his friend O'Byrne, "for all of us, I think."

"For the Old English, no doubt," O'Byrne said ruefully. "Whether that extends to myself remains to be seen."

"I think it does," answered Orlando. "If the king favours some Catholics, he must favour them all. Even here in Fingal," he added, "I can think of a dozen Catholic landowners who are of Irish blood—Conran, Dowde, Kennedy, Kelly, Malone, Meagh—all gentlemen like yourself, Brian. I cannot see how a difference could possibly be made between them and me. Not to mention the fact that amongst the ordinary folk in Fingal, from the servants in this house to the fishermen and tenant farmers, four out of five are Irish, you know. If we are allowed our religion, then so are they."

"If allowing us our religion will lessen the English desire to steal our land," said O'Byrne drily, "then no doubt we should be grateful."

"Well, I still think," Orlando responded, "that at this stage we should all be greatly heartened."

"Perhaps." It was Lawrence who spoke now. The Jesuit had been sitting silently, his long fingers resting upon the table in front of him. He looked at them all, seriously. "I do not share your optimism, however. In the first place, you seem to assume that the new king favours the Catholic faith."

"He married a Catholic," Orlando pointed out.

"That was statecraft. An alliance with France."

"He is hardly a Protestant."

"In manners and temperament, undoubtedly, he is closer to ourselves than to his Protestant subjects in England," Lawrence allowed. "But I can tell you that we have no evidence that he means to return his country, or even his own family, to Rome." He paused while the three men listening to him glanced at each other. Everyone knew that the Jesuit intelligence network had the best information in Europe.

"What does he believe, then?" asked Orlando.

"His father persuaded himself that kings rule by divine right, and it seems the son has taken up this belief. King Charles believes that he does not answer to men for his actions, but to God alone, personally and directly, and without reference to the wisdom of the ages or to Holy Church." He made a wry grimace. "Such a belief, you know, shows a massive conceit that no Catholic churchman would tolerate for a minute." He shrugged. "If he continues in this foolish belief, then he will surely prefer his own Church of England, of which he is the Head, to the Church of Rome, where in spiritual matters he would have to acknowledge the authority of the Pope."

"Yet he is ready to favour Catholics."

"In Ireland perhaps. But be sure," Lawrence tapped his finger on the table, "he will demand a quid pro quo."

"What will that be?"

"Money, Orlando. He needs money." Lawrence placed his fingers together, as he liked to do if he was delivering a little lecture. "Consider the recent history at the English court. A handsome young man comes to court and fascinates old King James, who promotes him far beyond his merits or capacity and makes him Duke of Buckingham. Charles, instead of sending Buckingham away, favours him even more. It is bad enough that all Christendom is split into armed camps of Catholic and Protestant; but Buckingham, who has no statecraft, has now involved England in expensive military expeditions for which no rhyme or reason, religious or otherwise, can be found. Twice now, the English Parliament has refused to grant the king any funds unless he gets rid of this wretched Buckingham, and Charles, who believes he can do no wrong, refuses. Now he has no money and is trying to raise it in any way he can. Titles of nobility, trading privileges, even public offices are all being sold. He's even forcing honest gentlemen in England, men like yourself, Orlando, to make him loans under compulsion, and threatening them with jail if they refuse." He shook his head in disgust. "We may be sure, therefore, that if the king offers to help the Catholics of Ireland, it is only because he wants a large payment of money in return."

When he had finished, there was silence for a moment. His view might be harsh, but Lawrence's opinion carried respect.

"I hope," said Orlando, "that you are mistaken. But if you are right, then that is all the more reason to take advantage of this opportunity and get as much as we can." He indicated a sheaf of papers on the table. "As you'd expect from a lawyer, I have some proposals."

The proposals that Orlando began to outline had not come from himself alone. For weeks, lawyers had been circulating ideas amongst themselves; all over Ireland, meetings like this were taking place. Cleverly, the proposals did not concern only the Catholics. "There are a number of small reforms here which not even Doctor Pincher of Trinity would object to," Orlando explained. But also there were measures, modest enough individually, that taken all together would profoundly transform the lives of Ireland's Catholics. These would include the abolition of the recusancy fines for practising the Catholic faith. "And Catholic lawyers like myself would no longer be barred from holding public office," Orlando said. "I have nearly thirty proposals here. If we could get even the majority accepted, it would mark the beginning of the end of Catholic isolation here."

The business of considering the proposals now began. The five men went through them all, one by one. Each man had useful ideas to contribute. Walter Smith showed himself canny in seeing how each would play out in practice with the officials as well as the merchants in Dublin. Doyle could foresee the objections of the Church of Ireland. Several good suggestions were made concerning inheritance. It was the final proposal which caused O'Byrne some amusement.

"You want to raise a militia?" In times past, when the English government wanted to raise troops in Ireland, funds would be transferred from London to help pay for them. But some of the men drafting the proposals had cleverly suggested that the Old English of the Pale should save the government this expense and maintain a militia of their own. "The government will be fools if they let you do that," O'Byrne laughed. "You'd take over Ireland again."

"All the more reason to ask," said Orlando with a smile. But more seriously, he continued: "Whatever we can persuade the king to grant now, however, we must then make sure that we prove to him that we are loyal. Our greatest hope for the future lies in demonstrating to the government that, given the right to worship according to our faith, we are not planning to rebel, or seek help from foreign powers; the king must see that the loyal Catholic gentlemen of Ireland—and that would include you, O'Byrne, and others like you—are to be trusted. Out of that trust will come any further recognition of our rights." He glanced at the new clock he had proudly installed in the corner of the parlour the year before.

"It's almost noon," he said. "Let us have dinner."

❖

Anne had enjoyed the morning. She had spent much of it in the kitchen with the servants who were preparing the midday meal. The eldest of them, Kathleen, had been there when she was a child, and they greeted each other warmly with a kiss. It was good just to listen to the women talking in the local Fingal dialect. She was glad to help with the setting of the table, and to handle the old household items familiar from the past: the heavy container for the salt that stood in the place of honour on the dining table, the brass candlesticks, the pewter dishes, and the silver tankard with the family arms engraved upon it, from which their father and now Orlando would drink. All in all, she thought, a pleasant journey back in time.

There had also been the opportunity for several hours of talk, so that by noon she knew all the gossip about every family in the locality. Nor did this talk exclude her own family. And as far as the Walsh family was concerned, she discovered, there was only one subject of discussion.

"It's a baby we're waiting for," Kathleen told her, "in this house."

It was strange and a little disappointing that her sister-in-law Mary had still not conceived. Orlando and she had been married three years now, and Anne knew how passionately her brother wanted children. The Walshes had never had trouble producing heirs, and Mary was one of a large family. Anne had no reason to suppose her brother wasn't having a normal family life.

"It's why she isn't here," Kathleen confided to Anne when they were out of hearing of the other women. "Only last month it was, we were standing together in the kitchen and suddenly she turns to me and says: 'Why haven't I a child, Kathleen? Can you tell me that?' I didn't know what to answer. 'It's not for lack of trying, the Lord knows,' she says. And then the poor soul starts to cry. She never said a word about why she was going to see her mother, but you may be sure it's to talk to her about that subject, when her mother has ten grown children of her own."

It seemed to Anne that the older woman was very likely correct. She felt sorry for her sister-in-law and resolved to make an effort to come out to see her more often and keep her company in future. Though whether I can really help her with good advice about marriage is a little doubtful, she thought. She also felt a great concern for her brother. He had given no indication, even to her, but if his wife was so upset about the subject, she could imagine the pain Orlando himself must secretly be suffering. She wondered whether to bring the subject up with him, or whether to say nothing unless he did.

The meal to which they all sat down, a little after noon, was Fingal cooking at its best. The area was especially rich in seafood: there were splendid oyster beds in the estuary at nearby Malahide; cockles and mussels were gathered at Howth; salted herring was landed at Clontarf, just a little farther south. For the main course, there were offerings of salted pork, beef, and duck, accompanied by black pudding, peas, and cabbage. Another vegetable was also served, which greatly interested O'Byrne, since the Irishman had never eaten it before. This was the potato, a new vegetable from America.

"I planted a quarter acre a few years ago," Orlando told him proudly. He liked to think of himself as being in the vanguard as a landowner. "Nobody else in Fingal has tried it. Yet there's more nourishment per acre from the American potato than from any other crop."

It was half past two when Walter Smith pleasantly remarked: "If we don't go for a walk after this, I shall go to sleep."

"We shall walk," Orlando announced, "to the sea."

⁘

Anne was glad to join the men in their walk. They took the path that led across the fields towards Portmarnock and the sea. It pleased her that nothing ever seemed to change there— fields of wheat and barley near the house, then the open spaces shelving down to the sea where sheep and cattle grazed.

Orlando and O'Byrne led the way, followed by Lawrence and Doyle. Despite the fact that he was wearing a soutane, her elder brother had taken Orlando's fowling piece—a splendid flintlock made in France—with which he hoped to shoot some duck to take back to the Jesuit house in Dublin. She and Walter came last. They talked quietly. Walter described to her all that had passed in the morning's discussions, and she told him what she had heard about Orlando's wife. "Should I speak to him about it, do you think?" she asked.

"You might give him the opportunity to bring the subject up, I suppose, but I wouldn't do more than that," Walter advised. "You're his sister, though, so you're probably a better judge than I would be." He sighed. "Thank God that we have our own dear children," he said with feeling.

"Yes," she said. "Thank God."

Out of respect for Lawrence's views, Orlando did not take them by the holy well at Portmarnock but went straight through the dunes to the beach. There they all walked together as a single group along the strand towards Howth. The afternoon was warm. After a while, they came upon a fisherman sitting by a small boat, mending his nets. As they paused to exchange a few words with him, O'Byrne turned to Orlando to ask about the little island out in the water below the Ben of Howth.

"We call it Ireland's Eye," Orlando replied. "Nobody goes there but the fishermen."

O'Byrne turned to the fellow by the boat.

"Would you take me there for a shilling?" he asked. It was a handsome offer, and the fisherman gladly accepted. "Who goes with me?" O'Byrne turned to the group. There was not much enthusiasm from the men, but Anne smiled.

"I'll go—if Walter doesn't mind. I haven't been since my father took me out there as a child."

Walter glanced at the water. It was perfectly calm. The fisherman was grey-haired, but looked strong enough to handle any currents. "As you like," he said evenly.

The crossing was easy enough. She and O'Byrne sat in the stern facing the fisherman, who pulled slowly but firmly on the oars. As they got out of the shallows, O'Byrne remarked to him pleasantly, "It's the Eve of Bealtaine."

"It is," the old man said quietly. "There'll be people out on the hills tonight."

The old Celtic May Day festival was not forgotten. In many areas, people would still go up hills to watch the rising sun, and Anne had heard that in some places, the cattlemen still drove the cattle between two fires that day, in the ancient pagan manner. She asked Brian O'Byrne if he had ever seen such a thing.

"I've seen it done," he answered.

Perhaps it was because his green eyes reminded her of her son, or perhaps that his fair hair made him seem younger, but there was something almost boyish, and very appealing, it seemed to Anne, in this pleasant Irish gentleman.

"I believe you do it yourself up in Wicklow," she teased him gently.

"We're not pagans at Rathconan," he answered with a smile, though she noticed that he hadn't actually denied it.

"As for what happens to the girls . . ." she continued. She'd heard that not every virgin who went up the mountain at Bealtaine came down in the same state.

"I cannot answer for my ancestors," he laughed.

The island was coming closer. They could see the rocks on the beach. They watched it in silence. Anne was enjoying the feel of the soft air and the sun on her face.

The fisherman landed the boat on a small shingle beach. Anne went up a grassy knoll from which she waved across the water to her husband, who waved back. Having satisfied themselves that she was safely across, the men were setting off down to the southern point of the strand where there were some marshes. No doubt Lawrence would be hoping to shoot some wildfowl there. Meanwhile, she and Brian O'Byrne began to inspect the island.

They looked at each of the little beaches. At the base of the cliff with its high cleft, Anne pointed out the natural shelter the rocks had formed. "A hermit could live here," she remarked. They went all the way round until they came to the fisherman again. He had brought one of his nets with him and was quietly at work on it. He seemed in no hurry to return. They continued round again and sat down by one of the rock pools. The sun was dancing off the water. They stared down at a crab making its way across the bottom, and Anne felt a sense of peace as if she had returned to her childhood again.

"It's strange," she said after a little while, "to find myself with a man who has my son's green eyes." And she smiled at him.

"Mwirish still doesn't know of our relationship?"

"No. His father doesn't wish it." She reached down to the rock pool and trailed her hand thoughtfully in the water for a moment. "My husband's very cautious," she said with a little shrug.

He shot her a glance.

"Your husband's a sensible man," he said. "I'd do the same in his place, I think." He paused for a moment. "When the first Mwirish changed his name to Smith, he made a decision for his descendants. They're to be English now. As for the green eyes, they turn up from time to time in many families." He chuckled. "Your husband wouldn't be the only natural descendant of Sean O'Byrne, I can assure you! We're all cousins up in Wicklow, anyway, like the Old English in Fingal, I dare say." He stretched comfortably. "Everybody's related somehow, I should think. I've the blood of the Walshes of Carrickmines in my own veins, come to that."

"You have?" She was delighted. "We are related?"

"It's centuries ago." He laughed. "Which means that you and your husband are related through the O'Byrnes, too."

"I never knew that." She stared down and looked rather thoughtful for a moment; then she brightened and looked up again. "I was already related to my husband, but now I'm connected to you as well. So that's a gain."

Why did she like Brian O'Byrne so much? Was it the eyes? Did he remind her of Patrick, that she had lost? She wasn't sure.

"So, can you see me living up in the wild Wicklow Mountains?" she asked.

"Oh yes," he said quietly. "I can see you."

He told her some stories then, about the O'Byrnes and the O'Tooles in times past, of the life in the wild, free spaces of the mountains, and also of the fighting between the Irish chiefs and the Tudor troops from England. She knew many of these things as history; but she had never heard them told by an Irishman before, and for the first time she gained a sense of the Wicklow Mountains not as a treacherous, dangerous territory, but as a great haven, a land of ancient freedoms and holy places which the English had not only invaded, but defiled. And she found herself strangely moved.

After a while, he said, "We should go back," and she said, "Yes, we should," but neither of them moved. Finally, after what still did not seem so long a time, he glanced up at the sun, which was getting lower in the sky, and rose, and gave her his hand to help her up. And so they walked slowly back, still talking, to the boat where the fisherman, having mended his nets, had fallen asleep.

When they got back across the water, they found only Walter and Orlando waiting for them. Neither was smiling.

"Where are Lawrence and Cousin Doyle?" she asked. "Did he shoot any duck? I didn't hear the gun go off."

"They got tired of waiting and went home," said Orlando bleakly.

Brian O'Byrne immediately apologised for keeping them waiting.

"We weren't so long," said Anne.

Orlando and Walter glanced at each other.

"You were two hours out there," Orlando said quietly.

"Oh, I don't think so. We can't have been. It didn't seem any time at all," Anne answered brightly. "He told me all about Wicklow."

"You could see a hermit like Saint Kevin living out there," said O'Byrne quickly. He turned to Walter. "I took Orlando up to Glendalough once, you know. He prayed for nearly an hour at the shrine of Saint Kevin."

"I'll walk with you now, Brian," said Orlando as soon as O'Byrne had paid the fisherman. "Anne and Walter will want to walk together."

On the way home, Anne took Walter's arm and squeezed it gently.

"I didn't realise we were so long," she said. "I thought you were looking for duck down on the marshes."

"We were," said Walter.

"You know, I should like us all to visit Rathconan one day," she said.

But Walter did not reply.

‡

On a bright Sunday morning in June 1627, Doctor Simeon Pincher made his way from Trinity College to Christ Church. It was normal for the doctor to walk with a stern purpose in his step; but today he strode like a champion of old, a Hector or Achilles, going into battle. And indeed, he was going into the greatest battle of his life, from which, he had no doubt, he would emerge victorious.

For today Doctor Pincher, by a single daring action, was going to place himself at the head—the moral head, at least— of the entire Protestant community of Dublin, and even perhaps of all Ireland.

As he passed through the eastern city gate and started up Dame Street, he noted with approval that the great bell of Christ Church had already begun to toll. "I shall be ringing the bell an extra ten minutes, Your Honour, on your account," Tidy had promised him the day before. "It'll be a great day when you preach your sermon, Sir." He must remember to give Tidy a shilling for his kindness, Pincher thought. Perhaps even two.

If Pincher was committing himself to a mighty battle, he had also, like a good general, made careful preparations. Firstly, his timing was excellent. For months now, the Church of Ireland's senior men had been aware of the growing hopes of the Catholic community for some help from the king; and in recent months, while men like Orlando Walsh were drawing up proposals, concern in these Protestant circles had turned to alarm. Something had to be done—they all agreed.

Next, Pincher had chosen his battleground carefully. He was not mounting an invasion into unknown territory. The bridgehead had already been established when, during the month of April, no less a person than the uncompromising Protestant Bishop of Derry had come down to Dublin and preached a scathing sermon on the sinfulness of tolerating Catholicism. "To tolerate Catholics," he had firmly announced, "is to dishonour God." The sermon had been much admired, but had not been followed up with anything practical. Pincher had also made sure that his troops were all prepared and his allies in place. For a month now, he had been quietly talking to friends in Trinity and the sympathetic administrators in Dublin Castle. The Lord Deputy himself was away that week, but many of his officials would be attending the service, and the congregation would be judiciously packed with supporters. Word had also been leaked to men like Doyle that something dramatic was going to happen in Christ Church that morning, for to achieve the effect he wanted, Pincher needed a large audience.

As he came in sight of the cathedral precincts, he was pleased to see that a number of the Catholic aldermen—the very fellows who would normally be drinking at the inn until the sermon was over—were also gathering there out of curiosity. By the end of the service, some of those men would be his mortal enemies. So much the better. That was exactly what he wanted. He wanted to be the one they hated. That would make him the leader.

The Protestant army was waiting to be led. If his sister in England still had doubts about him, if perhaps he had even once or twice had doubts about himself, his actions today would put those doubts to rest forever. This, it must be, was the predestined role for which the Lord had kept him in waiting. He was chosen not only to be one of the Elect, but to lead them.

Yet when, a little later, Pincher took his seat in the cathedral, even he was astonished by the success of his preparations. The church was packed. It was one of the largest congregations he had ever seen—from loyal souls like Tidy's wife and his Trinity friends, and the Church of Ireland regulars like Doyle, to such frankly Catholic merchants as Walter Smith and his wife. Dublin Castle, as he'd hoped, was well represented, too. The plan had worked. They had all come to hear him.

The morning service at Christ Church was an impressive affair. The choir was excellent. As well as the modern organ, which had been installed a decade ago, the precentor and organist also employed other musicians to enrich the sound. Today there were viols, sackbuts, and cornets. Pincher could not entirely approve of these extra embellishments, which he thought too rich and pompous for a Protestant service; but in other respects the arrangements at Christ Church were to be commended. The communion table was plain and simple and stood modestly in the centre of the choir. There were few candles, little ornament. And above all, there could be no doubt about where the true focus of the whole proceedings lay: not in the choir, not upon the altar, not even in the prayers, important though these were. The focus of a Protestant service was the pulpit. Catholics might go to church to see flickering candles and the sacred host, miracle and mystery; but Presbyterians came to hear the preacher preach.

And a preaching they should have. When the appointed time came, Pincher rose from his seat and ascended the stairs to the pulpit. His face was pale, his Geneva gown all black as ink. During an expectant silence, he surveyed the multitude. Having done so, he opened his arms wide, like an avenging angel, then, lowering them, he clasped the edge of the pulpit in front of him and, leaning out into space towards the congregation as though he were now a bird of prey straining forward from its perch, he cried out in a terrible voice:

"I come not to send peace, but a sword."

The word of the Lord. The tenth chapter of Matthew. The Saviour's most fearful words. The congregation gave a collective shudder.

A sermon in the Stuart age was an impressive thing—a mighty structure, constructed like a building. First came the foundation, the biblical text. Then, like so many columns and arches, transepts and chapels, came related texts, learned allusions, and subsidiary themes—for the congregation liked their preachers to be learned—stated and repeated, amplified, piled one on top of the other, and all set forth with the muscular magnificence of Protestant prose. And thereby was raised up a rhetorical temple so huge, complex, and echoing that by the end it might almost be wondered whether the authors of the sacred texts themselves could have imagined the mighty structure of which their humble words were now a part.

Why, Pincher asked his hearers, why was it that Our Saviour came not to send peace? Because such a thing was impossible: by the very fact that He was good and holy—here followed several learned allusions—it was impossible that He should do so. Were not all things possible to God? All except one, for He had established it so, and that was that He should sin. But we know sin. He looked sternly at the congregation. They knew sin. Mankind had known sin from the first, since the Serpent—here followed several allusions to the Prince of Darkness—since the Serpent had beguiled Eve and she had tempted Adam. "Since Man's first disobedience and the fruit of the forbidden tree brought death into the world," he cried, "we have no peace." Peace will come only at the end of the world, when the devil at last is vanquished by Our Saviour. Sin shall be destroyed. There is no other way to deal with the devil but by striking him down.

"I come not to send peace, but a sword."

Man had fallen, he continued, Paradise was lost. Like Adam, we wander the world, where the devil has set snares and temptations for us—forbidden trees—at every turn. Eat of their fruits, and we shall be snatched away to everlasting hell-fire, with no further hope of salvation. Adam was warned by God not to eat of the tree, but that benefit has been removed from us now that we have fallen, and often as not, the devil has made the forbidden trees to be fair-seeming. "The serpent is sapient and subtle," he informed them. "He speaks sweetly and softly." He makes use of Eve, the eternal temptress. She shows us fruit, fair without, yet corrupt within. How, therefore, shall we know the temptress and the fruit for what they are? He would tell them, he declared. A tree is known by its fruits: that was how they could know. And now he paused and looked around them all.

"There is a tree in the world," he cried out loudly, "whose fruits we know." Superstition, idol worship, blasphemy, hypocrisy: of what tree was he speaking? What else could it be? What yielded these fruits, if not the Church of Rome?

"The Church of Rome," he shouted, "the painted whore, with her incense and images, her liturgies and lurries. Beware, I say, of the papist Eve, the harlot and the Jezebel. Turn your face from her. Strike her down!

"I come not to send peace, but a sword."

The congregation had given a little gasp at this. The sentiments were familiar enough, but to hear such a virulent attack, in the presence of so many Catholic gentlemen of Dublin, was more than a sermon. It was a declaration of war. Pincher was in full flood, however, and was moving inexorably to his next topic.

The sword, he reminded them, was a weapon that made clear divisions. Good was divided from evil, and the distinction was absolute. Let them beware, he cried, let them not believe that any man can serve two masters. Those who compromise with evil—he gave his audience a terrible look—partake of evil, and are divided clearly by the sword from the good. They shall be damned. Damned utterly, damned eternally. There were some—he let his eyes travel round them all accusingly—sinners here present who were willing to compromise, and who counted the devil amongst their friends. What did he mean? he asked rhetorically. Had he examples in mind? And now came the moment he had prepared for. Yes, he had.

The list of sinners was long. Apart from his supporters, there was scarcely a person in the congregation who was without blame. There were those who tolerated the presence of Jesuits living openly near the cathedral itself; those who winked at the keeping of papist priests in chapels, private houses, and even city churches. Church land was being let or sublet to Catholics who kept their priests upon the proceeds. Recusants were escaping fines. The entire way of life that had made the religious division in Ireland bearable was mercilessly exposed, and condemned. "Our Lord has promised that the meek shall inherit the earth," he thundered, "but in Ireland, instead, it is inherited by traitors."

The congregation understood all too well. A shocked silence seemed to roll through the sea of faces like a wave. But Pincher had prepared for this also. For now, from twenty or thirty Protestant lips came an echoing "Amen."

"Repent!" he cried back in answer. For what, he demanded, would be the fate of the city of Dublin if they failed to enforce the Protestant faith? Had not the Lord foretold the fate of the cities which heard the word but repented not? He had indeed, in the Gospel of Matthew. "Woe unto thee," Pincher called out in a loud voice, "it shall be more tolerable for the land of Sodom in the Day of Judgement than for thee."

"Amen," called back his chorus.

"I come not to send peace, but a sword."

"And yet . . ." The doctor paused, and to the congregation's surprise, gazed at them benevolently. "The way is hard." What if, perhaps, a Catholic is our neighbour, a man to whose company we have grown accustomed, to whom we are bound by daily courtesy, even affection? What must we do then? We may preach the true faith. There can be no harm in that. We may reason with our neighbour, urge him to repent and to forswear his foolish ways. We may pray for him. We should pray for him. But if after all this, if still in his obstinacy he continues in his sin, then no matter what the ties, we must sever them, we must turn from them lest we be contaminated ourselves; we must divide them utterly from the body politic and even strike them down. For what did Our Lord say?

> If thy right eye offend thee, pluck it out. And if thy right hand offend thee, cut it off and cast it from thee. For it is profitable for thee that one of thy members should perish and not that thy whole body should be cast into hell.

"Take thy sword, then, Christian pilgrim," cried Pincher in ringing tones, "and cut off that which doth offend thee."

"Amen," intoned the chorus.

The congregation was now in a state of some perturbation. Most were sitting in shocked silence. Others were beginning to murmur, some with approval, others not. The sense amongst the latter—that the business was going too far and that it was time to end—was palpable.

But if they thought he was done, he was not done.

For now, dropping his voice as a prelude to the climax, Pincher leaned towards them almost confidentially. We must not suppose, he reminded them, that the devil was ever passive. He was scheming all the time, not only to save his evil empire from destruction but to regain the upper hand. Even now—Pincher's voice began to rise—the servants of the whore of Rome were plotting to undermine the Protestant cause, to reinstate the Bishop of Rome, who was the Antichrist, amongst the godly in Ireland. These servants of the whore would try to seduce the king himself, to change the godly laws of the land; and if they were allowed to succeed, it would be Protestants, soon, who were trampled down. Trampled and cut down by the Catholic Irish hordes—Irish hordes who, he pointed out, would be led by the very men whom the congregation now called friends and neighbours. Would his hearers permit such a thing to happen?

"Will you," he cried, "make yourselves part of that droiling carcass of conformity and comfort, that takes its ease and sleeps while the devil is at his work and the godly are destroyed? Or will you, like soldiers of Christ, arise, put on armour, and buckle thy sword?" For if they did not, he warned, let them be in no doubt as to the consequences. They risked eternal hellfire. God was watching, he cried, his voice rising higher. The Lord was testing them. Would they be seduced, cheated of their birthright and their everlasting souls by the Catholic whore who, even now, would seduce the king to do what he ought not? Or would they take up the cross, and the sword Christ had given them, and strike down the Catholic whore? "Strike!" he shouted. "Strike down the whore!"

"Amen," came the chorus.

"Strike down the Jezebel, the harlot."

"Amen. Amen."

"I come not to send peace," his voice resounded a final time around the cathedral, "but a sword."

"Amen. Amen. Amen."

And furling the black wings of his gown around him, Doctor Simeon Pincher stalked like a raven down from the pulpit.

✢

At the end of the service, he did not join the crowd that gathered in the precincts. Too proud, or too wise for that, he departed privately by another door and strode quickly down Dame Street and out to his lodgings.

Behind him he left a scene of some confusion. The Puritan elements who had provided the chorus were exultant. The sermon, they all agreed, easily surpassed the Bishop of Derry's diatribe in the spring. And Pincher was a local man. Now that they had such a spokesman, they said, it would go hard with the Papists.

The Catholics, naturally, were horrified. Two questions in particular were asked. Did Pincher speak only for himself and his friends—or were there others, more powerful, behind him? And was this a signal that the king, instead of helping the Catholics, had changed his mind and was about to turn on them?

But a large party, some Catholic, some Church of Ireland men, had a different view. They did not share Pincher's contempt for compromise, and were disturbed at this attempt to worsen a political situation that was already tense. Walter Smith, in particular, was deeply distressed, and was quite surprised therefore, on meeting Doyle outside, to find that the Church of Ireland merchant, who certainly believed in compromise, was taking things so calmly.

"What is to be done?" Smith asked anxiously.

"Done?" Doyle looked at him quizzically. "There is nothing to be done. Pincher has just destroyed himself."

"How so? There are many in Dublin Castle, and in London, who would agree with every word he says."

"No doubt. But he's destroyed all the same." Doyle smiled grimly. "You did not listen carefully enough," he continued quietly. "His sermon was fearful, certainly. But he also made one fatal mistake."

❖

In the chilly month of January in the year 1628, a delegation sailed from Dublin on a journey to London. It consisted of eight members of the Old English community and three Protestant settlers. Orlando Walsh was not a member of the delegation, although his name had been considered; but his cousin Doyle was.

The purpose of the delegation was to negotiate an agreement with the English Privy Council. During the summer and autumn, the proposals which Orlando had discussed with his family in the spring had been further worked upon by many hands and finally refined into twenty-six "Matters of Grace and Bounty to Ireland" to be presented to the king; and it was these "Graces," as they were called, which the delegation carried with them.

The situation they left behind them in Dublin had not changed greatly from the way things were after Pincher's sermon. The doctor strode about Dublin now like a man who has been marked by destiny. To many of the Protestant faction, he was a hero; to most Catholics, he had become a figure of hate. For men like Walsh and Doyle, he was contemptible: a man of learning who had turned into a rabble-rouser; the poorer Catholic folk watched him pass with murder in their eyes. All this the doctor relished. He had never experienced fame before.

But most gratifying to Pincher was the sense that his life was now justified. It is a fine thing for a man to know that he is right; but it was finer still to know that he had stood up for what was right, and that all Dublin, all Ireland, knew it. Even his sister knew it, for he had written her a full account of the business the very day after the sermon. And if she had not yet sent word of her approval, he was in imminent expectation of a letter from that quarter.

Meanwhile, no further action had been taken by the authorities at Dublin Castle. Everyone awaited the outcome of the negotiations in London.

A new English Parliament had been called, and the king and his advisors were fully occupied trying to wrestle grants of taxes from its unwilling members. Doyle was able to learn much about the character of the English. It was easy enough to encounter some of the gentlemen who had gathered from all over the country for the Parliament. Some of these were solid country landowners and professional men like his cousin Walsh. They were Protestants, though few of them struck him as deeply religious. But they all seemed to have a great fear of the Catholic powers, who they believed would like to bring the Inquisition to England. Nearly all of them also quite honestly believed that the native Irish were little better than wild animals. Doyle thought their fears of Catholics unnecessary and their views of the Irish laughable. Their political concerns were another matter. They were furious that the king's irresponsible favourite, Buckingham, was plunging the country into senseless wars; and feared that King Charles, with his open contempt for Parliament and his illegal methods of raising money, was deliberately trying to undermine their English Liberties. On these matters, the Dublin merchant decided, he'd have felt the same as they did.

But among some of the other Parliament men, and still more in the city tradesmen, Doyle encountered a tone that was far more strident. Puritans and Presbyterians, these men dressed soberly and looked at the world with stern disapproval. They reminded him of Doctor Pincher, only more so. Once, when he chanced to say that he had been across the river to see a play, a Puritan merchant asked him in all seriousness if he did not fear for his immortal soul. "The theatres are for the idle and the corrupt," the London man explained. "They should all be closed." Doyle explained that the play had been instructive in its way. "It was by Shakespeare. Would you close his plays down, even?" he had asked. "His especially," the man replied. With these men, Doyle could find no common ground at all.

"They hate the king not so much for his tyranny," a friend at the Exchange explained, "but because he is not a Puritan. And their party is growing." Then his friend had smiled. "If your mission here succeeds, King Charles will have better friends in Ireland than he has in England." It was a remark Doyle was to remember.

As the weeks passed, and King Charles and his Parliament remained at loggerheads, it seemed to Doyle that the Privy Councillors became more interested in coming to terms with the Irish delegation. They would meet, usually, in a chamber in the old palace of Westminster, or in the nearby royal palace of Whitehall. Often, the Irish party would dine together in a tavern afterwards. As a member of the Protestant Church of Ireland, but one who always took a sympathetic and moderate line on Catholic matters, he found that his voice was listened to with increasing respect; and one day late in March, just as he was leaving the chamber where the discussions had been taking place, one of the English councillors, an elderly gentleman with a white beard, drew him to one side for a private talk. That evening, gathering the Catholic members of the delegation together at his lodgings, Doyle summarised his meeting as follows.

"The king would like to do as much for you as he can. But he faces two difficulties. One is the general strength of the Puritan party in his realm. The other is that any subsidy from Ireland will have to be raised from all the parties there, including the Protestants in the plantations. He cannot give the Catholics all they want, but he will do as much as he can to help."

"How much?" asked the youngest of the delegates.

"He cannot and will not give Ireland her own militia. The Parliament men here in England would see that as a threat—a Catholic army to be used against them. That's how they'd see it. And I can vouch from my own observations that this is true. However," he went on, "the king is prepared to let us Catholics bear arms. He is, if you like, acknowledging your loyalty, and that is important."

"What about the recusancy fines and the Oath of Supremacy?" asked another Catholic gentleman.

"The Oath remains for those seeking office. The Protestants won't stand for anything less. As for the fines, he dare not publicly remove them—at least not at present. But he will give you a private assurance that they will not be collected. And further, he will see to it that Catholic priests, so long as they remain discreet, will not be troubled. In other words, he will maintain the status quo, and will not yield to the demands of Pincher and his like."

"We'd hoped for an advance from that position."

"One is offered. The question of inheritance and the threat of making heirs take the Oath of Allegiance. So long as your family had held their land for sixty years, there will be no question of applying any awkward tests." This would help a great many Old English families; even Irishmen like O'Byrne of Rathconan, Doyle had noted with satisfaction, would now be secure, once and for all, under such a ruling.

"It's a move in the right direction, at least," the gentleman who'd asked the question agreed.

"There is one thing, however," Doyle continued, "and that is the question of money." He paused. "They will not ask for it. But they are hoping we might offer."

"And how much are they hoping we might offer?"

"Forty thousand pounds."

"Forty?" There was a collective gasp.

"For each of three years, paid quarterly. From the whole of Ireland, of course, Protestant settlers and all."

"That is a very large amount," the Catholic gentleman remarked.

"The king," said Doyle drily, "is very short of money."

He himself wrote the very next morning to both Walter Smith and his cousin Walsh to seek their advice on raising such an amount. Three weeks passed before he heard back from them that they thought it could be done.

It was early in May that the old councillor took him to one side again and asked him to come to a private meeting with some friends of his the following day. Naturally, Doyle agreed, and the following morning met the old man by the little monument of Charing Cross, which stood a short way north of Whitehall. Walking southwards with the old man towards Westminster, Doyle was surprised when his companion suddenly turned in at a door of Whitehall Palace. "This way," he said, leading Doyle down a passage. At the end of the passage was an impressive entrance, guarded by two soldiers who, on seeing their approach, immediately opened the doors.

And a moment later, the Dublin merchant found himself in the presence of the king.

King Charles of England could not be mistaken. Doyle had seen his picture often enough, with his long hair, his neatly pointed beard, and his Stuart eyes, brown, very fine, and some-what sad. But one thing Doyle had not quite realised.

The man was tiny. Beautifully dressed in doublet and lace collar, but tiny. He remembered a painter he had once encoun-tered in a tavern telling him: "They wanted me to paint a pic-ture of the king that would look heroic. I told them the only way to do that was to put him on a horse." Even wearing the built-up heels that were now the fashion at court, the king only came up to the Dublin man's chest. But if Doyle had been sur-prised by his stature, he was equally struck by the royal hands. They were quite extraordinary: very fine, and with the longest, tapering fingers that the merchant had ever seen. Who would have imagined, he thought, that this elegant, spidery little fel-low had not long ago informed his Parliament, in no uncertain terms, that their only purpose was to do what he told them, and that if they argued with him, he'd send them all home? Yet he was about to discover one other feature of the king's strange personality: in private, King Charles was always very polite.

Having presented Doyle to the monarch and let him make his bow, the elderly gentleman had drawn back, leaving Doyle standing alone with the king. King Charles, with a faint smile, courteously thanked the Dublin man for his patience and help as a member of the delegation during the long negotiations.

"I have heard many reports of your conduct, Master Doyle," he said quietly, "and I know you to be well-affected to us, and a man of wise judgement."

"I thank Your Majesty." Doyle bowed again.

"You believe, Master Doyle, that an accommodation can be reached with the Catholics of Ireland?"

"I do," Doyle answered honestly. "I have many Catholic kinsmen, Your Majesty, to whom I am bound by close ties, who are well-affected to you and whose families have been faithful to the British crown four centuries and more. Such people, and many like them, are Your Majesty's loyal friends."

"I know it," the king said with a thoughtful nod, "and in time to come, be assured, I shall count upon that friendship.

I should have liked to do more for them now, but there are gentlemen in England of a Puritan persuasion who are not so well-affected and who place difficulties in the path." The king now glanced across to where Doyle's elderly companion was discreetly waiting. It was a signal that the interview was about to end.

But before he parted from the monarch, Doyle realised that he had one more thing to do. He had been looking for a chance ever since the previous summer. Once or twice in Dublin he had raised the issue, but never with much success. Now, he saw, he had just been granted the best opportunity he could have dreamed of.

"The loyalty of many in Dublin—and the raising of a grant of money," he shrewdly added, "is made more difficult by certain of the Puritans there, who cannot, I think, be any friends of Your Majesty."

The royal eyes returned to him quickly.

"How so?"

"I speak of those who openly preach against Your Majesty's government and even against those closest to you. For they stir up discord amongst the people," he explained gravely, "which those of wiser counsel amongst us are unable to allay."

"Pray tell me more."

It did not take the merchant long to give an account of Pincher's sermon. The attitude it represented not only made an accommodation with the Old English impossible, he pointed out, but in its virulent Puritanism, it was a long way from the moderate Church of Ireland to which he had supposed he belonged. Was this truly what the king wished? he respectfully asked.

The king had listened gravely to all this.

"It is not our wish, Master Doyle," he replied, "and this shall be made plain. But I fear there are many in Dublin who hold such opinions."

"Some, Your Majesty. But there are many more who may follow where Doctor Pincher leads." Doyle paused, while the king nodded thoughtfully. He was ready, now, for his master-stroke. For a moment, he pretended to hesitate. Then he struck. "It is not only the attack upon Your Majesty's Church and government that I find seditious, but the words touching the person of the queen."

The king's eyebrows raised.

"The queen?"

Doyle looked embarrassed. The fact was, he explained, that Pincher had repeatedly referred to the Catholic influence in the most insulting terms: the Catholic whore, the harlot, the Jezebel. And he had said that this whore should be struck down.

"Perhaps he did not intend it so, Your Majesty, but I took it he was referring to the queen." There was an awful silence. "It may be," said Doyle, with an insincerity that did not need to be disguised, "that I mistook his meaning. But so it was widely understood."

Had Pincher intended the queen herself by his phrase? Not directly. Doyle didn't think so for a moment. By implication or inclusion? Perhaps. He might not have called the queen a har-lot, but he certainly loathed her Catholicism, felt outrage at her marriage to the king, and saw her as an agent of evil. Was he urging his audience to murder her? Of course not. But that construction could be placed upon his words. And when the royal councillors made enquiries about the sermon, and the phrases had all been confirmed, Doyle had no doubt what King Charles would think.

That night, he wrote with some contentment to his cousin Orlando Walsh: "Doctor Pincher, I think, is now destroyed."

The Holy Well

F ATHER LAWRENCE WALSH loved to be with his brother and sister. He also loved the autumn season, and the golden leaves were falling by the path as the family rode across to Malahide Castle that Sunday morning.

Orlando was accompanied by his wife Mary. Anne and Walter Smith had brought their son Maurice.

When they arrived at the Talbots' little castle, they found a knot of people gathered outside. Some were household servants, some folk from the village of Malahide, others from farther away; two local gentry families had come over from their estates. Several members of the Talbot family were there to greet them, and when they saw Lawrence, they asked if he wished to assist the priest, who was already inside. But Lawrence indicated that he would be happy to sit with his family unless the priest had need of him. Soon after this, they all went inside.

From the small hallway by the entrance, the little congregation made its way quietly up the big staircase, and from there into the chamber known as the Oak Room, in which they could all just be accommodated, and which served every Sunday as a chapel for the local community. Father Luke, the elderly priest, a little thinner and more bent than when Lawrence had seen him last, was waiting for them and greeted the Jesuit with a smile. A scent of incense pervaded the room. Though there was light from the window, the candles on the side tables made a pleasing glow on the dark wood panelling. But the room's finest feature, in front of which the little altar had been set up, was the big oak panel over the fire, upon which a magnificent depiction of the Assumption of the Blessed Virgin had been carved in low relief. Lawrence looked at it with affection. It had been there as long as he could remember, and he had been coming to the Sunday Mass at Malahide Castle since he was a boy. As soon as they were all gathered in, and had sunk to their knees for a few moments of silent prayer, the old priest began to say the Mass.

What was it, Lawrence wondered, that made these occasions so special? He had so many commitments in the city, and there was no doubt that they were all worthwhile. His faith had never been stronger. But there was something about these gatherings in country houses, an intimacy and warmth in which, he was sure, the pure flame of the faith burned especially bright. The nature of the Mass itself was intimate and intense, of course. And to be welcomed by a family like the Talbots into their home: that also made a difference. But the fact that, like the congregations of the Early Church, they were compelled to meet like this in secret—perhaps, he reflected, this very persecution was a kind of blessing. For here, in the Oak Room at Malahide, he always felt that he was, truly, in a direct communion with those early days of the universal Church.

As he looked at Orlando and his wife, both deep in prayer, and at Anne, her eyes a little dark and haggard nowadays, with her solid, grey-haired husband Walter, he thanked God for their quiet, determined piety. Even young Maurice, an eighteen-year-old youth now—though he did not seem to have experienced the sense of religious urgency that had marked his own life and Orlando's at the same age—even young Maurice surely felt gratitude for the embracing religious atmosphere in which he had been brought up.

The Mass proceeded. *Agnus dei . . . Ora pro nobis . . .* The kindly Latin of the liturgy flowed seamlessly on, the Latin words that had brought comfort to men all over Western Christendom, and given structure to their lives, for a millennium and more . . . The host was elevated, the miracle of the Mass was achieved. Yes, Lawrence thought, the Church of Rome was the universal church, its pillars were moral precepts, its arches gave shelter to every Christian family. Once within, there was no valid reason to leave. It was with a profound sense of peace that he rose from his knees at the end of the service.

The congregation did not leave the Oak Room immediately. Father Luke came round to say a few words to each of them. The old priest was delighted to see Anne, who had not been there for some time, and to learn that the last of her daughters had also married that summer. "That leaves only this young man," he said with a twinkle in his eye to Maurice, "who has no need to think of such things yet." Orlando and Mary he greeted warmly. It was clear that he had a special feeling for the devout couple.

The couple were still childless. Though Lawrence knew better than to question divine providence, it nonetheless puzzled as well as grieved him that his brother and his wife had never been blessed with a child. At first, he had not been too concerned. He remembered when Anne had raised the issue ten years ago, that afternoon when they had all walked out to the sea at Portmarnock: even then, he had believed that with a little patience, all would be well. But the years had passed, and no child had come. Why, he wondered, should God have witheld His normal blessing in this way? It could not, surely, be that the couple were being punished for some transgression. Both were deeply devout, and devoted to each other. Indeed, their failure to have children, he guessed, had probably caused their religion to be even more intense. Lawrence sincerely loved his sister-in-law. She had one of those faces that, to the superficial eye, do not improve with the years. As a pretty, brown-haired girl, she'd had a button nose and soft cheeks. Those cheeks had become a little coarser and redder now, and her nose seemed somewhat shapeless, like a smudge. Her brown eyes looked out at the world seriously, with a slight bulge. But to the keener, religious gaze, her goodness made her more beautiful than ever. Hers was a quiet soul. She ran her household perfectly and her servants were contented; her husband lacked nothing that a good wife could provide, and he cherished her as a good husband should. But under the calm, unruffled surface that she presented, he could only guess at the pain that she must feel.

For although Orlando had never spoken of it, Lawrence knew very well the intense grief his lack of children caused him. His religious faith might tell him to accept the will of God; and as a devout man he doubtless did—in his head. But in his heart, the desire for a family, for an heir, and above all, to fulfill that vow to their father—in the secret places of his heart these must have eaten at him every day. "He goes out by himself to the holy well at Portmarnock, you know, every week," Anne had confided to him some years ago. "He doesn't tell Mary, but he did tell me." And whatever his own views about such superstitions, Lawrence could hardly blame his brother. "I dare say," he had remarked charitably, "that a man may pray there as well as any other place." And no matter how carefully and kindly Orlando concealed it, Mary must have known what he did. She must have known his secret anguish and, with a pain of her own equal and even greater, surely blamed herself. Dear God, the Jesuit thought, if I supposed it would do any good, I'd go on my knees to pray at my father's old well myself.

When they finally came down and emerged into the open air, the sun was shining and the golden leaves on the trees in the park were gleaming against the bright blue sky. Just before they mounted their horses to return, Orlando indicated to his brother that he would like to speak to him in private on the way.

They rode back in pairs. Anne and Walter led; Mary rode beside young Maurice, who, as he usually did, kept up a pleasant chatter; Orlando and Lawrence followed a little way behind.

For several minutes, they went along in silence. Orlando seemed to be deep in thought, and Lawrence, not wishing to disturb him, waited for him to begin the conversation. He supposed it would concern the political situation.

As far as the Jesuit was concerned, nothing much had changed. There had been some quite striking events. In England, the king's favourite, Buckingham, had been murdered. Nobody was sorry about that, and English diplomacy, at least, had been more rational since then. In Dublin, they had watched the eclipse of Doctor Pincher. Their cousin Doyle had given them a gleeful account of how he had ruined the preacher's reputation in his interview with the king. After the return of the delegation from London, the Graces had been promised and the king's money, with some difficulty, raised. But the promised concessions to Catholics had not been followed through, and for a couple of years the English Protestant party had even begun to persecute the Irish Catholics again. True, things had finally started looking up when, a few years ago, the king's trusted lieutenant, a blunt and powerful man called Wentworth, had come to rule Ireland for him. Wentworth favoured a formal and ceremonial Church and had made short work of the Puritan nonconformists. "I think we may take it," Orlando had told him, "that the king is showing that he really is a friend to Catholics, just as he said."

But Lawrence saw no reason to alter his original assessment. "Wentworth is King Charles's trusted man. Of that there is no doubt. As such, he has only one interest, which is to increase the royal power. He will support or attack Catholics or Puritans with equal impartiality to further those ends. But that is all." Recently, plans had been announced for a new, western Protestant plantation, in Connacht. "Nothing has changed," said Lawrence. "Even so," Orlando had pointed out, "Catholics are still left to worship in relative peace."

So Lawrence was surprised when, just after they had left the Talbots' land, Orlando turned to him and quietly said:

"I am worried about Anne."

"Anne?" Lawrence was surprised. "I thought she looked a little pale today," he remarked, "but nothing more. Is she unwell?"

"Not exactly." Orlando rode on a few paces. "In a way, it's worse." He took a deep breath. "I think she's in love."

"In love?" Lawrence was so taken aback that he almost gasped the words, and glanced forward quickly to make sure that he had not been heard by the riders in front. "With whom?"

"Brian O'Byrne."

The Jesuit digested this startling information in silence for a few moments.

"Are you certain?"

"Yes."

"You surely do not mean that she would . . ."

"Yes," said Orlando. "I do."

⋄

When Jeremiah Tidy had looked at his son Faithful that morning, he had felt a sense of justifiable pride. The boy was turning into a young man, and he was shaping very well. "He's taller than me," he would remark to his wife with pleasure. Faithful's hair was brown where his father's was fair; his eyes were broad-set and intelligent. He had studied hard as well. True, he had not always wanted to study. "I could be earning money instead of reading books," he would complain. And Tidy's wife was not always helpful, either. "Look at that poor Doctor Pincher, and what all that studying has done for him," she would sometimes say. "I'm sure he'd have been married if it wasn't for all that studying." Privately, Tidy mightn't have disagreed. But he wasn't allowing any of this talk to distract his son from what needed to be done. "It's his future I'm thinking of," he would tell them. His vision was larger than theirs.

And now, he thought, the boy was ready. The moment he had been waiting for all these years had finally arrived. When the morning service was over, he informed his wife:

"It's time I took him to see Doctor Pincher. I want you to arrange it today."

✜

Doctor Pincher was glad to see Mistress Tidy.

He had been feeling rather low of late. Until recently, it had not occurred to him that he was getting old. It was a toothache that had reminded him. In an age when so many men were staining or rotting their teeth with tobacco or molasses from the New World, Doctor Pincher's austerity had protected him from these vices, and as a result, he had kept all his teeth, which were long and the colour of old ivory. But a month ago he had suffered a raging toothache and had one of them pulled; so that now, on this right, lower jaw, a gap had appeared that his tongue would sadly explore every waking hour, to remind him of his mortality.

But this little *memento mori* had only added to a more general sense of failure that had pervaded his life for the last ten years.

He had never recovered, really, from his time in jail.

It had been the strangest business. He could never put his finger on what had gone wrong. In those first, heady months after his great sermon, he had enjoyed a degree of fame. Important men—some of the larger plantation landlords, even his patron Boyle, newly made Earl of Cork—had written to him or sought him out to express their unequivocal support. "It needed to be said," they warmly declared. But then, shortly after the delegation to England had returned, the unspeakable thing had happened.

Soldiers had come marching into Trinity College, when he was in the middle of a lecture. They'd arrested him in front of his students. Before he knew what was happening, he found himself before men in Dublin Castle, men he knew, with grim looks on their faces.

"Sedition, Doctor Pincher," they declared. "Possibly treason. You have spoken against the queen."

"How so? When?"

"Your sermon in Christ Church. You called her a harlot and a Jezebel."

"I did not."

"The king thinks you did."

The thing was absurd, monstrous, untrue. But there was nothing he could do. There was no trial, no chance to clear himself. He was taken forthwith to jail, to remain there at the king's pleasure. It was hinted that there might even be further consequences. Fatal perhaps. In an agony, he passed his days in his small stone cell. And in that time he also discovered one other thing. If he thought he had friends, he had none. Or scarcely any. The Castle men, his admirers from the congregation, his colleagues at Trinity—not one of them came by. No word was spoken for him. He was a man marked by disfavour, dangerous to associate with, to be avoided. Only two people gave him any hope.

The first was Mistress Tidy. She came every day. She brought him broth and cakes, a little ale or wine. Like a ministering angel, she never failed him. Nor did she ask for anything, though of course he paid her. He wondered if Tidy himself might come, but he did not. Never mind: she was enough. Without her, he freely confessed to himself, he might at times have come close to despair.

The other was Boyle. Without the new Earl of Cork, for all he knew, he might have stayed in jail until the end of his days. But by God's grace, the mighty landowner had, in 1629, become the Lord Chief Justice, and at Christmas that year, Boyle had been able to order his release. By way of consolation, his patron had even found him some land in south Leinster where, Pincher had discovered to his gratification, there was some extensive woodland to cut down.

So he had resumed his life again. His Puritan friends, although they had never come to see him, treated him as something of a hero. Hadn't he been imprisoned for his faith? His students applauded him when he next came in to lecture. He tasted, as every public man must, the bittersweet fruit of hollow affection, and learned to be grateful for the gift thereof.

Only one thing still puzzled him. How had the charges ever arisen in the first place? He did wonder whether perhaps something might have been said by one of the Catholics in the delegation that had gone to the court in London, and he once even asked Doyle about this.

"If they did," Doyle answered him truthfully, "I can promise you I'm not aware of it."

The thing remained a mystery.

Nor had his hopes for the Puritan religious cause been satisfied. At first, at the time of his release, there had been some further clampdowns on the Catholics. But his hopes for the Protestant Church had been smashed less than three years later when King Charles's new governor had arrived.

Wentworth. The name came like a curse to his lips. He would never forget that terrible Sunday, not long after the new Lord Deputy's arrival. He had been delayed and left late for the morning service at Christ Church. By the time he got there, the congregation had gone inside, and Wentworth and his large entourage were already seated in their royal pews. Entering hurriedly, Pincher had unobtrusively found a place at the back of the nave. In his hurry, he had scarcely looked around, but quickly sank to his knees for a moment's prayer, before slowly raising his eyes to gaze eastwards towards the choir. And then he had started in horror.

The eastern end of the cathedral had been completely rearranged. The communion table, instead of being in its usual place in the centre of the choir where all might easily approach it, had been removed to the eastern end where, raised on a dais, it had been converted to a high altar. Over this altar was spread a magnificent altarcloth, threaded with gold, and upon it, in splendid silver candlesticks, burned six tall candles. Standing before the altar in a surplice so gorgeous that it might have come from some popish church in Spain, or even Rome itself, was the officiating clergyman. Pincher stared, stunned, at the terrible sight. He half rose. Only a residual spirit of self-preservation held him back from crying out: "Popery! Idolatry!"

The cursed Wentworth was responsible. There was no doubt. This was exactly the kind of High Anglican ritual that King Charles and his Catholic queen favoured. The distant high altar, the candles, the priests in their rich vestments—forms and ceremonies over preaching, the power of king and appointed bishop over true teaching and moral authority. It was worldliness and corruption, popery in all but name: it was everything the Puritans despised and hated. Here, before his very eyes, Christ Church—the place where he had preached, the centre of Protestant Dublin, the veritable Calvinist temple in the wilderness of Irish superstition—was now made into a den of papists and idolators. And with Wentworth's arrival there was not a chance he would ever be asked to preach there again.

And there had been nothing he could do about it. The cathedral that was the centre of English rule had remained the same ever since. He would have liked to avoid the place, but in his position such a refusal would have caused endless difficulties. Humiliated, he went to church now with just as much reluctance as the Catholics had gone in the years before. The changes at Christ Church had gone hand in hand with a toleration of Catholics for which not even the prospect of a new Protestant plantation in Connacht could compensate. It seemed he had to witness the destruction of everything he had worked for.

He'd even thought of leaving Ireland and returning to England in disgust; but that would have meant giving up his position at Trinity, where, despite all these changes, he still remained a person of consequence. And besides, who was there in England to welcome him if he did return? Nobody, it seemed.

His sister had never written to him. Twice more, over the years, he had sent letters to her, but there had been never a word in reply. He had even made discreet enquiries in case she had died or moved away. But he'd learned that she was still living in the same place, and in excellent health. Of Barnaby he heard nothing at all. Indeed, if there had been any other choice, he might by now have considered looking for another heir. He could leave Trinity a handsome endowment: something, perhaps, that would carry his name. But even this idea, it had to be confessed, was an admission of family failure. At the service this morning, it had struck him rather forcibly that he was old and lonely.

So he was secretly rather grateful when Mistress Tidy appeared.

There had been times when he had felt a little aggrieved at Jeremiah Tidy. He knew that this was unreasonable. Tidy had not been disloyal to him. Whenever they met, the sexton and verger would shake his head and tell him: "Things have come to a pretty pass in Christ Church nowadays, Your Honour." But somehow, fairly or not, Pincher never felt that this expression of disapproval was quite enough. But faithful Mistress Tidy was quite another matter. When he thought of all her goodness to him, he could only marvel that she herself, humble soul that she was, seemed to set no great store on her own good works. "I am not learned, Sir," she would say. "I cannot even read." And he would smile. "God values us according to our calling," he'd assure her. Once, she had come to him in genuine distress. A woman she knew in the city, a simple woman like herself who had never done any harm in her life, had fallen sick and seemed near to death. But the woman was a Catholic. "You have always said, Sir, that God has chosen some to be saved and others to be condemned." Was it possible, she asked, that unknown to everyone, God might have chosen her poor Catholic friend to be saved, despite her religion? Not wanting to disappoint her kindly soul, he had answered: "It is true, Mistress Tidy, that the mind of God is not known to mortal man." Then, touched by the relief on her face, he had quite ardently declared: "But I think

I may say with certainty, Mistress Tidy, that you yourself will go to Heaven."

She came to him today with a small plum cake, in the making of which she told him, if it was not a sin, she had added a little brandy. He received it with gratitude and asked after her family. And when she told him that her husband and Faithful would like to call upon him that day, he answered pleasantly:

"By all means. Let them come at four o'clock."

❖

It was early that afternoon when, having eaten two slices of the plum cake, Pincher decided to take a brief stroll to wake himself up.

Leaving Trinity, he went through the gate in the old city wall and up Dame Street towards Christ Church. Passing one of the three public clocks that the city now boasted, he heard a bell strike and saw that it was the hour of three. Continuing westward, he passed out through another gateway and turned down the slope towards the ancient bridge across the Liffey. He calculated that he had just time to walk across it and return in good order before the arrival of Tidy and his son at his lodgings. As he reached the water's edge, he noticed that the breeze was stirring up the surface of the river into a thousand tiny, frowning waves.

Pincher stepped onto the bridge. It was deserted. He began to stride across. His long, thin legs, thank God, were still strong. The breeze over the water felt cold upon one cheek. He relished the bracing tingle it produced. After a few moments he noticed that, on the other side of the river, two gentlemen had also stepped onto the bridge and were coming in his direction. No doubt their purpose was to take some exercise, too. The taller was dressed in dark green; the shorter in russet. He reached the midway point. They were approaching him rapidly. Then he saw that the shorter man was Thomas Wentworth.

There could be no mistaking the Lord Deputy of Ireland. Short of stature, he had a moustache and a neat little triangular beard that did not entirely mask the sensual, petulant mouth. His eyes, which were puffy, glared at you bellicosely when he spoke, and were sulky in repose. His dark, curly brown hair was kept clipped into order, but it seemed that it might spring up aggressively at any time. A surly boy, thought Pincher, made masterful by a king. Wentworth had recognized him and was coming straight towards him. He could not be avoided. He stopped, three paces from Pincher, and stared at him. His companion in green, one of the Dublin Castle officials, stopped also.

"Doctor Pincher."

Pincher stiffly inclined his head. Wentworth continued to stare at him rudely. He seemed to be thinking of something.

"You have a lease on some lands down in South Leinster?"

"I have."

"Hmph."

And with that, the Lord Deputy walked straight past him. The man in green followed after.

Pincher stood speechless. He went on a few paces and then stopped. He wanted to turn round and go home, but that would mean following close behind Wentworth. So instead, he continued across the Liffey and did not turn back until Wentworth was safely off the bridge and out of sight. Then, shaking with fury and vexation, he started home.

He knew what it meant. Wentworth had been insulting, but Pincher did not take that personally. It was all part of the man's infernal scheme of things. The Lord Deputy was busy enriching himself, of course—what else would a man in public office do? But probably for the first time since Strongbow had come to Ireland four and a half centuries ago, the king's representative there was actually interested in improving the revenues of his royal master.

Not a month went by when Wentworth didn't grab land or rents from somewhere. Often as not, it was the new English settlers who suffered. It was certainly true that the plantation men had often taken many times the land they had legally been allotted; now Wentworth was making them pay the price. Some of that extra land was going to be taken back to produce crown revenue, or for resale. And if this rule applied to the lands of the king, then it applied to the lands of the king's church, too. Church leases were being called in or renegotiated with a new and ruthless efficiency. And now, evidently, the greedy eye of the Lord Deputy had lighted upon the lease of his own little estate down in South Leinster.

In the last years, Pincher had been active upon the land. Ever since he came out of jail, he had made a trip south once every year, when the weather was fine, to pass by the land he leased in South Leinster, and, of course, to visit his living down in Munster, where he would preach a sermon and do the accounts. In both places, he had certainly let in the light. The Munster living had been cleared for a good profit, and was now so productive that he had even been able to give the poor curate a small increase in his little stipend. In Leinster, so far, he had only cut down some of the woodlands, just enough to pay the lease and give him a modest profit.

His lease was perfectly legal. It was signed and sealed, and it had years to run. The rent was outrageously low, of course, but it was legal. Not that he supposed for a moment that this legal nicety would matter to the blunt and brutal mind of Wentworth. He means to attack me, Pincher thought, and he has just told me so. And if Wentworth succeeded and Pincher lost this income, what would be the result? He'll have more money to spend on his cursed candles, his golden altarcloths, and his popish ceremonies in Christ Church, the doctor thought bitterly. He was so upset that he could not even bring himself to walk back past the cathedral, but returned along Wood Quay instead. One thing at least was certain. Before Wentworth gets it from me, he thought, I'll strip the place bare.

So he was not in a very good temper when, upon reaching

his lodgings, he found Jeremiah Tidy and his son Faithful dutifully waiting for him.

÷

It certainly wasn't Tidy's fault if Pincher heard his request without enthusiasm. The sexton could hardly have presented his case better. He began very humbly. The doctor had honoured him with his acquaintance all these years and Pincher knew that he and his wife were only simple people. Though loyal, he added quietly—a fact that Pincher acknowledged with a slight inclination of his head. But thanks to their admiration of the learned doctor, young Faithful had not only been brought up in strict adherence to Calvinist doctrines but had also received an education. In fact, he had excelled at his studies. Pincher had been aware that the boy had gone to one of the little Protestant schools in Dublin, but knew little else of his attainments.

And now, it seemed, Tidy was desirous that his son should make the greatest step of all and go to Trinity College as a young scholar. His father could undertake to meet the costs involved—though naturally for a man like himself it would be a sacrifice. He had thought that Doctor Pincher might think it a lack of courtesy if he did such a thing without consulting him first, and he hoped that perhaps the learned doctor might give young Faithful his support for his candidacy.

It was the sort of request that had been made at Oxford and Cambridge for centuries. Sons of prosperous yeomen and merchants, and even of humble craftsmen and peasants, had gone to those hallowed colleges and risen, through the Church or the law, to great heights. The teaching fellows of the colleges themselves might well have started life as poor scholars. And though Trinity was intended first for the sons of the new Protestant settlers who called themselves gentlemen, there were humble young men there, too. Why, therefore, should Pincher have given the verger and his son a frown of disapproval?

Partly, of course, it was because he was already in a state of fury about Wentworth. But as he gazed at Tidy now, he felt a certain sense of aggrievement. Tidy might bemoan the state of things at Christ Church, but he was still snugly embedded there while he, Doctor Simeon Pincher, was utterly excluded. Tidy no doubt continued to enjoy all the fees and other benefits from the cathedral, which allowed him to send his son to university. And now he wanted him to put in a good word for the boy. Faithful Tidy would go to Trinity under his aegis—the very thing he had failed to accomplish for his own nephew Barnaby. It was decidedly irksome. He turned to the boy.

"You have studied hard?"

"Yes, Sir."

"Hmm." He had, had he? Pincher suddenly addressed him in Latin, with a question about his reading of Caesar.

To his surprise, the young man replied readily in Latin, gave him quite a full answer, and ended with a quotation from the great man. Pincher tried some more questions. All were well answered in Latin. Pincher gazed at the boy and found himself scrutinised in turn, respectfully but intelligently, by a pair of bright eyes set wide apart. He was impressed but did not show it. Had the boy a recommendation from his school? Tidy produced a letter, which Pincher tossed on the table but did not read. However annoyed he felt, he had already decided to take the young man, for the sake of his kindly mother as much as anything. But he wasn't going to let these people think he was an easy touch, so he stared at them so sternly that it almost seemed like a scowl. And it was this bleak look that caused Jeremiah Tidy to play his final card.

"I wouldn't be troubling you, Your Honour, if you hadn't always been so good to us, a great scholar and a Cambridge man such as yourself."

A Cambridge man. That strangely obsequious tone. Despite himself, Pincher involuntarily winced.

"We shall see, Tidy, what can be done," he said with resignation, and waved them away.

✛

The Tidys had gone about a hundred yards when Faithful turned to his father.

"What was that about Cambridge?" he asked.

"Ah." His father smiled. "What did you notice?"

"As soon as you said Cambridge, he looked as if something had bitten him."

"It's my secret weapon, you might say. I noticed it years ago. Must've been something he did at Cambridge, I suppose, that he doesn't want anyone to find out. But he suspects I know it. Makes him nervous. So I let him think that I'll take care of him if he takes care of me."

"But what was it?"

"His secret? I've no idea."

"Don't you want to know?"

"I don't need to know. Better if I don't. All that matters to me is that if I say Cambridge, he'll do what I want."

Faithful digested this piece of wisdom thoughtfully.

As they came near to Christ Church, his father indicated that Faithful was to follow him into the cathedral. There was no one else in there. They had the place to themselves as Tidy led his son to where the long rope hung down from the bell, hidden far above, which summoned the people to prayer. Tidy stopped beside the bellrope and looked at his son carefully.

Jeremiah Tidy had been saving up this little lecture for many years. Now it was time to deliver it.

"You see this bellrope, Faithful?" Faithful nodded. "What is it?" his father went on. "Just a length of rope. That's all. Nothing more. A man could hang himself with it, or he could climb up it. For myself, my son, I have made my life by pulling on it." He paused and shook his head in wonderment at the strange simplicity of the thing. "By pulling this bellrope, Faithful, I earn the right to live in the precincts of this cathedral. And what sort of place is the precinct of Christ Church?"

"It is a Liberty," answered his son.

"A Liberty," echoed his father. "Like the Liberty of Saint Patrick's Cathedral or any of the other great cathedrals of Ireland. And what is so special about a Liberty?"

"We live under the rule of the Dean."

"Correct. We do not answer to the Lord Mayor of Dublin, nor to the king's sheriff, nor even hardly to the Lord Deputy. The Liberty is like a little legal kingdom, Faithful, in which the Dean is the only lord. And we enjoy all the privileges of the Liberty. I have lodgings which are almost free. I can trade from my house—which I do—without needing to belong to a city guild or having the freedom of the city, for both of which you have to pay. Nor do I pay any of the profits of my trade to the Dublin corporation." He smiled. "I enjoy all the privileges of the city, yet I pay no taxes. And all because I pull this bellrope."

These were by no means all the benefits of being a servant of the cathedral. Like all such ancient foundations, Christ Church took care of its own. All kinds of folk, from the verger and the vicars choral who sang in the choir, to the humblest sweeper and scavenger, found shelter and sustenance in its nooks and crannies. All kinds of perquisites and customary charity were given out, from shoes and gowns to food and fuel. When the great candles on the altar reached a certain low point, for instance, Tidy would replace them and take the remains home. His family enjoyed the finest wax candles, but never had to pay for them. Above all there were the innumerable little fees which the laity paid for every service he performed, the greatest of which, of course, was the ringing of the bell.

"It makes no difference, Faithful, whether they are High Church or Calvinist, papist or Puritan, they will always wish the bell to be rung," Tidy declared. "And all I have to do is pull this rope. A fool could do it. But it has made my fortune." Though he was careful never to let anyone guess it, Tidy had by now amassed a fortune that was quite equal to that of Doctor Pincher.

"And now, Faithful," he concluded, "you are going to climb up this rope to a higher sphere entirely. You could become a lawyer and even a gentleman; and one day you'll look down upon me as a humble, ignorant sort of fellow. But remember: it was this bellrope that got you there."

While this homily was in progress in Christ Church, Doctor Pincher, who had not stirred from his seat since the Tidys left, was engaged in some deep thoughts of his own. But these did not concern the Tidy family at all.

If Doctor Pincher had more cause than ever to hate the king's Lord Deputy, he was not alone. The Puritan party hated him for his High Church; the New English settlers hated him for attacking their land titles. The Earl of Cork himself, meeting Pincher in Trinity College, had confided to him: "We'll bring this cursed Wentworth down one day, I promise you."

Over in England, Pincher was aware, the situation was different but even more tense. There, the Puritans were so disgusted with Charles's Church that they were starting to leave for the new American colonies—not just in a tiny trickle, as in the previous decade, but in regular convoys. A little army of useful craftsmen, small farmers, and even some educated men was removing itself from England's shores forever. Even more significant politically was the fury of the gentry. With the help of new taxes which he had been able to extract through the law courts, Charles had found that, so long as he stayed out of costly wars, he could get by without calling a Parliament to vote him extra funds. As a result, England had now been ruled by the king alone, without any Parliament, for the last seven years. Parliaments had been called, and listened to, for centuries. They might be collections of country gentlemen and lawyers, but they represented ancient English Liberties, and to many of the solid, landed class who led the community, this was clear evidence that King Charles, who believed he had a divine right to do what he liked, was on his way to imposing a tyranny. Gentlemen in Ireland might be at some remove from all this, but they were well aware that politically this represented a powder keg.

Sooner or later, Pincher mused to himself, Wentworth would fall. The English governors in Ireland always did. But even more important, when finally something forced Charles to summon a Parliament, then there would be a reckoning. The Puritans of England and Ireland would have their revenge. What form that revenge would take, Pincher did not know. But he would work towards that day of reckoning from now on. If he was an enemy of Wentworth, then he must also, henceforth, be an enemy of the king.

Though he was not entirely aware of it, Doctor Pincher had just taken the first step down the path towards treason.

⁘

If it hadn't been for young Maurice, Brian O'Byrne would never have seen them. Anne had told him so. It had been shortly after midsummer. Walter Smith and his wife had been staying two days with a merchant in Wicklow that Walter knew. As well as young Maurice, Orlando had also accompanied them. Returning home early in the morning, they had all decided to go up to Glendalough. They had walked all round the ancient ruins, admired the round tower and the silence of Saint Kevin's two mountain lakes. By noon, they had started home. The days were long. Even proceeding at an easy pace, they could be back at Dublin before darkness finally set in. They had just passed the track that led to Rathconan, and Orlando had just told them what it was, when Maurice had cried: "Rathconan. I should like to see that."

"If you ride along the track as far as that tree," Orlando had pointed to a tree at a short distance, "you can see the old tower house. But don't go any farther or you might be seen, for I never told Brian that I was coming up here."

But of course, Maurice rode farther, and O'Byrne himself had caught sight of him and, recognising the youth, had waved for him to come over. And a minute or two later, Brian was out at the main track, reproaching Orlando for riding by his house in such an unfriendly way, and courteously inviting Walter and

Anne to come in. It would have been rude to refuse, although Walter said, "We can't stop long." Anne had smiled, however, and remarked, "I should like to see your house." Maurice, meanwhile, was already headed back towards it.

As they had approached the old tower, Brian had given Walter a sideways look and murmured: "Your family home."

"Ah." Walter had only allowed himself a half-smile.

"Your son seems to like it, anyway." Maurice was already riding round the old tower with evident delight. O'Byrne had glanced across at Anne. She was looking around appreciatively.

"You take the cattle up there?" She pointed to the wild mountain slopes above.

"In summer."

He remembered Orlando's sister very well; he and Orlando had continued to see each other from time to time, but he hadn't seen Anne since that day they had gone out to the island together—it had to be more than ten years ago. She had changed remarkably little. A few more lines, some grey hair, but still a very attractive woman. She was a little older than he was, so she must be in her midforties. And still locked, he thought privately, in the same life with her dull husband.

His own life at Rathconan had not been so eventful. He had a brood of children now. The two boys studied with the priest; the girls were taught to read and write, but no more. His wife had died a year ago, giving birth to a seventh child. It had caused him much grief; but a year had passed, and it was time to think of finding a replacement. Handsome Brian O'Byrne of Rathconan would have no difficulty finding a young Wicklow woman happy to share his bed, manage his fine estate, and take over his lively children.

At Anne's request, he took them round the place. They appreciated the old stone house and admired the magnificent views. Maurice, in particular, was enthusiastic. Every time one of Brian's children appeared, he inspected them to see if they had their father's green eyes, but none of them had. He wanted to walk up the hillside with O'Byrne to see the summer pastures, and Brian was perfectly agreeable. Anne also wanted to go. "So we'll all go up together, then," Walter agreed with a faint sigh. By the time all this was accomplished, it was past midafternoon. Brian had pressed them to eat with his family and stay the night. And since it was clear to Walter that everyone except himself wanted to do so, he had agreed with good grace.

The big evening meal at Rathconan was a communal affair. The entire household ate together, in the old Irish manner. Neighbours or travellers often joined them. The priest blessed the food. Like as not, someone would strike up a tune on a fiddle, or tell a tale or two when the eating was over. As it happened that evening, there was a lively company. Several tales were told that long summer evening, of Cuchulainn, or Finn, or of local ghosts; there was music and some dancing.

Brian O'Byrne had watched his guests with interest. Orlando was quite at home, of course, tapping his foot contentedly in time to the music. Walter Smith looked less comfortable. He must have been as familiar with the stories and the music as anyone else born in Ireland; yet though the solid, grey-haired Dublin man sat there, smiling politely, you could tell that he wasn't really happy. You'd never guess, O'Byrne thought, that the man was his own flesh and blood. Young Maurice, on the other hand, the handsome young fellow with the green eyes, might be a son of his own. Those eyes were dancing, his face was flushed; he'd already taken an interest in a pretty young farm girl. Young Maurice belonged at Rathconan without a doubt. It all showed, O'Byrne considered, that whatever a man's ancestry might be, a man's character was entirely individual.

As for Anne, he observed her all evening. She was certainly enjoying herself. Like her brother, her foot was tapping to the music. At one point, when people were dancing, he saw her lean across and say something to her husband, and when he gave a slight shake of the head, she shrugged with a trace of irritation. A few moments later, young Maurice was summoned over to lead her to the dance. She moved with grace, and

O'Byrne would have liked to join her himself, but he decided it was wiser not to do so. And even though she glanced across in his direction once or twice, he pretended he had not noticed.

It was Maurice who had brought his mother over to him from the dancing, with a request. Her son liked Rathconan so well, she explained, that he wondered whether O'Byrne would let him spend a week or two there. Could the young man come to stay with him?

"By all means, Mwirish," Brian replied genially. "You'd be welcome here whenever you please. But first you'll have to ask your father, I should think."

It had been in the moments that followed, while Maurice had gone to interrupt his father, who was deep in conversation with the priest, that O'Byrne had known that Anne Smith might be his. She had been standing there in front of him, a little flushed from the dance. He had remarked with a smile that all the local girls would be hanging round the place if her handsome son were there, and she had laughed and put her hand on his arm. "I envy him being up here in the mountains with you," she had added, looking straight into his eyes. And at that moment, all the unspoken intimacy they had felt that afternoon on the island long ago came flooding back. He looked at her and nodded. "I wish you could come here with him," he replied, quietly and seriously, and she had looked thoughtful.

"I don't know if that would be possible," she had responded in the same tone. "Perhaps . . ."

He could see out of the corner of his eye that the boy was talking to his father. Walter Smith was glancing in his direction with a slight frown. Excusing himself from Anne, he moved across to the Dublin merchant and addressed him politely.

"Your son has just asked me if he might come and visit me for a little while. He's welcome here at any time at all. But I told him it's his own father he should be asking first, not me."

"You're very kind," Walter acknowledged at once. "I was afraid he might be troubling you."

"Not at all. We've people coming here all the time. I'd rather have him than most of them."

"He couldn't come at the moment," Walter said, "as I've things for him to do in Dublin."

"I come down to the city myself from time to time. When I'm next there, I'll call upon you at your house. If you care to send him back with me then, he can accompany me. Or if not, then he can always come another time. Meanwhile," he turned to the youth with a smile, "you had better give your father no cause for complaint, Mwirish, or I'll not be wanting you in my house, I can assure you." He looked at Walter Smith with a grin, as one father to another. "Isn't that right?"

"It is indeed," agreed Walter, with evident relief.

Brian O'Byrne was usually up at dawn, and the next morning he awoke to find the sky already a sparkling azure and the sun about to appear. Making his way outside, he went to a gate a short distance from the house, from which there was a fine view down to the coast and the distant sea. He liked to watch the rising sun.

He had been gazing at the eastern horizon so intently that he had not been aware he was being approached until, suddenly, he felt another person at his side. It was Anne.

"What are you doing?" she asked.

He pointed, and at that moment, the first gleaming edge of the sun's golden orb began to break over the horizon. He heard her give a little intake of breath as she watched it part from the waters. They stood together as it began to rise majestically into the sky. Neither spoke. He felt her arm resting lightly against his.

"I saw you from my window," she said quietly. "Everyone's asleep. Do you often watch the sun rise?"

"Usually. If it's clear."

"Ah. That must be good."

He nodded, and glanced back towards the house for an instant. The sun's rays were striking its walls, but the old tower-house seemed impervious to them, as though it, too, was still asleep. He allowed his arm gently to encircle her waist. She did not tense at all. He gave her a sideways glance. She turned her head a fraction towards him and smiled.

"Perhaps I shall come to Dublin soon," he said.

"I think you should." It was just then that a sound from somewhere behind caused them both to spring apart. But when they looked, they had seen no one. All the same, Anne had walked back alone and returned to the chamber where her husband was sleeping, while O'Byrne had gone to see the horses in the stable.

Neither, therefore, was ever aware that the sound had been made by Orlando and that he had seen them guiltily moving apart.

O'Byrne had not made a visit to Dublin until late August. As promised, he had made a visit to the Smiths' house and been sorry to discover that Walter and his son had already been away in Kildare for two days and were due back that afternoon. A pity, he'd thought. A missed opportunity. For several minutes, however, he and Anne had been quite alone in the parlour; and standing together, he had turned to look down into her face, and, as she looked up into his, they had kissed as if it had been the most natural thing in the world. The sound of someone coming to the parlour door had caused them, once again, to move quickly apart, but before he left, he had suggested: "Next time your husband is going away, send me a message."

And now, the evening before, a messenger had come with a missive from Anne to say that Walter was about to go away again. With some excitement, Brian O'Byrne was setting out for Dublin.

✢

As Anne Smith sat in her house the following morning, she wondered if Brian O'Byrne would come that day. She was also in some agony of mind. What was she going to do?

What had she been thinking? Why had she ever allowed the business to come so far? At times she hardly knew. Had she been aware of O'Byrne's assessment of her inner motives, she would have agreed that they were broadly true. But even he could not guess at the effect of the long years of self-denial and tension, the frustration followed by a sense of deadness that had enveloped her until, at times, she scarcely remembered what it was to feel alive. Nor how, with his sudden reappearance in her life, she had felt as if a magical light had transfigured the world. Morality, even religion, had seemed to be swept aside by something that had the force of destiny itself.

In the few encounters she'd had with O'Byrne so far, however—on the island long ago, up at Rathconan, or even here in her own house—the two of them had found themselves together, and events had seemed to unfold with a momentum of their own. Whatever was destined to be, she could tell herself, had happened. The thing was—almost—outside her control.

But now she had taken the step herself. She had summoned him. There could be no escaping that fact. And she was having second thoughts.

Was it fear of discovery? She wasn't sure, but she suspected that Orlando might have guessed. The day she had kissed O'Byrne, the Irishman had only been gone a few minutes when Orlando had appeared, looking strange. He was in Dublin for the day, he told her, and had come round to see if Walter was back. Then, with a slight frown he had asked: "Was that O'Byrne I saw, coming away from the house?" And like a fool, just for a moment, she had hesitated. Then, quickly recovering, she had replied with a laugh that was just a little nervous: "Yes. He was coming to ask about Maurice." She had seen the look of suspicion that had crossed her brother's face, the concern in his eyes; and he had seemed about to say something when, thank God, she had been called to the kitchen and been able to avoid any further conversation. Two weeks later, when the whole family had gathered up at the house in Fingal and gone to Mass together at Malahide, he had said nothing; but she wasn't sure that meant his suspicion had gone away.

Even so, it wasn't really fear of her brother that held her back. It was her affection for her kindly husband.

Last night had been everything that Walter Smith loved. As well as his wife and son, his daughters and their husbands and children had all been together at the house. They had eaten and drunk, spent a happy evening together, and played foolish family games. Walter had been wreathed in smiles. Several times he had given his irritating chuckle, and in the midst of so much happiness, Anne had hardly minded. And watching him, she had thought: this is a good man who loves me, and who, for his goodness, I love also. That morning, when he had parted from her with great affection, she had watched him out of sight and then turned indoors, thinking: no, I can't do this to him. Her married lot was not so terrible. She must draw back, stop this business with O'Byrne before it was too late.

She had wondered whether to send O'Byrne another message, telling him not to come after all. But that wouldn't do. He might be on his way already. And anyway, if she couldn't go through with it, she should at least tell him so to his face. That, she decided, was the only thing to do.

⁜

She was sitting in the parlour in the early afternoon when she heard someone arriving. She rose, and found that her heart was beating wildly. She started towards the door. But it wasn't O'Byrne.

It was Lawrence. Her elder brother came into the parlour and sat down, indicating that he wished to speak with her alone. For a few minutes, he chatted quietly about the family, and remarked that she might feel lonely while Walter was away. He said all this very kindly; then he paused. Clearly, he had something else on his mind. She waited.

"I wondered, Anne . . ." his voice was soft, "if there might be anything you feel you'd like to tell me?"

"I'm not sure I understand, Lawrence." She kept her face expressionless.

"Is there," he gave her a gently questioning look, "anything that you wish to confess?"

"I have a confessor, Lawrence."

"I am a priest, Anne. I could hear your confession if you wish."

"But I don't wish, Lawrence."

She saw a shadow of annoyance pass across his face. Just for a moment, the old Lawrence of her childhood seemed to have reappeared—strict, censorious. No one but a sister would have seen it. Then the Jesuit smoothed his face again and resumed.

"As you wish, Anne, of course. But let me, as your brother who loves you, say just this. Years ago, I urged you to marry Walter rather than his brother. You may recall."

"You told me: 'Head over heart, the better part.' I remember very well."

"Well, now I say something different. I beg you, Anne, to consider the heart: your husband's heart. You cannot be so cruel as to break it." He had spoken earnestly and with feeling. Now he paused, and his look became severe. "Whatever the devil has tempted you to do, stop now. Draw back. You are on the path towards eternal hellfire, and if you go down that path, it is hellfire you will deserve. I beg you, therefore, draw back before it is too late."

She stared at him in silence. She guessed at once that Orlando must be the source of his information. The fact that some of what he said was true didn't make it any better, nor even that she had already come to that very decision. It was Lawrence's playing the elder brother which annoyed her.

"Of what are you accusing me, Lawrence? Speak plainly," she said, dangerously.

"I have not accused—"

"I am glad to hear it," she cut in icily. "It almost sounded as if you were accusing me of betraying my husband." There was a cold contempt in her voice. Lawrence was stung.

"Are you prepared to swear," he demanded with some anger, "that you have committed no impropriety with Brian O'Byrne?"

"O'Byrne has kindly offered to have Maurice to stay with him," she answered firmly. "That is all. As for your suggestion, it is an outrage and an impertinence."

"I hope I can believe you."

"Do you call me a liar now?" She was white with fury. "Leave my house, Lawrence. And do not come back until you have learned some manners." She stood up and pointed to the door. "Go at once," she commanded. She was shaking with rage. Equally furiously, her brother rose and turned to leave.

"You use me very ill, sister," he said as he left the room.

After he had gone, she remained standing, enraged and defiant. Was she the same girl who had been in love all those years ago, for him to be giving her lectures like this. And accusing her, too, of something she had not even yet done. And then to call her a liar.

In that case, she thought in her fury, I might just as well do it.

And she was still in the same mood when, late that afternoon, Brian O'Byrne arrived.

✛

It had been shortly after the Smith family's visit in September that Orlando had confided to his wife his fears about Anne and O'Byrne. He had shaken his head and confessed: "I can't believe that my own sister would do such a thing." Mary too had been shocked, but perhaps less than her husband.

Whether or not her sister-in-law was having an affair with Brian O'Byrne, the business had one other effect upon Mary. It brought to the forefront of her mind another idea which, over the years, had come to her from time to time. And one evening, early in October, as they sat by the fire together, she looked across at her husband and said quietly:

"You should have an heir, Orlando. It's quite clear that I shall never have a child."

"I have you, Mary. That is enough good fortune for any man," he said with quiet affection.

"You're good to say it. But I should like you to have an heir." The room was silent apart from the faint hiss of the fire. "You could have a child with another woman, you know. I'd bring it up as my own. He'd be a Walsh and you could leave him the estate. I shouldn't mind." She sighed. "I dare say we should have done it long ago."

He gazed at her.

"You are a remarkable woman," he said. She shook her head. Then, in his kindness, misunderstanding and supposing she needed reassurance, he declared: "If you imagine that I could ever consider another woman, Mary, you are quite mistaken. There is not a woman in all the wide world for me but you."

"I was speaking of a child, Orlando."

"We must bow to the will of God, Mary," he replied. "If we did not do that, our life would have no meaning." He came over to her and took her hand in his. Then, overcome with the thought that she had offered such a sacrifice for his sake, he kissed her hand with great emotion.

The next Sunday they went to Mass at Malahide together, and it seemed to her that Orlando went through his devotions with a special intensity. That afternoon, he walked out alone to Portmarnock.

And so, while she was touched by her husband's kindness, he had not helped her at all.

✢

Anne and O'Byrne were very discreet. O'Byrne had a merchant friend who had a house in which he'd lodged before.

Conveniently, it lay near the western market where there was usually a throng of people. Passing through the market and making a few small purchases, Anne could slip in there without attracting any notice. If the highly respectable wife of Walter Smith the merchant was gone for a few hours in the afternoon, and remarked on her return that after the market, she had gone to visit a poor woman, or stopped to pray in a church, no one gave the matter another thought. From October 1637 until the following spring, O'Byrne made numerous visits to Dublin, usually for two or three days at a time, and each time, Anne and he met to make love in the afternoons, without exciting any suspicion at all. Once O'Byrne encountered Orlando in the street, asked after his family, and said, with perfect truth, that he had not had time to go round to the Smiths' house. Twice he saw Walter, who greeted him and invited him to visit them. On each occasion, he made an excuse but did not fail to add: "I'm still waiting for you to send young Mwirish to me. Send him for a week, a month, a year—whatever you like."

For O'Byrne, it was an exciting adventure. It pleased him especially because, after some initial shyness, Anne had become an eager and adventurous lover. For Anne, after waiting so long, it was the one passionate affair of her life.

The affair had its limitations. It could only take place in secret, behind closed doors. The lovers could never stroll out in each other's company, or even spend the night together. But Anne did not greatly care. "The only other place I want to be with you is up in the mountains above Rathconan," she declared. "I wish we could arrange that." But unless there was some valid excuse to go into the mountains, she couldn't see how this could come to pass. The opportunity came unexpectedly, however, in the spring.

At the end of March, after repeated begging from Maurice, Walter finally agreed that his son might go to stay with O'Byrne for a month. Her husband had been somewhat preoccupied with his business of late. Sometimes he had seemed a little depressed, although he assured her that there was no cause for concern. He had also put on weight. When she had remarked upon this, he replied with a sad smile that it was to be expected at his age. "My father was the same," he said. She had not thought this was a sufficient reason, but forbore to say so. He had also been keeping his son hard at work, so she was pleasantly surprised when he let Maurice go.

She and O'Byrne discussed whether she might accompany Maurice to Rathconan for a few days, but decided it would invite suspicion. "I don't want Lawrence knocking on my door again," she declared. So O'Byrne came to collect Maurice and took him up to Rathconan alone. "I shan't come down to Dublin while he's with me," he told her.

A week before Maurice was due to return, however, one of O'Byrne's cattlemen appeared at Smith's house with a message that Maurice had broken his leg and that his departure from Rathconan might be delayed.

"I think I ought to go to him, Walter," Anne declared, and her husband did not disagree. Taking the groom with her, she set off for Rathconan with the cattleman.

On her arrival, she found her son in good spirits. He was confined to a large bench in the hall and his leg was in splints. "Like a fool, I slipped off a rock in a mountain stream," he told her, "but I'm all right." O'Byrne was firm, however. "He must keep absolutely still for a week," he commanded. "I don't want it setting crooked." The main problem seemed to be keeping O'Byrne's younger children from crawling all over Maurice.

Privately O'Byrne told her: "I'm not sure it's broken at all. It may be just a bad sprain." He grinned. "But I thought it might bring you up here."

Anne sent the groom back to Dublin to report the situation to Walter. Remaining at Rathconan, she fell into a simple regime. During the day, she would sit and read to Maurice or otherwise keep him amused. In the evening, O'Byrne would play a game of chess with him. At nights, Maurice slept in the kitchen, where the cook kept an eye on him, while his mother slept upstairs in the guest chamber, to which, when the household was all asleep, O'Byrne would secretly come. Once, when she was afraid that their lovemaking might have made too much sound, he laughed quietly. "No sound carries through these stone walls, I can assure you. A lion could roar."

During the day, from time to time, she would walk about outside to stretch her legs, but as O'Byrne was busy, she seldom saw him. On the fourth evening, however, he turned to her son and remarked: "We're taking cattle up the mountain tomorrow, Mwirish. It's a pity you can't join us."

"Couldn't I come?" Anne asked. "I've always wanted to roam up there."

O'Byrne looked doubtfully at Maurice.

"We need to make sure that Mwirish here doesn't move."

Maurice smiled. It was clear that by now he regarded O'Byrne as practically a favourite uncle.

"I'll answer for my safety if cook will keep your children away," he laughed.

And so it was agreed that Anne should go up with the cattlemen into the mountains for the day.

The next morning was delightfully warm. It was almost May. The cattle drive was a slow process, with the cattlemen calling out and occasionally prodding the cattle with their sticks as they urged them up the tracks; and although they set out early, it was noon before they reached the high pastures. But as far as Anne was concerned, it was worth it. All around them stretched a huge, high tableland. The sky was blue. The views over the distant coastal plain were magnificent. Just below them, in the passes, the little mountain streams tumbled down towards richly wooded slopes.

After a little rest, some of the cattlemen were returning, and O'Byrne asked Anne if she wanted to go down with them.

"I should like to stay up here," she answered.

O'Byrne stayed with the cattle for a time, until he was satisfied that everything was in good order; then, turning to Anne in front of the remaining men, he remarked:

"It's a beautiful walk towards Glendalough. Would you like to see it?"

"What do you think?" Anne asked the men.

"It is. It's a fine view. Well worth the walk," they told her.

So telling the men that he'd be back, O'Byrne escorted her politely along the path that led southwards. He strode at a good pace, but she had no trouble keeping up. When they were well out of sight of the men, however, he slowed a little and put his arm around her waist, and they proceeded like that.

As they went across the open spaces and the winding ravines, Anne knew that she had never been so happy in her life. With the wild mountain landscape before her, the warm sun on her face, the delightful sensation of his arm around her waist, she felt so wonderfully free and confident. It was exhilarating. She gave a laugh of sheer happiness. A little farther on, she murmured something without even knowing that she had done so, and was quite surprised when O'Byrne asked her what she meant.

"You said: 'Heart over head,'" he explained.

"I did?" She laughed again. "It was just something my brother Lawrence once said. He was wrong, though." She had never been more glad to be alive.

They had gone a couple of miles when they came upon the place. A bend in a ravine had formed a natural little grassy arbour beside a mountain stream, protected and hidden by the surrounding rocks and trees. Without waiting for O'Byrne, Anne climbed down to the water's edge. After standing there a moment or two, she took off her shoes and stepped barefoot into the stream. It was colder than she expected, and when she stepped out, her feet were tingling. She laughed. She took a few steps towards the shelter of the rocks. She could feel the grass between her toes. O'Byrne was sitting on a rock above, watching her.

She half turned away. It was not difficult to loosen the clasp at her shoulder. A moment later, her clothes were falling to the ground and she was naked. She took a deep breath and felt the faint caress of the breeze on her breasts. She closed her eyes. The soft air was brushing lightly round her back, her legs, every part of her. She gave a tiny shiver. Then she turned to face O'Byrne. He was still sitting quietly on the rock, watching her. She smiled.

"Are you coming down from there?" she enquired.

"I think I may as well."

She watched him as he came easily down. He was strong, she thought, but lithe as a cat. Then he was standing in front of her. She could smell the light sweat on his chest.

"Do I have to undress you?" she asked playfully, and he smiled.

"Do you want to?"

"I do," she said.

She had never made love in the open air before. The hard ground under her felt good as the long strands of grass pressed against her harshly, leaving their imprint and little green smears on her skin. The scent of the grass was in her hair, and the tinkling sound of the stream was their accompaniment. Once, as they rolled together over the ground, they almost tumbled into the water, and both burst out laughing. She had never felt so alive before. They remained there, making love and caressing, something over half an hour.

Afterwards, as they walked back, it seemed to her that, here in the great open wildness of the Wicklow Mountains, something special had taken place within her; as if, on that day, the sense of deprivation, the anger that had blighted her life for so many years, had been assuaged and that she was free and whole again.

Two days later, a careful inspection of Maurice's leg satisfied everyone that although the ankle was badly sprained and the muscle torn, the leg was not broken. And so, after a last night with her lover, Anne set out with her son back to Dublin.

"I shall come to Dublin again," O'Byrne secretly promised her, "in three weeks."

"I hardly know how I shall do without you for so long,"
Anne told him.

And indeed, all the way down from the Wicklow heights
to the Dublin plain, she thanked the fates that she had found
O'Byrne, and that her husband knew nothing.

⁙

On a hot July day in that summer of 1638, Walter Smith made
a discovery.

He had just come out of the Post Office in Castle Street,
from which he had despatched a letter to a merchant in
London, when he met Orlando. The Post Office was one of the
several improvements in Dublin that Wentworth could point
to as benefits of his firm English rule. Others included the
lanterns that now lit the dark streets of old Dublin at night
and, most recently, a playhouse. But the Lord Deputy's blunt
bad manners had offended almost everyone by now, and his
attempts to get his hands on more Old English land in Leinster
and Galway had left him few friends amongst the Old English
Catholics, and so Walter Smith was rather surprised when his
brother-in-law, falling into step beside him, remarked cheerfully that the political situation was looking up. How so?
Walter enquired.

"Oh, I'm thinking of Scotland," said Orlando, as if the
thing was obvious—which, as far as Walter could see, it wasn't.

For to most Englishmen, the last year of royal government
had been a disaster.

It was typical of King Charles that he failed to understand
even the land from which his family came. The people of
Scotland had made it plain enough to his grandmother, Mary
Queen of Scots, that they overwhelmingly wanted a
Presbyterian church. So it was folly to imagine that the Scots
would now accept the sort of High Church services that had
been imposed on England and Ireland. Yet this is exactly what
King Charles had recently tried to do. If Doctor Pincher had

been shocked by the popish ritual in Christ Church, the Scots were outraged when the king ordered such things in their own land. There had been a riot in the cathedral in Edinburgh and resistance all over Scotland. To these heartfelt protests, Charles was deaf. He was the king, so he must be right. By the spring of 1638 the Scots, from the richest aristocrat to the humblest labourer, had formed that great protest movement bound together by the National Covenant, and Scotland was out of control. King Charles was now trying to raise an army to march north against the Covenanters.

"And don't you see," Orlando said to Walter, "that this may be good news for us?" In the first place, he explained, it would more than ever make the English government turn away from the Puritans—and that must include the Presbyterians, many of them Scottish, up in Ulster. "The king may come to regret that there were ever Protestant plantations in Ireland at all." Beyond that, he pointed out, it would make the king more than ever grateful for the solid support of the English Catholics of Ireland. "This is the time, Walter, for the Old English to remind the king, as often as we can, that we are his loyal friends."

"You believe that he may grant further concessions?"

"You have not seen my meaning, Walter," Orlando continued. "I mean more than that. I think it possible, if these troubles with the Protestants go on, that the king may even turn the control of Ireland back to us, the Old English. The old gentry families that he can trust." He smiled. "We Catholics may control Ireland again if we play our cards well."

It seemed to Walter that his brother-in-law was a shade too optimistic. But you never knew. Political reversals had happened before. Orlando could turn out to be right. They had reached the precincts of Christ Church.

"Won't you come to the house now?" Walter asked.

"I would. But I've an appointment," said Orlando.

"I'll give your greetings to your sister, then," said Walter.

"Ah. Please do," Orlando said quickly. And then he was gone.

Walter continued slowly towards his house. There was no question, he had to admit, that he had put on weight during the last year. Not that he felt any the worse for it. Indeed, the extra layer of fat he had acquired was comforting. Sometimes, when he was sitting alone, it seemed as though his body had grown, like a friend, to keep him company and, as a good friend should, protect him from the attacks of a cruel world.

He was sorry that Orlando had not accompanied him home, because he loved his brother-in-law. But he was not surprised. He had noticed for a long time now Orlando's strange reluctance to encounter Anne. If asked to come to the house, he'd make some excuse, as he'd done today, and swear he'd come soon. Or if he came, though he greeted his sister with a kiss, there was always in his manner towards her a faint reserve. With himself, Walter had observed that sometimes, without meaning to, or when he thought he did not see, Orlando had given him a look of pity or concern; and if they were standing together without speaking, Walter could sense in the silence a hint of awkwardness. With Lawrence, too, he had perceived a thin veil of discretion, like a coat of varnish, upon the Jesuit's courtesy.

It was very understandable. They thought he did not know.

He knew. He had known almost from the first. He could remember the evening—it seemed so long ago—when he had noticed his wife looking at him thoughtfully. Nothing so strange about that, perhaps. Yet something unusual had struck him: her look hadn't been critical or unfriendly; it was just that she seemed to be contemplating him, as if from a distance. Was she wondering how he would react in some situation or other? Was she considering some aspect of his character? She might have looked at him that way if she were comparing him with someone else, or even trying to decide how she felt about him. Surely such things were not to be thought of. But whatever was in her mind, her look suggested that some hidden separation had occurred; there was a dispassionate distance between them. He saw it, but said nothing. What should he say? In the days and weeks that followed, however, he had watched. And he had seen.

A careful glance at her figure in the looking glass, when there was no need to do that for him. A momentary look of impatience at something he said, which, if she felt, she had never let herself show before. Sometimes she seemed preoccupied, her mind elsewhere. At other times, her body had a wonderful glow. And somewhere in all this, he had noticed the behaviour of Lawrence and Orlando. Even then, he had scarcely been able to credit such a thing. Until one day he had followed her to the western market and saw her enter the lodgings and not come out. By that night, he knew it was O'Byrne that she had seen.

Even then, for a time, he could not quite believe it. His loving, virtuous wife acting in such a way? For several days, he remained stunned, in a state of shock. He must have looked terrible, for as she came in one afternoon, Anne looked at him in surprise and asked with a mixture of alarm and impatience: "Are you ill? You look like a ghost." He told her he was tired, and that it was nothing, and pretended annoyance over some trifling piece of business. After that, he was careful to conceal his feelings. He was not ready to have a confrontation yet. Instead, he had forced himself to consider the matter as dispassionately as he could.

Did she mean to run away with O'Byrne, or if he forced the issue, might she do so? He did not think so. She was taking pains to be discreet. She could hardly wish to bring disgrace upon herself and scandal to her children—especially Maurice, who was still at home—by such an action. And yet, he reminded himself, he'd never have thought she would do what she had already done in the first place. Could he himself put an end to the matter by confronting one of the lovers? Probably. Whatever this was for his wife, O'Byrne was a younger man who would soon be looking for a new wife. For O'Byrne, he guessed, this was an interlude that could be ended. But what then? He'd have a wife at home who could only resent him. Most men would still opt for that, he supposed. But for him, the thing was not so simple.

He loved her. But he could never forget that it was his brother that she had loved originally, not him. All these years, he had tried to be a good husband to her and make her love him, and he had supposed he had succeeded. She had said that he made her happy. But now it seemed that, after all, he had not. He had failed, and she, out of kindness, must have concealed from him all this time that she did not love him as he did her. What must that have been like for her?

For the fault was surely his. She was not a flighty woman. There was no question of that. She was moral; she was good. She was everything a wife and mother should be. He loved her passionately, but it seemed she did not love him. The pain was almost more than he could bear.

He had no one to talk to. Of his father's family, there was nobody left. He certainly wouldn't mention it to any of his children. Dishonour their mother in their eyes? Never. Anne's family obviously knew. Would he be the husband that comes whining to his wife's family when she's unfaithful? He'd too much pride for that. No, he must bear his anguish, and his rage, alone.

For rage he felt. Rage, as a man, at being mocked: mocked by his wife, mocked by O'Byrne. Mocked even in a sense— because they knew—by Lawrence and Orlando. And his rage set limits to his love. The affair was still not public. He was fairly sure of that. Anne's brothers might know, but they were hardly likely to let their sister's shameful secret out. Were any of O'Byrne's people aware? Quite likely not; and if his guess was right, O'Byrne would be discreet. If the matter became public, however, if all Dublin were to know of it, and therefore his children, too, then for all that he loved her, he'd send Anne from his house. Of that he was resolved.

But what if it remained a secret, though? Was there a glimmer of hope? When the affair were to end, as it surely must, and Anne resume her life again—what should he do then?

How would he feel? Was it possible that Anne would feel some love for him? Might she not, at least, see some fineness? For he deserved that much. He thought about it. A word even, if she meant it, would be enough.

It was the role of wives to wait for straying husbands to return; but he had known of cases with the roles reversed. For the time being, therefore, for the good of the whole family, he'd pretended he knew nothing. Their marital relations still continued, in a desultory way; but if he fell asleep at night, saying that he was tired, she didn't seem to mind. Their lives continued quietly as usual. Sometimes, lying in bed beside her, he had fancied that he smelt the scent of another man upon her skin, or in her hair, but closed his eyes and seemed to sleep. Only one thing more had offended him. And that had been that Maurice loved O'Byrne. He understood the boy's fascination, of course. The handsome Irishman with the same green eyes would have to have been a fascinating figure to the boy. But even my son thinks O'Byrne a finer figure than his father, he thought bitterly. O'Byrne has taken even that from me. It was a final resignation, then, when he had let the boy go away with him. The boy wants to leave me, too, he thought. What can I do? How can I blame him? But when Anne had followed him up into the mountains, upon a somewhat specious pretext, he had almost burst out in vexation, and was held back only by the knowledge that, if he protested too much, he would tell her that he knew the truth. But that had been the final blow. He would keep silent for the family's sake; but he was not even sure, after her departure for the mountains, that he could ever entirely resume his intimacy with her again.

Then and afterwards, however, he had continued to drag himself through the days. He went about his business and, at close of day, sat in his chair in the parlour and felt his body silently growing its layer to soften the arrows of pain. To his wife he was quiet and mild, watching her sometimes and wondering, did she never guess he knew? But then, that was the misery of it. She did not see because she did not want to. She did not want to since she did not care, and did not care because she loved another. Such was the circularity of his life, as he grew stout.

The house was quiet when he reached it. The servants were busy in the kitchen. Neither Anne nor his son was indoors. Normally, he would have sat down in his chair and, perhaps, taken a short nap; but after his conversation with Orlando, he did not feel sleepy, and casting about in his mind for something to do, he decided to go up to the attic and look through the documents of the Guild that resided in the chest up there. He'd been meaning to sort through them for years, but never got round to it. Grunting a little to himself, he climbed the stairs.

The attic space was quite large. The ceiling had been covered with boards, so it was quite warm and dry, even in winter. He was rather proud that he had the records there at all. Most of the old Guild's accounts had been taken away by Wentworth and given to a new Protestant guild that had been set up. But he'd managed to keep these ones, and he had no intention of letting them go. The big, brass-banded strongbox stood in the middle of the floor, and he unlocked its three locks carefully with three different keys. It was with a certain sense of medieval mystery that his own father had kept them. And he had always meant to go through them himself one day.

At one end of the attic was an opening covered with shutters. He unfastened them and a stream of sunlight entered. He dragged the chest towards the big rectangle of sunlight and, sitting down on the floor beside it, began to take out papers.

As he had expected, most of the contents were records of minor events and disbursements, contracts with craftsmen for the upkeep of the fraternity's chantry and tombs. Nothing of great interest. As he delved further, however, he came upon documents that were quite old. He found himself in the reign of Elizabeth, Catholic Mary, the boy king, Edward VI. In that reign, he saw, a chalice and a number of the guild's candlesticks and other religious objects of value had been removed to a place of safekeeping in case the Protestants should try to seize them. It was as he reached the reign of Henry VIII that he caught sight of a somewhat different document. It was on thick paper, carefully folded and closed up with a red wax seal that had evidently never been broken. He took it out and held it in the light. Judging by the impression in the wax, it looked as if one of the Doyle family had sealed the document. On the outside, in a bold handwriting that he thought he might have seen somewhere before, he saw the following words:

DEPOSITION OF MASTER MACGOWAN CONCERNING THE STAFF

He wondered what it meant: What staff? Some implement belonging to the Guild, he supposed. MacGowan would obviously have been one of the Dublin family of merchants and craftsmen. Whatever it was, someone had thought it important enough to seal it. Many letters and documents were sealed, of course. But all the same, the thing might be of interest. He fingered it.

Should he break the seal? There was no reason why not. He was the keeper of the chest, and the thing was probably a century old. He slid his finger along the edge of the wax.

"Walter?"

He turned. It surprised him that he had not heard her come up the narrow stairs, but there his wife stood, staring curiously at him.

"The door to the attic stairs was open," she remarked. "I wondered why. What are you doing?"

"Just looking through some old papers." A year ago, he would have shown her the document he had found. Now he just let it fall back into the chest. "Why? Were you looking for me?"

"I was." She hesitated, gazing at him, and for a moment it seemed to him that he saw the same look he had noticed that first time he had guessed that something was amiss between them. She was considering him now. But then he saw something else. She was trying to conceal it, but she could not quite do so. It was fear.

"And why was that?" he asked mildly.

"Come down to the parlour. We can sit down there."

He did not move.

"Is this bad news?"

"No. Not bad, I think." She smiled at him, but in her eyes there was still a trace of fear. "Good news, Walter."

"Tell it to me now."

"Let's go down."

"No." He was mild, but firm. "I've things to attend to here. I should like you to tell me now."

She paused.

"We are going to have another child, Walter. I am with child."

✣

It was a cause of rejoicing when, at the end of January 1639, Anne Smith was successfully delivered of a baby son. All the family visited. Her daughters had been coming in and out almost every day for months; they had taken great delight and amusement in their parents' unexpected good fortune after so many years, and showed a gentle concern for their mother's health, as well as teasing their father a little about his continued potency—all of which he accepted with a show of cheerfulness.

The previous August, Walter had gone to see Lawrence and had a long and frank conversation with him. "It's for the honour of your sister," he'd concluded, "for the sake of the children, and for my own dignity, too." And not without admiration, the Jesuit had agreed to all he asked. After that, both Lawrence and Orlando had made regular visits to the house; and presented with this united family front, it had never

occurred to anyone, at least in Dublin, that the child in virtuous Anne Smith's womb could belong to any man but her
husband.

✛

For Anne, the months of her pregnancy had been a strange
mixture of joy and loneliness. The stage had been set by that
first interview with Walter in the attic. She had gone for a walk
beforehand to prepare herself, to prepare for the part that she
must play.

"It must have been in April, just before Maurice was hurt,"
she had said.

"Ah." He studied the strongbox in front of him. His face
had registered neither pleasure nor pain. "That would be it."

He had not looked up at her at all. Slowly, almost absently,
he had replaced the papers one by one in the box. Then, carefully, he had locked the three locks one by one. Only after that
did he get up, and as he rose he gazed straight into her eyes and
gave her a single, terrible look that told her at once that he
knew everything. Before that look, she quaked.

"The children will be glad to know that we are to have
another child." He said it quietly. It was both an act of mercy
and an order, and she hardly knew whether she felt relief, or
that a knife had been stabbed, deservedly, in her heart. And as
he gazed down at her, for he was still by some way the taller,
she thought: Dear God, but he is terrible. Terrible, and fair.
You had to admire him. She did admire him. But she felt nothing. She saw him, as never before, for the fine and noble man
he was. And felt nothing. She could think only of Brian
O'Byrne. The child was his. She was sure of it.

All the time the baby was growing, she had longed for
O'Byrne. She had imagined him at his house and up in the
mountains. How she wanted him to be with her, to put his
hands on her and to feel the little life within her, to share it
with her. His absence was like a nagging pain. She wanted to

write to him, and discovered she could do so through the new
Post Office. Making the letter look like a business communi-
cation of some kind, she sent him a carefully worded message,
indicating that she hoped he would come to call at the house
of Smith the merchant soon. And then she waited.

Heart over head, as Lawrence would have said. She had
not reckoned with this agony of separation and uncertainty;
and yet, she told herself, she'd have done it all again, for the
wild release the affair had given her, and for the new joy it
had brought into her life. She saw the irony—that her joy
was only by courtesy of her husband's kindness—but she
could not be answerable for that. Life was as it was. There was
no more to say.

He came at last, with Maurice. He had waited, cleverly, at
a place in the town where he knew her son would pass. And
with a cry of joy at seeing him, Maurice had brought him to
the house. When they were alone for a moment, she had
reminded him: "The child is yours. I know it." And he had
smiled.

"I've dreamed of running away with you," she told him.
"Running off to the mountains with you in the old Irish way."

"You would, too." He laughed softly. "You would if you
could. I think you're even wilder than I am."

"Perhaps I will," she said.

He stroked her hair affectionately.

"You're better off here."

"Do you love me?" She looked at him in doubt.

"Is your memory so short?" He was still stroking her hair.

"I'm getting very big."

"You are magnificent." It was said with real feeling. Then
he continued softly: "You are so beautiful, you know. So
beautiful."

They had heard Walter enter the house. O'Byrne had
kissed her lightly and left the room. She heard his voice outside
in the passage as he encountered Walter, and gave him the
usual congratulations. She heard Walter reply quietly but

firmly: "She is with her family now." And she knew that O'Byrne would not visit the house again.

You are so beautiful—those meaningless words had brought her joy and comfort many times in the weeks ahead.

When the baby was born, everyone had made a fuss of it. Maurice in particular had looked again and again to see if the baby had his green eyes. "Babies' eyes often look blue for a little while," she had told him. "You can't be sure of the colour at first." But the tiny boy's eyes were not green. They were blue.

It was only a little while after the birth that she realised that something was wrong.

✢

If Lord Deputy Wentworth considered the Ireland under his charge in the spring of 1639, he could feel some satisfaction. True, he had by no means done all that he wanted to do. The plantations were nothing like the ordered Protestant colonies that they were meant to be. The one he'd planned for Galway was not even begun. If he went into the house of any merchant or craftsman in Dublin, or any gentleman in the country, he'd probably find scurrilous pamphlets about himself. But it was an age of pamphleteering; and if he was hated by Catholic and Protestant alike, he did not care. He wasn't interested in being popular. He was interested in raising money for the king. And in order. "I believe in being thorough," he liked to say. "Thorough." And he had certainly proved it. They might hate him in Ireland, but they were still cowed, and the island was quiet—which was more than could be said of the rest of the king's realm.

King Charles's attempt to bully the Scots had proved a disaster. Having pledged to their Covenant that they'd have none of Charles's popish church north of the border, the Scots had stuck to it. Charles had blustered, then tried to negotiate. The Scots had watched him impassively. "He'd like to compel us, but he hasn't the power," they correctly concluded. And they sat tight. By the spring of 1639, therefore, King Charles had decided on a show of force. He began to collect troops, and tried to find gentlemen who'd be willing to lead them. It wasn't proving easy.

⁜

On a mild day in April, down on the old Wood Quay, the people watching the boats bringing passengers from a vessel anchored out in the stream saw a curious sight. For clambering with surprising agility from a boat, at the very spot where, over forty years before he had first set foot on Irish soil, came the tall, spindly figure of Doctor Simeon Pincher. He was dressed, as always, in black. But today, instead of the stiff Puritan hat that he normally favoured, Doctor Pincher was wearing a large, floppy cloth hat of the kind that, in a later age, would be called a tam-o'-shanter. And when the boatman, hoping for a tip, asked him, "Are you all right, Sir?" he answered very cheerfully, in a voice that the boatman could have sworn sounded Scottish:

"Aye, man, I'm well enough."

Doctor Pincher had been to Scotland.

There were many in Trinity College who believed that Doctor Pincher had become a little eccentric. There was no harm in this. Elderly university teachers were supposed to be eccentric. So the sight of the strange hat would only have brought smiles of pleasure to the undergraduates as he strode past the college gates to his lodgings. And if the Calvinist firebrand who had electrified the congregation at Christ Church years before was now seen as harmless and a little mad, this suited Pincher very well.

Before reaching his lodgings, Pincher sent a college servant on two commissions: the first to fetch a pie from Tidy's wife; the second to find young Faithful Tidy and tell him to come to his lodgings at four o'clock precisely. As soon as he was home,

Pincher poured himself a small glass of brandy and then sat down to write.

When Faithful Tidy came to the lodgings, he made sure to be on time. In doing so, he was carefully following his father's orders.

It had become clear, as soon as he arrived at Trinity, that having personally guaranteed his presence there, Doctor Pincher regarded Faithful as his personal property. The young man, who still referred to the learned doctor as "Old Inky" behind his back, had somewhat objected to being used to run errands, but his father had counselled him to be patient.

"How often does he call upon you, Faithful?"

"Maybe once a week."

"That's not so much. You owe him something. Just do it with a willing manner." His father nodded. "He may be old, Faithful, and not the man he was in Dublin once, but you never can tell how he may be useful to you in good time, if you serve him well."

More recently, Faithful had come with another complaint.

"He has me take letters to a place down by Saint Patrick's and leave them in a doorway."

"No harm in that."

"The letter's always sealed. Addressed to Master Clarke."

"Why shouldn't it be?"

"I never see the man. I just leave it there. Once, I asked a neighbour who Master Clarke might be, and he said he never knew such a person. There's something strange about the business, in my opinion. I'd like to wait one day and see who takes the letter. Or break the seal and read it."

At this, however, his father had become very agitated.

"Don't do it, Faithful. This is none of your affair. And if it's anything it shouldn't be, the less you know the better." He looked at his son urgently. "You carry a letter from Doctor Pincher of Trinity College. You know nothing of the contents or who receives it. You've done nothing wrong. Do you understand?"

"Yes, Father."

And it was a letter to the possibly fictitious Master Clarke that Pincher put into his hands at four o'clock precisely that afternoon, with instructions to take it to the usual place. Faithful set off at once.

When Faithful had gone, Pincher stood up, stretched, poured a glass of wine, and cut himself a large slice of pie. He felt contented with the world.

His visit to Scotland had been a great success. He had travelled to Edinburgh and met numerous learned preachers and Presbyterian gentlemen. He had liked them, and the place, so well that he had reflected to himself: I should have come here when I was a young man, instead of Dublin. It was soon clear to him that the great National Covenant to which the Scots had sworn was a formidable instrument indeed. King Charles might march northwards with whatever following he could gather, but the Scots weren't frightened in the least.

"God's on our side," one gentleman had told him. "Also the numbers."

It was also clear that these gentlemen had been in correspondence with some of the Puritan gentlemen in England. The king would not find it easy to get support against the Scottish Covenanters from his English subjects. Pincher had returned more than ever determined to pursue his own secret war.

The document which Faithful Tidy had just taken would be collected by a third party, whose name was not Clarke, and thence delivered anonymously to a printer. Within days it would appear in Dublin, the Ulster plantation, and many other places besides. It was a vigorous little pamphlet. Late in life, Pincher had discovered a talent for journalism. Its object was to attack no less a person than the Lord Deputy himself.

Would Pincher be in danger if he were discovered as the author? Possibly. In England, seditious writers had even been known to have their ears cut off. But having lived so long, having been repressed in his personal life and blighted in his ambition, Pincher hardly cared. His mission in life was to keep the pure flame of the Calvinist faith burning brightly in

Ireland, to proclaim God's word and the Puritan cause, and to attack the evils of popery. He was careful not to attack the king, but he could and did insult the cursed Wentworth.

But of course the thing was deeper and more dangerous than that, and here his visit to Scotland had greatly encouraged him. For in Scotland he thought he saw a potential parallel. What if the Presbyterians of Ulster—many of whom were Scots—were to form a Covenant like their kinsmen across the water? There would be others, from the powerful Earl of Cork to the Puritans in Dublin, who would put pressure on the government. If Wentworth could be removed, the case would be even better. How this might come about, and where it might all lead, he could not yet foresee. But the general direction was clear. The men of God were on the march, and the popish King of England sooner or later would have to give way.

That evening, he wrote a letter to a Presbyterian gentleman in Ulster whose name had been given him when he was in Scotland. When he had finished, he smiled to himself. He would send it through Wentworth's own Post Office.

❖

She had not known at first. She might have been alerted when Maurice remarked, "His face looks strange," and Walter had taken him by the arm and said, "The child's just born." She might have realised, but in the first flush of her happiness, she had seen what she wanted to. The others had all known, too, but it was Walter who had decided when she should be told, and he had done it himself, very gently, as soon as he judged she was ready.

"Anne, it seems the child is . . . sickly." He paused. "Not whole."

"Not whole? Misshapen? The child is misshapen?"

"It will be a simpleton."

For a moment she had not wanted to believe it, but she had looked carefully and seen the truth of it: the broad face, the tilted eyes, the flat back of the baby's head—the mongoloid features left little doubt. She had seen children like that before. In old times, in some countries she had heard, such babies were held to be the offspring of werewolves and were burned at the stake. In Ireland, more often than not they were treated with kindness. But they grew up slowly, never to full height, clumsy of speech. Often as not, they died before they were adults. Was her lovely child, the baby given her by O'Byrne up in the wild beauty of the Wicklow Mountains, such a one? Was it possible? How could it be?

After he had told her, Walter had kissed the child and placed it in her arms.

"He is God's creature, and we shall love him all the same," he remarked quietly. It was typical of his generosity, and she could not but be grateful. But after he had left her alone again, she had held the baby close to her, and after she had quietly cried for a while, she had been overcome with a sense of passionate protectiveness which the thought that she had failed, and that his life would be short, only made the more intense. Sometimes, these children were almost normal. When Walter had come back again, she had looked up at him defensively.

"He's only a little imperfect," she said.

In a sense she realised, for Walter, it had been a relief. The presence of a healthy, handsome child of O'Byrne in his home, to mock him into his old age, could not be something he looked forward to very much. Indeed, her husband might secretly have hoped that the baby would be stillborn. In his eyes, at least, this defective child could in some sense be discounted, especially when set beside his own, handsome young Maurice. She had no doubt also that, though he had too much grace ever to say it, Walter must consider the baby's condition a sign of God's displeasure at her conduct. Most people would have thought the same. And if her husband was too kind to say it, she certainly expected something of the kind when Lawrence came to see her a week after the discovery. She was greatly surprised when the Jesuit picked up the baby and, having examined it closely, remarked:

"It has been noted by physicians that these children are usually born to older women. It is not known why." After a short pause, he continued: "If you wish, later, for the child to be looked after with kindness, I can make arrangements. I know of such a place."

"I should rather care for him myself."

"That is between you and your husband." He had given her a searching look. "Your husband, Anne, is beyond all praise. I speak as a simple Christian."

"I know, Lawrence."

"I am glad." Mercifully, he had left it at that.

They called the baby Daniel.

✣

To be fair, it wasn't often that Maurice Smith gave his father any trouble. But that didn't prevent Walter from worrying about him. Like any parent, he worried about what might happen as much as what had.

It was a curious feature of Walter's mind that, despite his awareness that he was, by ancestry, an Irish O'Byrne, he always considered that he was entirely English, and that the Irish strain in his blood was like red hair, green eyes, or madness—that might or might not show up in some family member. His fear, which he never expressed to Anne, was that Maurice might turn out like his brother Patrick: handsome, charming, but weak. This Walter considered the Irish streak. All through the boy's childhood, therefore, he had kept an eye out: if he thought that Maurice was not attending to his studies, or had not finished a task he'd been set, he would quietly but firmly see that the work was done. As Maurice approached manhood, his father thought that, on the whole, he was sound.

Only one thing worried him. Maurice worked hard. But was there a certain wildness about him? If this was just the high spirits of a young man, well and good. Walter could understand. But if it was something more profound, then there were two possible explanations: it might be the Irish blood in him; or it might be the inheritance of the Walshes. Had the centuries of living cheek by jowl with the O'Byrnes and the O'Tooles down on the borderland of Carrickmines affected the family? Perhaps. They might have been representatives of the Old English order—that was certainly how he had thought of them when he married Anne—but he had realised since that there was a strain of wildness and unreliability in them which their piety had masked. Wasn't it just this instability that had recently come out in Anne?

Even without his discovery of her affair, therefore, his fear that his son might be attracted to Irish life would have made him discourage his friendship with Brian O'Byrne. Only the boy's endless pleading, and the fact that he could not tell him the true reasons for his objections, had finally worn Walter down to the point where he had shrugged his shoulders in secret despair and allowed Maurice to go up to Rathconan. And what a catastrophe that had turned out to be.

So when, in the spring of 1639, Maurice had said that he wanted to ride over to Rathconan to see O'Byrne, his father at first tried to dissuade him and had then forbidden it. Maurice had protested: "But he's our friend, and my uncle Orlando's, too. I was living in the man's house." But Walter was quietly obdurate. Maurice had appealed to his mother. He had sensed that she wasn't in agreement with his father, but she only told him: "You must obey your father."

Late in April, just after the return of Doctor Pincher from his travels, Walter announced: "I'm going into Fingal on business in a couple of days. I'll stay the night at Orlando's house and be back the following evening."

Anne didn't give the matter much thought until, on the morning that her husband left, she came upon her son about to leave also. When she asked him where he was going and when he'd be back, he said he had to see a friend and would return the next day. She thought he looked evasive, and she questioned him further. What friend? "No one you know," he said, but her instincts told her it was not true. She insisted, and told him that if he didn't tell her the truth, he should not leave. So finally he admitted that he was going to Rathconan. "I'll be back before Father returns," he said. "He needn't know."

Anne stared at him. She knew what she ought to say: he must not go. It was her duty to support his father. Yet she had received no word from O'Byrne since his visit. She longed for something, even a word from him. If Maurice were to see him, he could at least bring her word of him, how he was, some covert message from him perhaps. "You should not disobey your father," she said weakly.

"Are you going to tell him if I go?"

Now he was making her his accomplice. He had no idea what he was doing, of course. If only the circumstances had been different. She could have sent a message with him. But at least she would hear something this way. She hesitated. Then she took the coward's way out. "You're to obey your father," she said. "And if ever you don't, I have no wish to hear anything about it. I don't want to know." Then she turned on her heel and left him. A few minutes later, she heard him ride away.

At dusk that day, Walter returned. His business had finished early, and so he'd had no need to stay at Orlando's. It wasn't long before he asked for his son. Anne was sitting in the parlour, the baby Daniel in her lap.

"He rode out this morning. He told me he mightn't be back tonight," she answered with perfect truth.

"Where was he going?"

"He didn't want to say."

"You let him go?"

"I thought perhaps . . . I had a feeling it might be some girl . . ."

Walter was silent. It was obvious what had happened. There was one place he knew the boy wanted to go. So Maurice had waited until he thought he could slip up there without his father knowing. He was furious that his son should have been so deceitful, but he had enough good sense not to be morally outraged. Boys did these things. His wife was another matter. She claimed not to know? He stared at her accusingly. She quailed, and dropped her eyes. He slowly nodded. So that was it. She'd let their son go to see her lover, in open defiance of his wishes. A deep, sullen rage welled up within him. He gazed at the baby for several long, terrible moments. Then he walked out of the room.

The next day when Maurice returned, his father was very calm. He did not even ask where he had been. But he informed Maurice that he was not to disappear for the night at any time without his permission, and he also informed him that he no longer had a horse, and that it would not be restored until the following Christmas. He immediately sent him upon some errands in the town.

Later, Anne learned from Maurice that O'Byrne was as well and as cheerful as ever, and that he would be visiting Dublin in due course.

"Soon?"

"He didn't say. But he sent his best remembrances to you."

In the weeks that followed, Walter Smith was very busy. It also seemed to Anne that she detected a change in him. Whether or not he had actually lost a little of his extra weight she wasn't sure, for they were not physically intimate. But there was a new briskness and hardness about him as he conducted his business each day, as if, in his own mind at least, he no longer needed her.

She waited, meanwhile, for some word from O'Byrne.

✤

When Wentworth's officials asked Doyle to join an important Commission, he assumed that he must have been remembered with favour after his dealings in London a dozen years ago in the matter of the Graces. "You're seen as a dependable Church of Ireland Protestant," one of them told him. "I suppose," Doyle remarked wryly to his cousin Orlando soon afterwards,

"I must take that as a compliment." And though he had no desire to desert his family to go on the mission, he continued, "I'd be a fool to refuse." So it was, one summer morning, that he set out with a large party of gentlemen and officials from Dublin Castle on a journey northwards. He would be gone almost a month.

The purpose of the Commission was simple: to ensure there was no trouble in Ulster.

When King Charles and his reluctant army arrived at the Scottish border late that spring, the Covenanters had come out to meet them. There had been a few skirmishes, but King Charles had got nowhere and concluded a truce. The government of his realm was now at a stalemate. Meanwhile, the royal council had been looking at Ulster and asking the obvious question:

"Are the Scots in Ulster going to start trouble, too?"

As Doyle rode northwards, he couldn't help being impressed. The Commissioners and their entourage were a considerable party, but accompanying them was a military force of mounted men, foot soldiers, and musketeers that was like a little army. These were not like the raw levies that the king had led so uselessly against the Scots. They were trained soldiers. When he confessed his admiration to one of the officials, the fellow smiled. "Even the Presbyterians will find them persuasive," he replied.

Once in Ulster, the procedure they followed amazed him. The way that Wentworth intended to ensure peace was to force the Ulster Scots to take an oath of loyalty. There was nothing new in this. King Henry VIII of England had done the same when he broke with the Pope in Rome, and some loyal Catholics who refused, like Sir Thomas More, had gone to their deaths. It was their refusal to take this same oath that was keeping Orlando Walsh and the rest of the Old English Catholics out of public office now. In traditional Ireland, the swearing of loyalty oaths was a normal procedure—although, wisely, it had usually been accompanied by the taking of hostages as well. The oath they were to administer now was called the Oath of Abjuration. The swearer had to abjure—to renounce—the mighty Covenant of Scotland and to give their loyalty to King Charles. Doyle had supposed that they would be going to the men of substance and obtaining the oath from the head of each household. He should have known Wentworth better.

"Thorough: that's my motto." They went to every house, every farm, every field and barn. "Wherever there is a Scotsman, be he never so mean, even a pauper," they were told, "if he has attained the age of sixteen he shall take the oath." And that is what they did. Most of the Scots lived in the eastern, coastal region of Ulster, but the Commissioners went wherever they needed to. Arriving in each area in force, they split into smaller parties, though always accompanied by troops, and went from door to door. Any Scot, resident or visitor, was forced to take the oath. Doyle himself took the oath from hundreds, holding out a small, bruised Bible for them to swear upon. They did not like it. "The Black Oath," they called it. But they had no choice. After three weeks, Doyle was thanked and allowed to return home. He spent a few days on his own, travelling around the province, before he did so.

On his way home, as he passed through Fingal, he turned aside to stay a night at the house of his cousin Orlando.

He enjoyed an affectionate family supper with Orlando and his wife, then Mary left the two cousins to talk. Orlando was eager to hear about the Commission, and Doyle was equally glad to share his thoughts with the intelligent Catholic lawyer. Were the Ulster Scots minded to form a Covenant, or cross the sea to join their kinsmen across the water? Orlando enquired. "While you've been gone, the sending of the Commission north has had the effect of frightening many people in Dublin who were not afraid before," he explained.

"I do not think there is much danger," Doyle replied. "There is traffic across the water between Ulster and Scotland, of course. All the time. But the situation in each place is entirely different. The Scots Presbyterians are a minority in Ulster. They have to live quietly, although they'll no doubt be glad to help the Scots if they can, and they are delighted to see the king's Church humiliated there."

"I try to imagine a whole community full of Doctor Pinchers," Orlando said with a smile.

"I found them upright, proud, hardworking. In some of them, despite the circumstances, I thought I saw a grim humour. To tell the truth, Orlando, I rather liked them—far better than I do Pincher." He paused to consider. "And yet there is a force in them that Doctor Pincher lacks, and which frightens me more."

"More frightening than Pincher?"

"Yes. How can I put it? Pincher believes in his religion. I may not like his belief, and as a Catholic you must abhor it. But I do not question his sincerity. He believes passionately. They are not so strident. But they do not just believe. They *know*." He shrugged and smiled wryly. "You can't really argue with a man who knows."

"But I know also, Cousin Doyle. As a Catholic, I know that my Church is the true and universal voice of Christendom."

"That is so, yet there is a difference. You have not only the apostolic succession but a millennium and a half of tradition, to fall back upon. Catholic saints have given testimony. Catholic philosophers have argued their case painstakingly, and the Church has reformed itself from within time and again. The Catholic Church is huge and ancient and wise, and it can justify itself upon those grounds. There is a place for all humanity in it, a flexibility in many matters, a spirit of kindness." He paused and grinned. "At least, it is to be hoped."

"I look forward to your return to it, then," Orlando said drily. "Did you find these Scots unkind?"

"No. Though any people will become unkind if they are threatened. I found them not unkind, but certain. They *know*. That is all I can tell you."

"We must be grateful that we have peace there, at least."

Doyle nodded thoughtfully before he went on. For there was another matter in his mind, which was the real reason why he had turned aside to visit his Catholic cousin.

"There is something else, Orlando, I saw in Ulster that worried me more. It does not concern the Scots at all."

He had caught a glimpse of it a few times in the intervals during his Commission work. But it was the series of visits he had made after finishing and before returning home that had left him so thoughtful. It had not been difficult for him to see anyone he wanted of the important men of Ulster. The English knew of his trusted position; the Irish were aware of his connections to the Catholic families. Some were politely guarded, others more frank. Nothing explicit was said, but he had come away with a clear impression.

"What concerns me," he went on, "is the effect of all this upon the Irish." He saw Orlando's eyebrows slightly raised. "I am speaking of the most well-affected Irish men—of the landowners like Sir Phelim O'Neill, Lord Maguire, and the others. They are heirs of the old Princes of Ireland, men who after the Flight of the Earls saw the English government take most of their lands and the land of their friends, certainly. But they have still more or less made peace with the new regime. They sit in the Irish Parliament. They keep their dignity and some of their old state still. I talked to some of these men, Orlando, and I observed them."

"And what did you think?"

"I think they are watching. They see that Wentworth is powerful but that King Charles is weak. The Scots with their Covenant have proved it. Equally important, they see the Protestants now quarrelling amongst themselves."

"And what conclusions might they draw?"

"I can see two. The first, and the less dangerous, is that they will use the king's weakness to press their case for better treatment. Indeed, they may well be delighted at this Presbyterian rebellion in Scotland, for it will make the king have need of loyal Catholics even more."

"The other?"

"The other is far more to be feared. They might ask them-selves, why should we not make a Covenant of our own, a Catholic one? The king's so weak, perhaps he cannot stop it."

"Wentworth could stop it."

"Probably. But one day . . ."

"Wentworth will not be here." Orlando nodded. "And you wonder, perhaps, if I have information." He smiled. "As a Catholic, that is. A loyal Catholic."

"Quite." That was exactly what Doyle was wondering. He watched his cousin. Orlando sighed.

"As to the first—put pressure on the king to recognise his loyal Catholics—it's what I've said all along. There are many Irish gentlemen who, I am sure, for the sake of order, would join such a cause. And we can only rejoice if the Scots force him to it. As to the latter—which would, in effect, be another rising like Tyrone's—I can tell you with my hand on my heart that I have heard nothing. Such a hope may exist, for some future time, but nothing's been said. And if it were, you can be sure I should oppose it. The Old English must stay loyal to the king. It's what we were created for."

His words comforted Doyle somewhat, and soon after this, he went to bed. But Orlando sat up alone a little longer. And as he thought of all that Doyle had said, his mind travelled back to the days of his childhood and the memory of those ancient Irish chiefs whose names had been like magic. They had fled across the water, to be sure. But their magic had not died. Their heirs lived on—O'Neills, O'Mores . . . Princes of Ireland. And as he mused, a thought came into his mind.

I wonder if Brian O'Byrne knows anything?

⁜

It was Mary Walsh's idea, in September, to ask Walter Smith and Anne to spend two days with Orlando and herself in Fingal. The baby Daniel came with them, but Maurice did not come. "As he has no horse," his father said blandly, "he will have to walk, or stay in Dublin." And to make quite sure that his son was fully occupied, he gave him a mass of work to be completed before his return.

Mary had been wanting to arrange this visit for some time. It was not that she was so close to the Smiths herself. She wasn't. But however bad Anne's conduct might have been, it seemed to Mary that it was unhealthy for Orlando and his sister not to be friends, and she hoped that in this way she might also be helping her sister-in-law.

The Smiths arrived in the evening, and the family had supper together. The two men, in particular, were clearly fond of each other. Mary knew that Orlando felt some responsibility himself for having brought O'Byrne into Anne's life in the first place, although she'd told him: "You can hardly blame yourself for something that she did all by herself." He'd seen little of O'Byrne either, in the last year, despite the fact that he had always enjoyed the Irishman's company. But she had been sure that Walter's affection for Orlando had never faltered; and to see the two men contentedly talking and laughing together, Walter with a little food on his tunic, and Orlando with a large wine stain on his lace cuff, gave her much pleasure.

Anne was another matter. Mary was glad to see Orlando greet his sister warmly, and she observed Anne sitting side by side with her husband, smiling quietly. But she seemed to be somewhat apart from everyone. Before the meal, Mary took her into the parlour, and they sat together while Anne played with the baby. After a little while, Anne had asked if she would like to hold Daniel herself.

How wonderful it had felt to cradle the warm little life in her arms, to feel the baby nestling against her. She had taken his tiny fingers and counted them out, just as she remembered seeing her own mother do. And gazing down at his broad head with its slanted eyes, she felt a longing like an ache, and thought: how glad I'd be if I had only this.

As they sat in bed together that night and discussed the evening, she asked her husband what he thought of his sister and her husband. They seemed, he replied, to be getting along well enough.

"Do you think so? Didn't you see, when they were sitting together, the way they leaned apart?"

"They were smiling."

"They were leaning apart. In all the evening, they never touched each other once."

"I hadn't noticed." Orlando sighed. "No doubt you're right. It must be hard, I should think, to have the child between them, reminding them every day of what has taken place. Do you suppose the child's condition makes it worse? A child like that grows more slowly, needs more attention—that would make it worse, I'd say."

"She dotes upon the baby."

"I was thinking of Walter." He glanced at her. "Can anything be done, do you think, to bring them back together?"

"Couples can be reconciled."

"Anne would have to make the first move. It's she who has wronged him."

"I agree."

"Could you talk to her, Mary?"

"I don't know her so well. And she's more than a dozen years older than me. It's you who should speak to her."

"I cannot." He shook his head. "Lawrence tried. She lied to Lawrence, you know."

"Wouldn't you have? In the circumstances?"

He looked at her in genuine surprise.

"No. I wouldn't."

She was silent for a moment. Then she leant over and kissed him on the head.

"I shall pray for her, Orlando." God knows, she'd prayed often enough on her own account. Perhaps her prayers for another would be accepted.

"We must pray, certainly." He sighed. "We shall pray, Mary."

In the morning, the two men paid a call upon the priest at Malahide. The two women remained in the house together. Though some of her time was occupied with the baby, Anne was able to help her and the women in the big kitchen. Mary could see what pleasure it gave Anne to be in her old house, and she was glad of that. The baby seemed to be happy, too. Once or twice during the morning when they found themselves alone, she had almost raised the subject of Walter; but somehow the moment had never seemed right, and she had said nothing.

The midday meal went well. The two men were in cheerful mood, delighted with their visit to the old priest. The joint of pork the women had prepared was judged a great success. During the meal, Mary again observed the interchanges between Anne and her husband, looking for signs of intimacy between them; but though they were as polite and friendly as ever, it still seemed to her that there was an invisible barrier between them, as though they were two people walking on opposite sides of a boundary.

It was Mary, after the meal, who made the suggestion.

"Let us walk over to the well at Portmarnock," she said. Orlando glanced at her in slight surprise, but Walter was quite agreeable. "You should come with us, Anne," she continued. "The women in the kitchen can look after Daniel."

On the way out to Portmarnock, Mary walked beside Walter, while Orlando and Anne went a little way in front. She wondered if Orlando was saying anything to his sister about her marriage, but she guessed that he was not. As for herself, she did not feel she could allude to her brother-in-law's marriage directly, but she could drop a hint.

"Orlando goes to the holy well to pray, though he does not tell me." She smiled at Walter sadly. "He prays for the child that God has never yet granted us." She sighed. "Do you think God sometimes sends us misfortunes to test us?"

"Probably."

"If we pass the test, however, if we continue to pray, I believe our prayers are always answered. Do you also believe that?"

"In this life? I do not know."

"I believe it, Walter. Truly. We may not foresee the outcome ourselves, but in some way our prayers are answered."

"I shall pray for you, then, Mary," he said with a kindly smile.

"And I shall pray for you, Walter," she said in a quiet voice. "You have shown such Christian forgiveness, I shall pray that you are given the respect and happiness you deserve." And she touched him softly on the arm.

He did not reply, and she did not presume to say more, but after a short while he murmured, more to himself than her: "Have I forgiven?"

When they reached the well, it was quite deserted. The afternoon sun was hazy because of some high, feathery cloud, but the faint breeze was quite warm.

"The well of Saint Marnock," Orlando announced. "Our father used to come here to pray."

"The place lends itself to prayer," Walter observed.

They moved about the well for a few moments, inspecting it in silence. After gazing into it for a short while, Orlando quietly knelt down in what was evidently his usual place and bowed his head in prayer. Anne, perhaps less willingly, knelt down at the other side of the well in a stiff, upright posture, like a praying effigy on a church tomb. Walter seemed to hesitate a moment, then placed himself at a short distance and a little behind his wife, as though he did not wish either to be too close or to distract her. Mary knelt a little farther off, from where she could see them all. But though she watched she tried, also, to pray with all her heart that Anne Smith and her husband might be reconciled. They remained like this, each in their different supplications, for several minutes.

Mary was the first to hear the horse's hoofs. They were pounding along the path from which they had come. She looked up in surprise. So did Anne. Just before the rider reached them, Walter looked up and then, reluctantly, Orlando, his rosary in his hand, raised his head also.

It was Maurice. His face was flushed. He looked excited. He scarcely seemed to notice that he was interrupting their devotions, or to care.

"I came from the house," he cried. "They told me I'd find you here."

"I gave you no permission to ride," said Walter bleakly.

"Forgive me, Father," Maurice called down. "But I know you will when you hear what I've to tell you." He looked round them all triumphantly. "Wentworth is recalled."

The effect was certainly what he had wished.

"Wentworth recalled?" Orlando looked stunned, then turned to Walter. "That is news indeed."

"He's recalled to England, to save the king in his difficulties. He's the only man King Charles will trust, it seems. He leaves at once. I heard it at the castle this morning. The news is all over Dublin. There now, Father, was I right to ride out to tell you?"

"You were." Walter nodded, and young Maurice grinned.

"I've another piece of news for you as well. Just before I left, who did I see in the street but Brian O'Byrne?"

Mary saw Anne stiffen. Walter's face was motionless. Only Orlando responded.

"And what of that, Maurice?"

"Only that he's to be married again. To a lady from Ulster. One of the O'Neills, no less. A kinswoman of Sir Phelim O'Neill. Isn't that a fine piece of news?" And he beamed at them all.

Mary watched. Just for an instant, she saw Anne wince and then almost topple forward as if she had been struck by a blow in the stomach. Then she saw her steady herself and recover with an almost stately calm, like a nun smoothing down her habit. But Anne did not speak, and the blood had drained from her face, which suddenly looked white and gaunt as a death's head.

The two men saw it, too. Orlando was the first to collect his wits.

"A kinswoman of Phelim O'Neill?" One of the most important men in Ulster.

"So he said."

"A fine marriage, certainly." Mary realised that her husband was trying to deflect Maurice's attention from Anne, for he went on quickly. "And Wentworth? Is it known who's to take his place?"

"I heard nothing as to that," answered Maurice. "Are you all right, Mother? You look pale."

"Your mother was tired after her walk," said Walter firmly. "Indeed, as you've brought us a horse, Maurice, you can give it to your mother now, and you can walk back to the house with your uncle and aunt."

Maurice dismounted at once and gave his father the reins.

"Walk with us, Maurice," said Mary. "We haven't seen you in far too long." And she and Orlando linked arms with the young man and started back along the path at once, leaving Walter and Anne alone.

Anne had risen very slowly. She did not look into her husband's face, but stared away to one side.

"I'd like to ride on the beach," she said. "You should go with the others. I'll catch you up."

"I'll wait for you here."

"I may be gone a little while."

"I'll wait for you."

‡

Anne rode slowly through the dunes and out onto the open strand. There was nobody there. She started to go slowly southward towards the Ben of Howth. Out in the water, lit by the pale sun, the little island with its cleft rock seemed like a ship about to depart. She gazed at it and thought: I shall grow old alone.

She rode farther. A curlew was skimming over the shallows. Several times, she heard the seagulls cry. The sea was still, but tiny waves were breaking on the sand. She could see the tide was going out.

He has left me forever, she thought. He has left me, and he has left our child. He has left me without a word.

And the pain was so great that she could not ride on. She had to get down, and sank on her knees in the sand. And there she remained, hearing the little waves break with their small, repeating, retreating sound, as the sea slowly withdrew, like life itself, withdrawing.

What was it Lawrence had said?

> *Heart over head,*
> *Better dead.*

Was he right after all? Yes, she thought, he was right. And, sagging, almost doubled over with the pain, she stared at the blank, withdrawing sea, and heard the waves as they said: Better dead. Better dead. Better dead.

⁜

A long time passed before she slowly arose and rode back to the well, where Walter was waiting.

CROMWELL

NOBODY HAD TOLD Maurice what they were doing with the baby. So it came as a complete surprise.

Shortly after Christmas, he had accompanied his mother and the baby Daniel back to Fingal, where they stayed for three pleasant days. Maurice spent most of the time with his uncle Orlando; his mother and his aunt Mary were occupied with looking after the baby. But then, just as they were departing for Dublin again, his mother told him that they would be leaving the baby behind.

"It's best for little Daniel," she said with a smile, though he could see there was a tear in her eye. "It's best for everyone." More than that she wouldn't say.

Maurice had to ask his father to get a proper explanation.

"It was your uncle Orlando's idea," Walter explained to him. "It's hard for your aunt Mary, having no child, you see. He wrote to me late in the year asking if they could bring up little Daniel, and after I discussed it with your mother, we thought it would be for the best. It will bring joy to your aunt and uncle, and I'm quite certain little Daniel will be happy there." Maurice was sad to lose his baby brother but supposed that his parents knew best.

"Can I visit him?" he asked.

"Of course you may," his father answered.

The first months of the year passed quickly. News came of O'Byrne's wedding. Maurice would have liked to go, and asked his parents if they were not going, but was told that they were not. "Could I go with my uncle Orlando?" he asked. "I'm sure he must be going." But Orlando was not going. A little while after this conversation, he saw his mother sitting alone, staring out into space, and looking very sad. He was just about to go in to ask her if something was wrong when his father came up behind him and, taking his arm, told him quietly that he needed his help outside. When he remarked that his mother looked sad, Walter said: "Your mother just needs to be alone for a little while." Later that day, he saw his father quietly put his arm round his mother, which was not a thing he often did; and it seemed to him that in the days and weeks that followed, his mother looked happier than before.

In March, Dublin became busy, because the Irish Parliament was called. Wentworth briefly came back to preside over it. The king was so pleased with him that he had given him a title, Earl of Strafford. The Parliament brought all sorts of important figures into the city. There were the New English landowners who had taken up the big land grants in Ulster and Munster, together with the Protestant gentlemen representing new boroughs, who would guarantee Wentworth a majority of Church of Ireland Protestants. But there were still plenty of Old English gentlemen, and some Irish aristocrats, too. One day as he was walking with his father in the street, Walter Smith pointed out one of these Irish princes, Sir Phelim O'Neill himself. Knowing of his connection to O'Byrne, Maurice looked at the Ulster aristocrat with interest. But if he was expecting a brooding, impressive presence, a figure from the days of the Flight of the Earls, he saw only a fellow in his late thirties, whom he might have taken for a Fingal gentleman like his uncle Orlando, sharing a joke with two similar fellows as they sauntered along.

"The two men with him are Rory O'More and Lord Maguire," his father murmured. "O'Neill is a kinsman of the great Tyrone—distant, of course—but they say he's up to his ears in debt. Truth to tell, the other two don't amount to much either. They're hardly the Irish chiefs their forbears were."

"But they're important in the Parliament?"

"They speak for old Ireland, you could say, and for the Catholic cause. They're also in the Parliament to see what they can get out of it."

"I thought most of the Parliament men were here for that reason," said Maurice.

"Probably." His father smiled. "Though they and their class have had so many of their lands taken from them in the past," he continued more seriously, "that they are hardly to be blamed if they try to protect themselves from losing any more."

Wentworth's object was simple: to get the Irish Parliament to raise money and troops for the king to use against the Scots. It didn't take long for the Parliament to comply. "They voted the money to get rid of Wentworth," his father remarked drily. And indeed, by April, Wentworth was back in London, where the English Parliament was called.

But the English were in no mood to help King Charles. For eleven years he had ruled without a Parliament; he had abused them with illegal taxes and petty tyranny; he had forced upon them a Church that was hateful to his mostly Puritan subjects. In the last decade, almost a fiftieth of the population had left for America. Now was the time of reckoning. The parliamentary leaders were in league with the Scots, and they knew their hand was strong. Meeting Doyle one day, the Smiths had discussed the situation in London.

"They'll hold the king's feet to the fire," Doyle had told them with a grim smile. And so they had. King Charles was furious. In less than a month, word came: "He's sent them all home."

That month, Maurice saw the first of the new troops that the Irish Parliament had agreed to raise. He had met Doyle near the entrance to Dublin Castle when a troop of about a hundred men came marching up the hill and in through the gates.

"Those will be the men they raised in Kildare," the merchant remarked. Maurice could see that the troops were mostly poor fellows, Catholic labourers and the like. At their head, however, rode a small, hard-faced man who looked foreign to Maurice. "That's the colonel, the man who raised the troops," Doyle explained. "The men are Catholic, but the officers will be Protestant. Some of them, like that fellow, are mercenaries from the continent whom Parliament has paid to recruit and train the men." He sighed. "That's how armies are raised, Maurice. It's a business like any other. For the moment, Maurice learned, the troops would be garrisoned in Ulster.

They had turned away from the castle and were walking towards Christ Church when Maurice noticed the old man and the girl approaching. The elderly man, to whom Doyle made a polite bow, and who returned a discreet smile of recognition, was a distinguished little figure, hardly higher than Maurice's shoulder, but very neatly dressed. He had a narrow face, snowy white beard, and kindly eyes, the palest blue that Maurice had ever seen.

"That's Cornelius van Leyden," Doyle murmured as soon as they were past. "A Dutch merchant." Maurice knew of several Dutchmen in the town but was quite sure he had never seen the old man before. "He only came here recently," Doyle explained. "His son had been doing business here, but he died and the old man came over to look after the business. He says he likes it here and has decided to stay. I hear he's just taken a lease on an estate up in north Fingal."

"He's a Protestant?"

"Yes. Like most of the Dutch. And he has some big connections. He knows the lord of Howth, and it seems he's an old friend of Ormond himself." Of the two great Old English dynasties of Ireland, the Fitzgeralds had mostly kept their Catholic faith, but the head of the Butlers, the rich Lord Ormond, had joined the Protestant Church of Ireland. "The Dutchman's a gentle old fellow," Doyle concluded. "And wealthy."

"And the girl?" Maurice asked.

"His granddaughter." Doyle gave him a quick look. "Pretty, don't you think?"

Maurice turned to stare after her. The old man had one hand resting upon her arm as he walked stiffly along the street. Maurice wondered how it would feel to touch her arm like that. She was a bit younger than he was, he had guessed. Her body was slim and elegant. She wore her golden hair long so that it framed her face. She had creamy skin and perfect white teeth. She had glanced at him with a hint of interest. She seemed quiet, but something told him that her nature was sensuous. He continued to stare until he felt a nudge from Doyle, and looked up to see the merchant looking at him with amusement.

"She's Protestant, Maurice," he said quietly. "You can't marry her."

"Of course not," said Maurice. But he wondered if he'd see her again.

✧

The summer was a gloomy one. There were frequent rains. In the Dublin region, the harvest was bad; up in Ulster, he heard, it was ruined. As for the girl, there was no further sign of her. He supposed she might be up in Fingal, unless she and her grandfather had sailed back to the Netherlands.

He did not see much military activity. The recruiting of troops had been quite successful. An army of over nine thousand men had been raised. But they and their colonels were up in Ulster, where they were being billeted on the farmers and townsmen. "With the harvest ruined, there's a lot of bad feeling up there at having so many troops to house and feed," his father told him. At the end of the summer, however, came further news. The Scots had advanced across the English border. The royal army had retreated. Soon afterwards, the merchants coming into port announced: "King Charles has had to cave in to the Scots. They're to keep their religion, and he's got to pay them an indemnity, too."

"They've humiliated him," Walter Smith remarked. "He cannot let that stand."

In September, Maurice was allowed to go to visit his uncle Orlando and see the baby Daniel. It was a successful visit, and he stayed several days. It was evident that Daniel was happy. There was no way of telling whether he remembered his mother, but it was obvious that he thought of Mary Walsh as his mother now, and it was a joy to see her play with him and cuddle him like her own. Orlando was very friendly, and took Maurice to visit several neighbours. One morning, they called upon the Talbots at Malahide, and made a visit to the village and the oyster beds in the estuary just above the castle. As they were leaving, Orlando said: "I have to ride into Swords, Maurice, if you want to come."

The small town of Swords lay four miles inland from Malahide village. Formerly the home of a monastery, on the road that led north towards Ulster, it was a rich little borough that returned two members to the Irish Parliament. While Orlando was seeing a merchant there, Maurice inspected the place. The busy main street boasted a cheerful inn called The Boot. There was a small castle keep, two old chapels, and, in a churchyard, a fine old round tower that surely dated back to Viking times rose impressively into the sky.

Maurice was just going back along the main street when he saw the girl. She was waiting outside a saddlers. This time her hair was braided and scooped up inside a hat. It made her look a little older, more womanly. He went up to her.

"You are the granddaughter of Cornelius van Leyden?"

"Yes. If you want him, he is in there." She indicated the saddlers.

"I'd rather speak to you," he said boldly.

She looked at him coldly.

"And who might you be?"

He explained quickly who he was and added: "I am a kinsman of Doyle the merchant, in Dublin."

"Oh." Her face brightened. "We know him."

He learned that her name was Elena, that their estate was only a few miles to the north, near the coast, that she had been there with her grandfather all summer, but that they would soon be returning to Dublin.

"Perhaps I shall see you there," he said.

"Perhaps."

At this moment, her grandfather came out, and Maurice introduced himself.

"The son of Walter Smith? Ah, yes." The old gentleman was polite but reserved, and as he indicated that he and his granddaughter had business to attend to, Maurice withdrew. But he noticed that, when she thought her grandfather wasn't looking, Elena glanced back at him over her shoulder.

✛

As the year of 1640 approached its end, Faithful Tidy had had enough. "I shall be glad when I'm finished with Trinity," he told his father, "just to be rid of the old devil." Indeed, he was even starting to wonder if Doctor Pincher was right in the head.

During November, it was clear that Pincher was in a state of suppressed excitement. King Charles, humiliated by the Scots and short of the funds to pay the indemnity to them, had been forced to call the English Parliament again. As soon as they assembled, its angry members had moved decisively. Convinced by now that the king and his minister were planning a Catholic coup, and that the Catholic troops raised in Ireland would be used against them, they struck by impeaching the newly ennobled Wentworth. "He's been imprisoned in the Tower of London," Pincher told young Faithful with glee. It was a devastating blow at King Charles. The Parliament was out to destroy his chief advisor. "Give him to us," they effectively said, "or you won't get a penny." Some people suspected the Parliament men would like to keep the king under their thumb on a permanent basis.

Since the impeachment was a court proceeding, evidence of Wentworth's misdeeds would be needed, and soon there were messengers going back and forth between London and Dublin. With his domineering ways, the Lord Deputy had no shortage of enemies in Ireland, Catholic and Protestant alike, and now that it was safe to do so, Pincher made no secret of his loathing for him. One morning, Faithful saw one of the men preparing Wentworth's prosecution coming from the old man's lodgings.

In December came further news. Some of the London Puritans in Parliament were openly proposing that all the bishops should be abolished, and that England should have a Presbyterian Church instead. After hearing this, Pincher's face seemed to be transformed into a kind of ecstasy.

So why, with all his enemies in retreat, should Doctor Pincher have been so obsessed with a sense that he was under threat?

"There are dark forces approaching, Faithful," he would insist, "and we must prepare to meet them."

Christmas passed. During January and February of 1641, Dublin was fairly quiet. As the trial of Wentworth approached, it was clear that, by whatever legal means, the English Parliament was determined to destroy him. There was proof, it was said, that he meant to bring over the troops raised in Ireland and use them against the English Parliament itself. "He won't come out of his trial alive," his enemies declared. But none of this seemed to satisfy Pincher. Once, when Faithful dared to remark to the doctor that he couldn't see why he was worried, Pincher admonished him.

"You must look beyond this day, Faithful Tidy," he explained. "Wentworth is evil. But he is strong. Once he is gone, the ship of state will be without a master. And then there will be everything to play for."

"But if the English and the Scots force the king to give them a Presbyterian Church," Faithful began, "then here in Ireland . . ."

"Look beyond England. Look beyond Scotland. You must look to Europe, to all Christendom, Faithful, if you wish to understand what is passing in Ireland," the doctor urged. And as usual, he added: "The forces of darkness are gathering."

It had been early in December when the doctor had started to give Faithful the most tiresome of his errands. At certain times—the young man never knew how Pincher chose them—he would be told to loiter near the home of a known Catholic. Often it was the lodgings of the Jesuit, Father Lawrence Walsh. Sometimes he would be told to go out in the early morning, sometimes after dark. "But I always get frozen," Faithful complained to his father. If someone came to see the Jesuit, for instance, Faithful was to take note and try to establish his identity. If Father Lawrence went out, Faithful was to follow him, report where he went and, if possible, whom he saw. Sometimes a week or two would go by without the doctor bothering him. "But it's only to be raining for him to send me a message," Faithful declared. "And always, when I tell him what I saw, he tells me I'm doing the Lord's work."

"You must do it all the same," his father said.

As the months of 1641 continued, Pincher gave no sign of ending these demands.

"I tell you," Faithful told his parents, "I think the old fool's gone mad."

⁜

Easter had just passed when, in the house of Orlando and Mary Walsh, something wonderful occurred.

During the last year, Orlando's work had kept him very busy, and while he had followed political events closely, he had not taken any active part. But the greatest change had been in his home life.

At first, the presence of the baby Daniel in the house had seemed disruptive. He had no doubt that he and Mary had done the right thing in offering to give the child a home away from the Smith household, where his presence could only cause distress. Even so, the baby seemed to need so much attention that several times Orlando had secretly wondered if the whole business had been a mistake. As time went on, however, he came to another way of thinking.

It was the change in Mary. For, as the months went by and she became accustomed to motherhood, there could be no doubt that an alteration was taking place. Her face seemed to soften. When he watched the mother and child together, she radiated a gentle glow. She became more relaxed, laughed more. A cloud of warmth and softness descended upon the house. At Christmas, she had confided to him: "It's strange, yet I feel as though the child's my own."

"I feel the same," he answered with a smile, as he put his arm around her. And if this was not quite true, his love for her was so great that, feeling the rush of happiness that went through her when he said it, he believed it for her sake. He felt no sense of lack anymore. They were a happy little family just as they were—small, but complete. He even gave up going to the holy well at Portmarnock.

As Easter approached, the Lenten fast had begun. For Orlando, the forty days of Lent was always a very special time. He went about his business on the estate and in Dublin as usual; but in the privacy of his home, he tried to create a place apart, upon which the events of Dublin or London would impinge as little as possible. It was his hope that this would be the case all the year round, but it always seemed to him that the days of Lent, that great mirror of the forty days Christ spent in the wilderness, provided the opportunity to rebuild, as it were, the spiritual walls of his house, to ensure that it remained, as it should be, a still and silent centre in a turning world. And this he shared with Mary. So this year, as in years before, meat and fish, eggs and cheese, milk and wine were banished from their table, except where the dispensations of the Church allowed—though the baby Daniel, of course, was fed as normal. But beyond this ordinary fasting, he and Mary chose to observe a further fast—one of abstinence from marital relations. For over forty nights, they would occupy the same bedchamber yet abstain from all things carnal. And as the years went by, this almost six-week period of abstinence shared, by no means easily, had become for both of them a time of extraordinary tenderness.

Holy Week arrived. On Palm Sunday, prompted by an impulse, he walked out to the holy well at Portmarnock. But once there, he felt such a surge of love for his wife, and the peace of his house, that instead of asking the saint to intercede for him, he asked for nothing, but only gave thanks for the blessing of the baby Daniel and the happiness of Mary, before going home.

During the rest of the week, through the dark and awesome days of Good Friday and Easter Saturday, he and Mary maintained their life of quiet fast and prayer. Then they went to Malahide Castle for the lighting of the Paschal candle and the Easter Vigil, and attended the Easter Mass. They both felt tired that night, Mary especially. But on Easter Monday, their fast of food now broken, they dined together late in the afternoon and then retired to their chamber. And that evening, as he took his wife in his arms with great love and tenderness, Orlando had an intimation that something extraordinary had occurred.

⁘

When Brian O'Byrne caught sight of Father Lawrence Walsh, he hesitated. Meeting him might be awkward.

Although it was a late-summer day, a steady drizzle was falling. It seemed to have been raining for weeks. The summer of 1641 was going to be even worse than the summer of '40. Two years of harvests ruined.

He hadn't been into Dublin for months, but a message from his wife's kinsman, Sir Phelim O'Neill, who was still attending the Irish Parliament, had brought him down from Rathconan. Sir Phelim had written to say that he wished to see him at once. O'Byrne had already spent the evening before with him, and was due to see him again later that day. Meanwhile, he was whiling away a few hours, visiting the markets and attending to a little business. He had avoided the Smith house. He had no wish to encounter Walter; and with his new wife to think of now, Anne was relegated to the past. He would have been glad to see young Maurice, but that couldn't be helped.

As for Anne's two brothers, he wasn't sure how matters stood. He hadn't seen his friend Orlando for a couple of years. He'd heard that Orlando and his wife had adopted the child he had given Anne; but what their feelings might be about himself, he didn't know, nor was he sure he wanted to inquire. But he knew very well that Lawrence must have disapproved strongly of the affair.

So he was rather surprised to see Father Lawrence coming towards him now with a smile, and proclaiming: "Just the fellow I wanted to see."

O'Byrne instantly became watchful. His instincts were excellent. There had to be some ulterior motive for this friendly greeting. As he greeted the Jesuit politely and glanced at his clever, ascetic face, he found himself silently asking: "What is it you want to find out?"

"You have been with Sir Phelim, no doubt?" A question. Brian inwardly thought: "You know very well that I have." He allowed himself to be taken to the side of the street, where the copious wooden overhang of a merchant's house kept the drizzle from their heads and provided a damp enclave. "These are interesting times for Catholics, O'Byrne," the Jesuit said.

In May, the English Parliament had got their way. The trial of Wentworth had actually been a travesty, but they'd forced the king to sign Wentworth's death warrant, and his head had been struck off while the crowd cheered. For the time being, there was no new Lord Deputy in Ireland, but two lesser men, each called a Lord Justice, administered the island from Dublin. Next, the delighted English Parliament had disbanded the nine thousand recruits in Ulster who had looked such a threat to them. King Charles had almost no military forces in Ireland anymore.

So it was hardly surprising that the members of the Irish Parliament were also wondering what they could get out of the king's weakness. "Let Ireland be a separate kingdom," some of the Old English said. "King Charles will be king, of course; but we shan't have to answer to the London Parliament anymore. Ireland will be ruled by the Irish." By which, of course, they meant themselves. It was an attractive idea to loyal gentlemen like Orlando Walsh, who might reasonably have hoped that any such government would end up being Catholic. At the least, the king would surely be forced to grant all the Graces and to end any plans for further plantation—in return for their support.

O'Byrne wasn't sure what he felt. Native Irish aristocrats like Sir Phelim would no doubt form part of the governing class; thanks to his wife's connections, he might benefit himself. But he doubted whether many of the lesser Irish landowners would gain much.

Besides, would these Catholic hopes ever come to anything? Both were anathemas to the New English Protestants in the Irish Parliament, let alone the Puritans in London. The king might give way, but the Protestants never would.

The meeting yesterday evening had been a very secret affair. Only when he had arrived in Dublin had he discovered how his wife's kinsman wanted to make use of him. "I want you to go in my place and report back," he'd explained. "This business is too dangerous for me to commit to it yet. Go therefore, take note, and tell me what you think." Given their relationship, O'Byrne had not been able to refuse. Following instructions, he had gone to the house of a Catholic gentleman in the parish of Saint Audoen's. At intervals, during three hours, other people had slipped in, arriving one by one. Lord Maguire had appeared. Then three or four others. Then O'More. Their discussions had been wide-ranging. Some of the things he had heard were frightening. Before leaving, with everyone else, he had taken an oath never to divulge what had been said.

"Interesting times? I suppose so," O'Byrne therefore replied.

"Sir Phelim's views would be interesting," the Jesuit quietly led again.

"He's a very good man. There can be no doubt of that," O'Byrne replied blandly. "His relationship with my wife is quite distant, you know, but he has done her many kindnesses." And he gently bored Father Lawrence for a minute or two with a story of O'Neill's good nature.

"All Europe is watching us, you know," the Jesuit said, eyeing O'Byrne carefully.

On this subject, Father Lawrence undoubtedly knew more than O'Byrne did. And the Jesuit had cause for satisfaction. It was not just a question of influence and education.

All over Europe, during the last few decades, the forces of the Catholic Counter-Reformation had scored significant successes. In France, the Calvinists were a threatened minority, permitted to exist, but in retreat. The mighty Lutherans of Germany, though helped by sympathetic English, Danes, and Dutch, had been driven out of many areas, and saved from total collapse only by the Protestant army of Sweden. In the east, half the Protestant churches of Poland were already gone. In central Europe, the Protestants had been thrown out of Austria; and a powerful coalition of Spanish, German, and papal forces had smashed the great Protestant communities of Bohemia and Moravia, and returned those lands to the Catholic faith.

"There are good Irishmen on the continent who are ready to serve the holy cause," Father Lawrence continued quietly. For two generations, Irishmen who had left their native shores had been enlisting in the armies of Catholic Europe. Irish chiefs and princes had become skilled continental commanders and attained high positions. "And perhaps," the Jesuit said, watching O'Byrne carefully, "the opportunity will arise for them to serve the cause in their native land."

O'Byrne took a moment before replying. He did not know what hopes the Catholic powers of Europe might entertain for Ireland at present, or what the dreams of Irish exiles might be. No doubt Father Lawrence did. He certainly had no wish to insult the Jesuit. But it was not his place to bring him into the counsels of the other men, and he had taken an oath to divulge nothing of what he had heard the evening before. If they wished Father Lawrence to know something, they'd tell him soon enough. So he wisely took refuge in innocence.

"Do you think so?" he asked. In return for which he received an exasperated look. It was time to change the subject. "What news of Orlando?" he enquired.

And it was then that he discovered, to his great astonishment, that Mary Walsh was pregnant.

"It must have occurred just after Easter," the Jesuit explained. "They told no one, not even me, until quite recently. If all is well, she will have the child in December, I believe." He smiled. "After so many years, it is indeed a gift of God." And with that O'Byrne could only agree.

He wondered whether he should go and see his former friend.

⁘

When Faithful Tidy saw them part a few moments later, he made a note of the time and then followed the Jesuit back to his lodgings. Once he was safely inside, Faithful could go home himself. He couldn't see that a street encounter between the Jesuit and O'Byrne of Rathconan could be of much interest. But he carefully noted it for old Pincher all the same.

Walter Smith was an honest man, but he believed he was shrewd. His business dealings over the years had left him rich. When Anne had fallen in love with O'Byrne, he had perceived it a great deal sooner than she had realised. As for public affairs, he followed them closely. And on most counts, in the autumn of 1641, he was modestly hopeful.

Was Anne still in love with O'Byrne? Probably. But she had been hurt by him, and disappointed. She had yearned for the wild freedom of the Wicklow Mountains, but they had turned out to be a harsh terrain. O'Byrne might be a romantic figure, but in Walter's estimation, he was ultimately cold. With O'Byrne's baby safely out of sight in Fingal, the warmth and security of her loving family and the comfortable house in Dublin may not have looked so bad. That, her sense of guilt, and her gratitude for his forgiveness had helped to reconcile his wife to him, and they were now, he supposed, as happy as many couples at their time of life.

He was also pleased about Maurice. His son was turning into a hardworking young man. If his green eyes sometimes flashed splendidly, they made him look handsome, and no doubt that would be attractive to women. But he always attended to business in a thorough manner, and Walter was really becoming rather proud of him.

As he looked at the political situation, Walter believed that there were grounds for cautious optimism. Dublin was quiet. In August the Parliament was prorogued, and Phelim O'Neill and his friends had gone home to their estates to salvage what they could of the harvest. King Charles was still getting nowhere with the Scots. With the king so weak, it still seemed to Walter that he might be induced to grant the Catholics of Ireland some concessions. Even failing that, he supposed that the usual uneasy tolerance would continue.

One thing worried him a little. The troops that had been sent home in the summer had not all been paid, and bands of them would appear from time to time. "It's a pity the government won't allow them to be recruited by some of the mercenary commanders in Europe," he told his son. "At least it would get rid of them." But his greatest concern as October began was the food supply for the winter. On the land he still held above the Liffey, he had been able to save part of the harvest, and according to Orlando, most of the Fingal farmers had been able to do the same. Farther north, in Ulster, the situation was worse. In Dublin, bread prices, which had been rising since last year, were even higher. Rich men like himself would get by, but the poorer folk would need help. "In my grandfather's youth, before the Protestants abolished the monasteries," he liked to say, "it was the religious orders who fed the poor in time of trouble." He, Doyle, and several other merchants had already discussed what measures might be proposed to the city council if things got too bad.

❖

Saturdays were market days in Dublin. Carts with all kinds of produce rolled in from the surrounding countryside, and a stream of people came to buy, or to enjoy themselves, too. Saturdays were cheerful, busy days. And Saturday the twenty-third of October 1641 began like any other. Almost.

The rumour started early in the morning. Maurice, who had gone out to the market, brought it to the house.

"There are troops at all the city gates, and the castle is closed and guarded. There's been a revolt up in Ulster. They say that a plot was discovered here in Dublin, too. Nobody knows what's going on." Shortly afterwards, Doyle looked in with further news.

"A fellow got drunk at an inn last night and started boasting that he and his friends would be taking over Dublin Castle in the morning. Someone went to the justices, and he was taken in for questioning late last night. At first nobody took him seriously, but then fires were seen up in Ulster. We're still waiting for news. The Castle men are in a ferment. They're rounding people up. It's a Catholic plot, apparently," he added, with a sidelong glance at Walter. "Though it seems to have been poorly planned."

"I know nothing of it," Walter replied with perfect truth.

"I did not suppose it," Doyle said pleasantly, and went on his way. Maurice went back to the market at once to try to learn more.

So it was with great surprise that, half an hour later, being told by Anne that a gentleman had arrived at the door asking to see him privately, Walter entered the parlour to find an old man sitting there whom he had never seen before, and who, rising stiffly to his feet, bowed politely and informed him:

"I am Cornelius van Leyden."

⊹

Maurice had been in the market for less than an hour when he heard the news. A merchant he knew came up to him. Looking worried.

"They've arrested thirty people. And can you believe it? One of them is Lord Maguire."

A parliamentary leader. The plot might have miscarried, but if a man of that importance was involved, then the business must be serious. And Maurice had just begun to question the merchant further when he saw his mother, accompanied by one of the servants, hurrying towards him.

"Maurice," she told him urgently, "you must come home at once."

He had never seen his mother look so distraught before. There was little time upon the way, but she told him what he'd been accused of. "Tell me it's not true," she begged. How could he explain?

"It's true," he said. Yet strangely, she hardly seemed to hear him.

"It's me your father will blame," she cried with a sad shake of her head—which made no sense at all.

"Oh, you and Father would never have done such a thing," he said with some bitterness. "I know that."

"You know nothing," his mother snapped, and spoke no more until they were home.

⁘

His father was white with anger. His eyes were blazing. But the eyes of the old Dutchman were even worse. They gazed at him silently, but with an awful, pale blue certainty that, before his family and before Almighty God, he stood accused and guilty. Maurice cast his eyes down before them.

"You have been paying court to this gentleman's granddaughter." His father's face was tight with suppressed anger. "Without our knowledge. Without any reference to me. Or to you, Sir." He turned to old Cornelius van Leyden.

"It is true, Father."

"That is all you have to say?"

"I should have spoken to you."

"But you deceived me, because you knew very well what I should have said. Do you not see the disgrace you have brought upon yourself and upon us all? And worse by far, do you not understand the terrible wrong you have done to this gentleman and his family, not to mention his granddaughter herself? Do you not see the wickedness of it, Maurice?" The Dutchman might be a Protestant, but it was clear that Walter had already conceived a respect and liking for old Cornelius van Leyden, and that he was hugely embarrassed as well as angry. "How long has this been going on?" his father demanded.

In fact, it was not so long. Maurice had encountered Elena several times in Dublin the previous autumn, but it was only in the spring that they had started walking out together. They had kissed. Matters had gone a little further. He had hesitated to go beyond that. Marriages between Catholics and Protestants might not be uncommon in his class, but it depended on the family. If Elena had been the daughter of Doyle, whose Protestantism was entirely pragmatic, and who wouldn't have cared much what church his daughter's children belonged to, then things might have been different. But the van Leyden family were as sincere in their faith as Walter Smith and the Walshes were in theirs. It had been Elena who had been less bashful, more eager to experiment than he. For much of the summer, however, she had been away in Fingal, and they had only had the opportunity to meet a few times.

"We became friends in the spring, but we hardly saw each other all summer." In so far as it went, this was true.

"How far has this matter gone?" Cornelius van Leyden's voice was quiet but insistent.

Maurice gazed at the floor. How much did the old man know? How much had Elena told him?

"Not too far." Cautiously, he allowed his eyes to lift and observe the two men. He saw that his father was about to ask him what he meant, but then thought better of it.

"You will wait outside, Maurice," his father said. "I shall speak to you later."

As soon as the door had closed behind his son, Walter Smith turned to Cornelius.

"No words can tell my shame, Sir, for the wrong my son has done your family."

"The girl was at fault also," the old man said simply. "It was ever thus."

"You are generous."

"If there had been a child . . ."

"I know. I know." Walter groaned. "I give you my word, he shall never come near her again. He shall also keep silent about the matter," he added meaningfully.

"It would be best." The old Dutchman sighed. "Were we of the same faith, our conversation might have been different."

It was true, Walter thought, that if only the girl had been Catholic, she might have made an excellent match for his son.

But there was nothing to be done about it, and soon afterwards, old Cornelius van Leyden went upon his way.

✦

Alone with his son, Walter Smith did not hold back. He accused Maurice roundly of seducing the girl. It was bad enough that she came from a respectable family; that they were Protestant only made it worse. "What will they think of us?" he cried. Had matters gone further, he pointed out, had she conceived a child, there would either have had to be an impossible marriage, or Elena would have been ruined. Maurice was lucky not to be cast out of his family forever, he went on. "To think that your mother and I . . ." he began; but then, suddenly remembering Anne's behaviour with O'Byrne, he fell silent and threw up his hands in despair.

"You are never to see her again. Swear to me."

"I swear," said Maurice reluctantly.

And Walter Smith might have had more to say, but just then, from outside, came the sound of the great bell of Christ Church ringing out, not as it usually did, in a sonorous manner, but with a wild, urgent clamour. Tidy must have been hauling on the bellrope with all his might and main. Turning to the door, they both rushed out into the street.

People were running by. There seemed to be a general panic. Walter stopped an apprentice and demanded to be told what was going on.

"It's war, Sir," the young man cried. "The whole of Ulster has risen. And they're on their way here."

✦

Though the news of the revolt in Ulster was certainly disturbing, and though within weeks it would spread across all Ireland, at no time in the months that followed did it ever occur to Walter Smith or any of his family, or anyone they knew, that one of the great watersheds of Irish history had just been passed. For centuries to come it would be portrayed as either a mass, nationalist uprising of the Catholic people against their Protestant oppressors, or else as a wholesale massacre of innocent Protestants.

It was neither.

On October 22, the Irish gentry of Ulster began a series of coordinated operations. In the absence of any trained commander, Sir Phelim O'Neill had assumed the leadership. He had, after all, the blood of the old High Kings in his veins. The aim of the rising was quite limited. Having decided that neither the Irish nor the English Parliaments would ever give them the security for their lands or the concessions to their Catholic faith as matters stood, Sir Phelim and his friends had decided to put pressure on the government by taking over the province and refusing to budge until some concessions were granted. Well aware that if the Scottish settlers in Ulster were harmed, the mighty army of the Covenanters might come over from Scotland to punish him, O'Neill had given strict orders that the Ulster Scots were to be left alone.

But it didn't work. Sir Phelim O'Neill was not a soldier. A few small inland towns let him in, but Ulster's strongly defended ports were all in the hands of tough Scottish Presbyterians; he led his men up to their walls, but the citizens weren't impressed and he couldn't take a single one of them. Worse, out in the countryside, he couldn't control the people or even his own troops. Soon bands of looters were roving the land. Quite often they were helped by O'Neill's ragtag troops. Falling on Protestant farmsteads—English or Scots were all the same to them—they looted, stripped, and, if the people resisted, they frequently killed them. Nor was it long before Protestant settlers sallied forth from their walled boroughs to take their revenge in a similar manner. There was no single massacre; but day by day, week after week, there were scenes of scattered chaos and killing. Protestant deaths mounted: hundreds, a thousand; still it continued and spread beyond Ulster.

The settlers, some of them stripped even of their clothes, were soon straggling into the ports to leave for England, or making their way south to the safety of Dublin, fifty miles away.

Meanwhile, the Justices in Dublin hastily called upon the head of the mighty Butler dynasty, the rich and powerful Lord Ormond, who, thanks be to God, was a member of the king's Protestant Church of Ireland, to take command of whatever forces the government could muster to deal with this terrible threat.

⁜

All through the month of November, the refugees were streaming into Dublin. And it was no surprise that some of them should seek sanctuary in the great cathedral of Christ Church. Still less was it surprising that they should find a ready welcome from the verger's wife.

Tidy's wife had never been busier. If one of the cathedral clergy should see a cluster of children's faces staring unexpectedly from the window of some underused lodgings in the precincts, or suddenly come upon a family camping by some old tomb in the crypt, and should ask the verger, "Is it really necessary, Tidy, for these people to be in the cathedral?" Tidy would only sigh and answer, "I can't stop her, Sir." And since every Protestant in Dublin was united in outrage at what had been done to the godly folk in the north—and Christian charity should in any case have stifled any criticism—there was really nothing to be done. Nor could they very well complain at the substantial bill that the verger submitted for ringing the great bell for several hours when news of the rising had first come.

In all these ministrations, besides, the Tidys had one powerful champion.

If people had formerly considered Doctor Pincher an eccentric, if young Faithful Tidy had even thought the old man was going mad, nobody thought so now. Hadn't he warned of the Catholic menace? Hadn't he believed a Catholic conspiracy was brewing? He had. And now he was revealed as a prophet.

Doctor Pincher emerged into his new role like a swan. Every day he came to Christ Church, where he was received by Tidy's wife as a hero and taken to see the new arrivals. His thin, inky-black figure strode among them, but to each one he would bend kindly and say: "Take heart. I know what it is to suffer for the cause." He was especially gratified one day when a grim Scots Presbyterian declared: "The fault was our own. It was a judgement of God upon us for taking the Black Oath."

In the middle of November, the doctor even preached in the cathedral again, to a congregation swelled to capacity with Ulster refugees. Once again, he took for his text the words, rendered so timely now:

> *I come not to send peace, but a sword.*

But there was no need for him this time to warn his congregation of the Catholic menace. They knew it all too well. His theme, on this occasion, was more inspiring. If their suffering had been terrible, he told them, they should not despair. For had not Our Lord declared: "The Son of man must suffer many things"?

The sword of Christ, he reminded them, divided the elect from the damned.

"Ye are the salt of the earth," he cried. "Ye are the light of the world." A quiver of grateful recognition passed through the congregation. "Be glad, therefore," he admonished them, "for your suffering."

The Catholic idolators might wield the sword and seek their blood. But in due time, the sword of Christ should strike them down.

"The unrighteous shall perish, and we, God's chosen, shall be brought into Israel, and there we shall build a new Jerusalem," and now the doctor's voice grew in strength so that, despite his age, it thundered, "from which we shall never be driven out again, no, not in a thousand years."

It was, by universal agreement, one of the finest sermons ever heard.

✢

During this period, the Catholic forces of Sir Phelim O'Neill were laying siege, without much success, to the port of Drogheda, fifty miles up the coast from Dublin. The Justices in Dublin, meanwhile, were still taking Depositions from anyone who could give them evidence of who was behind the original plot. Informers were coming forward regularly, though it was hard to know how much of their evidence was true and how much invented. In the last week of November, the Dublin administrators did manage to send out a force of six hundred poorly trained troops to relieve Drogheda. Two days later, however, the news came back: "The Catholic rebels have smashed them."

It was time for the Justices in Dublin to take more serious measures.

✢

It was at this juncture that Tidy's wife witnessed a curious meeting. She was taking Doctor Pincher to visit a family lodged in Dame Street when they saw Father Lawrence Walsh coming towards them. She expected the two men to ignore each other; but after the triumph of his recent sermon, Doctor Pincher was in no mood to avoid anyone. He began to reprimand the Jesuit from ten paces.

"I am surprised, Priest, that you show your face in the street after the evil that you papists have done," he cried.

"I do not condone the killing of innocents," Father Lawrence calmly replied. But Pincher took no notice.

"O'Neill and his friends are traitors. They'll pay with their lives," he announced grimly. "And you, too, Priest. You, too."

"Yet I hear," Father Lawrence mused, "that Sir Phelim is acting with the king's support."

Nothing about the Ulster rebellion was more infuriating to the Protestants than this. Partly to confuse the opposition, and partly to induce the loyal Old English Catholics to join him, Sir Phelim had announced that he was acting on the king's behalf. He had also produced a written commission to prove it. The document was a forgery, as it happened. But was the king capable of using this Catholic army against his own Protestant Parliament? Nothing was more likely, in Doctor Pincher's estimation. He gave Father Lawrence a look of pure hatred.

"Do not imagine that I am ignorant, Priest," he answered bitterly. "All over Europe you papists have been planning this for years. You would convert or kill us all."

Father Lawrence regarded him dispassionately. In a sense, what Pincher said was partly true. Holy Church meant to recover Christendom. For a generation and more, brave souls in Ireland, many educated on the continent, had patiently awaited the chance of deliverance. Outside Ireland's shores, Irish soldiers in Europe's Catholic armies, the huge network of priests and friars, and watchful Catholic rulers had all looked for an opportunity. Over the years, Father Lawrence could remember a dozen hopeful plots and plans, some plausible, some absurd. To his certain knowledge, the plan to take Dublin Castle had originated on the continent. But in his own estimation, none of these dreams, and none of the vague promises of help from overseas would ever materialize until there was a Catholic army with a proper organization and plan, on the ground, in Ireland itself. That was why, the moment he had received hints of what Sir Phelim and Lord Maguire were planning, he had shown such an interest. For the first time, it had seemed to him, there might be a realistic chance.

Faced with Pincher's accusation, however, he gave no ground at all.

"I am surprised at what you say," he replied blandly. "For as far as I can see, Sir Phelim O'Neill, who proclaims his loyalty to the king, asks only for a promise that the lands of loyal Catholics will not be stolen and that the Graces, granted long ago, should be honoured. True, he has occupied Ulster to force the government's hand. But where did he learn that trick—if not from your own friends the Scottish Covenanters?" There was nothing that Pincher could say to this. It was well known that Sir Phelim had already stated, "It was those Scots who taught us our ABC?" And Father Lawrence could not resist gently asking: "Or would you call the Covenanters traitors, too?"

Pincher could only scowl. But he was not going to let the Jesuit get the better of him.

"I know a traitor when I see one, Priest, and I see one now. No doubt your brother is another. Your whole family is a nest of vipers. But be assured, it will be crushed underfoot."

Father Lawrence turned. There was no point in continuing the conversation.

After he had gone, Pincher stared after him with loathing. And the doctor had almost forgotten Tidy's wife, when he heard her voice beside him: "I know the Jesuit is wicked, Sir, but I am sorry all the family are traitors." Pincher glanced down at her and saw there was no trace of irony in her words.

"There can be no truth in a papist," he muttered irritably.

⁜

Any day now. It would be any day. For Orlando Walsh, awaiting the birth of his child, his house was now a private haven—specially blessed, and quite apart from the angry sounds of the world, which seemed far away, almost unreal, and hardly important anymore.

There had been no difficulty with the pregnancy, no alarms. His wife was healthy, and he had no doubt the child would be born healthy, too. Had he, once or twice, wondered whether the baby might not turn out like little Daniel? Not really. Whatever God gave, he would accept it gratefully. But in his own mind he was sure that, after so many years of faithful waiting, God's gift to him would be perfect in every way.

"If it's a girl, I think we should call her Donata," he said to Mary. Donata: the one given. "And Donatus if it's a boy," she said, to which he readily agreed.

At the start of December, several small Catholic foraging parties raided Protestant farms in Fingal. They wanted provisions, but when some of the farmers resisted, there were some scuffles and a few people were hurt. At Orlando's estate, however, everything was quiet.

On the second day, a man he knew slightly from Swords came by with a message. "We've got to defend ourselves, Orlando Walsh," he announced. "The men in Dublin won't do anything for us." It was true that during the whole of the last month, the men in Dublin Castle had ignored most of the Fingal gentry. Orlando hadn't been surprised. He knew the mentality of the government's Protestant servants. "We're Catholic, so they don't really trust us," he mildly remarked. "That's all it is."

"And they can't defend us, either," the man from Swords declared. "Or won't. The only force the government has sent out so far was smashed. We can expect nothing from that quarter, and we've farms to protect. That's why you have to come with us." A party of gentlemen from the area were planning, he told him, to meet with some of Sir Phelim's men. Given his wife's condition, Orlando explained, he couldn't come; but he agreed that the parley was probably sensible. "With luck, as we're mostly Catholic, Phelim O'Neill and his troops will agree to leave us in peace," he told Mary.

On the third day of December, he received a summons from the Justices in Dublin. It seemed that they were taking an interest in the Fingal landowners after all.

"They're calling us all to meet in Dublin," he told Mary. "In five days' time." He saw the anxious look on her face. "I shan't go if the baby's not born," he promised, and saw her look of relief. He wasn't inclined to go anyway. He had no wish to be involved in their military operations, either, if he could avoid it.

It was midafternoon on the fourth day when Doyle arrived. He was looking grim.

"You must both come to Dublin at once," the merchant told him.

"Mary can't travel in her condition, and I don't want to leave the estate when everything is so uncertain," Orlando explained. But Doyle shook his head.

"You don't understand the mood in Dublin," he declared. "The castle men are in a state of panic, and the city's being stirred up by men like Pincher." And when Orlando mentioned that he knew some of the Fingal gentry had gone to meet Phelim O'Neill's men up at Tara, Doyle almost exploded. "No, you don't know. You know nothing, Orlando. Do you hear? The very fact," he went on more quietly, "that they came to you at all places you under suspicion." Orlando had received a short letter from Lawrence describing his passage of words with Pincher, but until now he had not supposed that the old man's threats and talk of treason should be taken so seriously. "Come to Dublin," Doyle urged him, "and prove your loyalty. Otherwise you will be under suspicion." It annoyed Orlando that anyone would seriously question his loyalty, but he still didn't see that he could leave at present.

"Tell the Justices," he replied, "that I shall come to the meeting in Dublin if my wife is safely delivered of her child."

"I shall tell them," answered his kinsman, "and I pray that the child comes in time."

The next morning, the gentleman from Swords came again. He was in a hurry and did not even dismount. "It's been agreed," he cried. "We're joining with Phelim O'Neill."

"In rebellion?"

"Not at all. That's just the point. Every Catholic gentleman in Ireland will come together in a grand league and proclaim our loyalty to the king. There's to be a big meeting at Swords on the eighth of December, three days from now. I'm going round every estate in the area to spread the word. Mind you're there."

"But that's the same day we're all supposed to be in Dublin," Orlando objected.

"You can ignore the damned Protestants in Dublin," the Swords man cried impatiently. "Stick with your own."

"I shall come," Orlando told him also, "if my wife is safely delivered of her child."

"And what," Mary asked him when he told her afterwards, "if the baby has come before then?"

"I shall go to neither meeting," Orlando said quietly. It seemed to him the safest thing to do.

❖

Two days later, a servant arrived from Doyle with a letter begging him to come to Dublin at once, without delay. He did not go. That night, Mary went into labour.

The next day, the eighth of December, early in the morning, the child was born. It was healthy, and it was a boy. They called him Donatus.

❖

Maurice Smith was delighted with the news that his aunt had had the baby. He had been wondering what to do for nearly a week—ever since the letter from Elena had come.

It had been handed to him in the marketplace by one of van Leyden's men, who had asked him to give an immediate reply, as he must return at once to the Dutchman's estate in Fingal. Maurice had never received a letter from Elena before. He noticed that although her English was still imperfect, her writing was firm and regular. The letter was not long. She wrote that her grandfather had kept her in Fingal for two months now, and that although the old man went into Dublin quite often, he refused to take her with him. Now, with the rebels getting closer, she was afraid. What did Maurice think she should do?

Taking the letter into a scrivener, where they lent him pen and ink, he wrote his reply onto the letter. She was in no danger, he told her. The rebels might come to forage; they might even take some valuables. But though they might turn nasty if they encountered some of the hated English Protestant settlers, he thought it unlikely they'd hurt a harmless old Dutchman and his granddaughter.

It was clear to him that the real message in Elena's letter was that she was frightened and wanted him to come and comfort her, and he felt a great urge to do so. Yet how could he? It had been wrong to court her when he had. He'd given his father his word never to see her again.

So what could have possessed him, at the end of his message, to add "I shall come to see you as soon as I can"?

+‡+

For when Orlando's message had brought the glad tidings of the birth, there had also been a request that Maurice should go to his uncle's straightaway, so that he could be godfather to the baby, whose christening would be performed by the old priest from Malahide as quickly as possible. Walter was delighted. "It's a great honour, Maurice," he told him. He also saw it as a useful opportunity. "While you are there, you must do everything you can to persuade your uncle to come to Dublin. He failed to appear on the eighth, but that can be explained by the birth of Donatus. Your cousin Doyle has seen to that. But as soon as the child is christened, your uncle should go in to the castle at once and establish his loyalty. I, too, as a Catholic, would be under suspicion if I were not here in Dublin. Tell him all this and that I join my voice to Doyle's, and urge him to come."

It was a charming little ceremony. It was held in the house. Present were just Maurice, a lady from a neighbouring estate who acted as godmother, the happy parents, the old priest from Malahide, and little Daniel, who, miraculously, kept quiet throughout the ceremony. Maurice stayed with them until the following day; and that evening, when he found himself alone with Orlando, he delivered his father's message. His uncle listened carefully, nodded thoughtfully, and thanked him, but made no further comment.

In the morning, Maurice left. But as soon as he was out of sight, instead of riding south, back towards Dublin, he turned his horse and took the track towards Swords. From Swords he turned north-west, and an hour later, he was in sight of van Leyden's stone and timber farm.

Here he had to pause. He could not go up to the door, for fear of encountering the old man, so he waited for a long time in the cold until he saw a farmhand coming towards him. Telling the fellow that he was a scout sent out from Dublin to look out for rebels, he quickly learned that none had been seen, that the old man was in Dublin, though expected back that afternoon, and that Elena was in charge of the house in his absence. Asking the man to fetch her, he rode slowly towards the farm. And moments later, Elena appeared.

She seemed pleased to see him. Despite the cold, they walked together so that they should not be heard. If at first she seemed a little constrained, he could well understand it, for he felt the same. But more than anything, she seemed to need reassurance that they would not be attacked by Phelim O'Neill's men. "I told my grandfather that we should go to Dublin for safety," she complained. "But he does not want me to be there." She made a wry face. "Because of you."

Maurice told her again that the rebels had no quarrel with the Dutch. "These are not criminals or animals," he reminded her. "I promise that you and your grandfather will be safe."

He had never seen her afraid before. Their relationship had been several things. He'd enjoyed her company, for they made each other laugh. There had been the excitement, with the added thrill that their relationship was forbidden. He had found her wonderfully sensuous. But if the truth were told, neither of them had felt real love or passion. Now, however, seeing her afraid, he felt a sudden wave of tenderness. Putting his arm around her, he did his best to comfort her and stayed with her for nearly an hour. They kissed before he left, and though he didn't say it to her then, he found himself wondering seriously whether—he did not yet know how—they might be united after all.

It was midafternoon when he entered Swords again. To reach Dublin before dark, he needed to press on. The city gates would be closed at dusk, and it would certainly be hard to explain himself to his parents if he were locked out. But he also felt uncommonly thirsty, and as he passed down the main street and saw the inn, he couldn't resist turning in there for a small tankard of ale. There was time, surely, for that.

It was gloomy inside the tavern. The windows were small and the day outside was grey. A large fire at the end of the place provided what light there was. A narrow table with benches ran along one side of the room. The floor was covered with rushes. There were only a few people in there. The innkeeper soon brought Maurice his ale, and he sat at the end of the table nearest the fire, drinking it quietly. At the far end of the table, in shadow, two men were playing at dice, small piles of coins on the table between them. One was a small, wizened man; the other had his back turned to him. After a few minutes, this fellow gave a sad laugh and pushed his coins towards the small man.

"Enough." He spoke in Irish. "I've lost enough for one day." His voice sounded familiar. The small man rose, scooped up the coins, and started to move away. The other turned, glanced at Maurice, and then stared. "Well, Mwirish," he said in English, "what brings you here?"

And Maurice found himself a moment later sitting beside his friend Brian O'Byrne.

They talked for a long time. Maurice told him everything: about the birth of Donatus, at which O'Byrne was greatly delighted; about Elena, at which the Irishman shook his head. "Leave that, Mwirish. Your father is right. You can do no good there."

O'Byrne himself, he explained, had been on a visit to Rathconan and was now returning to Drogheda. He had been with Phelim O'Neill since the start of the rising. "I'd have joined him anyway, Mwirish," he said, "but with my wife being his kinswoman . . ." He shrugged. "It was fate."

O'Byrne ordered more ale. As they drank together, it seemed to Maurice that his old friend was uncharacteristically moody. At one point, O'Byrne turned to him and suddenly remarked: "You belong at Rathconan, you know. I saw it from the first."

"I feel at home there," Maurice acknowledged, though he did not know what had made O'Byrne say it just then. In any case, the Irishman hardly seemed to be listening.

"It's where you belong," he said, almost to himself. He gazed at the fire and sighed. "Perhaps that's how it will be," he mused. And he seemed so intent upon his own thoughts that Maurice did not like to interrupt.

Glancing out of the window, Maurice saw that the afternoon light was waning. He looked back at the handsome Irish chief, whose green eyes he shared. The firelight was catching his face, giving it a brooding, romantic quality. And whether it was the fear that he might be late back to Dublin and his visit to Elena be discovered, or whether he was suddenly overwhelmed by a desire to be in the company of this man he loved and admired, fighting for the sacred Catholic cause that was their heritage, he burst out:

"I want to come with you. Take me with you to Drogheda."

O'Byrne gave him a long look and slowly smiled. But he shook his head.

"No, Mwirish, I've brought enough trouble to your house. I'll not take Walter Smith's son away as well." This didn't make sense to Maurice, and he wanted to ask him what he meant;

but O'Byrne had not finished. "Tell me, Mwirish," he asked, "do you like to gamble?"

"I don't know."

"Every Irishman likes to gamble, Mwirish," said O'Byrne. "It's in the blood." Perhaps it was the play of the firelight on his face, but it seemed to Maurice now that his friend looked strangely sad. "This rising, Mwirish, it's just a gamble, you see. A roll of the dice."

"Gamblers can be lucky."

"True." O'Byrne gave a wan smile. "Though few are lucky all the time. I was rolling the dice when you came in, Mwirish. But I lost."

"I want to come with you."

"We'll meet again, Mwirish. But go back to Dublin now. You must leave, for I've other business."

So Maurice left, and rode as fast as he could back to Dublin, arriving there just before the gates were closed.

After he had gone, O'Byrne sat alone at the table for a little while. If he had other business, there was no sign of it. He sat moodily, rolling the dice on the table by himself.

At last he got up. He would be going north in the morning, and who knew when he would pass this way again? He had been much moved by what young Maurice Smith had told him about Orlando and Mary. How truly wonderful that after all these years God had granted them a child. He had heard of such cases but never encountered such a case himself. It was like a biblical story: a holy thing. He felt a great desire to see his friend again, to take his hand in friendship once more and congratulate him. If he left now, he could be at the Walsh estate before dark.

It was not long before he was riding south towards Orlando's house. His mind was occupied by many things as he rode through the gathering December dusk.

It did not occur to him that he was being followed.

✦

Faithful Tidy had not been best pleased when Doctor Pincher had made him follow the priest to Swords. Though he had tracked him dutifully, he hadn't been able to discover anything except that the priest had gone to spend the evening in the house of an old lady who turned out to be his mother. All the same, since the meeting of the Fingal Catholics at Swords the other day—of which everyone in Dublin had been immediately aware—the town almost counted as enemy territory. So when Faithful had stopped for a drink at the inn there, he had sat quietly in a corner and kept his eyes open.

✢

And his vigilance had been rewarded when he saw the handsome Irishman he knew to be O'Byrne of Rathconan entering the place. Faithful had watched him carefully, observed his conversation with young Maurice Smith, and then followed him until he saw him go into the estate of Orlando Walsh. As it was dusk, he had returned to the inn at Swords. But the following morning, he rode back to Dublin to report to Pincher.

The worthy doctor listened avidly to his account of the evening.

"And you saw O'Byrne ride off alone?"

"He'd been talking to Maurice Smith for a long time."

"Never mind the Smith boy," cried Pincher excitedly. "He's nothing. Do you not see? O'Byrne's the key. He's connected to Sir Phelim O'Neill, the greatest traitor of them all. And he went straight to the house of Orlando Walsh?"

"There isn't a doubt of it."

"Then I have him," shouted Pincher with a glee he did not trouble to conceal. "I can destroy Orlando Walsh."

✢

All through that December, Orlando Walsh stayed on his estate with his little family, as quiet as a mouse.

There was no question, the winters were colder, now, than they had been when he was a boy; and this year turned out to be the coldest anyone could remember.

As midwinter approached, a howling blizzard swept down from the north. For a day and a night, the snow fell on Fingal until there was more than two feet of it. After that, the storm moved on and the landscape froze.

Some days, the sky was blue and the landscape sparkled. But if the sun melted the surface, the frost turned every drop of water back to ice. Soon there were icicles, tall as a man, hanging from the eaves of the big barn. By Christmas, Orlando heard that down at Dublin, the River Liffey had ice upon it.

Around the Walsh estate, the countryside was quiet. To the north, there were still stories of Protestant farms being raided. To the south, the Protestants in Dublin Castle sent out parties to burn the property of local Catholics they suspected. "They want to provoke them to rebel," Orlando explained to Mary, "to prove that Catholics are all traitors." Meanwhile, the powerful Lord Ormond, the only man of real stature in the government's camp, was reportedly drawing together a military force which he had promised to bring to Dublin.

✛

The morning after Christmas, the gentleman from Swords came by again.

"We're arming our men, Walsh," he told Orlando. "There's bound to be a fight. Are you joining us?"

"I am not," Orlando told him.

"Afraid?" The man sneered. "We've already smashed them once."

"I've no wish to fight Ormond," Walsh answered simply.

For a start, the great magnate had probably assembled a fighting force to be reckoned with. But as he also pointed out: "Ormond's our best hope." The mighty head of the Butler dynasty might have sworn to uphold the king's Protestant church, but he was a moderate man with dozens of Catholic relations himself. "We should be talking to him, not fighting him," Orlando said.

"Everyone else is with us," the Swords man declared. This was quite untrue. Orlando knew very well that a number of Catholic landowners, including his neighbour Talbot of Malahide, were holding back. Others were allowing younger sons or brothers to go while they themselves stayed cautiously at home. So Walsh made him no further answer and let the man depart.

A few hours later, a dozen fellows arrived at the house. They were labourers, but not from the locality. Orlando didn't like the look of them but was careful to be polite. The man who was their leader said he was a friar of the Franciscan order. Orlando wasn't sure he believed him, but thought it best not to argue. Having established that this was a devout Catholic house, they were civil enough. When Orlando asked their business, the friar told him they were scouting accommodation and fodder for when O'Neill's army came that way. This was almost certainly a lie. Nonetheless, Orlando brought them inside and fed them, and secretly prayed that they would not wish to stay. Mercifully, they decided to move on. The friar said they were heading north for the territory above Swords. As they departed, he heard one of the men remark: "When we find some Protestants, we'll stretch their necks."

After this visit, all was quiet.

⁘

Maurice Smith gazed down at the scene from the bridge. The Liffey was a remarkable sight. Big sheets of ice covered most of the stream. The sun had made the surface gleam. Children were sliding on the edges, and an enterprising fellow had organised horse-drawn sled rides upstream along the bank.

The first of January. Amongst the Protestants, at least, there was a festive mood. The day before, Ormond and his well-drilled men had marched out across the bridge onto the icy plain of Fingal. Reaching Swords, they had found the untrained brigade gathered by the local Catholic gentry and easily crushed them in a short skirmish. By that evening, Tidy was ringing the great bell of Christ Church to announce the victory, and Doctor Pincher was out in the streets proclaiming that the Protestants in Dublin could take heart at this proof that God was on their side.

Maurice had been standing there for some time when he noticed the little cortege enter the bridge from the northern end. Five riders, heavily muffled against the cold. As they came closer, he saw that their covered heads were encrusted with ice, suggesting that they had made a long journey across the snows. He wondered who they were. On reaching the bridge, they had slowed their horses to a walk. As they brushed by, he observed that the rider in the centre was a woman. Her face was half covered, but it looked familiar. She caught sight of him and seemed to give a start, but they were already past when he realised that it was Elena.

Her grandfather was not one of the party. He was sure of it. So he called out: "Elena."

If she had ridden on, he would have understood that she needed to be discreet. But instead, after a momentary pause, she pulled up, and the men accompanying her did the same. He ran over and came level with her. He was excited.

As she turned to look down at him, she unwrapped the black scarf that had covered the lower part of her face. Though flushed from the cold, her face looked strangely pallid and drawn, as though she had suddenly grown older. She gazed down at him, stonily, saying nothing.

"So your grandfather has changed his mind," he said, and smiled. She continued to smile at him. "I mean, you are in Dublin." He stopped, fell silent. At last she spoke.

"My grandfather is dead." Her voice was cold, as if he were a stranger.

"Dead?"

"Yes. Dead. A party of your friends came," she said bitterly. "They were led by a priest."

"A priest?"

"Priest, friar." She shrugged contemptuously. "What does it matter? One of your unholy orders. They came to steal. They started looting. They even took my mother's locket. Tore it from my neck. My grandfather protested and they killed him. In front of me. I was lucky they did not kill me, too. Or worse."

"But this is terrible." He felt the blood draining from his face as he remembered the advice he had given her, assuring her she was safe.

"Yes. It is terrible." He heard the pain in her voice; but in her eyes he saw only rage and contempt. He gazed at her helplessly. She seemed to be another person. The sensuous girl he knew had gone. There was not a trace of her. In her place was a young woman who was looking at him with loathing. "It is true, what they say," she went on with a cold fury. "You Catholics are not just ungodly. You are animals. Cut open a papist and you will find the devil."

She let the words fall. They lay there between them, worse than a curse. For a moment, he was too shocked to reply.

"Elena," he pleaded. "I am as shocked as you by what has happened . . ."

She did not let him continue.

"I do not wish to hear what you feel. Do not come near me again, you dirty papist." She kicked her horse into a trot, but as she left him behind, she cried out the word a final time: "Papist."

⁜

When the grey-bearded merchant arrived at the house late in January and asked to speak with Orlando Walsh, he was politely shown into the hall. And until he was within two feet of him, Orlando himself did not realise who it was.

"I have come to say farewell," explained Lawrence.

The situation for the Jesuit had been getting worse by the day. The political situation was in a state of great confusion. In England, King Charles and his Parliament had reached a point of complete rupture. The king had left London; Parliament was effectively ruling the capital. Across the water in Ireland, Lord Ormond continued to keep military order for the government in the region around Dublin—but whether the government now meant king, Parliament, or both, nobody was sure. In Dublin itself, the Protestant authorities were behaving as if the city were under siege. The gates were guarded. No strangers were allowed in without permission. "Even you couldn't get in now, Brother," Lawrence told him, "because you're a Catholic." As for his own position, he explained, Pincher had been agitating constantly at the castle. "Any day, he'll have me arrested. I grew my beard for ten days and slipped out in disguise."

"We can hide you," Orlando offered at once, but Lawrence shook his head.

"No, Brother. You and your family shall not be put in danger on my account. In any case, I have a boat waiting for me at Clontarf. I'm going abroad."

"You're leaving forever?"

"Not exactly." He paused. "Sir Phelim is a good man, Orlando. But he is not the military commander that we need now, and he'd be the first to say it. There is, however, another O'Neill who has just the qualifications, if he will come."

"You mean Owen Roe O'Neill?"

"I do."

Of all the princes of Ireland who had risen to high command in the great Catholic armies of the continent, none was more famous than this scion of the house of the old High Kings. The nephew of the Earl of Tyrone himself, rumour said that he had been privy to the plans to take Dublin Castle the previous autumn. But a man living the princely life of a great European general still needed some inducement before he would leave all that to risk life and fortune in a rebellion, even

in the sacred land of his fathers. If he did decide to come, however, neither his kinsman Sir Phelim, nor anyone else in the
Catholic cause, would hesitate in yielding him command.

"You think he will come?"

"I am going to add my voice to those which are begging
him to come without delay. If I am successful, I shall return
with him." Lawrence smiled. "And now, if you will give me a
glass of wine, I shall greet your wife, and bless your son, and be
on my way."

Shortly afterwards, as he watched his elder brother depart,
Orlando felt a surge of affection for him. Lawrence could be
stern and unbending—but he had always acted for the best.
He was a loyal servant of the true Faith. There was no doubt
about that. If necessary, he would die for it.

✣

Two weeks passed. The weather grew warmer. The snows
melted, and after nearly a week of sunny days, Orlando saw a
sprinkling of snowdrops, and even a crocus or two in front of
his door. News came of scattered skirmishes elsewhere, but
Fingal was now quiet. Lord Ormond had done his work well.
Several of the local gentry who had taken up arms were fleeing the country; others had surrendered to him personally and
had been sent to Dublin. Orlando heard that the gentleman
from Swords was one of these. So far, however, no one had
come to trouble Orlando, and he was beginning to hope that
they wouldn't.

It was early one afternoon, when Mary and the baby were
both asleep, and he was quietly playing with little Daniel, that
Doyle arrived. His cousin's large, burly form filled the doorway
as he entered the house and strode into the hall, where he
threw his cloak impatiently on a bench and announced the bad
news at once.

"They're passing sentence on you tomorrow. I had the

whole thing from Tidy the sexton, who knows it, of course, from Pincher. You're to be outlawed."

"Outlawed?" It was an old medieval English sentence, and a vile one. An outlaw had no legal protection at all. He could be robbed or killed with impunity. An outlaw could only run for his life or turn himself in. It was the way the ancient state made its enemies destroy themselves.

"You're not the only one. Half the gentlemen involved in the rising are being outlawed. Some of them have already fled the country, as you know. The estate will be taken, of course. You must save what valuables you can."

"But I was never in the rising," Orlando protested.

"I know. But your brother is a Jesuit who's disappeared. You're a Catholic. You didn't come to Dublin . . ." Doyle shook his head furiously. "I spoke up for you and I thought I'd convinced them you were innocent. But I underestimated Pincher. The man has spies everywhere. It seems you were visited by O'Byrne, who's in the thick of the rebels, at the very time when you should have been in Dublin. Pincher had a spy out at Swords who followed O'Byrne to your house. I didn't discover who the spy was, but it doesn't matter. The whole thing has been reported to the Justices, who want to dispossess every Catholic they can. The men at the castle aren't concerned with legal niceties at present. Pincher's accusations were enough for them." He paused. "You know those men who surrendered to Ormond?"

"Yes." Orlando thought of the gentleman from Swords.

"Well," Doyle continued, "when Ormond sent them to Dublin, do you know what the Justices did? They've put one of them on the rack." He shook his head again, in disgust at the cruel torture. "They're out for blood."

"But if they take the estate, we'll be almost ruined," cried Orlando, aghast. "What shall I do?"

"If you flee the country or go to the rebels, you proclaim your guilt. If you stay here, they'll arrest you. I'll try to persuade the men at the castle to take a different view—and of course we'll all take care of Mary and the children—but in the meantime, I think you should hide." He looked at Orlando thoughtfully. "Is there anywhere you can think of?"

※

There was still smoke in the distance when the soldiers came—several hundred of them—on a mild March day.

Mary Walsh was waiting at the door of the house, with a baby in her arms and little Daniel beside her, as the cavalcade of officers at their head rode up.

She had known they would be coming and, after a long talk with Orlando in his hiding place, she had prepared herself carefully. The soldiers were a frightening sight, and she might have found it even harder to conceal her fear if she had not seen, riding at the centre, the unmistakable figure she had been hoping for.

James Butler, twelfth Earl of Ormond, was a well-set man with a broad, intelligent face. Though still only thirty-two, he was born to such great wealth and position that he obviously wore his command easily. Dismounting, he came towards her courteously and asked for her husband.

"He is not here, Lord Ormond," she answered politely.

His eyes rested on her.

"You know he is to be arrested?"

"So I have heard, my lord. But I do not know why, since he is loyal. Perhaps," she added drily, "the Justices in Dublin know something that we do not." Though he said nothing, at the mention of the Justices, she saw a flicker of aristocratic contempt cross his face, which told her what he privately thought of the Dublin authorities.

"I should like to step inside," he said quietly.

Two officers accompanied him, and half a dozen men. The officers and men began to search the house from top to bottom. Outside, she had no doubt, the troops would be combing the farm buildings also for Orlando. While the search went on, Lord Ormond himself remained in the big hall, where she politely offered him a glass of wine, which he accepted. As they waited, and knowing that she must use the time well, she probed a little further.

"Tell me, my lord: we still see smoke in the distance, and we have seen it for days. It seems that the Justices have given orders for Catholic farms to be destroyed. Their men have said they will burn all the crops as they grow. But if they do that, how will Dublin and your own troops be fed?" It was another example of the vicious stupidity of the men in Dublin Castle that they should have ordered this pointless destruction. They had even wanted to destroy the local fisheries as well.

"You are correct," he answered without looking at her. "I have persuaded them to stop. By tomorrow, I hope, you will see no more smoke."

"This is a sad business," she remarked. "We are to be ruined for no offence. How many other honest Old English gentlemen are to suffer in this way?"

"I have no wish to make traitors of the Fingal gentry," he told her frankly. "But whatever they or Sir Phelim may claim, the fact is that they went into rebellion against the king's government. That is what the king thinks, I assure you."

"And I can assure you that my husband did not join them. He was here with me at all times, I give you my word. You will find no one of the rebels who will tell you he was there."

"He did not give them aid?"

"Not unless you count the party of ruffians, attached to nobody, who came by once. We fed them and prayed they would leave, which they did, thank God. That is all."

Ormond indicated that, as far as he was concerned, this was not an offence.

"Your husband has gone to the rebels now?"

"He has not."

"Has he fled overseas?"

This was a dangerous question. If they thought he had done so, the authorities might stop looking for him; but it would also indicate his guilt.

"No, my lord, he has not fled overseas."

"Shall we find him here?"

"I do not think so."

"Then where is he?" Ormond asked quietly.

This was it. The moment she had been dreading. But they had agreed what she must say.

"My lord," she answered gently, "I am his wife, and I shall not tell you." She held her breath. His eyebrows rose. "Unless," she added softly, "you mean to put me on the rack." She watched him. Had she gone too far?

But thank God, he did not turn on her in fury. Instead—she saw it clearly—he winced with embarrassment. They fell silent.

A minute later, the men came back and the officers reported: "Nothing." Ormond indicated that they should wait for him outside.

"The Dublin men are eager to confiscate this estate, Madam," he remarked to her when they were alone, "so that they can get their hands on it themselves. However, I find that I shall need to garrison some of my troops here. About a hundred," he added bleakly. "The estate will need to be properly farmed, to ensure that they are fed. Do you understand?"

"I think so."

"If your husband is loyal to the king and the king's government, then he must be loyal to me."

"That," she said with feeling, "you could depend upon, my lord."

"I cannot reverse the proclamation against your husband. It is not in my power. But if he is here, supplying my troops on my orders, he will not be touched—for the moment. That is all I can promise you."

"I am grateful." She hesitated. "For how long might this last?"

"Who can say?" He sighed. "Everything is uncertain. I scarcely know from whom my own orders will come next month. We must live from day to day." He gave her a long look. "Find your husband by tomorrow, Madam."

She nodded. He gave her a brief bow, and before she even had time to curtsey in return, he was gone.

✣

There was a light mist over the sea, early the following morning, as Mary came down to the shore. So at first, as he looked out from the little island with the cleft in its cliff, where he had been hiding for the last three weeks, Orlando did not notice her.

But then, as the rays of the rising sun came racing over the sea and burst upon the shore, he saw her, waving to him from the beach. And he pushed out the little curragh he had been using and rowed towards her with the rising sun behind him, to learn what tidings she brought.

✣

Doctor Simeon Pincher gazed at the letter. He was still astonished.

The month of April 1642 had not been encouraging. In England, the split between King Charles and his Parliament had grown so wide that it seemed likely to develop into civil war. Here in Ireland, though Ormond had done good work around Dublin, the rising was spreading even wider. Leaders of the Old English and Irish gentry, with ancient names like Barry and MacCarthy, were now taking up arms down in Munster and beyond. Even Ormond's own Catholic uncle had joined the rebels. Still more disturbing were the rumours, growing more persistent with every passing day, that the great general Owen Roe O'Neill had finally agreed to come to Ireland and command the Catholic forces.

Yet all these troubles seemed to melt into the background as Pincher read, and reread, the letter.

In the first place, it informed him that his sister was dead. He was not sorry, and had the honesty to admit it. He had received no word of kindness from her in the last forty-five years; and though he trusted that she was predestined for Heaven rather than Hell, he caught himself hoping that the heavenly regions were large, so that their future meetings could be infrequent.

The rest of the letter was even more heartening.

He looked at the handwriting: it was firm and manly. That, he thought, augured well. The style was not learned, not even elegant, perhaps, but rather that of a plain, devout gentleman. Such was the conclusion he was able to draw by his third reading. Of the writer's religious conviction there could be no doubt. He was a vehemently godly man.

So this was his nephew, Barnaby Budge.

It gratified him that his nephew wrote to him in terms of such respect: and he could not help wondering whether perhaps the departure of his sister might have removed an invisible barrier to what might, long ago, have been a closer family relationship. Why, it was possible, he supposed, that with acquaintance his nephew might even feel affection for him. After all, Barnaby was his heir.

Despite his years, Doctor Pincher was prepared to brave another sea voyage, if necessary, to visit his nephew. But it seemed there might be no need. For at the end of the letter came the most wonderful news of all. Barnaby hoped to come to Ireland soon. Indeed, he might even be coming to live there.

"For trusting in God's providence," he wrote, "I have taken up the Parliament's cause, and have invested five hundred pounds."

It was only the month before that the English Parliament, wondering how it could finance both Ormond's troops in Ireland and a possible armed conflict with the king at home, had hit upon a new ruse for how to make use of Ireland.

Settlement and plantation had been tried; Irish chiefs had rebelled and friends of the government had been able to buy their land at cut prices; but the Act for Adventurers of March 1642 was a new advance in English ingenuity. It was inspired.

For now the English Parliament invited all good Protestants: "Give us cash today, and in due time, we will give you Irish land." The promised land in question, though not available yet, would be confiscated in time from those who had just rebelled. By this means, the English Parliament men hoped to raise a million pounds—a stupendous sum. On looking at the terms, Pincher had calculated that they would require no less than two and a half million acres: four thousand square miles, almost a quarter of Ireland, and many times the holdings of all those who had rebelled so far. "Don't worry," one of the castle men assured him when he asked about it. "If they can raise the money, we'll find the rebels."

On such terms, five hundred pounds could secure Barnaby a thousand acres, a gentleman's estate. With help from his uncle, he might do even better. Doctor Pincher had been disappointed when Orlando Walsh had been allowed to remain on his estate. But now it seemed to him that there might be another hand at work in this. For it was only a stay of execution. Ormond would not need Walsh forever. By the time Walsh was kicked out, Barnaby Budge might be able to get the place. Could it be that this was, indeed, the divine plan?

He wondered how soon Barnaby would come, and what he would be like.

⊷ 1646 ⊶

Brian O'Byrne and his wife stood in the empty street. The town of Kilkenny was quiet. It was a December afternoon. It was cold. And he didn't know what to do.

He had experienced many things in the last five years. Danger. A little joy—his wife had given him a fine new son two years ago. Some loneliness, even moments of depression. But nothing had been harder than the choice before him now.

He glanced at his wife. There was nothing very special-looking about Jane O'Byrne. She was a pleasant, light-haired young woman with small, neat teeth, who might have been a landowner's wife in any one of the four provinces. But she had brought Brian O'Byrne money and some fine connections, and she knew it.

They had been together in Kilkenny for three days now. Tomorrow he was due to go down into Munster; she was returning to Rathconan, which was safe for the moment. They had been busy days, and happy ones, but he had not been able to tell her what was on his mind. And he was still wondering how to bring the subject up when he heard a voice, calling his name, behind him. He turned.

Father Lawrence Walsh was in his early sixties now. His sparse grey hair was clipped short. His face was thinner, striated with deep vertical lines; but his wiry body was vigorous. He greeted Jane, and looked at O'Byrne keenly.

"We last met here in Kilkenny, I think," he said.

Four years ago. It seemed more like an age. The meeting had drawn Catholic leaders from all over Ireland. O'Byrne had gone there with Sir Phelim. That was when they had decided that if the revolt begun in Ulster was to have any chance of success, then the Catholics of all Ireland must form a single, disciplined organization, like the Covenanters in Scotland. They had set up a Supreme Council—Sir Phelim was one of its members—and a network of local leaders in every county. The Catholic Confederation, they called it, and made their headquarters in the town of Kilkenny, in South Leinster. While the English government had held Dublin, and the Scottish settlers had held the ports of Eastern Ulster, the Kilkenny council had controlled huge tracts of Ireland for most of the time since.

"I also saw you again, here in Kilkenny," the Jesuit continued, "the day the Nuncio arrived. But you didn't see me in the crowd."

The twenty-fifth of October 1645. A symbolic day, never to be forgotten: the arrival of the Nuncio, Archbishop Rinuccini, the personal emissary of the Pope to the Catholic Confederation at Kilkenny. The rebirth of Catholic Ireland.

They had received him like the Holy Father himself. O'Byrne remembered the crowds lining the road outside the town for miles. The finest scholars of the region had come out to greet him; one of them, crowned with laurels in the Roman manner, had made a Latin address. Then, holding a canopy over the Nuncio's head, they had led him through the doors of Saint Patrick's church, where the clergy of Ireland awaited him. Afterwards, Archbishop Rinuccini had been conducted to the castle, where the Confederation's Supreme Council were gathered. Thanks to Sir Phelim, O'Byrne had been allowed into the castle's great hall, where the Nuncio, seated on a throne covered with a rich damask of red and gold, addressed them all in Latin, and gave them a message of encouragement from the Holy Father. It had been a magnificent occasion.

And as he'd looked around the great concourse of gentlemen, soldiers, and priests, O'Byrne had been struck by a thought. Here were hundreds of men, some Irish like himself, others Old English like the Walshes. Nearly all of them spoke both languages. Whatever their ancestry, they belonged to Ireland and were united by their Catholic faith. Many of them, moreover, had been educated in the great schools of France, Spain, or Italy, or served, like Owen Roe O'Neill, in the great Catholic armies of continental Europe. And here they were, a government in waiting, being addressed by the Nuncio in the same Latin that Saint Patrick himself had spoken. This was the true Hibernia, he'd thought: an ancient member of the great, universal family of Catholic Christendom. This was what the sacred land of Ireland should be.

Though he and Father Lawrence had never been particular friends, he was glad to get some news of Orlando.

"I cannot go to see him, of course," the Jesuit explained. "The Dublin Protestants have complete control of Fingal. But he remains at the estate. He has a hundred government troops to feed. But he is left in peace, and Lord Ormond protects him."

Despite the fact that Parliament and the king he served had gone to war, Ormond, since he had more prestige than anyone else, had been left as the representative of the Protestant English government in Dublin. O'Byrne was glad that his friend Orlando had a powerful protector.

"And the Smiths? Young Maurice?"

"They remain in Dublin. They are tolerated, though the city council has become entirely Protestant. Maurice is his father's trusted partner in the business now. My sister Anne is also well," he added without further comment.

"I am glad of it," O'Byrne said.

Father Lawrence was regarding him thoughtfully. He glanced at Jane.

"So, Brian O'Byrne," he asked quietly, "may I know whose side you are on?"

✛

It had all been so much easier at the start. When he'd accompanied Sir Phelim to Kilkenny, the objective of the Confederation had been clear—to force King Charles to end the persecution of Catholics in Ireland. When the native Irish chiefs from the provinces had joined in, they might not have shared the enthusiasm of the Old English for the king, but they had gone along with the Royalist line for the sake of a strong Confederation. As a result, the Confederation had gained two fine generals with European experience: Owen Roe O'Neill, the returned Irish prince, in the north; and Thomas Preston, an Old English Catholic, in the south.

The Protestant opposition had been far more confused. Lord Ormond, the Old English Protestant grandee, was in

Dublin. Up in the north, General Monro led ten thousand ardent Scots who had crossed the water to aid their Presbyterian brethren in Ulster. Yet down in Munster, the Protestant forces were led by Lord Inchiquin, a native Irish prince descended from Brian Boru himself, but who had taken the Protestant faith and who personally hated the Church of Rome.

At first, the Confederation had done well, and Lord Ormond had gladly agreed to a truce. In England, meanwhile, King Charles, having gone to war with his Parliament, had also appeared to be winning. Even in Scotland, a Royalist group had emerged.

Those had been good days for O'Byrne. Sir Phelim had favoured him; his wife had given him a child.

But then things had begun to fall apart. Across the water, the Covenanters crushed the Royalists in Scotland; and in England, new Parliamentary generals, Fairfax and Oliver Cromwell, had emerged and smashed the king's armies. This year, Charles had been forced to surrender and was now held a prisoner by the Scots. The Royalist cause seemed to be finished.

Or was it?

"Kings have their uses, even captured ones," Sir Phelim liked to say. And now that King Charles was a captive, it seemed there was more to bargain about than ever. The Scots were ready to put him back on his throne—so long as he took the oath to their Presbyterian Covenant. The English Parliament was prepared to do the same—so long as he let them control him. The Catholic Confederacy in Ireland would sign a peace so that Charles could use Ormond's army in England—why, they'd even come to England to help him themselves—if he'd give Catholic Ireland its rights. As for Charles himself, he had no wish to oblige any of them; but he was playing for time, in the hope that if he could divide his enemies, he could still climb back on his throne.

But here in Ireland, there was now a problem of a different kind. The Confederation had been successful. Ormond and Inchiquin were both pinned down, and Owen Roe O'Neill, the dashing Irish prince, had scored a stunning victory over Monro and his Scots up in Ulster.

"Now is our chance," O'Byrne had told his wife, "to sweep down upon Dublin and take it. Then we could probably drive the Protestants out of the strongholds of Ulster."

But nothing had happened.

Partly the problem was the vanity of generals: Irish O'Neill and Old English Preston refused to take orders from each other. They could hardly even be persuaded to act together. But behind this lay a deeper rift, in the heart of the Confederation. The Old English still wanted to drive a tough bargain with King Charles. "Better him than a Presbyterian Parliament," they said. And Sir Phelim had taken this view. O'Neill and his Irish friends were more radical. "Let's kick the Protestants out once and for all, and their king too, and run Ireland ourselves," they declared.

Dashing Owen Roe O'Neill: an Irishman after his own heart. Brian O'Byrne knew where his secret sympathies lay. For six weeks now, he had been planning to desert Sir Phelim and attach himself to Owen Roe O'Neill.

✢

But it was Jane O'Byrne who answered Father Lawrence.

"We are with Sir Phelim, of course."

O'Byrne said nothing. Father Lawrence smiled.

"You are loyal to your family. But there is a higher authority than the family. I mean Holy Church."

"Not everyone agrees with the Nuncio," Jane remarked.

"He is harsh," Father Lawrence acknowledged. "But unfortunately, he is also right."

Archbishop Rinuccini had not been in Ireland long before his clear Latin mind saw the weak logic of the Old English position. "For a start," he pointed out, "King Charles is a heretic whom nobody trusts. Secondly, he is never going to give you what you want."

Since its formation, the Confederation had evolved quite an impressive list of demands that included not only the freedom to practise the Catholic religion, and equal legal status, but the return of many Catholic lands. They also wanted the Irish Parliament to be independent. In effect, Charles would be king of a separate country. "We know we won't get all we want," the Old English party told the Nuncio.

"You won't get any of it," he'd replied. "King Charles would like to use Irish troops against his enemies. But he can't grant your Catholic freedom, because his own Protestant Parliament will never let him. Your entire position rests upon a fallacy." Yet since a Protestant Parliament would give them even less than the king, they countered, what were they to do? "Sever your connection with England," he told them. "You've no alternative." And who would protect them from England after that? they had demanded. For the English Parliament would always see an independent Catholic Ireland as a threat. "You will defend yourselves," he ordered. "But help will be forthcoming. From France, or from Spain. From Rome itself."

They were the Old English of Ireland, they reminded him. Their families had been loyal to the English monarchy for centuries. "This is hard for us."

"If you are Catholics," the Nuncio had replied, "your faith will come first."

Now, backed by Owen Roe O'Neill, the Nuncio had taken over the Supreme Council. He was even threatening to excommunicate anyone who opposed his uncompromising view. The Old English, and Irish moderates like Sir Phelim, were still refusing to go along with him. The Confederation was split.

"And what does he want in the end?" Jane demanded. "Are we to drive every Protestant out of Ireland?"

"The Protestants of Ireland are a mixed group," the Jesuit replied. "There are men like my cousin Doyle, who has no strong religious feelings, and who would probably change back to Catholicism as easily as his father turned Protestant. There are the planters, some of them strongly Protestant. At the end of the day, they are adventurers. They'll either grin and bear it, or they'll sell up and leave. As for the government men at Dublin Castle, they are the most strident." He smiled. "But my guess is they'd run like rabbits." He paused. "The real problem is elsewhere."

"You mean Ulster."

"I do indeed. The Scots. They are another matter entirely. Look at the mighty Covenant they made in Scotland. They are implacable for their faith. They would not tolerate an English Prayer Book; they will surely never tolerate a Catholic government. The others will crumble, but the Presbyterians of Ulster will not."

"We'll have to drive them out, then?"

"I think so."

"Where would they go?"

"Back to Scotland perhaps. Or to America."

Father Lawrence left them after that. When he had gone, Jane O'Byrne turned to her husband.

"When I think of all that you owe my kinsman—the friendship and promotion he has given you—I hope you do not think of deserting Sir Phelim." Her eyes were fixed upon his in a hard stare. She was not afraid of him in the least.

He said nothing. He had always done as he pleased with women before. To be nervous of his wife was a new experience.

✢

Nor did Brian O'Byrne make any move in the weeks that followed. Christmas came, and the month of January. Owen Roe O'Neill had gone to winter quarters anyway, so there was nothing to be done.

It was in the month of February, when he was up at Rathconan, that the news came.

"Lord Ormond has handed Dublin over to the English Parliament. He's leaving Ireland." He gave the news to his wife himself.

"But that's impossible. Ormond is the king's man."

"He's the king's man still. But he feared he couldn't hold Dublin. He's gone to King Charles. They hope to gather more forces and return. Meanwhile, the English Parliament men are sending troops over to strengthen the garrison."

"The Parliament men have Dublin?" The Puritans?

Sir Phelim and the Old English, it seemed, had miscalculated.

Jane O'Byrne looked at her husband with a new uncertainty in her eyes.

"So what will become of us now?"

✧

As Doctor Pincher considered the world in the Year of Our Lord 1647, he knew that God's Providence alone had allowed him to live so long, and he was grateful. When Dublin was handed over to the English Parliament, he was seventy-five, and one of the oldest men in the city. Considering his age, his health was good. Perhaps, he thought with some secret pride, I shall outlive them all. He was determined, at least, to live to see the Protestant cause triumph.

And to see his nephew well settled.

Soon after the start of the war between King Charles and his Parliament, Barnaby Budge had written to say that he had taken up arms against the king and joined the Roundheads, as the Parliamentary army was nicknamed. Some time later, Barnaby had written to tell him about the new force that was being formed—a model army filled with godly men, ready to train themselves to new heights of discipline. Led by their generals, Fairfax and Oliver Cromwell, this New Model Army had soon swept all before it. Subsequent letters had described their military actions, and Doctor Pincher had experienced elation and also some fear.

"I pray that God may deliver my nephew to us safely," he confessed more than once to Tidy's wife, to which she had comfortingly replied, "Oh, Sir, I'm sure He will."

During that year of 1647, the signs were certainly encouraging. Parliament sent battle-hardened troops and seasoned commanders to Dublin. The Confederate forces in Leinster and Munster were now driven back; and when Owen Roe O'Neill made a move towards Dublin, he was soon chased away. Equally gratifying, the Protestant city authorities had made life so unpleasant for them that several prominent Catholic merchant families, including that of Walter Smith, decided to leave. Pincher chanced to meet Smith on the day of his departure, and asked him where he proposed to live now.

"With my brother-in-law Orlando Walsh," Walter replied. Though Ormond's Protestant troops at the Walsh estate were under the control of the Parliament men in Dublin now, the arrangements protecting Orlando had still been continued. "At least your Protestant troops will protect us," the merchant remarked wryly.

Only one development caused Doctor Pincher concern. It was something which he would never have foreseen, and it took place in England. It worried him so much that he wrote to Barnaby about it.

"The army," he began, "seems to forget that it is the servant of government, not the master."

There was no question that Doctor Pincher was right. The Puritan army, having fought their way to victory, had grown impatient with the Presbyterian gentlemen of the English Parliament, who sat in comfort and were still trying to strike a deal with the fallen king. "Put him on trial," they demanded. They had swept into London and overawed the citizens; and Oliver Cromwell had sent one of his most trusted young officers, Joyce, to grab the king and transfer him to army custody. If King Charles in prison was still nominally king, and Parliament still sat, it was the army which was really taking charge.

But what shocked Pincher were some of their other views.

If King Charles's Church, with its bishops and its ceremonies, seemed no better than papism to most Puritans, one might argue about what should replace it. But one thing was certain: there must be order. The gentlemen in Parliament and the solid London merchants now favoured an English version of the Presbyterian Church. Instead of clergymen, each congregation would choose its elders, and they in turn would elect a central council, whose authority would be absolute. This would be the new, national Church.

But while they had been risking their lives together, turning the world upside down, the army men had been discussing such matters, too, and they had come to quite different conclusions. They had had enough of the Parliament men. If they could fight the authority of an anointed king, why should they bend the knee to Parliament? "By what authority," they demanded, "would a Parliament tell us how to worship God? God speaks to every man directly." So long as they were godly and not papist, the congregations should be free to follow their own consciences and set up independent chapels in any manner they liked.

Such doctrines were infectious. Pincher discovered it one morning when he encountered Faithful Tidy. He had been a little disappointed that since leaving Trinity College, the young man had scarcely ever come to see him; but as Faithful was now assisting the Chapter Clerk, they met from time to time. The Parliament men in London had already made clear that they intended to legislate a Presbyterian Church for Ireland, too, and Pincher was glad to hear it. For if those army fellows were given their way, he remarked to Faithful, there'd be chaos—a breakdown of all religious and moral order.

"Yet when you think of it," Faithful had answered easily, "isn't that just what the Catholics said when the Protestants challenged Rome's authority?" He shrugged. "What's the difference?"

Pincher stared at him in stupefaction.

"The difference, young man," he thundered, "is that we are right."

Since leaving Trinity, Pincher thought, young Faithful was getting impertinent. But Pincher was profoundly shocked that he should even think such a thing.

Some of the civil ideas of the army men were just as bad. One group of these insolent fellows had started a new and hideous argument. According to them, all men were equal. Levellers, these villains called themselves. Their ideas varied, but they wanted all men to have the right to choose their government, and some of the most extreme were even questioning the right of men to own private property. So appalled was Doctor Pincher by what he heard that he even wrote to Barnaby about it.

"These Levellers," his nephew wrote back, "are dangerous and ungodly men." They would be dealt with, Barnaby assured him, in due course. But every report reaching Dublin suggested that the number of Levellers was increasing.

And if Doctor Pincher was alarmed by the radical spirit of the Roundhead army, he was not alone. All over Britain, as that year progressed, people were beginning to ask: did these soldiers recognise no authority but their own? Was power only to be maintained by the sword? "Are we to exchange King Charles's tyranny for an even worse one?" In Scotland especially, the Presbyterians looked at the army's religious independence and did not like what they saw.

In Dublin, Doctor Pincher spent an uncomfortable winter, afflicted with chilblains. The spring of 1648 came, but still he felt depressed.

And then an astounding series of events occurred. All over England, people started rising for the king—not because they liked him, which they didn't, but because they had no wish to be ruled by the army. Even some of the ships of the royal navy mutinied. In Scotland, one of the great lords was gathering a Royalist army. Lord Ormond, with the help of the queen, who was in Paris, and King Charles's son, a gangling but cunning youth also called Charles, had agents active in Ireland. For the Catholic Confederation, Lord Inchiquin now declared firmly that he was for the king. Within a month the Supreme Council had met, voted out the Nuncio, and declared for King Charles also. Only Owen Roe O'Neill held out. It seemed that the Civil War was about to be fought all over again.

So distressed was poor Doctor Pincher that twice in one week he took to his bed, to be ministered to by Tidy's wife, who brought him healing broth.

Only a letter from Barnaby gave him any comfort.

I am with General Cromwell now. He is not only our finest commander, but a wise, kindly and godly man. He is strong in the Lord. And he will deal firmly with the Royalists and the levellers alike, I promise you.

Though he had heard a good deal of this rising general, Pincher had not been especially impressed. The man sounded solid enough. A Member of Parliament who had turned soldier, Cromwell had inherited large estates and was a wealthy man in his own right. As a rich squire, Cromwell would have no patience with the social ideas of the Levellers. But his religious ideas were less clear. He had grown so close to his men that Pincher was not sure he was a Presbyterian at all. Certainly, he'd lent his name to one pamphlet which had argued for religious independence. Pincher had read it with disgust.

As the weeks went by, however, Cromwell's generalship could not be disputed. As the main Parliamentary forces ground down the Royalist risings on the eastern side of England, Cromwell stormed up the west, from Wales to Scotland, and every opponent he met was smashed by the iron hammer of his battle-hardened troops. By autumn, it was all over. The Roundhead army had won.

And now the army had had enough. Sweeping down into London and finding a large part of the Presbyterian Parliament men still trying to negotiate with King Charles, they kicked them out and announced: "We'll try King Charles after Christmas."

In January 1649, the trial took place. At the end of the month, they executed him. In the weeks that followed, the monarchy and the hereditary House of Lords were abolished, a Council of State was chosen, and England was declared a Commonwealth.

It was an extraordinary business. To execute a king, with all the forms of legality: such a thing had never been done before. The world was turned upside down, and Pincher was not at all sure he liked it. But he also noticed before long that Cromwell, who increasingly dominated the Council, was taking quite a conservative line. He'd even been reluctant to execute the king, according to Barnaby. Sound Presbyterian gentlemen were being brought back into the Parliament; the army radicals were being quietly ignored. Having given them the head of the king, Cromwell was returning England to a state of normalcy. Perhaps, Pincher dared to hope, Cromwell could provide a godly order in Ireland, too.

For at Easter that year came the letter from Barnaby that Doctor Pincher had been living for.

Cromwell is to come to Ireland. He will come this summer.
And I shall be coming with him.

Several parties of men had arrived at the camp that day. From his position on the slope, O'Byrne observed the small group of horsemen as they came up the track below, but he paid them no special attention.

The August sun was hot on his face. It was midafternoon. In the distance lay the walls and steeples of Dublin. To the right, clearly visible through the slight haze, he could see the soft blue waters of Dublin Bay. Here on the slopes of Rathmines, a few miles south of the capital, thousands of men were waiting, just as they had waited all day before. They were waiting for Cromwell. O'Byrne turned to the young soldier standing beside him.

"Go and see who those men were that just arrived," he said. He didn't really care, but the youth had been getting restive and it would give him something to do.

The armies waiting to confront Oliver Cromwell as he sailed to Ireland were a strange collection. For a start, they were partly Protestant. Overall command was in the hands of

Protestant Lord Ormond, who had returned to the island now on behalf of the late king's son. The troops he had gathered at Rathmines today contained a large number of Old English Catholics, but many Protestants also. Also in the Royalist coalition, Lord Inchiquin the Irish Protestant had added his forces from Munster. And up in eastern Ulster, the coalition had been joined by an army of Ulster Scots who, as Presbyterians, had declared themselves the enemies of the religious independents of Cromwell's army. Only the main army of native Irish had failed to join the coalition, because Owen Roe O'Neill was still holding out, in splendid isolation, in western Ulster. Altogether, Lord Ormond had over fourteen thousand men.

And the coalition was formidable. They had already boxed in Owen Roe O'Neill up in Ulster. The Parliamentary garrison in Dublin was now pinned down again. And Lord Inchiquin had surprised everyone by sweeping up from the south and taking over the fortified port of Drogheda, the gateway to Ulster, and then nearly all the Ulster strongholds except Derry. Just recently, a squadron of Royalist ships had come to Ireland's southern coast, where, together with the local privateers, they hoped to harass Cromwell's fleet.

Ormond had chosen his position well. If Cromwell landed in the south, Ormond blocked his path to Dublin. If Cromwell's fleet sailed into Dublin Bay, their ships would be in range of the artillery that Ormond had placed on the coast nearby.

Yet as Brian O'Byrne gazed down at the camp on the slopes below him, he had only one question to ask himself: why was he here?

He scarcely knew. His wife and son were with her family, in the relative safety of Ulster for the moment. He'd been up at Rathconan only days ago, and wished he were back up there now, skulking and trying to stay out of trouble. There was nothing fine about war: he'd seen enough to know that. If he had to fight, he'd sooner have been with Owen Roe O'Neill.

But he'd made too many commitments to the Confederates and his wife's relations now. He must fight with them, even if his heart wasn't in it.

Nor was the reluctance only on his side. For the greatest opposition to the coming of Cromwell to Ireland had already come from another quarter entirely: Cromwell's own troops.

It was the Leveller element, of course. But this was just a matter of radical individuals: whole companies, entire regiments of his iron-willed model army, had refused to serve in Ireland. Cromwell had threatened, he had cajoled, but his faithful English soldiers would not come. They had refused for several reasons. Some had demanded their back pay; others wanted political reforms in England. But the most powerful argument advanced, which came from soldiers in all ranks, was the most astounding.

"A man's religion is a matter of personal conscience," they said. "Why should we force the Irish to be Protestants?"

Nobody had ever heard such an argument before. Rulers, from personal cynicism or for political reasons, might sometimes tolerate other religions within their realm—though, of course, a Catholic king would know that his Protestant subjects were bound for hellfire, just as the Protestant communities knew the same about the Catholics. But no political body, since the days when the Roman Empire had made Christianity the state religion, had ever supposed that a man's church could be a purely private matter, of no business to anyone but himself. The idea was shocking both in its novelty and its blinding simplicity. And even to a sympathetic army general like Cromwell—who was disposed to allow that the Protestant revelation might be celebrated in different ways by the congregations—to suggest that the great evil of Catholicism could be treated as if it were just another godly sect, and that the great divide between Catholic and Protestant could be ignored, was anathema.

But although Cromwell and his fellow generals had moved swiftly to crush the Leveller mutinies, he was still obliged to allow numerous companies of English soldiers to go home, because they could not see why the Irish should be forced to be Protestants.

And as O'Byrne gazed sadly at the encampment below, and considered the blood that had been shed during even his own short life in religion's cause, he shook his head and allowed himself to wonder whether, perhaps, those heretic English mutineers might even have had a point.

The young fellow he had sent to check on the new arrivals came riding back.

"A party from Fingal came to join us. All Catholics. I heard one was a Dublin man named Smith."

"Smith?" O'Byrne's face creased into a smile. "Did you say Smith?" His sadness was forgotten. "It's young Mwirish," he cried happily, and began to ride down the slope.

So he was greatly surprised, having ridden through the camp, to find himself face-to-face not with Maurice at all, but his father.

❖

Something had happened to Walter Smith. He had changed. Not to look at. He was still the same stout family man with balding grey hair that he had been before. But something had happened to him, and he was changed within. That was how it seemed to O'Byrne as they sat by the campfire that evening.

The merchant had not been especially pleased to see O'Byrne, though he must have known that the Irishman might be in Ormond's camp. He appeared to accept O'Byrne's presence as another fact of nature, like the weather, in an existence which, after a lifetime of seeking order, he had now ceased trying to control. And so when, out of courtesy, O'Byrne had invited him to eat at his tent that evening, Walter had nodded briefly and answered: "As you wish." So now, as they ate, O'Byrne gave him a good account of the military state of affairs, the strength of the various parts of Ormond's forces, and the likely tactics if they engaged Cromwell's army.

That afternoon, Ormond had decided to place a forward battery right down at the mouth of the Liffey. But the battery would be dangerously close to the Dublin defenders, and as dusk fell, he prepared to send a large contingent, some fifteen hundred men, to secure the position first, under cover of darkness.

"It's an excellent move," O'Byrne told Walter, as they saw the men gathering to leave. "A battery there could wreak horrible damage on Cromwell's ships if he tries to sail into Dublin."

For his part, O'Byrne was eager to learn the latest news of his friend Orlando, of young Maurice, and of the household in Fingal where the Smith family was still living. Walter confirmed that young Maurice was now running the family's business affairs, although trading was not easy. He was often impatient, and had wanted to come and fight with Ormond; only the fact that the family needed him had kept him at home. Anne was well, but suffered from a stiffness in her joints. The person who had been most ill at ease, it soon became clear, was Walter himself.

O'Byrne could imagine it. Walter did not say so in so many words, for neither of them wished to refer to the matter that lay between them, but O'Byrne could imagine it all too well.

The barn, the outbuildings, the house itself, all filled with Protestant soldiers. That would have been bad enough. But to be crammed in close, as a permanent guest in his brother-in-law's house—no matter how much Walter and Orlando liked each other—must have increased the strain. And then, to be sharing rooms each day with a family that included the simple boy, Daniel, the ever-living reminder to all of them—except Maurice, who knew nothing—of his humiliation . . . For myself, thought O'Byrne, I couldn't have borne it.

But borne it Walter had, month after month, because he was a good and decent man; until at last, having done all he could for them and knowing that the coming of Cromwell was the one mighty threat to all their lives, he had taken his decision. Putting his wife in Maurice's charge at the Walsh estate, and telling them that he was going on business into Connacht, he had quietly ridden down to take up arms, for the first time in his life, as a soldier in the army of Ormond. And so this solid, peaceable family man, well past his sixtieth year, had walked secretly out of his family's lives, and in some strange way he seemed to be free. I wonder, thought O'Byrne, if he means to return?

And as he listened to the merchant, and reflected upon the innate decency of the man, and the fact that it was he himself who had brought all this misery upon Smith, O'Byrne, besides feeling guilt and shame for what he had done with Anne, found himself suddenly struck by the realization, quite common in those who have played the game of adultery, that they have more affection and respect for the husband they have wronged than for the wife they stole.

How strange, O'Byrne considered, as he poured them both more wine, that this fellow, who has none of our looks—those had gone to Maurice—is nonetheless my kinsman, more Irish than English. And he's come to fight at my side, though God knows whether he knows how to use a sword. He'll be butchered, of course, when the fighting begins. But that is his choice. He drank his wine and fell a little quiet.

And perhaps he had drunk too much, but later that night, when the fire had burned down to glowing embers, and Smith rose to depart to his own tent, O'Byrne suddenly took him by the arm and softly cried, "Don't seek your death here. There is no need." And as the merchant slowly shook his head: "You're a far better man than I am, Walter Smith. You're worth ten of me."

But the merchant did not reply, and walked away in the darkness.

⁜

Since he awoke at dawn, and was higher up the slope, O'Byrne was one of the first to notice. For a short time he imagined that they had concealed themselves; but as the sun began to rise, and his keen eyes scanned the coastal position selected for the cannon, he became increasingly alarmed. The troops who had left during the night were not there, nor anywhere else that he could see. Fifteen hundred men had disappeared.

News spread through the camp. Soon people were staring out, eyes against the sun. Where were the troops? Had they marched into the secret halls under the mountains, like the shining heroes of Irish legend? Sometime around eight o'clock the answer became clear, as the long column appeared in the distance, making hurriedly for the coast.

"Dear God," O'Byrne murmured, "the fools got lost in the dark."

But if O'Byrne could see the Royalist men, so could the garrison in Dublin. The column reached its objective. The sun was well up in the sky. Then he saw what he had feared.

A large column was coming out of Dublin. He could judge the numbers by the dust in the distance. It was almost a mile long. Perhaps five thousand men. Against fifteen hundred troops who'd just spent the night lost in the dark, and who hadn't had time to entrench their position. They were going to be massacred.

Moments later, Ormond sounded a general attack.

⁂

They were moving too quickly. There was no time to lose, but as they moved across the open ground towards the hillock, O'Byrne could see that the forward companies were almost breaking into a run. His own cavalry troop was well trained. He kept them in close formation. But he saw another company breaking into a gallop. They were anxious to save their comrades. But what were their commanders thinking of?

He wondered where Walter Smith was. He hadn't caught sight of him.

A young officer came up with orders.

"Wheel." They were to join a concerted charge on the enemy's right flank. A sensible move, thank God.

During the next minutes, O'Byrne had little time to think. He could no longer see the enemy. There were two waves of cavalry in front of him, thundering forward. The first wave broke upon the enemy line. But the troops from Dublin were in perfect formation, presenting an impregnable wall of pikes. As the second wave crashed, he saw ahead of him a churning mass of fallen horses and men, into which the enemy was pouring musket fire. There was no hope of getting through. Seconds later he was wheeling, streaming along the line, the forest of pikes gleaming horribly on his right, through the acrid smoke. A musket ball hissed past his head. He saw one of his men go down. "Back," he cried. Time to regroup.

All the rest of the morning the battle continued. The fifteen hundred men who got lost in the night were mostly wiped out. Again and again, Ormond's men tried to take the enemy positions. Finally, around the middle of the day, the enemy made a lightning advance. Ormond's men were fighting back, but to left and right, O'Byrne could see them giving ground. Then, suddenly, the lines collapsed. Whole companies were turning to flee. The enemy were harrying them. O'Byrne saw a cavalry regiment racing round the right flank to cut them off. It was going to be a bloodbath. Ormond's army was going to be destroyed, and there was nothing to be done.

"Save yourselves," he told his men, and wheeled his horse round.

Some way off, he could see open ground. From there, tracks led westward. If he could work his way to reach the open ground, he might be able to get away. From there he should be able to travel south, then up to Rathconan. It was worth a try. He started off.

Men were fleeing across his path. He encountered two skirmishes but rode swiftly round them. It seemed to him that he might be getting clear. He had gone about half a mile when he saw Walter Smith. He was held at bay in front of a stand of trees by three enemy horsemen. The first was upon him, hacking at his leg. A red gash appeared on Walter's thigh. The merchant had drawn his sword, flailing wildly, but in another few moments they would have him down.

Just then, by some miracle, he caught his assailant in the face and the man fell back, howling. But the other two were racing up. It would be all over for Walter Smith.

O'Byrne let out a shout and spurred his horse forward. The men saw, and one of them veered round to meet him. O'Byrne drew his sword and they came together. He could not look out for Smith now, as they parried and thrust. The Englishman was skilful. For a moment, O'Byrne thought he might lose. But by the grace of God, the fellow's horse missed his footing, the man's head jerked back, and O'Byrne caught him with a thrust to the neck that split his windpipe open.

As the Englishman fell, O'Byrne saw Walter. Amazingly, the merchant was still there. The remaining horseman, distracted by the fight between his comrade and O'Byrne, had not yet struck him down. Now the Englishman hesitated. Walter came at him, brandishing his sword. O'Byrne made straight for him, hoping to reach him first. The fellow thought better of it and fled.

"Come." O'Byrne was beside Walter now, taking his arm. "We must go." He nodded at Walter's leg. "You're wounded."

Walter Smith stared. In the heat of the battle, he had hardly noticed the wound in his leg, which was bleeding considerably. He was flushed.

"We beat them."

"We did." O'Byrne smiled. Does the man realise that I've just saved his life? he wondered. Apparently not. "We must get away now, though," he said kindly. But to his amazement, Smith shook his head.

"We cannot leave the field of battle." He said it with a stubborn determination.

O'Byrne gazed at him, then grinned.

"You're too brave for me." He chuckled. "But we're obliged to go, you know. It's orders. The retreat has been sounded."

"Oh." Smith looked confused, but allowed himself to be led.

It took them an hour, skirting the remains of the battle. O'Byrne didn't say so to Smith, but it was obvious that the broken forces of Ormond were being caught piecemeal and butchered. He wondered how many would be left at the end of the day. After a couple of miles, with the battle behind them, O'Byrne thought it was safe to stop a few minutes so that he could look at Walter's leg. Fortunately, the wound was not deep, but Walter had lost a good deal of blood. O'Byrne tore a strip off his shirt and bound the leg tightly.

It was late afternoon as they began to go up the track that led to Rathconan. Walter by now had grown pale and quiet, but O'Byrne wasn't too concerned about him. The merchant might not be much of a soldier, but he was surprisingly strong. When they reached the house, they found the old priest, who was still in residence, and a couple of the serving women. They carefully bathed Walter's wound and bandaged it. He seemed grateful, and well enough to eat the evening meal with them.

"We have to hope that Cromwell doesn't come here for a few days," O'Byrne remarked.

"What will you do now?" the priest asked him.

"I hardly know," O'Byrne answered. "It will depend upon the military situation." He did not add what he was sure of—that there was nothing, now, between Cromwell and Dublin.

After the meal, they helped Walter up to the chamber, where they put him in the bed which once O'Byrne and Anne had occupied. He lay there, gazing around him.

"It's a fine place, Rathconan," he said sleepily.

"It is. And your own home, too," O'Byrne reminded him. "For you're still an O'Byrne."

"I know." Smith nodded and closed his eyes.

O'Byrne waited a moment, then, thinking the merchant had fallen asleep, turned to go.

"We fought bravely today, didn't we?" Walter murmured, his eyes still closed.

"We did," said Brian O'Byrne. "You fought like a lion." And seeing the merchant smile, he bent down and kissed him.

That night, he slept deeply and awoke long after the sun had risen.

Going to the chamber where he had left Walter Smith the night before, he was surprised not to find him there, and still more to discover, after searching the house and stable, that both Walter and his horse had vanished.

✣

Doctor Pincher was now in his seventy-seventh year, but he hadn't been so excited since he was a boy. For Barnaby Budge had arrived, and they were to meet today.

Doctor Pincher had been greatly pleased that, even while Cromwell's fleet was disembarking, Barnaby had courteously sent him a message by a soldier to ask where and at what time it would please his uncle to receive him. Doctor Pincher had already given much thought to the manner of their meeting. He had hoped to find an excuse to arrange it within the hallowed precincts of Trinity College, so that his nephew should first see him in those august surroundings rather than his more humble lodgings. The matter was solved by the soldier, who informed him that General Cromwell himself was to be taken in a carriage to College Green, where he would address the people of Dublin.

"I shall be there to receive General Cromwell," the doctor told him. "Let Captain Budge," for so he now learned Barnaby was styled, "walk into the college beside the green afterwards, and he shall find me."

It couldn't have been better. A speech from Cromwell, whom Parliament, besides giving him military command, had also designated with the title of Lord Lieutenant of Ireland. Then one of his brave officers and the distinguished Trinity professor would have a public family reunion. It would do honour to the family. Within the hour, he had made sure that several of the lecturers, a selection of the best young scholars, and even the Tidy family would be there to witness the event.

So pleased was he that, in the privacy of his lodgings, Doctor Pincher actually hugged himself.

The arrival of Oliver Cromwell and his Roundhead army in Ireland was an impressive business. A hundred and thirty ships came into the Liffey estuary and began to disembark their troops: eight thousand foot soldiers, three thousand ordinary horse, twelve hundred dragoons. There were also the several thousand English troops already in the Dublin garrison. These numbers, though large, were not awesome, but they belonged to what was probably the best fighting force in Europe. The ships also brought quantities of artillery, and last but not least, the sum of seventy thousand pounds to pay for any supplies they might need.

Against them would be arrayed a coalition of forces. Ormond's army had been shattered at Rathmines. Four thousand men had been killed, and another two and a half thousand taken prisoner. Others had melted away to their homes. Ormond still had about three thousand men, however, camped on the edge of the Midlands. There were also the Royalist forces down in Munster, and the town garrisons in every province— some of them protected by mighty walls. But the coming of Cromwell had also provoked one other important figure.

Owen Roe O'Neill might be proud, but faced with the arrival of Cromwell himself, he had finally agreed: "We must forget our differences and combine the Confederates again." The papal Nuncio might have been furious, but the Irish prince was now rejoining the Royalist cause. He was sick with a gangrenous leg, but he had five thousand men with him and could call on as many again.

The numbers were with the Royalists. In addition to that, neither the native Irish, nor the Old English in the countryside, nor the Presbyterian Scots of Ulster had any wish to see him there. Cromwell was entering hostile territory.

It was while his army was being received by the Dublin garrison that Oliver Cromwell was taken by carriage to College Green.

✣

The day had started badly for the Tidy family. Perhaps it was Tidy's fault.

The two Roundhead officers who arrived at Christ Church that morning were looking for quarters where troops could be billeted. Considering all that Tidy's wife had done to house the Protestant refugees eight years before, it was not surprising that they should have come to the cathedral precincts.

But they did not understand about the bell.

There was no question, old Tidy had given it his best. Hour after hour, as Cromwell's fleet came into the Liffey, the great bell of Christ Church had tolled its Protestant welcome. For seven whole hours the old sexton had pulled on the bellrope, only letting his son take a short stint each hour while he drank a tankard of ale to revive him, and attended to the calls of nature. And it had been his intention to ring the bell again today, to mark the entrance of Cromwell into Dublin.

So delighted had he been with these efforts that he had not hesitated, as perhaps he should have done, when he saw the two officers, but presented them with a bill for the princely sum of forty shillings. This had not been well received. Indeed, blunt words had been spoken by the officers when, not knowing the custom of the place, they had refused to pay. The sexton having then informed them that they'd be quartering no troops in the precincts of Christ Church, the larger officer, who seemed to be under the impression that this was a papist church, had remarked: "General Cromwell will quarter his horses in this cathedral if he pleases." To which Tidy had riposted that the general might put his horses in the nave of Saint Patrick's, but not Christ Church. They had parted on no good terms, despite the efforts of Tidy's wife and Faithful to reassure the officers of their loyal intentions.

It was not a happy Tidy family that walked, while no bell tolled, to listen to Oliver Cromwell.

The crowd at College Green was impressive. The aldermen and city councillors were all there; the great men of Trinity College, old Doctor Pincher easily visible among them; the city's Protestant parish clergy, still a small and unimpressive collection; and a large gathering of citizens. They all watched with interest as, with a cavalry escort, the general arrived in a simple open carriage.

When the carriage stopped, Cromwell did not leave it. He took off his hat and stood up. He was a strongly built, soldierly man, an inch or two under six feet. His greying hair was parted in the centre and hung to his shoulders. His face was not ugly, but plain, and seemed to have warts on one side. When he spoke, his voice was rough and his manner blunt. And the message which Oliver Cromwell now delivered to the people of Ireland was plain and brief.

He had been brought there by Almighty God, he told them, to restore them to liberty. Those who, recognising God's Providence, were amongst the godly—by which he meant any good Protestant—could be assured that the barbarous and bloodthirsty Irish would be subdued, and that the Parliament of England would protect them. Those who opposed the authority of the Parliament with arms would be crushed. Let there be no doubt of that.

But let them also understand, he continued, that he had no desire to hurt tender consciences. Those who were well-affected need not fear. The watchword of the army of God was justice: punishment for those who were guilty of shedding innocent blood, but for the rest, gentleness. Virtue and order should be their guide.

"Civil liberties for peaceful people," he announced.

Then he sat down, put on his hat, and was driven away.

✣

Doctor Pincher frowned. This was not what he had expected at all.

The message was carefully calculated. That was to be expected. And the tactical situation in which Cromwell found himself was well understood. He was a general. He had come to Ireland to protect the Parliamentary forces' western flank. Those opposing the authority of Parliament with arms—in other words, the Royalist forces—would be crushed. This was clear. Of course.

Those who had shed innocent blood would be brought to justice. Did he mean the Irish bands who had run riot when Sir Phelim and Lord Maguire had begun the rebellion in 1641? Presumably. The memory of those massacres, and the refugees coming into Dublin, was still fresh, though identifying the remaining culprits now would not be easy.

But what was this talk of "tender consciences"? The phrase was a code, well known to every listener. It meant those of another faith. If those with tender consciences were "well-affected," the general had announced, they had nothing to fear. The political language was unmistakable. The hint to the townsmen gathered on College Green was clear. As far as this blunt English general was concerned, respectable Catholic merchants like the Smiths of Dublin, if they gave him no trouble, could be left alone. It sounded suspiciously as if Cromwell might even let them continue to worship if they did so discreetly and out of sight. Doctor Pincher was appalled.

Was this the general of the army of God? Were the Catholics not even to be forced to convert? Were they not to be dispossessed? Pincher had been waiting for this all his life. Perhaps this speech was just a tactic to keep the Catholics quiet until they could be properly dealt with. He hoped so. But another possibility also occurred to him: could it be that General Cromwell, beyond smashing the Royalists and punishing the guilty, had no plan for Ireland at all? Pincher glanced around the crowd. Everywhere, people were looking at each other with surprise.

It was in some confusion, and with disquiet in his soul, that Pincher prepared for the meeting with his nephew.

✦

By the time that the Tidy family had entered the sanctuary of Trinity College, Pincher had already set the scene. He himself was standing alone, black-gowned and erect, looking towards the gateway where a group of students was watching. By a doorway on the right, several of his fellow lecturers had gathered, waiting to be introduced. The Tidys stood just inside the gateway.

Through which, moments later, a large figure, dressed in the leathers of a Roundhead officer, strode with a heavy tread. He saw Doctor Pincher at once and made straight towards him. And Tidy groaned.

"God's blood," he muttered. It was the officer with whom he'd quarrelled that morning.

✦

Doctor Pincher stared. The figure coming towards him was tall, but there all family resemblance ended.

Barnaby Budge was burly. His chest was broad, his big breeches clearly housed legs like tree trunks, his leather riding boots were huge. But it was the sight of his face that transfixed the doctor.

Barnaby Budge's face was large and flat. It made Doctor Pincher think of a saddle of mutton. Was it really possible that this brutish fellow lumbering towards him was really his sister's son?

"Doctor Pincher? I am Barnaby."

The doctor inclined his head. Words would come, no doubt, but at that moment he could think of none. Meanwhile, he realised that the big soldier was studying his physiognomy with interest. Then Pincher heard him mutter to himself: "My mother was wrong."

"Wrong? How so?" Pincher asked sharply.

Barnaby looked surprised, then embarrassed. He had not

imagined that his uncle's hearing, at such an advanced age, would be so keen.

"I see, Sir," he answered heavily but truthfully, "that you are not ill-looking at all."

Pincher gazed.

"Come, Nephew," he said quietly, with a glance towards where the lecturers of Trinity College were watching, "let us discuss family matters at my lodgings." And giving the Tidys not even a nod, he passed stiffly out through the college gateway with Barnaby striding at his shoulder.

Once at his lodgings, it did not take long to dispose of the necessary family enquiries. The doctor learned that Barnaby had been solidly set up in the drapery trade before joining the army of Cromwell, that he had inherited a little property and a good house. He spoke dutifully of his mother but, it seemed to Pincher, without much affection. He also spoke of the matter of his investment in Ireland.

"I have come here to do the work of the Lord, Uncle, and I am owed five hundred pounds."

"Quite so," said Doctor Pincher.

For seven years, he explained, the five hundred pounds he had contributed to the Parliamentary cause had naturally been much in his mind. And as it was now to be repaid handsomely with confiscated Irish land, he would be glad to hear his uncle's advice. He looked forward, he told the old man, to settling in Ireland and becoming his friend. "We shall turn this into a godly land, Uncle, I promise you," he said, and clapped the old man on the back. To all of which Doctor Pincher, who was beginning to wonder if he really wanted this large relation to embarrass his declining years, replied:

"All in good time, Barnaby, when the battle is won."

Nor did it take Pincher long to take the measure of his nephew's intellect. Barnaby was not a scholar. Indeed, though familiar with many parts of the scriptures, it did not appear to the doctor that Barnaby had ever read a book in his life. His religious faith, as a solid, God-fearing Protestant, was commendably strong. When asked if he believed he should be saved, he answered firmly: "I serve in the army of God, Sir, and hope to be saved." But when it came to church membership and Calvin's understanding of Predestination, Barnaby seemed less certain. "Only God knows, I suppose, whom He has chosen," he remarked—which, while undoubtedly being true, was not very satisfactory. And probing further, Pincher came to understand, as he had never really done before, how, quite apart from their English dislike of being told what to do by Scottish Presbyterians, the godly men of Cromwell's army had come to believe that it was their years of fighting fellowship that proved they were of the Elect, rather than belonging to any church. While it pleased Pincher that his nephew should know himself to be chosen of God, it irked him that he should know it for the wrong reason, and he hoped that once peace was established, Barnaby should be led to a better understanding.

He was interested, however, to hear more about the puzzling figure of Cromwell. He quickly learned that his nephew, and the entire army, revered the blunt general.

"He is a godly man," Barnaby assured him. "If he has a fiery temper, he shows it only in the cause of righteousness." No man in his regiment, the doctor was glad to hear, could blaspheme or even swear an oath, on pain of punishment. Cromwell had been content with his lot as a country squire and Member of Parliament, according to Barnaby. Only the impossible tyranny of King Charles had forced him into opposition; and only Parliament's complete inability to bring the business with the king to any conclusion after the war had forced him, with the other army men, to take control. "He had no wish to execute the king," Barnaby declared. "Only cruel necessity made him do it. He told me so himself." Though whether this was the agonising of a plain man or the self-justification of a politician, Doctor Pincher did not know. But one other piece of information was encouraging.

"Cromwell is strenuous for the Lord, and he knows that the Catholic priests are the greatest devils of all. Any priests he catches, I can promise you, he will kill."

Whatever the general said about tender consciences, therefore, it did not seem that the Catholics could hope for much. Pincher was relieved to hear it.

It was when Barnaby spoke about the feelings of the army who marched with Cromwell, however, that his statements became startling.

"We know why we have come, Uncle," Barnaby assured him. "We have come to punish the barbarous Irish for the massacres. We'll avenge the rebellion of '41, I promise you."

"It was a terrible thing," Pincher agreed. "I preached to the survivors in Christ Church Cathedral," he added with some pride.

But Barnaby was scarcely listening.

"I am fully informed, Uncle," he assured him. "The whole Irish nation rose," he recited. "They turned upon the Protestants, man, woman, and child, and they butchered them. There was no mercy given, no limit to their Irish cruelty. They killed them all, except the few who got away. Three hundred thousand innocent Protestants died. There has been nothing like it in all the history of Man."

Doctor Pincher stared at him. The actual loss of life in the rising of 1641 was somewhat uncertain. He believed that when it was all done, perhaps five thousand Protestants lost their lives across the whole of Ireland, though it might well be less. Another thousand or two Catholics had been killed in reprisals. Since then, of course, the figures had swollen in the telling, but Barnaby's statement was astounding. Pincher wasn't sure there were even that many Protestants on the island.

"How many?"

"Three hundred thousand," said Barnaby firmly.

Pincher despised the Irish and hated Catholics, but he was not a dishonest man.

"That number," he ventured, "may be somewhat high, you know."

"No, I assure you," said Barnaby. "It is so. The whole army knows it."

And now Doctor Pincher understood. The army of Oliver Cromwell, having questioned the need to convert Catholics, had been fortified by these reminders of the atrocities to avenge. And he sighed. Every army, he supposed, has to be told a story. Sometimes the story is true, sometimes not. No doubt, he supposed, this story would serve its necessary purpose.

ÐROGHEÐA

WALTER SMITH moved slowly round the side of the great mound. It was a blustery day at the start of September, and it seemed that the winds might turn into gales. Along the low ridge, the huge, grassy tombs lay grimly under the cloudy sky. At his feet, the scattered shards of white quartz took their tone from the dullness of the day, like so many bleached bones. Below, gusts of wind angrily ruffled the slate-grey water of the River Boyne.

It was said, he knew, that the legendary inhabitants of the island long ago, the Tuatha De Danaan, still lived and feasted in their bright halls under the magic mounds. Perhaps it was the weather, but to him the old sacred site seemed cold and vaguely threatening. He continued to ride eastwards.

A month had passed since he departed Rathconan. Why had he left so abruptly? Perhaps it was ingrained in his nature that he must finish any task he had begun. Having committed himself to fight, he had to look for the battle. He had found Ormond and the remains of the forces of the crown and rested with them in camp for three weeks. During that time, his wound had nearly healed, although his leg still hurt him and he walked with a slight limp.

After Cromwell's arrival in Dublin, the news of his preparations had come quickly. He had picked the best men of the garrison and added them to his army. He had also imposed his usual iron discipline. His troops were quartered on the city, but they were forbidden to give any trouble. There was no looting, on pain of instant death. He had even insisted that all provisions from the surrounding countryside, from Catholic and Protestant farmers alike, were to be fully paid for. Not only was this unheard of, it was also very clever. So far at least, not a hand had been raised against him or his men.

Presumably, Walter thought, Orlando was being fully paid for his grain. More than once, he had felt the urge to visit the estate in Fingal, but he knew it was impossible. Even if he were not arrested, it would only cause trouble. He must stay away until this business was over.

It was not long before a rider came with definite news.

"Cromwell's preparing to move north." This made sense. If he could take back the Ulster garrisons held by the Royalists and smash Owen Roe O'Neill, then he would have broken the backbone of the opposition. But it was also a strategy with risk. The garrisons were strong, and before entering Ulster, he must take the greatest stronghold of them all.

Drogheda. Tredagh, the English were calling it, as their best approximation to the way the Irish pronounced the name. Soon after the news came, Ormond had strengthened the garrison with some of his best troops, under the command of Aston, a veteran commander. Walter, as an unskilled volunteer, had not been chosen to go. So he had quietly slipped away from Ormond's camp the previous day. Once he arrived there, he considered, they would hardly turn away an extra man.

He had only to ride a few miles along the northern bank of the River Boyne before he came in sight of his object.

It was a grim old place. Occupying two hills on each side of the river, Drogheda's medieval walls towered up in massive masonry that was almost impregnable. As the second great port after Dublin in that region, its importance was obvious, and it was the guardian of the coastal gateway into Ulster. Like most Irish towns, its citizens had been both Catholic and Protestant, but when forced to choose, it had closed its gates firmly against Sir Phelim and his Catholic rebels, who had besieged it for months and got nowhere. As a stronghold loyal to the government, it had recently been garrisoned by Ormond's Royalist forces. Today, under a sullen, windy sky, its grim defences and grey steeples seemed to say: "We did not yield to Sir Phelim and his Catholics, and we shall not yield to Cromwell, either."

As Walter got near, he encountered a little stream of townspeople leaving, some on foot, others with carts. Evidently, Cromwell was expected soon. Entering through a gateway in the north-western wall, he passed into the town.

Soon after making himself known to one of the officers, he was summoned to the commander's headquarters, where, to his surprise, he found himself face-to-face with the commander himself. He knew a little about Sir Arthur Aston. A short, fiery man who had lost a leg in action, he had been one of the few Catholic officers in King Charles's army. The men respected him. He was also wealthy. "They say his wooden leg is filled with gold," Walter had been told. Hearing that Walter had come from Ormond's camp, Aston was eager to talk to him.

"I had hoped you were bringing ammunition," he told the merchant. "Lord Ormond has promised to send me both powder and shot." He shook his head. "Owen Roe O'Neill has promised me troops. They haven't arrived either." He gave Walter a quick look. "Don't worry. The walls here would protect us if we never fired a shot."

Aston quickly gave orders that Walter should be attached to a small mounted company, whom he found lodged at an inn that lay in the northern half of the town. Though Ormond's coalition contained both Catholics and Protestants, most of Aston's men were Catholic, and the little company Walter joined was entirely so. The innkeeper was an English Protestant

who had genially informed them that he had no particular preference between themselves and Cromwell's men. "But I'd
sooner stay here and be paid for my ale than have you gentlemen drink it for nothing when I'm gone." He'd been widowed
the year before and had a three-year-old daughter with golden
curls, with whom the soldiers played to pass the time. Amused
to find themselves with a comrade who was so much older, the
soldiers immediately called Walter "Granddad." When the little
girl asked why, they informed her: "Didn't you know, Mary,
that this is your granddad? He's everybody's granddad." And
when she turned to her father, the innkeeper genially answered:
"Most children only have two grandfathers, Mary, but you are
so lucky—you have three." The child insisted on sitting on
Walter's knee all evening after that.

Cromwell's army appeared from the south the following
day. Walter watched their movements from the city walls. As
they pitched their tents on the slopes opposite, the watchers
estimated that Cromwell had brought about twelve thousand
men. By the next morning, it was also clear that his artillery
had not yet arrived.

"He's probably sent it by sea," Aston told them. With the
continuing winds, the coastal waters were treacherous. "With
luck," the one-legged commander remarked, "his transports
will have been sunk." Faced with the high walls of Drogheda,
and without an artillery bombardment, there would be nothing Cromwell could do.

The succeeding days were strangely quiet. Walter's comrades tried to teach him some of the rudiments of swordplay
and military tactics, though without much success. He spent
the rest of his time wandering about the town.

The two sections of the town, on each side of the river,
were completely self-contained and walled. The river between
them was deep, and could only be crossed by a stout drawbridge on the northern side, which could be quickly raised. In
the southern sector, which was somewhat smaller, there was a
high mound with a small fortification on top, and a church

with a high steeple which had commanding views. The sector on the northern bank, with its medieval streets and neatly walled and hedged gardens, was agreeable. Sometimes Walter would put little Mary on his shoulders and take her with him on his walks.

During these days, Aston sent a number of raiding parties out to harass the enemy. One day, Walter was ordered to go on an errand for the commander, only to find that his company had been out on a raid in his absence. Nothing was said, but he realised that they had wanted to spare him, and felt humiliated, especially after several of his comrades failed to return. Another day, a large party went out, but they were ambushed by Cromwell's men and annihilated. There were fewer raids after that. But Aston remained confident. Meeting Walter and some of his comrades on the wall one afternoon, he surveyed the tents opposite thoughtfully, then turned to them briskly.

"They can't breach the walls, and winter is coming. After that, gentlemen, I have two allies who will surely defeat them." He smiled. "Colonel Hunger and Major Disease. They will attack Cromwell for me, I assure you, while he sits out there in the rain. That is what always happens, sooner or later, with a siege in Ireland."

Meanwhile, life within the walls of Drogheda was surprisingly calm. Cromwell was on the south side of the river, and there was no easy crossing place nearby. Many of the remaining townspeople now left, which meant that the food supplies, which were still being brought in through the gates on the northern side, would last much longer. Aston had brought several Catholic priests with him, and they celebrated Mass for the Catholic troops in the big church. It was good, Walter thought, to see the old medieval church being used by the true faith again.

On the seventh day, the transport ships with Cromwell's cannon sailed into the Boyne. Walter watched the lumbering pieces being dragged into position—some on the slopes overlooking the town, some on the lower ground facing the southern walls. The next morning, a horseman came down from Cromwell's camp with a message.

It was brief and to the point. To prevent what the Puritan general called "the effusion of blood," he invited the garrison to surrender. If they refused, "You will have no cause to blame me."

There was no mistaking the meaning of this message. The rules of war were ancient and cruel. If a besieged town accepted the chance to surrender, its garrison could save their lives. If they refused and the town fell, no quarter need be given. The attacking general had the right to kill all combatants. Usually, the two sides cut a deal during the proceedings; but the defenders knew they ran the risk that if they refused the first offer, they might all lose their lives.

But Aston was confident. The walls of Drogheda had not been breached before. Soon they all heard:

"The offer has been rejected."

Walter was up on the wall, gazing at the gun emplacements, when the first cannon shot roared out. He felt a little rush of fear and excitement as he heard the cannonball hiss past. To his surprise, it did not hit the wall at all but smashed into the tall steeple of the church behind, sending down a little shower of masonry. A few moments later came another roar, and the same thing happened again. They seemed to be using the steeple for target practice.

"They'll bring down the church tower first," an old soldier beside him calmly remarked. "They'll not want any musketeers shooting at them from up there." He sniffed. "But those cannon won't make so much impression on the walls."

For a short time there was silence. Then they heard another roar. But this one was different. It was louder and ended with a deep, harsh growl. There was a great crash, and a gaping hole appeared in the lower part of the spire.

"What was that?" asked Walter.

"I'm not sure," the soldier replied. "It may have been a thirty-pounder." He shook his head and fell silent. Another roar was heard.

There were two types of siege artillery in Europe at this time. There were mortars, which lobbed a large iron shell filled with gunpowder in a high trajectory, and which exploded with horrible effect. And there were the cannon, which fired a solid cannonball that knocked down masonry. The largest cannon seen in Ireland usually fired a twelve- or fourteen-pound ball. The great walls of Drogheda, though they'd be damaged, could withstand a pounding from shot of this size. But there were greater beasts than these. The demicannon, whole cannon, and cannon royal fired balls several times larger.

Lord Ormond and his commanders had not realised that Cromwell would bring some of the great cannon of Europe to Ireland. And the artillerymen aiming them were experts.

All morning the cannon continued their surly sound. The steeple began to look as if some unseen raven had been savagely pecking at it. Then, suddenly, it came down with a crash.

The cannon did not even pause, but pounded the church tower below instead. By noon it looked like a jagged, broken tooth, and the cannon began to bombard the nearby bastion at the corner of the city wall. This was a sturdier structure by far. But the cannon kept up their steady work, hour after hour, never pausing, all afternoon and into the evening. As the acrid smoke drifted across from the battery towards the city, Drogheda's mighty corner tower, which had withstood every assault for centuries, slowly crumbled down. Shortly before dusk, the gunners turned their attention to the walls and made two breaches high up in them.

That night, Aston had parties of men repair the breaches in the walls, replacing the stones and pouring on extra mortar. At dawn, however, a much larger work began in which half the garrison joined in with urgency. The men dug three big lines of trenches a little way back from the wall that had been breached. Behind each trench, the earth thrown up was formed into a parapet, behind which the musketeers could take cover.

Though such work was normally done by the infantry, Walter joined in and nobody stopped him. Spade in hand, working alongside men who were mostly half his age, his portly form unused to such exertion, the early morning found him red-faced and sweating, but happy that he could make himself useful. The trenches ran to the walled churchyard. Behind the lines rose the steep, high mound, topped with its little fort.

Early in the morning came news that a small group of aristocrats had urged Aston to surrender. He had thrown them out of the town by one of the northern gates.

"How can he surrender?" one of the officers cried. "If mighty Drogheda gives up, what other town would stand and fight?"

At that moment, the thunder of a cannon was heard and the first salvo of the day thudded into the wall.

✢

All morning, as grey clouds crowded into the sky above, and the crash of cannonballs sent small showers of masonry down from the wall, they dug the trenches and raised the parapets.

The walls of Drogheda did not come down easily. In places they were six feet thick. But the medieval mix of stone, rubble, and mortar, strong though it was, could not rebuff the steady pounding of the cannonballs—hundreds of them—that went on hour after hour. Gradually, they crumbled into great, untidy heaps at the base. By midafternoon, the men at the trenches could see through the big, jagged chasm to the enemy camp on the slopes opposite.

Shortly before five o'clock, Aston came down amongst the diggers, hobbling about on his wooden leg and telling them to prepare.

"They'll make their assault through the gap," he announced, "but they'll have to climb across the rubble on foot. It's too high for cavalry. You'll shoot them down easily enough. Mark my words."

Behind the trenches, Walter's cavalry troop had appeared. Cleaning the mud off his face and clothes as best he could, he went back to join them. As he did so, he realised that the cannon had ceased to fire. A strange quiet hung in the air. Aston was behind the trenches now, placing the men.

He placed musketeers behind the two back parapets and in the churchyard. In the first line were the men with pikes. It took a powerful man to handle a pike, which was sixteen feet long, with a heavy shaft and a fearsome steel spike. Walter had once asked a burly pikeman to let him try one, and had almost fallen over with the weight of the thing. But in the hands of an expert, it was a terrible weapon to encounter. As the enemy troops clambered up to the first parapet and were stopped by the pikes, they'd either be gouged by the spikes or cut down by musket fire from the churchyard and the two parapets behind. And that fire would be deadly. Even with their cumbersome matchlocks and flintlocks, each trained musketeer could fire three times a minute.

The silence continued. As he waited, Walter could feel his heart beating. To his own surprise, he found he was almost too excited to be frightened.

There were shouts outside the wall. He saw the metal helmets of the Roundheads coming into the breach and over the mound of rubble. A hundred, two hundred—he was not sure. He heard Aston's voice cut through the air.

"Wait, musketeers. Wait." The first wave was over the rubble; the second was in the breach now. He saw their officer, a handsome, grey-haired man. "Fire."

It was well done. The first salvo caught them and brought fifty men down. The grey-haired officer fell as a musket ball shattered his head.

"Fire." Another salvo from the third parapet, and another mass of men going down. There were screams and cries everywhere. He saw half a dozen men horribly caught on the pikes. No wonder the advance guard of an attack like this was known as "the Forlorn Hope." The soldiers coming over the breach now and seeing the carnage before them seemed to be hesitating.

"At the breach. Fire." Another deadly salvo caught them.
And now, suddenly, the Roundheads were turning back. The
men in the breach were already scrambling to safety, but the
musketeers in the churchyard, firing freely, were picking them
off. A cheer went up from the Royalists. The Roundheads were
on the run.

"Reload. They'll come again. Cavalry, load your pistols."
Aston's voice, clear and precise.

Like most of the mounted men, Walter had been given two
pistols, which sat in holsters on each side of his saddle. He
primed them now, and kept one in his hand. Several minutes
passed before the Roundheads came again. They came faster
this time, and there were more of them. The first wave came
right up to the line of pikes before Aston called out: "Fire."
And again they were caught in the withering hail of musket
balls. "Cavalry, fire at will. Aim for your man."

Walter rested the long barrel of his pistol on his spare arm
to steady it. In practice with his comrades, he had discovered
he had an aptitude for this. He saw a fellow who had just
reached the pikes, took careful aim, and pulled the trigger.
He had aimed at the chest but struck the head. With a surge
of triumph, he saw the man go down. I wish, he thought
proudly, that my family could see me now. Moments later,
another cheer went up. The Roundheads had been broken
again.

"Reload," called Aston. But this time there was a length-
ening silence. Perhaps the Roundheads, having been mauled
twice, had given up for the day.

There were two batteries opposite the breach. One lay on
the level ground and had been directing its fire up at the walls.
The other was on the slopes behind and looked down towards
the breach. From this battery Walter now saw a puff of smoke.

A tremendous hissing. A jolt as his horse was struck.
Ripping sounds, terrible screams. Then he was falling. As he
hit the ground, he heard another terrible hiss. More screams.
Horses were rearing.

Cromwell's cannon on the slopes had been filled with half-pound shot, and they were pouring it through the breach into the cavalry. Walter had hardly got to his feet before he saw a mass of men rushing through the breach. Clearly, they meant to overwhelm the trenches by sheer force of numbers. The muskets rang out, but in the confusion now, their volley sounded more ragged. He looked down. His poor horse was already dead. All around him were writhing horses and men. There was blood everywhere. He felt light-headed, though he was sure he hadn't been hit. A hand was pulling on his arm.

"Come on, Granddad. We're falling back."

He understood, but for a moment he stood there stupidly. And as he did so, he saw on top of the breach a single officer in a leather coat, sword in hand, his long, greying hair blowing in the wind. And he knew at once who this must be.

Oliver Cromwell himself had got off his horse and come to lead his men in person through the deadly breach of Drogheda.

His pistol. It was still in the holster by his saddle. He dived down to where his horse lay and retrieved it. Then, with the pistol grasped in his hand, he rose again. Cromwell was still there, waving his men forward with his sword. Walter took aim.

And, as though in a dream, he stood paralysed. His finger was pulling the trigger, but nothing seemed to be happening. How could that be? He tried again. Something in the simple mechanism had jammed.

"Granddad. Come quickly." The fellow pulled him so hard, he almost lost his balance, and as he did so, the pistol went off, sending a ball high into the air. He cursed, and staggered to where he was being led. Some of the rest of his troop had gathered on foot. As soon as he reached them, they took him in charge and started to leave. The first parapet was being overrun. The musketeers were discharging their weapons and then falling back. As he was hurried away from the scene, Walter saw Aston hobbling on his wooden leg with a company of his men back towards the high mound with its little fort. He wondered if he should join him, but two of his comrades dragged him on. They were hurrying up the street towards the river. The drawbridge was ahead.

"We'd better get across the drawbridge before they raise it, Granddad," one of his companions cried. Once that was up, those left behind would have to fight as best they could, but Cromwell's men would be unable to follow them. The river was deep and the walls of the northern town were stout. It would be a safe refuge, for a while at least. As they reached the drawbridge, however, a great crowd of musketeers and pikemen caught up with them, and glancing backwards, Walter could see the leather jerkins and metal helmets of Cromwell's troops close on their heels. They thundered across the drawbridge pell-mell.

Only as he ran into the main street of the northern town did Walter realise. No one had raised the drawbridge. As the defenders fled over the River Boyne, into the northern sector, Cromwell's men were crossing, too. He turned and cried out, "Raise the drawbridge," but nobody took any notice, and the press of men made it impossible to do anything as he was swept along.

Some way ahead rose the big church of Saint Peter. His companions swung left into the cross-street that led to the western of the northern sector's two gates. A short way along this street lay a turning down to the inn where they had lodged. Two of his companions had left money at the inn, so they hurried to reach it. "At least we'll have the money if we have to run," they told him. The innkeeper, having heard the commotion but unaware of exactly what was happening, was busy closing the shutters. When Walter quickly told him, the fellow cried: "I must get Mary." She was at a neighbour's house down the same street.

"Close up your inn," Walter told him. "I'll get the child." And he hurried away.

It only took a minute or two to extract little Mary from the neighbour's house. Holding her hand firmly, he started back the short distance towards the inn. He had almost forgotten that he still had a sword banging at his side until he realised that it had nearly banged against the child; so, scooping her up, he carried her towards her home.

The mass of the soldiers were still in the main street. They had not come that way as yet. His companions were standing with the innkeeper by the door. He was fifty yards away when the party of Roundheads in their heavy leathers came bursting from the street into the lane. Seeing the Royalist soldiers, they set up a roar and rushed towards them, so that his friends only just had time to draw their swords. He heard one of the Roundheads yell, "Papist dogs," and heard the innkeeper swear a curse before the Roundheads fell upon them. There was a ringing crash and bang of swords, more bangs, shouts, a terrible cry, and a scream. It happened so fast, he could scarcely believe it. He saw his friends go down, and the innkeeper, too. No doubt they thought he was one of the soldiers.

Instinctively, as the soldiers appeared, he pulled back into a doorway and held little Mary close, with her face to his chest, so that she should not see. He waited there for several moments, wondering if the Roundheads would come that way, but they did not. At last, carefully looking out, he saw that they had gone. But he could hear shouting from the street from which they'd come. Her father's body lay with the others in front of the inn. He could hardly leave her there, then. He began to retrace his steps towards the neighbours where he had found her. No doubt they would take her in. But now he could see Roundhead uniforms in the street at the end of the lane near the neighbours. He dared not go that way. There was an empty alley beside him that led westwards. He stepped into it and began to make his way along. The only thing to do was to keep the child with him until he could find a place of safety for her.

Perhaps it would still be possible to get out of the western gate. Had Cromwell's men reached that yet? Or had he now managed to send troops across the deep waters of the Boyne to encircle the town and cut off such retreats? He did not know.

"Your granddad's taking you for a little walk," he whispered to little Mary. "Then we'll meet your father." And he forced himself to smile.

Cautiously, he went along the alley, wondering where it led.

⁜

Barnaby Budge pulled up before the breach. He was not afraid. Why should he be? Yet again, God's general was carrying all before him. A day of victory for the Lord.

He knew who lay behind Drogheda's dark walls. The barbarous, bloodthirsty Irish, the papists and their lackeys. Three hundred thousand they had murdered: Protestants, godly folk, men, women, and children, without mercy or distinction. But the day of reckoning had come at last. Justice would be done. *Vengeance is mine, saith the Lord.* And the army of saints was the Lord's right hand. Had not the Saviour Himself declared: *I come not to send peace, but a sword.*

And when it was over, and the papist Irish were scattered and driven out, then the soldiers of Christ should receive their recompense and inherit the earth. The five hundred pounds that, seven long years ago, he had ventured in the cause would be repaid with Irish land; and upon that land he'd build his portion of the holy city, and take a godly wife, and settle down, and look after his uncle in his old age. His sword, his wealth, his life: he had offered all. He was a soldier for Christ, an adventurer for God. If, as he dared to hope, he had been chosen as one of the Elect, he had also paid for his salvation. It was knowing all this, as he did, that Barnaby Budge with a courageous heart approached the breach in the dark walls of Drogheda.

He felt a faint tap of wind on his cheek and glanced upwards. The wind seemed to be changing. The grey clouds were churning in the sky, as if they might fly apart.

Cavalry forward, the order had come. Cromwell himself had summoned them. And who could refuse when the leader himself showed no fear? Twice his men had been driven back from that breach. The dead were lying in heaps. But Cromwell had dismounted, unsheathed his sword, and led the third charge himself. Cromwell, valiant for God.

"Will we follow him?" Barnaby shouted to his men.

"Into the mouth of hell!" they roared.

There was only one way to get over the pile of rubble that was the breach, however.

"Dismount," he ordered quietly. And taking his horse's reins, he led them across on foot. A couple of musket balls hissed by, but he ignored them.

The scene before him on the other side was terrible. The fighting had moved past the trenches to the high mound behind. He walked his troop through the churchyard, which was strewn with bodies. Coming to the foot of the mound, he paused. Aston and a company of men had gone up into the little fort at the top but, seeing their position was hopeless, had decided to give up. If they had hoped to save their lives, however, they were mistaken. The Roundhead troops were in the tower already, and a series of furious shouts were coming from above.

"They want his wooden leg," the officer standing at the base explained. "It's supposed to be full of gold."

Now there were cries of rage from above, followed by a series of sickening cracks. It sounded to Barnaby as if the troops were beating Aston's brains out with the wooden leg.

"They didn't find the gold," the officer remarked drily.

At this moment, from the other side of the mound, Cromwell himself appeared. He nodded to Barnaby.

"Take your men across the drawbridge and secure the northern gates," he ordered. He gave him a stern look. "We have the main enemy force trapped in the town, Captain Budge. Break Drogheda and we break all Ireland. Let none escape. Do you understand?"

"I do, Sir."

"No quarter, Captain Budge. They have deserved none; they shall receive none." He paused, glanced up at the tower, and looked thoughtful for a moment before gazing hard at Barnaby again. "It is the Lord who has brought us here and delivered to us this town. Victory belongs to Him alone."

"God's will be done," answered Barnaby firmly. And as his troops clattered over the drawbridge a few moments later, he gave the order: "Draw your swords."

The onslaught of the Roundheads across the drawbridge had been so sudden that the defenders had no time to regroup. There were street battles going on all over the northern section of the town.

And the scattered Royalist troops were being cut down like grass. Riding up the main street, he had to pick his way over the fallen bodies. Coming to an open yard which gave onto a little garden, he found a young officer and his company. They had captured a dozen of the Royalists, who had surrendered their weapons.

"No quarter," he told the young fellow. "General Cromwell's orders." And when the officer started to protest, "I gave them my word," Barnaby said, and shook his head. "Remember what they have done to Protestant women and children. Kill them all." And he stayed there a few moments while the Roundheads went to work with their swords, to ensure that it was quickly done.

Two hundred yards ahead, a huge battle was in progress around the big church of Saint Peter. There were shouts, bangs, crashes, and the constant crack of musket fire. But Barnaby had his instructions, which were clear. He must secure the gates. There were two gates to the northern part of Drogheda, and he knew, from a map the officers had studied the previous week, exactly where they were. They lay at each end of a long cross-street, one in the eastern and one in the western wall. The eastern being closer, they rode quickly towards that. Here and there, he saw faces peering through half-closed shutters from the upper floors of the houses along the street. But they seemed to be ordinary townspeople who had remained behind. That could be checked later. The enemy, however, appeared to be all in the streets. Reaching the eastern gate, he found it was already secured, with a troop of infantry on guard. Instructing them on no account to open it, he turned back, therefore, towards the western side.

As they crossed the main axis of the town, he glanced up towards the big church where the battle was taking place. There were shouts and cries from that direction, but he did not hear the same sounds of battle as he had done before. Something had changed. Then, glancing down at the roadway, he realised that the open gutter that ran along the centre of the street was running with a shallow stream of blood. They were putting the Irish papists to the sword. He had seen streams of blood before on the battlefield, but never quite like this. They must have slaughtered several hundred already.

It was a bloody business, but he knew it must be carried through. And when he thought of the huge and bloody slaughter of innocents of which these accursed people were guilty themselves, he hardened his heart, knowing the Lord's work was being done.

The western gate lay less than four hundred yards away. But the broad street that led to it was not empty. A band of infantry troops had just gathered there. There were pikemen and musketeers, and they were quickly getting into battle order. There looked to be a hundred men or more. From a side street now, half a dozen cavalry came out, making a screen in front of the troops. He glanced back. He had twenty men, mounted and armed like himself. And the enemy, who must realise what was being done up at the church, were doubtless determined to sell their lives dear. To one of his men he called back, "Find reinforcements." The enemy might be desperate, but his troops were battle-hardened veterans, and soldiers of Christ besides. Cromwell himself had ordered him to secure the gate. God would protect them. He measured the enemy before him with a practised eye.

And just at that moment, a rift opened in the clouds and a great shaft of evening sunlight burst down upon the very place where the enemy horsemen were, flashing its sudden fire, blinding them for an instant. And seeing this, Barnaby knew with an utter certainty that this was a sign from God, lighting his way like a pillar of fire to the promised land.

"Not my arm, O Lord, but Thine," he murmured, and raising his sword high in the air so that it caught the sun with an answering flash, he called his men to charge.

Then Barnaby Budge fought for the Lord, as his horse bounded forward and he crashed into the enemy, striking this way and that as the blood of the Irish beasts burst out. The horsemen were down, the footmen were falling, the papists were parting before him as he hacked, and slashed, and struck for the Lord.

Shouts behind him. He glanced back. Roundhead reinforcements had come. So be it. The enemies of the Lord were scattering. He spurred forward and cut them down as they ran.

They were fleeing into yards and alleys, running down the street. He could see the gate, a hundred yards ahead. It was open. He started towards it.

As he did so, he saw a papist soldier at the side of the street, dressed as a horseman but without any horse, cowering by the entrance to an alley. The villain had snatched up a little child and was clasping it across his chest, his round red face gazing up at him, seemingly transfixed. Did he think to escape justice by such means?

He wheeled his horse and struck him with a single, slashing blow that burst through the wretch's collar and chest and carved through the child as well.

No doubt the child was a papist, too. No matter. He wheeled his horse again. There were still papist soldiers between him and the gate. There was still much work to be done.

And as he turned and raced at them, and struck again, and saw them fall, and felt the sun's rays upon his face, Barnaby knew the glory of God, and that the strength of the Lord was in his arm, and that he should receive the promised land of which he was owed five hundred pounds.

⁘

So it was, that evening in Drogheda, that the Royalist garrison perished, English and Irish, Protestant and Catholic. Two thousand five hundred were put to the sword, many after surrendering their weapons.

Rumour was that the townspeople also were slaughtered, and doubtless some few of them were, though the evidence is dubious.

But who should say, even if it were true, that the slaughter was shocking? When kings and parliaments decided men's faith, to differ meant bloodshed. It could not be otherwise. For a hundred years, since Luther and Calvin split Christendom, it had been the same; for generations to come, the bloodshed would continue. All over Europe, the faithful were falling, Catholic to Protestant, Protestant to Catholic. It was all one and the same.

The Staff of
Saint Patrick

⊰ **1689** ⊱

MAURICE SMITH gazed at the ancient chest. He'd been meaning to open it for years.

Outside, it was a bright March day, and the breeze made its way to Rathconan with a faint hiss, like the whisper of faith itself coming up from the sea.

The chest had belonged to his father. It had been kept in storage since Walter Smith had disappeared. Maurice knew it contained some old papers, but that was all he knew; and his father had not been there to ask.

No one had ever known what happened to Walter Smith. It had been supposed that he must have been robbed and murdered somewhere when he had gone away. One or two people had suggested he might even have joined the Royalist forces; but that seemed out of character, and there was certainly no proof of such a thing. It was just as well. Had he been involved in the fighting, things might have gone harder with his family after Cromwell's victory.

Whatever had become of Walter, his papers and other personal effects had been stored. When life in Dublin had become impossible for a Catholic merchant, Maurice himself had left for France. The Doyles had kindly taken in his mother, Anne; and the chest of papers, together with the other effects, had been transferred to their attic. There they had remained, even after his return, until he had collected them a few years ago.

He had to admit, it had really been laziness on his part not to have sorted the chest before. But now, with such wonderful events taking place—and the promise of so many good things for the Catholics of Ireland—it had occurred to him that if, by chance, there were any deeds or other documents in his family's favour hidden away in the chest, this would be the time to find them. He'd discovered that the chest was locked with three different locks; but amongst his father's effects there had been quite a collection of keys, and he had found the ones relating to the chest easily enough. Having unlocked it, therefore, he dragged it near to a window and, sitting himself on a stool, opened the lid.

At first, he was a little disappointed. The documents all seemed to relate to the old Guild of Saint Anne and not to the family at all. But finding that they went back to the days of the Reformation itself, he started to read them and found such a rich history of the life of the faithful in those days that he soon became quite engrossed. An hour passed before he came to a document on thick paper, carefully folded and closed with a red wax seal, on which was written in a bold hand:

DEPOSITION OF MASTER MACGOWAN
CONCERNING THE STAFF

The seal had never been broken. He broke it, and began to read. And as he did so, he gasped.

It was clear that the merchant had given his Deposition verbally, and that it had been written down by one of the members of the guild. Sometimes it was in the first person; in other places it strayed into the third: "Master MacGowan swears that the events took place in exactly this manner." But the subject was what mattered. For the staff of which he spoke was the Staff of Saint Patrick himself.

The *Bachall Iosa:* the most sacred relic in Ireland. He knew the story of its destruction of course. Everybody did. Back in 1538, when the heretic monster King Henry VIII had ordered the holy relics of Ireland to be burned, the sacred Staff of Saint Patrick, that had been held in the hands of the saint himself more than a thousand years before, had been taken from Christ Church Cathedral and thrown on a public bonfire there, in the middle of Dublin. No greater sacrilege, no greater insult to Ireland, could have been imagined. The dark deed had never been forgotten. The Staff was gone.

Or was it? There had been rumours since—occasional, muted whispers in the land—that the Staff might have been saved. There had been a claim that it was still in existence, some twenty years after its burning. Then nothing more had been heard. Maurice had always taken the claim to be a legend, and no more. Three years ago, a story was current in Dublin that the Staff had been seen in County Meath. But Maurice had never met anyone who'd actually set eyes on it. He suspected the story was a hoax.

The Deposition of Master MacGowan said otherwise. On that terrible day, while the soldiers were bringing cartloads of sacred objects to the fire, he had run into the cathedral, seen the Staff already out of its case, and in a brief moment, when the attention of the king's vandals was directed elsewhere, seized it and fled. He had taken the Staff to his own humble house. The following day, in the company of Alderman Doyle, he had gone quietly out of the city and conveyed the Staff to a devout family "known to the members of this guild," in Kildare. No name was given. The matter was too secret for that. Maurice supposed it was probably one of the ancient families, the guardians of monasteries and providers of priests whose service to the Church sometimes stretched back almost to the days of the saint himself.

The Deposition was corroborated and sworn to by Alderman Doyle. There was no doubt of its authenticity. And as he held it in his hand, and contemplated the implications of the document, Maurice began to tremble.

For a start, the sightings of the Staff were surely genuine. One of the most sacred objects in all Christendom was residing, quite likely, within forty miles of Dublin. But more than that: for the bruised and humiliated Catholics of Ireland, here was a religious and national symbol, an object of pride, of veneration, of inspiration, waiting to be raised on high in their very midst. And now, if the Staff were held up before the people, and their heretic rulers dared to say that it was a fraud, here in his own hand was the living proof that it was genuine.

That he should have found such a document, at such a time as this, could only mean one thing. It was a divine intervention, a sign from God. He quickly said a prayer.

Next, he had to consider what to do. For the moment, it might be best to keep the matter confidential. The document had huge value, both to the Catholic cause and its enemies; but nobody knew of its existence. It would be perfectly safe locked in the chest. He ought to share the knowledge with someone, though. Someone he could trust. And he might need help as well. It did not take him long to think of an answer. Whose family was firmer in their faith, who had more discretion, than his own cousin Donatus Walsh? That afternoon, he wrote a short and carefully worded letter. He gave no details, but he told his cousin that he had a matter of the utmost importance to discuss concerning the faith, and asked to meet him urgently, by the old Tholsel in Dublin, in three days' time, on Sunday. Then he gave it to a servant. The fellow could ride down and be in Dublin by nightfall. He could deliver it to the house in Fingal the next morning. As for the meeting in Dublin, the timing could not have been better. They would both be there anyway.

For here was the reason why his discovery was so clearly a

sign from God: Ireland had been given a Catholic King—and he was arriving in Dublin, on Sunday.

❖

The letter arrived while Donatus Walsh was out. He had gone to Saint Marnock's well. Now, sinking to his knees, he gave thanks for Ireland's deliverance.

Forty years had passed since the terrible coming of Cromwell: forty years, during which the Walsh family had never lost faith, not even in the darkest days. And proof of God's Grace had not been lacking. Yet who could have imagined the wondrous events unfolding now?

❖

Donatus loved this holy place. How often he had come here with his father, Orlando. And it was thanks to his father that he had been able to spend so much of his childhood in Fingal, on this estate he knew and loved so well. His father's watch-words had been simple: keep faith; and hold on. He had never lost faith. For a while, he had been able to hold on.

For after the terrible massacre at Drogheda, however much he had disliked doing it, Orlando had continued to supply Dublin Castle with rent and the Dublin troops with food. Cromwell had smashed his way through Ireland; but he had not remained long, and left his commanders to mop up. Despite the ruthless efficiency of their military operations, it had still taken them another couple of years before every corner of Ireland was completely subdued. During that time, when cash and food were scarce, the authorities had little reason to trouble themselves with the Walshes. But it could not last forever.

Donatus had been nearly twelve when his father had returned from Dublin one day, looking grim, and announced: "They mean to transplant us."

"What do you mean—transplant?" his mother had asked.

"The Catholics. They mean to send all the Catholics to the west—into Connacht. The rest of Ireland is to be given to the Protestants."

Later, Donatus had learned that his father, and thousands like him, had thought for a time that they might be executed. Several hundred executions were carried out, including the killing of numerous priests. Many others fled. But fortunately, the executions had been curtailed. Once the godly men of England had gained their victory, it had soon appeared, it was not the death of the Irish rebels that they sought. It was their land.

Soldiers, adventurers, friends of Cromwell, governments officials, men like Pincher, godly men all—it was land that they had come for, and land they must be given. "It'll take two-thirds of Ireland to satisfy them all," Orlando had remarked. But that didn't worry the English. "The more land we take," they pointed out, "the more Protestant Ireland will be."

The procedure decided upon had been simple. Many of the greatest rebels had fled. Most of them were Catholic, of course; though some, like the great Ormond, had been Royalist Protestants. Their land was taken at once. But after these came the hundreds of lesser men, including many of the Fingal landowners, whose part in the rebellion had been slight. What should be done with them? A handful of gentlemen, including some Catholics who had turned informer or aided the English cause, were left with their land as a reward. But for the rest, a novel solution was found. "If they're Protestant, let's fine them," the government men suggested. "If they're Catholic, kick them out." But rather than completely ruin them, Cromwell's administrators decided that, depending on their degree of guilt, they might be given a half or a third of the value of their estates in the poor land of Connacht, in the west. To leave his land in Fingal, where his family had been for centuries, to go to the wilds of Connacht? It seemed to Orlando to be a monstrous idea. But one of the new men in Dublin

Castle had put it to him very simply. "You have a choice, Master Walsh. You can go to hell, or Connacht."

It had taken some time even so. The scale of the operation was huge, and they couldn't move everyone at once. Continuing his services to Dublin as before, Orlando had managed to remain on his Fingal estate for another year and more.

It was in 1653 that old Doctor Pincher had arrived. There had been an outbreak of plague in the city, and he came with orders that he was to be accommodated on the estate until he wished to return. Donatus had been rather fascinated by the thin, black figure who looked at him so coldly, occupied the best bedroom, and expected to be waited on, hand and foot. His father told him that the scholar preacher was over eighty years old. But the old man's visit had also been educational.

Doctor Pincher had been there ten days when his nephew Captain Budge came to visit. He stayed only one night. Usually, the old man ate alone in his room, but on that occasion they had all supped together, and Donatus had observed the big, flat-faced officer with interest. Captain Budge was an important man, with an estate of his own. For when Brian O'Byrne had wisely fled for his life from Ireland, Rathconan had been given to Budge. So when his father had politely questioned Budge about the coming transplantations, Donatus had listened carefully. Did the policy not seem a little harsh, Orlando had gently enquired.

"No, Sir. Necessity," Budge had answered. "The Irish natives, of course, are averse to all civility. Incapable of self-government. Mere beasts."

Living on the estate in Fingal, Donatus had never heard the Irish described in this manner. The servants, the tenants, and men in the fields, the fishermen by the shore, the oystermen at Malahide, the craftsmen at Swords—the gentle, hospitable Irish folk he had grown up with were not so dissimilar, he had supposed, to country folk in other lands. But Budge had not finished.

"They must be kept down. They killed three hundred thousand innocent Protestants, remember."

"That's quite untrue, you know," Orlando had answered mildly, and he had glanced at Doctor Pincher. But the preacher only put a piece of bread in his mouth and chewed upon it. He still had most of his teeth.

"It is true," Barnaby said. "It was in a book."

"Books can lie," Orlando remarked.

"Papist books can. This was a Protestant book." Barnaby nodded to himself. "And it was the papist gentry who led them into revolt before," he pointed out, "so we'll make sure it never happens again. Every Irish chief, all the priests, every man with knowledge of arms, every Catholic gentleman of repute, they will all be removed, out of this land. Then the Irish dogs will have Protestant masters who will keep them docile. That is the purpose of the transplantation."

"So I must go to Connacht?"

"Most assuredly," said Barnaby.

It was the first time that Donatus had really understood the mind of the English settlers who were now to rule the land.

The following spring, the Walsh family had been transplanted. Taking four carts piled high with their furniture and possessions, their jewelry, and coins of gold and silver sewn into their clothes, Donatus and his parents had set out on the long road westwards. Daniel, though unable to understand why they were leaving, had naturally been with them, too. They were accompanied by only three family retainers; the rest of the servants, the tenants, the cottagers, and labourers had all remained on the estate in Fingal. In this, the Walshes were repeating the pattern found everywhere else. The great mass of the native Irish stayed exactly where they were, to till the land for their new Protestant masters, while their hereditary landlords went to Connacht.

"We are in good company, at least," his father had remarked wryly. By the time they left, so many neighbours and friends had already gone the same way. Some had Irish names:

Conran or Kennedy, Brady or Kelly. But often as not, the transplanted families bore Old English names: Cusack and Cruise, Dillon and Fagan, Barry, Walsh, Plunkett, Fitz this or Fitz that.

Most of the land around Dublin had been taken over by the government directly, to be let out on leases. It did not come as a great surprise to learn, upon their way, that Doctor Pincher had secured a lease on their own estate—at a rent of only half of what Orlando had been forced to pay to stay there himself.

There was only one problem that his father, by holding on to his land as long as he could, had not foreseen.

It had never been clear what size of land grant would be allowed to Orlando Walsh. After numerous enquiries at Dublin Castle, he had realised that even the Dublin men did not know. "It's all being arranged at Athlone," they had told him. "You'll have to wait till you get there." It was not until they had been travelling slowly westwards for five days that they reached Athlone. The court administering the land grants to the transplanted gentry was in a large house in the main street. On arrival, they found an inn; and the next morning Orlando had gone to the land offices, taking Donatus with him. The man in charge, a small, bald-headed fellow with a businesslike air, gazed at Orlando with genuine regret.

"It's a pity you didn't come a few months earlier," he sighed. "Then you might have done better."

"You have instructions concerning me?"

"Not really. We are to find something for everyone, if we can. But it's all at our discretion." He shook his head. "Cromwell, you know, has a general idea of what he wants, and he knows what he hates; but he is not an administrator. He issues instructions; but details . . ." He spread his hands to indicate that there were none. "The transplanting to Connacht has been . . ." Again, he indicated with his hands that the process had been chaotic.

"I'm only here to clean up," he went on. "The men who allocated the land are mostly gone, now. Nothing to keep them. They've made their fortunes, you see." He gave Orlando a meaningful stare. "There's a little place down in Clare," he said. "It's only about thirty acres. Not what you've been used to at all. But you could subsist there I think. It's the best of what's left."

A few inquiries had corroborated the truth of what the fellow had told him. The transplanting had not only been a shambles; it had been a scandal. Men who were supposed to receive nothing, but who came early, with handsome bribes for the officials running the court, had secured large tracts of land. Others, due hundreds of acres, had been lucky to receive fifty. Chaos and official bribery were to be expected when any conqueror reallocated the resources of a country—how could it ever be otherwise? But the transplanting to Connacht had been an unedifying sight.

So had begun the seven long years in County Clare. Their little farmstead had a small dwelling, which Donatus and his father had slowly rebuilt. The land at least had given them subsistence. Their neighbours had been kindly. The Walshes worked hard, and they had survived. But the first two years in the cramped and leaking cottage had been especially hard. They had sent two of their retainers back to Fingal, since they could scarcely keep them and there was nothing for them to do. Though she had tried to put a brave face on it, Mary Walsh had been depressed. But the person who had suffered most had been poor Daniel. If his understanding was limited, he had seemed to sense the unhappiness of Mary more strongly than the others. He clung to her, almost fretfully sometimes; and this too was hard for her to bear. After a year, he had grown sick, and died. Orlando had warned Donatus, long before, "The simpletons, you know, seldom live to twenty," and so he knew he must not grieve too much. But a cloud of sadness had hung over the family for many months after they had buried Daniel.

One thing Donatus did count as a blessing however was that, because of this exile, he came to know his father better than he might otherwise have done. He knew the humiliation his father felt at their poor conditions; and he admired the fact that he never showed it. Together they worked their little piece of land—kept pigs, a few cows, grew cereal crops. And Orlando also took his education upon himself—as a result of which, by the time he was twenty, Donatus already knew most of what the University of Salamanca had to offer, together with a general knowledge of Irish legal practice. Perhaps, by keeping constant company with an older man, he acquired an outlook somewhat middle-aged for a boy of his years. But this was hardly a time for the enjoyment of childhood things; and it gave him great joy to know that he stood, in all things, side by side with his father.

Every year, they had made a pilgrimage to Fingal. As transplanted men, it was illegal for them to travel; but they went discreetly, and they were never caught. Those were times of reunions. The tenants on the estate would welcome them and hide them in their cottages. One of them would even give Orlando part of the rent. "I tell that old devil Pincher that I can't afford to pay him the full amount. Damned Protestant. He doesn't know one way or the other," he would say with glee. Their cousin Doyle would also come out from Dublin to meet them. Before leaving, Orlando had left a hundred pounds in his safekeeping; fortunately, he seldom had to draw down much of this. And Doyle would give them the latest news from Dublin. Often this concerned the latest goings-on amongst the Dublin churches.

If there was one aspect of Cromwell's rule that afforded the Catholics—and the Old English Protestants like Doyle—some light relief in the darkness, it was his ordering of the churches. Of course, papist priests were to be killed; the high Anglican church of King Charles, with its bishops and ceremonies, was firmly abolished. But beyond this, like most army men, Cromwell believed that the congregations should be free to choose their own, godly preachers. The results, even in Christ Church itself, had sometimes been startling. Baptists, Quakers, sectarians of various kinds, and above all, Independents, each with his own, particular vision, had all appeared in Dublin.. Some of their services were sombre; others ranted; a few had even induced hysteria. Doyle, with his cynical mind, would take a quiet pleasure in attending these services and reporting their excesses to Orlando. "You see, my dear son," he would remark to Donatus, "how right our priests are when they tell us: the trouble with these Protestants is that they are completely confused."

It was their third return to Fingal when they'd learned that old Doctor Pincher had died. His nephew Captain Budge had taken over the lease. But the circumstances of his death had been somewhat remarkable. It was their tenant, when he gave them their rent, who told them. "Just before the end, he was delirious. Screaming he was—about a man attacking him with a sword. And when they came to dress his body, what did they find but a scar? Right the way across his back, from his shoulders down to his ribs. So there must have been some reason for his words. Then in comes Captain Budge, and they tell him about it. And he looks thoughtful for a while. Then: 'It was in the rebellion of '41,' he says. 'It was the Catholics that attacked my dear uncle. He was lucky not to be martyred.' Do you suppose it was true?"

"I never heard it before," said Orlando.

Before Donatus and his father left Fingal, their routine was always the same. Together they would go to the holy well at Portmarnock to pray together there. "I do it," Orlando used to remind him, "just as my father did before me." And while they were there, he would also say: "I am sorry, Donatus, that you should see your father brought so low. But we must never lose faith. It was God's Grace that, after so many years waiting, gave you to us. And in time, after we are tested, He will restore us again, as He sees fit."

And so, in the end, it had come to pass. God had restored them.

Their deliverance had come from England. For while Cromwell had been successful in crushing Ireland under colonial rule, England itself had been another matter. For all his military might, Cromwell had never been able to find a satisfactory government to replace the monarchy he had destroyed. Rule by Parliament, a Protectorate in which he was king himself in all but name, military rule by generals— all had been tried, none had worked. And when, after a decade, the exhausted tyrant had died, his son hadn't even wanted to fill his shoes. In 1660, the English Parliament and the late king's son had come to an understanding. King Charles II was restored to the English throne—on certain conditions.

One of these was that the Protestant settlers in Ireland should keep their land. But there had been some minor exceptions. And when Ormond had been returned to Ireland as the new king's Lord Lieutenant, he had graciously remembered the unlucky Walsh family. His word had been enough to assure the royal officials that Orlando had committed no crime; and somewhat grudgingly, Barnaby Budge had been persuaded that he should give up his uncle's lease. Unlike many of their friends, the Walshes had returned to Fingal. It was proof, indeed, of God's Grace towards them.

By God's continuing Grace, he had lived here ever since. He had seen both his parents live to old age. He had known the joy of having a family of his own, and recently married both his daughters to good men. Five years ago, his wife had died, and he had supposed that this part of his life was over. But rather to his surprise, he had found happiness again. Even more wonderful, this last December, his new wife had given him his first son. In a mood of great celebration, they had named the baby Fortunatus.

And now, in a series of events that could never have been foreseen, the continuing faith of the Walshes, and countless families like them, had been granted a new hope. King Charles II of England, a man who loved building, the sciences, and his many mistresses, had suddenly died four years ago, and been succeeded by his brother James. And James II was a Catholic.

He had arrived in Ireland ten days ago, and was coming to Dublin to hold a Catholic Parliament. The situation was by no means without danger. Nobody knew what was going to happen next. Perhaps the Catholics of Ireland would be tested again. But this much was certain, Donatus would be in Dublin that Sunday to welcome the new king, come what may.

❖

When he got back to the house and found the letter from his cousin Maurice, he read it with curiosity. But also with a smile. Maurice Smith was a good man of business. He had done well enough during his time in France. And when the more easygoing rule of Charles II finally encouraged him to return with his family to Dublin, he had managed, despite being a Catholic, to prosper there. Yet there was something of the romantic in his cousin too. He'd be swept away by sudden enthusiasms.

The purchase of his estate was a case in point. When Brian O'Byrne, along with most of the other Irish gentry, had been forced to flee from Cromwell, and the Rathconan estate had been granted to Barnaby Budge, it had been a sad thing, to be sure. Budge had taken over, and though the people up in the Wicklow Mountains hated him, there wasn't much they could do. Budge had lived in the old fortified house, called himself a gentleman, and obtained other property and leases whenever he could. He'd kept Rathconan through the restoration of Charles II, and lived there until he died a dozen years ago. But when his elder son had come into the place, he'd had trouble. His father and his younger brother Joshua were made of sterner stuff, but Mr. Benjamin Budge was a peaceable fellow, and it wasn't long before he'd been troubled by Tories.

It always amused Donatus that the two political camps in the English Parliament should be known by such curious names. The party that believed Parliament should control the King, and that was generally more Protestant, were known as the Whigs, which was a term of gentle scorn. A member of the

King's party, on the other hand, was known as a Tory—which meant an Irish brigand.

And it was certainly Irish brigands—local men, mostly, who loved the freedom of the Wicklow Mountains and hated the Puritan settlers there—who had made the life of poor Mr. Benjamin Budge so miserable. By the latter part of the reign of Charles II, that genial monarch had eased the restrictions, so that a Catholic could once again buy land. So when Maurice Smith had made him a fair offer for the estate, Benjamin Budge had taken the money and been glad to be rid of the place. He resided in Dublin, at present, and seemed to have no desire to purchase another estate.

But why had his cousin Maurice been so anxious to go up into the mountains like that? Donatus had often wondered. He knew that Maurice had always had a liking for Brian O'Byrne, and felt an affinity for his mountain estate. Certainly, since living up there, he'd always claimed to be very happy; and since he was a Catholic, with some vague connections to the place, the local people seemed to have tolerated him well enough. But he'd put all his fortune into Rathconan, and Donatus doubted that he was getting much of a return. It was just like Maurice, after years of saving, to do such a thing.

So as he read the letter his cousin had sent from Rathconan once again, and considered the mysterious excitement of its language, he wondered what new idea Maurice might have got now.

✣

Sunday, March 24. Palm Sunday: festival of the Saviour's entry into Jerusalem. Was the date, also, a sign from God? King James came in through Saint James's Gate, in the west.

Outside the gate was set a stage, upon which played two Irish harpists. A chorus of friars gave joyous song; and a company of townswomen from the markets, all dressed in white, performed a charming dance before him. The mayor and corporation came out, with pipes and drums, and gave him the key of the city before he entered. Then, through the gate he came, with his gentlemen and cavalry, his footmen and fifes, and made his way along streets that, if not strewn with palms, had at least been freshly gravelled. King James II had come into his own again. At the gates of the castle, he wept.

He came modestly. He was not a bad-looking man: his complexion pale and reddish, where his brother's had been swarthy and dark; his face, once proud, now somewhat humbled by exile and disease. He thanked the good people of Dublin as he passed. He came, he seemed to wish to say, with friendship to all the people of his Irish kingdom, and enmity towards none. Yet as Donatus Walsh and Maurice Smith stood side by side and watched him pass, they knew, each of them, that it would not be easy. For the fact remained, the people of England had already kicked him out, and his rival for the kingdom might invade at any time.

.÷.

As far as the Protestant people of England were concerned, they had never expected James to be King. His brother Charles II had always seemed to be in rude good health. There had been suspicions that Charles might be a secret Catholic. But if he was, he had been far too clever to be caught. Instead, he had kept his mistresses, attended the theatre, joked with the ordinary folk at the horse races, and generally applied common sense whenever the religious extremists seemed in danger of getting too excited. But if he tried to encourage his Protestant subjects to be more tolerant towards the Catholics, his task was not made easier when at the end of his reign, his cousin King Louis XIV of France had brutally kicked out the Huguenot Protestants from his kingdom, and forced them to flee—some two hundred thousand of them—to Holland, England, and anywhere else that would take them in. London received tens of thousands. But in doing so, the Londoners remembered the Inquisition, the Irish rebellion, and every other outrage, real or imagined, of Catholic against Protestant. So it was a great shock to all England when, quite suddenly, Charles II had died, and his younger brother, an open Catholic, unexpectedly came to the throne.

They were prepared to tolerate him, however, for a single reason. Catholic he might be, but his heir was his daughter, Mary; and she, thank God, was both a Protestant herself and married to another—Prince William of Orange, the ruler of the Dutch. They might have to put up with James for a while, therefore; but once he was gone they could look forward to William and Mary.

So when James started promoting Catholics to high positions, the English gritted their teeth. When he started placing Catholic officers in the army, they looked on in alarm. And when—despite the fact that he hadn't fathered a child in years, and rumour had it that venereal diseases would prevent him from doing so—the king suddenly had a son by his second, Catholic wife, the English exploded. Was it his? Had the queen even been pregnant? Was it a changeling? Was this another devious Catholic plot to steal the English throne for Rome? The rumours flew. Whatever the truth, the English weren't having it. With scarcely any loss of blood at all, they simply threw him out. William of Orange arrived, to be offered a kingdom. James fled to France.

But Ireland was another story. Both Protestants and Catholics in turn had been alarmed at the events across the water. But King James's favourite, the Catholic Lord Tyrconnell, had done well for his royal master. He'd managed to overawe the Protestants with his troops, but at the same time assured them: "King James means you no harm." The Presbyterians in Ulster were highly suspicious; the walled town of Derry was refusing to submit. But most of the Catholic island hoped that King James would come as a deliverer.

And now, with money and troops supplied by his cousin, King Louis of France, he had arrived to be welcomed by his Irish kingdom.

✛

Once King James had gone into the Castle, Donatus and Maurice had gone to an inn to take some refreshment. Donatus had already gathered all the news.

"He's going to call a Parliament. It will meet here in Dublin early in May. They want the old Catholic gentry as members. Think of that, Maurice—a Catholic Parliament."

"And our religion?"

"He has been cautious, and wise, I think. This last ten days, all the way from Cork to Dublin, he has been meeting the Protestant clergy and assuring them that the Protestants will be free to practice their faith. All Christians are acceptable. That's the word. So long as they are loyal." He smiled. "But Ireland will be Catholic, of course."

Then Maurice told him about the Staff and was gratified that Donatus entirely agreed with him about the importance of his discovery.

"The power of such a thing would be great indeed, if we could just put the Staff and the Deposition together. A symbol for Ireland. And if it comes to a fight with King William, to have the true Staff upon the field of battle . . ."

"You will help me then?"

"Most certainly. We must find it."

✛

It was not until early May, just as the Parliament was assembling, that Maurice set out upon his quest. He knew that he might be gone for some time. He left Rathconan in good hands. His son Thomas was not a man of business, but he loved the land and everything on it. Thomas would run the estate very well in his absence.

Donatus Walsh, in the meantime, had been busy. His enquiries in Dublin had yielded nothing. But some careful research had produced the names of numerous families who might have information about the Staff; and it was armed with this considerable list that Maurice went out, like a pilgrim or knight errant from olden times, in quest of his Grail.

He went first to County Meath. That was where, if the reports were true, the Staff had last been seen. For two weeks he went from house to house, wherever there was a Catholic of any consequence or a priest. But though he made the most diligent enquiry, he could discover nothing definite. Several said that the Staff had been shown in a house or chapel. It seemed that it might have been brought there by someone from outside the area. But more than this he could not learn.

From Meath he passed into Kildare. The Deposition, after all, had made mention of Kildare. Again, he conducted his search in the same manner, for another two weeks. But in Kildare, he could find nothing at all.

There remained, however, an obvious possibility. There had been so much movement of people since the Deposition was made. In particular, almost every faithful gentry family had been transplanted into Connacht. From Kildare, therefore, he went westwards, and searched out any old Kildare families who might have been sent there. This was a larger and more difficult task; but he was a man on a mission, and the further he went, the more determined he became not to give up.

It was a distressing experience: to travel from farm to farm, even cottage to cottage, and see the ancient Catholic families reduced to poverty after the Transplanting. Many of them hoped that with the new Catholic Parliament, they might be restored to their former estates. Maurice hoped and prayed that it might be so. But none of them had any knowledge of the Staff. Week after week passed. Only when he had used all the money he had brought with him did he leave off his quest and return to his home, with the promise to himself that he would resume his search again, as soon as he could.

It was on a day early in July that he came over the pass in the Wicklow Mountains and descended towards the old house at Rathconan that he loved so well.

He was somewhat surprised, as he came towards the door, to see that he had a visitor. As a horse was tethered by the doorway, it was clear that the visitor must have arrived only just before him, coming up from the opposite direction. His wife was standing by the new arrival. So was his son, Thomas. They were looking at him strangely. He rode up and dismounted.

The visitor was a tall, dark-haired, handsome man. He had the air of a military captain. He was middle-aged, perhaps a decade younger than himself, but he looked fit and athletic. He gazed at Maurice, then moved towards him.

"So you are Mwirish, the son of Walter Smith?"

"That is so."

"I am Xavier O'Byrne. The son of Brian O'Byrne. I just came up to look at the place," he indicated the house and the land of Rathconan, "now that it's to be returned to me." He smiled. "I was about to ask your family here: where will you be going to live yourself?"

⁘

Maurice was to learn stranger things than that, as he sat at table with O'Byrne that evening. So engrossed had he been in his quest that he had hardly bothered to follow the detailed deliberations of the Dublin Parliament. He had known that land might be restored to those transplanted, but he was not aware of the mechanism by which such a thing might be accomplished. And to tell the truth, he had never thought of the O'Byrnes.

"King James is against the whole business," O'Byrne explained, "because he fears that it will stir up too much trouble, but the Catholic gentlemen in the Parliament are absolutely determined. They want all the lands confiscated and given to Protestants by Cromwell to be returned to their owners. Including those who left the country, if they wish to return. So you see, that includes Rathconan."

"But I am Catholic, and I bought the estate," Maurice pointed out.

"You are one of many. But you bought it from Budge, you see, who should never have had it in the first place." He smiled. "You aren't alone. There are numerous people in your position, and the latest idea is to pay compensation. There are quite a few Protestants who sent aid to King William when he came to England. Their lands will be taken, and you'll be paid out of that."

"But I love Rathconan."

"I'm glad to hear it. But my own family have been here for centuries."

Maurice sighed. He couldn't deny the justice of what O'Byrne said; but he wished it were otherwise.

"Nothing will happen for a long while," O'Byrne assured him. "The Parliament men will go on arguing about it for years, I dare say. And besides, we haven't secured Ireland yet."

When he discussed the military situation, O'Byrne was both interesting and cynical. "I am a soldier of fortune, Mwirish," he declared. "I look upon these things with a cold eye. The Irish troops that Tyrconnell has raised—and he has thousands of them—are poorly armed. Some of them haven't even got pikes. They've no training. Brave as lions, of course: it makes me proud to be Irish. But useless. There are Irish officers like myself, men whose families fled Ireland long ago, and who've come back to see what they can get. We train them as best we can. French troops are coming, too. They'll be tough professional soldiers. But if King Billie comes over, he'll bring an army that's fought in every major campaign in Europe." He sucked on his teeth. "Most of your boys have never seen anything like that."

"Will he come?"

"That's the question." O'Byrne shook his head. "I don't know. So far he doesn't seem to want to. That has to be the hope—that he'll leave King James to keep Ireland. It's a family business: James is his father-in-law, after all; and they were always on friendly terms as long as William and Mary were to inherit England. Perhaps they can come to a new agreement." He paused to reflect. "Mind you, whether the English Parliament could live with a Catholic Ireland on its doorstep I'm not so sure."

"At least we have secured Ireland itself," Maurice said.

"Probably, Mwirish. Probably. Those Protestant boys up in Ulster are still waiting for King Billie. It's a powder keg up there, in my opinion. And you know, we still haven't taken Derry." It was one of the most remarkable features of that summer. The obstinate defenders of Derry had closed their gates and refused to surrender to James's forces. They'd been trapped and blockaded inside their walls since April, but they still hadn't given up. "They must be eating the rats by now," said O'Byrne, with a soldier's admiration. "And even when the place does fall, it's very difficult to subdue people like that."

But the real surprise for Maurice Smith came when they turned to family matters. He had already ascertained that his old friend Brian O'Byrne had passed away—on a campaign, he'd learned, fighting for the King of France. It was only late in the evening, when he remarked sadly that he'd never known what had become of his own father, that O'Byrne said: "After he fought at Rathmines, you mean?"

"Rathmines? My father was never at the Battle of Rathmines."

"Oh, but he was," answered O'Byrne. "My father was with him and he told me the whole business." And he related all that had passed. "He was no soldier, you know," O'Byrne added with a smile. "But he fought like a hero, my father said. He never knew for certain, but my father always wondered if he'd gone up to Drogheda, and perished there."

For some moments Maurice digested this extraordinary piece of news. Then, suddenly overcome with a wave of affection for his vanished father, he felt his eyes fill with tears, and had to look away. "I had no idea he would do such a thing," he said at last.

"He was a true Irishman," O'Byrne said quietly.

Then Maurice told him about the Staff of Saint Patrick.

⁓

For Donatus Walsh, the autumn and winter of 1689 was a trying time. To everyone's astonishment, Derry had not only held out; late in the summer it had been relieved. To the Protestants of Ulster it was an inspiration; to King James, a bitter blow. Despite the fact that he was a Catholic King on a Catholic island, it showed his enemies that he could be beaten.

Not that King William had fared so much better. He sent over his long-time commander General Schomberg. But instead of sweeping down towards Dublin, the old veteran got stuck up near the Ulster border. Many of his men fell sick during the cold and damp of the Irish winter. The months that followed were, for the most part, a grim stalemate.

Grim for the troops, grim for the people. The winter was cold. The Irish, determined to do nothing to support the English across the water, gave orders that all English imports, including the usual coal for heating the houses of Dublin, should be turned back. They needn't have bothered. The English didn't send any. Shortly before Christmas, Donatus tore down two of the hedges on the estate, to provide fuel for his people. At the start of the new year, going into Dublin, he discovered that half the wooden posts and railings in the city had already been taken for firewood.

He saw Maurice Smith several times. His cousin also introduced him to O'Byrne. Nothing was being done about the land settlement for the time being, and it seemed that, whatever the outcome, the two men were quite resolved to remain friends. As for Donatus, he was intrigued to meet the soldier of fortune, and enjoyed the soldier's clever, worldly mind. As for the news that the soldier had brought to Maurice of his vanished father, it seemed to have had a strange effect. The solid, punctilious merchant of whom Donatus had always heard, evidently was a far more romantic soul than anyone had realised. Maurice never said so, but Donatus was sure that his cousin felt a new sense of closeness to the parent he had lost. There was a look of peace and joy in his eye when he spoke of Walter now. And Donatus was glad that Maurice should have found such a wellspring of unexpected emotion in the latter half of his life. If anything, the knowledge that his father had sacrificed himself for the Catholic cause seemed to have made Maurice more determined than ever to pursue his quest for the Staff. He spoke of returning to Connacht again in the spring.

But the military stalemate could not go on forever. By February, the rumour was that William, having given up on General Schomberg, might be coming over himself. In March, a force of several thousand Danish soldiers, hired from the King of Denmark, were landed in Ulster. "The Vikings are being used against us again," the Catholics of Dublin complained. Yet in a way, the forces sent to help them by the King of France were almost as bad. In the first place, they marched into Dublin with every sign of arrogance and contempt for the Dubliners. And they had no sooner arrived than another discovery was made. Several thousand of the mercenaries were Protestants!

Through the month of April, English, Dutch, and German troops were starting to arrive in the north. One of William's naval commanders even made a cheeky raid into Dublin Bay and took away one of James's ships. One way or the other, it seemed to Donatus that matters must come to a head that summer.

Only one piece of cheerful news came during this time. A little before Easter, Donatus learned from his wife that she was pregnant again.

✢

The priest came to his door one day in the middle of May. He was an old man. The cloak he had wrapped around him was spattered with mud and torn in several places; but his blue eyes were keen.

"You were inquiring about the Staff?" In fact, during the winter, Donatus had not been inactive. It had occurred to him to write to the several Irish colleges on the continent, explaining the recently found authentication and asking whether they had any news concerning the Staff. So far, the replies he had received had been courteous and evinced every sign of interest; but sadly there had been no positive news. One never knew, however, what further conversations such an enquiry might provoke in the great Irish Catholic network of the European world. And it seemed that just such a thing had now occurred. "I had a letter," the priest said, "from a dear friend in Douai. So as I was passing through Dublin on my way overseas, I thought to call upon you."

"Have you seen the Staff?" Donatus asked eagerly.

"I haven't. But a certain Father Jerome O'Neill, who died two years ago, told me that he had. Some time ago, he assured me, it was kept where you might expect it to be."

"Expect?"

"In the centre of Saint Patrick's ministry. I think you might expect it to be there."

"The centre of his ministry has always been held to be in the north. At Armagh."

"Quite so. Well, that is where it was."

"This is remarkable."

"I cannot tell you more. I wish I could. But I haven't the least reason to suppose he was mistaken. He was a most precise and scholarly man. It is possible that it has been moved since, of course. But the likelihood would be, I should say, that you might find it there."

Donatus had begged the priest to stay, but he had been anxious to be gone. "I shall take a glass of brandy, if you will be so kind, but then I must return to Dublin. I leave tomorrow."

That very evening, Donatus sent a message to Maurice. They met in Dublin three days later.

✢

It seemed to Donatus that his cousin was a little feverish. He wondered if Maurice was sickening for something. But when he told him the details of what the priest had said, it was all he could do to stop Maurice leaving at once. "I was going to Connacht again very soon," he cried. "But this . . . This . . ."

"The Staff may not be there. And even if it is, you may not find it."

"It's more information than we've ever had before," Maurice pointed out. And this could not be denied.

There was also the problem of geography. Armagh lay in enemy territory. King William's forces were spread all over that part of Ulster now, and there was every sign that they were getting ready for battle. "If you go up there at present, looking for the Staff of Saint Patrick," Donatus warned him, "you are courting great danger."

"Set against that the effect upon our own troops," replied Maurice, "if I could bring the authentic Staff to them, before they go into battle." He nodded with satisfaction. "I shall return to Rathconan to get ready. Then I shall go north." It was quite evident that nothing would stop him.

"At least come by my house then, when you set out," Donatus begged. "It's upon your road. Perhaps I shall come with you, part of the way." This Maurice promised to do.

But in any event, his journey was delayed. Donatus had been right in thinking that his cousin was feverish. A message from Rathconan a few days later informed him that by the time Maurice got back home, his head was throbbing and his wife had to put him to bed. The next day he had a raging pain in his throat; by the sound of his sickness, it might be a week or two before he was ready to travel.

It was in the last week of May that Donatus chanced to

meet Xavier O'Byrne in Dublin. He had gone into the city on some business, and was just walking by the Castle when he saw O'Byrne coming out. As they were both going eastwards, they walked together, and fell into such easy conversation that, passing an inn in Dame Street, they decided to continue their talk in there. As he took a glass of wine, O'Byrne was in a meditative mood. He expected to go north with King James before long. "For I've no doubt," he told Donatus, "that the battle proper will begin within a month." When Donatus told him about Maurice's plan to search for the Staff at Armagh, O'Byrne smiled.

"He is a well-meaning fellow, this cousin of yours," he remarked. "I am sorry at the thought of taking Rathconan from him, you know, even if the place is rightfully mine." Then he grimaced. "Though if King Billie beats James, there won't be any Catholics getting their estates back, we may be sure."

"You think that William will win?" Donatus asked.

"It is hard to say. Last year, we had more men than we could use. Every Catholic gentleman and merchant in Ireland was turning up with recruits, none of them trained. We were turning them away. I dare say we'd take some of them now; for our numbers are down. But the troops that we have are professional. And so are King Billie's." He sighed. "I am a mercenary, Donatus. I have fought for years for the King of France. But I could still end my life fighting for the Holy Roman Emperor or for Spain. I'd have to fight for a Catholic, I think. I'd not fight for a Protestant. But I'm still a mercenary. I've a son nearly grown. He'll probably do the same in his turn. We are mercenaries, and so are many of the professional troops in Ireland now. King Billie has Dutch and English troops, but also his Danes and Germans. We have Irish recruits, of course, but we have Frenchmen, Walloons, and our own Germans, too—who are mostly Protestants, God help us. It's a mercenary's war."

"Maurice sees it as a Catholic crusade. Actually, I thought I did, too," said Donatus.

O'Byrne took another sip of wine, stretched his legs, and gazed towards the window through half-closed eyes.

"For Ireland, it is. I agree. For England, too, you might say. This little war will decide whether Ireland is to be Protestant or Catholic, that is certain. But a crusade?" He paused. "Consider the chief participants, Donatus. King Louis of France seeks to dominate Europe. Against him is ranged a grand alliance of countries: King William with his Protestant English and Dutch; Austria and Spain, both devoutly Catholic; even the Pope, do not forget. The Pope, in this conflict, is not on King James's side at all: he supports Protestant King Billie. This business in Ireland is just a little skirmish in that wider war. There will be *Te Deum*s sung in Catholic churches all over Europe if King Billie wins. I can't call that a crusade. Can you?"

"Well, at least we and King James are fighting for Ireland," Donatus said.

"It would be comforting to think so."

"You will not allow me even that?"

+‡+

"Oh, the Irish are fighting for Ireland." O'Byrne smiled. "The Old English like yourself included, of course. Perhaps I am fighting for Ireland too, Donatus. I think that I am. King James, however, has a different mind. He is Catholic, of course. But why is it that he has been so insistent on granting complete religious freedom to Protestants ever since he came here? He is courting the English. Even as we speak, there's a plan being considered for James to take part of the army to England as soon as King Billie arrives, while Tyrconnell keeps Billie at bay here in Ireland. I know it from Tyrconnell himself. The French think he's mad, and they'll stop it, I'm sure. But King James wants England, not Ireland. He can't wait to be gone."

"So does nobody care about Ireland?"

"Nobody. Neither King Louis, nor King Billie, nor King James." He nodded thoughtfully. "The fate of Ireland will be decided by men not a single one of whom gives a damn about her. That is her tragedy."

Donatus parted from O'Byrne an hour later, on the most friendly terms. But he returned to Fingal with a sense of sadness and misgiving. He hoped that the cynical soldier was wrong.

⁙

Maurice Smith arrived at his door at the end of the first week in June. He was fully recovered from his illness, and eager to go into Ulster. Proudly he showed Donatus the Deposition, which he kept in a special pocket he had made, hidden inside his coat. With his sword at his side, he had an almost martial air. His eyes glowed with enthusiasm and excitement. Donatus tried to persuade him to rest at his house for a day, but he wouldn't hear of it.

"I will ride with you, then," Donatus said. They left early in the afternoon.

How happy Maurice looked as they rode along. His face was radiant with a sense of purpose. He truly believes, Donatus thought to himself, that he will find the Staff. His heart went out to him.

What was he to say? Had he hoped to dissuade Maurice from his quest? Most certainly, it was madness. With the armies gathering now, there wasn't a chance of Maurice getting safely through. He was sure of it. Was there even any point? He thought of his conversation with O'Byrne. Should he share that with Maurice? Would his cousin even pay attention if he did? Probably not.

And what if, by some miracle—and one should never turn one's face away from such a possibility—God should grant that Maurice found the Staff and brought it safely down to the army of King James? Would it make a difference? Yes. Whatever O'Byrne might say, it probably would. The conflict would become a crusade. Who knew what the effect upon Ireland might be? Not only the Staff itself, but the fact of its being brought forth, the fact of the Deposition being found at such a time, would be taken as signs. In his way, Maurice was right. Dreamers and visionaries had won battles before. The chances were slim, the dangers obvious; but he had a feeling that Maurice did not really care about that.

"Your chances are not good, you know," he did bring himself to say. "You are courting great danger."

"No greater than my father faced," Maurice replied, with contentment, "when he fought alongside Brian O'Byrne."

Donatus nodded. He thought he understood. They rode all afternoon together and camped that evening within sight of the Hill of Tara. The night was warm. Early in the morning they continued, until they came in sight of the River Boyne. "I shall leave you now," said Donatus. And he embraced his cousin warmly. He watched, for a short while, as Maurice rode northwards, then he abruptly turned his horse's head and made his way back. He had a strong presentiment that he would not see Maurice again.

⁜

In the second half of June, news came that William had arrived up in Belfast with a large fleet. James and his forces set out for the north at once. A week passed. Soon reports came that they had gone up into Ulster. Then, some time later, that they were being driven back, towards the River Boyne.

Donatus heard no word from Maurice. It was a July evening when the first men came riding past his house, heading south in a hurry.

"King William has broken through. At the Boyne. He's on his way down."

⁜

The letter from O'Byrne did not come until three weeks later. It was affectionate in tone. He was writing to Donatus, he explained, because he felt that he knew him, and he asked Donatus to convey the news, as he saw fit, to Maurice's family.

The Battle of the Boyne had been more like a big skirmish, really. But it had been decisive. King William himself, bravely wearing his star and garter for the enemy to shoot at, had led his own cavalry against the Irish troops. They had broken through. James, having done nothing, had fled. He had spent one night in Dublin, where he had blamed the Irish for his own failure. Then he had left for the safety of France. The remains of the Irish army who, like him or not, had respected William's courage, and felt nothing but disgust now for James, had regrouped in Limerick. It was from Limerick that O'Byrne wrote. The story he had to tell was quite surprising.

Maurice Smith had gotten to Armagh. How he had managed it, even O'Byrne could not imagine, but so he had. And there, for days, he'd searched for the Staff. "Without success, alas," the soldier wrote. Only when William's army was on the move southwards was he forced to ride south again. "They drove the good man, so to speak, into our arms," wrote O'Byrne, "and the rest, I dare say, will not surprise you."

The soldier had urged Maurice to return home. There was nothing useful, he assured him, that he could do. But Maurice wouldn't hear of it. He had shown the Deposition to numerous people. Even to Tyrconnell, who'd mentioned it to the King. But without the Staff itself, the document could not inspire great interest.

> He felt he had failed, and for that reason, I should guess, was all the more determined to fight. I kept him in my sight, you may be sure, so far as I could. But it was a stray musket ball that carried him off, during the business at the Boyne. He was, I should say, as brave a man as I have ever known; and in his own way, I believe, he died as he would have wished.

It was not until the end of the following year that Donatus heard from O'Byrne again. Without the presence of King James, the remaining Irish forces had acquitted themselves well, maintaining a resistance in the west. King William had gone about his other business, but sent a good Dutch general, Ginkel, to complete the pacification of the island. The Catholic forces were led by Sarsfield. Donatus knew him slightly. On the mother's side, Sarsfield was the descendant of Irish chieftains; on his father's, an Old English gentleman like Donatus himself. Conducting his campaign with considerable daring, he had kept the Dutch general busy for another year. Finally, in the autumn of 1691, he had held out in Limerick for months until he could conclude the best and most honourable terms.

Amongst these was the promise that the Catholics of Ireland might continue to practise their religion without persecution.

After this, Sarsfield and some twelve thousand men were permitted to march out of Limerick and take ship for France. Donatus had heard that O'Byrne had stayed to the end, largely, he suspected, from feelings of loyalty to Ireland. He was touched, nonetheless, that the soldier of fortune should have taken the trouble to send him a final word of parting.

> It is over, Donatus, and I am departing. There is nothing more for me here. I shall roam the world, as I have done before for so long, and as my son, I dare say, will do after me.
>
> But I am glad to have come home to Ireland, and to have seen Rathconan, and to have made the kind friends that I have.
>
> And now we who leave Limerick—Irishmen, soldiers, Catholics that we are—will fly away on the wind, like the wild geese, and I do not believe that we shall ever return.
>
> I am sorry that Maurice never found the Staff.

Yet if, in the years that followed, Donatus often turned to that letter, it was with increasing sadness. Within a year the Protestant Parliament had overturned the terms of the Limerick agreement—though King William was quite happy to leave the Catholics in peace. Those who had fought in the Battle of the Boyne—and alas, the name of Maurice Smith had been found—were to lose their land. The Flight of the Wild Geese, as the departure from Limerick came to be called, assumed the character of a recessional: the last, echoing cry of a noble, Catholic leadership, lost to the island forever. Of the Staff of Saint Patrick, he never heard another word.

It was when his son Fortunatus was a boy of seven that one day, after going to the well at Portmarnock and remaining there longer than usual, Donatus returned and made an unexpected announcement to his wife. Their second child had been a boy also, whom they had named Terence; but there had been no more children after that. Looking at the two boys now, he quietly announced: "I have promised the saint—and my dear father also—that Terence shall always be brought up a good Catholic."

"I should hope so," his wife replied.

"There is something more, however, which may at first be harder to bear, yet which I believe, for the preservation of the family, and of the faith itself, may be necessary."

"And what is that?"

"Fortunatus shall be brought up a Protestant."

Ascendancy

"You're very good to offer," Terence Walsh said to his brother Fortunatus. "But I should warn you that he may cause trouble."

The sun was dipping over St. Stephen's Green. There was a soft glow in the air.

"I'm sure," Fortunatus replied with a smile, "that young Smith can't be so very bad."

You've no idea how bad he can be, Terence thought, but he didn't say so.

"If only I weren't going away." Terence had been promising himself this little retreat to the monastery in France for a long time now, and they both knew it. "You're so good-natured that it's almost a fault," he continued. "I really shouldn't be asking you."

"Nonsense."

How delightful the evening was, thought Fortunatus. Dublin was certainly a pleasant city—so long, of course, as you were a member of Ireland's ruling elite. And even if my dear brother is not, Fortunatus reflected, that is what I am. A handsome city, too. For in Dublin, at least, the Protestant Ascendancy over Ireland was expressed in bricks and mortar.

It was astonishing how the place had changed in his own lifetime. Inside the walls of the old medieval city, the narrow streets and alleys, and the landmarks like Christ Church and the old Tholsell town hall, were not much changed, except for a few repairs. But as soon as you looked beyond the walls, the change was striking.

For a start, the River Liffey was not only crossed by several stone bridges, but it was noticeably narrower. The marshes that had started just downstream from the Castle, and skirted the ancient Viking site of Hoggen Green where the precincts of Trinity College now lay, had been reclaimed and the riverflood contained within walls. Upriver on the northern bank, the Duke of Ormond had encroached on the water further when he laid out the Ormond and Arran quays, with lines of warehouses and buildings that would have graced any city in Europe. Outside the city's eastern wall, the former grassy common of St. Stephen's Green was now surrounded with fine new houses, with subsidiary streets leading down to Trinity College. The curving line of the little stream that had run from the common down to Hoggen Green and the Viking long stone, had disappeared under the roadway of one of these, a pleasant crescent called Grafton Street. On the western side of the city, not a mile from Christ Church, the huge Royal Hospital at Kilmainham had been modelled on the stately, classical Invalides of Paris; and on the northern riverbank, opposite, stood the gates to the Phoenix Park—the enormous tract that Ormond had landscaped and stocked with deer. The Phoenix Park was bigger and grander than anything London had to offer.

But what was truly striking was the appearance of the new houses.

The British might not be original in the arts, but in their adaptation of the ideas of others, they would often show genius. And during the last decades, in London, Edinburgh, and now Dublin, they had perfected a fresh method of urban construction. Taking simplified classical elements, the builders had discovered that they could endlessly repeat the same brick house, in terraces and squares, in a way that was both economic and pleasing to the eye. Elegant steps led up to handsome doors with fanlights above; outside shutters were not needed in the colder northern climes, so nothing broke the stern brick surface of the outer wall; severe, rectangular sash windows stared blankly out at the northern skies, like the shades of Roman senators. Over the doorway, like as not, there might be a modest classical pediment, for decency's sake—to omit that might have seemed like a gentleman emerging without a hat—but all other external ornament was avoided. Austere and aristocratic in style, yet domestic in scale, it satisfied lord and tradesman alike. It was, without doubt, the most successful style of terracing ever invented and would make its way across the Atlantic to cities like Boston, Philadelphia, and New York. In time, it would come to be known as Georgian.

All around St. Stephen's Green, Trinity College, and behind the quays north of the Liffey as well, these classical brick terraces and squares were spreading. As the city's wealth and population continued to grow, it seemed to Walsh that a new street sprang up every year. Dublin, after London, would soon be the most gracious European capital in the north.

"What's wrong with him, anyway?" asked Fortunatus, as they reached the corner of the green.

"He is Catholic."

"So are you."

"He carries a deep resentment."

"Ah." Fortunatus sighed. "He has not been as lucky as we."

Looking back now, he could only be amazed at the foresight of their father. Dutch King William might have promised tolerance to the Irish Catholics, but his parliaments, especially the Irish Parliament, had other ideas entirely. The English Parliament, after all, had gone to all the trouble of throwing out King James just to keep England free of Catholicism. But James was still at large with his young son, supported by his bellicose Catholic cousin, King Louis XIV of France, and Ireland, as always, looked like a perfect base from which to harass England. The western island was to be kept garrisoned, therefore, and under the iron control of English administrators and the established Protestant Church.

As for the new, Cromwellian settlers like Barnaby Budge, hadn't God sent them to Ireland to humble the papists and ensure the triumph of His Protestant faith? And weren't they, besides, occupying the land that the papists would still like to claim back now? Not only their consciences, but their very survival, depended on keeping the Catholics down.

So they had started to pass laws for the purpose. Through the reigns of William and Mary, then of her sister Anne, and now of their German cousin, George of Hanover, the list of anti-Catholic laws had grown longer.

A Catholic could not hold public office or sit in the Dublin Parliament. He could not become a full member of a city guild. Most of the professions were closed to him. He could not attend university himself, or—at least legally—send his children abroad for their education, either. He could not buy land, or even hold it on more than a thirty-four-year lease. Any land he already owned at his death would be divided up equally amongst his sons, unless the eldest converted to the Protestant faith, in which case the Protestant son was to inherit all and his brothers get nothing. And so the list went on.

It was an iniquity; it was an insult; above all, it was calculated to destroy Catholicism in Ireland.

Donatus had died late in the reign of Queen Anne, but he had seen enough to see the wisdom of his decision that Protestant Fortunatus should protect his Catholic brother. Other families since had made similar arrangements, but the early conversion of Fortunatus Walsh had stood him in good stead. He'd married well. Friends in high places, pleased with his loyalty, had several times given him those genial government posts—inspector of this, collector of that, or some other position in the sought-after Revenue—with which, for very little work, a gentleman could handsomely increase his income. Thanks to all this, Fortunatus had been able to add several hundred acres to the family's holdings. Why, when a member of the Dublin Parliament had died recently, he had even gotten a seat in the Irish House of Commons. He had been in a good position to help his brother Terence, therefore.

And Terence had needed it.

"I'd have liked to be a lawyer," Terence had always said. But although, as a Catholic, he might have been a lowly attorney, the profession of barrister—the gentleman lawyers who argued the cases in court and made all the money—was for Protestants only. For a time, he had tried to be a merchant in the city and had joined the Merchants Guild. As a Catholic he had to pay fees every quarter, higher than those a Protestant paid, and was denied any voting rights in the guild elections; he was also unable to become a freeman of the city. But he could trade.

"Swallow your pride and make money," Fortunatus had advised him. "Even a Catholic may get rich." And he had gladly staked Terence with some capital so that he could trade. But after five years, though he had made a living, Terence returned the money and told him: "I'm not cut out for this."

"What will you do, then?"

"I've been thinking," Terence had replied, "that I might practise medicine."

Fortunatus had not been pleased. The practice of medicine was not, in his judgement, a very respectable business. True, anatomy and medicine were studied at the great universities. But the surgeons who pulled your teeth or amputated your leg shared a guild with the barbers—indeed, the surgeon might be the same man who cut your hair. And there was nothing to stop anyone in Dublin setting up as a medical man, whose methods were mostly confined to cupping and bleeding you, or applying herbal remedies of their own invention. Most of these physicians, in his private estimation, were quacks.

But a Catholic could be a physician. There were no restrictions at all.

So after a period of intense study with one of the better medical men, Terence had set himself up near Trinity College, and Fortunatus had recommended him to everyone he knew, with the cheerful injunction to his brother: "Try not to kill all my friends."

And Terence had done uncommonly well. He had a pleasant manner; the fact that he had gone prematurely grey, and wore a little pointed beard, gave him a look of kindly authority that his patients found reassuring. "It is even possible," his brother allowed, "that you may do your patients some good." But above all, Doctor Terence Walsh was a gentleman. The whole of fashionable Dublin agreed. The fact that he was Catholic and that most of his patients were Protestant was not an issue. Old ladies asking him to come to their bedside, aristocrats who might need to confide some medical embarrassment over a glass of claret, could feel that he was a discreet and trusted member of the family. Within three years, he had all the patients he could handle. And being an honourable man, he also set aside time for the poor folk living near him, whom he treated without charge.

The family had been able to help him in other ways. His father might not be allowed to leave him anything directly, but by making use of family trusts, it had been easy enough to give him the use and the income of a small estate out in Kildare. Other families they knew had done the same. If the authorities in Dublin Castle were aware that the law was being quietly flouted, they never said anything. And last year, Fortunatus had seen another way to help his brother.

"Terence," he announced, "you're going to become a Freemason."

There had been craft guilds of stonemasons since the Middle Ages. It was not until sometime after 1600, and for reasons unknown, that some gentlemen in Scotland had decided to form what they called a Freemasons' lodge, which used the ceremonies and "mysteries" of the medieval guild but was dedicated not to the building trade, but to general good works. Only gradually did this new Freemasonry, which was run as a friendly secret society, spread to England and Ireland. But in the last two decades it had suddenly become fashionable, and Fortunatus had joined the most aristocratic of the new Dublin lodges.

"We must get you in, too, Terence," he had explained. "The Masons make no religious distinctions. Your being a Catholic is not a barrier. And it will be good for your career." Indeed, they were on their way to a meeting of the brethren that very evening.

Having enjoyed so much support from his own loving family, it was natural as well as commendable that Terence, in turn, should have wanted to help a kinsman himself.

Like young Garret Smith.

If old Maurice Smith hadn't been killed at the Battle of the Boyne, his descendants might not have fared so badly. For King William's Treaty of Limerick was generous to those of King James's army who had surrendered. But for those who had been killed back at the Boyne, there was no such provision. They were judged to be rebels and their estates were confiscated. By the time it was all over, the Smiths were ruined.

Fortunatus remembered the family at that time very well. Maurice's son Thomas had been philosophical, but his grandson Michael—a boy a few years younger than himself—had not taken it well, becoming bitter and withdrawn. The Walshes had done all they could to help. After all, Fortunatus remembered, old Maurice was actually my father's first cousin. But Thomas had died, Michael had been resentful, and the two families had drifted apart. Michael had clung to a heroic picture of his family's role and of the character of King James, and always swore that the Stuart king, or his son, would return and restore the Catholic faith to Ireland.

The Jacobite cause, as this longing for the Stuarts was called, might not have been entirely hopeless. When the unpopular German, George of Hanover, had come to the English throne, there were many who wanted to have the son of King James back instead. There were even scattered risings. But they soon fizzled out, and nobody rose for the Stuart Pretender in Ireland. Soon after that, Michael Smith had lapsed into disappointment and drink. Two years later, he was penniless and dead.

But he had left a little son. And it was young Garret Smith that Terence had determined to help. He had found lodgings for the boy and his mother—modest certainly, but cleaner than the ones they'd had before—in Saint Michan's parish on the north side of the Liffey. At his special request, the priest there had ensured that the boy received some education. Then, a few years ago, he had made the necessary payments for the boy to be apprenticed to a respectable grocer in the parish. And once a month, without fail, he would bring the young man to dine with his wife and children in the friendly comfort of their family home in the hope that, in due course, when he had set himself up in business and found a sensible wife, young Smith might follow a similar, if more modest, path himself. In short, he had done everything that a kindly member of the Walsh family might be expected to do.

It was hard to say exactly when the trouble had begun. He had not taken the boy's scrapes or his brushes with authority too seriously. "It's just a young man's devilment," he would say genially. More problematic had been the day when his wife had found Garret teaching their children to be Jacobites.

"I'll not have him bringing trouble of that kind into this house," she had protested to her husband. And it was only after much pleading, and the promise that young Garret should never be left alone with their children, that Terence had been able to bring him to the house again. "He shall not come here while you are away in France," she had declared.

During the last year, there had been some complaints from his master the grocer, as well. Terence had encouraged the good grocer to take a firm hand.

"I must confess that I'm concerned," he told Fortunatus. "I shall be away a month, and there's really no one to keep an eye on him, or take charge if there should be any trouble. But I feel that I'm taking advantage of your good nature in turning to you."

"The young man is just as much my kinsman as yours," his brother pointed out. "I'm probably at fault for having done nothing for him before." He smiled. "I'm sure I can handle him." Fortunatus prided himself on his ability to manage people.

"I may tell his master, and the priest, that you will act for me in my absence, then?" Terence said with great relief.

"I shall go to see both those gentlemen myself. Set your mind at rest." Fortunatus put his hand on his brother's shoulder. "And now," he continued cheerfully, "we are about to enjoy a dinner with our brother Masons at that excellent tavern in Bride Street. And since I intend to consume at least three bottles of claret, I shall expect you to carry me home."

⁜

The sun was already high the next morning when the servant girl drew back the long curtains. Fortunatus blinked, and wished that he had not. The sunlight hurt his eyes.

"Will you close them again, for the love of God?" he groaned hoarsely. His throat was a desert, his head a cavern of pain. "Too much claret," he said shakily to the girl.

"We heard Your Honour singing when your brother brought you home last night," she answered amiably. "You have visitors, Sir," she continued, "waiting below."

"I have? Send them away."

"We can't, Sir. It's Mrs. Doyle."

⁜

She was waiting for him in the front parlour. Like all the houses on St. Stephen's Green, the main rooms were very tall, and like most Irish houses, sparsely furnished. The hanging on one wall, and the dark and clumsy little portrait of his father on another, did little to add cosiness to what might otherwise have been mistaken for the stately anteroom or a public Roman mausoleum.

She made no comment upon his haggard appearance as he gazed at her with hollowed eyes and wondered why it was, even on the best of days, that his cousin Barbara made him nervous.

It was getting on for two centuries since his ancestor Richard had married the Doyle heiress. How many generations had passed since then? Six or seven, he supposed. But the families had always kept on close terms. "Our Doyle cousins were uncommonly good to me and to your grandfather," Donatus had always told him. If the Walshes were generous to relations less well-placed than themselves, they prided themselves on remembering favours received as well. And Barbara Doyle was not only the widow of one of these kinsmen, but she had been born a Doyle herself; so she was a kinswoman on two counts. "Cousin Barbara," the whole family called her. When her husband had suddenly died, leaving her with a young family, they had been there at once to support her, and she recognized the fact. Anyone less in need of support, Fortunatus considered, it would be hard to imagine.

God knows what she was worth. She'd been left a rich woman, and she'd made herself richer. Every year, as a new terrace of houses would spring up in Dublin somewhere, you could be sure that Barbara Doyle owned one of them. Indeed, she owned the very house they were in now, since Fortunatus rented it from her. He wondered nervously why she had come.

Hastily, he urged her to his best armchair—for her comfort, no doubt, but chiefly because she wasn't quite so infernal sitting down as standing up. Even her little son John, whom she had brought with her for some reason, was quickly offered a silk-covered stool.

Yet even if she was richer than he was, she was still only the widow of a merchant, whereas the Walshes, since time out of mind, belonged to the landed gentry. So why was he afraid of her?

Perhaps it was her physical presence. She was large, stout in leg and body, and undoubtedly weighed more than he did. In the enduring fashion of the Restoration, she wore a low-busted dress, from which her breasts swelled out mightily. Her hair was thick and black, her face was round, her cheeks a blotchy red. But it was her basilisk-brown, cold-staring eyes that always disconcerted him. Sometimes, under their bellicose glare, he would even find himself stuttering.

"Well, Cousin Barbara," he said with a forced smile, "what can I do for you?"

"Now that you're in Parliament," she answered firmly, "a good deal."

And his heart sank.

If it hadn't been for the seat in Parliament, he probably wouldn't have rented the house. Usually, a country gentleman would rent a Dublin house for the social winter season if he had a son or daughter to marry off—and Walsh had no children of that age at present—or if he had parliamentary business to attend to. Having got his seat, Fortunatus, who was usually careful with his money, had decided that if he was going to do the thing, he'd do it in style. So he had taken a big house on fashionable St. Stephen's Green. But it had cost him dear, for rents in the best parts of Dublin were scarcely less than those in London, and he was paying Mrs. Doyle the princely sum of a hundred pounds a year—which was almost more than he could really afford.

Barbara Doyle fixed Fortunatus with a baleful gaze. Then she made her announcement.

"It's time," she said, "that Ireland stood up to the English."

There was hardly a person in Dublin who would have disagreed.

For if the English Parliament wanted the Irish kept safely under Protestant rule, that did not mean that they were interested in the welfare of the rulers. They weren't.

After all, Ireland was a place apart. True, many of Cromwell's English followers had obtained Irish land. But often they had sold it, taken their profits, and returned to England. Some of the largest English landowners held huge tracts there now, but engaged middlemen to extort the highest rents they could and remit the money to England, where these great men preferred to live as absentees. As for the Protestants who actually lived in Ireland—and their number was large—even the new arrivals had mostly been there a couple of generations now, and time and distance had bred forgetfulness. The English wished them well, of course, so long as they weren't a nuisance.

"But these Irish colonists need to be kept in their place," the English judged. Even back in the days of Charles II, the English Parliament had found it needful to restrict Ireland's time-honoured exports of beef, for an obvious cause: "Their beef competes with our own." During the reign of King William, it had also been necessary to embargo the Irish wool trade for the same excellent reason. And when Ireland's almost entirely Protestant gentry and merchant class had protested, the Parliament men in England knew what to think: "There's something about that damned island that makes people disloyal."

Indeed, a few years later, the English Parliament had been obliged to remind the Protestant Irish Parliament somewhat firmly, "The troops you have raised and paid for are by no means to be considered under your control." And just a couple of years ago, King George had even had to promulgate a Declaratory Act to remind them, once and for all, that London could and probably would override any decision or legal judgement they made.

"We are loyal to the king and his established Church," the Irish Parliament concluded, "yet we are regarded as inferior subjects." They were exactly right.

The Catholics, though affected by anything that damaged the island's trade, were not really part of the quarrel. They had their own problems to worry about. It was the Protestant ruling class, the Ascendancy—the Anglo-Irish as they were starting to be called—who felt so badly used by London. Why, even the best-paid government jobs, the sinecures, the best-endowed

livings for the clergy—the expected perquisites of government
in that genial age—were being given to men sent over from
England. "Why should it be only the second-rate jobs that are
left for our own boys?" the Irish gentry wanted to know. And
if the oppressed Catholic peasants hated the absentee landlords and their grasping middlemen, the Ascendancy often
disliked them almost as much. "This rent money flooding out
of the country to the absentees is stealing away Ireland's
wealth," they complained. The amounts that left were not in
fact large enough to do serious damage, but both Barbara
Doyle and Fortunatus Walsh were convinced they did.

The final insult, however, had just occurred this very year.

"What are you going to do," Mrs. Walsh demanded,
"about those damned copper coins?"

It has always been the prerogative of rulers, in all countries and in all political systems, to look after their mistresses.
King George of England, naturally wishing to do something
for his mistress, the Countess of Kendal, had had the happy
thought of giving her a patent to mint copper halfpence and
farthings for Ireland. The gift of such a license to a charming
royal friend was such a normal thing that nobody had even
thought about it twice. She in turn, not being in that business, had very sensibly sold the patent to a reputable iron-
master named Wood. And now Wood's copper change had
arrived in Ireland.

"Why should we take these cursed, clipped coins in
Dublin?" Barbara Doyle fixed Fortunatus with a bellicose eye.

In fact, when Walsh had inspected some of Wood's coins,
it had seemed to him that their quality was perfectly sound,
but he did not say so now.

"What is so foolish about the business," he remarked with
perfect truth, "is that we're actually short of silver coinage these
days. It's silver we need, not copper." The various outflows of
money to England had produced a shortage of the higher-value
currency on the island recently—which was one of the reasons
why even the English placemen in the Revenue Commission

had warned London that this copper issue was a bad idea. But if he hoped to deflect his cousin's assault by changing the subject, Walsh was out of luck. Barbara Doyle had never been deflected in her life.

"Do you think Ireland should be governed by the favours given to a jezebel?" she threateningly enquired.

That his cousin was actually shocked by the king having a mistress was doubtful; as for royal favours, Ireland had been familiar with those since before Saint Patrick came. "The whole thing was done behind our backs," she cried. "That's what turns my stomach."

And that, thought Fortunatus, was the rub. It was the casual insult implicit in the transaction that had infuriated everyone. Time and again, the English Parliament had refused to let the loyal Irish mint their own coins, since that would have smacked of too much independence; now, without even a word to the Irish Parliament, and against the advice of the authorities in Dublin, this private coinage had been foisted upon them.

"It's shameful," he agreed.

"So what are you and the Parliament going to do about it?"

The Irish Parliament met from the autumn to the following spring, every other year. After a gap of eighteen months, a new session was just about to begin. Fortunatus had no doubt that there would be a big protest about the coins, but whether it would do any good was another matter.

"I shall speak out on the subject, you may be sure," he answered firmly.

"Damn your speech," she answered. "Those coins must be withdrawn. And you and your friends must see to it." She stared at him. Her eyes were not in the least friendly.

"We shall do our best," he said guardedly.

She continued to stare.

"The lease on this house is up for renewal soon," she remarked. "I could get a hundred and twenty for it. More, I dare say."

He gazed back in horror. Was the woman actually trying to bully him into a parliamentary action, which he probably couldn't accomplish anyway, by threatening to raise his rent? Or possibly evict him? The naked brutality of the thing was appalling. And in front of a child!

He looked down to the stool where the little boy sat, and found the child staring at him coldly. His eyes were just like his mother's. Good heavens, he realized, the widow Doyle had deliberately brought the child along to show him how to conduct business. And she's teaching him, he thought with despair, how to bully me.

And then, suddenly, he almost burst out laughing. The dreadful woman was right, of course. The boy had to learn. For wasn't this exactly how all public life was run? Indeed, he didn't suppose that parliamentary politics could be organized in any other way. In England, government ministers and mighty aristocrats with control of patronage commanded small armies of parliamentary men, who did their bidding in return for favours, or the fear of losing them. Even in the Dublin Parliament, powerful men like Speaker Conolly, or the Brodrick family in Cork, controlled large factions with promises and threats. In her crude way, Cousin Barbara was just trying to do the same.

The problem was that he had no idea how the business would go once the Parliament met; to imagine that a new and insignificant Member of Parliament like himself could promise anything was absurd. Yet as he gazed at her, he had no doubt that she would carry out her threat.

"We shall have to see, my dear Barbara," he said carefully. "I shall certainly do my best."

But when she left a few minutes later, he shook his head and wondered—was he about to be evicted from his house?

It was partly to take his mind off this tiresome subject that he decided, that very afternoon, that he'd walk across the Liffey to see about young Smith.

Having crossed the Liffey, he made his way into the parish of Saint Michan's. It was one of the more ancient parishes, lying on the western side of the old Norsemen's district of Oxmantown, and there had been a church there since time out of mind. Making his way through several handsome new terraces, he came to a more modest quarter still occupied by gabled houses which dated from the century before. And entering Cow Lane, he was soon directed to the premises occupied by Mr. Morgan MacGowan, grocer.

He liked what he saw. A yard with stores around it. From an open door in one of these came a faint and pleasant malty smell; inside, he could see smoked hams hanging from hooks, and sacks of spices—cloves, garlic, sage, peppers—on a low wooden shelf that ran along the wall. There seemed to be children everywhere, running barefoot in the yard, buzzing in and out of the house like bees around a hive, peeping from rafters. Ushered inside the house by the tradesman's pleasant wife, he found an old-fashioned parlour with a wooden floor, a scrubbed wooden table, wooden benches and stools, all spotlessly clean. When he explained that he was the brother of Terence Walsh, his welcome turned from politeness to warmth, and the smaller children at once made it clear that they expected to be swung around in the yard. When he mentioned the name of Garret Smith, however, he was informed that the young man was out, and, it seemed to him, a cloud passed over Mrs. MacGowan's face. Soon after this, MacGowan himself arrived.

The tradesman was a small, round, comfortable-looking man. The grocer's trade in Dublin was a pleasant one. Unusually, there was no guild, and therefore no discrimination against Catholics. A Catholic like MacGowan could engage in the grocery business without a sense of inferiority, and could prosper. Grocers were among some of the richest merchants in the city. And though MacGowan was not rich, Walsh had a feeling that he probably had more money than he cared to let you know.

They talked amiably for a few minutes, about Terence, for whom the grocer clearly had a high regard, and his forthcoming journey. Though he had not travelled abroad himself,

MacGowan was clearly well-informed about the trade and ports of France, and Fortunatus liked him.

"So I hear," he said after a little while, "that you have had some trouble with our relation, young Garret Smith."

MacGowan was silent for a moment. He looked at Walsh carefully, as if he were considering something.

Walsh noticed that the grocer had a curious stare. He didn't think he'd ever seen one quite like it. As he cocked his head slightly to one side, his left eye drooped half closed, but his right eye remained fixed upon the person he was speaking to, and opened so wide that it seemed as if it had grown, staring at you with a gaze of such intensity that it was startling.

"He does his work well enough," MacGowan said quietly. "I sent him to Dalkey on an errand this morning, or you'd have seen him here."

"He gives no trouble, then?"

"He has a headstrong spirit, Mr. Walsh, and he thinks highly of his own opinions, as many young people do." He paused. "He's a clever young fellow, Sir, and I think he has a good heart. But he is subject to moods. He can sing you to sleep, or make you laugh till you cry. But then something will make him angry . . ." He paused again. "He's fallen into bad company recently. That's my opinion, Sir."

"What sort of company?'

"You remember the trouble in the Liberties the other week?"

As in other cities, there were sometimes fights between different gangs of apprentices. In the poorer sections of Dublin, especially the old Liberty areas which had been under the feudal rule of the medieval Church, there had been some altercation between the butcher boys and the Protestant Huguenot immigrants from France. Recently, some Huguenot boys had taken a savage beating.

"A bad business," said Walsh.

"It was a terrible thing they did," MacGowan continued. "He's been spending time with the butchers—though I have told him not to keep bad company—and he was there when it was done. I don't say he had a hand in it. Please God he didn't. But he was there. And when I told him he must never go there again, all he said to me was: 'It was only some Protestant Frenchmen that they beat. They deserved no better.' Those were his words." The grocer continued to fix Walsh with his one-eyed gaze.

"That was very wrong of him," Fortunatus agreed. "Though I dare say he only spoke in the heat of the moment."

"Perhaps." MacGowan's gaze travelled slowly round the room until his eye appeared to fix on some distant point outside the window. "He worries me, Sir."

Fortunatus nodded.

"And is there anything else," he gently enquired, that you think I should know?"

MacGowan's eye stared at him once again, then looked down at the floor.

"No." He paused. "But you could ask Doctor Nary, the priest," he suggested quietly. "He might know more than me."

✢

As the house of Doctor Cornelius Nary lay not far away, when Fortunatus left the grocer's, he decided to see if he was at home. Indeed, he was quite glad of the chance to visit him, for the parish priest of Saint Michan's was one of Dublin's more notable figures.

So he was delighted when, arriving at the door of the house, he was greeted by the worthy divine himself.

"I am Fortunatus Walsh, the brother of Terence Walsh," he began politely, and got no further. For the priest beamed.

"I know who you are," he cried. "I know your brother well, and I know all about you. Come in, Fortunatus, and welcome."

Like other priests of that time, you would not necessarily have known that Doctor Nary—it was an odd spelling of the usual Neary, which the doctor pronounced "Nairy"—was a priest at all. Sometimes, to be sure, he wore the flowing gown and tabs of an academic and divine, but today he was simply dressed in the long buttoned tunic, cravat, breeches, and stockings of an ordinary gentleman, and his wig was off. Fortunatus was especially struck, however, by the priest's noble features. His face was a perfect oval, with fine, almond-shaped eyes and only a slight loosening of the flesh under the chin. As a youth, thought Walsh, he must have looked like a renaissance Madonna. When he smiled, the eyes creased with humour in a pleasant way. Though now in his sixties, the priest looked fit and energetic. He led Fortunatus inside to a modest study, neatly crammed with books, offered him a chair, and, sitting down at his table, enquired, with a mischievous twinkle in his eye:

"So what may a Catholic priest do for a good Church of Ireland Protestant like yourself?"

If the English did not like Catholicism and did all they could to discourage it, the native Irish had ignored the Penal Laws and kept steadfastly to their faith. So the government had been forced to compromise. The religious orders—the Franciscans, the Dominicans, the Jesuits especially—were all strictly outlawed. Bishops were also forbidden. But ordinary parish priests were tolerated, as long as they had registered with the authorities and taken an oath of loyalty to the crown.

Cornelius Nary had been at Saint Michan's for a quarter of a century. He ran a busy parish with the help of several junior priests. Having studied theology in Paris, he was a noted scholar; he had written a thousand-page history of the world, and even translated the New Testament into everyday English. He was widely liked by the Protestant clergy. Fortunatus knew that the vicar of his own Church of Ireland parish held Nary in high esteem. "What I find admirable," he told Walsh, "is that he stands up for his faith in a manly way: he writes pamphlets against us Protestants—and you have to admire his courage— but he's always reasonable, never discourteous." It might be that the Catholic priest was merely diplomatic, but he was careful always to present these religious disputes as an honest disagreement between well-meaning parties. "If matters between Protestants and Catholics could always be conducted in such a manner," the vicar had confessed, "I personally would see no need for the Penal Laws at all."

Fortunatus told the priest that he had come from Morgan MacGowan and explained his mission at once.

"You'll be aware that Terence has taken an interest in our relation, Garret Smith."

"It does your brother credit. I placed the boy with an excellent little school in this parish, you know." Under the Penal Laws, Catholic schools were not supposed to exist. But the English administrators had long since discovered that, instead of being the barbarian beasts that they had supposed, many of the native Irish regarded education as a birthright, and it had been quite impossible to keep them from it. Officially, therefore, they did not exist; but behind closed doors, Dublin was full of them. "He proved to be very intelligent," the scholarly priest continued. "I gave him instruction myself."

"He is a fortunate young man, then," said Fortunatus politely.

Nary gave him a wry look.

"Oh, he doesn't think so, I assure you. He has the greatest contempt for me. He told me so himself." Observing Walsh's astonishment, Nary laughed. "I'm not nearly good enough for him, you know."

"How can he possibly . . . ?"

"Oh, he's a most furious young Jacobite, you know. He despises me because I am registered and do not flout the law—much as I dislike it—and because some of the Church of Ireland clergy are my friends." Nary shrugged. "I like to think he does me an injustice."

In fact, as Walsh knew very well, the priest had done more than write some fearless pamphlets. Ten years ago, he had been forced into hiding and then arrested after illegally helping some poor nuns who'd been dispossessed. Only two years ago, when a Catholic in Cork had been unfairly condemned to death, Nary had openly rebuked the authorities by draping his entire chapel in black mourning cloth. There was no question about the man's courage. He had simply calculated that he could achieve more for the faith by making friends than by making enemies.

"I had been intending," said Fortunatus a little doubtfully, "to keep an eye on him while Terence was away."

"You were?" Nary clearly found this quite amusing. "And you a Protestant. Brave man."

"He sounds a monster," Walsh ventured, "and yet it seems to me that you like him."

The priest nodded.

"You are right. I even discussed him with the bishop." Catholic bishops might not be allowed in Ireland officially, but of course they were often there, and the authorities usually ignored them. "Yet neither of us was certain how to help him. The bishop wondered if he would make a priest. He has the brain, but no vocation." Nary gazed thoughtfully at Fortunatus. "You might say that he is both the best of young men," he continued, "and the worst. His mind is very keen. Give him a subject to master, and he will swoop down upon it like a falcon. He will master it with an intensity at which I marvel. I lend him books. He has read prodigiously. But he lacks a centre. I'm not even sure of his convictions. Just when you suppose you have engaged his attention, he'll turn from you—it's as if he's been swept up by a whirlwind into the sky. And suddenly you've lost him." He paused. "He has a terrible, dark passion," he added regretfully.

"I asked Morgan MacGowan if there was anything in particular I should know," Fortunatus remarked. "He said I should ask you. I'm wondering what it might have been."

"Ah." The priest sighed. "That would be the girl."

"He mentioned no girl."

"How like him. He wouldn't because, in his eyes, she belongs to me." Doctor Nary stared up at the bookcase where three unsold copies of his translation of the New Testament kept each other company. "Kitty Brennan. A servant girl in this house. Her family live down in Wicklow. Poor farmers. I feel responsible for her. So I take it unkindly that young Smith has made the girl his sweetheart."

"He has seduced her?"

"I don't say that. For all I know, it was the other way round. But I have asked him to promise not to see her anymore."

"Has he done so?"

"No. And I shall have to send her back to her family. We can only hope there have been no unfortunate consequences."

"Terence said nothing of this."

"He doesn't know. It has all come about this last week or so."

"Surely the girl should go at once, then, for everyone's sake."

"I fear so. She's not a bad little soul, and I'm sorry to send her back to her wretched home. But . . ." The priest shook his head, then suddenly burst out: "The young fool. He could go far. As far, at least, as a poor Catholic boy can go in Dublin nowadays."

Fortunatus watched him thoughtfully. It was clear that Nary was frustrated with his difficult protégé.

"You say he has read a great deal."

"He's been through half my library."

"He comes to dine with Terence and his family every month, as you probably know. I suppose I could do the same. But I have to go up into County Cavan for a few days shortly. I wonder if I should take him with me. It would keep him out of trouble."

"I could send the girl away while he's gone," Nary said thoughtfully. "That might do very well. Though you're a brave man to take him. What do you mean to do up there?" It was clear from his tone that to Nary, who came from the rich farm-land of County Kildare, the northern county of Cavan with its bogs and little lakes held no attraction.

"I'm to visit an old friend, a schoolmaster. He's a learned man, and a wit as well. It might interest the boy."

Doctor Nary was listening carefully. Now he gave Fortunatus a sharp look.

"A schoolmaster, you say, with a house in Cavan? And what would be the name of this place, might I ask?"

"The house is called Quilca."

"Quilca?" Nary slapped his hand on the table. "I might have guessed. Quilca." He shook his head. "And tell me this— will there be other company there, from Dublin?"

"I believe there will, yes. Another old friend of his." He grinned. "I think you know already. The Dean of Saint Patrick's."

"I knew it," cried Nary, in only partly mock vexation. "The intolerable unfairness of the thing. It's me you should be taking, Walsh, not young Smith."

"I'm sure you'd be very welcome."

"Perhaps. I hope so. But I've other duties here." He sighed. "I feel, Fortunatus, like the worthy brother in the parable of the Prodigal Son. Here I am, labouring faithfully in the service of the Lord, and it's that young rascal who's to go to Quilca. Why, man," he burst out, "you'll be in the finest company in all Ireland!"

"I would not disagree."

"Take him to Quilca, then," groaned Cornelius Nary. "Take him for the good of his soul. Though I hope you do not live to regret it."

"I'm sure I can manage him," said Fortunatus.

"Perhaps. But I warn you," said the priest, "that you are taking a considerable risk."

✛

It was some hours later that the three brothers met in the family house in Belfast. They came together in sadness.

Outside, it was raining. If Dublin was still bathed in evening sunshine, up here, eighty miles to the north, a wet wind from the west was dragging a pall of grey cloud over the Mountains of Morne, and a dreary rain was falling over the great port of Belfast beyond.

A month had passed since their father had died, that sound, God-fearing old Ulster Scot. They had buried their mother ten years ago. There was nobody left in the family now but Henry, and John, and Samuel Law.

Henry observed his brothers. We are decent young men, he thought. We love each other as best we can; and when love is difficult, loyalty always remains. We cling to that.

"Well, Samuel, no doubt you've made up your mind. What's it to be?" John, the eldest, straight to the point. Tall and dark-haired like their father. Hardworking, the undisputed head of the family now.

Samuel smiled. Perhaps because he was the youngest, he was the most easygoing. He was built differently, as well. He was considerably shorter than his brothers, even a little chubby. His hair was sandy, flecked with red—an inheritance from their mother's side, Henry supposed. But he knew what he wanted. Always had. In his genial way, considered Henry, he's just as stubborn.

"I'm going," he said. "There's a good ship leaving next week. I'm going to America."

John nodded. If a man left for America, the chances were that you would never see him again.

"We shall miss you," he said quietly. That was a lot, coming from John, the man who never gave way to his emotions. Even then, Henry noted, he did not say "I shall miss you," but "we." That made it a statement of family duty rather than personal feeling. Henry smiled to himself. John never changed. Just like their father. "But I think you are right, Samuel," John continued gravely. "I believe I'd go myself, except for . . ." There was no need to finish the sentence. John was the only one married as yet, and they all knew that his wife had made her feelings very clear. She had a large family in Ulster and no intention of being parted from them. "I am sure that it's God's will, and that you'll prosper there," John added.

"It isn't just for myself that I'm leaving," said Samuel. "But if God grants me a family one day, I'll not bring them up in Ireland."

And no one could blame him for that, thought Henry. For under Ireland's English rule, the Law family lived under humiliating disadvantages. Not because they were Catholic but, on the contrary, because they were Protestant.

If there was one thing the Ascendancy believed it had learned from the past, it was that religious disputation led to bloodshed. The disputes must therefore end. The official Church, with its compromise liturgy and its bishops, might not be perfect, but it represented order. It was to be established once and for all, and any other groups, whether papist, dissenters, sectaries, or anything else, were to be rendered impotent. Even the stern Elect of God were now to be humbled. "We had enough of those damned Presbyterians before, especially the Scotch ones," the gentlemen of the Ascendancy parliaments declared. So their legislation was directed not only against Catholics but all dissenting Protestants as well. "Join the established Church," they were told, "or be second-class subjects." And so the Scots Presbyterians who formed the most vigorous part of the Protestant community in Ulster were therefore debarred from civic and public life, and humiliated.

It was three generations since the Law family had come to Ulster. Hardworking, respectable Lowland Scots, their great-grandfather had proudly taken the Covenant; it had been a younger son, looking to make his fortune, who had come over to Ulster. There he had prospered in the wool trade, conducted through the growing port of Belfast, and raised his family in the Presbyterian faith. The Law family had been horrified when Catholic King James came to the throne, and delighted when King William beat him. And after the Battle of the Boyne, they had assumed that the new Protestant regime would be the end of their troubles, not the beginning of them.

When the English showed their loyalty to their fellow Protestants in Ireland by destroying their wool trade, the Law family had suffered a grievous financial blow. But it took more than that to defeat their sturdy Scottish enterprise.

None of the three brothers would forget the day—they had still been boys at the time—when their father had called them into the cobblestone yard and shown them a small barrel.

"This was just landed, from America," he told them. "And it will save us. Do you know what is in it? Flaxseed."

For from flax came linen.

There had been linen in Ireland from time immemorial. But the opening of the New World had now provided a vast potential supply of cheap flaxseed. As the wool trade declined, enterprising men like Law saw an opportunity. They started making linen instead of woollen cloth, and since the English themselves were not much engaged in that commodity, they had no need to destroy the livelihood of their Irish friends in this new trade.

And no one was more active in promoting the linen business than the Law family. They did not simply trade in finished linen. Soon Mr. Law had a network of a dozen farmers whom he provided with seed, spinning wheels, anything else they needed for making the yarn. With supplies guaranteed, he devoted himself first to making the linen and then to selling it. By the time King George came to the throne, Law had his own warehouse on the wharf at Belfast, and shares in half a dozen ships. He also had three sons who were thoroughly trained in the business.

The Laws were a typical family of their kind. Their faith, though it derived from the Calvinism of the century before, was of a gentler nature. They found inspiration in the simple affection of their family, in praying, or better yet, singing, the beloved Psalms together. And they were not without humour.

Nonetheless, they were tough Scots, with a strict Presbyterian church, and they believed firmly in the virtue of hard work and frugal living. They had, all of them, a sharp eye for profit and a dislike of unnecessary costs. Mr. Law had been able to acquire a handsome town house in Belfast; but when his wife had suggested she'd like some fine silk curtains for the parlour, she had been told that the old tapestry ones left by the previous owner, with only a small amount of mending—her husband kindly got down on his knees to show her how easily the thing could be done—might perfectly well be made to serve another twenty years. And since a display of silk would, in any case, be vanity and ostentation, religion dictated what her husband desired, and so there had been no need for the matter ever to be raised again.

Close-knit, churchgoing, sober, healthy, frugal, debt-free: this was the Law family. And, there could be no doubt, the Presbyterian faith was of particular assistance for a manufacturer of dry goods. But since that heritage meant that they would not bow the knee to a bishop, the Ascendancy could not accept them; and so, in a strange irony, the fact that they were strict Protestants meant that they must be treated, almost, like papists.

It was hardly surprising, therefore, that the Presbyterians of Ulster had been leaving. Being intrepid Scots, whole families would often go together, so that thriving colonies of Ulster Presbyterians had sprung into existence in the New World with remarkable speed—colonies where a new arrival like Samuel Law would find a ready welcome in a godly congregation.

Not that the Law brothers were blind to the other reasons for going. They were businessmen, after all. "Land is to be had cheaply in America," Samuel had pointed out. "The opportunities for trade are sure to grow." They had also discussed where he should go. Many families they knew had settled in New England, others in Delaware, New York, or even down as far as southern Carolina. There were Ulster settlers all the way down the Eastern Seaboard. But Samuel had expressed a preference for Philadelphia.

"You are still determined upon Philadelphia?" John now enquired. He had not entirely approved of Samuel's choice, objecting: "The place is run by Quakers."

"There are Presbyterians there," Samuel reminded him.

Henry decided to come to his aid.

"Philadelphia is a good choice," he agreed. "It has a fine future. The city has many attractions." It had not escaped Henry's notice that a family they knew who had emigrated there some months before had a very pretty daughter. And he gave his younger brother a wink that their brother John failed to see. "But I shall miss you," he added. "And if you ever change your mind and return, I shall rejoice to have you back again."

Samuel grinned. If he secretly preferred Henry to their older brother John, it was understandable. As tall as his brother, Henry had thick brown, wavy hair and was always judged to be the most handsome of the three. He was the athlete, too. Hardly any of the young men in Belfast could keep up with him in a race. Though he worked just as hard as John, Henry was easygoing. Yet he was also more adventurous. The women all liked him. Samuel knew a dozen girls who'd be glad to marry Henry, and several times he'd thought his brother was going to choose one of them; but it had seemed to Samuel that something was holding Henry back. It was as if his brother had a plan—no one knew what it was—but something that he meant to accomplish before he settled down.

"With the two of you here, I'm not really needed," Samuel remarked. "But once I'm established in Philadelphia, I hope we may conduct business together across the Atlantic."

Henry nodded. Though Samuel did not know it, he and John had already agreed to stake him by sending him a shipload of free goods. As for the business in Ireland, it was true that he and John made a formidable pair. They both knew every aspect of the linen trade, but in recent years John had attended to the supply and manufacture, and Henry to the selling, which reflected their particular talents. If Samuel wants to trade in other commodities, Henry thought, it'll be me that sees the opportunity, and John who'll need persuading.

"I must return to my lodgings soon," said Samuel. "It's amazing how much there is to do before I leave."

"Let us pray together, then," said John Law, "for God's blessing upon your journey, and all that you may undertake."

And so, with quiet affection, the three brothers prayed together for a little while, as they had always been taught to do.

After Samuel had gone, Henry remained with his brother.

⁘

It was quiet. Neither man spoke for a time. Henry watched his brother thoughtfully. Though John never showed his emotions, it was clear that he was melancholy. Perhaps he had been secretly hoping that Samuel would not go. Henry had never been in any doubt that Samuel was leaving, but you never knew with John. He stayed awhile, therefore, to keep him company.

And for another reason, also.

He had been wondering all day whether to give his brother the other piece of unwelcome news, or whether to wait. On balance, he thought it was kinder to let him absorb all the bad news at once.

"We shall have to consider how best to carry on the business when Sam is gone," he said at last.

"Yes." John nodded.

"I believe Dublin will be important for us."

The linen trade had been growing rapidly not only in Ulster, but down in Leinster also. The new Linen Hall in Dublin was already a thriving centre of the trade, and in recent months Henry had made a number of visits to the capital. "There is even more linen being shipped out of Dublin nowadays than out of Belfast," he had reported. "I think we should have a second business down in Dublin as well," he now continued. "You have everything so well in hand here, John, that you scarcely have need of me; but if I went down there, we could greatly expand our affairs."

Since all this was entirely true, there was no need to say that, without the presence of Samuel to act as a buffer between them, Henry would have found his brother's solemn and sometimes overbearing presence too difficult to live with.

"So you, too, are leaving me." John nodded slowly.

"Not leaving, John."

"There is much truth in what you say," John continued quietly. "I don't deny it." It was clear that he was not deceived. He knew very well that, behind his brother's genial charm, there was also an ambitious mind, just as ruthlessly determined as he was, and who would find it irksome to take orders from an elder brother. He knew he should not be hurt. "I should come to Dublin to help you set up the manufacture," he could not help adding.

"Ah." Realising the hint of reluctance in his own voice, Henry added quickly: "There is no man who could give me better advice, John, in all Ireland."

"It will be strange not to have you here," John said sadly.

"Dublin is not far from Belfast. I shall be coming back and forth all the time."

"There is another consideration." John's voice showed his concern. "It is easier by far to be a Presbyterian in Ulster than it is in Dublin. Here we are many, and strong, whereas in Dublin . . ." He looked at Henry searchingly. "It will be hard for you, Brother."

Henry returned his gaze evenly. He had given this part of the matter much thought. He gave him a reassuring smile.

"I shall be in God's hands," he said.

It wasn't exactly a lie.

✠

It was Tidy who saw them coming down the lane. He recognised Walsh at once. Fortunatus was riding a handsome chestnut gelding and leading a packhorse. He wore a long coat and a battered old three-cornered hat. But you could see at once, thought Tidy, that he was a gentleman.

Of all the seventeen living grandchildren of Faithful Tidy, Isaac Tidy was one of the poorest. He was short, with oily, crinkly yellow hair, and he stooped forward. But he had his standards. As a youth he had tried several occupations. He had worked for a printer, for he could read and write, but he had disliked the long hours of drudgery and the smell of printer's ink. He had looked for a position as a verger or sexton in a church. And it was while doing so that he had encountered no less a personage than the Dean of Saint Patrick's Cathedral, who had taken him on as his manservant. The position, it might be thought, was somewhat menial for a man whose grandfather, he quietly let you know, had been Chapter Clerk of Christ Church. "I would not have done it," he told his family, "for any other man." Nobody in Dublin would have denied that Dean Jonathan Swift was a man of quite particular stature. And so completely did Tidy identify with his master and his exalted position, so indispensable did he make himself, and so well aware was everybody of his own, not-to-be-sneezed-at ancestry, that when even the junior clergy addressed him as Mr. Tidy, he took it as no more than his due. And if there was one thing Isaac Tidy liked, it was a gentleman.

For Irish society, as far as Tidy was concerned, was divided into two, and only two, classes. There was "the quality," or "the gintry," as he, like many Irishmen, pronounced it; and there was the rest. This single line of demarcation, as mighty and defensive as the Great Wall of China, crossed many social terrains. Dean Swift, a man of birth and education, was gintry, and Tidy wouldn't have served him his claret otherwise. Fortunatus Walsh, the Old English, Protestant member of the Dublin Parliament, with his Fingal estate, was also, obviously, gintry, and so, therefore, was his brother Terence the doctor, despite being a papist. Indeed, even a native Irish Catholic, so long as he was a landowner, or a man of wealth with some plausible claim to princely ancestry, might qualify. But most people you met in the street did not.

He could always tell. He himself didn't always know how he did it. But Tidy usually needed only a few seconds, or at most a minute or two, with any man to sniff him out. And if that man was putting on airs and graces, but he didn't really belong to the gintry, Tidy would know it. He'd be civil enough, usually; he mightn't say anything. But he'd let that man know by subtle means that, even if the Duke of Ormond or the Lord Lieutenant had taken him for a gentleman, he, Isaac Tidy, knew him for the impostor he really was. Under his seemingly subservient gaze, even the boldest intruder began to feel awkward.

As the new arrivals approached Quilca now, Tidy's attention was fixed upon the dark-haired young man who was riding beside Fortunatus. His clothes were carelessly worn. You couldn't tell by that, though. He also was wearing an old three-cornered hat. But where did he get it? Was it his own, or had Fortunatus lent it to him? The strangest thing, though, was that while Fortunatus looked perfectly happy, this young man appeared to be paying him no attention at all. For while his horse walked beside Walsh's, he himself was busy reading a book. Now, would a member of the gintry do that? For once, Tidy wasn't sure.

❖

As they came to Quilca, Fortunatus felt rather pleased with himself. He knew very well that, before going to France, Terence had impressed upon young Smith the need to behave himself. But it had been a stroke of genius on his own part, he considered, to keep the young man occupied with a book.

Having discovered that Garret was not yet acquainted with them, he had brought two small volumes from his own collection of the plays of Shakespeare, thinking that if the young man got bored during his time at Quilca, nobody in that household would be offended if he sat down in a corner to read. Garret, however, had begun the process a little earlier than he had intended. They had ridden quietly enough on the first day of their journey; but when they had stopped at an inn last night and sat down for supper, Garret, after allowing Fortunatus to engage him in conversation for a while, had not considered it necessary to continue their talk, but had taken out *King Lear* and proceeded to read it for the rest of the meal, remarking only at the end of that silent repast, "This is very good, you know."

He had finished it that night. This morning he had enquired if there would be books at Quilca, and when Walsh had answered, "Undoubtedly," he had nodded, then taken out and proceeded to read that play during their journey. He had just come to the end of the third act when they arrived.

If some people might have thought Garret a little rude for so entirely ignoring the kindly gentleman who had brought him there, Fortunatus, on the contrary, was delighted. For if the young man had such a thirst for literature, he thought, no matter what his views, he would be welcomed, and enjoy himself at Quilca.

"Put up your book now, young Garret," he cried happily. "For you are at the gates of heaven."

✢

Quilca: the country retreat of Doctor Thomas Sheridan, Church of Ireland clergyman, friend of Dean Swift, Irishman, and the greatest educator in all Ireland.

It lay beside still waters. A habitation had existed there a long time, for the grass-covered circle of an ancient rath still occupied the site, and was used by Sheridan as an outdoor theatre. But at some time more recently, a modest gentleman's house had been constructed next to the rath, with a commodious stone-walled garden down to the water, where you might almost have supposed yourself at the house of some scholarly canon in one of the great cathedral closes of England, rather than in County Cavan, surrounded by miles of bog land. This was Sheridan's temple of the muses.

It was not in good repair. The roof was missing several slates, the gaps having been obligingly filled by the birds with what appeared to be permanent nests. On the walls, ivy had hastened to make good the many deficiencies of the masonry, covering the crevices which, it was clear, Sheridan himself was never going to trouble about. Whether his head was too full of the classics of Greece and Rome, or whether he had inherited a fine carelessness as to small things from the Irish chieftains from whom he was descended, it would probably never have occurred to Sheridan to dislodge the birds from the roof, which, he doubtless considered, was as much theirs as his own.

And it was Sheridan now, accompanied by the Dean of Saint Patrick's, who came out to greet them.

They were a striking pair. Swift was the older man by twenty years, in his midfifties now. His face, which had once been round with a jaunty chin, had been drawn down to a longer, graver repose. His mouth, once puckish, was thin and ironic; his eyes, still humorous but somewhat sad. Something in his manner indicated that, though disappointed in his hopes of higher English office, he was still Dean of Saint Patrick's, and conscious of the dignity of his office.

Sheridan, beside him, though a person of some consequence himself, was too vague to remember it, and so full of good humour that you suspected he might dig the Dean in the ribs at any moment—which would cause the Dean affectionately to reprove him—or at least attack the older man with an outrageous Latin pun, at which the dean's gravity would probably collapse. With bright eyes and a broad brow, he looked what he was, a merry scholar.

"Who's this, *O Fortunate*?" he cried, indicating young Smith.

"A kinsman of mine," replied Fortunatus cheerfully, and introduced young Garret to the company.

"He reads while he rides," said Sheridan. "But what, when he rides, does he read?"

"*Macbeth*, today," said Walsh after Garret had failed to answer.

"Indeed?" Doctor Sheridan turned his kindly eyes upon Garret so that he could not escape them. "I have never known anyone to read *Macbeth* on a horse before, Mr. Smith. The sonnets perhaps, but never *Macbeth*. Might I enquire if you like it?"

Garret eyed him warily. He wasn't going to be patronised into any kind of submission.

"It's English, but it's good enough to be Irish," he said quietly. His even gaze offered neither respect nor friendship.

Swift gave Walsh a bleak look. But Sheridan seemed delighted.

"It is," he cried. "It is. Spoken like a true Irishman." He turned to the others. "It really ought to be translated into Irish, you know." He turned back to Garret. "Are your own abilities enough, do you think," he asked him seriously, "to attempt such a task yourself?"

"Perhaps," allowed Garret. "I suppose I might try."

"Capital!" cried Doctor Sheridan. "A young Irish scholar. Welcome, my dear Mr. Smith, to Quilca. Let us go in."

As the party entered the house, only Isaac Tidy remained outside. He had been observing the young man closely.

With his sallow face and his mass of dark hair, this young fellow had not impressed him at all. He must be about twenty, but he had no manners at all. He might be related to Walsh, but even a fine gentleman like that could possess a kinsman without quality. Besides, he'd seen through the young man easily enough. Why was he rude? Because he was defensive. Always a giveaway, that. No, Tidy gathered his observations together, totalled them, arranged them in order, and, in his mind, put young Smith in a box and closed the lid. He was not a gentleman. Never was and never would be. There was something else he didn't like about him, too. He had strange green eyes.

And he'd bear watching. Like as not, Tidy thought, he'll try to steal the silver.

Fortunatus was watching him, too.

As soon as they had been shown their chamber, with an oak bed for himself and a couch on which Garret could perfectly well sleep, it was clear that Sheridan was anxious to take them round his domain, and so they soon gathered outside again with Sheridan and the Dean, and proceeded into the walled garden. As they walked down to the water's edge, Sheridan was in a bubbling mood.

"Those roses, Walsh, are new since your last visit. The lavender has a powerful scent, does it not? I had it from a gentleman in London. Over there, Mr. Smith, I mean to plant a cedar of Lebanon, when I can get one."

Indicating the landscape of woods, drumlins, and bogs all around, he informed Garret:

"All this was Sheridan country. The name is one of the oldest in Ireland, you know. The O'Sioradains came from Spain, they say, soon after the time of Saint Patrick. We had the great castle of Togher before the coming of Strongbow, and our lands extended," he gave a fine wave of his arm, "right across Cavan." It was clear to Fortunatus, from a faint look of irony on Swift's face, that the Dean had heard this speech before. "We are descended from the O'Rourkes, princes of Leitrim, the princes of Sligo and Tyrone, from O'Conor Don. . . . I tell you this so that you may know that here you will find the very heart and soul of ancient Ireland."

"I can't see how, when you're a Protestant," said Garret Smith rudely.

Fortunatus was ready to intervene and rebuke the young man, but Sheridan waved him back.

"You are right. It is strange, for most of the Sheridans are Catholic. But I'll tell you how it came about. More than a century ago, my ancestor Donnchaid O'Sioradain was orphaned and taken in by a kindly English clergyman who brought him up in his own religion. My forbear became a clergyman himself, and a close associate of Bishop Bedell of Kilmore." He was in full flood now. "Did you hear of Bedell? He was the only English bishop who preached in the Irish tongue, and even translated the Old Testament into Irish as well. He was a good man, and well loved in Cavan. So much so that when the great rebellion came in '41, not a hair of his head was touched. When the rebels came to his house, they told him he had nothing to fear and that he should be the last Englishman ever put out of Ireland. When he died, half of those who walked beside his coffin were Catholic Irish chiefs." He smiled. "Our history, you see, Garret, since it is the story of people, is not always as simple as we might suppose it to be. And it was inspired by him that my Protestant branch of the Sheridans, which has included several clergymen, tried to make the Church of Ireland a Gaelic church here in Cavan." He sighed. "But circumstances were against us."

Garret said nothing, and Fortunatus had no idea what he thought of the Sheridan family history.

"Come," said Sheridan, "let me show you the rath."

Garret seemed to like the rath. Sheridan's enthusiasm for the theatrical possibilities of the old earthwork was infectious, and he even managed to draw the young man out a little.

"Come, Garret, stand by me here, and let us recite the great speech from *Macbeth*. No need for the book. I'll teach it to you. 'Is this a dagger that I see before me?'" And he proceeded to recite the next thirty-three lines from memory—a feat which quite impressed the young man. "Shakespeare's very well," he announced after they had finished, "but it's Greek drama that should be performed in a circular space like this. So you know Sophocles, Euripides? No? Read them. I'll lend them to you. They say the ancient Irish were a Mediterranean people," he went on, "and I believe it to be so. Look out at the waters of Dublin Bay, Garret, look south down the coast past those volcanic hills, and whom do you see arising from the soft waters? Manannan mac Lir, our Irish sea god. And who is he, if not Poseidon himself, sea god of the Greeks, under another name? We are Greeks, Garret, Greeks," he cried, adding in a lower voice, "taken over by Jesuits." He gave the young man a sly glance when he said this. "I suspect you are a Jesuit in spirit, Garret," he said, gently teasing. "You have a mind like a knife."

Though Fortunatus watched a little anxiously, Garret did not seem to take offence at this banter or the shrewd perception that lay behind it. He merely inclined his head silently, which seemed to satisfy Sheridan.

As they went back to the house, Garret and Sheridan went side by side, talking quietly now, while Fortunatus walked beside the Dean.

Swift had remained half smiling but taciturn during most of this performance. As they strolled, Walsh engaged him in conversation.

"I've admired Sheridan for so many years," he remarked. "He seems to me the best sort of clergyman—and he has the finest school in Ireland. I send my son to him. His school plays are famous. But I never realised until today what a passion for the theatre he has. He'd make a fine actor."

"True." Swift gave a wry smile. "The pulpit and the theatre, Walsh, are never far apart."

"It's clear he loves Quilca. I never saw a man so obviously delight in his house."

"So do I, Walsh. 'Tis a pity," Swift raised his voice just enough to carry, "that the place is falling down. Last time I was here, there was a crack in the wall of my room that let in such a draught I had to stuff it with my coat. The roof leaks abominably, too."

"I heard that," called out Sheridan. "There is nothing wrong with the roof."

"You wouldn't notice if it was off," retorted Swift.

"Occasionally," the Irishman replied airily, "it flies away like a bird to visit an uncle in Cork, but it always returns. It only complains," he added with a certain emphasis, "if swifts nest beneath it."

"Ha."

"Besides, you've been perfectly dry."

"It has not been raining."

Entering the house, Sheridan led them to a large, long room. The shutters were nearly closed, so that the room was in deep shadow, but Fortunatus could see the central fireplace, in front of which stood a large upholstered bench, a pair of tattered wing chairs, and a small table covered with papers. At the far end of the room, against the wall, stood a refectory table, doubtless taken from some monastery in Tudor times; and it was only when he noticed young Garret staring at it that Walsh realised, with a start, that it was occupied by what appeared to be a long, thin corpse, as though laid out for a wake. Sheridan glanced at it.

"That's O'Toole," he remarked. And he opened one of the shutters. Then, turning to Swift and indicating the papers, "Come, Jonathan," he said, "let us resume. Perhaps our friends can help us."

Earlier, it seemed, the two men had been busy with a composition that the Dean was preparing—not a sermon or a religious tract, they learned, but a literary composition. Walsh had explained to Garret that, before taking up his position in Ireland, Swift had already made a reputation for himself in London as an editor and writer of powerful poems and satires. "He's a close friend of the great poet Alexander Pope, you know," he had told him. Swift liked to write up at Quilca, Fortunatus knew, because he found his friend Sheridan's fanciful flights of language and imagination a useful foil to his own mordant irony. And the work upon which he was engaged was a strange one indeed.

It seemed to be a satire on the popular travel books—a curious tale of a man named Gulliver, who would make a series of voyages to imaginary lands—one island inhabited by tiny folk, another by giants, yet another ruled by rational horses; he even had a series of sketches about a visit to a flying island.

"We were choosing names for some of the curious places and creatures encountered in these travels," Sheridan explained. "For names are important. We already have, for instance, Lilliput as the island where the little people dwell; and our rational horses are called Houyhnhnms—doesn't that sound just like a horse's neigh? But come, Jonathan, set us some more challenges."

Encouraged by his friend's enthusiasm, Swift obligingly read out a few passages, and the company set their minds to work.

"We should ransack every corner of our imaginations," Sheridan declared. "Words from English and French, Latin or Greek, onomatopoeia, even Irish. Did you know that Dean Swift has some Gaelic, Garret? He does not speak it so well as you or I, but he has studied our native tongue, to his credit."

The flying island Walsh and Swift thought should be Laputa. They also prevailed when, for the loutish creatures who annoy the rational horses, they chose the name of Yahoo. Sheridan, however, came into his own when a name was required for the small, mouselike creatures that the Yahoos like to eat."

"The Latin for mouse is *mus*, and the Irish word is *luc*. Therefore, I propose that these unfortunate little fellows be called *luhimuhs*. Can't you just see the poor things?"

Swift was delighted with this. But the most ingenious choice was made a little while later.

"There is a land which Gulliver visits," he explained, "where all those who wish to be received by the king must not only, in an oriental fashion, prostrate themselves, but must crawl towards him as he sits upon his throne, licking the dirt from the floor as they do so. What are we to call that?"

This was followed by a profound silence. Walsh knitted his brows; Sheridan gazed into space, lost in thought. Finally, Garret Smith spoke.

"The Irish for slave—and any man who does such a thing is a slave—is *triall*, and the Irish for evil and dirt is *droch* and *drib*. So you could call it Trildrogdrib."

They all looked at each other. It was brilliant.

Then, at the far end of the room, a sudden chuckle came from the table by the wall, and the corpse sat up. "Excellent!" said the corpse.

"By God," cried Sheridan, "you've woken O'Toole."

‡

When Sheridan had told Garret that he was in the very heart and soul of ancient Ireland, he had not entirely misspoken. It was a genial party that sat down to eat that evening. The talk, admittedly, was carried on mainly in English, but if O'Toole, for instance, quoted some Irish verses, Sheridan would like as not join in, with Dean Swift and Walsh nodding approval; and for a few minutes thereafter, the conversation of the whole table might transfer into Gaelic, during which the two women who had appeared with the meal from the kitchen would like as not join in. Only Tidy, who had been deputed to act as butler, would remain silent, as he himself had never wished to speak the Irish language and could never understand why the Dean troubled to do so. He also managed to give Garret a few contemptuous looks, which clearly conveyed his opinion that the young man should be waiting at the table, not sitting at it—and which nobody noticed except Garret himself.

The centre of attention was O'Toole.

Fortunatus had not encountered Art O'Toole before. The man was quite young, still in his early thirties. A fair, rangy fellow, eyes like pools of blue water, a long, thin face with a wide mouth and high, protruding cheekbones: in Walsh's imagination, he took shape as a fair-haired violin. During much of the year, he lived with his family up in the Wicklow Mountains, but in the summer and early autumn he would take to the roads, as the poet bards of Ireland had done since ancient times, and be welcomed with respect wherever he went. Usually, in modest farms and hamlets, he would perform his art for the native Irish, who could only provide him with food and shelter for the night—and he surely only did what he did for the love of the thing. Sometimes at such *ceili* gatherings, he would sing, tapping his foot to the rhythm while a fiddler or two accompanied him. Or often he would tell stories from the old Irish folk tales. But best of all, if he was in the mood, accompanying himself on a small harp he carried with him, he would quietly sing verses of his own composition.

There were a number of poets of this kind on the island. The greatest of them was Turlough Carolan, a poet musician who had been blind from his birth. "Blind as mighty Homer," Sheridan had once described him to Fortunatus, "and with the most phenomenal memory I have ever encountered. As for his verses, as one who is familiar with all the classical Greeks, I should rank some of them with Pindar himself." Carolan lived in the region and had been to Quilca several times. O'Toole was his junior by twenty years, but in the opinion of many, might one day be his equal.

During the meal, the poet talked sparingly, reserving himself for his performance afterwards; but when he did speak, it was in a pleasant, easy manner, and it was clear to Fortunatus that, as well as an encyclopaedic knowledge of Irish poetry, he was well acquainted with classical literature and even some recent English authors. He drank a little aqua vitae. "I offer you wine, Art," Sheridan said, "but I know you prefer usquebaugh."

"I do," confessed the poet, "for I find that if I drink wine, my brain becomes clouded, whereas the water of life has little effect upon me, except somewhat to sharpen the faculties."

"That," Sheridan responded happily, "is exactly what claret does for me."

O'Toole spoke to Swift with a marked respect, and to Walsh in a courteous manner, saying that he had heard much good of his brother Terence. He also spoke a few words to young Garret, who only replied in monosyllables, and Walsh supposed that the young man might be shy. But at one point, he did address the poet directly.

"What part of Wicklow do you come from?" he asked.

"From up in the hills. On the road to Glendalough. Rathconan is the name of the place."

"Would you know the Brennans there?"

A faint cloud seemed to pass across O'Toole's face.

"There is a family of that name there." He looked at Garret carefully. "Have you a connection with Rathconan?"

Garret stared at him.

"You could say so."

"Ah." O'Toole nodded thoughtfully. "The green eyes. That would explain it." But he made no further comment.

When the meal was done, he moved to a chair apart and took up his harp.

"First," he announced, "some music."

First he played a short jig, then a soft old Irish tune, so that Fortunatus assumed this was a prelude to an Irish tale. But then, to his surprise, O'Toole suddenly began to play a lively Italian piece which, to his even greater astonishment, he recognised as an adaptation of a violin concerto by Vivaldi. Seeing his amazement, Swift leant over to him.

"I have heard blind Carolan make an Italian composition of his own in just the same style," he whispered. "Your Irish musicians could be the equal of any in Europe."

Having proved a point, O'Toole skilfully returned to some Irish airs, and after three or four of these, he paused, while Sheridan brought him some usquebaugh. By this time, the women from the kitchen had also come back into the room, together with the boy from the stable and the men from the farm, so the whole household was present. "Now," the poet said quietly, "a tale or two." And sometimes singing, sometimes reciting, he wove the magical tales of old Ireland, of Cuchulainn, and Finn Mac Cumhaill, of ancient kings, and saints, and mysterious happenings. Most of the time he spoke in Irish, but once or twice in English, and always with the greatest ease. Apart from the occasional sip of his drink, he did not pause for over an hour.

"You will be celebrated, Art, long after we are forgotten,"

said Sheridan warmly when he paused at last. For several minutes, the company drank quietly, the conversation little more than a murmur. Then O'Toole ran his fingers lightly over his harp again. "A composition," he announced, "of my own. I call it, 'The River Boyne.'"

For if the Irish Catholic cause had been utterly lost at the Battle of the Boyne, it had certainly not been forgotten. How could it be, when Protestant landlords occupied all the stolen Catholic land, and the law added insult to injury every day of a Catholic's life? Small wonder, then, that the poets sang haunting, mournful songs to the Ireland that was lost, conjured visions of Ireland restored to its ancient glory, and dreamed dreams of the day when that should be. Above all, however, it was the sadness, the tender yearning for the Jacobite cause, that the harpers like Carolan expressed. And it was just such a lovely lament—for the bloodshed by the magical River Boyne, for the loss of Limerick, and the Wild Geese long since fled—that Art O'Toole sang now.

And it touched them all, Irish and English alike. Fortunatus looked around him and saw the serving women with tears in their eyes; Swift, silent but clearly moved; Sheridan, eyes half closed, half smiling, like an angel; even Tidy seemed thoughtful, aware, perhaps, of the beauty of the music. But it was Garret Smith's face that Walsh's eyes rested upon.

The transformation was remarkable. Gone was the self-absorbed, sulky look that he had mostly worn before. His face had relaxed; he was gazing at the poet with shining eyes, his mouth half open, rapt.

Whatever the young man's faults, thought Fortunatus, young Garret had genius: there was no question. He really belongs at Trinity, he thought, and Terence and I could send him there if only he weren't a Catholic. But as a Catholic he can't go, nor enter the learned professions for which nature so obviously intended him. Instead, he must be a frustrated and discontented grocer's apprentice. He shook his head at the terrible waste of it all. He thought of the conversation he'd had with the worthy priest and wondered what Garret's feelings might be for the servant girl, illiterate no doubt, that he'd been busy seducing. At this very moment, very possibly, the poor girl was being taken back to her family up in the Wicklow Mountains. To the very place, it now turned out, where O'Toole himself lived. What strange coincidences. Was there some hidden meaning here? What did it all mean?

⁘

Nobody rose early the next day. In the middle of the morning, Fortunatus came down to find Garret sitting on a bench outside, reading *Macbeth*, and eating an oatcake. Sheridan and Swift were talking quietly down by the water.

At noon, O'Toole appeared, took a little light refreshment, and said that he must be on his way as he had ten miles to walk to the village where he was next expected. Sheridan and he had a brief talk together at which, Fortunatus had no doubt, a guinea or two had been bestowed. Then all the party said their farewells and gave the thanks that the poet rightly took as his due. Garret murmured something to him in Irish, which Walsh did not catch, and the poet answered with a calm nod. Then, with a long, loping stride, he was gone.

They were not to dine until late in the afternoon. Sheridan and Swift clearly wished to continue their conversation alone, so when Garret had finished his reading, Walsh took him off for a short walk. He tried to draw the young man out about his reactions to O'Toole the night before. Garret said little, but it seemed to Fortunatus that there was a suppressed excitement in his manner, as though he had made some secret discovery or made a great decision. What that might be, however, Walsh could not guess.

It was later, during the meal, when Fortunatus brought up the other matter that had been on his mind.

"I need your advice," he told Swift and Sheridan.

"And why is that?" his host asked amiably.

"To avoid eviction," Walsh replied with a laugh. And he told them about the visit from his cousin Barbara Doyle, and her fury over Mr. Wood's copper coins. "I haven't the least idea," he confessed, "how to satisfy her."

"From all accounts," remarked Sheridan, "there will be protests in the Dublin Parliament from every side."

"Which the government in England will ignore," said Swift bluntly. "For I have it upon excellent authority that they mean to do nothing at all."

"Yet surely," said Fortunatus, "after the scandal of the South Sea Bubble, the London men will know that their reputation is at a low ebb. You'd think they'd be anxious to avoid any financial transaction that looks improper."

The great crash, three years ago, of the entire London financial market, in a staggering series of overblown expectations and bogus stock offerings, had left the reputation of the City of London and the British government in tatters. Walsh could only be glad that his own savings, and those of most of his friends, had been safely in Ireland. There was hardly a town in England where someone hadn't been ruined.

"You underestimate the arrogance of the English," Dean Swift replied grimly. "The government believes that the complaints from Ireland are due to political faction. They suppose that those who raise objections do so only because they are friends of members of the opposition party in the English Parliament."

"That is absurd."

"The fact that a proposition is absurd has never hindered those who wish to believe it."

"I wish, Dean," said Fortunatus fervently, "that you would use your satiric pen in this cause. Even an anonymous pamphlet would be a far more powerful weapon than any poor speech I could make." The Dean's satires in the past had been published anonymously—though no one ever doubted who'd written them.

The Dean and Sheridan glanced at each other. Swift seemed to hesitate.

"Were I to consider such a thing," he said guardedly, "it could only be after the Dublin Parliament has debated the issue and had a response from London. For me to write, even anonymously, must be a last resort. As Dean of Saint Patrick's, I may speak out on a moral question, but not a political one."

Fortunatus nodded.

"If it should come to that, however," he smiled, "you must let me tell my cousin Margaret it was only thanks to my prompting that you did so. If I can take the credit, I may keep a roof over my head."

"Very well. As you wish," Swift answered. "Yet the truth is, Fortunatus, that I not only share your view about this business; my indignation surpasses your own." He frowned, before continuing with some heat: "For this man to flood Ireland with his debased coinage, I find the most insupportable villainy and insolence. Then, when we complain, Wood and his hirelings represent it as disloyalty. It is infamous. Yet it is believed. And the reason for it," he continued angrily, "I must acknowledge as an Englishman, is that while the English have a contempt for most nations, they reserve an especial contempt for Ireland."

Walsh was quite taken aback at the sudden anger of this outburst from the taciturn Dean, but Sheridan smiled affectionately.

"There, Jonathan, you are a wise and circumspect fellow, yet your passion for truth and justice will suddenly come out and make you quite as reckless as I am."

"Ireland's wool trade is ruined," Swift went on, "she is vilely treated at every turn, and it is done with impunity. Let me say, Walsh, what I think the Dublin Parliament should do. It should forbid English goods to enter Ireland. Perhaps then the English Parliament, and these operators like Wood, might learn to mend their ways."

"That is strong medicine," Fortunatus said.

"A necessary cure for a national reproach. But even this would be just a little bleeding, Walsh, a temporary cure. For the underlying cause is this. Ireland will be mistreated so long as its

Parliament is subservient to that of London. We elect men as our representatives, yet their decisions are set at naught. London has not the moral or constitutional right to legislate for Ireland."

"A radical doctrine."

"Hardly so. It has been said in the Dublin Parliament for more than twenty years." Indeed, leading Irish politicians of the previous generation like Molyneux had advanced just such a case. But Walsh was still surprised to hear it coming from the Dean of Saint Patrick's. "Let me make clear," Swift said emphatically, "it is my opinion that all government without the consent of the governed is the very essence of slavery."

And it was now that young Garret Smith suddenly burst into the conversation.

The truth was that, for some time now, the other men had forgotten him. He had been sitting on Swift's right but had not said a word, and while he was talking to Walsh and Sheridan, the Dean had had his back to him.

"Welcome," he cried quite loudly, "to the Jacobite cause."

The Dean turned sharply. Fortunatus stared at him. The young man's face was flushed. He wasn't drunk, but he'd evidently been drinking quietly by himself all through the meal. His eyes were shining. Was there genuine excitement, bitter irony, or outright mockery in his tone? It was impossible to say. But whatever it was, there was more of it to come.

"The Catholics of Ireland will bless you." He laughed a little wildly.

And Fortunatus felt the blood drain from his face.

The boy didn't understand what he had said. That was evident. But it was too late now. Dean Swift was turning upon him, and his face was black with fury.

"I am not, Sir, a Jacobite," he thundered.

For, strangely, it was not the suggestion of Catholic sympathies that was so damaging to the Protestant Dean of Saint Patrick's: it was calling him a Jacobite.

How could Garret understand? In the complex world of English politics, a man like Swift had to be careful. Though his sympathies had originally been with the Whigs, who had supported the new Protestant settlement after throwing out Catholic King James, Swift as a literary man had found friends and patrons who belonged to the Tory party. So in the minds of the Whigs, who were in power now, Swift was in the Tory camp. And since some of those Tories had formerly been supporters of King James, there was always the suspicion that any Tory might secretly desire the return of the hated Stuart royal house. Any Tory whom they desired to destroy, therefore, they'd try to expose as a Jacobite—a traitor to King George and the Protestant order. Guilt by association.

Hadn't the Jacobite cause died when the Stuart Pretender had so utterly failed to make any headway back in 1715? You couldn't be sure. King George and his family were hardly popular. In the cockpit of Westminster and the great country houses where rich English lords wove their political webs, intrigue was always in the air. Every man had enemies, even the faraway Dean of Saint Patrick's, and there had been whispers from them that Swift was a Jacobite.

Did it matter? Oh, indeed it did. You could complain about Wood's copper coins, you could argue that Ireland should be ruled from Dublin, you could even mock the government in a satire, and probably get away with it because, in the political world, that was considered fair game. But if they could prove you a Jacobite, that was treasonable, and they could bring you down like a pack of hounds upon a fox. It didn't take much, either. A careless word in print, a sermon that could be misinterpreted, even an unwise choice of text, and your position in the church or university, your chances of preferment, the very bread upon your table, could be gone. These niceties were well understood by Walsh and Sheridan, but obviously not by young Garret. Under no circumstances could Swift allow himself to be labelled as a Jacobite.

"But you are!" cried Garret Smith cheerfully. "And if Ireland is to be ruled with the consent of the governed, then you'll have Catholics sitting in Parliament, too."

Swift glowered at him, then turned a furious look upon Walsh, as though to say, "You brought him here."

The trouble was, thought Fortunatus, that the boy was actually right. When Swift spoke of the governed, Walsh knew very well that he meant the members of the Protestant Church of Ireland. Swift entirely believed in the need for the Ascendancy, and for the exclusion of Catholics and Dissenters alike. But the man's innate passion for justice was leading him farther than he himself realised. That's it, thought Fortunatus: he's a good man, at war with himself, who doesn't entirely know it. Perhaps that was the wellspring of his strange satire, of his love for stern classical order and Irish exuberance all together.

"You are impertinent, young man, you are ignorant, and you are wrong," Swift shouted in a rage. "The Jacobites are traitors, and as for the Catholic religion, Sir, I must tell you very plainly that I abominate it. I abominate it utterly." And he rose from the table and strode from the room.

"Damn," said Sheridan. "Damn." He sighed. "You'd better take your kinsman away, Fortunatus, first thing in the morning."

⁜

It was a clear, crisp morning as they rode away from Quilca, but Walsh's mood was hardly cheerful. Sheridan had spoken to him briefly before he left.

"I'm truly sorry that your stay is cut short, Fortunatus, but I can't have Swift annoyed," he had said. "Your young kinsman has genius, undoubtedly, but I fear he has much to learn." What upset Walsh, however, was the thought that because of this, he might not be asked to Quilca again.

Young Garret seemed in better spirits. Though Walsh was not aware of it, Garret too had received a parting word, not from Sheridan, but from Tidy. The Dean's factotum had skilfully waylaid him by the corner of the house where no one should see them.

"Well, young Smith, you've been thrown out on your ear, haven't you?" he said nastily.

"I suppose I have," said Garret.

"This isn't a place for the likes of you," Tidy continued, "sitting down at table with the quality. You don't belong in the company of the gintry, and you never will."

"I go where I'm asked," Garret replied reasonably. "It's rudeness to refuse hospitality, you know." To this, Tidy made only a sound in the back of his throat as though he were about to spit. "Anyway," said Garret, "Art O'Toole was welcome here, and he isn't gintry, I should think."

Since Tidy privately had no use for O'Toole either, he confined himself to silence; but something in his look suggested that, as a performer, O'Toole belonged in the servant class.

"Don't give yourself airs and talk back to your betters," he replied. "You should have been whipped last night, and thrown out into the stable yard where you belong. Now, get along with you."

"Thank you," said Garret.

As Garret rode beside him on the road south, Fortunatus wondered what his destiny would be. Would he settle down quietly as a grocer in Dublin? Would he get in trouble with the law? Would he do something entirely different and surprise them all? And what, after all, had he made of the last two days' events? After they had gone a mile or so, he ventured to remark:

"I'm sorry you fell out with Dean Swift. He is a great man, you know."

"Of course he is," said Garret obligingly. "I admire Swift."

"Indeed?" Fortunatus was surprised.

"At least he's honest." They rode on a few more paces. "It's you and Sheridan," he resumed cheerfully, "that I despise entirely."

"Ah," said Fortunatus.

But if Garret Smith did not even glance at him to see how he received this insult, it was because he did not really care. He had already made up his mind what he was going to do.

GEORGIANA

⇥ 1742 ⇤

THE TRAP WAS SET.

As he walked swiftly across the bridge towards the north bank of the Liffey, Doctor Terence Walsh smiled to himself. He was glad to be useful to his kindly brother—assuming, of course, that the trap worked, and snared its prey. But the thing had been so carefully and cunningly devised that, in his own estimation, there was a very sporting chance it would. Like cattle raiders from old Ireland, Fortunatus and he would lead the prize home together, and the family would rightly applaud.

The Walsh brothers were going to trap a young lady. The trap was set for that evening.

It was a fine April morning. As usual, whenever he could, Terence liked to walk. Though middle-aged, his wiry body might have belonged to a younger man; there was a spring in his step, and his eyes were still keen as a falcon's. He gave a smile and a nod to each of the people who greeted him as he strode along—for he was a popular fellow—but he didn't stop to talk, as he was going about his business.

He couldn't remember when MacGowan the grocer had last complained of any ill health, so when one of the grocer's many children arrived at his door to say that his father was poorly, Terence had sent the child back with the assurance that he'd be there within the hour.

Approaching the house and entering the yard, he noticed that the place seemed strangely quiet. He was met at the door by MacGowan's wife. He observed that she looked pale and that there were hollow rings around her eyes. She murmured something he didn't catch, and motioned him towards the fire.

The grocer was slumped in a chair. His face was ashen, his spine bent as if he were a little old man. He'd lost so much weight that his clothes hung on him like rags. As he looked up at Terence, his eye seemed full of pain and hopelessness.

The previous summer, Terence had been down in Munster. In the winter of 1740–41, there had been a terrible winter all over Ireland, and there had been widespread crop failures every season since. The failures varied by region, however. The area around Dublin had not suffered much, and supplies had been maintained in the capital; but Munster had been very badly hit. He had been shocked by the state of the countryside, where the poorer folk were literally starving. As always at such times, it was the elderly and the infants who were being carried off, but the numbers were large. He had never seen a famine before, and the memory of the people he encountered in the villages through which he passed had haunted him ever since. Many of them had looked as MacGowan did now.

But it was surely not starvation that was affecting the Dublin grocer.

"Have you any pain?" he asked.

"Just in my back, Doctor." MacGowan indicated the hollow between his shoulder blades. "Just a dull pain, but it keeps coming on."

Had the poor devil a wasting sickness of some kind, or was he declining towards a crisis?

"Are you short of breath?"

"Not really."

"No other pains? Do you sleep?"

"He does not," broke in his wife. "He tosses and turns all night, and then he'll sit like this for hours. He hardly moves." There was both concern and a trace of anger in her voice. "He hardly attends to his business."

Over the years, within the limits imposed upon his profession by the almost complete lack of any medical science, Terence Walsh had become a good doctor. The reason for this was that he had the two most important qualities for a general practitioner in any age: a knowledge of human nature, and a sense of his patient's health that came from intuition—for he rightly believed that a doctor without intuition is useless.

"And how is your business, Mr. MacGowan?" he asked.

"Well enough."

His wife, however, was shaking her head.

"It was that shipment of wine, Doctor. He was well enough before that."

Terence gazed at the grocer thoughtfully.

"Mrs. MacGowan," he said, "I shall need two small cups, and then I shall need to be left alone with the patient."

When this was done, Terence produced from inside his coat a small silver hip flask.

"Brandy, MacGowan," he remarked. And he poured some into each cup. "I'll have some, too." He watched while the grocer swallowed his, and took a sip himself. "Now," he said quietly, "why don't you tell me all about it?"

It did not take long for Doctor Walsh to concur in Mrs. MacGowan's diagnosis. The cause of the grocer's condition, almost certainly, was a cargo of wine.

In a way, the grocer's problems were the result of his success. His business had always been sound, and as the years went by, he had been able to expand his activities. He had enlarged the size of his market stall. He had engaged in some modest wholesale activities, buying in quantities of grain, flour, and butter from the region's farmers and selling these commodities on to other traders. In these activities, his being a Catholic was an advantage, for just as Catholic tradesmen in Dublin employed fellow Catholics to work for them, the Catholic farmers in the region preferred to do business with other Catholics. He had built up quite an extensive network. With his older children all apprenticed to other tradesmen, or set up on their own account, and with his younger children helping him in the grocery business, MacGowan in his fifties was a vigorous man on the verge of entering that coterie of grocers whose names appeared amongst the merchant fraternity of the city.

Indeed, he had calculated, if he invested all the money he had on hand in one big shipment, a valuable cargo of the kind the city's leading merchants handled any day of the week, he would be able to take that step. And then he had made one fatal error. Having proved his competence in one business, he had been tempted to go into another he did not know. He had invested his entire capital, and half as much again that he'd borrowed, in a shipload of wine.

It had come from Bordeaux, through a merchant in Galway. The price was good—too good. Had he consulted any of the wine merchants in Dublin, they'd have told him not to deal with the Galway man or the Bordeaux shipper. But because he was poaching business where he didn't belong, he had kept his activities dark. He'd paid for the wine; the ship had delivered; the wine was undrinkable; and the Galway man was nowhere to be found.

His capital was gone. He owed a large debt. He'd been able to get some credit from his usual suppliers and continued to trade. But no matter what he did, the weight of his debt was like an incubus upon his back that could not be shifted and that was crushing the life out of him. As the weeks passed, he could see no end in sight. No matter what he did, he could not seem to lessen the debt. It was going to destroy him. Worse. After pressing him down into the ground, it would leave a great pit into which his poor family would fall as well. He could not bear to think of it. He sagged. He lost the will to do anything.

And if no remedy is found, thought Terence Walsh, this man will either waste away or suffer a crisis and drop dead. The question was, what could be done?

The wretchedness of the thing, he considered, was that if it weren't for his debt, the grocer had an excellent business. He might not have enjoyed being a merchant himself when he was young, but he knew enough thoroughly to understand how MacGowan was situated. Not only had the man a large stall and any number of loyal customers, but thanks to the farmers who were his suppliers, he was in an excellent position to take advantage of the opportunities offered when food supplies were short and prices high. Indeed, he considered, this would be an excellent time for him to expand, rather than contract, his trade. If the debt were smaller, and I didn't have my own family to look after, he thought, I might take a chance and make him a loan myself.

"I can promise nothing, but do not give up hope," he told the grocer. "I do not think your debt is as hopeless as you suppose, and I shall call again in a few days. In the meantime, you are to eat, to take a glass of brandy each day, and to walk to Christ Church and back each day. I shall tell your wife to make sure you perform each of these. Then we shall see." And having given these instructions to Mrs. MacGowan with some emphasis, he went upon his way.

It would be the first time that he had set out to cure a patient's illness by raising money, but he looked forward to the challenge. He liked MacGowan, and if he possibly could, he was determined to save him.

It was as he reached the end of the street and glanced back towards the grocer's house that the memory of another person he had tried to help, long ago, came into his mind. It was a very long time since he had arranged for young Garret Smith to be an apprentice there; almost twenty years since the young man had suddenly disappeared out of Dublin. God knows what had become of him now.

✛

The evening sky was pink. The carriages had poured out their passengers by the precincts of Christ Church, and the fashionable world of Dublin was flowing, like a glittering stream, down to the handsome structure of the Music Hall, which now stood squarely on one side of the old medieval thoroughfare of Fishshamble Street. As they reached its wide doors, it might have been noticed that the ladies had omitted to put in the hoops that would normally have caused their skirts to balloon out like so many beribboned battleships, and the gentlemen had put off the jewelled swords which were the mark of their order. These reductions had been made at the special request of the stewards of the Musical Society, since the audience was so large that they could never have been packed in otherwise.

Inside, it was a brilliant scene. The Music Hall seemed to be lit by ten thousand candles. At one end, upon a dais, sat the combined choirs of Christ Church and Saint Patrick's Cathedrals—the most powerful chorus to be found in Dublin. As the nobility and gentry came in to find their allotted places, members of every great family could be seen: Fitzgeralds and Butlers, Boyles and Ponsonbys, bishops, deans, judges, gentry, and even the greatest merchants. Seven hundred people had been issued tickets—even more than had filled the hall for the triumphant rehearsal five days before.

They were all inside when the party of the Lord Lieutenant made its entrance, coming last, as befitted the royal representative. And upon seeing the stately duke, the whole place burst into applause—not only out of respect for his office and person, but because it was he and his magnificent patronage that had brought the renowned composer to Dublin in the first place, as a result of which it was the *beau monde* of Dublin, rather than of London, who were now to hear the first performance of what was already being hailed as the composer's greatest work.

They had come to hear Handel present his new oratorio: *The Messiah.*

So magnificent and so joyous was the scene that it would have been a churlish spirit indeed who could not forget, at least for the evening, that there was anybody starving in Ireland. But as Fortunatus awaited this encounter with the sublime, his face was anxious. He had paid a good deal of money for his seats. His wife was beside him; so was his son George. And so was a gentleman he knew slightly named Grey. But the next five seats in the row remained empty. People were still moving about, taking their places. He dared not look round.

The trap was set. But where the devil was the quarry?

❖

Terence had started it all, one evening three months ago, when he had looked up at Fortunatus as they were sitting with a bottle of claret between them in the parlour and remarked:

"I heard of something that might interest you the other day. Do you know Doctor Grogan?"

"Slightly."

"Well, he has not as many patients as I, but he does well, and he's not a bad fellow. And he was telling me that he visits a family named Law."

"Henry Law?"

"The same. You know him?"

"He's a linen merchant from Belfast. That's all I know about him."

"That doesn't surprise me. He lives quietly and attends to his business. But there is more than that. Grogan has overheard things when in the house, and he has made enquiries. He's a most enquiring man, Grogan." He paused for effect. "Henry Law is one of the richest men in Dublin."

"The devil he is. And?"

"He has daughters. No son."

"I see. Heiresses."

"Better. There are three: Anna, Lydia, and Georgiana. But Lydia is sickly, and Grogan gives me his assurance that she won't last more than a year or two. So the entire fortune will be split equally between her sisters."

"You are thinking of George?"

"I am."

"He is still only twenty."

"Georgiana is sixteen. By the time she is eighteen . . ."

"And we should get in before the competition, you mean." Fortunatus considered the matter. His son George was a handsome and intelligent boy. He seemed to be easygoing. People liked him. But Fortunatus was a good enough judge of character to see where his son's interests lay. His other son, William, would be perfectly happy running the family estate in Fingal. When he'd brought William into the splendid new Parliament building that now looked down upon College Green, William was wellmannered enough, but Fortunatus could tell that he was bored. Not so George. His broad-set eyes took in everything. He didn't just listen to the speeches; it was clear to his father that he was carefully studying each speaker's style. "I should like to come here," he told his father after his first visit. And he would ask searching questions about the leading politicians, and their families, and who held power over whom. "I can give you a start, George," Fortunatus had told him frankly, "but if you want to make a figure in the world, then you must find a rich wife."

"What religion are the Laws?" Fortunatus now enquired.

"The family was Presbyterian. But after he came to Dublin, Henry Law joined the Church of Ireland."

"I should not like," he said slowly, "to be seen to be fortune-hunting."

"You must not. It would destroy your chances."

"You have a plan in mind?"

"Perhaps. But first, there are things that you should know."

❖

Barbara Doyle had been delighted to oblige. Apart from the fact that her hair was grey now, it was remarkable how little she had changed. And Fortunatus had been in high favour with Cousin Barbara for many years now, ever since the affair of Wood's copper coins. ·

It hadn't been his speeches in Parliament; those had been excellent but useless, since the English government had refused, on this matter, to take any notice of Dublin's opinion. But then Swift's printed attacks had begun.

The *Drapier's Letters* had come out over a period of months. They were anonymous, but everyone knew that Dean Swift was the author. Who else could have written such magnificent, excoriating prose, so laced with irony? By the time Swift had done, the government of England had been made to look contemptible, and being no less vain than any other political men, Swift's ridicule proved more than they could bear. The coins were withdrawn. The Irish were triumphant. Having told Cousin Barbara that the whole business had been his idea, hatched with Swift up in County Cavan, Walsh had experienced a moment of near panic when, chancing to meet Barbara outside the Parliament building, he had seen Dean Swift emerge from Trinity College and come straight towards them. Mrs. Doyle hadn't hesitated to accost him.

"I hear that it was my cousin Fortunatus who put you up to those *Drapier's Letters*," she challenged him.

"Indeed?" The Dean looked at her, and then stared at Fortunatus. *He's remembering young Smith's impertinence at Quilca,* thought Walsh with a sinking heart, *and he'll deny me.* He imagined his rent doubling. But whether it was the sight of his anxious face, or just his own good nature, the author of *Gulliver's Travels* decided to be merciful. "I wrote them only after his persuasion," he confirmed—which, strictly speaking, was not even a lie. It was good enough for Cousin Barbara, anyway. She'd beamed at Fortunatus, and never given him any trouble since.

Her encounter with Henry Law the linen merchant, some six weeks before the performance of Handel's *Messiah*, could not have been more natural, since they both happened to

attend the same parish church. Henry Law's wife was not close
to the widow Doyle, who she thought had grown even bigger
and more forthright over the years. They had little to say to
each other. But Henry Law had no objection to talking to her,
and also had a shrewd respect for her business brain. They
would often chat for a few minutes after the service, while Mrs.
Law attended to more social affairs. So it had been quite easy,
that Sunday, for Barbara to steer the conversation towards the
subject of families split by religion.

"That is the case with my own family, you know," Henry
Law had remarked. "In Ulster, I was a Presbyterian, but when
I came to Dublin and married my wife, I changed to her reli-
gion, which is Church of Ireland."

"I didn't know that," Barbara Doyle lied.

"Well," he sighed, "my brother in Ulster has never spoken
to me since." He shook his head sadly. "I can well understand
how he feels, but I have never felt so strongly myself. So far, all
attempts by me to heal the rift have failed."

Did he know Doctor Terence Walsh? she asked. By reputation only, he replied. A distant kinsman of her own, and a
Catholic, she explained. Yet his brother, the Member of
Parliament, and a solid Church of Ireland man, never let religion come between them. "He does everything he can to help
Terence, and the two of them are bosom friends. They are very
good people, I have to say."

"Ah, that is how it should be," said Henry Law. "I wish I
had achieved the same. Those Walshes have an estate in Fingal,
I think."

"An old gentry family. But simple people. No foolish airs
and graces there," she said firmly. "Work hard and stick by your
family."

"I'd be glad to meet Mr. Walsh someday," Henry Law said
thoughtfully.

"And he'd have come to your house that very moment,"
Cousin Barbara reported to Fortunatus afterwards. "But I know
that's not what you want. So I just said nothing, and we parted."

"He really feels so strongly about the matter of family?"

"He does. He has made a fortune in the linen trade, but he's always been ready to share what he has with his family. I learned this through the vicar, but he has twice saved his brother in Philadelphia from ruin, to his great cost. Your treatment of Terence would be all-important to him."

"He must regret his lack of a son."

"There was a boy, born after the girls, but he died. The vicar told me that as well. He never speaks of it. After that, it seems, he changed. He loves his daughters, I'm sure, but he hasn't the same ambition for them." Cousin Barbara grinned. "It's the mother who's ambitious for those girls. So tell me," she enquired genially, "how are you planning to get the mother into your net?"

❖

Isaac Tidy surveyed the room. There were three weeks to go before the grand performance of *The Messiah*. He did not imagine that the duke would require him for that event, but tonight the Lord Lieutenant was giving a Saint Patrick's Day Ball in Dublin Castle, and Tidy had been working hard on the preparations since the morning.

There were some, he knew, who had thought ill of him for deserting Dean Swift. But it had not been easy. The Dean's health had been in slow decline, and with it his temper. He had even quarrelled with Sheridan and turned him away. As Swift's life became restricted and morose, Tidy had concluded that there wasn't much he could do for him. "Unless I want to finish up his nursemaid, which I don't," he told his relations. At this very time, he heard of a position opening up in the household of the new Lord Lieutenant, and he had applied for it at once. To his amazement, the duke himself had interviewed him.

"I won't have it said that I took you from the Dean of Saint Patrick's," the duke had told him plainly.

"You have my word, Your Grace, that I have left his service already," he had firmly replied. For guessing that this might be a condition, he had taken his chances and left Swift's employment that very morning.

Some people might have thought that his new position was quite a step down. He was certainly not the butler. The duke had a butler. But he was an under butler, well above the legion of gilded footmen who strutted about the duke's mighty household. He was no longer the valued retainer, either, but a newcomer. And certainly nobody dignified him with the name of Mr. Tidy. But he was prepared to suffer these minor indignities because, by going to the duke, he had gone from a small private house to the palace of a mighty potentate. "Higher than the duke, in Ireland," he told his family proudly, "you cannot go." If he ever got the butler's position, he would tower over every unfree man in Dublin. He walked carefully, therefore, abandoned his contemptuous glances for those who were not of the "gintry" for a suavity that was haunting, and made himself useful to those above him and below. Within his limitations, he was really very clever.

Isaac Tidy was happy. In a while, the dancing would begin. The great hall of Dublin Castle looked magnificent. The grand redesigning of the Irish capital as a classical masterpiece was still a work in progress but now it had reached the shabby old Castle, too. Work had already begun on a magnificent ceremonial staircase and a set of staterooms that would rival anything in Europe. For the moment, the huge old hall was used for functions such as this, but even the hall, tonight, had been transformed by the decorator's art into a vast classical pantheon. And the company itself was equally splendid. Lords, ladies, gentlemen—here was the quality indeed. Many of the faces he knew; for once a person had visited any of the ducal residences, Tidy made it a point to remember him. As his eye travelled round the room, he even noticed, at the far side, the cheerful face of Fortunatus Walsh.

As for himself, here he was, where the entire company could

see him, standing discreetly only feet away from, and awaiting the personal instructions of, the Duke of Devonshire. He permitted himself a tiny smile and glanced down at his exquisitely polished shoes. And in that tiny moment of bliss, he did not notice that Walsh had just given a nod to one of the ducal party.

A few moments later, the duke was indicating that he needed him. Tidy glided swiftly and smoothly to his side. And was most surprised to be told he was to fetch Fortunatus Walsh.

You couldn't fail to notice Tidy as he crossed the great hall. Partly this was because, out of the corners of their eyes, everyone was watching the ducal party; and also because, as the sleek and powdered servant stalked from the duke across the centre of the room, with ladies and gentlemen parting before him, you couldn't possibly miss him. Everyone at the ball, therefore, was wondering who was about to be approached.

Not least Eliza, wife of Henry Law, linen merchant.

It had surprised Eliza when a lady, whom she did not know particularly well, had asked if she'd accompany her to the Lord Lieutenant's ball. The lady's husband had to be away from Dublin, "And I don't want to go alone," she'd said. The Lord Lieutenant's office had no objection to her making the substitution, she assured Eliza.

"But what if someone asks me to dance?" Eliza wanted to know.

"You dance, of course," the lady laughed.

If the invitation was unexpected, it was hardly to be refused. It was one of Eliza's greatest regrets that, as the years went by, her genial husband had become less and less interested in going to parties. It was not something she had been able to understand. "How can you be bored," she had once asked him, in genuine astonishment, "when there is dancing?" He'd go to a theatre or a concert, or even to an assembly, to please her, and she had given him fair warning that he must soon do more for his daughters. But that was as far as she could get him. At least he had raised no objections to her going to the ball this evening.

Her companion was smiling. As it happened, though Eliza Law wouldn't have known it, her companion's closest friend was the wife of Doctor Terence Walsh.

"It's a fine scene, isn't it? The duke is looking very well tonight."

The Duke of Devonshire was the second great aristocrat to be sent as Lord Lieutenant in the last decade, and his own huge wealth and standing conferred a sense of stability on the Dublin scene. Standing there in all his magnificence, in a blue and gold coat, the broad, intelligent face under a powdered wig gazing lazily but benignly out at the gathering, he was a symbol of magnificence and peace. Europe might be split into rival dynastic camps for much of the time; invasions might occasionally threaten, though they never seemed to materialise; even the Jacobite cause might still be alive here and there; but in Dublin, one could look out upon a scene of modestly increasing prosperity—except for the native Irish, of course—and political peace.

But it was not the duke, whom she'd seen before, that fascinated Eliza. It was his party. What a glittering crowd they were.

"The Ponsonbys are all there," her friend remarked. Eliza gazed at them avidly. The Ponsonby family—or "Punsinby," as it was fashionable to pronounce the name—had been a family of Cromwellian settlers not so very much greater than her own. But two generations of careful intrigue and some important political patronage had brought them to a point where they were even more important than the rich Boyle family down in Munster. By the time that the Duke of Devonshire had come to Ireland, the Ponsonbys could already undertake, with their followers, to deliver the government the votes it needed to pass legislation smoothly through the Dublin Parliament; and it had added to their own prestige—and suited the duke's political convenience—that one of their sons had now married one of his daughters. Best of all, as far as Eliza Law was concerned, these activities had brought the family not only wealth but a title.

Ah. A title. There were plenty of them going in Ireland nowadays. If the head of the Ponsonby family could be Earl of Bessborough, lesser men could hope for simple peerages. Irish peerages, in particular, were often given for political services. A man had only to be in the right place at the right time, and deliver a vote that the government needed, to get himself made a lord—a reward that was almost eternal, since it passed down to your heirs forever. If you sought status for your family—and who at that assembly did not?—then a peerage was the thing to have.

A title. Ah. A dreamy look came into Eliza's eyes at the thought of it. She mightn't ever be called Lady Law herself, but she would fain have such a thing for her lovely, her dear, her swanlike daughters. Young gentlemen with the prospect of a title: that was what she dreamed of for her girls. It was not a subject she discussed with her husband, for his own ambitions were more down-to-earth. But in her own sweet way, she was quite determined about it. And here they were, in the hall before her, concentrated in particular in the blessed group around the Lord Lieutenant. How wonderful it was. She did not know when she had been more delighted.

And now she saw Tidy returning. He was leading a handsome, middle-aged man behind him. They were crossing the floor, straight towards the ducal party, while everybody was looking, the gentry and the lords and ladies, and the future lords, all looking, in that great hall with ten thousand candles blazing. Oh. She gave a tiny quiver of excitement; she couldn't help it. They were all watching, and all their murmurs had died away to a little silence as he'd reached the duke, and the duke had put out his hand and, oh, the duke was smiling.

As Walsh approached, the duke had turned to his son-in-law.

"What's this all about, by the way?" he mildly enquired.

"Fortunatus Walsh. Member of Parliament. Old Fingal gentry. Wants Your Grace to make much of him. Needs to be seen. Won't take a minute."

"And there's no reason we shouldn't?"

"None at all. Loyal man. Always helpful. Good friend."

"Then we'd better oblige him." Behind his sometimes lazy exterior, the duke was a very shrewd operator, and an expert at little courtesies like these. He extended his hand. "My dear Mr. Walsh, we are very glad to see you."

It was easy enough to make small talk for a moment or two. He spoke to Walsh of Handel, for whom Fortunatus expressed a well-informed admiration. They touched upon a few plays they had seen at the Smock Alley Theatre. Indeed, the duke quickly decided that he liked Fortunatus very well, and even—ultimate mark of distinction—proffered his snuff box. They actually went on talking for five minutes, while all Dublin watched.

"We must speak again," the duke said to close the interview, but with a nod to his son-in-law to indicate that he really meant it. After which Fortunatus retired in discreet triumph. "So tell me," the duke murmured to Ponsonby after Walsh had gone, "what's the game?"

During the whole of this time, Eliza Law had been so captivated by the honour bestowed within the glittering circle that she had watched without saying a word. Now she turned to her companion.

"Who is that gentleman?"

"Oh, didn't you know? That's Fortunatus Walsh. Fine old family. And in high political favour, so I hear."

All these careful preparations, together with the intelligence that the Law family was going to the performance of *The Messiah*, would not have been enough to bait the trap this evening had it not been for one other, propitious circumstance.

This was the fact that, just at that moment, young Tom Sheridan had nothing much to do.

Despite the unfortunate business at Quilca all those years ago, Fortunatus had been able to keep up his friendship with Doctor Sheridan and with his family. Tom was the good old doctor's most lively son, in Walsh's opinion. A godson of Swift's, he had shown a marked literary disposition himself, and gone to Trinity College. Now he had just come down from that institution, and expressed a wish to act—unusual for a young gentleman, though not unknown—and to write plays.

"Smock Alley's the place for me," he had cheerfully told Fortunatus.

Dublin's Smock Alley Theater was certainly a lively place. Not only did it put on plays old and new during the winter season, but in the summer, the best productions from the London theatre would tour there. This year, the new sensation of London, the actor Garrick, was due to come.

"If you can get a play put on at Smock Alley, Tom, I promise you we shall all come," Fortunatus had told him. "But how are you keeping body and soul together in the meantime?"

A variety of small jobs, it turned out, including one with the Musical Society. And it was this fact that had come into Walsh's mind when he considered how the desired arrangements might be secured for *The Messiah*.

"Do you have any part in the allocation of places for the concerts, Tom?" he asked him when he met him in the street one day.

"I could certainly arrange something."

"How would you like to make two guineas?"

"I should like to make two guineas very much indeed."

"Then at *The Messiah*," Fortunatus said, "I should like you to place us next to the family of Mr. Henry Law."

❖

And now, here they came at last. Evidently, Eliza Law had delayed them by talking to someone in the audience. Fortunatus hid his relief.

There could be no mistaking them. The merchant, spare and handsome, his hair still fair, was smiling quietly. He looks a gentleman, too, Walsh noted approvingly. His wife, fussing over her daughters, gazed around with pale blue eyes. Her figure was still trim. Quite passable. Then the three girls. It was obvious which one was Lydia: she must be the one with the long neck. She certainly looked very pale and sickly, just as Terence had said. But as for the other two, his eyes opened wide. What beauties. One was fair and smiling; the other, with a dash of burnished red in her hair, was bold and buxom. Was she Anna or Georgiana?

How would they sit, though? Would it be as he had hoped? He gazed forward, smiling vaguely and holding his breath. Yes. It was perfect. Himself, then Grey, and then Henry Law just on the other side of him.

And now the purpose of Grey would appear. For turning to his right, that worthy gentleman smiled.

"Mr. Law, I see."

"Why, Mr. Grey. I am delighted to see you, Sir. My dear, you do not know Mr. Grey, I think, but he and I have business together." Smiling greetings were made.

Then Mr. Grey, rather quietly, to Mr. Law:

"Do you know Mr. Fortunatus Walsh, the Member of Parliament? I am in his party."

"Oh. I don't, but have heard of him."

"Should you care to be introduced?"

"Indeed," with some warmth, "I should."

"May I present Mr. Henry Law? This is the Member of Parliament Mr. Fortunatus Walsh."

"Mr. Law. I have the honour."

"Mr. Walsh," Henry Law was smiling with some excitement, "I am most honoured, Sir, and delighted to make your acquaintance."

⁜

The performance was sublime. For Handel, for the duke, for the Musical Society, indeed for everybody, it was a triumph.

As the Law family walked home—for, the weather being dry and the distance not great, Henry Law had not seen the point of using their carriage—he turned to his wife.

"If we gave a dinner, I think we should invite Fortunatus Walsh and his wife. He is a most sensible man, and I think he would come."

For just a moment, his wife was about to tell him that not only was he a sensible man but in high favour with the duke himself and, for all she knew, in line for a title; that he appeared to have a handsome unmarried son; and that given the chance she would lie down on the ground and invite him to walk over her to the front door of her house, but she thought better of it. Better not to share that information with her husband, who might not approve. She'd keep it to herself and the girls.

"As you wish, my dear," she said. And thanked God for sending not only Handel but Fortunatus Walsh to the Music Hall of Dublin that sublime evening.

⁜

Both Cousin Barbara and his brother arrived at the house in St. Stephen's Green the next morning, anxious to know how the evening had gone.

"It was magnificent. You really should go to listen to Handel, you know," he remarked to Barbara.

"A hymn I can sing in church is enough music for me," she stoutly declared. "Now, none of your nonsense. What about Law?"

"We shall see. But I think," Fortunatus said honestly, "that he's hooked. By the by, those girls are exceedingly handsome. The red one I especially admired. That's Georgiana."

"And George, which does he prefer?" enquired Terence.

"I haven't asked. But in the circumstances," said Fortunatus with perfect reasonableness, "I trust he will like the one who likes him."

"I like the sound of George and Georgiana," said Barbara Doyle cheerfully.

"It has symmetry," Fortunatus agreed. "But whether anything comes of this or not," he added, "you are both of you to be thanked." He smiled at his brother. "I shall not forget, my dear brother, that you have repaid any kindness received by so greatly helping me."

Then they spent a happy twenty minutes going over the whole business, episode by episode, and congratulating each other on their cleverness all over again.

It was only after this that Terence Walsh remarked:

"I'll tell you who needs help at present far more than any of us, and that is my poor patient MacGowan the grocer. And he told them the whole sad story.

"What will you do?" asked Fortunatus.

"I intend to go, this very day, to visit some Catholic merchants of my acquaintance. I hope that perhaps we can put a small company of merchants together who could save him and his business, which, as I say, could still be very profitable."

"You should do so," said Cousin Barbara firmly. "The Catholic merchants quite often stick together."

"I hope so most sincerely," answered Terence.

Soon after this, Barbara Doyle had to leave, but Terence remained with Fortunatus a little longer.

"Do you know who else came into my mind as I was leaving MacGowan?" Terence said to his brother after a pause.

"Tell me."

"Our kinsman, Garret Smith. I wonder where he is, and how he does."

"By all accounts, when he left Dublin without even completing his apprenticeship, he went up into Wicklow. I consider that he treated you very badly."

"He was young."

"He has never made any attempt to see you again, either to apologise or explain."

"Perhaps he is embarrassed."

"Put him out of your mind, Terence. Nothing good will ever come of it. You have better things to do."

"I suppose you're right." Terence got up. "I've MacGowan to think about today."

The grocer was worth saving, Fortunatus thought. Garret Smith, probably not.

⁜

It would have surprised both men very much if they could have seen their Cousin Barbara at that moment. After leaving the house, she had directed her coachman to drive north-wards. After passing Trinity College and the splendid new Parliament building that, with its huge classical façade, almost seemed to suggest that London was commanded from the Irish Parliament, and not the other way round, the coach swung over the bridge across the Liffey and proceeded towards Cow Lane.

Barbara Doyle supported the Protestant Ascendancy and had few dealings with Catholic merchants, but the chance of a profit was always uppermost in her mind. And it'll be at least a day or two, she judged, before Terence can organise a collection of Catholic merchants to do anything. She always believed in getting in first.

So, a few minutes later, the discouraged grocer was much astonished to find himself accosted by this unlikely and rather frightening saviour.

"Tell me it all," she ordered, "and we'll see what we can do."

She listened carefully as he gave her all the details of his transactions, then announced: "I shall be your partner, and want a third of the profits from now on, but we'll pay off all your creditors. In six months, the debts will be cancelled. Take it or leave it."

"I'd take it," he answered nervously, "but . . ."

"But what?"

"The debt is large. I don't see how we'll pay it off."

Then Barbara Doyle smiled.

"I shall talk to your creditors. We'll come to an agreement. Who says," she asked quietly, "that we shall repay it all?"

⊰ 1744 ⊱

In the autumn of 1744, George Walsh and Georgiana Law were married—an event that seemed as natural and inevitable as the long peace that Ireland had now enjoyed for nearly a lifetime. Yet a certain anxiety hung over the proceedings, as if a wicked witch had been spotted in the distance, making her way towards the wedding feast.

"The French are coming." That was the rumour.

Of course, rumours of invasion were hardly new. In the never-ending rivalries between the European powers, Britain was now in league with France's enemies, and naturally, therefore, the French would be tempted to invade Ireland to annoy the English. Such was the way of the world in the eighteenth century. But now another rumour was growing. The heir to the lost Stuart crown, a vain young man whom the Scots liked to call Bonnie Prince Charlie—and whom the French had been protecting for years—was planning to come to Scotland to claim his birthright. A Jacobite rising in Scotland and a French invasion of Ireland: it was exactly the combination the London government dreaded.

For once, even the unflappable Duke of Devonshire was rattled. Orders flew. The troops in the Irish garrisons were to be readied. Any suspicious characters were to be reported. Any suspect priests were to be rounded up. And all Ireland waited. Would the threatening clouds on the horizon disperse, as they had always done in the decades before? Or would they gather together into a single dark mass and come racing across the sea towards the Irish shore?

⁘

O'Toole rested his back against the wall and felt the sun on his face. There were a dozen children sitting on the grass in front of him. He handed over the book—*Caesar's Wars*, in Latin—to one of the boys.

"Construe."

The boy began. He wasn't bad. But after a minute or two, he floundered. O'Toole winced.

"No. Anybody?" Another boy offered. "Worse." Silence. "Conall." Reluctantly, the boy answered. "Very good."

The dark, tousle-haired boy with the wide-set green eyes never offered unless he was asked. O'Toole didn't blame him. While the others were all on the grass, Conall Smith had perched himself on a small, flat outcrop of grey stone. Any attempt by one of the others, whatever their size, to dislodge him from that spot and they would have been sent sprawling, because nowadays young Conall was unusually strong. But it embarrassed him that he always had the answer to the master's questions when his friends did not, and sometimes he would pretend he couldn't answer, and O'Toole would stare at him, knowing very well that he knew, and finally shrug his shoulders and move on.

O'Toole loved the boy almost as much as he loved his own granddaughter. That was what made today's lesson so difficult.

The hedge school. Sometimes it was, indeed, a master and a few children huddled behind a hedge, or in a hidden clearing in the trees, or in a peasant's cottage—or, in this case, behind a stone wall with a delightful view down from the Wicklow Mountains towards the Irish sea. The hedge school was illegal, of course, because giving an education to Catholic children was illegal. But they were all over the country, hundreds of them.

It was soon after his visit to Quilca, almost twenty years ago, that O'Toole had become the hedge schoolmaster at Rathconan. He was considered a good master, but not one of the very best. For although his knowledge of the classical languages, of English, and of history and geography was excellent, his knowledge of philosophy was only moderate, and his mathematics no more than adequate. And it was mathematics, above all, that the native Irish prized: arithmetic for keeping accounts;

geometry for surveying and even astronomy. The best hedge schoolmaster mathematicians would proudly write "Philomath" after their names. One old man he'd met, named O'Brien, had a reputation for mathematics that spread even to Italy, and he was known all over Ireland as The Great O'Brien. Such was the illegal education system for Catholics all over Ireland.

If O'Toole was only a moderate mathematician, he had other strengths. His poetry and music had brought him a reputation, if not quite on a level with blind Carolan, as an important figure all the same. When his pupils translated from Latin, they had to give their version first in Irish, then in English. He even taught them a good deal of English law, since it would be useful to them. Already, he had produced three pupils who were making their way successfully in the merchant communities of Dublin and Wicklow, and another who had gone to France to study for the priesthood—not a bad record, he considered, for a little village up in the mountains.

Not that all his pupils did so well. With the Brennans, for instance, he found he could do practically nothing. But he must try. He sighed.

"Conall. Go and stand on watch."

As long as the little school kept out of sight, Budge generally left it alone. But as the local landlord and magistrate, he would sometimes ride out and see if he could spot their proceedings—of which he strongly disapproved—and if he caught sight of them, there would certainly be trouble. Like most hedge schools, therefore, when O'Toole taught, he usually posted a watch.

"Now then, Patrick," he said, as kindly as he could, to the eldest of the Brennan boys, "let me hear you read."

As the boy stumbled his way through a simple passage—O'Toole had sent Conall off to watch so that he would not have to listen to this painful process—the master could only marvel: how was it possible that young Conall Smith, the child with a mind as fine as, perhaps finer than, his own, could be half a Brennan?

Sometimes he wished he had intervened to prevent Conall's birth. It was a foolish idea, no doubt, but was it possible that he could have said something to persuade the boy's father to lead a different life and choose another wife?

There was just one day, it seemed to him, when he might have had the chance to do so. That day, almost twenty years ago, up at Quilca. He'd marked out young Garret Smith at once as a fellow with genius. He'd guessed the young man's anger and his frustration, too. How could an intelligent Catholic boy like that feel any other way? But if only he'd guessed what was in Garret's mind when he'd asked if he knew the Brennans, and then informed him, as he was leaving in the morning, that he'd come to see him at Rathconan. If only he'd known.

What could he have done? Used any influence he had, begged the young man, at least, to follow another course. Anything to prevent him running off after that illiterate girl and making himself part of the worthless Brennan family up at Rathconan. Had he been able to do that, then Garret Smith would surely not have fallen into his present wretched condition; and Conall—another Conall, of course, perhaps even a finer one—would have been born to a different mother, and under far different family circumstances.

But by the time he'd returned to Rathconan that autumn, he'd found young Garret already there, living with the Brennans, his heart dark with anger and contempt for Nary, who'd sent her away, for Sheridan, the Walshes and all their kind, believing foolishly that up there in a hut in the mountains, he would be somehow a freer, purer man than he would be working for MacGowan the grocer in Dublin. Had it just been a question of living in the mountains, he might have been right. A man might find himself up in the wild and open spaces, or in the great sanctuary of Glendalough. But in a hut with the Brennans? O'Toole didn't think so. Within a year, the slut of a girl had given him a child; then another. Young Smith should have walked out on them all, in the high old way, in O'Toole's opinion. But Garret was too good for that. He'd gone before a priest and married her. After that, he was doomed.

He should have become a hedge schoolmaster. He'd have had to study more, but he had the brain to do it. I'd have helped him, O'Toole thought. But he'd have had to move, since the position in Rathconan was filled and there was no need for another. A local priest had given him some work. But then he had quarrelled with the priest. Was there something in the man that craved his own destruction? It had often seemed to the schoolmaster that there was. For look at the man now. A labourer. A carpenter and carver of images, commissioned but never delivered; a maker of poems never finished; a dreamer of Jacobite dreams that had no chance of becoming real. A drinker. Every year, more of a drinker. A husband of a wife he'd buried now, and whose family, in his heart, he must have come to despise—for they were dirty, lazy, and stupid. A father of children left unkempt, while he talked to them of the Jacobite cause and the shabby way he'd been treated, or cursed them and sank into moroseness.

There had been three daughters that lived. Two, sluts like their mother, in O'Toole's opinion, had married down the valley. The third was a servant in Wicklow. Two little boys had died in infancy. And then, miraculously, had come Conall.

"He'll die like the other boys, I fear," the priest who'd performed the baptism had said to O'Toole. And most people in Rathconan had thought so, too. He remembered him when he was three—so pale and fragile, with those wonderful green eyes. Such a poetic-looking little fellow that it broke your heart to think how little time he probably had to know life. When his own little granddaughter Deirdre, who was only months younger than the boy, had become his friend, O'Toole had tried gently to discourage her from becoming too close, for fear of the pain it would cause her when the boy died. But he could hardly stop her playing with him, or walking with him hand in hand when he wandered up the mountain to where the sheep were grazing, or sitting beside him on a rock overlooking a pool formed by the mountain stream, sharing her food with him, and talking by the hour.

"What do you talk about, Deirdre?" he had asked her once.

"Oh, everything," she had answered. "He tells me stories sometimes," she had added, "about the fish in the stream, and the birds, and the deer in the woods. I do love him so." And though his heart had sunk, he had not known what to say.

It had been Garret who had brought the boy to him, when Conall was six. Surprisingly, he had even come with the requisite money.

"Teach him," he had asked O'Toole simply. "Teach him all you know."

"You could teach him yourself, for the moment," O'Toole had pointed out, "for nothing."

"No," Smith had shot back with sudden vehemence. And then, after a pause: "I'm not fit to teach him." A terrible admission, but what could the schoolmaster say?

So he had started to teach the boy. And he had been astonished. The little fellow's memory was astounding. Tell him a thing once, and he remembered it forever. His thought process, O'Toole soon realised, was also entirely out of the ordinary. He would listen quietly, then ask a question that showed he had considered every aspect of the matter already and found the thing that, for the time being, you had thought it simpler to leave out. What delighted O'Toole most, however—and this was a gift that could never be taught—was the boy's use of language: his strange, half-playful formulations which, you suddenly realised, contained an observation that was new yet stunningly accurate. How could he do such a thing at such a tender age? As well ask, how can a bird fly, or a salmon leap?

He also noticed that his young pupil had a busy inner life. There would be days when he seemed moody and preoccupied during the lesson. On these days, often as not, O'Toole would see him afterwards wandering off alone, enjoying some communion with the scene around him that no one could share.

By the time the pale little fellow was eight years old, the schoolmaster loved him almost as much as Deirdre did.

If only it had not been for those other days, when Conall would fail to come to the hedge school and word would come that he was sickly; and O'Toole would go to Garret Smith's house and find little Deirdre sitting by his side, feeding Conall broth, or quietly singing to him, while the little boy lay there so pale it seemed as if he might be taken from them within the day.

But then, suddenly, two years ago, he had started to get stronger. A year later, he seemed as robust as the other children; soon after that, one of the toughest. And now, he could physically dominate them all. At the same time, O'Toole detected a new toughness in the boy's growing mind. He did not just excel at his lessons; he stormed through them, so that the schoolmaster was often challenged himself to set work that Conall wouldn't find too easy.

Little Deirdre also watched these developments with evident delight. "Isn't he strong?" she would cry. And it seemed to O'Toole that his granddaughter felt she could take a personal responsibility for Conall's new condition. At the same time, from her looks, and from occasional words that she let fall, her grandfather could guess that she still saw the same, pale little boy that she had loved beneath this new incarnation; and indeed, Conall would still sometimes fall into his strange, melancholic moods, and the two of them would still go off for walks together in the mountain passes.

Deirdre was Conall's only close friend. He was often with the other children, and joined in all their games. But it was clear that he did not share his confidences with them. There were only two other people nowadays to whom he might be close. One, perhaps, thought O'Toole, was himself. In their studies together, master and pupil had developed a degree of intimacy. The other was his father.

O'Toole suspected that Garret Smith had little enough to live for these days but his son. The man's drinking was getting worse, and he looked twenty years older than he actually was; but if it hadn't been for the boy, he'd surely have been far worse. And if this love did not always extend to paying the modest fees for the hedge school on time, he usually managed to make them up sooner or later. In the evenings, when he was sober, he would sometimes spend hours in deep conversation with the boy. O'Toole had often wondered what it was they talked about, and once he had asked Deirdre if she knew. But she didn't. All she knew was that Conall had once told her: "My father and your grandfather are the only two men I truly admire."

Did the boy know that his father was not held in high regard? The villagers were usually polite about his father to his face. "Your father's a great reader," they'd say. "He knows many things." But if, behind his back, they added, "He knows more than he works and less than he drinks," Conall was beginning to guess it. Once, when a boy was rude about his father, he knocked him down. Though afterwards, when no one could see, he burst into tears. And to Deirdre he sadly remarked: "No one understands him but me."

So it was only his father and Deirdre that Conall really loved and trusted. And after them, O'Toole considered, I dare say it would be me.

And so now, as Conall kept watch for the hedge school, and the schoolmaster thought of the conversation he'd had the day before, he felt a terrible sense of guilt.

It weighed heavily on his conscience that he might have to betray the boy.

⁜

At shortly after noon, Robert Budge, landowner and magistrate, set out from his house to see Garret Smith. When Walter Smith's family had been dispossessed, the Rathconan estate had been offered for sale at a knockdown price. Benjamin Budge had had no desire to return there, but his younger brother, who was made

of sterner stuff, had been glad to buy it. The Budges could claim
to have been at Rathconan for four generations now.

He hadn't decided what to do about the Smith boy yet.
O'Toole wouldn't give any trouble. He'd already seen to that.
As for the boy's father . . .

But the boy could wait. Today he had other business with
Garret Smith. It concerned Rathconan House.

If the old chiefs of the place could have seen Rathconan
now, they might have been rather surprised. They might even
have found it comical. Yet it was like scores of other old houses
in Ireland. For, finding the accommodation of the old tower
house insufficient, Budge's father had added, across the front of
it, a modest, rectangular house, five windows wide. The house
was of no particular style, though the plain windows might
have been called Georgian. No attempt had been made to alter
either the house or the old keep that loomed up behind it, so
that they would blend together. The new Rathconan looked
like what it was: a house stuck onto the front of an old fort.

But it was where Robert Budge had been born and raised,
and he was proud of it.

He'd been only twenty when his father had died, five years
ago, leaving him lord and master of the place, and, with a
young man's vanity, he had even considered changing the
house's name. He had thought, as some of the grander settlers
had done, of calling it Castle Budge, but that seemed over-
reaching. More reasonable might have been another English
formula favoured in Ireland: Budgetown. But that was hardly
euphonious. Better-sounding was the Irish version:
Ballybudge. In the end, however, considering the fact that the
Budges had hardly built the place, and fearing the mockery of
the local Irish and his neighbours, he had thought better of it
and left the name as it was—Rathconan—to which he liked to
add the appellation "House," to make it sound more like an
English manor.

To Robert Budge, Rathconan House was home. True, like
all the rest of the Cromwellian settlers, he was still viewed by

the native Irish as an unwanted colonist. True, also, that he was proudly English and Protestant. For if the Cromwellian families were not there to uphold the Protestant faith and occupy the confiscated estates of the former Catholic owners, then what was their justification for being in Ireland in the first place? Indeed, his father, a man of far less religious conviction than old Barnaby Budge, had firmly taken his more or less Presbyterian family into the royal Church of Ireland exactly because, as he had put it: "We must all stick together."

"Always remember," he had advised Robert shortly before he died, "the good people here have known you all your life, they work your land, and they'll probably call you 'Your Honour' and give you a daily greeting. But if ever our order breaks down, my son, they'll put a knife between your ribs. And don't you forget it."

All the same, it was nearly a century since Robert's great-grandfather Barnaby had first come there. And during that time, the Anglo-Irish settlers had evolved to blend, in certain ways, with the surrounding environment. If the men in the Irish Parliament felt themselves treated as a different breed by their compatriots in London, out here in the country, the lesser Anglo-Irish landlords had produced a type that was entirely their own.

His own father had exemplified the breed. He'd lived almost all his life at Rathconan and knew all its ways. He spoke English with a pronounced Irish intonation, and he treated many of the details of his life, including his children's education, with a certain fine carelessness. In this he had been joined by his wife, who came from a similar family with identical views.

Some Anglo-Irish families, of course, sent their sons to Oxford, Cambridge, or Trinity College in Dublin. But not the Budges. Basic education the children were given, boys and girls, but much more was considered superfluous.

"My father had a whistle which he would blow to summon his dogs," Robert would cheerfully tell his friends. "But if he blew two blasts, that meant he wanted me." When his mother had caught his sister reading a book when she could have been healthily out of doors, she had locked her in a dark closet for two hours and told her she'd give her a whipping if she caught her behaving like that again. The Budge children were brought up to be strong, to run estates, and, if need be, to fight. In their love of the open air, the Budges had something in common with the Irish chiefs who had gone before them. It would have surprised them to know that they were less educated.

It was a matter of education that had caused him to speak to O'Toole so firmly.

Robert Budge was only twenty-five, but he was often treated like an older man. Perhaps it was his large, imposing presence, but as the owner of Rathconan, he was considered a useful local man by the authorities, and a year ago he had been made a magistrate. So long as he could stay in the country at Rathconan, he was glad to cut a bold figure in this local world, and he had recently been a guest at several houses in Counties Wexford and Kildare to look out for a suitable wife; he had also been to Dublin a few times, so that the people at the Castle and the Parliament should know his face.

His reason for visiting Dublin the previous week had been to obtain the latest news on the threat of invasion from France. The garrisons at Wicklow and Wexford were all in readiness, he knew very well. And he was impressed with the numbers of smart, red-coated troops with their muskets that he saw in the handsome streets of the capital. Like every other magistrate, he had been on the lookout for suspicious characters or signs of sedition at Rathconan, but he couldn't honestly say that he'd found any—a pity really, as he'd have been glad to have something to bring himself to the attention of the authorities.

He hadn't learned anything particularly new in Dublin about the threat from overseas, but towards the end of his visit, he had gained one quite interesting piece of information. He'd been standing in a group of similar fellows around the Member of Parliament Fortunatus Walsh when he'd heard it.

"There's a growing feeling," Walsh had told them, "that something has to be done about our education of Catholics. The hedge schools are everywhere, as we all know, but our own Church of Ireland has made only the most pitiful attempts to challenge them. We've started Protestant Charter Schools for poor children in some parishes, but as we all know, they have attracted few pupils."

"The Catholic families won't send their children to them," someone remarked.

"Exactly. But there are some in the government who are recommending that a new method be tried. Take some promising young Catholic children from other areas, and place them, away from home, in the better Charter Schools."

"So they become Protestants?"

"That is the hope, certainly. I am not sure it would work, but the idea is to help the gradual spread of Protestantism that our penal system and our Church of Ireland have so far entirely failed to accomplish."

"An interesting idea," said Budge, not because he thought so, but so that Fortunatus would take note of him.

"Well, Mr. Budge," Walsh smiled, "if you have any candidates for such a project, you will find at least some at the Castle who will be grateful to you."

Budge had said nothing, but he had made further enquiries in Dublin, visited a school, and pondered the matter all the way back to Rathconan.

If he were to do such a thing, there was only one possible candidate.

"I'm thinking of sending young Conall Smith," he had told O'Toole. "And," he had given the schoolmaster a careful look, "I shall be expecting your support."

"But . . ." O'Toole was about to say, "He's my best pupil," then remembered that this would be admitting the existence of the hedge school. "Why would I support such a thing?"

"You know very well that he's practically an orphan. His father's not fit to look after him."

"But he's still his father. And he has family besides."

"The Brennans? Fit guardians for a boy of such intelligence?"

Since O'Toole's opinion of the Brennans was, if anything, even lower than the landlord's, the schoolmaster found it difficult to say anything to this.

"But to force a boy away from his family and into a Protestant school at such a time," O'Toole said carefully, "would create bad feeling."

"Is that a threat?" Budge gazed at him evenly.

"It isn't. But I believe it's the truth," O'Toole said frankly.

"That is why," Budge answered with equal care, "I am counting upon your support. Your word carries influence here. As much as if you were the priest."

It was a curious fact that in villages all over Ireland, the Protestant landlords often relied upon the Catholic priests to help them keep order. Not that the priests were happy about it. If they were unlicensed, however, the landlords could always have them expelled; and even if they were entirely legal, any sedition or trouble—which was never going to do their parishioners any good anyway—could always be imputed to their influence and lay them open to prosecution. By and large, therefore, the priests encouraged their flocks to stay out of trouble.

Up in Rathconan, where the nearest priest lived some miles away, O'Toole, as the most educated man, had a similar influence. His own religious convictions were not strong, but he dutifully taught his pupils their catechism and gave them a good grounding in the Catholic religion. The priest would soon have made life difficult for him if he didn't.

"And the penalties for teaching a hedge school," Budge added, "as we both know, are severe."

There was the threat, delivered quietly, well understood.

If the hedge schools were everywhere, they were still illegal; and if the magistrate chose to find the hedge school and prosecute the master, O'Toole could be in serious trouble. In theory, he could even be transported to the American colonies.

"Are you decided upon this?" O'Toole asked.

"No. But I am thinking about it."

In fact, Budge was still uncertain. Did his conscience trouble him about taking the boy from his father? He wasn't sure that it did. He hesitated to cause bad feeling in the area at such an uncertain time politically—O'Toole was right to warn him about that. And while he had no doubt that the Smith boy, of whose talents he was aware, would be welcomed as a promising pupil, he also had another minor concern. What if the boy, bright though he was, should turn out badly like his father? That would reflect poorly upon himself. He meant to weigh the matter for a few more days before he finally decided.

"My conscience troubles me," the schoolmaster said quietly.

"It shouldn't. I am right, you know."

"I am troubled, but not for the reason you think."

Now what, the landlord wondered, did he mean by that?

As he strolled towards Garret Smith's small dwelling, he passed several others. They were all mostly the same—low, stone-built cabins with turf roofs. Some had only two rooms, one of which was often shared with the livestock; but most of the inhabitants of Rathconan had a low-ceilinged room with a fire and some wooden furniture—a table, benches, and stools—together with one or two other rooms. Some even had a bed, though nobody would have thought twice about sleeping on straw. Their fires, in which they burned wood or turf, sometimes had a rudimentary chimney, but usually, the rooms filled with smoke until it escaped under the eaves. To the eyes of English visitors, these low and narrow shacks seemed to be filthy and degraded—although they observed that the women and barefooted children who emerged from them were surprisingly clean. But they would have observed more accurately had they realised that the conditions before them were simply those which had been prevalent in much of Europe through the Middle Ages. To Budge, the dwellings didn't look especially mean. He knew places a lot worse.

He passed the house of Dermot O'Byrne. God knows how many O'Byrnes there were in the Wicklow region, but he felt sure that even if he met them all, he'd still like Dermot the least.

For a start, he never paid his rent.

It was not unusual in Ireland for rents to go unpaid. The fault lay mainly with the English settler landlords who had continued to demand rents that were far too high. To keep what they could of their native land, the Irish would agree to pay and then inevitably fall short. Some landlords blamed the primitive agricultural methods of the island. Down in Dublin, some well-meaning gentlemen had formed a society to raise Irish standards to those of England, where, it was true, farms had recently become far more productive. Budge had heard of some interesting experiments with new crop rotations up in County Meath. But the basic problem stemmed from the settlers' original fear and greed, and they had no one but themselves to blame.

Up here at Rathconan, however, the situation was different. "My grandfather Barnaby," his father had told him, "undoubtedly demanded rents that were too high. But I've lowered them all, and you'll find our tenants mostly pay." Not Dermot O'Byrne, though. He would promise anything, with expressions of loyal emotion so fulsome and insincere as to be insulting. Excuses would follow, and finally, long overdue and delivered grudgingly, just enough of the rent to keep Budge from throwing him off the land. "The truth is," his father had once remarked, "he doesn't think he should be paying us anything at all."

Robert Budge sighed. He would never like Dermot O'Byrne.

And now there was Garret Smith's house, just ahead of him.

If his ancestor Barnaby Budge had considered the Irish slow and unreliable—if many gentlemen in London believed that now—the Budges had been in Ireland far too many generations to hold such foolish notions themselves. If an Irish craftsman said he would come to work on the door of your house, you did not necessarily ask him to name the day. He would come upon a day that seemed good to him, but he would come, and the work would be well done.

So when Robert Budge had agreed with Garret Smith that the latter would make him a new front door to his house—which was demonstrably in need of it—and when Smith had taken careful measurements and stated that he would return with the door, and fit the same, Budge expected after six weeks that the work would be in progress. When he had gently reminded Smith of this, the latter had agreed, and assured him that he'd have it soon. Another six weeks later, another reminder had been given. Thereafter, plain questions. "Where's my door?" Six months had now passed, and Budge had had enough.

He arrived at the house.

÷

It was a pity that, there being no particular work to occupy them that afternoon, two of Rathconan's older inhabitants should have come to join Garret Smith and that, early though it was, all three of them had been drinking for some time—Garret Smith more than the others. They were sitting at the single table in his cottage.

As he quite often did when the drink began to hit him, Smith had reverted to the subject of the Jacobite cause and had given it as his opinion that if, as the government seemed to fear, the French came, and Bonnie Prince Charlie raised an army of Scots, Ireland might see a return of the Stuarts and of Catholicism before the year was out.

"So you say." Fergal Brennan had heard all this before. He had been impressed by the education and the fervent politics of the young man who had married his little sister twenty years ago, but the years had passed and nothing much had come of Smith and his fine words.

Dermot O'Byrne, however, nodded in agreement.

"And when that day comes," he said darkly, "it will be myself back in Rathconan, where I've the right to be, and Budge with his throat slit."

Fergal Brennan sighed. In a century and a half, the resentment of Dermot's branch of the huge O'Byrne family against the ruling chiefs at Rathconan had never abated. They still believed, in some way, this inheritance should have been their own. With Dermot, it was an article of faith. But it irritated Fergal that because of this nonsense O'Byrne seemed to imagine he was superior to the Brennans.

"The O'Byrnes of Rathconan flew away with the Wild Geese," he said quietly. "It's they who'll be lords here, if they ever return. It's he," he indicated Garret Smith, "who has more of a right to it than you." It was not much spoken of, but perfectly known in the village, that the forbears of Garret Smith had briefly owned Rathconan—and also that, albeit illegitimately, the blood of the O'Byrne chiefs flowed in their veins. "His family paid for it with good money, too," he added mischievously, "which wouldn't have been the case with your family, I believe."

"It was stolen from us. That's the truth of it, whether you like it or not," Dermot O'Byrne said grumpily, and took another drink.

And here this foolish conversation might have ended, as the three men drank on in silence. Several minutes passed before Garret Smith, who in an attitude he often adopted when a little heavy with drink, was bent forward, leaning his ribs against the table and staring down at it, suddenly gave a small laugh.

"What's that?" asked Brennan.

"I was only thinking of the absurdity of the thing," answered Smith, and shook his head with amusement. "I looked into O'Byrne's claim once, you know. Years ago. There's not a shred of a case he can make in either English or Irish law. His ancestors were passed over because they were worthless. And the O'Byrnes of Rathconan had a perfectly valid English charter for their land."

Dermot O'Byrne glanced at him, then spat on the floor.

But Garret wasn't done. There were times, when he was somewhat drunk, when the arrogance of his youth would still return to him. At this moment, though his tousled hair was grey and his face mottled with drink, he still resembled the self-absorbed young man who had gone to Quilca.

"So I just find it funny to hear two ignorant peasants arguing over whether one of them should be lord of Rathconan."

And now Brennan and O'Byrne looked at each other.

If Garret Smith was not entirely liked by his neighbours, it was not just on account of his unreliability and his drinking. It sometimes seemed to them that there was a pride in him that was unpleasing. Because of his learning, which was far less than O'Toole's anyway, he appeared to think he was better than they.

A silence followed this last statement, therefore, while the two men pondered.

It was Brennan who finally spoke.

"We were not so delighted, Garret, when you married my sister." He paused to let this sink in. "You seemed to have a great opinion of yourself. But we were not delighted. For it's certain that you did little enough to provide for my sister once you'd married her, God rest her soul."

"It's true, Garret." O'Byrne saw the chance now to take his own revenge. "You were never a worker. Nothing you do is ever finished. It's a wonder to me you can pay the schoolmaster what's owed."

"Not that he always does," muttered Brennan. "He has only the one son at home, and he takes no care of him at all. You'd think the boy meant nothing to him, the way he drinks and does no work."

And now he had struck home. He saw Garret, in his half-slumped position, wince as though he had been hit in the stomach. Brennan didn't care. So much the better, he thought. He half expected an outburst—for Garret could lose his temper sometimes—or a cutting remark. God knows the man had a cutting tongue when he wanted. But there was nothing.

Garret reached for his drink in silence. Whatever he was thinking, he was keeping it to himself. His head hung a little lower.
His shoulders hunched.

There was a knock at the door.

If he heard it, which he must have, Garret Smith didn't move.
The knock was repeated, louder, more peremptory.

"Garret Smith."

Budge's voice. Brennan and O'Byrne glanced at each other.
Why would he be calling? Brennan picked up the beakers and
the bottle and placed them discreetly in a corner. It looked better that way, he considered. O'Byrne, however much he despised
the landlord, also straightened up. Garret remained as he was.

"Better let him in," said O'Byrne, and went to the door.

"Is Garret there?" Budge's voice again.

"He is, Your Honour. Come in and welcome," said O'Byrne
with a warning look back at Garret, who still hadn't moved.

Budge bent his head and stepped through the low doorway
into the room. He stared towards Garret, who didn't look up at
him. Under normal circumstances, Budge would have asked
Garret to speak with him alone, but the apparent rudeness of
Garret's manner annoyed him. He began politely enough all the
same.

"I came to ask about the door, Garret. Do you have it for
me?"

He noticed the other two men exchange glances.

"I do not." Garret's voice seemed a little slurred. He was
still staring down at the table.

"It's been six months." Budge's voice was one of reasonable
complaint rather than anger. Again, he saw the two other men
look at each other. They appeared to be enjoying Smith's dis-
comfort. "You must be nearly finished by now."

"You are assuming," Smith said, thickly but calmly, "that I
have started."

"Started?" This was too much. "Good God, man, what are
you thinking of?"

"These gentlemen will tell you," Garret said coolly, "that I never finish anything."

"You mean you have deliberately kept me waiting this half year with not the least intention of completing the work?" Budge was becoming heated. "Is that what you mean?"

"To tell you the truth," Garret answered, "I cannot now recall whether I intended to finish it or not." Budge stared at him. There being no way that he could possibly guess at the secret anger, self-loathing, and despair that lay behind these words in the soul of Garret Smith, he could only think that the man was either drunk, mad, or, for reasons beyond his understanding, deliberately trying to provoke him. Well, the reasons didn't matter. He wasn't going to stand for it.

"You are a useless and a worthless man, Garret Smith," he shouted. "Is this an example to set your son?"

He could not know that he had just probed the same distressful nerve again. But now, stung twice, Garret suddenly leaped up.

"The only lesson my son needs now, damn you," he cried, "is how to fire a musket for the French when they come!"

Budge became very still.

"I see," he said. Then he turned upon his heel and, stooping quickly, went out the cottage door.

Inside, all three men remained silent. Then Brennan spoke.

"Jaysus, Mary, and Joseph," he said in shock and awe. "Whatever made you say that?"

÷

It was two days later that O'Toole watched Budge take Conall Smith away. It was only his assurances that Garret had been drunk when he spoke that had prevented Budge arresting Smith as a dangerous person and sending him in chains down to the garrison in Wicklow. The boy's fate had been sealed entirely. "You can choose," Budge had told Garret firmly. "The boy goes to Dublin or you go to Wicklow."

"He is not a fit person to bring up the boy, anyway," the landlord had announced so that several of the villagers had heard it. Whatever they thought of the landlord and his Protestant school, there were not a few of Garret's enemies who were glad to say, "He brought it on himself."

And on the boy, thought O'Toole. For in their different ways, it seemed to him, both he and Garret Smith had betrayed the boy. Garret by his drunken carelessness. And he himself? What else could he have done?

He answered that question by asking another. What if it had been Deirdre, rather than Conall, who was threatened? Wouldn't he have found a way to protect her? Relations elsewhere to whom she might quickly have been sent? Indeed, knowing what he did, he hadn't even warned Garret Smith of the danger.

And why? That was where his conscience troubled him. He knew very well.

Deirdre. She loved Conall. How could she fail to love him? There wasn't another boy in Rathconan, or in the whole area, like Conall. The boy was princely, magical. But also the son of drunken Garret Smith and the Brennan slut. Bad blood. He feared it. He'd seen such things before—a brilliant early promise followed by a disastrous manhood. No, he did not want his little Deirdre growing any closer to young Conall and one day—he could see it all too well—becoming his partner for life. He did not want it. He'd sacrificed the boy. It had to be done.

"It will all work out for the best," he'd told Conall when the boy came to bid him farewell. "Trust me that it will be so." A lie. "You'll only be in Dublin, you know, and be back to see us often." Two more.

And now, dear God, he was witnessing the boy depart. And suddenly Conall looked younger, and he was crying out like a little boy, clinging to his father, with Garret himself looking like a man before the gallows, so pale and in despair—worse than death, for certain, worse than death—and little

Conall was crying out, "Don't take me from my da, I want my da." But the men were pulling him away, dragging him to the cart that was to carry him to Dublin, placing him in it and holding him there while he turned round, his green eyes wide and streaming tears, looking pleadingly at his father, who could only stand there, stone cold sober, watching him like a dead man.

Then they flicked the pony with a little whip and the cart went down the track.

It was as the cart began to move that Deirdre stepped away from her grandfather's side. He'd been holding her hand, but as the cart started, she slipped her hand from his and walked alone, quite slowly, down the track behind the cart. At the first bend, there was rock beside the track, and she stood upon it, watching the cart's slow progress down the valley, standing very still, never taking her eyes off it, but watching, as it wound slowly away, until it was out of sight.

But even then, the little girl with her long dark hair stayed where she was, moving not at all, staring into the distance, and the great mountain silence, and the nothingness that was her future. And she remained there, as if she, too, had turned to stone, for over an hour.

GRATTAN

⚛ 1771 ⚛

O H , I T W O U L D B E a grand evening, an evening to
remember. The whole family was coming—brother,
children, grandchildren, cousins.

"It gives me great joy," old Fortunatus said to his wife,
"that during all my eighty years and more, our family has lived
without any discord. And," he added contentedly, "I've every
reason to hope this will continue for another eighty years."

They were coming to see him and his wife, of course. But
Fortunatus had also arranged a guest of honour—a personage
of such singular interest and fascination that they were all agog
to meet him—and who, with a proper sense of the dramatic,
he had asked to arrive an hour after the rest of the party. "He
will make, you may be sure, a remarkable entrance," he told his
wife with relish.

But even more exciting, to Fortunatus himself, was the
news of another addition to the party—news that had only
reached him at midday—and which caused the dear old man
more joy and anticipation than he thought it proper to express.
Hercules was back. "George and Georgiana will bring him. He

will be here with all the others. They will all be together," he allowed himself to say. "That is what pleases me so much."

And now the guests were arriving.

After mounting the dozen broad steps to the front door of the house on St. Stephen's Green, the visitor entered a stone-flagged lobby with a fireplace. Here Fortunatus, dressed in a gold-braided coat as red as his face, breeches and silk stockings that still showed a manly calf, silver-buckled shoes, and his best powdered wig, affably greeted his guests in turn.

First came his brother Terence, slimmer than Fortunatus, his face less florid, with his children and grandchildren. His first wife having died, Terence had married again when well into middle age, a widow from a Catholic family, and to everyone's surprise had produced another son, a delightful young man named Patrick, of whom Fortunatus would happily exclaim: "Mark my words, that boy will go far." The two brothers greeted each other with warm affection.

Soon after came the Doyles. If Fortunatus had spent years moving his family up the social world, now in his old age, he had relaxed. He was genial, even sentimental. And the fact that his kinsmen the Doyles, though rich enough to set up as gentlemen, had chosen to remain stolid Dublin merchants, with no trace of *bon ton*, was no reason to forget them when the extended family gathered. He was only sorry that his formidable cousin Barbara, dead seven years now, was no longer there to terrorize everyone. But here was her son, the boy he remembered her bringing to his house almost fifty years ago, a dark, rather taciturn man with grandchildren of his own, showing in the politeness of his greeting that he appreciated Walsh's kindness in asking not only himself but all his family to the house.

His granddaughter Eliza arrived next—George and Georgiana's eldest girl—along with her husband. He was one of the Fitzgeralds—another brilliant match that had raised the family's social status even further. He had Georgiana to thank for that. And Fitzgerald was a very decent fellow, too. He welcomed them gladly.

Then two of his own daughters and their families. Well, he saw them often enough, thanks be to God.

But where were George and Georgiana? And Hercules? Ah. He saw their carriage drawing up outside. Without knowing he did so, he pulled in his stomach and stood a little straighter. The past, wishing to make a good impression on the future. The footman was opening the door; the butler was bowing, more deeply that he had before. George and Georgiana came in first.

Lord and Lady Mountwalsh were a very handsome couple. Everything about them was handsome. The fine Palladian mansion they had built at Mount Walsh, their Wexford estate, was handsome. The big town house they had recently acquired in the nearby development of Merrion Square was handsome. Their fortune was more than handsome.

For when not only sickly Lydia had died, very properly as she was supposed to, but also Anna, quite unexpectedly, had succumbed to a fever just before she was supposed to be married, Georgiana had been left the sole heiress of her father Henry's fortune. And when Henry had quietly passed from life ten years ago, George had remarked to his father: "We've so much money that I scarcely know what to do with it."

He need not have worried. In no time at all, a host of charming people appeared—architects and artists, cabinet-makers, rug sellers, silversmiths, antique dealers, horse deal-ers—every kind of huckster. Even a philosopher. "Don't worry," they assured him, "we'll show you." And making only a modest dent in his fortune, he patronised them all. Dear God, the man was loved.

Easygoing, nonpartisan—it had surprised no one when soon after building his Palladian country house, George had obliged the government enough to be raised to the peerage. And so, while old Fortunatus remained very contentedly in the Irish House of Commons, his son now sat as Lord Mountwalsh in the upper chamber, where, it was universally agreed, he was a handsome ornament.

A rustle of silk beside him: Georgiana, grey-haired but still in the full flower of mature womanhood. A soft look came into the old man's eye. She had brought his family not only a great fortune but beauty and kindness, too, and he quite openly adored her. She kissed him tenderly on the cheek. Her two younger daughters he also greeted affectionately. But now came the moment. Here came the man.

"Hercules, my boy. Welcome indeed." The Honourable Hercules Walsh: heir to all the family's wealth and growing power, who had just stepped off a boat from England that very morning. Their hope for the future.

By God, the boy was good-looking. No doubt about it.

He was only twenty-two—they'd celebrated his majority down at Mount Walsh the year before—but he might have been a year or two older. He'd graduated from Trinity College, in Dublin, and was now at the Inns of Court in London. Not that he needed to follow any profession, of course, but these were useful parts of the education of an aristocrat with estates and a fortune to manage, and who would probably enter public life. He had a rather square, well-cut, manly face, which might have belonged to a young Roman general. His hair was light brown, thick, and grew forward, ending in curls. His eyes, set wide apart, were brown and even. He was quiet, though polite when he answered your questions; he smiled only when it was necessary, and he did not often seem to think it was. Clearly he thought it was now, for he smiled as well as making the old man and his wife a polite bow.

"Grandfather. Grandmother."

But already his grandfather had turned his face towards the inner hall.

"Patrick! Patrick!" Old Fortunatus called. "Bring Patrick here. Ah, here he is." The young man appeared, accompanied by his father. "Stand beside your cousin, Pat, so that I can look at you both together. There now. Did you ever see a more handsome pair?" he cried delightedly.

Though closely related, the son of Terence and the grandson of Fortunatus were an interesting contrast. In the great minuet of the genes, it seemed that, when each was formed, different music had played and different partners been selected. Patrick, though about the same height as Hercules, was of a thinner build entirely. His face was finer, and suggested a clever lawyer or a doctor, a man of ideas. His eyes were lustrous. When in genial company, he had a delightful, boyish charm. When listening to a serious conversation, he would incline his head, slightly tilted, towards the speaker, with a concentrated but kindly expression.

As Patrick stood beside his cousin Hercules, who had given him a brief nod, it did not escape Fortunatus that a tiny cloud had passed across his nephew's face. It would be understandable, of course, if young Patrick, the son of a Catholic doctor of comfortable but modest means, should feel a little constrained beside his Protestant cousin, whose resources must be a thousand times his own. But generations of family loyalty weren't to be troubled by such considerations.

"How I wish," Fortunatus exclaimed happily, "that our dear father could be here to see this, eh, Terence?" He turned to the young men. "When our father Donatus decided I should be brought up in the Church of Ireland and Terence remain in the Catholic faith of our family, he intended that one branch should always protect the other. He himself, let it be remembered, stayed a good Catholic until his dying day, God rest his soul. And in time it will be your turn to maintain that tradition, Hercules, as I know that you will. Let me see you shake hands now. There. That's it. Bravo." He looked round them all, beamed, then linked his arm in his brother's. "Come along, Terence, let's drink a bumper of claret." And the brothers went together towards the parlour, followed by the two young men. Hercules did not smile.

Georgiana watched it all. She liked Patrick. As for her relationship with old Fortunatus, her husband had cheerfully remarked, many years ago, "My father's quite in love with you," to which she had sweetly replied, "I know, my dear," and, giving his arm a friendly tap with her fan, "so just remember that you have a rival." The old gentleman himself, while freely admitting his affection, also had a more calculated assessment. "I love my son," he told his wife, "but Georgiana's got the brains."

Time had been kind to Georgiana. Her hair was grey, but the fashion for powdered hair and wigs was convenient for the middle-aged. Her face was not much lined, and those lines she had only made her more attractive. If her eyes were worldly, they were also quizzical, and seemed, upon occasion, to contain a wonderful light.

For if there was one thing Georgiana enjoyed, it was making people happy. And as a rich woman, with a husband in the Lords and houses where she could entertain, she had ample scope to do so. Her *demarches* were quite disinterested. A marriage to be arranged, a family quarrel to be adjusted, a job to be found for a nice man in difficulties: Georgiana's genius and kindness were a byword.

In recent years, her services had been particularly in demand. For decades, almost since the great days of the Duke of Devonshire, the Lords Lieutenant had usually held office only for short periods, and came to Dublin only for the parliamentary sessions. Irish rule, and therefore patronage, had been in the hands of their deputies in the Castle, and the great parliamentary managers like the Ponsonbys and Boyles. But finally, the London government had concluded, "We're spending a fortune on the Ponsonbys and their friends," and had sent over a clever aristocrat, Lord Townshend, to see if he could sort things out. In his fourth year in Ireland now, Townshend had quietly broken the grip of the old cliques. Patronage came through the Lord Lieutenant himself once more, and the favours became fewer. "It's English interference," cried the furious Ponsonbys. "Ireland is being subverted." And not a few agreed with them. But the change of regime never troubled Georgiana in the least. She soon became Lord Townshend's friend. And as Lord and

Lady Mountwalsh were so comfortably apart from political faction, and Georgiana only asked favours for people who needed help, it was amazing what she could get away with.

"How the devil do you do it?" her husband had asked.

"Quite simple," she answered. "Townshend prides himself on being rather honest, so I ask things out of kindness, and offer nothing in return."

Once, when relations with France were especially bad, she even persuaded him to release a young Frenchman who'd been detained, because, she blithely told the great man, his fiancée in France would be worried about him.

"Can this do you, or me, the slightest good?" Townshend had enquired with some amusement.

"None at all that I can see," she'd answered.

And if, once or twice, the Lord Lieutenant had secretly asked her to help him out of a difficulty, and she had gladly done so, not a soul in Dublin ever came to hear of it.

So now, as she watched young Patrick with Fortunatus, it was natural for her to wonder what good turn she might be able to do the charming Catholic boy.

But not just yet. She had another mission to accomplish this evening.

Sometimes Georgiana worried about her son. He'd been named after a friend of her husband's, who'd been the boy's godfather. Yet his name seemed to have decided his character. He had done everything that was expected of him, but he did it with a blunt, mechanical precision, like a general wiping out an inferior army, that was almost frightening. He played to win, and he took himself seriously. Too seriously. Perhaps it was her own Presbyterian ancestors coming out in him, she didn't know. But something had to be done.

The solution she'd come up with was simple enough. He needed a woman to take him out of himself. She didn't care whether it was a mistress or a wife, but if the latter, she'd have to be very carefully chosen. And just recently, she thought she'd found the very thing.

There was no greater family in all Ireland than the ancient house of Fitzgerald. Practically rulers of Ireland until the Tudors broke them, the mighty Fitzgerald Earls of Kildare were Irish princes in all but name. Two decades ago, in Dublin, it had been the Earl of Kildare who had led the development of the city into the Liffey marshland below St. Stephen's Green by laying out Kildare Street, and building beside it a splendid mansion, like a Palladian country house, which, since he had recently been given the even grander title of Duke of Leinster, was now called Leinster House.

The Leinster family was huge and extended. But a marriage into any part of it, for the Walsh family, was a final seal on their rise from the gentry into the aristocracy; and when their daughter Eliza had married one of the Fitzgeralds who was quite a close relation of the duke's, George and Georgiana had congratulated themselves and gone to the huge assemblies at Leinster House, as members of the family now, with joy in their hearts.

Young Fitzgerald had a sister. Not only was she therefore one of the Leinsters, but Georgiana happened to know that she was due to receive a large legacy from one of her aunts. She was doubly eligible, therefore. But this was only important, as far as Georgiana was concerned, to satisfy her son and her husband's family. Young Hercules had a fortune already. What mattered to her was the girl's character. She was clever, kindly, and full of humour. If anyone could turn her son into a relaxed and happy man, it might be this girl. True, that would be two of her children marrying a brother and sister, but that would not cause any more remark, in that day and age, than would the marriage of first cousins.

With the visit of Hercules, the gathering tonight provided the perfect opportunity to talk to Eliza about it. This was Georgiana's programme for the evening.

This, and one other thing. Everyone would be wanting to speak to the guest of honour when he arrived. But she had a particular reason for wishing to do so. For there was something she wanted to ask him. It concerned her family.

✢

Fortunatus was glad, having spent a very agreeable quarter of an hour with the various members of his family, to see Hercules standing alone. He wanted a private conversation with the young man.

The fact was that, excited though he was to see his grandson back from London, he did not really know him very well. It wasn't so surprising. When Hercules was a small child, his grandfather had always seen him with other children; then he had often been away on the estate down in Wexford. Nor had his grandparents seen much of him while he was at university in Dublin. But undergraduates are taken up with their own lives—Fortunatus knew that. And then the young man had been anxious to complete his education in London as soon as possible. Could it be, Fortunatus wondered, that Hercules was just a little too impatient?

"We were sorry not to see more of you, my dear boy," he began affably, "when you were up at Trinity. You made good friends and got into some scrapes there, I'm sure. Had to turn your cloak inside out a few times, eh? So tell me, how many windows did you break?"

So many of the young gentlemen at Trinity College were scions of important families that when they got up to drunken high jinks, as they often did, the authorities seldom did much about it. Since the sons of peers had to wear gold braid on their academic gowns, they would often discreetly turn them inside out before any window breaking began.

"If windows were broken, I don't remember anyone counting," Hercules quietly replied. In fact, although he had watched others do so from time to time, he had broken none himself.

"Ah, capital," said old Fortunatus approvingly. "That's the spirit. And London—you are enjoying that? Making friends? Going to plays and so forth?"

"Quite."

"What news of our friends the Sheridans?"

It had been one of the things with which his family had burdened Hercules on his going to London, this friendship with the talented Sheridan family. After a few years in Dublin, where Tom Sheridan had run the Smock Alley Theatre with brilliance, it had burned down and nearly ruined him. Taking a leaf out of old Doctor Sheridan's book, Tom had then gone to London, set himself up as an educationalist, and even persuaded King George to grant him a handsome pension to produce a pronouncing dictionary of spoken English, on which he was still working. His wife, meanwhile, had written a popular novel to bring in some extra money.

"The great Doctor Johnson says that Sheridan's dictionary will be a wretched thing," Hercules coolly related.

"Of course he does. He's making a dictionary of his own, and he's jealous," said Fortunatus loyally. "And Tom's son? Young Richard. About your age, isn't he?"

"Younger, I believe. They say he's already written a play." Something in Hercules's tone suggested that he did not really desire to have such theatrical and literary folk as family friends.

"His grandfather, Doctor Sheridan, was a man of great note, you know," Fortunatus observed gently. "Ancient family. Used to own most of County Cavan." He decided to change the subject. "Do you drink much?" he enquired.

"In moderation, Grandfather."

"Probably just as well," Fortunatus conceded. "You'll have noticed that half the gentlemen in Dublin suffer from the gout, which is no joke when you have it."

"In London, too."

"No doubt. My brother and I have always been spared, but I can't promise that the family is proof against it. Best to take a little care. Not," he added reasonably, "that a bottle or two of claret in the evening ever did harm to any man. You're drunk sometimes, though, I suppose?" He gave his grandson a slightly anxious look.

"It has been known."

"In politics," Fortunatus declared with a lifetime of experience, "a man who is never drunk will never be trusted."

"I shall bear that in mind."

"You know that in a few years, my seat in Parliament will be vacant. I shan't stand again, you may depend upon it."

Until recently, elections to the Irish House of Commons had been held only when the monarch died. It had suited the Members of Parliament well enough, since once in, they could stay in their seats without the trouble and expense of an election until they, or the monarch died; and it suited the government because, once they had persuaded or bribed a member to support them, there'd probably be no need to worry about that member's vote again for twenty or thirty years. But even in the grand old political stasis of eighteenth-century Dublin, things were changing. Elections were now to be held every eight years. In five years, assuming he lived so long, old Fortunatus's seat would be open to an election again.

"You'll take the seat then, I hope, my boy. It's a good thing for the family to be represented in both houses." He glanced at Hercules to make sure he was in agreement. "Good. You'll find," he went on, "that Parliament is very like a club. We may have different opinions, but party doesn't affect civility and friendship. We're all very congenial fellows. Otherwise," he gave his unsmiling grandson another quick glance, "it wouldn't do at all, you know." And then, quite firmly: "Not at all."

What was his grandson thinking? The young fellow seemed agreeable enough; so why did he feel a faint sense of disquiet? Did this determined-looking twenty-two-year-old understand the tradition to which he was heir? Surely he must. His mind returned to young Patrick. Yes, the Catholic question. That was important.

"There is talk, you know," Fortunatus continued, "of new legislation in the next session, to give the Catholics some property rights. Longer leases, at any rate. A sign of the times, Hercules. I shouldn't be surprised in a few years—not in my time, perhaps, but certainly yours—to see the Catholics of

Ireland with almost the same rights as Protestants. There's a growing feeling in the Commons, and in the Castle, too, that we're all better off with Catholic support."

This was not wishful thinking on the old man's part. The long peace of the Ascendancy had by no means taken away the old fear of Catholicism, but it had taken away its edge. There was a real sense of embarrassment in many quarters that decent gentlemen like Doctor Terence Walsh, or the solid Catholic merchants of the ports, should be treated so shabbily. Old Fortunatus smiled. "One day your cousin Patrick will take his place beside you, not just as your equal in the family, as of course he is, but in the public arena as well. That would have pleased my dear father greatly."

Hercules inclined his head politely.

"Well, you've listened to me long enough, I dare say," the old man concluded. "But I'm glad to see you friends with your cousin. Nothing can be more important than family, my boy." Then he left his grandson to enjoy himself.

A few minutes later, however, he was glad to see that Hercules and Patrick were speaking together.

Their conversation might not have been quite what he would have hoped. All Hercules wanted was a piece of information.

"Do you know a man named John MacGowan?"

"I may do. Why?"

"This one's recently joined a club I belong to. The Aldermen of Skinners' Alley. You may have heard of them."

"I see."

You had to hand it to Hercules—he never wasted any time. Within hours of arriving from London, he'd been out in Dublin and learned that there was to be a meeting of the Aldermen, a dining club dedicated to the memory of William of Orange, the very next day. Patrick knew of the club, of course: an unusual body, since all classes of society cheerfully mixed together at its meetings—so long as you were Protestant, of course.

"I thought the MacGowans were Catholic," said Hercules.

"I'm sure they would be, mostly."

"This one says he's Protestant."

Did young Patrick hesitate?

"There are so many of them," he replied after a moment. "It's quite possible that some of them could have turned Protestant."

"This one's a grocer. Do you know a John MacGowan who's a grocer?"

Patrick frowned.

"I believe I do. But there's a whole tribe of MacGowan grocers, you know, all cousins. If one of them says he's Protestant . . ." He shrugged. "I wouldn't try to stop him, if that's what you mean."

"Hmph," said Hercules, and turned away.

And he was still looking irritated a few moments later when his mother came up to him.

"Did you enjoy your talk with your grandfather?" she asked.

"He thinks I should help the Catholics. Give them the same rights that we have."

"And will you do so?"

Hercules shrugged.

"Why give up an advantage?"

To this, Georgiana didn't reply.

"Come and talk to your sister Eliza," she said instead.

✣

The honoured guest arrived at the appointed hour precisely. Fortunatus ushered him into the big parlour where all the family were waiting. As he entered, everyone fell silent. Georgiana was standing beside Hercules. As the visitor came in, she observed him closely.

He was a curious figure. An elderly man in a brown, homespun coat. He wore stockings and buckled shoes, but no wig. Long wisps of white hair hung down from his large, bald pate.

On his nose sat a pair of half-spectacles, over which he looked benignly at the company. What a dear old man, she thought.

Mr. Benjamin Franklin was making his first visit to Ireland.

Fortunatus conducted him round the room, introducing each member of the family to him in turn, while the American shook hands or bowed his white head in the simplest and most pleasant manner imaginable. But Georgiana had seen enough of public men to notice that the kindly old eyes were also exceedingly sharp. And when he got to her, and the eyes lit up with an unmistakable gleam at the sight of her own gently swelling bodice, she smiled to herself and concluded: this clever old fellow is not as sweet and homespun as he pretends. But he's a first-rate actor.

"Mr. Franklin has already paid a visit to our House of Commons, where he was invited to sit as a member, during a debate, and where I had the honour of making his acquaintance," Fortunatus announced. "As to his purpose in visiting Ireland, I shall let him explain that himself in a little while."

For about a quarter of an hour, Franklin conversed with several of the party and gladly answered their questions. Yes, he was a member of the Philadelphia legislature. Indeed, he'd been born in Boston. He had returned from America to London upon his present business, but had resided in London for many years in the past and had the warmest affection for that city. After a little while, however, Fortunatus led him to one end of the room, from where he could address them all.

When the old American spoke, it was in a very simple and friendly manner. He had come to Ireland, he explained, because he believed that their own situation here was rather similar to the case in the American colony.

"We have our legislatures, as you have yours, but they are not given the powers which, as plain free men, we should think reasonable. We can adjust local matters, but all decisions of importance are made in London, by men we never see. Troops are quartered in our towns—by London. We are ruled by government officials who are chosen and paid—by London—so that we have no control over them. Our trade is restricted and ordered—by London. It is London that controls our currency. Contentious taxes are imposed—by London. Yet in the Parliament in London that so orders our lives and our livelihoods, we have no representation whatever. We are subjects of the king, yet we are treated as something less than subjects; we are free men, yet we are not free. I should therefore say that while most of those in the American colony are well affected, they are nonetheless seeking an amelioration of these conditions.

"My purpose in visiting London," he continued, "is to negotiate some concessions on these matters; and my hope is that if we in America and those desiring similar changes in the Irish Parliament were to act together, we might both stand in better hope of equitable treatment. For if the American colonists receive no satisfaction," he added seriously, "then I do not know what troubles may follow."

This speech was received with differing degrees of enthusiasm, but Fortunatus was nodding warmly.

"The party in our Irish Parliament which seeks changes of this kind—and I am often of their opinion—are rightly called the Patriots," he declared. "For while they are steadfast in their loyalty to the king, they have an equal love for their native land. You will find many friends in Ireland, Sir."

Lord Mountwalsh now gently intervened.

"Granted what my father has just said, is it not also true that you have been prepared to take actions, harmful to Britain, to make your point?" he enquired. "How do you justify this?"

"We refused to buy British goods, and won concessions on some unjust taxes thereby," Franklin answered. "Now we are importing British goods again. Was that justifiable? I think so."

"As a matter of fact," Fortunatus remarked, "that's exactly what Dean Swift told the Irish to do fifty years ago." He noticed as he said it that his grandson was frowning. "So, Hercules," he called out, "have you a question to ask Mr. Franklin?"

Though it was clear that Hercules would sooner not have

been asked, Fortunatus was glad that his grandson responded in a manly way.

"The government in London would deny that the American colonies are not represented," he said. "The king himself, and the men of the British Parliament, who have America's interest always in their hearts, are your representatives. How would you answer that?"

"The phrase they use is that, if we lack elected representatives in London, we have, through their kindness, a *virtual representation*," Franklin replied with a nod. "And a very pretty notion it is. But if we allow this, then let me make you a proposal." His old eyes twinkled. "If we accept this *virtual representation*, then instead of paying taxes ourselves, we will also allow the English to pay the taxes for us; and this we shall call *virtual taxation*."

This raised a general laugh, although not from Hercules.

"We have heard of the loyal intentions of the colony," he pursued, "yet at the same time, you hint that if your demands are not met, other troubles may follow. Do you mean rebellion?"

"God forbid," said Franklin firmly. But it did not seem from the young man's face that Hercules entirely believed him, and so, to avoid unpleasantness, Franklin went on smoothly: "I also have hopes that our position will be well understood in Ireland because of the extraordinarily close links between our peoples. You will all know of the huge communities of Ulster Presbyterians in America now. Yet for every five Presbyterians, I estimate that there are at least two Irish Catholics also—since they are free to practice their religion without disability in America." Here he glanced with a quick smile towards Terence Walsh and his family. "Taking these two together, it is an undoubted fact that one out of every two people in our entire American colony has come from this island. We look to you as our family, therefore." And he smiled at them all.

This remarkable information was greeted with some surprised murmurs.

"So if there's a rebellion there, it'll be an Irish one," Hercules muttered, but luckily no one except his mother heard him.

After this, the party broke into groups and people came up to Franklin, who chatted to them very amicably. Georgiana waited a little, then joined the great man while he was talking to Doyle.

"What surprised me most, I confess," the old American was saying, was the noble scale of your capital. Your Parliament building is finer than the London Parliament." The building that now housed the Parliament, designed early in the century by a young architect named Pearce, was indeed of a magnificence to rival the Roman Empire. "When I was in that great domed hall of your Commons, I might have supposed myself in the Pantheon, or Saint Peter's Rome. As for your broad streets . . ." Franklin was lost for words.

"We have a body called the Wide Streets Commission," Doyle informed him proudly, "whose aim is to make our thoroughfares and squares the most spacious in Europe. Have you seen our Rotunda Hospital? That's another fine building, and the first lying-in hospital, exclusively for women giving birth, in all the world, so they say." The merchant was always glad to point out the splendours of his native city; and Franklin was not the first visitor to be impressed by the growing magnificence of Georgian Dublin.

"But there is one other discovery I have made in this fair city," the Philadelphia man went on, "that has given me particular delight. And that is a most excellent beverage. It is brewed by a man named Guinness."

"Ah now," Doyle declared, "as to that, I can give you some particular information. For my late mother Barbara Doyle, a remarkable woman, was a friend of Guinness when he first began his business. And it was she who gave him the name for his brew."

"Indeed?"

"Well, so she claimed. And it would have been a brave man who contradicted her, I can tell you. Guinness came to her one day—this would be a dozen years ago, when he first began—and he says to her, 'I've a fine dark beer I want to sell, but the devil if I can think of a name for it.' And she says to him, 'Well, if you want to sell to the city fathers, you'd better make sure the name will please them. So I'll tell you what to call it.' And he did."

"Guinness Black Protestant Porter," said Georgiana with a laugh.

"Guinness Black Protestant Porter, the very same," echoed Doyle with satisfaction. "Though there's plenty that drink it without being Protestant, I may say."

The contemplation of the excellent brew brought the conversation to a momentary pause, and Georgiana used it to put her question.

"I wonder, Mr. Franklin, whether in Philadelphia you ever heard of some of my family. My uncle there was a man named Samuel Law."

She was almost ashamed of it, but in the nearly thirty years she'd been married, she had quite lost contact with her father's family. After the rift between her father and his brother John, the Ulster and Dublin branches of the family had never had any contact with each other. Her father had kept up a written correspondence with Samuel, and then his widow in Philadelphia, but she had never known much about this, and been too busy with her own family to pay much attention. So the truth was that she knew nothing about her cousins there, assuming that they still existed. "If I wanted to send a letter, I wouldn't even know who to write to," she confessed.

"But I remember Samuel Law the merchant very well," Franklin told her brightly. "And I know that he had brothers in Belfast and Dublin, for he told me so himself. They are an excellent family."

And he proceeded to give her a most encouraging account of the family—lawyers, doctors, worthy merchants, with good houses and some excellent farms in the region. "Judge Edward Law would be considered the head of the family at present, I should say."

"How I wish I could see them," she exclaimed. "How I should like Hercules to meet them also."

At this last idea, Franklin looked a little doubtful. But he gladly made a suggestion.

"I shall be sending a packet of letters to Philadelphia in a day or two, Lady Mountwalsh. If you care to write a letter to the judge, and give it to me, I can promise that it will be delivered to him in person."

It was an offer she accepted at once.

And when the party ended later that evening, and the guest of honour was escorted out, she agreed with all the rest of the family that it had been a great success.

✢

The meeting of the Aldermen of Skinners Alley was well attended. More than forty cheerful fellows gathered in the upstairs meeting room of the city inn. As usual, the company was mixed. There was a wig-maker, two apothecaries, sundry other craftsmen and merchants, half a dozen lawyers, the operator of the Dublin-to-Belfast stagecoach, some clerks from the castle, a couple of army officers, numerous gentlemen, and a sprinkling of aristocrats, including young Hercules.

It was a convivial gathering. The Aldermen had been meeting like this each month for over eighty years, ever since the Battle of the Boyne. The business was light. A few new members were proposed and seconded, the sole qualification being that the applicant was a good fellow—and a Protestant, of course. News was exchanged. Hercules soon made the acquaintance of John MacGowan, who turned out to be a pleasant enough man, tallish, about thirty, with a receding hairline and a humorous caste of mind. Within an hour the business, which included collecting the sixpenny subscription that would pay for tonight's supper, was completed and the real object of the evening could begin.

The feast: everything was done to form. In the centre of the long table stood the hallowed bust of King William, the

Protestant liberator. Down the middle of the table were numerous jugs: blue jugs for rum punch, white jugs for whisky punch, pewter jugs for porter—Guinness Black Protestant Porter, of course. As the members sat down and began to eat, a great platter of sheeps trotters was brought in, a reminder of how Catholic King James ran away from Dublin as King Billie approached. The talk was jolly. Only when the main meal was done could the profound business of the evening begin.

That deep business began with the entire company singing "God Save the King." After which the master of ceremonies, duly elected and given the office of Lord Mayor, solemnly rose and announced: "Gentlemen, I give you the Orange Toast." And then, to as near as you can get to a hush when forty jolly fellows have already eaten and drunk a good deal together, he intoned the following awe-inspiring invocation:

"The glorious, pious, and immortal memory of the great and good King William not forgetting Oliver Cromwell, who assisted in redeeming us from popery, slavery, arbitrary power, brass-money, and wooden shoes. May we never lack a Williamite to kick the arse of a Jacobite! And a fig for the *Bishop of Cork*! And he that won't drink this, whether he be priest, bishop, deacon, bellows-blower, gravedigger, or any other of the fraternity of the clergy, may a north wind blow him to the south, and a west wind blow him to the east! May he have a dark night, a lee shore, a rank storm, and a leaky vessel to carry him over the River Styx! May the dog Cerberus make a meal of his rump, and Pluto a snuff box of his skull; and may the devil jump down his throat with a red-hot harrow, with every pin tear out a gut, and blow him with a clean carcass to hell! *Amen!*"

The language of the toast said it all. Part Shakespearean English, part seventeenth-century sermon: it was Protestant, antipapist, half-pagan, triumphalist. It was serious, yet not to be taken too seriously—so long as the freedom-loving Protestants were comfortably in control, of course. It was Ascendancy Dublin.

"Amen!" they all cried. "Nine times nine!"

And now, for those with the head for it, the serious drinking of the evening could begin.

It was some way into this latter process that John MacGowan committed his indiscretion.

Hercules had his own way of dealing with long evenings of drinking. Firstly, he was blessed with a head like a rock. If he had to, he could outlast most men in a drinking session. Secondly, it was easy for him to keep a cool head, because he was secretly bored—as he always was when no useful business was being conducted. But thirdly, he had become practised at drinking less than he appeared to. In convivial company with his friends, therefore, he was less of a companion and more a cold observer than they usually realised.

During the meal, he had been sitting across the table and a few places down from John MacGowan, and had the opportunity to observe the grocer from time to time. At first, MacGowan had spent most of his time listening and smiling, perhaps a little uncertain of himself as a newcomer to the company. Hercules had noticed a few beads of sweat on the balding front of his head, and wondered whether they came from the heat or from nervousness. Gradually, however, he appeared to gain confidence. He started to chat, even to tell a joke or two, and these being well received by his neighbours, he perceptibly relaxed. He drank more; his face began to glow. From time to time, when not engaged in conversation, he looked down at the table and laughed to himself—though whether because he was a little drunk or enjoying some private joke concerning the proceedings, it was impossible to tell. When the elderly man on MacGowan's left, having drunk his fill, quietly departed, Hercules walked round the table and took his place beside the grocer.

MacGowan greeted him with a nod, though Hercules wasn't sure if the grocer remembered who he was. After a moment or two, he said to him casually:

"You're in the grocery trade, I think you said. Family business?"

"Indeed it is. Several generations now."

"You won't mind my saying, I hope, but MacGowan being a Catholic name, I should think the family might have been a little put out, with you being a Protestant, I mean."

MacGowan gave him a cautious glance, but Hercules smiled and returned a look of great sincerity.

"In fact," the grocer replied with a slow nod, "it must be said that it was a Protestant who saved my family. A remarkable woman, old Mrs. Doyle: but for her, my grandfather would have been ruined, instead of which he died a very prosperous man. The business is split between us now, but it's thanks to her that we have it." And he fell silent for a few moments. Hercules noticed that, as he cogitated, MacGowan half closed his left eye, while his right opened very large as he stared at the table.

Hercules took a blue jug and poured punch for them both.

"Let's drink to her," he said.

MacGowan grew quite friendly after this. He cracked a few jokes, at which Hercules laughed companionably, and poured him more punch. The grocer's face was growing quite red and there was a slight slur in his speech, but he kept going very gamely, with Hercules encouraging him in a friendly manner at his side.

"I wonder," Hercules ventured at last, "whether you ever came to know a Doctor Terence Walsh."

"Doctor Walsh?" The grocer's face lit up with pleasure. "Indeed I do. That's a very fine old man."

"I quite agree. I have the honour to be a kinsman of his myself."

"Ah, indeed?" From the slight look of confusion on MacGowan's flushed face, it was clear to Hercules that the grocer had rather forgotten who he was.

"You'll know his son, my cousin Patrick, then?"

"I do. I do." MacGowan was looking a little fuddled, but delighted.

"He told me all about your being here tonight." Hercules gave him a grin and a wink.

"He did?"

"He's my cousin. A very good fellow."

MacGowan gave him a confidential look.

"He told you about the bet?"

Hercules nodded.

"I wasn't clear if the bet was made with himself, though," he said.

"No, it wasn't. That was with two other fellows. But he came to hear of it. You don't think he'll tell anyone else, do you?"

"Never."

"He's a capital fellow."

"He is indeed." He dropped his voice. "For a Catholic to get in here like this . . . into the Orange Aldermen themselves. What a thing to do. How much will you get?"

"Two guineas for getting in at all. Two more if I'm undetected. Then another two if I can do it next month as well." He grinned. "So I've two guineas already."

Hercules laughed. Then he got up, walked round the table to the lord mayor, and told him that they had been infiltrated.

The next few minutes were interesting. There was no precedent for such a thing, and so while they held him on the bench, and delivered a few kicks and blows to his body to pass the time, the company had to come to a decision—which, as the lord mayor pointed out, might set a precedent—as to what to do with the Catholic grocer who had dared to violate the sanctity of the proceedings and witness their secret counsels in this manner. Some of those present were very angry indeed and argued that, since there was, unfortunately, no law which could sent him to the gallows where he clearly belonged, they should at least, as decent citizens, beat him within an inch of his life. Others, their judgement perhaps clouded by drink, argued that since it was done for a bet, the punishment for the fellow's crime, heinous though it was, might be somewhat mitigated. Hercules himself, having performed his proper service by exposing the crime, took no part in these discussions. In the end, the moderate council of the lord mayor prevailed, and they only dragged him over to the window and threw him out.

The drop onto the cobbled street was hardly more than a dozen feet, but MacGowan did not fall as well as he should have, and the landlord informed them later that he had broken a leg. But not badly: the surgeon had set it well enough. So that was the end of the matter.

᛭

At least, for the rest of the Aldermen. But not for Hercules. There was one other matter to be attended to.

The next day he went to see his cousin Patrick and asked to speak with him privately. The conversation did not take long.

"You knew about John MacGowan cheating his way into the Aldermen. But you didn't tell me."

"It was difficult. I'd given my word. The thing was only a foolish wager."

"You lied to me."

"Not exactly. I said nothing, really. I hear the poor fellow was hurt."

"You can make all the Catholic equivocations you please, but you lied."

"I resent that."

"Resent it all you like, you damned papist."

Patrick shrugged contemptuously.

"If we have to meet at family gatherings," Hercules continued coldly, "I shall be polite. I shall not offend Grandfather. But stay away from me. I never wish to see your face again."

And so it was, unknown to Fortunatus, that the friendship between the two branches of the Walsh family, planned by his father and cherished for eighty years, came to an end.

᛭

For Georgiana, the years that followed Ben Franklin's visit were busy ones.

She was delighted some months after writing to Philadelphia to receive a courteous letter back from Judge Edward Law. From the tone of his letter, she had the impression that the judge was rather tickled to have a relation with such a fine-sounding title. Not only did he give her news of her American cousins, but kindly included a family tree. He also gave her an interesting account of the mood in the American colonies, which indicated that, in his opinion, the disputes between the colonists and the English government would not easily be resolved.

A year later, when news reached Ireland of the Boston colonists' destruction of a valuable cargo of tea, another letter from the judge arrived.

Here in Philadelphia, the governor avoided a similar conflict by persuading the captain to take his cargo of tea back to England. But now that such a challenge has been made to London, I fear that legal retaliation will follow. And resorting to law, alas, can only make this conflict worse. I have written also to our cousins in Belfast.

This last sentence, she supposed, might be a gentle hint to her that, having gone to the trouble of reestablishing relations with the family in distant Philadelphia, it might be a kindness to do the same for her relations in nearby Belfast. In this case, she knew that her uncle John had had a son named Daniel, so she knew whom to write to. And indeed, if she asked herself why she had never done so, she had to confess that it was probably a fear that her Belfast relations, who were not at such a safe distance as the ones in Philadelphia, might embarrass her in some way. Having decided that this was small-minded, and having made sure that her kindly husband had no objection, she wrote a letter. But she received no reply.

The following year, old Fortunatus lost his wife, and Georgiana made a point of going round several times a week to keep the old man company. She would often find his brother Terence there, and it was heartwarming to see the two brothers sitting so contentedly together. Though he complained of nothing more than a stiff leg, it sometimes seemed to Georgiana that Doctor Walsh was not entirely well himself. Occasionally, he looked gaunt and tired. But he was obviously content to sit chatting with his brother all afternoon. And if she didn't find Terence, then she'd often encounter his son Patrick there instead. "It's good of the boy to come," Fortunatus would say, "when he has better things to do." Yet she had no doubt that Patrick enjoyed the old man's company.

Though his father had suggested he follow in the medical profession, Patrick had chosen the wine trade instead, and was working hard at it. The more she saw of Patrick, the better she liked him. He was clever, humorous, and kind. And he was not without ambition. "I hope to make my fortune if I can," he told her frankly. And when she asked if there was anything else he desired: "I could never change my faith, but if it were ever possible for a Catholic to do so, then I should like to enter Parliament."

Though that still seemed a far-off hope, Georgiana was glad that there were now some small, but encouraging developments for the Catholics of Ireland. The Pope had opened the door. Some years ago, after two centuries of opposition to England's heretic monarchs, the Pope had compromised, and King George III was now recognised by the Vatican as the legitimate sovereign of Britain. That made things easier. "And with all this trouble in the American colony," her husband told her, "the government wants to keep every section of the community as happy as possible." In Ireland, Catholics were excluded from every office, because the Oath of Allegiance was worded in such Protestant terms that no Catholic could possibly take it. "So we're going to try to find a way round it," her husband explained. The Protestant Bishop of Derry, working with some of the Catholic hierarchy, devised a new oath. Not all the Catholic bishops liked it, but others urged their flocks to take it. This might, after all, open the way to further things."

"Will you take it?" Georgiana asked Patrick.

"I shall, at once," he declared. And old Fortunatus was equally enthusiastic.

"This is what the family always stood for back in my father's and my grandfather's day: loyalty to their faith and loyalty to the king," he reminded them. "I still pray," he confessed to her after one of Patrick's visits, "that you may live to see the two branches of the family—Hercules and Patrick—both in the Parliament together."

Hercules would also go to see his grandfather from time to time, of course, but Georgiana noticed that if he came and found Patrick there, one or other of them would soon make a polite excuse and leave. Once, she asked Patrick if there was anything amiss between him and her son, but he dodged the question, replying: "We both love Uncle Fortunatus, you know." When she asked Hercules the same thing, he answered briefly: "He has his life; I have mine." And he refused to say anything more. So she did not pursue the matter. But I like him anyway, she thought, whether you do or not.

Her project to marry Hercules to the Fitzgerald girl had miserably failed. The girl herself, according to Eliza, found Hercules cold. His own assessment was blunt and final.

"She has too many opinions of her own, Mother, to be of any interest to me."

Georgiana sighed. No mother wants to think poorly of her son. She would continue to try.

Early in 1775, her husband had taken her to London for a month. It had been a most successful visit. They had gone to the Houses of Parliament, heard Pitt, Fox, and Burke, the greatest orators of the day, watched Lord North, the Prime Minister, apparently half asleep in the House of Lords. "Actually," a knowing friend informed them, "Lord North is a much cleverer fellow than he looks, but he holds the position more from a sense of duty than because he likes it." They also spoke to numerous politicians. In the course of this, Georgiana had gained a clearer insight into the mentality of the London government concerning the Catholics in Ireland. "The fact is, Lady Mountwalsh," a cynical government supporter informed her with a smile, "this new loyalty oath has been a deucedly good thing. On the one hand, the Catholic bishops don't agree with each other about it. So that splits the Catholics and lessens the chance of them giving us any trouble. But at the same time, it's encouraging Catholic recruits into the army. You see," he explained, "for years now, about one in twenty of the troops in the British army have been Irish. They were all supposed to take the Oath of Allegiance, of course, but if they were Catholic, we just forgot about it. Now, however, with their priests encouraging them to take the new oath, we're recruiting two or three times as many. If this trouble in the colonies turns into armed conflict—and we're damnably short of troops—we can send these Irish off to fight in America." He laughed. "So I'm all for Catholics at present, my lady."

She had been around politicians for decades and was no stranger to political calculation, but when she thought of old Fortunatus and of young Patrick's honest loyalty, and the hundreds of Catholic Irish she knew, she felt a sense of sadness and disgust at the Englishman's shallow calculation.

The real purpose of their visit, however, was for pleasure. She had seen the latest London fashions, bought some fine silks and shoes, while George had acquired three Italian paintings in the sale rooms. But perhaps most delightful of all was the night they went to the theatre to see the new romantic comedy that had just taken London by storm.

As well it might: for *The Rivals*, with its almost dreamlike plot, its lively characters like Sir Lucius O'Trigger, Sir Anthony Absolute, and the novel-reading Lydia Languish—not to mention the ineffable Mrs. Malaprop, who always uses the wrong word—was obviously destined to become a classic of the stage. Even Garrick, the great actor manager, had already declared it a masterpiece. And to think that the author was still only twenty-three!

Having roared with laughter and warmly applauded, it gave Lord and Lady Mountwalsh particular pleasure to go backstage afterwards to congratulate the handsome playwright himself, none other than young Richard, Tom Sheridan's son.

"You know how happy my father will be that the grandson of his old friend, the great Doctor Sheridan, should have succeeded so brilliantly here in London," George said warmly. "And will you forgive me if I say that some of your language is so delicious, so brilliant, that it could only have come from an Irishman."

Both these sentiments seemed to give young Sheridan enormous pleasure.

"I remember your father, when I was a boy in Dublin," he cried.

"You may have known our son Hercules, when he was here in London," Georgiana added.

"Ah yes," said Sheridan.

The spring passed quietly for Georgiana. Then came news from America that fighting had begun near Boston. Soon afterwards, she received another letter from Judge Edward Law in Philadelphia.

After some hesitation, I am now inclined to what we here call the Patriot cause. My estimation is that about one fifth of our people are patriots, favouring a complete separation from Britain; two fifths are loyal to the crown, though they want reform; and another two fifths are undecided, uninterested, or afraid to commit to anything. The slave-owners in the south fear anything that might lead to a slave revolt.

I know that our cousins in Ulster, like most of the Presbyterians there, entirely favour the patriot cause and would be glad to see America—and Ireland—independent from England. I wonder if you are for us or against us?

After reading the letter carefully, she thought it better not to reply just yet. When her husband asked her if it contained anything of interest, she answered, "Not really, George," and later locked it in her bureau.

A year later, the American Declaration of Independence had gone ringing round the world, four thousand troops had been despatched from Ireland to quell the colony, and news had come that dear old Mr. Franklin had gone to France to get military aid from Britain's oldest enemy. It was just as well, she supposed, that she had never replied.

In that same extraordinary year, a more mundane event came to occupy her attention closer to home.

Hercules had found a wife. The girl's parents, who owned a good estate in County Meath, had brought her to Dublin to find a husband, and there Hercules had wooed her and won her heart. Not that—given that she had come there expressly for that purpose and he was the heir to Lord Mountwalsh— this was a task requiring more than common sense. But he had done it, and she was exactly what he wanted.

Nobody could object to Kitty. She wasn't the kind of beauty that everyone remarked upon, but she looked very well at his side. She had the same upbringing and outlook as scores of other girls of her class, and being still only eighteen, she clearly looked to Hercules for guidance. Once, when Georgiana asked her what she thought of the American colony's actions, she looked at once to Hercules, who answered firmly for her:

"They are rebels, and they'll pay for their treason."

"Even old Benjamin Franklin?" she'd pursued.

"Franklin?" Kitty seemed uncertain who he was.

"That old devil, especially, should be hanged," said Hercules, at which Kitty looked relieved.

"So do you prefer the country or the town?" Georgiana had then asked the girl.

But even here, Kitty had glanced at Hercules.

"Depends on the season, doesn't it?" he had suggested to her genially.

"Yes. It depends on the season," she had replied firmly. And Hercules had given his mother such a look that she had asked no more questions.

And since his marriage seemed to improve his temper somewhat, Georgiana supposed she should be grateful.

That same year saw another milestone in her son's life: his election to Parliament.

An election in England or Ireland was always an interesting business. Not that there was much voting. Most of the seats were controlled by a small number of prominent citizens or by a few local landowners. The citizens would normally expect to receive something for their vote, in cash or help with their business; the landowners usually put in one of their family members, or a friend. And in all cases, naturally, the government would attempt to bribe the electors to choose a candidate who'd support the government line. In the case of the election of 1776, the government succeeded rather well.

"No less than eighteen new peerages are given out," George told Georgiana with a laugh. "At this rate, I fear we Irish peers will soon be common as tinkers."

As promised, old Fortunatus gave up his seat to his grandson Hercules, and the next generation of the Walsh family glided smoothly down to be launched into the waters of politics. But the weather over the sea ahead looked stormy.

The Parliament Fortunatus had left had consisted of factional interests that were loosely organised in an informal fashion. The group calling themselves Patriots, who desired more authority for the Irish Parliament, fluctuated in number, and even their leader, a fine speaker named Flood, had accepted government office not long ago. The Walsh family had chosen a moderate course. In the Lords, George Mountwalsh could usually be relied upon to support the government unless they proposed something egregious. Fortunatus, on the other hand, sitting in the Commons, had been sympathetic to the Patriot cause ever since the days of Dean Swift and the copper coin scandal. But he was a genial fellow, and the officials in the castle had always considered him a reasonable man whose vote might be solicited from time to time.

But now, suddenly, the American Revolution had bathed the world in a new and dangerous light. Out in the colony, the American Patriots—respectable landowners, lawyers, merchants, and farmers—had taken destiny into their own hands. "And what," those who similarly called themselves Patriots in Ireland might ask, "have we accomplished by comparison?" At the very least, they decided, they should stick together and use the situation to win some real concessions. Other members, however, who might have been sympathetic to their cause, now decided that, in such a crisis, it wasn't the time to rock the boat. As the new Parliament assembled, the government men were making clear, "If you're not with us, you're against us," and it looked as if the Patriots might be isolated.

It was a Parliament that might have been made for Hercules. All his natural instincts were called upon. He was like a hound that has scented its quarry. Within hours of his arrival, he had sought out the government's sternest supporters and let them know that, whatever his grandfather's views might have been, he was of their party. He was for order; the Patriots were for disorder; the Patriots should be destroyed. Such enthusiasm was rare in politics.

But the Patriots were not without friends. Soon after the election, Georgiana met Doyle, who told her:

"Let the government learn from what's happening in America, and treat the free men of Ireland better. We're all Patriots in this family," he declared, "and I hardly know a merchant in Dublin who isn't." In towns all over Ireland, the Protestant merchants and craftsmen were saying the same thing.

One day, on a visit to the Parliament building to see her son, Georgiana had been rather astonished to find him in earnest conversation with his cousin Patrick. After Patrick had gone, she had remarked to Hercules that she thought he didn't like Patrick.

"I detest him," her son replied, as if it were the most natural thing in the world, "but we are on the same side. At the moment, anyway." And later that day, Patrick had called round at her house and explained to her:

"I'm organising a loyal address from the Catholic tradesmen of Dublin—pledging our support for the government and our opposition to the American rebels." He saw her surprise and continued: "The Catholic community is doing the same in towns all over Ireland. If we want to increase our influence, this is the moment to show the government that it can trust us—the better sort amongst us, anyway." He smiled. "So Hercules and I may not be in harmony, but we're singing the same tune!"

But if the government was getting support from the more prosperous parts of the Catholic community, they had also gained a vigorous opponent they had surely never thought of.

Fortunatus Walsh. Well into his eighties, without a wife, without a seat in Parliament, yet with all his mental faculties, old Fortunatus after a lifetime of genial, cautious calculation had apparently decided he didn't care what anyone thought anymore. Was he just bored, or deeply persuaded of the rightness of the cause? Even Georgiana wasn't sure. But whatever the reason, he had no sooner quit the House of Commons than he became a passionate Patriot. Not only did he denounce the government and cheerfully declare that the American rebels were in the right, but he turned the house on St. Stephen's Green into a meeting place for any of the Patriot party who cared to come by.

Many people were surprised. Her husband George shook his head affectionately. Hercules, however, had not been amused at all. "I have told everyone," he informed her, "that my grandfather is in his dotage and has lost his wits."

Georgiana continued to call on Fortunatus often, and she thoroughly enjoyed it. The house was livelier than she had ever known it before. Radical broadsheets like *The Freeman's Journal* were scattered on the tables. A copy of Tom Paine's

Common Sense, advocating American independence, even arrived from the colony. The Doyles would often look in, and once they brought with them a radical Member of Parliament named Napper Tandy, who told her: "When we mobilise the trade guilds as well as our Patriots in Parliament, the castle will be surprised at what we can do." It sounded ominous, but she also found it rather exciting. Charles Sheridan, the playwright's elder brother, also put in the occasional appearance. He had just entered the Parliament on the Patriot side, and Fortunatus had made a point of seeking him out and bringing him round. Charles also gave her an interesting piece of news: "My brother Richard is quite determined to enter politics in England if he can make enough money by writing plays. If he succeeds, we shall have one Sheridan in the Dublin Parliament and another in Westminster."

On another day, Fortunatus introduced a delightful young lawyer who had recently entered the Commons. A gentleman, but without the two thousand pounds needed to purchase a constituency, he'd been given a seat by a Patriot peer. His name was Henry Grattan.

She liked young Grattan at once. He had a thin, clever face. "You look like a lawyer," she told him.

"I know," he said with a smile. "But I must confess that all the time I was in London and supposed to be studying the law, I was at Westminster in the gallery of the House of Commons listening to the great orators like Pitt, and Fox, and Edmund Burke. Ah, what men! I studied politics there, Lady Mountwalsh, and I hope I may succeed in it, for I fear I should make a terrible lawyer."

They spoke for some time, and as they did so, she noticed that as well as looking clever, there was a delightful, kindly light in his eye that she warmed to. "He reminds me of Patrick," she told Fortunatus afterwards.

She had wondered if Fortunatus might be disappointed that Patrick, so much a favourite, had taken a view so opposed to the Patriot cause. But if there was any doubt about the old man's mental faculties, he quickly dispelled it by his answer.

"No, my dear. The boy's quite right. The Catholics should demonstrate their loyalty and support the government. Leave the opposition to us." He gave her a shrewd look. "Remember, Georgiana, my father told us brothers to help each other by sitting on different sides of the fence."

"You're a cunning old fox," she said with approval.

But about his grandson Hercules, he seemed to feel rather differently. Once, walking round to call upon George and Georgiana at Merrion Square, and finding Hercules there, he gave him a cross look and remarked:

"Young Grattan made a damn fine speech the other day." Then adding with a sniff: "'Fraid yours wasn't much good, though." In answer, Hercules had made him a curt bow and withdrawn from the room, but not before his grandfather had remarked, so that he could not fail to hear: "No gift for speaking. None at all."

The next day, Hercules had warned her: "I think it's unwise for you to be seen at Grandfather's house. It could embarrass the family." A warning of which she had taken not the slightest notice.

It came as a shock to everyone, early in 1777, when Doctor Terence Walsh suddenly had a stroke and died on the spot. "He didn't suffer," Georgiana comforted Fortunatus. "I know, and I thank God he lived to see Patrick grow into such a fine young man," he replied sadly. "But I'd always hoped to go first." Half Dublin gathered for the funeral at the Catholic chapel, including several Church of Ireland clergymen; and it was certainly gratifying to see in what universal affection the doctor had been held. "I fear, however," Fortunatus remarked to her afterwards, "that he leaves no great fortune behind."

In the months that followed, she was glad to see that Patrick never failed to look in once or twice a week upon his uncle, and she would often time her own visits so that she might encounter him there. She hardly liked to admit it even to herself, but she felt more at home in his company nowadays than she did in that of her own son.

Hercules, meanwhile, was starting to make a name for himself. The American war was taking a toll. The government had forbade the Irish to trade with America anymore—to the fury of the Irish merchants. But the war was depressing all business anyway. In Ulster especially, the linen industry was hit, and there were many bankruptcies. The Patriots blamed everything upon the government, and young Grattan spoke so well that he was already their rising star. But the government loyalists struck back, and of all the denouncers of the Patriots, none was more virulent than Hercules Walsh. He might not have Grattan's genius, but in his blunt way he could make a point. And as far as he was concerned, the Patriots in the Parliament, the complaining tradesmen, and the Ulster Presbyterians who sympathised with America were all the same: traitors. When news came that Ben Franklin and his colleagues had succeeded in bringing France in to fight for America against Britain, his attacks became even more scathing. It was soon after one of his more insulting tirades that Georgiana received a letter from Ulster. It was signed: "Daniel Law."

> I did not reply when you wrote to me before, being uncertain what to say to you. Thanks to your government, the linen trade has been in such a desperate condition that, upon this day, the business of Law of Belfast will exist no more. Yet I read in the journal that, according to your son, I and those like me in Ulster, who still profess the honest and godly faith of our forefathers, are nothing better than traitors, and dogs to be chained up and muzzled.
>
> I write to you now, therefore, being certain at last what I should say to you is, that I have nothing to say to you; and that this correspondence between our families, which you have seen fit to reopen, should henceforth cease, forever.

She put the letter down with a sigh and a sense of failure. There was no use in writing. Whatever she said herself, Hercules would be sure to make another offensive speech again. She wondered if there was something she could do for them if, as seemed likely, they were in financial difficulties, but concluded that any offer would be curtly refused. She locked the letter in her bureau, therefore, with the one from Philadelphia, and she prayed for better times.

Soon afterwards, she was able to do a good turn for someone else, however.

She had been on her way from St. Stephen's Green towards the Parliament when, halfway along the gentle curve of Grafton Street, she saw young Patrick coming towards her in the company of a pleasant-looking fellow, a little taller than he, and who walked with a slight limp. She greeted Patrick and asked if he was not going to present his friend.

"Ah yes." His hesitation was only momentary. "This is Mr. John MacGowan. Lady Mountwalsh."

The taller man bowed politely and said that he was at her service; but she noticed that, at the mention of her name, the smile had died upon his face. Some people might have passed on and put the incident out of mind, but Georgiana could never quite restrain her curiosity. So, as politeness made the two men captive until she let them go, she engaged them in conversation. She soon learned that John MacGowan was a fellow Catholic with Patrick, and that his grocery business had expanded rapidly in the last seven years. "He's gone into salted provisions," Patrick informed her, "and though he's too modest to tell you so himself, there are only two merchants in Dublin who export more salted beef that he does. But I must tell you that, unlike me, he is no friend of the government," he added with a laugh.

If the government had been determined that the Irish should not trade with the rebellious Americans, now that France had joined the war, they had become obsessed with the idea that Irish merchants like MacGowan might supply the

French army and navy with the salted provisions that would be so important to them. New restrictions had therefore been made. And they had not been popular.

"You don't like the restrictions, I'm sure," she said with a smile.

"That is true, my lady," he said with a cautious glance at Patrick.

"It's all right, John." Patrick laughed. "You can say anything to Lady Mountwalsh. She hears far worse at my uncle's."

"The fact is, Lady Mountwalsh," the grocer confessed, "that I have had an antipathy for the Protestant rulers of Ireland ever since they threw me out of a window and broke my leg."

"Oh Mr. MacGowan, I am so sorry."

"In a way," he went on calmly, "I suppose I should be grateful. For besides leaving me with a limp, it made me so angry and so determined to succeed that I drove myself to expand the business. Had it not been for their cruelty, I'm sure I shouldn't be where I am now."

"I was thinking," Patrick said with a grin, "that I should take him round to Uncle Fortunatus—now that the Patriots are suddenly taking such an interest in us Catholics."

It had been the latest turn in the turbulent river of Irish politics, and it had been Grattan's idea.

If the Patriots still couldn't get a majority in Parliament, they could still pile on the pressure outside the chamber. They had most of the Protestant tradesmen. They had plenty of the smaller country gentry as well. For although the big landed interests might have concluded that this wasn't the time to rock the government's boat, there were plenty of lesser men and farmers who couldn't give a damn whether they rocked the boat or not. But there remained the largest group of all, four-fifths of the population of Ireland—the Catholics. Respectable fellows like Patrick might be proclaiming their loyalty—in the hope of better treatment in future, of course—but this in no way prevented the Patriots promising to do

more for them than the government would. "Free trade for
Ireland. Then amend those vicious old Penal Laws, that insult
every Catholic," he now demanded. Not all the Protestant
Patriots were sure about this, but Grattan had persuaded them
to go along. "It'll frighten the government," he could point
out. "It puts pressure on them to satisfy at least some of our
demands." Moral conviction, or cunning calculation? It was
hard to say. But it was powerful politics.

"I'll support the Patriots," said John MacGowan.

The next day, she questioned Patrick further about his friend.

"I didn't like to ask him, but how did he come to be
thrown out of a window?"

Patrick gave her a brief account of the affair, leaving a few
things out.

"I wonder he didn't prosecute them," she remarked.

"And have every Protestant merchant in Dublin his enemy
for the rest of his life? He was wiser to say nothing. His revenge
will be to finish up richer than most of them."

"But doesn't Hercules belong to that club? Did he take part
in this business?"

"He may have been there," Patrick conceded. "A lot of people were. But he had no part in throwing John out of the window," he added to reassure her. "None at all."

That evening, Georgiana told her husband about her
encounter with MacGowan. "I feel guilty about him, George,
even if Hercules didn't do it. I wish we could compensate him.
I'm sure his trade must have suffered recently," she added.
"Perhaps you could arrange something?"

"I agree about his physical injury," he replied. "His trade,
as it happens, may not have suffered. The American restrictions are unpopular, but the men in the provisions trade have
had such large orders from the British army and navy that
they've actually done quite well out of this war so far. I know
some of the salted-provisions men down in Cork have been
making fortunes." He smiled. "All right. I'll speak to some of
those fellows at the Castle and see what can be done."

The following month, John MacGowan received a large contract for supplying the British army with salted beef. Some time later, seeing Georgiana in the street, he came up to her and made a bow.

"I am well aware, Lady Mountwalsh, whom I have to thank for that contract."

"Do you feel any better about us?" she enquired.

"No. But I feel richer," he replied with a smile.

She didn't tell Hercules.

"Patrick and his friend MacGowan may receive some satisfaction sooner than they think," George told her a little while afterwards.

Grattan's tactics had been working. The London government was becoming increasingly nervous. The war with the American colony was turning into a wider conflict, trade was suffering, troops needed to be raised: the last thing they needed was any more internal disorder. If Grattan was whipping up the Catholics, then it was time to make some concessions.

"They don't want it to look as if they're caving in to the Irish Patriots," George explained. "Since the Penal Laws are similar in all three countries, they mean to make a general bill at Westminster for England and Scotland first, then extend it to Ireland as well." But some time later, he came home one evening, shaking his head. "The English and Scottish proposals are dropped," he informed her.

"Have the English parliament men such a hatred for Catholics?" she asked.

"No. It's the ordinary people of England and Scotland. They're shouting 'No popery.' There has been rioting in the streets." The Irish legislation was still to go forward, however. "Burke believes he can get a modest Irish measure through the London Parliament, and I dare say we can do the same here in Dublin."

So it proved. In the summer of 1778, the Catholic Relief Act passed through both parliaments, but with opposition. In Dublin, despite the fact that it had government support, there were still many loyal Protestants who refused to follow their usual lead, including Hercules Walsh. The relief the Act gave was limited but deeply symbolic, for in an age when land was everything, it allowed an Irish Catholic, for all practical purposes, to purchase land of all kinds and bequeath it to his heirs. Fortunatus and Georgiana went with Patrick and the rest of Terence's family to watch it pass through the Irish House of Commons, where Grattan and the Patriots greeted the final vote with a great cheer.

The following evening, Fortunatus held a party at his house. Many of the Patriots came, including Grattan; George and Georgiana, though not Hercules; Terence's family were all there and, a kindly thought, Terence's old parish priest had been invited. Patrick had brought John MacGowan with him.

Georgiana had never seen the old man so excited. His face was flushed, his eyes were shining brightly, and he drank not a few bumpers of claret. He made a short, enthusiastic speech, to which Grattan made an elegant reply. And again and again, he would come over to wherever Patrick was standing and, putting his hand fondly on his shoulder, declare: "This is the beginning, my boy. This is what my dear father would have wanted." It was, he told them all as they left, one of the happiest nights of his life.

Looking back on it, Georgiana realised, she shouldn't have been surprised that, after such excitement, the old man had suffered an apoplexy late that night. By dawn, the whole family had been summoned to his bedside.

It was clear to them all, without the doctor saying anything, that Fortunatus was dying. His face was grey. There were little beads of sweat upon his brow, and he was breathing with difficulty. But he evidently knew who everyone was, and though he could not speak much, he indicated that he wished to say goodbye to them, each in turn. To George and Georgiana he whispered a few words of thanks; to Hercules he said nothing but managed a sort of handshake; he patted Kitty's arm; he spoke a word or two to Eliza and Fitzgerald and allowed her to kiss him. It was the same with Terence's family, though it was clear that he was getting very tired. He insisted nonetheless that Patrick should draw close again and, taking his hand, whispered: "So proud. So proud."

The doctor was moving to his side now, but Fortunatus was trying to say that there was a person to whom he wanted to communicate something more. He was looking at Georgiana.

As she came to his side, he took her hand and gave it a faint but affectionate squeeze. He clearly wanted to say something, and was summoning the strength to do so. Finally, he seemed to be ready.

"One disappointment." His voice was faint. She leant forward to hear him better. "One regret."

She tensed, almost drew back. She realised, of course, that he must be disappointed in Hercules—in her son's blunt and brutal nature, so unlike Patrick's fineness. But this was not the moment to say it, and she wished that he would not.

He was gathering his strength again. He wanted to whisper something. She could not very well refuse. She leant down.

"I wish," he whispered so that no one should hear, "that I could have been George." And with a final effort, he managed to kiss her hand.

A flood of relief came over her so that she almost laughed. With great affection, she stooped again and kissed his cheek.

The doctor was gently but firmly pushing her to one side now. He was feeling the old man's pulse. Georgiana moved back to George's side. They all waited. Fortunatus suddenly started to sit up. His eyes opened very wide. Then he fell back, and they knew that it was over.

"What did he say to you?" George asked as they left the room.

"Nothing really," she said.

"He was very fond of you."

"Yes."

Then, halfway down the stairs, she quite unexpectedly burst into tears.

⁘

It was several days later when the will of Fortunatus was read. The bulk of the estate, which was respectable though not large, passed to George, together with a letter recommending that, while he wished the old Fingal estate to remain in the senior male line, his son might, if he had no need of the money, distribute the excess to various members of the wider family. This, with Georgiana's entire agreement, George did at once. There were also some thoughtful personal remembrances for various people, including a ring for Georgiana and some handsome prints for Hercules.

But there was one other bequest: some property, worth about a fifth of the total, that was left free and clear to his nephew Patrick. No one had known of this, least of all Patrick himself. But as everyone knew of his affection for the young man, who had certainly received little enough from his own father, it certainly did not occur to anyone to complain about it.

Except Hercules.

Georgiana had seen her son irritated, cold, contemptuous, even brutal before; but she had never seen him like this, and she was glad that he had come to his father's house where only she was in the room to see it. He was beside himself with rage.

"How dare he leave those properties to Patrick?" he shouted. "They should have come to me."

"But you have no need of them, Hercules," she said gently. "The estate will come to you, and the fortune you're to inherit is huge."

"Can you not see the principle of it?" he cried. "That is Walsh property. Ours."

"It was his own to leave. And your cousin Patrick is a Walsh, anyway."

"Of the cursed Catholic branch, may they rot in hell!" he bellowed. "If that damned papist takes it, then he's a thief."

This was too much.

"You are jealous, Hercules, because of your grandfather's affection for Patrick. You would do better to hide it."

But to her shocked surprise, he turned upon her now with a look of terrible coldness.

"You do not understand, Mother," he said icily. "I have no interest in what my grandfather thought of me, and never had since I was a child. As for Patrick, I despise him. But anyone who takes property from me," he went on in a deadly tone she had never heard before, "is my enemy. And I destroy my enemies. As for Grandfather, I never wish to hear his name again."

"He left you some prints. You'll keep those, then, I dare say," she retorted in some disgust.

He gave her a blank stare.

"I sold them this morning. Fifty guineas."

Then, banging the door behind him, he walked out.

It was hard for her to feel the same affection for him after that, though, as his mother, she tried.

⁜

If Georgiana deplored her son's personal behaviour, there were times in the months that followed when she began to wonder whether some of his political views might even be justified.

The situation in Ireland was becoming increasingly tense. Despite the Patriots' success with the Catholic issue, nothing else had changed. The restrictions on Irish trade were still in place. While Grattan continued his blistering attacks in Parliament, his friend Napper Tandy was busy organising the tradesmen of Dublin: copying the American rebels, they were threatening to start refusing to buy English goods. "Pernicious rabble," Hercules called them. But he had a more serious objection. "It's one thing for Grattan to attack us in Parliament," he declared, "but he and Tandy don't seem to care what other means they use. Next thing we shall have people rioting in the streets."

Just as worrying was the problem of Ireland's defence. "France is now at war with Britain, and the best of our garrison troops have gone to America," George pointed out. "If France should decide to invade us, we're practically defenceless." Parliament had voted to raise a militia, but he wasn't impressed. "It's an empty gesture, since there isn't any money to pay for it." There was talk of raising private volunteers. In Ulster, they were already starting.

Georgiana was looking out of her bedroom window early one Saturday morning when she saw them—a troop of about a hundred men, marching through Merrion Square. They wore an assortment of uniforms; some carried muskets, some only pikes. At their head rode an officer, and just behind him, proudly carrying a Saint George's flag, marched a young man whom she recognised as one of the Doyles. They were more or less in step and looking rather pleased with themselves.

It was only ten minutes later when Hercules arrived.

"Did you see the Volunteers?" he asked. "They came past my house, so I imagined they'd come down here."

To her surprise, despite his feelings about Fortunatus, Hercules had recently moved into his grandfather's house. True, he had stripped out every reminder of the old man's occupancy, and painted and repapered every inch of the place. "It suits me to be on St. Stephen's Green," he had explained, "and Kitty likes it."

"They looked splendid," she said.

"Splendid? They looked like damn trouble," he retorted.

"But they're all good Protestants, ready to defend their country." After all, the Volunteers had been springing up all over the island. Protestant townsmen and country gentry alike had rallied to the cause. Whatever else his views, no Protestant wanted to be invaded by the French.

"And did you notice who was carrying the colours in that little troop? One of the Doyles, who are all thick as thieves with Napper Tandy. Don't you see?" he exclaimed impatiently. "It's Grattan's cursed Patriots—only now they're armed."

Was it so? As it happened, she and George were dining at

Leinster House that day. When they were talking with the duke before the meal, she asked him what he thought.

"I fear your son may be right," he replied. "Personally, I doubt whether these Volunteers would be much use against trained French troops. But we can't very well prevent them forming. So I think we should tell them we're with them, and hope to control them as best we can." He looked at George. "I hope I can count on your support, Mountwalsh." The great aristocrat's aquiline features creased into a grin. "After all, if you can't beat 'em, join 'em."

A couple of months later, Hercules and Kitty had their first child. It was a son. Georgiana was the first one round to see the baby and congratulate the parents. Everything passed off well. She gazed at the baby for a long time.

"We shall call him William," Hercules announced firmly. "After William of Orange."

Only when she was safely home did Georgiana burst out laughing.

"I almost came out with it in front of Hercules," she told her husband, "but thank heavens I didn't. You must see the baby's face." For in their endless minuet, the family genes had apparently decided to show a sense of humour. "He looks exactly like Patrick."

⊹

This happy domestic event could not distract Georgiana from the fact that life in Dublin was becoming quite alarming. Napper Tandy and his tradesmen were carrying out their threat and English goods were now being refused at the port. "The English cloth merchants are really feeling the pinch," Doyle told her with glee. Many of the newspapers were supporting the action. The Volunteers were growing in numbers every week. They mostly had proper uniforms and insignia now, and they drilled with real purpose. They might be there, in theory, to fight the French; but there was no doubt that many of them were Napper Tandy's men.

In the summer, Hercules made a brief visit to London. He returned looking sombre. He had met a number of political men, including Lord North, the Prime Minister.

"I never saw a man so miserable in office," he reported. "He longs to retire and only stays because the king begs him. The American business weighs him down; half the Members of Parliament seem ready to cave in to the colonists, and it's only the king who remains firm. As for Ireland, he despairs of us. He confessed to me privately that he wonders if it mightn't be better to dispense with our Parliament and rule the island direct from Westminster. I can't say I blame him." He shrugged. "There's no one in London with any backbone."

Not long afterwards, he came round to see his parents, this time in a furious temper. He was holding a paper in his hand.

"Have you seen this?" he cried. It was a pamphlet. The author was recommending that, like rebellious America, Ireland should break away from Britain entirely. "He even has the impertinence to call it natural justice. And do you know who this author is? None other than a Patriot Member of Parliament, that damned Charles Sheridan." He gave them both a bleak look. "My family still treats the Sheridans as friends," he grumbled, "when I could have told you those people were no good."

But for Georgiana, the event that forced her to concede that Hercules might have a point came in the autumn.

As soon as the new parliamentary session began, the Patriots were in full cry again. Once and for all, Grattan was demanding, give Ireland her own free trade and end the English controls. Meanwhile, the Volunteers held several small parades at which Patriot speeches were made. But the word on the street was that this was only a prelude.

"Wait for King Billie's Birthday," they said.

Of all the days in the Protestant calendar, none was more popular with the Dublin tradesmen than the anniversary of William of Orange's birth. Each November it was celebrated with dinners and loyal speeches. So when it was announced that the Volunteers would hold a parade in front of King Billie's statue on College Green, it was clearly going to be a large affair.

As it happened, George had gone down on business to the Wexford estate, and so Georgiana, who was curious to see the parade, asked Hercules to accompany her.

"You mustn't go near it," he told her. "You should stay indoors. Firstly, I don't trust the Volunteers. And even if they behave, I don't want you seen there."

"I could watch them perfectly safely, and without anyone misunderstanding, if I went with you," she pointed out.

"Certainly not. I forbid you to go."

Perhaps, if Hercules hadn't said that, she might have stayed away. He probably meant to protect her, but it wasn't for her son to give her orders. So Georgiana said nothing but prepared to go. All the same, as it would be foolish for a lady to go into such a huge crowd entirely unescorted, she wondered whom she should ask to take her. And then she realised that she knew the perfect person.

She was already eagerly waiting long before Doyle arrived. The merchant was in high good humour.

"We've a perfect day for it," he declared. "And I have made arrangements."

They walked around Merrion Square, past the huge façade of Leinster House, and turned left at the corner, proceeding westwards with the grey wall of the Trinity College precincts on their right. The street was full of people going in the same direction, and soon there was such a press that she was doubly glad she had Doyle to escort her. As they passed Kildare Street and came towards the main college buildings, she had to keep close behind the merchant as he firmly made his way through the throng. When they finally came out in front of the College, it seemed to her that she would see nothing of the parade at all, for there was a cordon round the edge of the Green, and the crowd was now so thick that she could only see the upper part of the huge parliament building looming over their heads. Doyle kept going, however, and suddenly turned in at a doorway.

"A friend of mine," he explained with a grin. And moments later they were climbing the stairs of a narrow merchant's house, past the parlour floor and the first floor of bedchambers. They came to an upper landing, where they were warmly welcomed by a prosperous tailor and his family and ushered into a simple bedchamber, where a table of refreshments had already been set up. She was immediately given hot chocolate and taken to one of the windows, from which the family, with all their servants, were preparing to watch the proceedings.

It was a remarkable sight. The broad space of College Green had been cleared. Though there was a subdued hubbub from the crowd around its edges, it was as though the Green itself was holding its breath, waiting for the time when it must echo. In the centre, upon a high stone plinth, King Billie sat upon his horse, looking like a Roman general about to lead a triumph. Behind, the learned, classical façade of Trinity College watched impassively, indicating no doubt that it knew all about this sort of thing, while the splendid, upstart new parliament building, brash as the Colosseum, clearly hoped it was going to see some games. As for the private houses, every rectangular window seemed to have been turned into a theatre box for ladies and gentlemen, and some of the servants had even sneaked up onto the roofs.

After a while, a roll of drums and the sound of fifes announced that the Volunteers were coming.

They certainly made a fine display. The cavalry came first. There were more than a hundred of them. Red coats, drawn swords, flashing helmets sporting plumes; well mounted, too: as they clattered onto the parade ground, the crowd sent up a cheer. Then came the infantry: tricorn hats, blue coats or green coats with white cross-straps, white leggings. The men carried muskets; the officers, who also wore sashes, marched with drawn swords. Each company had its own emblem and colours; they marched in perfect formation, their drums beating a sharp tattoo as they swung round the Green to form a great hollow square on three sides of the statue. But even more striking to Georgiana was the fact that, behind the infantry, came an artillery train of half a dozen field cannon. She didn't know the Volunteers had cannon. Whatever their intentions, they clearly meant business. "I've three of my sons down there," she heard Doyle announce with satisfaction.

To the delight of the crowd, the troops performed some simple drill in perfect unison; next, the officers and colour sergeants came forward to salute King Billie's statue and troop the colours respectfully before him. Then, upon the order, the three sides of the square alternating with one another, the troops fired volley after volley into the air so that the serried ranks almost disappeared in smoke as College Green echoed and reechoed with the din.

The smoke cleared. The Volunteers stood still as statues themselves. And then the astonishing thing occurred.

The first banner appeared in the central company, behind the statue. Raised between two poles, it was made of green cloth, carefully inscribed with Roman letters, in Latin.

PARATI PRO PATRIA MORI

Ready to die for our country. Well enough: a noble sentiment. The crowd applauded. But now the company on the left was unfurling another banner: white cloth, red letters, as well-produced as the first, but this time in English.

FREE TRADE

The crowd roared. Georgiana gasped in surprise and glanced at Doyle. He was nodding in approval. And now, on the right, she saw a third banner. Red cloth, white letters, slightly broader than the other two.

FREE TRADE OR REVOLUTION

She couldn't believe it. The crowd was roaring even more loudly than before. Revolution? The good Protestants of Dublin?

What were they thinking of? She stared at the officers in their sashes. Were they going to permit such a thing? Not only permit it, apparently, but approve. For they ordered the firing of another volley, while the three great banners were held high.

They were shouting more commands. The troops were wheeling. Led by the cavalry, they made a full circuit round the Green, flags and banners unfurled and waving above their heads. As they passed in front of the Parliament, Georgiana could see that many of its members, including her son, had come out in front of the building to watch them go by. There was no possibility that the message of the banners would be missed. Behind the troops, the ominous cannon trundled by.

As the Volunteers moved away down Dame Street towards the Castle, the crowd continued to applaud. They seemed cheerful, and there was no disorder. But Georgiana was left trying to understand: what did this all mean? Had she just witnessed the first step in a revolution?

Out of courtesy to their host, they remained some time in the house to talk, after the troops had departed. Listening to the conversation, it was clear to Georgiana that the tailor and Doyle both took it for granted that everyone they knew was a Patriot. As for the banner threatening revolution, they seemed to treat it easily. "That'll wake up the government, I should think," the good tailor remarked.

College Green was relatively quiet when they came out. The Volunteers had ended their parade and small groups were drifting back. Georgiana and Doyle were just about to retrace their steps past the Trinity College precincts when he caught sight of one of his sons coming from Dame Street. It was the youngest, a man of about thirty now, looking rather handsome in his sergeant's uniform. He was accompanied by two other Volunteers, though the uniforms they wore looked slightly different from his own. Doyle waved and motioned him to come over.

Bowing politely to Georgiana, Sergeant Doyle asked her amiably if she had enjoyed their display—to which she made a noncommittal reply—and informed his father that he and his brothers intended to meet shortly at the family house. "I'm bringing these two good fellows from Ulster with me," he also announced. "They came down from Belfast to take a look at us. So I hope we impressed them."

The two in question seemed quiet, pleasant-looking men, of about the same age as young Doyle.

"We were impressed," the taller of them said with a smile.

"Very impressed," the other echoed in the same northern accent. "Good drill."

"And the banner?" she couldn't help joining the conversation. "Free trade or revolution? Are you planning to fight the British, like the Americans?"

The two Ulstermen looked at each other.

"Our ancestors took the Covenant," the taller replied. "When a principle is at stake, it may be necessary to take up arms."

"But not if it can be avoided," chimed the other.

"No. Not if it can be avoided." The tall man gave Georgiana a frank smile. His blue eyes looked kindly. Had she seen him before?"

"I don't know your names," remarked Doyle.

"Andrew Law," the taller replied. "And this is my brother Alex."

"I'm delighted to make your acquaintance, gentlemen. This is Lady Mountwalsh."

The change in the two men was extraordinary. They glanced at each other, then became completely silent. It was as if they had turned to ice.

Georgiana gazed at them. That was why the taller had looked vaguely familiar. Indeed, as she searched their faces, she could see other likenesses—not striking, but clear enough—to her own dear father.

"You are the sons of Daniel Law?"

Andrew Law inclined his head just enough to acknowledge the fact, but did not reply.

She understood, of course. Yet for some reason—she did not know exactly why herself—she felt a great urge to speak with them, to know them better.

"I am sorry that our two families are not closer," she said quietly. She did her best to sound friendly, and also, she hoped, dignified.

But if she was making a peace offering, it was in no way accepted. The two men stood there in silence, as if they were praying that God would remove her presence from them. The two Doyles looked on in some surprise. The eyes of Andrew and Alex Law remained grave. There was no hatred in them; they were too good for that. But it was clear that, like two elders of the Presbyterian congregation, they regarded her as a person not to be touched: an adulteress; even a fallen woman. She had never been treated like this before. She found it strangely disconcerting.

"Well," said young Doyle, "I suppose we must be going." And the two Laws, bowing politely to his father, turned away.

Doyle did not allude to the incident as they made their way back to Merrion Square, and so Georgiana was left alone with her thoughts. She felt strangely disconcerted, as if her world had been turned upside down. And as they came into the great empty space of Merrion Square, which she normally loved, her heart was heavy. Whether it was the parade, or the rejection by her cousins, or—she hardly knew what—she was suddenly overwhelmed by a sense of desolation and of loss.

❖

Nor could she shake off this depression. If the events of that day had triggered the debilitating process, in the weeks that followed the sense of sadness clung to her, like some insidious water weed that wraps itself round a swimmer, dragging him down.

Within a month of the parade, Lord North and his government had decided that it was wiser to give the Irish what they wanted, and the restrictions on Irish trade had all been lifted. Grattan and the Patriots were triumphant. "But it will also quieten them down—and the Volunteers, too," her husband remarked to Georgiana. Early in the spring, the discrimination against the Presbyterians was also removed. She hoped that would please the Law family in Ulster. Certainly, as the first months of 1780 passed without incident, it seemed that her husband's assessment might be right; and as the weather began to grow warmer, she knew she should feel more cheerful. But she didn't, and in the middle of April, George suggested: "Why not go down to Wexford? The change of scene might do you good."

⁘

It was a pity really, she thought, how little, up until now, they had lived in the big Palladian house they had built: a month or two each summer, that was all. Often as not, they would use the more humble family house in Fingal. Perhaps it was indicative of her husband's genial nature that, having done all that was required to raise his family in the eyes of the world, he had been quite content, instead of living in Wexford as a great lord, entertaining on a grand scale, to continue as the kindly country gentleman he really was. For her part, she was perfectly happy to live this way.

If some of the new Irish mansions were being set, like the greatest English houses, in huge landscaped parks, Mount Walsh had not yet attained such rural splendour. The house, big and impressive enough, to be sure, was fronted by open grass, with a ha-ha against the encroaching deer. But beyond that, and to each side, the woods and coppices followed straight and simple lines. The Wexford landscape around was very pleasant, though, with the open fields and modest hillocks, typical of the region, that had felt so familiar to the English yeomen farmers who had settled there.

And as the summer began, and she woke each morning to the glorious sounds of the dawn chorus, and walked out into the fields where the cows were grazing, or visited the dairy and watched the dairymaids at the milk churns, Georgiana began to experience, if not a lightening of the spirit, at least a sense of peace.

Thank God for her husband. He could not be there all the time, but he spent many weeks with her. His behaviour was perfect. If she felt moody, he would know when to leave her alone; but quietly, reassuringly, he was always there. With his broad face and kindly manner, George might not be deeply ambitious; but he was nobody's fool, and she respected him. And when, walking alone with her down a country track, he would put his strong arm round her waist, she felt comforted, and thankful to have such a fine and understanding husband.

All the same, when he was not there, she might have been lonely. Several of the servants in the house had been with them in Dublin before; but to the people working on the estate, and to the tenant farmers, she and George were still newcomers, and seldom seen at that. She found them friendly and polite enough, in a watchful manner—for they knew well enough whose money had paid for the estate—but there were only a few with whom she was on terms of any intimacy. She was quite glad, therefore, to find that there was one person in the house who seemed to be far more lonely than she was.

Brigid was her name. She was only sixteen, a thin, pale, dark-haired creature. Like many country girls, she had been sent to work as a servant with a local farmer near her home, some thirty miles up the coast. It was a good way for a girl in a large family to earn her keep and learn to be a good house-keeper until such time, God willing, as she found a husband. But the farmer had not treated her well, and she had only been there a year when the local priest, hearing of the opening through a friend in the area, had spoken to her parents and arranged for the girl and her mother to visit the housekeeper at Mount Walsh, who had engaged her, pending Lady Mountwalsh's approval. To work in such a fine establishment was considered an opportunity, and on being assured that it was a kindly household, the mother had left the girl there.

But she wasn't happy. Not that she was mistreated: far from it. But Mount Walsh was too far from her home for her to make visits to her family more than once or twice a year. And though she did her work well enough, she hardly spoke a word. "She's pale as a ghost and thin as a rake," the housekeeper told Georgiana, "and I can't get her to eat more than a mouthful at mealtimes."

So Georgiana had taken the girl under her wing, used her as an occasional lady's maid, taught her how to brush and dress her hair, and persuaded her to talk a little as she did so. She learned that Brigid's father was a craftsman, and that she could read and write. Under such kindly treatment, the girl seemed to become a little more cheerful, and even put on an ounce or two of weight. But the unforeseen benefit of her kindness was that, because of her concern for the girl's welfare, Georgiana had a small project to occupy her attention, and it left her feeling less lonely and more cheerful herself.

She was already feeling better by the month of July, when Hercules and Kitty came down, accompanied by little William. She was glad to have them there. If Hercules sometimes inspected the estate as though he'd be glad when his parents were out of it and the place was his, if he pointed out that he, personally, would make better use of the house for political entertaining than they seemed willing to do, she knew that he meant no harm. It was just his nature. If he warned her that several of the local gentry and farmers to whom she had taken a liking were damned Patriots—and that he had proof of it— she did not let it disturb her.

Much of the time, he was quite pleasant. Kitty, meanwhile, came into her own. Her conversation might be limited, but she was entirely at home in the country; she knew exactly how everything should be done; and everyone there, from the farmhands to the scullery maid, soon treated her with a friendly respect, as though they had known her all their lives. She'll probably run the place, Georgiana thought without any rancour, far better than I. And watching her walk arm in arm with Hercules, clearly happy, she had to admit that perhaps Hercules had made the right choice for a wife.

But the great joy came from baby William.

He was a darling little boy; and as she was his grand-mother, no one seemed to mind how much time she spent with him. Indeed, if Hercules and Kitty were otherwise engaged, they were glad that she was there to sit and play with him by the hour. Sometimes she summoned Brigid to help her, and the girl proved to be rather good with him. He was such a merry child. And he still resembled Patrick, although she was careful not to say so.

Once the cook, who had worked for Fortunatus many years ago, remarked quite innocently to Hercules: "Doesn't the baby look just like Master Patrick did when he was that age?"

"Not at all," said Hercules coldly.

"Ah, but you'd have been too young to remember," she added kindly.

"He doesn't look like him at all," Hercules thundered, and gave the cook such a terrible look that she never mentioned the subject again. It was as well, Georgiana thought, that Hercules was not the master of the house, or the poor woman would surely have been sent packing.

For Georgiana, it was almost as if she'd had another baby herself; and the presence of the child, and the happy prospect of the years ahead while he was growing up, did much to restore her still further. By the end of the summer, George smilingly told her: "You look much more like yourself."

That autumn, she returned with him to Dublin for the parliamentary session. There were no dramatic developments during those months. News came that the Redcoats were doing well against the American rebels in the south, and that the newly arrived General Cornwallis had crushed a southern army under Gates. "The slaves are flocking to join us, too, as we've promised them freedom," George reported. Not that this news had discouraged Grattan and his Patriots. Having won conces-sions the previous session, he was urging an independent Irish

Parliament now; but his support was limited. News came that in England, young Richard Sheridan had got himself elected to the Parliament in London. By Christmas, they had a letter from him making clear that he was already close with some of the leading opposition Whigs, "who are quite determined to do something for the Patriots of Ireland," he wrote, "if ever we can turn out Lord North—who remains like the rock of eternity." At the end of the spring, Kitty gave Hercules another son. They called the baby Augustus. It pleased Georgiana to think that he was probably conceived at the house in Wexford.

And it was to Wexford that she went back, with no small pleasure, in the month of May.

⁂

It was George's idea that Patrick should accompany her. He himself had business to attend to and would not be able to come down for some weeks. Hercules and Kitty had decided to spend time with the new-born baby nearer to Dublin, at the house in Fingal. But Patrick, who had been working hard for several months without a break, had said that he'd be delighted to go down to Wexford with her for a while.

He was certainly a most delightful travelling companion. He seemed instinctively to know when to tell an amusing story and when to be quiet. Sometimes he rode beside her carriage, sometimes he sat in the carriage with her, as they made an easy journey down, passing through Wicklow in the afternoon and stopping for the night at Arklow, before leaving early to reach Mount Walsh comfortably before the evening. Once at the big house, he immediately went to greet the cook and the other servants he remembered from his childhood; the next morning, when she took him round the estate, he spoke so gently and kindly to all those he met, some in English, others in Irish, that by the end of that day, he clearly had won them all. He also paid a call on Father Finnian, the local priest, to let him know that, without embarrassing his Protestant cousins at the big house, he would come quietly to Mass during his stay. And two days later, to his great delight, he discovered that one of the local gentlemen, a Catholic named Kelly with a small estate only three miles distant, was a fellow he had known some years before in Dublin.

He also made one other discovery. The gentleman in question had an unmarried sister, a few years younger than himself. They came to call at Mount Walsh a few days later. Jane Kelly was charming, intelligent, and pretty.

"I should think," Georgiana said after they'd gone, "that you might consider getting married one of these days."

Indeed, there was no reason why he shouldn't. With the modest legacy he'd received from Fortunatus, and the profits he was beginning to make in the wine trade, Patrick Walsh was well enough established to look for a wife. He was a gentleman; his father had been much loved. And as long as George and I are alive, he'll have family connections to help him, she thought.

"You're always matchmaking," he said with an affectionate grin. But two days later, he paid a morning call upon his friend and did not return until after dinner.

They settled into a very pleasant routine. Once a week, his clerk would send him a messenger with a report of the business from Dublin. He would spend an hour or two on this and write a reply. Apart from this, he was at leisure.

Some days, they would pay calls in the area and entertain in return. At least once a week, she noticed, he would see the Kellys. On quiet days, he and Georgiana would go for walks, eat together, and read to each other in the afternoon. He also set to work in the library. George had asked him if, while he was at Mount Walsh, he would catalogue the books there and draw up a list of recommendations for purchases. He went about the job thoroughly. "There's an excellent core of books which have come from Uncle Fortunatus's house," he told her. "You also have a remarkable collection of beautifully bound piffle." Georgiana informed him that they had been sent by a book dealer. "Who was damn certain no one would ever bother to open them," he laughed. "Anyway, I'm drawing up a list." The only trouble, he told her, was that he would need to get the list fair-copied. "My own hand is so illegible that I'm quite ashamed of it. I'll ask Father Finnian if he knows anyone," he suggested.

He was surprised, the following day, when she brought the girl Brigid into the library and asked him to judge whether her copying might be satisfactory. He was astonished when she not only wrote a beautiful script but seemed to have no difficulty with titles in French or in Latin. "She can even decipher my hand," he laughed, "which is the most remarkable accomplishment of all. Your father sent you to a hedge school, I suppose?" he asked the girl, and she nodded. For an hour or two each day, thereafter, Brigid was told to sit at the great library table and work on the notes Patrick gave her. Georgiana had been pleased to see, on her return, that her pale young protégé had continued to put on a little weight, and was delighted with herself for thinking of this further stratagem to give the girl confidence.

Halfway through June, George arrived. He was delighted with Patrick's efforts in the library and thanked him warmly. He also urged him to remain, but Patrick announced that he would return to Dublin the following day to attend to his business. That afternoon, he went to see the Kellys.

He joined George and Georgiana for a family dinner that evening, however. It was a delightful meal. The three of them dined together, not in the big formal dining room, but in a small parlour. The talk was general, but it soon turned to politics, and George gave them all the latest news.

"Grattan and his Patriots are quite determined to press ahead with their demands in the next session. I've spoken to many of them in the last month. The independent Irish Parliament they want would still be under the king; they aren't trying to break away completely, like the Americans; but the English Parliament would have no further say in our affairs at all."

"But they can't get it," Georgiana said.

"No. In the Dublin Parliament, they haven't the votes. At Westminster, Lord North isn't going to give it to them. If our young playwright friend Sheridan and his Whigs ever get in, they've promised to do something; but there's no chance of that at present."

"And the Volunteers?" asked Patrick.

"Reluctant. They've won their free trade. Most of them don't want the trouble of a revolution." He paused. "Except up in Ulster. The mood there is different. The Ulster Protestants have no love for England, for they're mostly Scots Covenanters at heart. They'd be glad to go the American way any day of the week, I'd guess."

Georgiana thought of her Law cousins.

"For them," she remarked, "everything is a question of principle."

"Probably," said George, "but they can be contained."

When they came to the dessert, the conversation turned to a more pleasant topic.

Georgiana had been especially enthusiastic about Patrick's work in the library, and also rather pleased with herself at finding him his assistant.

"Do tell George about Brigid," she begged.

So Patrick gave an account of the girl's talents.

"Her father is a craftsman, but he can speak Latin, and she even has quite a few words of it herself. Sometimes, when she is waiting for me to give her some more to do, I see her quietly reading the books—and she chooses the better ones, too! I have had a number of conversations with her. And," he gave them both a serious look, "though she is an unusually intelligent example, she represents more of our Catholic Irish peasantry than many Protestants suppose."

George nodded.

"It was a point my father, quite rightly, never ceased to make." He smiled. "And now, Patrick, I have a further favour to ask you, and one which we both hope will cause you to make more visits down here. Your recommendations for the library are so excellent, I wonder if you would consent to make the purchases for us, as you see fit, and install them here. In other words, take over the library and build it up into something fine."

"Would you, Patrick?" Georgiana added her own plea.

Patrick pursed his lips. He could not help reflecting that his labour would actually be building up a library for Hercules: not an attractive prospect. George seemed to read his thoughts.

"If I do it myself, I know the result will be mediocre. Hercules will never bother at all, for he reads little. But I'd like our generation to leave something of excellence for little William and the generations to come. It would give me—and it would certainly have given Fortunatus—great joy to think that in a hundred years or two, future members of the family would show people a noble library and say, "Our cousin Patrick is to be thanked for this.""

After that, how could he refuse?

⁜

Patrick returned at the end of the summer, when George was also there, and the three of them had a very pleasant two weeks together.

Patrick had brought with him a list of the books he had already purchased, and four large, leather-bound volumes that were to become the library's catalogue. He spent an entire day in the library with Brigid, setting up the catalogue, showing her exactly how the entries were to be made, and checking all the entries on the list as she wrote them. At the end of this, he pronounced himself highly satisfied with her work and even took the trouble to talk to her for half an hour after she had finished, announcing to Georgiana afterwards: "You have a treasure there."

While it would have been an exaggeration to say that Brigid had filled out that summer—for she was still thin and pale—

Georgiana considered that she looked very much improved from her former state, and this well-merited praise from Patrick, she was sure, could only give the girl further confidence.

Indeed, a few days later, she came into the kitchen to find that Patrick had gone down there to see his old friend the cook. He was telling her and the other servants an amusing story. They had not observed her by the door, so she watched in silence, and it was a delight to see from all their faces that they obviously loved him. At the end of the story, there were peals of laughter; even Brigid smilingly joined in, and Georgiana realised that she had never seen the solemn girl laugh before. She quietly left, congratulating herself that, thanks to her own efforts and to dear Patrick, Mount Walsh was a happier place than it had been before.

But what about the Kelly girl? He had gone to the Kelly house the day after he arrived, and again a few days later. She invited Kelly and his sister to visit them for the day, early the following week. George performed his part as Patrick's loyal kinsman, and seemed to get on famously with Kelly, while she discreetly praised Patrick to the girl. In the afternoon, they inspected a garden George had started to lay out, which gave Patrick and Jane a chance to walk alone together. But at the end of the day, when the visitors had gone and she found herself alone with Patrick and asked him what he really thought of the girl, his answer was rather unsatisfactory.

"I like her very well."

"And how well is that, might I ask?" she enquired.

"I find it hard to say, to tell you the truth. It surprises me that I should find it so, but I do. We agree on many things."

"She is Catholic."

"Yes. Her mind, her manners, her person are altogether all that could be desired. My feelings for her are . . ."

"Tender?"

"Oh yes. Tender." The thought did not altogether seem to please him.

"You are perhaps not in love."

"Perhaps not." He paused. "Not quite, I think."

"Common interests, respect, and tenderness are the best basis for a marriage, Patrick. I do know that. Love often follows."

"Indeed. Quite so."

"Has she feelings for you?"

"I think so. She has indicated . . ." He hesitated. "The fact is, I find myself confused by my own feelings. I do not know . . ."

"There is no other?"

"Other? Oh. No." He shook his head. "No. No other."

Georgiana sighed. She felt sorry for the girl, but she said no more.

A few days later, they were all due to leave for Dublin. She and George rode in the big carriage, which was followed by a second cart containing two servants and several portmanteaus. Patrick rode beside the carriage with them as far as Wicklow. There he parted from them, as he wished to ride up into the mountains to visit the old monastic site of Glendalough. "I have always heard so much about the beauty of the place," he told Georgiana, "yet to my shame I have never been there." He promised to call upon her in Merrion Square the following week.

As they made their way back to Dublin, Georgiana turned to her husband:

"I've been thinking. If Patrick can't make up his mind about the Kelly girl, there may be an even better alternative." And she told him her idea.

"Good God," said George.

✠

It was some weeks before she was able to arrange a meeting, since the girl was away. The parliamentary session had started. As promised, the Patriots and their friends were issuing calls for independence, but making little headway. The party she held at Merrion Square, therefore, had a purely social rather than a political character. An elegant company was invited, including even the Leinsters. Her daughter Eliza and her husband came, but Hercules, having been told that Patrick would be there, decided to stay away. And with Eliza came the young lady.

Only a sad accident had put Louisa Fitzgerald back in play. About a year after Hercules had declared that she had too many opinions to become his wife, she had married a neighbouring landowner and they had had a daughter. Then her husband had been killed in a hunting accident, and for some time she had been inconsolable. But now she had recovered sufficiently to go out in society again; and with the use of her husband's estate, her widow's portion, and the inheritance from her aunt still to come, she might be regarded as one of the finest catches in Dublin.

"You're aiming very high," George had warned her. This was an understatement. It would have been one thing for Hercules, the rich heir of Lord Mountwalsh, to marry Louisa; but for his poor cousin to do so, decent fellow though he undoubtedly was, would cause general astonishment. And much as Georgiana loved Patrick, she wouldn't have denied that the challenge of the thing was part of its attraction to her. But Louisa was a young widow with a mind of her own. Who knew whom she might choose? "And he is Catholic, to boot," George had added, "when she is Protestant."

That, of course, was another huge objection. Yet not insuperable. Georgiana had several aristocratic friends with mixed marriages. As long as they could agree about the children—who were normally brought up Protestant—the rest could all be arranged. She even knew of one man who had married twice, had three Protestant children with the first wife and three Catholics with the second.

The party was a great success. Louisa met Patrick, and Patrick was charming. A few days later, Patrick received an invitation to attend an assembly at Leinster House; and though it might be that the duke and duchess, having met him, had thought to add him to their list, Georgiana thought it more likely that Louisa was behind it. Certainly, Patrick told her afterwards, she had been there, come up to him herself, and invited him to call upon her. "Which I hope you will do," Georgiana said. "Do you like her?"

"Yes," he replied, and this time without any hesitation. "I like her very much."

Still more encouraging, two days later Eliza called round and told her, "Louisa has taken a great fancy to Patrick."

"His lack of fortune?"

"Could be overlooked."

"His religion?"

"In itself, not of great concern. Though I'm sure she would not wish her children to suffer the disadvantages that must attend any Catholic, no matter what their birth."

"Well," Georgiana remarked, "we shall have to wait and see, now, what Patrick means to do."

He duly called upon Louisa at her house, not once, but twice, in the next two weeks. Then he announced that he wished to go down to Wexford.

He departed for Mount Walsh in a cart, loaded with books for the library that he had already acquired. "He is going about our business in a most thorough manner," George said with approval. Patrick spent a week down at the estate, and since his work in the library could hardly have taken up much of his time, Georgiana guessed that he might be spending time with Jane Kelly. Had his encounters with Louisa caused him to turn back to the Catholic girl in Wexford? Was he trying to make up his mind where his heart lay between the two? She heard he had returned, but he did not call round to see her for a while. And she might have become quite impatient for news had it not been for another event which, at that moment, swept aside all other considerations.

"We are beaten in America. Cornwallis has surrendered." It was Doyle who came round to the door with the news. George and Hercules arrived together from the Parliament an hour later.

What did it mean? Throughout the midwinter season there was scarcely another subject spoken of in Dublin. Was the surrender of Cornwallis at Yorktown the end of the whole business? Would the government raise fresh troops, or was the entire colony to be lost? From the moment he heard the news, George was certain. "They haven't the will to go on. America's lost." Hercules in particular was plunged in gloom. "If the American rebels have won, then the Irish rebels will follow close behind," he decided. Certainly, in Ulster news came that the Volunteers were holding triumphant rallies and issuing demands for independence.

Patrick did not appear at the house until January, when he announced that he was going to London on business. "Also to see some book dealers on your behalf," he told George. When Georgiana asked him if he had seen either Jane Kelly or Louisa, he answered that he had seen them both, but he was entirely evasive beyond that point. "Whatever he is up to, he doesn't wish you to know," her husband laughed—which, seeing that she had been so instrumental in promoting both causes, she thought very unfair. All her daughter Eliza could tell her, which she had from Louisa, was that Patrick seemed to be torn in his loyalties. It must surely, Georgiana thought, be over the question of religion.

He remained away for weeks. Was he avoiding them all by staying in London? Perhaps. Meanwhile, the Ulster Volunteers held a huge rally up in the town of Dungannon. "They've issued a manifesto calling for independence, and sworn not to vote for any parliamentary candidate who won't support it," George told her. "It's the Covenant all over again."

Then, late in March, came the news from London.

"Lord North and his government have resigned. The English Parliament is giving up America. King George is threatening to abdicate." And then, soon afterwards, an ashen-faced Hercules came round.

"The king will stay; but there's to be a new government in London. The damned Whigs are in. Your cursed friend Richard Sheridan is given ministerial office. And do you know what he has declared in the English Commons? That the rule of the English over the Irish Parliament is a 'tyrannous usurpation.' Those were his very words." He shook his head. "The world has gone mad."

Mad or not, it was clear at once to everyone that a great change was in the air. With the Whigs in power in England, and the Ulster Volunteers sending out representatives with their manifesto all over Ireland, the Patriots had never been given such a glorious opportunity before. To the disgust but not the surprise of Hercules, Grattan immediately introduced a motion into the Dublin Parliament demanding independence for the Irish Parliament under the crown. "We will share a king with the English," the Patriots declared, "but with the dignity of a separate nation." On the day of the great debate, Georgiana went to watch from the gallery. Grattan was sick that day, as it happened, but he rose from his bed to attend. No one, not even his enemies, could deny, Georgiana thought, that he cut a simple and noble figure as he overcame his sickness to give one of the finest speeches of his life. Members who would have voted with Hercules before, seeing that the wind was suddenly blowing the other way, voted with the Patriots now. To cheers, the motion was carried. The Irish Parliament, by a clear majority, declared its independence from England. And there was little chance that the Whigs in London, having always supported the Patriot cause before, could do anything but ratify it now. Grattan had triumphed; Ireland had triumphed. But in all fairness, it had to be admitted that Hercules was not entirely wrong when he declared:

"It's the damned Americans we have to thank for this."

❖

Patrick returned to Dublin a week after the debate, and this time he did not fail to call to see Georgiana.

"You missed all the fun," she remarked.

"I conducted some excellent business," he informed her. "I have also shipped over a prodigious quantity of books for your library."

"And have you come to a decision concerning the women in your life?" she asked.

"Yes," he replied calmly, "I think so." But he did not say more, and so she managed, with great difficulty, not to enquire further.

Two days later, he called upon Louisa. But what had transpired between them, not even Eliza could discover. Early in May, accompanied by two cartloads of books, he went out for Mount Walsh.

The English Parliament did not vote upon the Irish question until the middle of the month, and George and Georgiana remained in Dublin until news came that, as anticipated, the Whigs had given the Patriots what they wanted. Then they set out for Wexford themselves.

"By the time we get there, I've no doubt Patrick will have catalogued and installed all the new books," George remarked with satisfaction.

"And perhaps he'll also be able to tell me what he has decided about Louisa and Jane Kelly," Georgiana added. "What do you think he has done?"

"I think he has been tempted by Louisa and her fortune, but that his conscience has led him back to the Catholic girl," said her husband.

When they arrived at Mount Walsh, however, and asked if Patrick was there, they were told that he had left the day before. That was all they were told.

"I could scream with vexation," Georgiana confessed with a laugh as soon as they were alone in their bedroom.

But she noticed that her husband was looking thoughtful.

"Something's up," he told her. "Didn't you notice that all the servants are looking awkward?" A few moments later, he left her, returning ten minutes later. "The books are in the library, all beautifully catalogued. Everything's in perfect order. But I'm telling you, there's something going on."

"Leave it to me," she said with a smile, and went down to see the cook.

It did not take long. Only as long as it took the dear woman to lead Georgiana into the pantry, where they could be alone, and to burst out her incoherent tale. "Oh, my lady," she began, "such goings-on." The butler was only waiting until his lordship came down to acquaint him of the situation.

"Situation?"

"Of Mr. Patrick. And after him and Miss Kelly always seeming so respectable together . . . to run off like that."

"He has eloped with Miss Kelly?"

"Oh, my lady, if only he had. If it isn't the girl Brigid he's gone off with, and not a word to anyone. Him such a gentleman and she . . . whatever she may be. And always so quiet and thin as a rake . . . or not so thin now, God help her."

"He has taken Brigid? Where?"

"He's after taking her to Dublin to live in his house. It might be to the ends of the earth, for all the good it will do the one or the other of them. But it's to Dublin they went, sure enough."

"You knew nothing before?"

"Never a word. Under our noses, and not one of us knew it. With the two of them up there in the library hour after hour."

"He has behaved disgracefully," Georgiana cried. Though in her heart she was thinking: and like a fool.

"She must have bewitched him," said the cook stoutly. "I should have been on the watch for it." She shook her head. "I should have known she'd be sly the day that I first looked into her face."

"For what reason?"

"Why, did your ladyship never notice the strange green eyes that she has?"

It was true. The dark-haired girl had eyes that were green. But she had never thought much about it.

CROPPIES

⚜ 1796 ⚜

DEIRDRE GAZED DOWN from Rathconan towards the sea. She had been standing there half an hour and the damp spring breeze had left tiny droplets of moisture on her brow, but she didn't move.

She was sure he was coming.

How did she know? There had been rumours, of course, whispers that had quickly penetrated even the high valleys around Rathconan, and which might have suggested that he would come before long. But that wasn't how she knew. It was a sense of things she couldn't explain, an instinct she had learned to trust that told her, as it had done many times before, that he was drawing near.

Patrick Walsh: the man she hated more than the devil himself.

She had good reason. In the first place, he had stolen her daughter. Then he had used her shamefully. And now? She was afraid of something even worse. He was going to steal her husband, too. He would take Conall away and—her instinct told her this also—she would never see him again.

There had never been anyone else for her besides Conall. It seemed to her that their lives were set together eternally, like a pair of rocks upon the high mountainside which had been together since the beginning of time and would remain, in life or death, until the end. As a little girl, he had been her life; when he had been sent away, it had been as if her life had ended. And for ten years, she had lived in a sort of wilderness.

During that time, her existence at Rathconan had been as uneventful as it was quiet. If you went down to the coast, there was a good turnpike road with a stagecoach running between Dublin and Wicklow town, so that you could be in the capital in hours. But once you travelled up the steep passes into the mountains towards Rathconan and Glendalough, you entered a timeless zone, a world away, where nothing ever seemed to change. Her grandfather had continued to teach the hedge school, ageing so slowly it was imperceptible. If he never spoke of Conall, she supposed it was so as not to hurt her. Nor did anyone else at Rathconan speak of him—or not to her, anyway. Budge had made it plain that he did not wish Conall to return home, and since his father Garret seemed intent upon sinking ever further into drunken `despondency, not everyone in Rathconan thought the landlord was wrong.

But once a year, each spring, a change would come over Garret Smith. He would stop drinking. His speech, which had become careless, would become precise again. He would take pains to make himself presentable. And then he would walk down to the Wicklow road, where he would board the stage-coach to Dublin to see Conall. Sometimes her grandfather would accompany him the first few miles of the way, unless Budge had a cart going down that way, in which case he would offer Garret a ride. The landlord seemed to have no objection to these yearly trips. He had long ago gained his point; and besides, he had married a young lady from Kildare and had other things to think about.

Each time Garret returned, she would ask after Conall, and he would give her news of him and how he had grown. After three years, she learned that he was leaving the school to be apprenticed to a carpenter. This surprised her, but Garret seemed to be happy about it. He'd be remaining in Dublin. "It's better for him there," his father told her.

"Does he speak of me?" she once dared to ask.

"He does, Deirdre. He remembers you well," Garret replied. But it was hard to tell what this meant. In due course, she heard that the carpenter was so impressed with Conall's abilities that he had sent him to complete his apprenticeship with his brother, who was a cabinetmaker. "I think he'll do very well," Garret told her.

It was on his next visit that something had happened. He had been looking sickly all that year. Some days his face had been flushed, but at other times when Deirdre had encountered him, his skin had been a ghastly grey and his hands had shaken. This time, before going into Dublin, his preparations had been less effective. He had only curtailed his drinking a day or two before he left; he had shaved, cutting himself several times, and put on clean clothes. But as the carter took him down towards the Wicklow road, her grandfather had shaken his head and remarked that he didn't think Garret would get through it this time.

He'd returned five days later in a woodman's cart, his clothes dusty and covered with shavings, and having staggered into his cottage without a word to anyone, had not appeared until the following day. When she asked after Conall, he gave her a haggard look and answered, "He was well, Deirdre, but I was not," and he would not say more. But to her grandfather some time later he confessed: "I behaved badly in Dublin. I humiliated my son before all his friends. Then I quarrelled with him." He had shaken his head silently, but tears had formed in his eyes. "Perhaps that oaf Budge was right to send my son away."

"You must repair the damage. You must stop your drinking, then go down and be reconciled with him," O'Toole had told him. But though Garret had nodded his head, he had not done it. The next year, he was in no better shape, his courage had failed him, and he had not gone at all. By the following spring, he wasn't fit to go anywhere.

And all this time, Deirdre had wondered: what was to become of her? While Conall was away in Dublin, she was growing into a young woman. Some of the young O'Byrnes and Brennans were already wanting to court her, but she hadn't the least interest in them. Should she look for work in Wicklow, as a servant, probably? Or in Dublin? She'd see him, she supposed, if she went to Dublin. She spoke to her grandfather to ask his advice.

"You wouldn't be happy in Dublin," he told her. "You'd miss the mountains. Every day you'd be standing in the broad streets, looking up at the hills—they seem so close, you know, it's as if you can touch them. Yet they, and all that you love, would be out of reach."

"Perhaps," she ventured, "I shouldn't be too lonely. Conall would be a friend to me."

"You should not think of Conall." He had sighed. "He was your childhood companion, Deirdre. But that was long ago, and people change. You should forget him now."

But a year later, when Garret, after a terrible three-week drinking bout, was obviously dying, it was her grandfather who had written the letter summoning Conall to come.

He'd arrived half a day too late. She had seen him in the distance, coming up from the Wicklow road, a slim, handsome young man, striding up the mountain track with confident ease; and as soon as she saw him, her heart had missed a beat. She waited until he reached her.

"I'm sorry, Conall. Your father's gone."

He'd nodded, as if he'd expected it. Then they had walked into Rathconan together.

It was strange, after so many years, that it should have felt so natural, walking side by side with Conall, as though they had never been parted. Did he feel the same? she wondered.

The wake was a subdued affair. She and her grandfather helped Conall make the arrangements. Everyone at Rathconan came. Even Budge and his wife appeared for a little while, as a courtesy to the dead, and greeted the priest civilly enough. Before leaving, Budge had taken Conall to one side, but Deirdre had been near enough to hear what passed between them.

"Your father died a Catholic, of course," the landlord said quietly, "but may I ask what Church you belong to yourself nowadays?"

"Well, Sir," Conall answered politely, "in Dublin, as you well know, I was in the Church of Ireland school, and so I went to that Church; and many of my Dublin friends are Protestant. Here at Rathconan, all these good people, my cousins many of them, are Catholic. And to tell you the truth, I have no very strong feelings in the matter."

"I see." There was no church at Rathconan itself, though from time to time Budge and his family would go to the church a few miles away, to show solidarity. His support for the Church of Ireland was absolute, but no one would have called him pious. Judging by the careful look he gave Conall now, it seemed that Budge found this answer acceptable.

Deirdre had been studying Conall ever since he got back. It was already clear to her that the years in Dublin had left their mark. The Conall she had known and loved was still there, she was sure of it. But this young man had a quiet self-assurance about him, a dignified reserve far more like her grandfather than his own father Garret. Yet, as was now apparent, he had learned to combine this confidence with a respectful manner that was clearly pleasing to a man like Budge.

"You mean to return to Dublin shortly?" the landlord asked.

"I am told that I could do well as a cabinetmaker in Dublin, Sir," Conall replied. "But I miss the mountains of my childhood. I am wondering if I could make a living as a carpenter here." He gave Budge an inquiring glance. "If I can prove that I am sober and reliable."

Budge looked at him searchingly for several moments, then gave a brief nod and suggested he come to see him after his father was buried. He left soon afterwards.

"You would stay up here, Conall," she asked, "after being in Dublin?"

"I think of it," he answered. "I think of marrying and settling down."

"Oh." She fought to control herself. "And who is this lucky girl that you're thinking of marrying?" she asked lightly.

"Yourself," he said.

⁘

If Budge had entertained misgivings about having another troublesome Smith as a tenant, it had to be said that he had behaved well enough. The day after Conall had moved in, he had come to the cottage in person and informed him:

"I had a front door made some years ago, but it is not satisfactory. Would you make me a new one?" And when the work was done, in best oak, and Conall had fitted it, Budge and his wife had admired it, and he'd exclaimed: "That is beautiful work, Conall, I have to say. Beautiful." And Conall had been well paid.

Further commissions had followed, from the landlord and from his friends. Some time later, armed with a letter from Budge, Conall had gone down into Wicklow to see a cabinetmaker there, and from this had developed a long relationship. The Wicklow man would send out work to him, and every few weeks would see Conall going down into Wicklow in a cart with a table, or some chairs, or a well-made cabinet. To give the lie to his father's reputation, the work was always perfectly produced and never late. After a few years, the Wicklow man had wanted to take him into partnership, but though he could certainly have made a better living, Conall and Deirdre had always preferred to stay up at Rathconan in the mountains.

Conall drank a little ale, but always in moderation. He never said or did anything to offend Budge or his like. And as the years went by, the landowner would often at dinner cite Conall as proof that, with a little persuasion and a lot of firm treatment, "your Irishman can frequently be turned into a hardworking and respectable craftsman."

As for herself, Deirdre had found happiness, peace, her destiny. A few days before she and Conall had married, her grandfather had taken her to one side and asked: "Are you sure, Deirdre, that this is what you want?" She had been so surprised that he would ask such a thing, but she had assured him that it was, so he had said no more. And the early months of her marriage had entirely confirmed her choice.

If years ago Conall had been the little boy she had protected and made whole, in the young man he had become, she had found a prince. In their lovemaking, it seemed to her as if they were made from the same mould; in their life together, they were in tune like two strings upon the same instrument.

Yet there was always something mysterious about Conall. Occasionally, he would still sit alone in a state of abstraction from which she would have to wait for him to return. One day, they had gone over to Glendalough; and as they stood together in the mountain silence by the upper lake, she had suddenly had the strangest experience, as if they were floating together, like mist over the water. And she had thought to herself: I am married not only to a man but to a spirit. They had been married almost a year before he told her the truth about his time at school in Dublin.

"That was a terrible place, Deirdre. There were only a few of us Catholic boys, and we'd been brought there to be converted. As far as the masters were concerned, we were wild animals to be broken. And they treated us as animals, too. Kicked out of bed at dawn, to scrub the floors, before the Protestant boys had to wake. We were like slaves the rest of the day, too, whenever we weren't in the lessons. And a savage beating if you even thought of arguing about it. As for the teaching . . ." He shook his head in disgust.

"Was it so hard?"

"Hard? Not at all. It was laughable. Those Protestant boys were so far behind us: I knew far more from your grandfather's hedge school before I arrived than any of them knew by the time they left."

"Are all the Protestants so ignorant, then?"

"I wouldn't say that. Trinity College turns out scholars of the highest repute: no question. But the charity schools like mine are sinks of iniquity. That's why I left as soon as I could and became a carpenter."

"Did you tell your father?"

"No." He fell silent for a moment. "What was the point? The poor devil had troubles enough, I dare say."

He never spoke of the quarrel between his father and himself, and she never asked. But she thought she could guess his sadness and his shame at what his father had become, just as it was obvious that he was determined to prove that he suffered from none of the same weaknesses himself. "I remember him as he was when I was a boy," he once told her. "I wish," he added wistfully, "that he could have stayed as he used to be, and lived to see his grandchildren."

There was no shortage of those. Down the years, Deirdre had given birth to a dozen children, and though many had been lost to sickness or accident, seven had lived to be strong and healthy adults.

She and Conall had never regretted their decision to raise their family up at Rathconan. It was their childhood home; her grandfather, whom they both loved, was there; and above all, they and their children were surrounded by the huge, open spaces of the mountains. And if the Brennans, as her grandfather assured them, were neither more nor less stupid than in generations before, and the O'Byrnes still foolishly believed that Rathconan and all that was in it should rightfully be theirs, Deirdre and Conall had been used to them since they were born and, along with the other local families, they came with the landscape.

If her grandfather had had doubts about Conall as a husband, he had soon buried them. It had been only a few months before a routine had developed that was to last down the years.

Once a week, the two men would spend the evening together. A little drink would be taken, of course; but mostly they would recite poetry or read books together—so that Conall laughingly told Deirdre: "The best thing about marrying you is that I can complete my education." Meanwhile, the old man, somewhat gaunt but with a mind as sharp as ever, had continued to act as schoolmaster to the village, and to tell his stories and recite his poetry at a *ceili* from time to time. He had lived into his eighties, and continued to teach the school until a week before his death.

His wake had been memorable. People had come from five counties to honour the old man. Yet it had also been the occasion of one small unpleasantness.

It had come from Finn O'Byrne. He had never been a person of any great account. About the same age as Conall, he was considered a fairly good cattleman and he had a brood of children to his credit; but although he would spend time with the Brennans, he and Conall never had a lot to say to each other. Nonetheless, Conall had once made him a good oak chair, with which he had declared himself well satisfied. So Conall had not expected any trouble when he saw the figure of Finn—small, dark, a great untidy mop of shaggy black hair lying in matted coils about his shoulders, and clearly a little the worse for drink—come lurching towards him during the long evening of the wake.

"I suppose that you'll be the new schoolmaster now," Finn remarked, "with all your learning."

There was something vaguely offensive in his manner, though Conall couldn't see why there should be.

"I don't think so, Finn," he replied. "I've too much else to do." In fact, he and O'Toole had discussed the possibility a few times down the years, but he hadn't felt the desire to take it on, and he had quite enough work on hand anyway.

"He'd have wanted it, Conall, to keep it in the family— with Deirdre being his granddaughter and you spending so much time in his company. All those hours, reading together, every week." The words were harmless enough, but there could be no doubt from the way he spoke them, the way that he drew out the word "reading" as if there was something wrong with it, that Finn was trying to insult him. "No, Conall, it was only yourself that was good enough to be in his company like that."

It had not occurred to Conall that his sessions with the old man would have given offence to Finn O'Byrne, yet clearly they had.

"I'm sure you'd have been very welcome to join us," he said. A lie, of course, but it seemed polite.

"Ha! Finn O'Byrne with the old man and his favourite. The boy apart. The prince, we used to call you in the hedge school. Until you were sent away, of course." He grinned viciously. "On account of your father. Another great reader, they say."

It was hard to know which shocked him more—the discovery that this man, of whom he had no high opinion, but towards whom he'd never held any malice, should hate him so much, or the fact that, in all these years, he'd never guessed it. Conall remembered him perfectly well in the hedge school. Finn hadn't been much of a pupil, but perhaps a bit above the Brennans. And now the passing of old O'Toole, and no doubt a little drink, had suddenly resealed these childhood resentments. He didn't know how much Finn had been drinking, but this was hardly the time to enter into a quarrel. He must, unwittingly, have looked at him with disgust, however, for O'Byrne burst out bitterly: "Ah, look at his face. He thinks himself so much better than the rest of us."

"Can you not respect the dead, Finn?" he said as calmly as he could, and made to move away. But this turned out to be another mistake.

"Move away." Finn made a mock bow. "The great Conall Smith doesn't talk to any but his own kind." He spat. "Respect the dead. Respect your father, do you mean?"

This was too much.

"You were a fool then, Finn O'Byrne, and you're a fool now," Conall said angrily. "But you've no need to prove it, for I knew it already." Then he did walk away.

He had told Deirdre all about it a few days later, but Finn had never mentioned the incident again, and they assumed he had probably been so drunk he had forgotten about it.

For a few months after that, Conall had helped by taking the hedge school, on an occasional basis, while they looked for someone else. But he had sent for the priest down the valley to come to catechise the children, not wishing to do it himself; and in due course an elderly man from Wicklow was found to take the job on, and he returned to his furniture making. He had no doubt that Budge had been aware of his activities, but the landowner had never said anything.

That had been twenty years ago. Since then, there had been peace at Rathconan, where, whatever else might be passing in the world below, little seemed to change.

There was one change, however. It was gradual, but her grandfather had occasionally remarked on it as he grew older, and in the two decades since his death, Deirdre had noticed it increasingly.

There were more people at Rathconan.

Of course, families had produced children. Apart from her own seven, Budge and his wife had had three girls and two sons; the O'Byrnes, Brennans, and the other local families had all added to the numbers. But as in times past, once the children had grown they had often moved away. The landowner's three daughters were all married to other landowners; the younger son, Jonah Budge, had married a merchant's daughter and bought a small estate a few miles away, while the elder son, Arthur, spent most of his time in Dublin. Of her own children, only two were at home, the rest in Wicklow or Dublin.

In the last generation, however, other families, especially the Brennans, had followed a different pattern. Instead of the eldest son taking over the holding, several of the children had decided to remain at Rathconan and split the holding into smaller parts between them. By doing so, they were increasing the population of the hamlet. And there were signs that in a few years' time, one of the Brennans might subdivide his holding yet again. In times past, such small holdings could not have sustained a family, yet now it seemed they could. And the reason for this change was easy enough to see.

"For the increase in the number of my Brennan cousins," Conall remarked drily, "we must thank the potato."

Everyone in Rathconan grew potatoes nowadays. Budge had two large fields. But while they still grew other crops, and raised their sheep and modest herd of cattle on the mountainside, the Brennans had given over the greater part of their subdivided holdings to the potato crop. It was a logical decision. The New World vegetable was so nutritious that, if you desired, you would remain perfectly healthy if you ate nothing else. Not only that, the potato was intensely productive: a family could subsist on the crop from a single small field. There were twice as many Brennans living in Rathconan now than there had been when Deirdre was a child, and they could have subdivided their holdings several times more without going hungry. Moreover, with the population increasing, they could usually sell their produce at good prices. So although their turf-roofed cottages might have looked poor enough, the numerous Brennans and their neighbours were actually living better than they had done before. Even the O'Byrnes were paying their rent.

All over Ireland, the pattern was similar. The towns were growing—Dublin's population had trebled in three generations—and the country peasants were living more densely upon the land.

Deirdre and Conall had little to complain of materially. Two of their daughters had gone to Wicklow. Both were now married, one to a butcher, the other to a brewer, both quite prosperous men. Her two eldest sons had both gone to Dublin. One was a printer who did well; the other, a tobacconist, seemed to have less success and was living poorly in the Liberties on the west side of the old city. The two youngest children remained at Rathconan: the boy, Peter, was following his father as a carpenter; his sister was working in the Budges' house.

And then there was Brigid. And that devil Patrick Walsh.

She hadn't even known that Brigid had run off with him until a month after the event, when she had received a letter from the housekeeper at Mount Walsh which made reference to the fact. The letter didn't say so, but she had to assume that they'd gone to Dublin.

"What does it mean?" she asked Conall. "Are they married?"

"We'd have heard from Brigid if they were," he replied.

"We must go and find her. We have to save her before her reputation's ruined," she cried.

"It's a bit late for that," he murmured, but he made preparations to leave for the capital the same day.

Deirdre had never been to Dublin before, and she marvelled at its size. Arriving soon after noon, they went straight to the house of their son, which lay in a narrow lane off Dame Street, and he was able to tell them where they might find Patrick Walsh. Leaving their son, they wasted no time, but made their way towards College Green and walked across the bridge across the Liffey. To the right, a little way downriver on the northern bank, they could see the first stages of a massive classical building beginning to rise, which they learned would be the great new Custom House. It was evident that, as the capital continued to expand, the big streets and squares on the north bank were becoming almost as grand and fashionable as the area around St. Stephen's Green. Deirdre gazed in awe at the great aristocratic houses on each side of the wide avenue known as Sackville Mall, which ran northwards for almost five hundred yards up to the handsome façade of the maternity hospital and fashionable Rutland Square beyond. The house of Patrick Walsh was in a lesser but still pleasant street, a short distance to the west of the great mall.

The front door was slightly raised from the street level. The tradesman's entrance lay down a flight of steps at the basement level. Conall hesitated an instant, then went to the front door.

Seeing their country clothes, the maid who opened it looked a little confused and asked if they were tradespeople; but Conall sent in his name, and a few moments later, she returned and ushered them through the hall into a small parlour. They only had to wait a short while before Patrick Walsh himself appeared. He was smiling.

"You are looking for Brigid, I am sure," he said before they could even speak. "I have been telling her to write to you for a month."

"She is here, then?" Conall asked.

"Indeed she is, Mr. Smith, and she will be with us directly." He seemed quite at ease, and friendly, as if there was nothing wrong at all.

Deirdre gazed at him. A clever face, kindly eyes, a charming manner: a gentleman through and through. And she wasn't fooled for a second.

"What have you done with her?" she demanded.

"Your daughter hasn't been kidnapped, Mrs. Smith," he replied calmly. "She was employed in the house of my cousin, Lord Mountwalsh, as you know." If this reference to the importance of his family was designed to put her in her place, it did not succeed. "Now she has agreed to come here," he gazed at Deirdre steadily, "as a housekeeper."

"Housekeeper? At her age?"

"This is not a large house. Ah," he looked up blandly, "here she is."

As Brigid appeared in the doorway, Deirdre almost gasped. The thin stick of a girl she had left at Mount Walsh had vanished, disappeared like a sapling with tightly closed buds that breaks into flower in the spring. Standing straight, in a rather severe dress, with her black hair pulled back neatly, she looked the very pattern of an efficient young housekeeper. But her mother could see at once that she had filled out; she stood like a proud young woman. She also saw that Brigid's skin had a glow, and her green eyes a sparkle that was entirely new.

"I want to speak to my daughter alone," she said firmly.

Brigid had a pleasant room on the third floor of the house, below the attic floor where the rest of the servants slept. There was a rug on the floor, a counterpane on the bed, and an easy chair. The girl sat on the bed and motioned her mother to the chair.

"I'm sorry I didn't write."

"Never mind that," her mother cut her short. "You're not his housekeeper."

"I am. I swear it."

"Is that all you are?"

The girl was silent.

"What are you doing, Brigid?" her mother burst out. "Do you not see what this makes you? You must come away at once." Brigid was starting to shake her head in reply, but Deirdre did not pause. "What have they done to you? Did they mistreat you at that house? Were you so desperate? You only had to tell me."

"I was lonely at first, Mother. I missed you all so much. But they were very good to me. And later . . ." She laughed. "I think I was bored. Until Patrick came along."

The laugh. The way she called him Patrick.

"Dear heaven, child. You're his mistress." She stared at the girl. "Do you imagine you'll find a respectable husband when it's known what you are? This fine gentleman isn't going to marry you. He'll use you, Brigid, and when he's done with you, what will become of you then? Have you not thought of that?" She shook her head. "It's my fault. I should have warned you, but I thought you were safe in that house. I never supposed . . ."

"It isn't your fault at all, Mother."

"You're to come back to Rathconan at once."

"And what would I do there? Marry one of the Brennans?" She paused, then added quietly: "He's a good man, you know. I won't find a better."

"Do you imagine that he loves you?"

"I interest him, I think. He cares for me."

"He's making use of you. You're just a servant."

"I was a servant in Wexford."

"You must come away with us now, Brigid."

"I'm sorry, Mother, but I will not."

"Your father will order it."

"He cannot make me go." She sat there on the bed, calmly defiant.

Deirdre was too shocked and too angry even to weep. She rose.

"I have nothing more to say to you, Brigid," she declared. But as they went down the stairs, she continued nonetheless: "We'll stay at your brother's a few days. I hope you'll change your mind."

She did not wish to speak to Patrick, but signalled to her husband that she wished to leave immediately.

They were no sooner outside than she exploded.

"Do you realise what is happening? She's his mistress."

"It is what I supposed." His voice was calm.

"Are you not going to do anything? Would you not save your own daughter?"

"Is she there against her will?"

"She refuses to leave."

"Then what would you have me do, Deirdre? Am I to shoot him?"

"He is the devil himself."

"Perhaps." He did not seem convinced.

"What did he say to you?"

"About Brigid? Not a great deal. She helped him catalogue a library." He paused while his wife stared at him in disbelief. "He has read your grandfather's verses, you know. And it seems that his father, old Doctor Walsh, knew my own father when he was young. In fact, it turns out that we are distantly related."

"Do you mean that he would marry Brigid?"

"I don't think," said Conall thoughtfully, "that he's the marrying sort."

⁜

And so it proved. Though she sent Conall to see his daughter and Patrick once more before they left Dublin, the situation remained unchanged. A year later, Brigid had a child. Again, Conall was sent to see them, and told Deirdre that both mother and baby were well, and that they were living contentedly in Walsh's house, and that neither the gentleman nor Brigid seemed to have any plans for changing the situation.

The years had passed. There were more children. Nobody seemed to mind, and there was nothing Deirdre could do.

But there was one thing she had not foreseen, and this was the friendship between Walsh and her husband.

The first time Patrick had passed through Rathconan, he had been on his way to visit Glendalough. He'd arrived with Brigid and their infant child, intending to leave Brigid with her parents while he visited the old monastic site. Deirdre did not speak to him if she could help it, but when he casually asked if Conall would like to accompany him, Conall had said he would.

"I suppose," she had said to Conall tartly, "that you are anxious to spend the day with the man who ruined your daughter."

She never knew what had passed between the two men at Glendalough that day, but when they returned, it was clear that they had been deep in conversation. Patrick had come again every summer after that, and each time the two men would go off together to visit the twin lakes. It became a yearly ritual. Sometimes, if Brigid was not in a state to travel, Patrick would come alone and, little as she liked it, he would join them for their evening meals, sleeping in the cottage on the night of his arrival, and again at the end of his day out, and before departing in the morning. Always, after Patrick had gone, she would ask her husband what they had talked about during their day together, and he would give her some vague, unsatisfactory answer. But if she said anything harsh about Patrick then, like as not, Conall would quietly defend him. "Ah, but he's a man of great intelligence," he might say, or "His heart's in the right place." Once he had even remarked, "He's a good Catholic," and she had cried: "If he were a good Catholic, he'd have married your daughter instead of using her as a concubine." But he had only looked thoughtful and remarked: "He is a lover of Ireland, anyway."

She was glad he only came once a year; but as time went by, she had an increasing sense that her husband was, in some subtle and insidious way, being pulled away from her. It was not only his association with Patrick. One other change had come over their life.

At first she had welcomed it when, one evening, he had remarked to her: "You know, it's a pity that nobody is singing your grandfather's verses anymore. Some have been printed, of course, but I've many more of them written down. There were the stories he told, as well. Wonderful stories."

"Perhaps you should do it, Conall," she had said. "I don't know who else would do it better."

So in the evenings, he had begun to study the old man's work again, and after a while he had called in their neighbours and performed for them—just as the old man had used to do. And they all said it was wonderful. Word had spread. A month later, he had been asked to a place a few miles away. Then to a second, and a third. And before a year had passed, he was making a journey somewhere every month or so; sometimes he was away for several days.

She had hardly known whether to be pleased or not. She was proud of him, of course, and glad to think that her grandfather was honoured again. She was glad, too, for her husband. She knew that if a man has a gift, he must use it, and that his lonely wanderings had always been necessary to him. But he had never wandered so much before, and she couldn't help wondering if it might not have something to do with herself. Could it be that he needed to be away from her now, after all these years? Was it an excuse to avoid her? Once or twice she gently challenged him, and he looked distressed, and even offered not to go anymore. And this offer was enough at least, somewhat, to assure her. Certainly, whenever he was at home, there was nothing in his manner or in their marriage that was lacking in affection. So she'd decided to put a good face on it, and to be glad that, when her neighbours referred to her wandering husband, they seemed to do so with a new respect.

It was an incident just a few years ago that had really disturbed her.

Though the newly independent Parliament had kept itself busy enough, there hadn't been any great excitement in Ireland for some years, when, in 1789, news of the French Revolution had burst like a thunderclap across Europe. If the American Revolution that she remembered from her girlhood had been exciting, this French Revolution seemed to be cataclysmic. Back in 1776, Irishmen had watched the new world breaking away from the old; but with the revolution in France, it seemed that, in an orgy of violence and bloodshed, the old world was trying to remake itself entirely. In this huge experiment, which Deirdre found sometimes inspiring but sometimes terrifying, men spoke of a new age of reason, an end to the social classes, of religious toleration—even the rule of atheism.

And it was while those astonishing events were unfolding in France that Patrick had come, by himself this time, for his annual visit. As usual, the two men had gone to Glendalough; on their return, they had settled down for their evening meal. Under Walsh's influence, Conall had drunk rather more than usual when the talk turned to France. They had discussed the latest developments in the continuing revolution and what it might mean for Europe as a whole. It was clear that the other monarchies of Europe could not tolerate this overturning of the entire social order in their midst. Then, dropping his voice somewhat, Patrick had remarked:

"You know my views on what this may mean for Ireland."

And Conall, quietly but with a passion she had never heard in his voice before, gazed at him intensely and answered:

"I shall be ready, I can promise you, when the time is ripe."

When she had asked him what he meant by that phrase, the following day, he had shaken his head and said it meant nothing. She resented this, since it was obviously untrue; but he had still refused to discuss the matter, except to say, "There are things it's better you shouldn't know." This patronising answer had infuriated her still more, and it had created a small but definite strangeness between her and her husband.

A few weeks later, he had gone down into Dublin, to see their sons, he said; but she had the uncomfortable feeling that there was some other reason, and that it had something to do with Walsh. And she cursed the day that had brought such a devil into their lives.

Then the nightmare had begun. The nightmare in which she was still living now.

She gazed down the valley.

At first, in the distance, it seemed that the figure coming up the winding mountain track was changing shape. One moment she thought she could make out a single horseman; the next, it looked like a deer with two great antlers. Only gradually did she realise that it was not a single man but two. Patrick came first: it was him right enough. But behind him rode a taller man she did not think she had seen before.

And somehow she knew, infallibly, that whatever they had come for, it would take her husband away from her. Armed only with her instincts, she wanted to run back to Conall, hide him from them, take him away—an idea as useless as it was absurd. For at this moment, she realised that he had come out and was beside her.

"Why are they here?" Her voice betrayed her. It sounded high-pitched, nervous.

He put his arm around her.

"I could not say it before, Deirdre," he answered quietly, "but now it's time that you should know." He held her closer. "Because I am going to need your help."

❖

Patrick was always glad to be at Rathconan. He loved the sensation of being up in the mountains. But he wasted no time. As soon as he had entered Conall's house, he introduced John MacGowan. Then, seeing Deirdre was still with them, he glanced at Conall enquiringly—in answer to which Conall said quietly:

"It is time that she should know."

Patrick gave him a brief, thoughtful stare, then nodded. Although he knew very well that Deirdre didn't like him, he bore her no ill will in return.

"You know, perhaps, Deirdre, that for many years I was a member of what is called the Catholic Committee."

She shrugged.

"I never really knew what it was," she replied.

"It was nothing very defined, I grant you. We were just a group—a large group—who felt themselves responsible for the Catholics of Ireland. We hoped for Catholic freedom, but we were prepared to be patient. For me, I suppose, it was the continuation of what my Catholic family has stood for in the last three hundred years. When Grattan got his independent Irish Parliament, it was intended that this would lead to a gradual improvement in our Catholic position. So it seemed to all of us at the time. But we had reckoned without the Ascendancy men, and the Castle."

Grattan's triumph in making the Irish Parliament independent had not been all he had hoped. Despite the fine words, it had never been quite clear who was to decide foreign policy and, still more important, matters of trade. Endless arguments had followed, with London trying to exert its influence in the usual old ways of patronage and bribery, while the

Patriots tried to reform the system and to prise Ireland loose. They had not been entirely successful. And when it came to the Catholic issue, they had failed entirely.

For in the Irish Parliament, the core of Protestant settlers were determined to deny the Catholics any power, and few of the moderate Protestants wanted to do battle on the issue. The Patriots had been isolated. While in Dublin Castle, an inner group of three powerful officials known as the Troika—fine administrators, but all three of them ruthlessly anti-Catholic—had managed all government business for years. Viceroys might come and go, Parliaments might meet, but the Troika had kept the well-oiled stagecoach of government bowling securely along the Ascendancy road.

"Nonetheless, I had continued to hope that our quiet diplomacy would bring about change one day," Patrick explained. "Then came the French Revolution. People became excited. And some Catholics, especially amongst the city tradesmen in Dublin, started to call for radical measures, public campaigns—"

"We remembered what the Covenanters in Scotland had done long ago," John MacGowan cut in. "So why not a Catholic Covenant?" He grinned. "Patrick here was horrified. He wouldn't have anything to do with us."

"But just as important, it has to be said," Patrick continued, "was the effect the French Revolution had on the Protestants. I learned all about this from one of my Doyle kinsmen. He'd been in the old Volunteers, and he had a radical turn of mind. When the new group we call the United Irishmen started, he joined it. 'Patrick,' he used to lecture me, 'Ireland must be a separate republic like France, with freedom of religion, votes for all.' He loved to debate these things. And frankly, that's all the United Irishmen were down here in those days: a debating club. But through the Volunteers, he'd become friends with a family named Law, who were Belfast Presbyterians. And they invited him up there to visit the Belfast United Irishmen. He told me he'd never seen anything like it. They had a huge rally on

Bastille Day, and they set up a proper organization. They really meant business—for the Ulster Presbyterians dislike English rule even more than we do."

"Speak for yourself," MacGowan muttered with a smile.

"And it's a Protestant who has chivvied us all along. You have heard, perhaps, Deirdre, of Wolfe Tone. He's a man of remarkable charm. It's Tone who persuaded the Ulster Presbyterians that they should campaign jointly with the Catholics—if only because there are so many of us. And he began to persuade many of the Catholic Committee, too."

"But not you," John MacGowan reminded him.

"Certainly not. I thought they were dangerous fellows. It was not until that terrible Parliament of '92—which I'm sure you recall—that I came round." He sighed. "And I owe my conversion to my cousin Hercules."

All Ireland remembered that Parliament. Perhaps foolishly, he had allowed himself to hope that something might be done. In England, the Whigs were pressing for the relaxing of the old Penal Laws: Burke was even persuading Pitt's Tory government of the case. In Dublin, the Duke of Leinster and his friends were arguing the same thing. There was already an understanding that Catholics would be allowed back into the legal profession. So when the moderates on the Catholic Committee had presented a modest petition to the Irish Parliament, Patrick had expected at least that it would get a reasonable hearing.

The day before the debate, he had chanced to see his cousin Hercules coming along Dame Street from the direction of the Castle. He was walking with a sturdy figure whom he recognised as Budge's elder son Arthur. It was always unpleasant approaching a man who disliked him so much, but it seemed to him that the importance of the matter was so great that he must speak a word to his cousin; and so, approaching them and making a most courteous bow, he expressed the hope that Hercules would give consideration to the Catholic proposal, explaining: "For it seems to me that, if nothing else, this will deny to the more radical elements the excuse they seek to agitate further." Hercules had stared at him but said nothing, so that it was impossible to know what he was thinking. Then, with what might have been a nod, he glanced at Arthur Budge and the two men moved on. The next day, Patrick had gone early to the Parliament to hear the debate.

If he had not been there himself, he might not have believed it. If anything, the advice of the London Whigs and the aristocratic Leinsters seemed only to have infuriated the members. They were like a pack of hounds baying for blood. They threw out the proposals by an astonishing vote of 205 to 27, and they freely insulted the Catholics as well. It was as if nothing had changed since the Battle of the Boyne. But for Patrick, the speech that rankled most hurtfully had come from Hercules.

"No matter what tricks, what cheap persuasions the Catholics may attempt, they are never to be trusted. Ireland is a Protestant land, and so it shall remain—immutable, inviolate, triumphant—not for this century only, nor for the next, but for a thousand years!"

The speech had been greeted by cheers. Afterwards, as he had been leaving, he had caught sight of his cousin standing in one of the colonnaded hallways. A tall figure had just come up to him and was shaking him warmly by the hand. It was FitzGibbon, the most powerful member of the Troika.

⁜

"It was that vote and the insulting words of my cousin Hercules that made me realise that John MacGowan and his friends were right," he told Deirdre. "The Ascendancy will give the Catholics nothing, ever."

But if he hoped that he was making some impression, it was clear that Deirdre, who could not possibly have any love for the Protestants, still regarded him as something even worse.

"So you say. But the Catholics were given the vote the next year," she pointed out sourly. "Both my daughters' husbands have it." If she suspected that he was a devil trying to lead her into a trap, she had caught him out in a lie.

And indeed, in 1793 the government in London, now at war with a French Republic, and fearful of trouble in Ireland as well, had begged the unwilling Irish Parliament to do something to keep the Catholics happy. The resulting legislation, however, had been less than it seemed.

"But it was a travesty," John MacGowan burst out in reply. "Every man with enough property to yield forty shillings may vote. I may vote myself. And what good does that do me? None at all—since no Catholic may sit in our Parliament. I may vote, but only for a Protestant. And since the majority of constituencies are still controlled by a handful of Protestants anyway, nothing will change at all. They gave me the right to join a guild as a full member also—as long as the existing Protestant members invite me in. The thing was designed to make us think we had something, and to give us nothing. It was a mockery, a swindle."

"And now," Patrick added, "the Troika have gone to work on King George. The word from London is that he has now privately vowed never to let any Catholic into Parliament."

It had to be said that King George III of England, as usual, had meant for the best. But just as he had conceived it his duty to hang on to the American colony, he had now been persuaded, by cunning FitzGibbon, that his coronation oath, which obliged him to uphold the Protestant faith, also meant that he must deny political representation to the Catholics. Once he believed he had given his word, nothing would ever persuade honest King George to change his mind. It was one of the Troika's cleverer moves.

"And if that is what the king vows in private, his government in public has shown itself just as determined. When once a viceroy came here—Lord Fitzwilliam, a decent man as it happens—who wanted to meddle with the Troika, he was recalled at once."

"So if nothing can be done," Deirdre remarked, "why is it you're here?"

Patrick looked at her seriously. His voice became quieter.

"A little over a year ago, Wolfe Tone was arrested for agitating. He was thrown out of the country. He went to America—to Philadelphia. The home of Benjamin Franklin." He paused a moment. "There he made many friends: men of importance who had taken part in the American War. He also came to know the representative of the French government. Most people suppose that he is still in America. But he is not. Like Benjamin Franklin, he has gone to France— Revolutionary France—to see whether they will now help Ireland as they helped the Americans before."

"And will they?"

"We have no idea. But if they do, we must be prepared. If such a thing is done, it must be done quickly and effectively. The larger and better organised the rising, the less the bloodshed need be. The United Irishmen have already shown what it means to act together in brotherhood. I believe all Ireland will rise. We shall have an Irish republic. There will be freedom of religion, as there is in America and France."

"And what in God's name has this to do with Conall?" she demanded.

For the first time, Conall spoke.

"I am to organise this area, Deirdre. From here all the way down to the border of Wexford. In fact," he continued gently, "I started many months ago."

"You devil!" She turned furiously upon Patrick. "Can you leave none of us alone? Do you wish to destroy us all?"

But Conall was shaking his head.

"You do not understand, Deirdre. It was not Patrick who asked me to do anything." He smiled, perhaps a little sadly. "It was I who asked him."

She stared at him.

"Your travels . . . ? With my grandfather's verses? They were all for this?"

"No, Deirdre, I'd have done that anyway. But it was a useful excuse to move around the region, as well."

Deirdre made a gesture of despair.

"John MacGowan is one of our captains in Dublin," Patrick explained. "And as your two sons there will answer to him, I thought it good that you should meet."

"Our sons too . . . ?" Deirdre looked horrified.

"They both wished it," Conall said quietly.

"How many men have you now?" MacGowan asked.

"Around Rathconan, a dozen. In the whole area, a hundred that I can rely on."

"Who at Rathconan?" Deirdre demanded angrily.

Conall mentioned some of the Brennans and other local families. "Finn O'Byrne is especially eager," he remarked.

"Finn O'Byrne?" Deirdre gave a look of disgust. "He's the biggest fool of them all. And he hates you, besides."

"It doesn't matter." Conall smiled. "He will fight for us because he believes that if we win, Rathconan will be his."

"But why, Conall?" she cried suddenly. "When you've spent all your life avoiding trouble—why would you do such a thing?"

Patrick thought this was uncalled for. So, by the look of it, did MacGowan. Conall seemed to read their thoughts.

"No," he said quietly, "she is right." He paused a moment. "It is true that, seeing the foolishness of my father, I have always taken care not to make the same mistakes. I have never drunk more than a little; I have kept my thoughts to myself. I have made furniture, as well as I know how, for men I despise, and taken their payments politely." And now a certain edge came into his voice. "In Dublin, I was treated like a dog at school by Protestant boys who had neither my intelligence nor my education; as a man I have seen my fellow countrymen held in subjection by these same bigots and fools. And I have hated them all. But hatred is useless, and revolt is a crime, because, unless it has the means to succeed, it is stupid. So I said to myself: 'Wait. Wait a lifetime if necessary. But wait until the time is ripe.' And for many years I thought that I should never live to see that time. But now I think it may have come. And if every carving and every piece of furniture that I have ever made should need to be destroyed, as we burn their houses down, I should say: 'Light the fire and burn them all,' and say it gladly."

"Oh, Conall." His wife shook her head. "I hope to God you may be right. For if you're not, we shall all be destroyed."

"Then you will help us?"

"I am your wife, Conall." She sighed. "Just one condition I make."

"Which is?"

"Never ask me if I believe."

❖

After leaving Rathconan, Patrick took MacGowan to Glendalough, which the Dublin man had never seen before. They also took note of the hamlets they passed. Patrick was pleased with the day. Though Conall and his men up in the mountains could only be marginal to any action, he was proud that he had an organization in place up there. "Besides," MacGowan pointed out, "you never know whom you may need." At the end of the day, they made their way down to Wicklow town, arriving there at nightfall.

The next morning, they inspected the place. Conall had warned them that his two sons-in-law there had no interest in the cause, but Patrick already had a merchant in the town who had volunteered, and he gladly took them round.

Like most Irish towns of the time, it had a barracks with quite a full garrison: Protestant officers, Catholic men. They seemed well-disciplined and quite smartly turned out. "We've tried to persuade some of the troops to join us—secretly, of course," the merchant informed them. "But no luck so far." Nonetheless, he informed them, he had twenty good men in the town. By midmorning they had parted from him and started back towards Dublin.

They were both rather cheerful. Patrick certainly felt that they were making good progress in Wicklow. A month ago, he had been down in Wexford where his old friend Kelly had told him: "The gentry here are absolutely split into two parties, but many of us, including myself, are with you." In other parts of the island, however, that lay outside his own remit, especially in Munster and Connacht, little progress had been made. "We shall all have to work hard so that Ireland is ready," he remarked to MacGowan, "if the French do agree to come."

Yet whatever the uncertainties both men, for their different reasons, could express confidence. MacGowan's reasons were practical.

"The Ulster men are formidable," he observed. "They are the backbone at present. But if a proper military force arrives from France—I mean ten thousand men or so—then I believe the effect upon our Catholic population would be incalculable. Up to now, any protest has been crushed, and they have no hope. But once they see the French—we'll have a hundred thousand men the next day. Even the whole English army would find it difficult to move about the island with every man's hand turned against them. We'd harass them and wear them down, just as the Americans did."

Patrick's reasons were vaguer, yet perhaps even more strongly felt. It was not so much the Catholic generality in whom he placed his trust, important though they were. It was the involvement of his own, Old English class that moved him.

If the great ducal house of Leinster had been the patron of the Catholic cause in Parliament, it was no less a person than the old duke's handsome younger son, Lord Edward Fitzgerald, who had now emerged as leader of the cause in Dublin. He had been profoundly affected by the ideals of the French Revolution. "All men are equal," he would remind his friends, "the duke and the street sweeper, the Protestant and the Catholic. And all social systems which deny such an obvious truth will sooner or later be swept away." And he practised what he preached. He'd stop in the middle of a Dublin street and talk to some modest labourer with just the same, simple honesty with which he'd have spoken to a noble lord. He cut his hair unfashionably short; and in his manner of dressing, you might have taken him for a modest Paris tradesman rather than an Irish aristocrat. Seeing Patrick's unusual household with Brigid the peasant girl, he had taken him for a member of his own class who shared the same egalitarian outlook. "It's up to us, Patrick, to take the lead," he had once confided in him. "I feel better, having you by my side." And even if some of Lord Edward's ideas seemed a little too radical to Patrick, he warmed to the aristocrat's noble idealism.

Two weeks ago, Patrick had chanced to meet him at his cousin Eliza's house. Taking him to one side, Lord Edward had confided: "Patrick, I'm going to make my own approach to the French, to back up Tone. Between our two efforts, I'm sure we shall persuade them. But I beg you, not a word to anyone yet." If this confidence—and the fact that he had a slight family connection with the great aristocratic dynasty—gave Patrick a certain snobbish delight, the idea that they were fighting side by side for the cause of the Irish people was imbued, in Patrick's mind, with an almost mystical quality.

Not that his religion was intense. Brought up by a physician father of liberal outlook, and coming of age when the French ideas of rational enlightenment were all the rage, it wasn't surprising that Patrick's religion was kindly rather than devout. If Wolfe Tone and the Ulster Presbyterians, who were now so important to him, privately thought of their Catholic allies as medieval obscurantists, Patrick would not entirely have disagreed. "I believe that the world must have been created by an eternal, all-encompassing being that we call God. And Christianity expresses the divine nature. But I don't believe much more than that," he once confessed to Georgiana. "So I suppose I'm what people nowadays call a Deist."

"So are most of the clever men I know," she replied with a smile, "Catholic or Protestant."

This in no way prevented him from going to Mass or making his confession—and certainly not from fighting for justice for his fellow Catholics in Ireland. Yet if he had no interest in visiting the holy well of St. Marnock, as his grandfather had still done, when he thought of himself and Lord Edward fighting for the ancient Catholic cause, he felt that he was fulfilling a sacred trust, and he experienced a sense of rightness, as if this was what his ancestors, and no doubt the deity Himself, had destined him to do.

They were ten miles from Dublin when they met Hercules, in the company of Arthur Budge, riding towards them.

❖

It was many years since Hercules had spoken to his cousin. Even when Patrick had come up to him before the parliamentary debate of '92, he had not said a word in reply. But now, seeing him coming from Wicklow, together with that cursed Catholic merchant John MacGowan, he did not hesitate.

"What are you doing here?" he demanded roughly.

"I'm after taking Mr. MacGowan to see Glendalough," Patrick answered with a bland smile. "Did you never go there, Hercules? It's a lovely spot. St. Kevin's hermitage may still be seen."

Hercules looked at the two men with disgust.

They were all the same, these Catholics, he considered. Insinuating and deceitful. Jesuits to a man. He would never forget that John MacGowan had pretended to be a Protestant so that he could sneak into the Aldermen of Skinners Alley. Once a liar, always a liar, as far as Hercules was concerned. As for Patrick, his loathing for his Catholic cousin had only grown down the years. If as a young man he had been jealous of the love his own mother felt for Patrick—her preference for his cousin, he'd sometimes suspected—by the time his grandfather had left Patrick the legacy, it had become clear to him that his cousin was only preferred because he practised the Catholic arts of manipulation. Dishonesty: that was all it was. As for Patrick's attempt to persuade him to change his convictions before that parliamentary debate, it had been contemptible.

Did the devious Catholic really imagine he would be swayed by these hypocritical appeals to his better nature—from a man who, himself, had been living in sin with his concubine for years? No, Patrick was nothing.

But what was he doing here? This tale about Glendalough was obviously a lie, intended to taunt him. But what did it conceal?

If Hercules was suspicious of the two Catholics, it was not surprising. The fear of the suppressed Catholic majority was so endemic in governing circles that almost anything a Catholic did might be seen as evidence of a conspiracy of some sort. When tensions between Protestant and Catholic textile workers had flared up in Ulster, and the Catholics had formed groups they called Defenders, to protect themselves against Protestant mobs, the government had seen it as a conspiracy. As a result, the Defenders had spread, and turned into just the sort of disruptive secret society that the government feared. Before that, down in County Wexford, some rural disturbances against the high tithes and other exactions made by the clergy had soon been denounced as another Catholic assault on decency and order. The charge was absurd, but despite the fact that his own family estate was in the same county, and he should have known better, Hercules had chosen to believe it.

In the last three years, however, the usual fear had turned to alarm. The Catholic Defenders seemed to be spreading and merging with the United Irishmen. Wolfe Tone and his friends were clearly up to something—but what? The Castle men weren't sure. Would revolutionary France try to foment trouble in Ireland? Quite likely. But nobody could find any clear evidence. FitzGibbon and the Troika did not intend to wait meekly for something to emerge. They took action. In every barracks, military men were drilled. A series of raids on suspect United Irishmen served to frighten many of their friends. Landowners were told to be vigilant. New justices of the peace were appointed and given extra powers of search and arrest.

It was exactly this process that had caused the two men to undertake their present journey. Hercules was going to Wexford. None of the family had been down to Mount Walsh since the previous year, since his parents had decided to spend this summer in Fingal. And though his easygoing father had assured him that the Wexford countryside was quiet, Hercules had decided to go to see for himself. As for Arthur Budge, his journey was more official. His father had been urging him for some time to return to Rathconan and run the estate, and now he had also asked the government to appoint Arthur as local magistrate in his place. It was as a justice of the peace, therefore, with stern injunctions to watch out for trouble, that Arthur Budge was now on his way to spend a month at Rathconan. As they were on terms of friendly acquaintance in Dublin, Arthur had invited Hercules to accompany him and spend the night at Rathconan upon his way.

Having parted from Patrick and MacGowan, Hercules turned to his companion.

"I hate those men," he remarked. "If they had their way, Ireland would be plunged into chaos."

"You fear chaos," Budge replied grimly. "But don't forget, I fear something worse."

"What is worse than chaos?"

"Catholic rule. Remember, a century ago, when King James brought Catholicism back to Ireland, it only took months for the papists to start taking over everything. It can happen again, and it could be worse. If the Catholics come into power, they'll throw every Protestant settler off his land. We Budges will be lucky if we escape naked with our lives."

"And what about their allies, the Protestant Patriots, and the Ulster Presbyterians?"

"They will lead the Catholics to victory, then they will be overwhelmed by them. It is inevitable." He grunted. "You think you are fighting for order. But I know I'm fighting for my life."

"Don't worry," said Hercules quietly. "We'll destroy them."

✛

Patrick was glad to get back to his family. The household of Patrick Walsh and Brigid Smith was unusual, but it seemed to suit them both. The pretence that she was his housekeeper had been quietly dropped as time went on, but in its place had been substituted something else.

She had taken to the stage. The old Smock Alley Theatre had closed now, but the Crow Street Theatre, well-placed off Dame Street just halfway between the Castle and Trinity College, was a large and lively place which catered to an audience of all classes. Brigid's slim figure, her dark hair and green eyes, had created quite a stir when she first appeared there; her voice, when she had learned to project it, had a pleasing resonance; and she had shown an unexpected talent for comedy. She was a popular performer, and her appearances were all the more attended because they were occasional—for she always put the needs of her children first. There were four children now: two boys and two girls, the eldest thirteen, the youngest three.

With this change in role had come a change in status. Dublin society was genial. Even in the greatest aristocratic houses, the atmosphere was far more easygoing than in the proud mansions of London. In the public assemblies at such places as the Rotunda Gardens by the lying-in hospital, the fashionable world mixed freely with merchants and tradesmen. If she wanted to go about in her own right, as a beautiful and talented actress she would find a friendly welcome in many places; and if she happened to be a gentleman's mistress—well, such things were to be expected in people connected with the stage. More problematic, however, was her connection to Patrick. The difficulty for the respectable residents of Dublin's Georgian terraces and squares was well summed up by Georgiana: "People feel that they can't invite her as his mistress, and she can't go as his wife." In the convention of the time, it would have been easier if she were safely married to someone else.

As it happened, this hardly mattered, because Brigid had little interest in visiting people whom, for the most part, she secretly despised. Georgiana herself would visit her from time to time, and she liked her. She had her own friends whom she saw as she pleased. And if Patrick was asked to dine in this house or that, she was glad that he should go without her.

At first it had suited Patrick very well to have her as his mistress. If he had withdrawn politely from the courtship of two women, either of whom would have been a good marriage, it was not only because he had become obsessed with the green-eyed servant girl. Something within him had also rebelled against the bonds of matrimony. Perhaps it was only the normal selfishness of the bachelor; but perhaps, also, he was drawn to something beyond—a need for larger spaces, wilder shores—that the love of this strange girl from the mountains could satisfy in a way that the companionship of the others never could. His love affair with Brigid had been passionate, and still was. He had seen her transformed from a lonely girl to a confident beauty with a public face. Their children were handsome, and she had brought them up wonderfully.

"Do you not think, after all these years, that for the sake of the children you should marry Brigid?" Georgiana had occasionally taxed him. Yet to his surprise, when he had finally made the offer to Brigid, she had laughed at him and refused.

"People in Dublin tolerate me," she answered. "But they always remember who you are. To your friends, I'm still the servant girl whose father's a carpenter up at Rathconan. They'll never accept me as your wife. I'm better off as I am. Besides," she smiled, "as things are, Patrick, I'm always free to leave you and take the children back to the mountains if I want." And because of the streak of stubborn pride in her, he knew she meant it, every word.

So now, after his children had finished climbing over him affectionately, he gave her an account of his journey with MacGowan, and told her privately what had passed between himself and her parents.

Though Brigid had always been aware, in a general way, of his activities for the United Irishmen, there had been no need to tell her all the details. With the way things were progressing now, however, he felt that he ought to warn her that the business could become more dangerous. "At some point," he explained, "it's likely that we shall be issuing arms." She listened to him carefully, and when he had finished, she only asked him one question.

"Do you truly believe in what you are doing, Patrick?"

"Yes," he answered, "I do."

"Don't forget to give me a gun when it starts," she said. That was all.

✣

Georgiana's party took place early the following week. It had been arranged at short notice after she and her husband had come into Dublin earlier than expected. Like his father before him, Lord Mountwalsh had made it plain that, in his genial way, he intended to have an active old age, and some legal business had drawn him back into the city. Since he liked to entertain people at the house on Merrion Square, she had made it her business to discover quickly who else was back in town, so that she could find some congenial company for him.

As the morning of the party arrived, she felt pleased with the company she had invited. There would be her daughter Eliza Fitzgerald and her husband, a couple of political men, both of moderate opinions, an amusing lawyer, a clergyman from Christ Church, and one of the Talbots of Malahide—all with their wives. Patrick was invited, alone; also a charming old gentleman who resided on St. Stephen's Green, named Doctor Emmet, and a few other old friends. Twenty people would sit down to dine in all.

She had asked old Doctor Emmet for a particular reason. While Hercules was down in Wexford, his wife and two sons had remained up at the old estate in Fingal. His elder son

William, however, had wanted to come into Dublin with his grandparents. As he was about to go to Trinity College for the first time that autumn, Georgiana had thought to ask Doctor Emmet to bring his own youngest son with him to the dinner, since the boy had already been up at Trinity for several years. Her husband, who knew a number of the professors at Trinity, had already reported, "They say he's a quiet, studious boy, with a talent for mathematics—well-liked, but as he lives at home with the old doctor, he doesn't get involved in any of the wilder parties." Young Emmet would be a nice, quiet young man for her grandson to know, she thought.

Of all her grandchildren, she loved young William the best. She didn't want to admit it, but all the family knew. And so she was especially glad that it was he who carried her own dear husband's name. As a baby he had strongly resembled Patrick; but as so often happened with children, his face had changed as he grew up, and now, at fifteen, he was starting to look just like old Fortunatus. So strongly did he bring back the memory of the dear old man she had been so close to that, more than once, catching sight of the boy that summer, she had caught her breath and then, to hide her sudden emotion, been forced to turn away. But in particular, it was the boy's generous nature that she loved. Once, when still a young boy, he had encountered some youths hurling stones at a stray puppy in a Dublin street, and without a thought for himself, he'd bravely driven them off, rescued the animal, and taken it home. The dog had been devoted to him ever since. The previous summer, when his younger brother had been sick for several weeks, William, who loved to be active, had sat with him every day by the hour, reading to him, playing cards, and keeping him amused. The doctors said the young fellow's recovery was largely due to his elder brother.

The only moment of doubt she had experienced about the party, however, had been on William's account.

"Can I invite old Doctor Emmet?" she had consulted her husband. "He's the most harmless of men, but he was always a

Patriot. And what about Patrick? What would Hercules say about his son meeting people he hates at our house?"

But Lord Mountwalsh had been firm.

"Our house has always been a place where people of any persuasion are welcome, as long as they express their views with courtesy," he pointed out, "and we shall not change for Hercules. Besides, young William is going to encounter people of every kind of opinion at Trinity. As for Patrick, Hercules may not like him, but of course William should meet his cousin once in a while."

On the morning of the party, however, he complained that he had slept badly and felt unwell, and Georgiana had asked him if he wanted to cancel it.

"Not at all, my dear," he had announced stoutly. "I shall take a cure. I shall go to Mr. Joyce's Turkish Baths."

If the English town of Bath had become fashionable for setting up a spa on the site of an old Roman baths, Dublin now had a Roman bathhouse of its own—except that, in the modern fashion, it was called a Turkish baths. The colourful entrepreneur who had set it up had been a Turk, wonderfully named Doctor Borumborad, whose thick beard and oriental robes had caused quite a stir in Dublin—until he had finally abandoned the disguise and revealed himself as a Mr. Patrick Joyce from Kilkenny. His baths had continued to flourish, however. They contained the usual steamy rooms and a magnificent plunging bath. Having been persuaded by a friend to try it once, Lord Mountwalsh had become quite a patron of the establishment, and the management were always delighted, naturally, to receive a visit from him. By early afternoon, they had returned him to her looking rosy-cheeked and contented.

"And now, my dear," he announced cheerfully, "I shall enjoy our party."

And he certainly did. As the guests arrived that evening, it pleased her so much to see how delighted he was to greet them. Patrick he greeted with particular affection. And it was clear that he was also rather proud to show off his young grandson, whom he insisted on keeping by his side as the guests arrived, and then as he made his way round them all again as they assembled in the parlour before the dinner.

Doctor Emmet, grey-haired but sprightly, had duly obliged and brought his youngest son with him, and once young William had finally been disengaged from his grandfather, she brought the two boys together.

It was interesting to observe the two of them together. Her grandson was actually the larger of the two, for Robert Emmet turned out to be a small, somewhat swarthy fellow, with a mop of black hair and small eyes that seemed to look out on life with a quiet but sharp intensity. Standing beside him, her grandson, with his friendly, open countenance, reminded her of a broad-faced gun dog beside a dark terrier. Robert Emmet seemed to be talking to her grandson pleasantly enough, however.

Elsewhere in the room, her guests were all conversing happily. She had observed Patrick greet her daughter Eliza and Fitzgerald warmly, and talk to several of the other guests. Now he was deep in conversation with Doctor Emmet.

✠

Patrick liked old Emmet. Not that he was so old: he must be a little short of seventy, Patrick guessed. But he was in semiretirement now, spending a good portion of his time at a small but pleasant estate he owned just south of the city. For years he'd been the governor of the hospital set up by Dean Swift's kindly legacy, and he had known Patrick's father well, and he was always happy to supply Patrick with anecdotes of his father's younger days. It was well-known that the good doctor supported the Patriot and Catholic causes. "Though I dare say," he remarked to Patrick, "that we had better not speak too loudly of that in the present climate." He gave Patrick a meaningful look. "Dangerous times, Walsh. Dangerous times."

"Ah," said Patrick noncommittally. If old Doctor Emmet had been a supporter of these causes, his support, Patrick felt sure, had never gone beyond a florid speech or courteous argument. He couldn't imagine the good doctor in the streets with a musket. Also, he was not entirely confident of the older man's discretion.

"You've brought your young son with you," he remarked, to change the subject.

"Robert. You've never met him?"

"I haven't." He had not seen the boy before; but he knew his elder brother, Tom Emmet the barrister. And he also knew that Tom Emmet was a good friend of Wolfe Tone, and undoubtedly knew about his mission to France. But did the old doctor know of this? He guessed that he probably did not. So he listened quietly while the doctor pronounced upon Robert's mathematical abilities, and the importance of mathematics in general, until dinner was announced.

The dinner was a noble affair. The day before, a cart had arrived from the Fingal estate with every kind of produce from the estate. Vegetables, cheeses, a great side of beef, smoked ham, and fruits, fresh and potted, from which the chef had constructed several desserts, including a fruit jelly of such sumptuous architecture that all the company declared they had never seen anything like it. The meal was served by ten footmen; the dinner service from China, upon which the family's arms and baronial coronet were handsomely featured, added a touch of magnificence to the friendly occasion. The Mountwalshes certainly did things very well, and there was no reason why they shouldn't.

Lord and Lady Mountwalsh liked to sit opposite each other at the centre of the big table, and there being more women than men in the party, Patrick and young William found themselves sitting together at one of the ends. Patrick had no objection to this. Thanks to Hercules's antipathy towards him, he had scarcely ever had the chance to talk to William, and he was delighted to find him such a pleasant and open young fellow. He seemed to be intelligent, and his likeness to old Fortunatus was striking. He was careful to steer their conversation away from political subjects which might give offence to the boy's father, and he was sorry that, for the same reason, he couldn't invite the boy to visit him at home and meet Brigid and their children. They had just embarked together on the fruit jelly when, taking him by surprise, young William initiated the subject himself.

"Why is it that you and my father are not friends?" he suddenly asked.

Patrick hesitated. He wanted to be honest with the boy, but he had to be careful.

"Your father is a fine man," he began. It was, he considered, a necessary lie. "And I have a high regard for him." Another lie. "But I come from the Catholic side of the family, and I support a political cause which he strongly believes is not only wrong but dangerous. He has every reason to dislike me, therefore, and rather than come to blows, he avoids me."

"Are such differences enough to break apart the bonds of kinship?"

"They always have been. Yes."

"You don't seem so bad to me."

"You don't know me." Patrick smiled. "If a cousin offends you, it may be better to cut him off. Your father's probably right to do what he does."

It was at this moment that Hercules Walsh appeared in the doorway of the dining room.

❖

From where he was sitting, Patrick could see Georgiana's face display a sudden look of apprehension. From the doorway, Hercules did not notice it. Lord Mountwalsh, however, with half a century of genial politics behind him, remained unfazed. You had to admire him. Collecting himself at once, he positively beamed at his son.

"My dear boy. Did you just arrive? Welcome back. Join us. Bring him a chair," he called to a footman. "I am most delighted to see you," the old man splendidly lied.

"I went to my house and learned that my son was here," Hercules replied evenly.

"He is. Indeed he is. Come here, William," he cried, "and greet your father."

But it was too late. Hercules's gaze had already started to travel down the table. His eyes rested, just long enough to register disgust, upon old Doctor Emmet; then, ignoring the clergyman and one of the moderate politicians, they reached young William and Patrick and stopped, fixing them both in a terrible, adamantine stare.

"William, get up," he said coldly. "You are leaving."

The table froze.

"You are in my house, Hercules." His father's voice broke the silence in a growl. Hercules continued to stare at his son, ignoring Lord Mountwalsh entirely. He beckoned to William.

"I said," his father repeated, somewhat more loudly, "you are in my house, Sir."

"And I do not care," Hercules did not deign to look at his father, but continued to gaze at Patrick, "for the company I find here." Then, as young William, blushing with embarrassment and confusion, began to rise, Hercules suddenly turned to glare accusingly at his father. "Nor do I care for the manner in which you entrap my son into such company when you believe my back is turned."

"Hercules," his mother cried out, "that is quite unfair."

"I consider it," Hercules's voice rose, as he enunciated the word with venomous fury, "dishonest!"

Patrick saw Georgiana wince, but Lord Mountwalsh was not disposed to be so put upon. His face was puce.

"Do you come here, Sir, to insult your father and your mother in their own house—and in front of their guests? Leave us, Sir, at once." He rose to his feet. "Leave us, Sir," he shouted at the top of his voice, "and pray do not come here again!"

Making a contemptuous bow to the company, Hercules turned and stalked out of the door, followed, miserably, by his son.

After that the dinner continued, but not quite so well.

A quarter of an hour after midnight, while still pacing up and down furiously in his dressing room, Lord Mountwalsh suffered a sudden apoplexy and dropped dead on the spot.

⁜

When he went to Trinity College that autumn, young William Walsh made one request. "I don't want to live at home like the Emmet boy. I want to live in college like my father did." This was granted, and William was glad.

On the day of his departure, his father called him into his dressing room for a private word.

The death of old George had meant a change of status for Hercules. He was Lord Mountwalsh now. He would no longer occupy a seat in the Irish House of Commons, where the fact that he had to submit to election—albeit by three family friends and a dozen docile freeholders—had always offended his sense of propriety. Now he would sit in the Irish House of Lords by the ultimate sanction of hereditary right. From the day of his father's funeral, servants and tradesmen had addressed him respectfully as "your lordship" or "my lord." Even better, perhaps, he had received a letter from a fellow aristocrat, which charmingly began, "my dear lord." When he walked, his brutal stride had, in some indefinable way, become stately; when he talked, he had the comfort of knowing that his opinions were right—not on account of mere, vulgar reason, but because they proceeded from himself. If he was not a man to practise the soft speech of aristocratic courtesy, it could nonetheless be said that, in the space of only a few short weeks, the ermine mantle of pomposity had descended upon him and fitted, very snugly, around his shoulders.

He looked at his eldest son kindly.

"So William, you are off to Trinity."

"Yes, Father."

"I had happy years there myself, and I'm sure that you will, too." He smiled. "Before you go, William, there are one or two things I want to say to you, as a father." He motioned to a couch against the wall. "Sit down beside me, my boy."

William had never had a heart-to-heart with his father before, as Hercules had never been inclined towards intimacy. With a sense that he was about to discover something important, he listened attentively.

"You are going to be a young man soon," his father said. "Indeed, I think you are a man already. And I know you have a good heart."

"Thank you, Father."

"One day, I expect you'll go into Parliament, as I did. And eventually, of course, you'll succeed me." He rested his hand on William's shoulder for a moment. "These are the privileges of our position, William. But they come with responsibilities. And you and I have to be ready to accept those, too. I'm sure you're ready, aren't you?"

"Yes, Father."

"Very well. There is no one that I trust more than my own son, and I hope you know that you can always trust me."

"Thank you, Father."

"From now on, you and I shall work as a team." He paused. "There are some things that, for the time being, I cannot tell even you, William. But the latest information, I can promise you, is alarming. There is a body of men, many of them here in Dublin, which plans a course of action that would destroy this island. These men talk of freedom, and some of them may believe that is their object, but if they were ever allowed to succeed, the consequences would be entirely different. I speak of invasion by our enemies, of blood in the streets, and the death not of fighting men, William, but of thousands of innocents. Women and children. It has happened here before. It can happen again. Is that what we want?"

"No, Father." So far, William was a little disappointed, for he had heard such things before.

"Fortunately," his father continued, "our information is better than they think. All over Ireland, good men are keeping watch: gentlemen, honest tradesmen, even the poorer sort—men with good hearts. We know much of what is being done, and how, often as not I dare say, simple people are being led astray. And we also know, William, that there is a group of men connected with the university who are eager to entrap any young men they can. They mean to recruit amongst the undergraduates. They will approach with a friendly face, but in the end, their object is to make use of the unfortunate young men and finally to destroy them."

"I'll be careful, Father."

"You, of course, would never be taken in by them. But others might. So I want you to be more than careful, William. I want you to be vigilant. If you see anything that you think suspicious—and you never know what may be of significance—I want you to say nothing. But you should quietly tell me. I shall know how to make the right enquiries. Just by doing that, you may perform a great service for your country." He paused, looked at William earnestly, then put his hand again on his shoulder. "It might seem to you that this is not an honourable action. The person concerned might even be a friend. But we owe a higher duty, you and I. And I can promise you, the best service you could do for any friend is to save him from a course of action he would later bitterly regret."

"I see." He waited. "Is there more, Father?"

"No, William, I think that is all." He nodded and then, probably remembering what his father had once said to him, added: "God bless you, my boy."

Ten minutes later, his younger brother found William sitting on his bed, staring moodily out of the window.

"What is it, William?"

"Father wanted to talk to me." William continued to stare out of the window.

"Oh. What did he say?"

"He said that while I'm at Trinity, I am to spy on my friends."

"Oh, William. You would never do such a thing."

"I'm to be a government informer. It's my duty, he says."
William was silent for a moment. "That was all he had to say
to me, you know. Nothing else." He turned to his brother.
Tears were welling up in his eyes. "That's all there is, I think.
That is the love of my father."

⁘

During the months that followed, William enjoyed the life of
the college and attended to his studies. These occupied a good
deal of his time because, although the young men at Trinity
knew how to amuse themselves, the courses at Dublin were
often said to be more demanding than those of Oxford and
Cambridge.

As for the situation of Trinity, it was unrivalled.

For by now, after St. Petersburg, Dublin was the most
splendid Roman capital in northern Europe. The great court-
yards and buildings of Trinity itself were magnificent; step out
of the main gate onto College Green, and the grandeur of the
Parliament building greeted you immediately opposite. Past
that, Dame Street led past the theatre towards the Castle and
the Royal Exchange, another fine, classical structure. Stroll a
few yards to the banks of the Liffey, and there, just across the
stream, stretched the imposing façade of the completed Custom
House. Look upstream, and your eye would rest upon the
rotunda and dome of the Four Courts. And all around, on both
sides of the water, the wide streets and squares of Georgian
Dublin spread, in their gracious assemblage, beside the harbour
and under the timeless gaze of the Wicklow Mountains.

Professors and politicians, government officials and
lawyers, clergymen, merchants, actors, fashionable gentlemen
and ladies, they all converged on the area round College
Green, and the Trinity College men were in the centre of it all.
There was no better place to attend university in the world.

From time to time he would catch sight of his father coming from the Parliament. Two or three times, his grandmother

Georgiana came to see him. She would walk round the college with him. If they encountered any of his professors or acquaintances, she would ask him to introduce them; and it was obvious that her reputation preceded her, for even those of his fellows who usually avoided him seemed to smile when they saw the rich and kindly old Lady Mountwalsh.

Unfortunately, there were quite a lot of people who avoided him.

Not all the undergraduates had clear political opinions— about half of them, he guessed. He wasn't sure he had himself. But the two most fashionable camps were those who supported the French Revolution and its ideals, and those who opposed it. These were the great questions argued over at the Historical Society, as the university's debating club was known, where arguments were passionate and, this being Ireland, eloquence was prized. It had become the fashion for those who most passionately espoused the revolutionary cause to follow the example of Lord Edward Fitzgerald and crop their hair short. "Croppies," their conservative opponents contemptuously called them. With most of the students, however, their affiliation was not so obvious.

But as the weeks went by, he began to realise that there was an easy way of telling where someone's sympathies lay: if they were revolutionaries, they avoided him. In the end, he decided to ask Robert Emmet about it.

Despite the embarrassing incident at his grandparents' house, Emmet had been very kind, sought him out when he first arrived, and shown him around. Every week or two he'd have William round to his rooms, and he'd introduced him to a few pleasant fellows. When they were alone, he'd always talk to William in a very easy way, and even share personal confidences. "I'm still foolishly shy sometimes," he might confess; or, smiling ruefully at his hands: "Why do I bite my fingernails?" William noticed, however, that he always kept these confidences to trivial things. If ever William introduced any subject that might lead to a philosophical or political discussion,

Emmet would deflect him with some light remark and turn the conversation to another topic. Nonetheless, towards the end of November, he did manage to pin him down on this question, when he asked him bluntly: "Emmet, why do so many people avoid me?"

"Well," Emmet had responded after a pause, "why do you think it is?"

"I suppose they think that, because Lord Mountwalsh is my father, I must share his political views."

"And do you share your father's views?"

"I don't know," William answered honestly.

Emmet regarded him curiously.

"You're telling the truth, aren't you?"

"Yes."

"Do you want to know what they really think? They think you're a spy. Anything they say to you will go back to your father, and from him, straight to the Castle and the Troika."

William blushed and looked down.

"I see." He sighed. "And do you think that of me? Do you imagine I would do anything so low?"

"I don't know. You can't blame us," he added.

"No." He nodded sadly. He couldn't. "I'd rather die than be a spy," he burst out miserably. "What shall I do?"

"Nothing," his friend sensibly replied. "If you try to prove you aren't a spy, that will only make people more suspicious. You'll just have to be patient."

And so William went about his business as quietly as he could; and then the Christmas season came, and he spent some time at home. He still didn't know what he thought about the great political questions, and he wasn't intending to think about them over Christmas when, two days before the day itself, his father came hurrying back to the house.

"It's beginning," he cried. "I knew it would. The French have arrived. In Cork. The French fleet's been seen in Bantry Bay."

✢

History furnishes many tantalizing moments—turning points when, had it not been for some chance condition, the course of future events might have changed entirely. The arrival, on 22 December 1796, of the French fleet in sight of Bantry Bay, at the south-western tip of Ireland, is one of them.

God knows, the idea that the French might invade Ireland was nothing new. During the course of the eighteenth century, as the British Empire had found itself sometimes the ally but more often the enemy of France, the fear that the French might try to stir up trouble by sending troops to Ireland had come and gone many times. But now it had actually happened.

And the results of Wolfe Tone's efforts in France had been remarkable. So well had he impressed the Directory who governed the new, revolutionary republic that they had sent not a token contingent but a fleet of forty-three ships, carrying fifteen thousand troops. Equally important, the ships also carried arms—for forty-five thousand men. And perhaps most important of all, they were under the command of a general, named Hoche, who was the rival of the republic's rising star, Napoleon Bonaparte. If he could take Ireland, Hoche might eclipse the upstart Bonaparte entirely.

But the fates, that winter, with or without reason, had decided to deny the French general his chance of immortality. As the fleet made its way into the northern seas, it encountered veils of mist which soon enveloped it; the mist grew ever thicker, until half the fleet lost its way. Those who continued towards Ireland were met with gales, and by the time they came within sight of Bantry Bay, it was impossible to land. Day after day, Wolfe Tone gazed through the spray at the distant Irish hills, rolling and dipping tantalizingly upon the horizon. He even persuaded the captain of his vessel to make a run towards land, but the others would not follow him, and at last, on the fifth day, the fleet sailed away. Had the weather been better, and had so large a force landed, they might have been successful. But as it was, the forces of nature had preserved the Protestant Ascendancy that Christmas season, and the men in Dublin Castle were not slow to claim that they saw in this the hand of God.

⁂

The French invasion had failed. Yet when the news of Bantry Bay reached Rathconan, Conall was not downhearted. Quite the reverse: he felt a sense of elation.

"I never thought they'd come," he confessed to Deirdre. And late in January, when he paid a visit to Patrick in Dublin, he learned that he was not alone.

"They have come once. They will surely come again," Patrick told him. "The effect upon people is remarkable. Now that they see there is hope, men in every county are coming forward. By summer, we shall have an army of men right across Ireland, ready to rise. The only difficulty," he added, "is how to arm them."

Though the legislation of '93 had taken away the absolute ban, Catholics had been forbidden to own arms for a century; muskets and pistols were hard to come by.

"We'll do our best," Conall had promised him. And on his return to Rathconan, he had received help from a rather unexpected quarter.

For when he had mentioned this problem to Finn O'Byrne, the shaggy-haired little fellow had nodded eagerly, and a few days later had appeared at the door of Conall's cottage proudly bearing a bundle wrapped in a blanket.

It was a remarkable collection: an old ploughshare, two scythes, an axe head, even an old metal breastplate.

"What do you want to do with them, Finn?" Conall asked.

"Find a good blacksmith. Melt them. Make them into pikes. You're a carpenter. You could make the shafts."

"That's true."

"There'll be more," Finn promised. And hardly a week went by without the fellow turning up with some piece of scrap metal he'd scavenged from the area. It was extraordinary what he could find. Sometimes these items could be used, sometimes not; but every month, when Conall made his run down to Wicklow, he would take the scrap metal with his furniture and deliver it to a blacksmith in the town. By the summer, there were thirty pikes secreted in half a dozen hiding places around Rathconan.

But if the threat from France had brought a new hope to the United Irishmen and their friends, it also had two other effects.

Wolfe Tone and his friends might be happy to cooperate with the Catholics for the sake of a new and tolerant state, but there were still many Ulster Presbyterians of the old school who were outraged by such a collusion with papists—who, after all, were still agents of the Antichrist. To combat this growth of papist influence, they had recently begun to form their own secret associations, which, in memory of good King Billie, they called Orange lodges. With the growing threat of invasion, these lodges were spreading even beyond the enclaves of Ulster.

Of more concern to Conall, however, was the other development. For this was local. Though their British troops and Irish militia drilled in the garrison towns like Wicklow and Wexford, the Troika wanted something more. And so a third force had been set up.

"They call them Yeomanry," Conall remarked. "I call them bandits."

The purpose of the Yeomanry was to act as a local presence, something between a police force and a vigilante group. Their character and discipline depended on the local gentlemen who recruited and led them. They were manned, almost entirely, by Protestants. Budge's younger son Jonah commanded the force that covered the area between Rathconan and Wicklow. As Rathconan was frequently visited by Arthur Budge now, and his old father, though walking a little stiffly nowadays, still kept a sharp eye on the place, there was little reason for Jonah Budge and his Yeomen to trouble the quiet of the hamlet much. But it meant that there were more eyes that might be watching, and Conall was always afraid that he might be stopped and searched on his way down to Wicklow.

The spring passed without incident. The work continued quietly through the summer. In August that year, he went to Dublin to see his children for two days. He visited both his sons and stayed with Patrick and Brigid. The night before he returned, John MacGowan came round and the three men talked together for some hours. The mood was cautious, but Patrick was optimistic.

"Lord Edward estimates that by the end of the year we shall have half a million men in Ireland who have taken the oath," he told them. Since taking an oath to support the United Irishmen was now a criminal offence, this was a remarkable figure. But even if the figure was high, it suggested an entirely new level of commitment to the cause. "When the French come next time, so many will rise that no English force will be able to do anything at all."

MacGowan was less sanguine.

"The English are equally determined to crush us before that happens," he said. Certainly, a British army under a brutal commander named Lake was scouring Ulster in search of troublemakers, Presbyterian or Catholic. "They are terrifying Ulster," he continued. "In one family I know, the Laws, two have been arrested, and one of those, a respectable man, was flogged. Some of the Belfast men are having second thoughts. And it will be our turn next."

"All that will change when the French come and the rising begins," Patrick assured him.

"When will that be?" asked Conall.

"We shall hear from Wolfe Tone. Have no fear. In the meantime, prepare."

A part of MacGowan's prediction, at least, appeared to be

correct, for when Conall reached home the following day, he found that Jonah Budge and two dozen of his Yeomanry had arrived shortly before him. Jonah Budge was still mounted, watching while his men went from house to house. His father was standing beside him, looking cross. Jonah was a tall, square-faced man, a younger version of his father, though with the years, old Budge himself had mellowed somewhat.

"Where have you been?" Jonah asked Conall curtly.

"To Dublin, to see my children," Conall answered calmly.

"They've searched your cottage already, Conall," old Budge remarked, with an irritable look at his son.

"Did you find anything of interest?" Conall asked innocently, but Jonah Budge ignored him.

They found nothing in any of the other cottages, either. The weapons had been well hidden.

"I told them there was nothing here," old Budge remarked to Conall after Jonah and his men had gone. It was clear that he resented the idea that his son thought anything could have gone on under his nose.

"I'm glad you did," Conall answered, with perfect truth.

"Ah, Conall," the landowner remarked with something approaching intimacy, "quite apart from anything else, I know you wouldn't be such a fool."

When Conall related the conversation to Deirdre afterwards, however, she declined to be amused.

"We must thank God they found nothing, Conall," she said. "But it isn't only the Budges you have to fear. Haven't I said it to you before? It's Finn O'Byrne you should watch."

"You've a terrible prejudice against the man," he replied. "I've no great liking for him myself, but he's in as deep as any of us."

And indeed, as the summer ended and autumn set in, Finn remained assiduous in bringing him items that he thought could be useful, and Conall continued to make his journeys down to Wicklow unmolested.

✥

Even in the cloistered precincts of Trinity College, the new military aspect of affairs had permeated. The college had its own Yeomanry now. Students—and they were numerous—who desired to show their loyal convictions could now put on uniforms and parade up and down to their great satisfaction. On the other side, having now been outlawed, the United Irishmen could not form such an open faction, but it was quite the fashionable thing among the "Croppies" and their friends to take the secret and illegal oath: it was dangerous, romantic, and exciting. There were also students who enjoyed looking mysterious and let their friends suppose they were engaged in all kinds of revolutionary activity even if, in fact, they were not.

The position of Robert Emmet remained uncertain. Some believed he had taken the oath, some did not. As for William Walsh, he said nothing and he joined nothing. He listened to everyone, but he expressed no opinion that could be held against him.

It was in the second week of November that he received a visit at Trinity College from his father. Such a thing had never happened before. But having inspected his room, examined his books, and apparently approved of what he found, Lord Mountwalsh smiled quite amiably before addressing his son.

"I had a talk with Lord Clare this morning, William. We spoke about you."

FitzGibbon, the feared leader of the Troika, had also become Lord Clare. As well as governing Ireland, he was also the Vice Chancellor of Trinity College, which meant that, albeit from a lofty height, he kept his eagle eye upon, it must be supposed, even the least among the students. But why, William wondered, should FitzGibbon be interested in him?

"He spoke to me," his father continued, "as a friend—which was good of him. He was concerned about you. You are seen frequently with young Robert Emmet."

"Emmet has been kind to me, Father, but I cannot claim him as a particular friend."

"Quite so. His father, as you know, has abominable views but is relatively harmless. His older brother, Tom Emmet, is another matter. He is known to be a close associate of the leaders of the United Irishmen. He is dangerous, William. Do you know him?"

"No, Father." He didn't.

"I did not think so. Nor does Lord Clare suppose any such association, by the way. But you do know young Robert. It is feared that he might go the way of his brother. A natural fear, I'm sure you'll agree. Has he spoken of political matters to you?"

"He does not confide such things to me, Father. But he is rather quiet and studious."

"Perhaps. There was concern that he might try to lead you astray. I explained that there is no possibility that he could succeed. Your mind and character, I know, are far too strong."

"Thank you, Father."

"And Lord Clare accepts that such is the case. But I was able to give him a further assurance. I explained that you and I had long ago agreed that, should you see or hear anything that made you suspect the loyalty of anyone here, you would confide it to me. Is there anything you can tell me now, about Emmet in particular?"

"No, Father, there is nothing."

"You surprise me. However, I have assured Lord Clare that you will increase your vigilance. I should hope that we may be able to contribute something. Meanwhile, I do not think that you need curtail your association with young Emmet. Indeed, quite the reverse. It is entirely possible that, in an unguarded moment of friendship, he may let something fall that would be of interest, even of real importance to our country, William. I shall ask you, therefore, to be assiduous in your observations. I know how good your heart is, so I am sure you understand?"

"Yes, Father. Is that all?"

"Your studies progress well, I trust?"

"Yes, Father."

"Well done. I shall hope to hear something concerning Emmet. Goodbye, my boy."

"Goodbye, Father."

✢

There were a few days of November left when Patrick Walsh received an unexpected visitor. It was his kinsman, young William. The boy seemed to be in a somewhat emotional state and asked to speak to Patrick alone.

"Do you know what my father has asked me to do?" he burst out.

"I have no idea," Patrick replied kindly.

"He has told me to spy on my friends at Trinity. In case they are traitors—as he would call them. Isn't that despicable?"

"It's not a pleasant task, I grant you."

"My father is a villain."

"I do not agree," replied Patrick. "Your father and I dislike each other, but he believes that he is right, and he believes it deeply. Any man, William, will do such things for a cause he truly believes in. You should not blame him." Though I wonder, he thought to himself, if the roles were reversed, whether Hercules would have spoken so generously of me.

"Well, I won't make a friend of Emmet just so that I can betray him to my father and FitzGibbon. I'm not a Judas."

As Patrick received this valuable information, his face was a mask.

"Why are you here?" he asked.

"You know, at Trinity, I've heard every argument for and against the United Irishmen."

"I imagine you have."

"And I like the arguments of the United Irishmen better." William looked down. "In fact, I should like to take the oath. But not in Trinity. I don't want them to know."

"Why do you come to me?"

"Because I'm sure you must be one of them."

"I see. And even if that were true, how would I know you weren't a spy?"

The look of horror and mortification on William's face was so complete that Patrick almost laughed. The best actor in the world—which this innocent boy was not—could not have dissembled like that. He gazed at the young fellow who looked so like old Fortunatus, and felt a wave of affection.

"Your honesty and your courage do you credit," he said kindly. "But you are too young for such things, William. Come to me again, if you like, in a few years. Your friends at Trinity are young, too, and scarcely know what they are doing. The best course you can follow is to attend to your studies and wait. Your time will come. But I am flattered that you have confided in me."

"You will not give me the oath?"

"I won't. Leave it alone."

When young William had departed, crestfallen, Patrick sat back, closed his eyes, and smiled.

By the time the boy was of age, he thought, God willing, there would already be a new Ireland. And young William Walsh would be a natural leader, one of the finest. He felt a little surge of family pride.

✦

It is not an easy thing for a woman to hate her only son. But Georgiana did, and there was nothing she could do about it. She blamed him for the death of his father—the scene that Hercules had made in their house had undoubtedly caused his apoplexy. And it was no use anyone saying that if it hadn't been that, it would have been something else: her kindly husband had not been upset like that in years, and given his easy, tranquil life, he might have been good for another ten years or more. At the funeral, Hercules had looked suitably grave, but she didn't believe he really felt much grief; and when in a moment of anger a day or two later she had cried, "You killed him," he had curtly told her not to be absurd. Nor was the fact that the whole of fashionable Dublin agreed with her any comfort.

But it was no use dwelling on her feelings, and for the sake of the family dignity, she tried to hide them. No one seeing her and Hercules in public together would have guessed at the cold and bitter hatred in her heart.

For comfort, she had her daughter Eliza living nearby, Patrick, whom she saw quite frequently, and her grandchildren. And of these, of course, the favourite was young William. Perhaps her greatest joy was one of her visits to him at Trinity. But though the young fellow knew she was very fond of him, she took care not to burden him with the full weight of her affection. "I can't bother the boy all the time," she remarked to Eliza.

The death of her husband had occasioned one surprise. In frank admission of the source of the family's wealth, and also of her own good sense, he had not only left Georgiana with a handsome widow's portion and the right to reside as long as she wished in both the Dublin house and the Wexford estate, but he had also directed that she be shown all the accounts. These were a revelation.

For in his quiet, genial way, the first Lord Mountwalsh had shown himself to be a businessman of genius. Taking the large Law fortune at his disposal, he had used it carefully but with remarkable shrewdness.

Like others of his class, he had attended first to the land, and the last two decades had been kind to him. With rising population and a strong overseas demand, prices for Irish agricultural produce had risen sharply, and the great barley producers of Wexford had done particularly well. Reinvesting his income and speculating cleverly in land leases, he had greatly increased the family's land holdings in the county. Georgiana discovered that they owned thousands of acres more than she had realised.

More surprising had been his interest in trade. Though
Ireland's trade and commerce were notoriously subject to sudden fluctuations, the decades since their marriage had seen a
large growth. It had been normal enough for the younger sons
of the gentry to be set up in Dublin, especially as commission
merchants, where, with little risk, taking a small percentage on
import and export shipments, a man might hope in twenty or
thirty years to amass enough fortune to buy a modest estate
and revert to the free-living, free-spending life of an Irish gentleman. Yet Lord Mountwalsh had not been too proud to do
the exact reverse. He had a financial interest in two merchant
houses, one exporting cloth to Britain in return for sugar, the
other sending meat to sugar planters in America—best beef-
steak for the planters themselves, inferior "French beef" for
their slaves. Not only had he financed these houses, but she
discovered that he had discreetly involved himself in their day-
to-day operations. He had set up a Huguenot family manufacturer of silk-and-wool tabernet cloth; he had brought over
some English glassmakers whose skill matched those of the
Waterford glassmen; and more important by far, he owned a
third share in a thriving bank that was looked upon with
respect even by the mighty La Touche house in Dublin.

What pleased her most of all, he had gone back into her
father's trade, as a passive partner in a large Dublin linen factory. And with Ireland's linen exports leaping ahead recently to
a massive thirty-five million yards of linen a year, the profits
had been huge.

All in all, her kindly husband had left three times the fortune he had received, and as she scanned his cautious, canny,
and sometimes brilliant career, her father's soul within her
swelled with admiration and pride. Let brutal Hercules ever, in
his whole life, exhibit a fraction of such intelligence and talent
as his father had shown.

The death of her husband had changed her life in one
other way. She had not realised how much he had protected
her. Though she had always taken a lively interest in what was

passing in the world, he had always been by her side. The doings of the Troika, the radical ideas of Patrick and his friends, and the brutal outbursts of Hercules might have been exciting or disturbing, but in her husband's unflappable presence, and with his secure political position, she had always felt safe. Now, however, events seemed to impinge upon her more directly; she felt a new and disquieting sense of unease. And events themselves were taking an ugly turn.

She heard with horror, from Doyle, of the imprisonment and flogging of her Law kinsmen in Ulster. She was careful never to ask Patrick too much about his political activities—she guessed, yet did not want to know. But he did indicate to her that he fully expected the French to come again. What would that mean for them all? she wondered.

During the summer, she had not been sorry to retreat to Wexford. She had lived there quietly. Patrick had visited for a few days. He was proud of his library, and he had suggested some additions. She had enjoyed his company and been sorry when he left. Young William and his brother had also come down briefly. She had not been lonely, however. She had become better friends with many of her neighbours. A short distance from the house, she had set up a small walled garden for fruit and herbs. She had found peace.

Returning to Dublin in the early autumn, she had not been happy. The usual social round was beginning—nothing ever interfered with that. But the parties were less enjoyable when one was alone without a husband, and the political tension in the air had robbed the gracious Dublin squares of their usual charm. Early in November, she had quietly left the capital and gone back to Mount Walsh for the winter.

And yet, in that colder season, even the gentle Wexford countryside seemed to have changed, as though the troubles of Ireland, like chill winds, were exposing under the green fields and groves another landscape that was bleak and harsh.

To her surprise, it was life in Wexford that gave her a greater understanding of the political storms she had witnessed in the capital. Even during the summer, she had noticed one thing. It had been a trivial matter: there had been a position for a new maid in the house. As usual, the housekeeper had selected two or three girls for Georgiana to choose from, but had also remarked that she could have chosen any of fifty girls she'd seen; and when Georgiana expressed surprise, the house-keeper told her: "At least fifty, my lady, and at half the wages we offer. There are so many young people nowadays that employers may have them for almost nothing."

Georgiana had been watching Dublin grow in size and splendour all her life, and had seen the army of craftsmen, tradesmen, and servants that the great city had drawn in; but she had not fully realised the extent to which this supply of labour was serviced by a huge swelling of numbers in villages and hamlets all over the island. In the last five decades, the population of Ireland had doubled to five million souls.

"Are they in hardship?" she asked.

"They are angry, my lady, because of the high price of food, but they are not starving. But in my opinion," the house-keeper's voice took on a warning note, "it's a bad thing when the simple people are discontented and have nothing to do."

By November, it was the mood among the local farmers that was most noticeable. The Troika's military activity was costing money. New taxes were being raised. She knew very well from the accounts at Mount Walsh that the new levies on salt and malt were hitting the landowners and farmers. In Wexford in particular, the malt levies had driven down the value of the region's precious barley crop. Everyone was grum-bling. "If one of the Troika caught fire," a neighbouring landowner remarked to her, "I don't know a single local farmer who'd oblige him with a bucket of water."

Thinking of her dear Patrick, she was curious about the attitude of the local Catholics, and here it was Kelly who enlightened her.

It had rather surprised her that, after Patrick had appar-ently courted his sister and then dropped her, Kelly and Patrick should have remained on such friendly terms, but Kelly's sister had long ago been married, and the Wexford man had only good words for Patrick. During her visits, she had found him one of her most congenial neighbours. He was also perfectly frank with her.

"We Catholics have lost all hope in the Dublin Parliament now," he told her. "It's become impossible to hold the middle ground anymore. And the consequences of that could be serious."

"Yet the Catholic Church isn't stirring up trouble, is it?"

"No, it isn't. Because the Church fears the radicals. It fears anything that looks like a revolution. As far as Rome is concerned, the French revolutionaries are atheists who murdered a Catholic king—not to mention the massacres of priests, monks, nuns, and loyal Catholics—and who want to destroy the natural order. The Church would rather deal with Protestant King George. All the priests I know in this region preach patience and obedience. But that doesn't mean their flocks are listening to them." He grinned. "Half of them would rather hear a good ballad about a daring highwayman than a sermon. And if it comes to a rising, they will need little persuading."

Kelly provided a further insight in January.

One evening, Hercules had unexpectedly arrived at Mount Walsh and announced that he wanted to spend a few days there. She wasn't pleased to see him, but did her best to be pleasant and avoid any discussion of politics. But the next morning, unaware of Hercules's arrival, Kelly had come by. He was ushered into the library, where he found both Georgiana and her son.

Many people hated or feared Hercules, but though he could not possibly have liked her son, Kelly had seemed to be mildly curious about him and had engaged him easily in conversation. His lordship had been prepared to speak, had soon started upon his favourite subject of maintaining order; he had also, just as easily, made it clear that if he said anything to offend their guest, he couldn't care less. Indeed, it was not long before he had made an insulting remark concerning Catholic priests. Georgiana wouldn't have blamed Kelly if he'd struck her son, but the Wexford man preferred to say nothing and to listen patiently. "The problem with you Irish papists," Hercules went on, "is not so much your priests as the army of hedge school masters. They're the ones that cause the trouble."

At this, far from being angry, Kelly smiled and remarked to her: "He's absolutely right, you know."

"I'm glad you agree," Hercules continued. "They encourage the natives to have too high an opinion of themselves by teaching them in their native tongue."

But now Kelly laughed.

"There, your lordship will forgive me, you're entirely incorrect. It's true that, when I was a boy, the hedge schools made extensive use of Irish. But in the last generation there's been a change. The parents haven't wanted their children taught in Irish, because they think it a disadvantage to them. They want them taught in English. And do you know the result? Those of the native Irish that can read—and there are many—have been reading the revolutionary tracts from America and the radical English broadsheets out of Belfast and Dublin." He smiled at Hercules blithely. "If the revolution comes, my lord, and sweeps you away—God forbid—it will be French troops and the English language that bring it about. Of that I can assure you."

This did not please Hercules at all, and with a curt nod, he left Kelly and Georgiana in the library. Kelly did not stay long, but promised to return another day. After he'd gone, Hercules remarked: "That man needs watching." But that evening, he also said something else which, when she thought of Patrick, filled her with fear for him.

"This revolution won't happen. We are better informed than these damned people imagine."

Mercifully, Hercules had departed by the time Kelly called again. She had a pleasant talk with him, and was glad to have the chance to apologise for her son's manners. Before the Wexford man left, she asked him:

"If the French come, what do you think will happen to us here at Mount Walsh?"

In reply, he gave her a careful look.

"You are well-liked around here," he told her. "I don't think you'd be harmed. But you might be better in Dublin."

"I see." She felt herself go a little pale. "Do you think I should leave soon?"

"Truthfully," he told her, "I have no idea."

As she went into her garden after he had gone, and saw the snowdrops growing, she decided there was no hurry. February came and there were crocuses: purple, orange, and gold.

⁜

A March day and the afternoon was wearing thin, a wet wind slapping the windowpanes, while Brigid sat within.

Rat-a-tat at the door. Nobody heard.

She knew there were soldiers in the Dublin streets. Martial law had been declared a little while ago, whatever that meant. A curfew at night, supposedly, though the theatre was still playing and the inns were doing business. But today, she had heard, more patrols were out.

Rat-a-tat. She glanced through the window, saw a scatter of raindrops dashing against the grey stone steps, but no soldiers. Then, close by the door, she saw the corner of a hat.

She opened the door herself and the tall figure came in hurriedly. He was wearing a heavy cape; his large tricorn hat hid his face. Only when he entered the parlour did he remove the hat to reveal his fine, aristocratic features.

Lord Edward Fitzgerald stood before her.

"Is Patrick here?"

"I expect him shortly."

"Thank God. Nobody saw me come here. I took care." He took off his cape, but he did not want to sit down. He began to pace the room. "They came for me at a meeting. Some of us got out by a back way. But they'll be looking for me. I'll need to hide."

"Cannot your family . . . ?"

"No." He shook his head. "If the Troika mean to arrest me, even the duke can't help me. They'd tear down Leinster House if they had to." He continued to pace. "I'd better not stay for long. Do you think they'll come for Patrick?"

Brigid considered.

"Probably not," she said. Patrick was a useful man in the cause, and a friend of Fitzgerald, but he was not one of the council. There would surely be many others they'd want before they got to him. Besides, she had other information. She smiled. "I've spies in the Castle, you see."

She did not go about much; but all the same, as an actress, it was natural that she should have admirers. And, as an actress, she knew how to deal with them. She had never been unfaithful to Patrick, but she had skilfully developed romantic friendships with a number of men. She didn't flirt with them. She never gave them hope. But she allowed them to entertain the unstated thought that, if it hadn't been for Patrick, they might have had a chance. And there were several men who were glad to enjoy her company on that basis. They were men she liked, and whose friendship she valued, and if she made use of them from time to time, they wouldn't have minded. They also served another useful purpose: if Patrick knew that he could trust her, he could never for a moment forget that she was desirable.

It was an admirer from the Castle who had been good enough to caution her, a year ago, that Patrick was suspected of conspiracy. She had immediately turned her dark-eyed gaze upon him.

"Why?"

"His cousin, the new Lord Mountwalsh, says so."

"I suppose you know that Hercules hates him. He has since they were boys, the malicious devil." She smiled. "I'd never let him do such a thing." Then she'd laughed. "In any case, I can assure you, Patrick wouldn't hurt a fly."

Some time later, her friend had remarked: "By the way, about Patrick: I passed on what you said to FitzGibbon himself."

"What did he say?"

"He just nodded and said, 'I know.'"

The men at the Castle no doubt assumed that Patrick was sympathetic to the United Irishmen, but so were all kinds of people. He'd always been careful. It was unlikely that they had evidence for anything more. Indeed, she had thought wryly, the known malice of Hercules had probably made Patrick less of a suspect than he might have been otherwise.

All the same, she was relieved when the next sound at the door turned out to be Patrick.

He was glad, but not surprised, to find Lord Edward there. The news was already out that a number of the United Irish leaders had been captured together. He also agreed at once that Fitzgerald should not stay there long.

"I'd trust our servants not to give you away. But sooner or later, even if no one gives me away, there's a chance this house will be searched, and there's nowhere to hide you."

The two men considered, and discarded, several deserted places inside and outside the city. "There's no use looking for a ship, either," Patrick said, "because all the ports will be watched." It was Brigid who finally came up with the solution.

"The safest place isn't out of the way at all. It's right in the middle of Dublin, not a mile from the Castle itself." She smiled. "If you don't mind the surroundings, you should go to the Liberties."

The Liberties: the teeming, stinking warrens that once had been the Church's feudal enclaves and were now home to Dublin's poorest. You might be an honest Catholic weaver, a Protestant labourer, a whore or a common thief; you might love your neighbour, or plan to kill him; but whoever you were in the Liberties, there was one thing you had in common with everyone else there: a loathing and distrust of the authorities. Even the military patrols preferred to stay out of the Liberties.

Lord Edward asked only one question.

"How?"

"Leave it to me," promised Brigid. "But be ready before dusk." Then she went out, and did not return for more than an hour.

No one disturbed the two men as they sat together. There was much to discuss. Depending on how many the Troika had arrested, the leadership of the United Irishmen would clearly be a smaller group. "I shall rely upon you, Patrick," Lord Edward said, "to be my link with the world." An immediate question was that of arms. "There are so many caches in the city that I don't think they will all be discovered," Fitzgerald declared, "but I want you to keep this list in your safekeeping. Hide it well, for it has them all. If anything happens to you," he continued, "Brigid will have to pass the information on."

Above all, they both agreed, after today, it would be critical to keep up everybody's spirits, so that they would be eager and ready to fight when the time came.

But when would that be? Patrick wanted to know. Had Fitzgerald any news from Wolfe Tone in Paris?

"Nothing definite. But both Talleyrand, who is in charge of all their external affairs, and General Bonaparte are well inclined towards us. Tone hopes for an expedition before the summer."

"I see." To Patrick this seemed promising.

Lord Edward looked at him thoughtfully.

"No, Patrick. You do not see. In fact, it was that very matter we were to discuss at the meeting of the council today. My view, you see, is different. If the Troika continues to close in upon us, I believe that another course of action may be necessary." He paused. "We should rise very soon, with or without the French."

"By ourselves? Without a trained army?"

"Taking Ireland as a whole, I think we could arm a quarter of a million men."

"I had never considered such a thing," Patrick confessed. "The risks . . ."

"Have faith, Patrick," the aristocrat said.

When Brigid returned, she was feeling pleased. She was carrying a bundle under her arm. She had seen her brother, the tobacconist, and he had promised that by nightfall, he would have a room ready where Lord Edward could lodge, at least for the present. She noticed that Patrick, in particular, was looking concerned, and he asked her nervously if there were patrols in the streets.

"Everywhere," she answered cheerfully. "But don't worry. I know what to do." And she began to unwrap the bundle.

It was as well, she thought, that she belonged to the theatre. It took her half an hour to complete her work, but when she had finished, she was proud of the results. In place of the tall, dark-haired, and youthful-looking aristocrat was a stooped, grey-haired figure in a dirty shirt and a shabby old greatcoat. His boots were scuffed, and he had to lean upon her shoulder in order to walk. As for herself, she was clearly a lady of the night who had once seen better days. "You're my father," she instructed him, "and I'm taking you home. Tomorrow," she added, "we'll get your own clothes to you, but you must never wear them out of doors."

"Which way shall we go?" he enquired.

"By the one way that a fugitive would never choose," she answered. "We'll walk straight past the gates of Dublin Castle."

As dusk was about to fall, they set out upon their way, crossing the Liffey to College Green, thence along Dame Street and past the Castle where the sentries regarded them with pity but no interest. They had gone a little farther on when a patrol appeared, and the officer advanced to question them. But Brigid told him sharply that she wanted her father home in the Liberties before dark, and let off such a string of obscenities that the fellow backed away rather than hear any more.

Normally, neither Brigid nor Lord Edward would have cared to walk unguarded about the city at such an hour. For when darkness descended upon Dublin, the city would show its night-time face: like a huge stage set, its houses would turn into black masses, punctuated by candlelight, streets would become canyons, alleys cave-mouths, dark or lamplit—and humans appear like flitting shades. Dangerous shades: from Christ Church to Dame Street, or even the fashionable quiet of St. Stephen's Green, the figure slumped in an alley or by a tree might be a sleeping drunk or pauper, or it could rise up suddenly to rob you, with a knife at your throat. It was the same in every other great city—London, Paris, or Edinburgh was no different.

But as two poor folk themselves, Brigid and her companion seemed ready to merge with the tattered shadows as they continued westward and passed, unmolested, into the Liberties.

Turning down a small street, then into a stinking alley, Brigid led Lord Edward to a doorway where another shadow, this time her brother, awaited them. Taking them up a rickety stairs, he unlocked the door of a room, which, by the pale light of his lamp, was revealed to contain one wooden chair and some bedding on the bare floor. And here Lord Edward Fitzgerald, son of a duke, descendant of the greatest feudal dynasty and of half the native princes of ancient Ireland, and accustomed to life in the huge palace of Leinster House, prepared to spend a cold March night.

When young William Walsh heard, on the eighteenth of April, that every man in Trinity College was summoned to attend, without fail, a visitation of the dreaded Vice Chancellor in the great dining hall the following day, he was sure he knew why.

The arrest of the leading United Irishmen in March had been followed by a huge hunt for Lord Edward. Some said he was still in Dublin, others that he had fled abroad to France, or even America. Nobody knew.

But the arrests had also turned the harsh light of enquiry upon a fresh target: Trinity College. Several of those arrested, including Robert Emmet's older brother Tom, had been graduates of the place. Indeed, Wolfe Tone himself had been a

Trinity man, and had friends on the faculty still. To his fury, FitzGibbon found his colleagues telling him that the university of which he was Vice Chancellor appeared to be a seedbed of sedition. Redoubled efforts were made to weed out trouble-makers. Two undergraduates who could be proved to have taken the Irishmen's oath had already been expelled. Now, clearly, FitzGibbon meant to launch a public examination of the entire student body. So when, that afternoon, William happened to encounter his friend Robert Emmet, he was eager to know what he thought of it and what he intended to do.

"If the chance arises," William asked, "do you mean to make a speech?"

For in recent months, Robert Emmet had sprung a surprise on the world of Trinity College. He'd always been such a quiet fellow that, when he had joined the Historical Society, no one had expected to hear much from him in their debates. Yet the first time he had risen to speak, he had shown a remarkable talent as an orator. "He sits there quiet as a mouse," one of the members told William, "then gets up and turns into a lion."

But to William's enquiry, Emmet shook his head.

"FitzGibbon hasn't come to debate with us, William. This is a ritual trial and execution. And I'm sure to be one of the victims. He's always been suspicious of my family. Now my own brother's been arrested. He means to expel me, I assure you. But I shall deny him the chance to bully me in public. I shall not go. I shall force him to condemn me without a hearing, and show himself for what he is."

"You think him such a bully?"

"Isn't our whole Ascendancy just a vast system of bully-ing?" Emmet smiled grimly. "Be ready to witness it tomorrow."

There was one thing, however, that William was not ready for. The next day, as he prepared to go to the assembly, he received word that he was to report at once to the Provost's. On arriving there, he was immediately ushered into a room where, instead of the Provost, he found himself alone with FitzGibbon himself.

He'd never met FitzGibbon in person before, so he couldn't help observing him with some curiosity. The leader of the Troika was a formidable figure, yet for all the terror he inspired, William knew that as a lawyer he had earned a reputation as a fine advocate and judge, and even a fair one. It was as soon as he stepped into his governmental role that he became so dangerous. Strangely, this pillar of the Ascendancy had actually been born into a family that had converted to the official Protestant Church. However—perhaps because he came from a convert family—he seemed to have conceived a violent hatred of all Catholics as well as of radicals. As FitzGibbon stood before him now, in his academic gown, he might have been some grim Roman governor cast in bronze.

Yet seeing William, he held out his hand.

"Ah, William." His first name, though they had never met before. The tall man even smiled. "Your father assured me I could rely upon you, and I see from your honest face that I can. We have important work to do today."

"My lord?"

"I shall look to you for support."

"I see," said William, who didn't.

"You are still young." FitzGibbon spoke quite kindly. "But today, all will be tested. Today will be the day to stand up for what you believe. I count upon you." He gave a brief nod to indicate that the interview was over, and William withdrew.

As he entered the great dining hall, William found it already crowded. On a platform at the far end stood a table and two chairs, like a pair of thrones, awaiting FitzGibbon and his fellow judge. Below, in the main body of the hall, the entire college sat on benches in hierarchical order: first the Provost and fellows, the scholars, graduates, undergraduates, even the college porters. He made his way quickly to a place. When everyone was assembled, the doors were closed. They all waited. Then, with an awful majesty, FitzGibbon and his fellow judge entered and assumed their thrones. For a moment, they sat in silence; then FitzGibbon arose.

He spoke clearly, like a prosecutor outlining his case. Let them remember, he pointed out, their privileged position. They were the future leaders of their country. Most of the important positions in Ireland were filled by graduates of Trinity College. Privilege, he reminded them, brought responsibilities. And also—a note of warning could be heard in his voice—it brought risk. To attend Trinity was to open up a bright path; to be expelled from it would destroy all hope of a successful career. And some of those present were about to learn that terrible lesson. For he knew, he told them, he had positive and irrefutable information that some of those before him had flirted with treason.

As he said this, his lawyer's gaze travelled accusingly round his audience, as though he could see into the secrets of every heart.

So what did he want them to do? Why, only the simplest and most straightforward thing in the world. He would ask them all, one by one, to come up. "For a few of you, I may have some questions, which I advise you to answer honestly." As for the rest, he would ask only that they take a simple oath. He nodded to his fellow judge, who, taking out a Bible, held it up, then laid it on the table. They must swear loyalty to the crown, and swear that they would give any information about their fellow students that they might be asked. There must be complete openness, he declared. No loyal man, he was sure they would agree, could have any objection to such an oath. Again, his eyes scanned the room. They rested for a moment, William thought, upon him in particular; and as he gazed back, it seemed to him that the Vice Chancellor's eyes were like two dark whirlpools.

As the proceedings got under way, it was soon clear what FitzGibbon was up to. "He means to frighten us," whispered William's neighbour. Every one of the undergraduates he called up was widely believed to be connected with the United Irishmen, and each was publicly questioned.

The first man quietly denied that he was a member.

"Come, come, Sir," cried FitzGibbon. "I have witnesses." And he had backed up his claim. "On the tenth of February, you were seen entering a house in which, we have it from eye-witnesses who were present, a meeting of the United Irishmen was taking place. . . ."

The damning evidence met with silence.

"Will you now," the Vice Chancellor proceeded, "take an oath to reveal your activities and those of your associates?"

"I will not."

"You may sit down, Sir."

Others were confronted in a similar manner, and gave similar responses. One brave soul decided to defy FitzGibbon.

"Upon whose authority is this inquisition made?" he demanded.

"Upon mine, Sir. There is none higher in this college."

"You ask me to betray my friends?"

"I ask you, Sir, not to betray your country."

"I refuse to recognise these proceedings, and I refuse to take your oath."

"Then you shall be expelled, Sir."

But if these, and a dozen others, were frightening spectacles, there was one that was pitiful.

He was only a little fellow, not five feet tall. His name was Moore. His mother was the widow of a poor shopkeeper, and for her son, therefore, the college meant a way out of the mean streets of poverty. Most of the undergraduates, being people of means, rather despised this sort of student, who often had to perform menial tasks about the college to defray expenses. But many felt a mild curiosity: had this timid boy really joined the United Irishmen? Not so far as anyone knew.

But Moore was guilty of another crime: he was a Catholic.

Until five years ago, he would never have been admitted to Trinity at all. But when the British government had finally pressured the Dublin authorities to make some concessions to the Catholic community, FitzGibbon, much against his better judgement, had admitted a few Catholics into Dublin's university.

The poor little fellow stood before the tall Vice Chancellor. He was trembling with fear, and who could blame him? Towering over him, FitzGibbon took the Bible, held it out, and ordered him to take the oath. William wouldn't have blamed the boy if he'd done so. The thing was meaningless. Moore surely hadn't anything incriminating to tell FitzGibbon, anyway. Take the oath and be done with it, he prayed under his breath. But Moore was shaking his head.

Something like a smile had appeared on FitzGibbon's face. Was he amused? He pushed the Bible into the boy's right hand, but Moore snatched his hand away and put it behind his back. FitzGibbon considered him, as a cat considers a mouse it has caught. He pushed the Bible at the boy's left hand. Moore snatched that away, too, as though the holy book was infected. Both his hands were behind his back now. He was defenceless. But he wouldn't give in.

All around the hall, even amongst a few of the Yeomanry, a feeling of sympathy for the plucky little fellow was starting to grow.

FitzGibbon was still regarding him, his head cocked to one side. Now he thrust the Bible at his chest. The boy backed away. Again. The boy edged back farther. Again and again: the Vice Chancellor and the little Catholic moved across the stage, the tall man making thrusts with his Bible, as the boy retreated before him. Finally, Moore was trapped with his back to the wall, and the Vice Chancellor either had to make him eat the holy book or desist. Some of the Yeomen were laughing. But William did not laugh. He was not even afraid. He felt only a rising tide of disgust.

"Sit down, Sir."

FitzGibbon returned to the table and put down the Bible. Then he called out another name.

"Mr. Robert Emmet."

Silence.

"Mr. Emmet."

Silence.

"Mr. Emmet is not here?" FitzGibbon did not seem surprised. "We have ample evidence of his conspiracy." He paused and gazed at the Bible. A thought seemed to strike him. Having so far dealt only with recalcitrants, perhaps he thought it was time to call up someone cooperative. He gazed over the audience.

"The Honourable William Walsh." He looked straight at William. "Mr. Walsh."

William came towards the platform slowly. He could feel the eyes of the entire college upon him, and he could guess what their thoughts might be. Some, people who knew him, might be wondering if, despite his discretion, he had been led by Emmet into the revolutionary cause. Many more would assume that, as the son of Lord Mountwalsh, he must be close to the authorities. No doubt they imagined that this was pre-arranged, and that FitzGibbon had called him up to denounce someone. William took his time, because at this moment he hadn't the least idea what he was going to say.

But now he was on the stage, and FitzGibbon was looking towards him, though not with any threatening appearance. Indeed, as he approached, William thought he detected from FitzGibbon's fellow judge a faint but courteous inclination of the head.

"Mr. Walsh." FitzGibbon seemed to be addressing the audience rather than himself. "You have heard a number of members of this college refuse to take the oath that has been offered. And there has, in each case, been a reason why they will not do so: namely, that they are, and can be proved to have been, involved in treasonable activities. But these are, if I may so put it, the bad apples in the basket. There are many members of this college—by far the majority, I should say—who are sensible and loyal fellows. They can have no possible reason to object to an oath that only commits them to abhor treason and to expose traitors, should they discover any in their midst. I shall now proffer you the Scriptures, Mr. Walsh, and ask you to take this simple oath." And with a smile, he picked up the Bible and held it out, in a pleasant manner, towards him.

And still William did not know what he would do. He gazed at the book.

After a moment, seeing that he seemed to hesitate, FitzGibbon frowned, in puzzlement rather than in anger. He nodded towards the book, as if William had forgotten what he was about.

"Place your hand on the book," he said quietly.

Still William did not move. Strangely, he was not afraid. He was only wondering what he was going to say. Just for a second, he saw a flash of dangerous anger in FitzGibbon's eye. Then he knew.

"I cannot take the oath, my lord." He said it calmly, but clearly. Even the college porters at the back would have heard him.

"Cannot, Sir?"

"The oath, my lord, is not one that any gentleman could take."

"No gentleman, Sir?" The Vice Chancellor's voice was rising, partly in anger, partly in sheer confusion. "I myself, Sir, should be proud to take the oath," he cried.

"Then your lordship is not a gentleman," William heard himself declare.

There was a gasp around the hall. FitzGibbon stared at him in stupefaction. Then, slamming the book down upon the table with a bang that almost shook the rafters, he shouted:

"And you, young man, we shall see what you shall be. Infamy! Infamy! Sit down, Sir, for you shall never sit in this place again."

That day, about twenty members of the college were expelled. Before he announced their names, the Vice Chancellor explained to the assembled students what this expulsion would mean. They need not suppose, he told them, that the nineteen were denied attendance at the Dublin university only. Letters would go to every place of learning in England and Scotland as well, to ensure that they were denied admittance to those places also. All hope of a professional career was now closed to them, therefore.

The expulsions, which naturally included Robert Emmet, had all been planned in advance, and, in the opinion of FitzGibbon, they were necessary. But to these was added the name of an unexpected traitor, William Walsh. For the young aristocrat who had so unexpectedly turned against his class and so dreadfully humiliated him, the Vice Chancellor reserved a particular fury and venom. And he did not mince his words when he wrote to Lord Mountwalsh that evening.

❖

Georgiana could scarcely believe it. She had been back in Dublin for less than a month when her grandson came to her door. She had heard about the expulsion the evening it had happened and had hurried round to Hercules's house at once; but she had found only her daughter-in-law, who told her that Hercules had just received a letter from FitzGibbon and had left for Trinity College in a fury. There was nothing to do but wait until the next day, and she had planned to go to the house in St. Stephen's Green again. But before she could do so, young William had come to her door to tell her that he was homeless.

If FitzGibbon had been furious, the anger of Hercules surpassed all bounds. If the Vice Chancellor thought William had betrayed his class, Hercules told his son, "You have betrayed me." And if FitzGibbon expelled him from Trinity College, Hercules was still more implacable. "You will not return home. You may walk the world alone. You are no longer my son," he told him. Indeed, before the day was out, Hercules had even instructed the family lawyer to discover whether there was any way that William could be stripped of his right to inherit the family title. Even his wife, who loved her son and hoped to see a reconciliation, was just as shocked as her husband, and considered that any father was justified in acting in such a way. As for William's younger brother, he was told that William had committed a crime so terrible that it must never be spoken of.

So he came to live with Georgiana. She received a note from Hercules asking her to turn the boy out since, he explained, her misplaced kindness might be construed as disloyalty to himself, but she ignored it. In a way, she was glad to have William in the house. She loved his kind and honest nature, so like her dear husband, and his looks so like old Fortunatus: it was as if she had got both of them back. And she could see that the boy loved her, too. As for his feelings for his parents, he said little, but he did once reveal:

"I love my mother, but she only follows my father." And of Hercules, he'd said: "I love my father, because he is my father. But I do not really like him." To this she said nothing. What could she say?

But the young man also frightened her. What was she to do with him? At the best of times, she might have been uncertain. But at a time like this? The authorities had struck, but they clearly did not think they had removed the threat. More troops seemed to be gathering in Dublin. Local Yeomanry companies were being formed in every part of the city. In Merrion Square, some of the residents were setting up their own group. Not one of these elderly gentlemen seemed to be under sixty. As they patrolled the square, they mostly seemed to be drinking tea or making use of their hip flasks. Two of them were even carried round by their dutiful servants in sedan chairs. But they were all armed with swords or duelling pistols. And if this was a comical aspect of the city's preparations, many of the other military patrols were a great deal more fearsome.

Clearly, if the Yeomanry were preparing for action, so were their opponents. The United Irishmen might be invisible, but everyone sensed their presence. The tension was growing. And what, in all this, did her wayward grandson mean to do? He had insulted FitzGibbon, but had he been seduced into the United Irishmen? She asked him directly.

"No," he told her. "But I'd support them against men like FitzGibbon and my father."

"You mustn't go and do anything foolish, William. I forbid it," she told him. But to this he made no reply.

What should she do? Lock him in his room? She hadn't the power to do it. Two weeks, three weeks went by. He gave no trouble. He kept her company. Sometimes he would go out—to see friends, he told her—and be gone for many hours. But she had no idea what he did. By the third week in May, the city seemed like an armed camp before battle. The tension was unbearable.

Then one morning, something special seemed to be happening. The patrols were moving about the city with a new urgency and purpose. By noon she heard that a blacksmith had been caught in the act of making pikes. All that day and the next, the searches continued. They were going from door to door. She found one excuse after another to keep her grandson from going out. Then, like a thunderclap, came the news.

"Lord Edward Fitzgerald is taken." Confused details followed. He was wounded, in jail, dying. As soon as he heard, young William rushed out of the house. There was nothing she could do to stop him.

It took a few days for the details to emerge. The young aristocrat had been betrayed. He'd been taken in his hiding place in the Liberties; there had been a scuffle, and he'd tried to defend himself. Shots had been fired; he'd been badly wounded. Meanwhile, the searches had gone on. A cache had been found at Rattigan's timber yard in Dirty Lane. "They've taken all the furniture out of his house and burned it, to teach him a lesson," she heard. Someone else had been flogged. Were the revolutionaries going to counterstrike? Young William was out for hours each day, and she'd no idea where he was. She tried to question him, but he was evasive. Two more days passed. The curfew was being rigidly enforced now. Nobody could be on the streets after nine at night. On May 23, William seemed unusually excited. He went out early in the evening but did not return. The curfew passed. Not a sign of him.

Georgiana paced her room. There was nothing she could do, but she couldn't go to bed. Hours passed. Midnight came. And then she heard the drums, close by. They were beating the Yeomanry to arms in St. Stephen's Green.

And all over the city. It was starting. Soon, there was banging at the door, and she ran down to it herself. There she found one of the old gentlemen of the Merrion Square patrol. He was carrying a lamp. A pair of duelling pistols were stuck into his belt and he was looking pleased as punch. "Close up your shutters," he cried. "It's begun now. And it'll be the devil of a fight, you may be sure."

"Where?" she called after him.

"You'll see it from your high windows right enough," he called back. And having hastened to the top of her house, she saw from the window that fires were breaking out on the foothills to the south.

At dawn, the same old gentleman called by again.

"They've stopped the mail coaches," he told her. He seemed delighted. "There'll be risings all over Ireland. Not a doubt of it."

Two hours after the curfew ended, young William appeared. He offered no explanation of where he'd been, and she didn't want to ask. He went to his room to sleep. Half an hour later, she was with Hercules. "You must take him back," she begged. "I cannot answer for him, and I don't know what harm he may do himself."

But Hercules was obdurate.

"It's too late," he answered. "He is dead to me."

It was only then, in desperation, that she turned to the one person to whom she guessed the boy might listen.

❖

Brigid had hesitated only briefly before deciding: she would go with him, whatever the consequences.

The boy had been a surprise, though.

When Georgiana had come to Patrick for help, Brigid had thought it unnecessary; but Patrick had been understanding. "She is his grandmother, she loves him, and she feels she cannot help him. The responsibility is too much for her. I don't blame her for seeking my help at all. And she may be right. The boy will probably listen to me." He'd agreed to go round that afternoon.

His plan, which he had not told Georgiana, had been a little harsh and somewhat devious, but necessary. "I'll take him over to our kinsman Doyle," he told Brigid. "Then we'll throw him in the cellar, which can certainly be locked. Doyle can keep him there until the business is over, one way or the other." Unfortunately, when Patrick had suggested this plan, old Doyle had refused. "He says it's too much trouble," Patrick reported. So they would just have to do what Georgiana wanted—which was to take the boy down to Wexford with them.

He had warned Georgiana that there would be risks. He had even confessed to her that he was a United Irishman. But this did not seem to surprise her.

"You will know how to keep him from harm's way," she had said. "You could take him to Mount Walsh. If you are going to Wexford, that should suit you rather well."

For Brigid and Patrick, the weeks since she had taken Lord Edward to the Liberties had been hectic as well as dangerous. Meetings had been arranged, instructions delivered. The whole structure—damaged, but still functional—of the United Irishmen had been contacted from that bare room in a squalid alley; and miraculously, she and Patrick had never been discovered. By the middle of May, the decision had been taken: the rising would take place on the twenty-third.

Not that Patrick had been in favour. "It's madness to begin without the French, he'd told her. But though trusted, he was not one of those who made the final decision, and Lord Edward and some of the others were obsessed with the idea. The wheels had been set in motion. By the time of Lord Edward's capture, it seemed that the rising was destined to go ahead anyway.

The plan was grand—Dublin would be taken, and all Ireland would rise. But the coordination was still weak. The Ulster organisation, after being pulverised in the previous months, was still acting separately. The disruption of the mail coaches the night before had been intended as a signal— when the mail failed to arrive in various towns, the people there would know that the rising had begun. But the Wexford coach had got through. At dawn that morning, it had been agreed that Patrick should go south the following day to do what he could to see that the groups he had set up proceeded in good order.

Taking his kinsman down to Mount Walsh would actually provide him with an excellent excuse to travel, and Georgiana promised to furnish him with a letter that day. "If you stay at Mount Walsh," she added with a wry look, "you could protect my house from your friends. I'd be sorry if the library you created should be burned down."

When Georgiana had departed, he turned to Brigid.

"I have to go, you know."

"I know." She smiled. "But I'm coming with you." And although he argued against it, she would not be denied.

That afternoon, Patrick went to see young William. Once he had explained the role that he and Brigid had played with Lord Edward, and told William that he wanted him to accompany him in an important mission to the south, the boy was only too anxious to come. They all set off the following morning.

✢

She didn't have to go with him. She'd hesitated to leave her children: they'd always come first with her before. But she had spent the better part of her lifetime with this kindly, idealistic, and slightly self-centred man. Perhaps it was a deep and primitive instinct that prompted her, as women had done through the ages, to follow her man into war. But whatever the cause, after all they had been through recently, she knew that, for better or worse, this was the time when she must be at his side. "Shouldn't you look after the children?" he asked her. "No," she answered simply, "this time I'm looking after you." She left her children in the care of her richer brother, at his house off Dame Street.

They were all three well-mounted. They were challenged once, at the city's southern outskirts. But upon learning that they were members of Lord Mountwalsh's family going to secure the estate, the Yeomanry officer let them through with only a warning to be careful along the road. There was trouble to the west, he informed them, all the way through Meath and down through Kildare, and the military was already out in force in those counties. "But take care," he cried, "Wicklow and Wexford will be next."

They saw some burned buildings along the way, but little evidence of any organised rising. At one village, they were gleefully told the landlord had fled. A few miles farther, a small group of local Yeomanry informed them proudly that the rebels in the vicinity had been crushed. Taking the road up into the mountains, they saw fewer people and less sign of trouble.

They reached Rathconan late that afternoon and went straight to Conall's cottage, where they found Deirdre, Conall, and Finn O'Byrne. Brigid admired the easy way that Patrick asked William to see to the horses while the rest of the party went into the cottage. As soon as they were inside and out of earshot, the men began to confer urgently. Conall quickly confirmed what they'd suspected. There had been confusion. Wexford was still waiting, uncertain what to do. Down on the coastal plain, the rebellion was proceeding southwards piecemeal, parish by parish. "I thank God you're here," Conall continued. "Old Budge is alone at the big house. Arthur Budge went down to Wicklow and his brother Jonah has been out with his Yeomanry down by the coast. My fellows are all ready. We can take over Rathconan within the hour. If this fellow had his way," he indicated Finn O'Byrne, "we'd have done it already. But I've been holding them back until I was sure the rising had truly begun."

"You did right," Patrick confirmed.

"But it's started now." Finn's eyes were shining with excitement. "I'll have the men ready in a minute. The weapons are all close by." He gave a grin in which joy and malice were perfectly conjoined. "We'll have old Budge's head on the end of a pike in time for him to watch the setting of the sun." He nodded with huge satisfaction. "We'll warm ourselves tonight with the burning of his house."

It seemed that if Finn still believed that his family were the rightful heirs of Rathconan, they could do without the house.

But Patrick shook his head.

"That's not what is needed. Not yet. If we took it, Finn, we'd not be able to hold it. Even Jonah Budge with his Yeomen would probably overcome you, and God knows what other reinforcements his older brother would bring against you. It would all be to no purpose. You must wait," he told them "for the general rising. When Wexford has risen, that is the time to take Rathconan and to tell all the other villages to rise. Meanwhile," he pointed out, "if the Budges think the place is quiet, so much the better. When the time comes, you will take them by surprise. Do not move," he instructed, "until I send you word." He looked at Finn firmly. "It would be a pity to be killed for nothing."

Finn looked disappointed, but he held his peace.

The family and young William ate together quietly that evening, and lay down to sleep at dusk. At dawn they left. Before they departed, Brigid had a brief but earnest conversation with her mother, after which Deirdre kissed her. Their journey was uneventful. They reached Mount Walsh that night.

÷

It was strange to be back in the great house where she had once been a servant. She still knew some of the people working there. When young William had retired to his room, she and Patrick went to the library where they had first met. They lit some candles and perused the collection.

"Not enough plays," she remarked.

"There's Shakespeare."

"No Sheridan."

"You are right. When this business is over," he hesitated only for an instant, "I'll rectify the omission."

"Please do."

"My life began here, Brigid, when I met you."

"Mine, too."

It was eleven o'clock when they finally retired. They were only sleeping lightly when they were awoken by the flickering of torches outside and the sound of hammering upon the main door. Still in his nightshirt, Patrick ran downstairs with Brigid behind him. Young William and several servants were also gathering in the hall. From outside came a voice.

"Come out or burn."

"What is it you want?" cried Patrick.

"To burn down the house of the infamous Lord Mountwalsh," the voice called back. "You'll not be harmed if you come out."

Patrick told them all to stand back, then turned to one of the servants.

"Open the door," he said. "I'll talk with them."

It did not take him long to talk them round. They were United Irishmen, about fifty of them. They weren't local, but had come from some miles away. On their way to a great muster tomorrow, they had thought to turn aside and burn the house which they understood belonged to the hated Hercules.

"It isn't his," he told them. "It belongs to his mother, who's a Patriot. It's she who sent me here." And he gave them a quick account of who he was and the purpose of his journey. It wasn't difficult for him to prove the truth of what he said. "The house stands for our cause," he explained. "It shouldn't be touched."

The leader of the group did not seem entirely pleased. To judge by his accent, he came from Ulster.

"My name is Law," he said, "and I've no great liking for that lady either. But we'll do as you ask."

Patrick expressed some surprise at finding an Ulster man in Wexford.

"There are several of us arrived," Law told him. "For myself, I came down here for a change of air after I was flogged."

Patrick asked him how the disposition of the forces stood.

"Wexford has started late," Law explained. "There's been no difficulty recruiting. Some of the local gentry are like Lord Mountwalsh, and they've even started Orange lodges. Even the moderate Protestants hate them. But they've been quite effective up the coast around Arklow. They arrested quite a few people in southern Wicklow and north Wexford. That set us back a day or two. But we had whole companies of men out this afternoon. Some of them said they were going turf-cutting. By dusk they were all under arms. Tonight, the whole of Wexford is rising."

"And what forces oppose us?"

"Down in Wexford town there's a garrison of two thousand men, with artillery. There's another garrison farther away, guarding Waterford harbour, in case the French arrive. But apart from that, and a Yeomanry garrison at Enniscorthy, there are only small garrisons in the smaller places. We can overrun them easily. You should come with us to the big muster," he added. "You could meet all the commanders."

Since this was exactly what he wanted, Patrick agreed at once.

"Rest here with your men a few hours," he suggested, "and we'll go on together at dawn."

Law agreed, and Patrick retired with Brigid to get a little sleep.

Brigid did not sleep, however, but watched over him until first light.

At dawn, before he left, Patrick gave his orders to young William.

"Wait here and be at the ready for a message from me," he instructed him. "There may be things I require you to do. In the meantime, you are to guard Brigid." To Brigid he whispered: "Keep him here at all costs, and see that he comes to no harm."

✛

Brigid liked the peace of the great house. The huge quiet of the countryside was like a silent echo of her own childhood up at Rathconan. But comforting though this was, she could not escape the growing anxiety she felt about Patrick. She tried to occupy her mind with other things.

She spent a good deal of time with young William. It was pleasant for her that he took an interest in the library. "Though whether my father will let me enjoy my patrimony seems uncertain," he remarked sadly. He was quite happy to take turns reading a book aloud with her in the evenings. More difficult was the task of keeping him there. The first two days, he went for a ride to take some exercise. But by the third, he was fretting that he should go to join the Wexford rebels. "If Patrick has told you to wait," she reminded him, "you can be sure it's for a good reason. He has a very high opinion of you, so you mustn't let him down now." Unwillingly, he agreed; but she wasn't sure how long she could keep him reined in. Though she had no use for the order to which he belonged, she couldn't help liking him all the same.

The weather was dry. She spent a good deal of time outside, often in Georgiana's walled garden, which she found a pleasant haven. Sometimes she and young William would walk in the grounds. She had come to love the wide, classical streets of Dublin, but the massive Palladian structure of Mount Walsh, so grandly uncompromising, seemed to her eyes to be alien and out of place in that soft and gentle landscape.

Thinking of the poor folk with whom she had grown up in Rathconan, she could quite see why people might want to burn it down. But she did not say so to William.

On the evening of the fifth day, thank God, Patrick returned.

He arrived with his friend Kelly, the neighbouring landowner. Both men were looking pleased with themselves, like a pair of boys.

"You won't believe how well it's gone," Patrick said.

The progress of the United Irishmen had been astonishing. The very afternoon of the rally, they'd been attacked by a force brought in from Munster, the North Cork Militia. "And we saw them off," Kelly cried triumphantly. Thousands of them had swept round the local villages, and the little garrisons there had fled. One garrison in their panic had left a huge cache of arms. "We couldn't believe it," Patrick explained. "They'd left us a present of eight hundred carbines and cartloads of ammunition. The next day, having no artillery, the garrison at Enniscorthy had surrendered. More rebel contingents had arrived. "We all camped on Vinegar Hill, outside the town," Patrick went on. "It's a pleasant place." But the most extraordinary stroke of good fortune had come the next day when a military detachment had foolishly allowed itself to be ambushed and given up its cannons. For now the rebels were not only a huge horde, with firearms and pikes, but they had artillery as well. Faced with this, even the commander at Wexford, the one real garrison in the region, had panicked and withdrawn.

"As of today," Patrick informed them, Wexford shall be the model for the new United Ireland. We have a Senate of eight governors, four Catholic, four Protestant. Similarly, we have both Protestant and Catholic commanders, with about ten thousand under arms." He smiled. "Before I left Wexford, I already sent a messenger to Rathconan to tell them—it's time to rise."

There was not much time. Finn O'Byrne looked up at the sky. The afternoon was wearing on. The message from Patrick had come the evening before. Conall had been out since dawn, travelling around the area putting the word out. The rising was to take place in the middle of that night. On Conall's instructions, he had already organised the men to fetch the weapons from their hiding places once darkness had fallen. The signal would be given sometime after midnight. Then they'd strike.

The target would be the house. Old Budge would be in there, of course. He was to be taken prisoner and held. Finn had been against that himself. "Kill him," he cried. But Conall had only shaken his head. "You're too bloodthirsty, Finn. He could be worth more as a hostage anyway." The people working in the house had not been informed, but as they were all local, no one expected any trouble, and they'd just be told to get out. More problematic was the question of the landlord's two sons. If either was there, they'd certainly put up a fight.

"We capture them if we can, but we kill if we have to," Conall had told him.

Jonah Budge and his Yeomen had last been seen ten miles away. His brother Arthur was down in Wicklow. That morning, however, seeing Old Budge by his door, Finn had asked after his elder son and Budge had answered: "He'll be here this afternoon." It was a piece of information Finn had kept to himself.

For he had needed to decide. And he had been having second thoughts.

Finn O'Byrne had been waiting for this rising all his life. For months he had been savouring the thought. At times, he could almost taste it. He'd been furious a week before when Patrick had made them wait.

The idea of seeing all the Budges dead—and all Protestants, for that matter—was sweet indeed. Conall said that there were good Protestants in the United Irishmen. But what did Conall know?

Whatever his feelings, though, he wasn't a fool, Finn told himself. There were things, important things, to be considered about the present situation. Things to make a man pause.

The men down in Wexford might have had a big success. But they possibly did not realise that, elsewhere, the rising had not been going so well.

Dublin was held by the government in a viselike grip. Despite all Lord Edward's efforts, his scattered forces were not really ready. Munster and Connacht had not risen. The risings in Meath and Kildare had been contained, and almost collapsed now, after big defeats at the ancient sites of Tara and the Curragh. There were signs of a Presbyterian rising up in eastern Ulster now, but would that be enough to topple Dublin? The men down in Wexford had been lucky, but they were more isolated than they realised. And even if Wicklow joined them, the outlook was bleak.

Unless the French came. That might change everything. But the French had not come, and who could say when they would?

They'll take Rathconan, he thought, and places like it, and three weeks later they'll all be flogged or in chains. He could see it clearly. At Rathconan, Conall would be singled out as the ringleader, of course. But the next person after Conall would surely be himself. It was a frightening thought.

Well, now he had made his decision. It was the only logical thing to do. But it needed to be done carefully, and there wasn't much time.

He could go to old Budge, of course. That might have seemed the simplest way. But it carried risks. He'd be seen, almost certainly. He wasn't sure how the landlord would react. The old fellow might not even get away. The alarm would not be sounded. He could see the whole thing blowing up in his face.

Or he could leave. Go down into Wicklow himself. Perhaps too late to do much good. And they'd know he betrayed them. He'd be a marked man. A knife in the back, sooner or later. Or worse.

No. There was only one good way to do this.

He began to walk down the track that led down the valley. There was a cache of arms a short distance down there. A good excuse to be going in that direction, if anyone should see him. But he was not seen. There was a clump of trees by a turn in the track, and he concealed himself on a high bank, with the track below him. Then he waited.

An hour passed. Then another. If Arthur Budge did not come soon, then his plan would collapse. Perhaps his father had made a mistake or the man had changed his mind. Perhaps he wasn't coming.

Or what if someone had already betrayed the rising? What if both the Budge sons should come riding up the track with two dozen Yeomen this very minute? No words would be any use then. It would be too late. They'd take him as a rebel. Dear God, he could feel the rope around his neck already. He broke into a cold sweat. Maybe he should take his chances and run back to the old man. In an agony of indecision, he let another half hour pass.

Then the lone figure of Arthur Budge appeared, riding up the track below him. He scrambled down the bank.

"Your Honour. You mustn't be seen . . ." It only took him a few sentences to explain. Budge was staring at him with angry eyes. But he was listening.

"Who's the leader?"

"Conall Smith. He's out raising half the country now."

"Midnight, you say?"

"Or soon after. Your Honour, now that I'm after telling you, you must arrest me, too. If they know that it was me that warned you, I'm a dead man."

Arthur Budge grunted.

"I'm thinking," Finn continued, "it'd be better I didn't tell your father, in case he let anything slip and gave the game away."

"Why didn't you tell me sooner?"

"It was decided only this morning," Finn answered, with perfect truth.

Budge nodded curtly, wheeled his horse, and was gone.

Finn went down to the arms cache and inspected the pikes. He rearranged them, then covered them over again.

Conall was going to swing. They'd hang him right enough. They'd give him the works, cut him open first, like as not. That's what they did to traitors.

The man was like his father. Arrogant. With all their learning, those Smiths always thought they were better than the Brennans and the O'Byrnes. Even the man's quiet voice, his gentle laugh, had something of the condescending in it. Well, he wouldn't be so condescending at the end of a rope.

So who was the wiser man now? he thought, as he made his way back into Rathconan.

⁜

Rathconan was quiet that night. Soon after dark, as planned, fifteen men stole softly out and, under Finn's direction, took pikes from their different hiding places. Two other caches remained untouched. As agreed, they waited in their own houses until midnight. A little after that, a soft knock came at the door of Finn's cottage, and he came out. Together with Conall, he proceeded to seven other cottages, picking up men at each.

Two of the men carried lamps, covered over so as not to give out any light until it was required.

Silently, they made their way up to the big house. There would be no attempt upon the heavy oak door, which Conall had made himself. They were going to break in one of the windows. This would make a noise, but it hardly mattered. The men who would burst in knew every inch of the house and where each of the inmates would be sleeping.

Big strands of cloud passed across the stars, obscuring the sliver of the moon. The night was dark. There was not a sound as they stood in front of the house.

Then, suddenly, there were torches and lamps behind them. Figures were looming out of the darkness. The door and the windows in front of them burst open with a bang and a clatter, and by the sudden lamplight they saw musket barrels pointed at them.

"Stand fast. One move and we shoot." The voice of Jonah Budge, harsh and peremptory.

Then his brother Arthur's voice, from the doorway.

"You are all arrested. Conall Smith, come forward."

❖

They were all held in the house until dawn. Soon after that, manacled and in chains, they were marched out and down the long track towards Wicklow.

As they left Rathconan, Finn O'Byrne saw the figure of Deirdre standing by the roadside. She had been gazing miserably at Conall, but now Finn realised that her eyes were upon him. She stared at him fixedly.

She had guessed. He saw it in her eyes. A terrible look. He turned his face away. How she knew, he could not tell. She could not have seen. It must be by instinct. But she knew.

❖

Though exhilarated from his exploits, Patrick had looked rather tired on the day after his return. Brigid wasn't sorry.

"There's nothing for you to do anyway," she pointed out. "You've done all you can."

It proved fairly easy to occupy young William. One day he was sent over to see Kelly at his estate nearby. He could also be sent down to Wexford town to obtain the latest news without much danger. So Brigid had Patrick to herself. The weather was dry and warm. Spring was turning into early summer. For several days, they enjoyed the huge mansion and its grounds like a pair of young lovers.

It was at the end of the first week in June that William returned from Wexford town with the bad news.

Perhaps it was not surprising that after such easy initial success, the rebels should have been a little too confident. At the town of New Ross, guarded by a modest but well-trained garrison of government troops, they had been utterly routed. In the confusion, they had lost two thousand men. Even worse in a way, in Patrick's eyes, was the sequel. During the retreat, a company of the rebels had taken the law into their own hands, rounded up two hundred people whom they took to be Protestant loyalists, and burned them alive in a church at a village called Scullabogue.

"Catholics burning Protestants! We might as well be back in the time of Cromwell," Patrick cried in anguish. "This is everything we stand against."

But there was more news, this time from the north. He was grieved to hear that in Dublin, Lord Edward had died in jail. But when he heard the news that the rising in Rathconan had been betrayed, and that Conall was to be tried for treason, he buried his face in his hands.

"This was my doing," he moaned. He looked up miserably at Brigid. "I have destroyed your own father. Full of grief though she was, she tried to comfort him and point out that Conall had chosen this path for himself; he listened to her, but the pain on his face remained.

She was not surprised when, the next day, he started a fever.

Part of the difficulty, it seemed to Brigid, was that there was nothing they could do. She knew he would have liked to go up to Rathconan with her, but with the Yeomanry scouring that area, and the likelihood of his own involvement in the United Irishmen being known by now, that was out of the question. Nor was there anything he could do about the disasters that had taken place in the south. This feeling of frustration and helplessness, she was sure, contributed to the worsening of his fever, so that by the fever's third day, she was quite alarmed about him. Young William was wonderful. He made no demands, and did all he could to support her. After a few days, Patrick seemed better, but still very weak. She let William go out for news again, and learned that another section of the United Irish forces were trying to work their way northwards up the coast, commanded by Father Murphy, a priest who, despite the disapproval of the Church, was taking part in the rising.

The weather was still dry. Strangely for that time of year, some of the grass was looking quite parched.

A week went by. She encouraged Patrick to spend time in the sun, and he was getting stronger now, almost his old self again. But the news continued to be bad. Father Murphy had been killed. The United Irishmen were under pressure on the Wicklow border. A big military force, it was said, was coming down from Dublin.

It was a day of rain, the first for weeks, when Kelly came riding up to the door. He was trying to look cheerful, but she could see he was flustered.

"Is he better?" he asked her. "Can he travel?"

"Why?"

"The government army's pushing down from the north. Everyone's withdrawing. He'd better get out. They know who he is. If they find him here . . ."

"Where can he go?"

"He can come with me. There's still a huge force down at Wexford. He should be safe enough there." He grinned. "Don't worry, Brigid. If need be, I'll put him on a boat at Wexford and send him to France."

"I shan't worry," she said, "because I'm coming too."

But to this, as soon as he appeared, Patrick refused to agree.

"You've the children to think of now," he told her. "You aren't involved in the rising. It'll be me they want. And you'll surely be safer here than anywhere else." He turned to young William. "I count upon you, William, to protect her. Will you promise me that?"

In this strategy, Kelly strongly supported him.

"As long as they don't find Patrick here," he said, "they'll be satisfied." He turned to William. "Your quarrel with your father may or may not be known, but you've only to say that you're the son of Lord Mountwalsh and that there are no rebels here, and they won't dare to give trouble in such a place."

She knew they were right. It was the only way. She gazed at Patrick for a long moment and said:

"I'll help you get ready."

Ten minutes later, he was ready.

They stood at the door. His horse was being brought round from the stable. The rain was falling, obscuring everything beyond the broad expanse of grass in front of the house, falling quietly like a veil. She could scarcely believe it had all come about so suddenly.

"I shall be safe enough," he said, and turning once again to William: "You have promised."

"I shall await word from you." She reached up on her toes and kissed him on the cheek, feeling the rain on her face, and whispered into his ear: "Thank you for my life."

He pretended not to understand.

"You will see the children before I do, perhaps. You'll give them every tenderness from me."

Then William gave him a leg up into the saddle, and wheeling about, he rode away beside Kelly without looking back.

Brigid did not move for a time, but stared into the pale, blank shroud of the rain, falling almost silently—like a curtain, it seemed to her, at the end of a play.

⚜

Night. It was almost the midsummer solstice. Below lay the little town of Enniscorthy, shuttered but watchful, where United Irishmen were encamped in their hundreds. Certainly enough to defend the place. But the main army had come up here, onto the pleasant slopes of Vinegar Hill.

It had been Kelly's idea.

"We'll go up the hill, Patrick," he'd said. "Safety in numbers."

And Patrick was glad of it. The summer night was warm and clear. Above his head, a crowd of stars sparkled: bright, eternal for a few brief hours, until dawn came to wash them all away.

It was a good place to make a stand. As General Lake and his army pressed down from the north, the advance detachments of the United men had given ground; but at Enniscorthy the British would be facing a much larger force, getting on for twenty thousand strong, with carbines and artillery. "We'll outnumber them by two to one," Kelly had pointed out. "The terrain's in our favour, too." For Vinegar Hill was an excellent defensive position. On every side, the British would be forced to mount steep slopes to reach the United forces entrenched above. It was from a similar hilltop, a month ago, and before they'd even had the firearms, that the United men had driven off the well-trained North Cork Militia. With some confidence, therefore, they waited through the night.

Patrick was happy. He had come there by choice. He could probably have travelled on to Wexford and found a ship, or even gone up into the mountains a dozen miles away to hide. But having been absent for all the setbacks of the last three weeks, he would have felt guilty indeed if he had deserted his comrades now. And what good fellows they were, most of them. He felt a surge of affection for Kelly and for all the thousands of unseen faces upon the hill. He even felt affection for the enemy. They were his fellow human beings, after all. He was sorry that so many would probably have to lose their lives during the day to come. It was a sad necessity that blood would have to be shed and sacrifices made for the creation of the new order in Ireland.

He had no doubt that the new Ireland was coming. Not because of the present rebellion, whose issue was still in doubt, but because, before long, the thing was inevitable. All over the world, the old tyrannies were being set aside: the tyrannies of outworn authorities over the body and the mind. In America, in France, men would be free to choose their governments, make their own laws, and worship, or not worship, as they pleased. The reign of oppressor and oppressed, of Catholic and Protestant, would pass away at last. The age of reason had arrived, and surely now, all that was needed was a kick or two, and the rotten old structures of the past would collapse of their own accord. He was grateful that he should have had the chance to be a part of the dawning of this new and better world.

A better world for his children. He thought of them with affection. It was almost a month since he had seen them last. How he wished it were possible for him to take wing, to fly through the night and spend an hour or two with them, to comfort them. He thought of Brigid also. When all this was over, the world would be changed. And once again, but with more insistence, he would ask her to marry him, and perhaps now she would agree.

How strange it all felt, he thought, up here. It was as if, when the evening had thrown its noose of orange light over the hill, it had magically drawn it away to some place beyond time; and that this huge crowd of thousands had been transformed into some ancient Irish gathering, waiting to welcome the rising in the east of the midsummer sun.

✢

General Lake did not wait until dawn. He was a brutal man. He had hanged and flogged his way through Ulster in the spring to break the spirit of the rebels there. But he was a competent general. And faced with an army which outnumbered his own, defending a round hill, he did what any good general would do. He took advantage of his strengths.

Placing his cannon carefully, as close to the hill as he could, he did not wait for the dawn, nor even the first hint of light in the eastern sky. The number of defenders on the hill actually worked against them, for they were so thick on the ground he did not need to be particularly accurate. He filled his cannon with balls and with grapeshot, and then, with a flash and a crash, he let rip in the night.

"I'll blast them to pieces in the dark," he declared.

⁘

At his side, Kelly was as startled by the bombardment as Patrick was. As the cannonballs hissed overhead, and dark splutterings of detritus burst up from the ground into the night sky, they heard screams from all around.

"Does he really mean to charge up the hill in the dark?" he wondered.

But General Lake had no such intention. He didn't move an inch, but let his beasts, the cannon, do his work for him. They pounded the hill in the dark; they pounded it during first light; they roared at the rising sun; and their rough logic, which knew nothing of freedom, of ages ancient or to come, chopped, and carved, and dissected Vinegar Hill until its green sides were splattered and running with blood.

The English artillery had another trick, too. Patrick witnessed it when a shell landed about fifty yards away, bounced, and came to rest by a group of pikemen, who looked at it with distaste. Then, suddenly, they were no more, but transformed into a flash and a bursting of bodies as the shell, with its new delayed fuse, exploded. The Irishmen had not seen the delayed-fuse shells before. Soon, there were eddies of panic all over the hillside as men tried to fling themselves pell-mell away from the shells when they landed.

There was only one thing to do. A huge charge was begun, to sweep the English from their positions. The sheer weight of their numbers should have done it. Patrick and Kelly were towards the rear of the charge, both with pistols and drawn swords, behind a line of pikemen. But they never got to the base of the hill. So devastating was the enemy fire that the charge was brought to its knees and recoiled up the slopes. As they drew back, Patrick saw to his horror that the English were using the confusion to move their cannon forward. He discharged his pistol towards them, but he did not see anyone fall.

Soon afterwards, they tried another charge, but with the same result.

Down in Enniscorthy, English troops were trying to seize the bridge that led into the town, by which they supposed the Irishmen might try to escape. But down in the town at least, the United men were having better luck, and it looked as if the British were beaten back.

Time passed. And still the bombardment went on. The heat was terrible. It was only now that Patrick realised that, while the cannon continued to roar, he scarcely heard them anymore. A strange kind of silence and unreality seemed to have settled upon the day. Glancing around, he wondered how many of the army on the hill were left. Half of them? He supposed so. Everybody seemed to be moving more slowly, though, as if there were all the time in the world. Come to that, what time was it? He didn't know that either. The sun was high.

Something new was happening now. Kelly was shouting something at him. He was priming his pistol. The English were coming. They were coming up the other side of the hill. He'd be ready for them. He nodded and held his pistol firmly, pointing it up the hill. He'd be ready for them, sure enough.

He heard a hiss and a cry. He felt Kelly's hand grabbing him unceremoniously by the collar, trying to haul him off away somewhere. He stumbled, then saw a flash, and found himself lying on the ground. He blinked. On his left, a couple of men were writhing on the ground. Kelly was on the other side of him. He sat propped oddly, as if he were trying to read a book just to the side of his chest. But there was a gaping, bloody mess where one side of his head was supposed to be. He stared. Kelly was dead. He didn't feel too bad himself. But when he started to get up, his left leg didn't seem to be moving properly. That was odd. He put his hand down, and frowned. It felt wet. He looked down and saw there was a great gash

down one side of his leg, with blood seeping from it and a
piece of metal sticking out. He didn't feel much pain. He'd
have to attend to that shortly, he supposed, but there were
other things to do first.

He looked up the hill, and there, silhouetted against the
skyline, was the line of English troops advancing. In front of
them, some brave fellows were standing their ground, others
fleeing. He pushed his pistol forward and tried to keep it
steady. Now he was going to get a shot at them. This time he'd
bring a man down.

✛

Jonah Budge hadn't wanted to miss this battle. He and a dozen
of his Yeomen had attached themselves to Lake's forces as they
came south. The rest of his men he'd left under his second in
command, a solid merchant from Wicklow who could be
relied upon.

He'd learned a valuable lesson today, and he was the first to
admit it. When he'd scoured the hamlets on the Wicklow
Mountains after the affair at Rathconan, he'd earned a reputation for swiftness of which he was rather proud. If he saw a
group of men preparing to give him a fight, or a barn burning—and there had been a few of those—he had always dashed
straight for the object in question. His speed and aggression
had always carried the day, and twice he had certainly saved
some unfortunate Protestants from being murdered or burned
alive.

"These papists will usually scatter if you go at them
quickly," he told his men. For whatever other people might
say, it was clear enough to him what this business was about.
The papists were trying to rise and up to all their old tricks.
"Give them half a chance, and they'll repeat the massacres of
1641 all over again," he would say. It was up to decent
Protestants like themselves to crush them. "Crush the croppies," he'd cry. And though he used the abusive term for the

modern revolutionaries, what he actually meant, and what his men clearly understood, was: "Crush the papists." Speed was the thing. Treat them like animals.

But Lake, tough though he was, had been more circumspect. Where Jonah Budge would have been up the hill and at them by dawn, Lake had held back, and held back again, battering and wearing them down with his artillery, as though they were a walled fortification to be reduced to rubble.

"They are an army, and they will fight like an army," he had cautioned. "Attack too soon, and I'll lose half my men." And, it had to be said, the croppies in the town had done well and given the trained troops a bloody nose. Lake knew what he was doing, therefore, and you had to respect him for it. While the poor devil on the hill had been blown to bits, Lake had hardly lost any men at all.

But now at last, Budge thought, I can do things my way. As he marched up the hill, the exhausted croppies put up a stiff fight. Some of the fresh government troops were falling. But the croppies could hold them. They were pulling back.

As he came over the crest of the hill, he saw to his irritation that there was one flaw in Lake's battle plan. There was a gap in the English lines at the base, where one of the commanders had failed to reach his station. The croppies knew it, too. There was a stiff fight up at the top, but once the English troops could gather to move down the slope in formation, the croppies had started to scatter and flee. They were making for the gap. Some squadrons of cavalry were aiming to cut them off, but it looked to Budge as if some of them would get away. His job was simple, though. Deal with those on the hill. Finish them off.

He was descending with his men down the slope when he saw the fellow lying on the ground twenty yards ahead to his left. He had a pistol. He was pointing it, with painful slowness, towards him. Evidently, the croppy was wounded. He was going to take a final shot. Budge didn't hesitate. He kept walking straight towards him. He had fought a duel once, some years ago, and this reminded him of it. As he came closer, he was not afraid—not because of bravery, but because, having a very good eye, he could see that the fellow was going to miss. The pistol went off with a puff of smoke. The ball hissed by, above and to the right. He kept walking. The man was looking at him, slightly surprised. A gentlemanlike face, it had to be said. When Budge was a few paces away, he took out his own pistol, paused, and aimed carefully. The man didn't flinch.

"Croppy, lie down," Budge said quietly, and fired, and Patrick Walsh was no more. Then he moved on.

❖

Brigid knew what it meant as soon as she saw the woman. It was Kelly's sister. Her husband had sent her a letter from Wexford.

The two women greeted each other quietly. It was many years since they'd met. The letter from Wexford had given a brief account of what had happened at Vinegar Hill, and how both Patrick and Kelly had been lost.

"I am sorry for your loss," said Brigid. "It was good of you to come. I should like to bury his body," she continued, but Kelly's sister shook her head.

"That's done already," she told her. "Don't go near the place. You should stay here, out of sight."

The English victory had been complete. General Lake had hardly lost a hundred men. Quite a number of the United men had managed to get away, though, and regroup at Wexford. Some of them were now marching west into Kilkenny, hoping to reignite the rising there; others were planning to slip past Lake and head north into Wicklow.

"Don't think of going north for the present," her visitor cautioned Brigid. "There'll be trouble all over Wicklow and beyond."

After this, Mount Walsh was silent. The days passed, and nobody came there. Brigid was resigned to waiting. Only young William was fretful, wanting to join the remaining United men. But Brigid was firm. There was nothing useful he could do there, she told him flatly, and he had promised Patrick that he'd look after her. "Would you leave me to go back to Dublin all alone?" she asked. And so, reluctantly, he stayed where he was.

A week passed, then another. News came of incidents in various parts of the region. A Protestant house burned by Catholics; an Orange lodge beating up some Catholic families. As the central network of the United Irishmen broke apart, the rebellion was sinking into ugly sectarian strife. They heard that the northern section of the United men had got into the mountains, that they were passing near Rathconan, and finally that they had dropped down into the plain of Kildare. Only then, some three weeks after the news of Vinegar Hill, did Brigid say to William: "We're going home."

Finn O'Byrne watched the arrival of Brigid and William with care. He'd only been back in Rathconan a few days himself.

The business at Rathconan had been swiftly dealt with. Acting as magistrate under martial law, Arthur Budge had not hesitated. Having marched them down to Wicklow, he'd tried, sentenced, and hanged Conall upon the same day. The rest of them had been held in prison for almost five weeks, while Jonah Budge and the Yeomanry cleared the mountains. They hadn't known what would happen to them until, upon Arthur Budge's authority, they were released. One move from any of them in the future, they were curtly informed, and they could expect death.

On their way out of Wicklow, they saw Conall. He'd been hanged from a bridge, and the blackened remains of his body were still dangling there. They had paused to pay their respects.

"It might have been any of us. Especially you, Finn," said one of the Brennans.

"I know it," Finn said gravely.

"It's a terrible thing to see."

"It is," he'd agreed, with secret pleasure in his heart to see Conall Smith so utterly destroyed. "A terrible thing."

They came back subdued, but as heroes.

Only two people in Rathconan failed to treat Finn as he would have wished. Surprisingly, one of them was old Budge. He knew that Finn had saved his estate, perhaps even his life; and it seemed to Finn that he should have been grateful for it. Yet despite the fact that he hated everything the rebels stood for, and despite the fact that he wouldn't have hesitated to hang Conall Smith for what he'd done, there was something in his eye that Finn did not like when the old Protestant landlord looked at him now. It was masked, of course. No word was ever spoken. But the look was there: the ancient, instinctive distaste that men feel for a traitor. And that from an Englishman. It was intolerable.

There was nothing unspoken about Deirdre, however. As soon as he was back, she sought him out.

"Do you think I don't know what you are?" she had whispered. "I know what you did."

He'd faced her down.

"You know nothing." She couldn't. It was absolutely impossible that she could know. But she did.

"Judas," she said. It didn't matter. Nobody believed her. They all thought she was confused by her distress. But it didn't stop her when she found herself near him, hissing: "Serpent."

He didn't feel guilty. He'd done what he wanted to. But for the contempt she showed him, he hated her.

Her youngest son and daughter, still in the village, also looked at him angrily; but other people there, including those who had been in prison with him, were telling them that Deirdre was mistaken. Soon he saw doubt as well as anger in their eyes. The accusation, he suspected, would die away. But since she was obviously out to poison the minds of the whole

Smith family against him, he knew very well that when Brigid arrived, she'd do the same with her.

He wasn't sure what he felt about Brigid. She had gone away so many years ago, and he would only see her briefly, once a year or so when she came up to see her parents. She wasn't the wife, but only the mistress, of Patrick Walsh: that didn't make her so important, he supposed. She was a well-known figure on the Dublin stage, of course. That had to count for something. After living in Walsh's house all these years, she also carried herself like a lady—though it would be the stage, no doubt, that would partly account for her manner. But whatever the reason, he concluded, he didn't like it, not one little bit, that she should arrive in Rathconan looking as if she was altogether of a different sort from the people like himself who, in the eyes of God and every reasonable person, were certainly better than she.

As for William, he still wasn't sure where the young man fitted in. He'd been down at Mount Walsh, his own family house. God knows what money he must have. And now he was returning to Dublin. He'd never heard any mention made of the boy by Conall, or even Patrick, and he'd noticed that when they had discussed the rising, Patrick had made sure the boy was outside. This young aristocrat, he concluded, belonged to another world entirely, outside his knowledge, and therefore of no interest to him.

It was evening when they arrived, and they went into the cottage. After a little while, the young man came out. Finn watched him. He wondered if, being an aristocrat, he'd go up to the big house. There was only old Budge there at present, although Jonah Budge, back from his adventures in Wexford, was somewhere in the area with his yeomen. But the young man just walked to the track that led down the valley and stood there for a while, staring down towards the coast. Then Brigid came out to fetch him. As they returned, they passed not far from where Finn was standing. As she did so, she turned to look at him. And so it was that he received the full force of her stare.

Finn almost gasped. The flash of those magnificent green eyes as they fixed upon him: they'd take any man's breath away. He had expected hurt, anger, rage even that he had killed her father. But though all these were present for a fleeting moment, they coalesced into something else.

Disgust. She was looking at him as if here were some filthy, loathsome creature that had come up from the ground. He, Finn O'Byrne, to be looked at in such a way: as if she wouldn't soil her shoes with treading on him. Then she and the young man were gone.

All that night, Finn O'Byrne brooded about how he had been treated.

Brigid and William left in the morning. The countryside between Rathconan and Dublin was not entirely quiet, but Brigid was so anxious to get back to her children now that she was determined not to delay any longer. Since it was deserted, they decided to take the track that led over the high ground. In the unlikely event of their seeing any troublemakers, William had his sword and a pistol, and Brigid herself carried an ornamental dagger, small but effective, secreted in her riding coat. More to the point, however, the ground was firm and they had good horses.

⁘

It was only an hour after their departure that providence smiled upon Finn O'Byrne. Jonah Budge and a dozen mounted yeomen appeared. It took Finn only a couple of minutes to realise what this could mean. And thinking of an excuse to go over to the big house, he managed without much difficulty to find an opportunity to speak a few words to the officer unseen. When he had finished, Budge asked a few quick questions.

"The young Protestant, Lord Mountwalsh's son, is not involved? I shouldn't care to arrest the son of such a powerful man."

"There's no need. He knows nothing. I noticed that they did not discuss anything to do with the rising when he was in the room. I think they were using him as an excuse to travel down to Wexford," Finn added.

"So Brigid Smith is Conall Smith's daughter, and also the woman of Patrick Walsh?"

"And it's he that gave the order for Conall to start the rising here at Rathconan."

"Can you testify against her? Have you evidence of her active involvement?"

Finn hesitated.

"Testify? No. For you promised to keep me out of it. Besides, I've nothing I can swear to beyond her being with him. But I'm sure she was in it. She must have been. If you take her in for questioning," he added with relish, "who knows what you might shake out of her?"

"I'll think about it," said Jonah Budge. Soon afterwards, he and his men left.

Behind him, Finn O'Byrne smiled to himself. He wondered what they would do to her. That would teach her to scorn him.

✛

Brigid and William were almost at the point where the great plateau of the Wicklow Mountain range falls sharply down into the Liffey basin when they saw the three horsemen approaching.

They could see that the men had uniforms, so they were not unduly concerned. They had taken their time crossing the mountains. The day was pleasantly warm. As the three men came close, they drew to one side from the track to let them pass. But they did not pass.

The three yeomen had been travelling for some hours. They were hot, and tired, and somewhat irritated. There were several ways to go over the mountains, and having failed to find anything, Jonah's men had split up into smaller groups to try each path. They knew little about their quarry, except that the young man was a Protestant from an important family and mustn't be harmed, and that the woman was the papist daughter of Conall Smith and wanted for questioning.

The yeomen varied widely. Even in Jonah Budge's little force, some were solid citizens, others merely fellows looking for an excuse for violence.

They ordered William and Brigid to dismount. As they were armed, it seemed better to comply. One of the yeomen, a sandy-haired man a little older than the others, dismounted also. He turned to Brigid.

"You are Brigid Smith?"

"I am the Honourable William Walsh," William cut in firmly. "My father is Lord Mountwalsh, and this lady is under my protection. I advise you to let us pass."

"You're free to go, young gentleman," the fellow replied gruffly, "but it's this woman that Captain Budge wants for questioning. Those are my orders." He gave Brigid a crude look of appreciation. During the last weeks, there had been several occasions when, turning the papist rebels out of their hovels, he'd come across some handsome females. There had been one young wife he particularly remembered. It had been a night raid and he'd got her alone in an empty cowshed. She'd screamed, but those of his companions who'd heard had only laughed. A tasty morsel that had been. This green-eyed woman was dressed as a lady, but wasn't she only the daughter of the fellow hanging from the bridge at Wicklow? And this was a quiet place. "We'll wait for the captain here," he said to the other two. "You escort the young gentleman down to the Dublin road."

"I refuse to leave," said William.

"What'll you do about that, Nobby?" one of the others asked with a smirk.

In any sane world, Nobby thought, he'd just kill the young man and do what he liked with the woman. But because of

Budge's orders, this aristocratic young whelp was making a fool of him.

Then he thought for a moment. If this young man was claiming responsibility for a papist rebel woman, then something wasn't quite right with the young man either. So he'd teach these people they couldn't make a fool of him. He looked at his companions and gave them a meaningful nod.

"Help the young gentleman on his way."

William started to protest, but the two mounted men were grinning. One of them had the reins of William's horse. Suddenly, they wheeled together and came one each side of him. Scooping down so fast he had no time to resist, they seized him one by each arm and started to ride away, carrying him between them. William was struggling wildly, looking back over his shoulder. As much as anything to show him who was boss, Nobby now lunged forward and grabbed Brigid by the breast.

"We'll have to find a way to pass the time," he said.

Brigid screamed. William, with a sudden wrench, managed to break free. The two riders, laughing, went on a few paces and turned. But he was running back towards Brigid as fast as he could. As he came close, he drew his sword.

With a curse, Nobby ripped open Brigid's coat, then let go and turned to face William. Brigid, her eyes blazing, reached into her coat and pulled out her knife. But this Nobby did not see. William stood before him, panting, his sword drawn.

"Leave her alone, you filthy brute, or you'll hear of it," he cried.

Nobby's face suffused with rage. He wasn't going to be insulted like this, in front of his fellows, by this cursed boy. Forgetting his instructions, he swore another oath, drew his own sword, and rushed at William.

William was white with anger. He had never fought for his life before; but unlike Nobby, he had received fencing lessons. As the Yeoman rushed and swung at his neck, he instinctively took up his stance, deflected the blow, and lunged. And Nobby stopped, his mouth falling open, the sword through his heart. He sank to his knees. William pulled out his sword. Nobby pitched face forward onto the ground.

Behind, the two Yeomen looked at each other in amazement. This was not supposed to happen. Should they kill the young man? They weren't sure. William had already turned to face them. He was very pale, but quite collected. His sword, red with blood, was in his hand, but he did not offer battle. He waited. Brigid was straightening her clothes. The dagger was in her hand. For a moment there was complete silence.

Then, half a mile away, they caught sight of another party of horsemen coming up the track behind them, and one of the two Yeomen announced with relief:

"It's the Captain."

When Jonah Budge arrived, he took in the scene at once. He scarcely needed to ask what had happened. He knew Nobby. He saw the confusion and awkwardness upon the faces of the two Yeomen, the outrage of Brigid and the righteous indignation of young William.

Jonah Budge was a tall, somewhat brutal-looking fellow. But he was capable of thinking very fast. He dismounted. Walking calmly to William, he made a slight inclination of his head and asked for his sword, which William tendered. Then he stepped over to Brigid and politely held out his hand for her dagger, which, reluctantly, she gave him.

"Thank you," he said.

He went to Nobby's body and turned it over. Stooping down, he inspected it. Then, with careful deliberation, he inserted Brigid's dagger in the open wound and pressed it home. Leaving it there, he wiped William's sword clean on a tuft of grass and stood up. He faced Nobby's two companions.

"It seems the woman stabbed him when he tried to arrest her."

They gazed at him, and then the light of comprehension dawned in their faces.

"Yes, Sir. That's right, Sir."

"No!" William cried. He looked at them in amazement and horror.

"You'll swear to that, no doubt?" Budge continued, ignoring William entirely.

"Oh yes, Sir. No trouble at all."

"That's not what happened at all," cried William. "The fellow tried to rape her, and when I challenged him, he came at me. It's I who killed him."

Budge looked at the two men hard, and also at the other Yeomen nearby.

"There must be no doubt, you understand? From this moment on."

"No doubt, Sir," they said quickly. "She stabbed him, all right."

"Well, there it is," said Jonah Budge coolly. "I cannot believe your testimony, Mr. Walsh. Nor, I assure you, will any court." He gave him a curt nod. "You may go, because we shall know where to find you. Your sword will be returned to you in due course." He told the two Yeomen to pick up Nobby's body and strap it to his horse. "Troop," he then called to the others, "place the woman on her horse and keep hold of the reins. She comes with us to Wicklow."

"You are nothing but criminals," she told him with disgust.

"And you, Madam, are accused of murder." He mounted and signalled the Yeomen to move off. As they did so, William was still furiously protesting. Budge waited until his men had gone a short distance before he turned to him again.

"Your gallantry is all very fine, young man. Commendable, I'm sure. But the fact is, I have just done you a most signal favour."

✢

For Georgiana, the summer of 1798 was a time of disillusion.

While Patrick and his friends were busy down in Wexford, she had watched sadly as news came in also of the

United Irishmen's other rising, in Ulster. Protestants and Presbyterians mostly, idealists for a new world, people like her dear father's family, they had succeeded briefly; but the government forces had been too much for them, and even before Vinegar Hill, they had been smashed. She mourned them.

The end of the summer brought one more, bitter irony.

The French arrived. They came too late and they came in vain. In August, a small force headed by a certain General Humbert landed upon the western coast of Ireland, at Killala in County Mayo. They were good troops. They even gave General Lake a bloody nose. For a little while. But they were isolated. The United Irishmen had only a meagre organization to offer in the west, and though some brave souls rose in support, most of the population, having already seen the failure in the east, left the little French force to conduct its business alone. By the time he reached the Midlands, Humbert saw he could get no farther, and wisely gave up.

Two months later, a larger French fleet appeared farther north, off Donegal. Six of its ships were captured, and on one of them, the authorities discovered Wolfe Tone himself, dressed as a French general. Court-martialled at once, he took his own life in his prison cell. And that was the end of the rising of '98.

Yet if these great events were depressing, it was an aspect of the rising nearer to home that made Georgiana truly uncomfortable.

When William arrived back, she had been relieved that he was safe. But the news he brought of the death of Patrick and Conall, and the arrest of Brigid, filled her with grief; and when he told her that it was he, and not Brigid, who had killed the Yeoman, she was horrified.

"She is innocent," he declared, "and I mean to speak for her at her trial."

"Do you want to be accused of murder yourself?"

"It wasn't murder. I was defending her."

Georgiana could see why the court would be ready to sentence Brigid, the daughter and mistress of known revolutionaries. But young William must be somewhat suspect, since he'd been expelled from Trinity. If he irritated the authorities by trying to intervene in her trial, might they not turn upon him?

She tried to persuade him to change his mind. He was shocked that she should even suggest it.

She had no choice. She went to see Hercules.

If she had come to despise her son, she still found it hard to believe his reaction. He was furious that his son should be mixed up with such a business, and when she pointed out that he had only defended Brigid, he seemed to feel that William should have left the yeomen to get on with their work. "If I help him today, he'll only disgrace me tomorrow," he said.

"You will do nothing for your son?"

"Nothing."

Yet if Hercules was a monster, what could she say of herself?

Georgiana had always thought of herself as a good person. She had never known what it was to feel moral guilt. But she knew what she had to do now. Young William must be removed from the scene. Sent away again. Kidnapped if necessary. He must not testify in court. Brigid might tell her story and hope the court would accept it. But William was not going to be there. Georgiana was too honest to hide the awful truth from herself. Brigid was her protégé and her friend, but William was her grandson. Brigid would have to be sacrificed.

Yet how could she get him away?

Help came from an unexpected quarter. Two days after her interview with Hercules, he turned up at her house.

"The trial of Brigid Smith will not be for many months," he informed her. "So many thousands of rebels have been captured that the courts-martial will extend far into next year. In the meantime, therefore, I'm arranging for William to visit England. He will not know it, but once there, he will be detained. He will never get back for the trial."

"Why this change of heart?"

"Arthur Budge came to see me. It was his brother who arrested Brigid. They would be glad if William didn't raise the matter of the arrest. It might be . . . embarrassing."

"So you'll help your son so as not to embarrass the government and its minions?"

"I think it's for the best. But I shall need your help. I want you to persuade William to visit London with you. After that, arrangements will be made."

She agreed to do it, of course. She was actually in London with him when they heard the news of the second French appearance and the arrest of Wolfe Tone. She stayed in London until mid-November, after which William, having been assured in a letter from his father that the trial of Brigid would not take place before the spring, was taken by an obliging landowner to stay with his family in the depths of the country.

The trial took place the day after Georgiana arrived back in Dublin.

She would have liked to go. She would have liked, at least, to see Brigid. But she couldn't. How could she face the woman she had just betrayed?

"What will become of her?" she asked Hercules.

"An offer has been made to her," he answered. "She maintains her innocence, and though the judges would not accept her defence against the word of the Yeomen, the court-martial could be embarrassing. As an actress, she has quite a following in Dublin. It was thought best to keep matters as simple as possible by offering lenience. If she pleads guilty, she will not be sentenced to death."

"Thank God for that."

"She will be transported to Australia."

"Australia? The penal colony? Even if she survives the voyage, never to return: isn't that almost a sentence of death?"

"Not at all. The climate there is excellent. And she will not want for company. We shall be transporting considerable numbers of rebels down there."

Georgiana still didn't go to the trial. It was very brief.

One concern she had was the fate of Brigid's children. They were Patrick's, after all. She was aware that they were being cared for by Brigid's brother; but now she wondered whether she could make amends to Brigid, and to Patrick's memory, by doing something for them. But she heard that Brigid's mother Deirdre had been at the trial and that, at Brigid's particular request, she had taken charge of the children. It seemed that Brigid wanted them to spend the rest of their childhood away from Dublin, up in the purer atmosphere of the Wicklow Mountains.

It was another six weeks before William discovered that he had been duped. He wrote her a letter of some bitterness, although, fortunately, he laid the deception entirely at the door of his father. Then he continued:

> I have decided not to return to Ireland for the present, but to go to Paris. And I am hopeful, Grandmother, that since I have only small funds of my own, that you might furnish me with some money, which I am certain that my father will not.

She sent him a hundred pounds the very next day. But she did so with misgivings. What did he mean to do in Paris?

EMMET

⊱ 1799 ⊰

B Y T H E S T A R T of the new year, Georgiana realised
that she was rather lonely. She loved Mount Walsh, but
she did not want to go there now. She wanted to stay in
Dublin; she missed the lively company she had enjoyed
when her husband was alive. Could she, as a widow, have
that again?

To her surprise, she found that she could.

After the rebellion, people with liberal views were out of
fashion. Sympathizers with the United Irish cause tried not to
draw attention to themselves. Old Doctor Emmet had closed
up his town house and left the city. So when, early in 1799,
Georgiana opened her house once more, those who remembered the kindly hospitality of old Fortunatus and of her husband were only too glad to find a haven there. Congenial
people of every political persuasion were welcome; she even
found that people from the Castle came to her.

For if Hercules and his friends were eager for revenge upon
the revolutionaries and their Catholic friends, there were
calmer voices in the British government who took a different

view. And the most influential of these was the new Lord
Lieutenant himself.

Lord Cornwallis might have had to surrender to the
American colonists, but he was a fine general and he had
become a wise statesman. With the Irish revolt under control,
he looked for solutions, not revenge; and Hercules and his
Ascendancy friends did not impress him.

What solutions were available? Firstly, he wanted to reduce
the tension. Large numbers of rebels had been captured. The
leaders had to be tried, but executions should be limited, and
most of the rank and file could be pardoned. Leading United
Irishmen like Tom Emmet, who had been held before the
revolt, would have to stay in custody, but negotiations were
started for their eventual release. More significant, however,
was another, growing perception.

"The biggest problem in Ireland," Cornwallis and his colleagues were concluding, "is the Irish Parliament."

Grattan's Parliament: seventeen years ago it had seemed to
bring hope of a new and liberal Patriot regime, but the reality
had been so different. It was Hercules and his friends, and the
Troika, who had triumphed. And what had been the result? A
huge revolt and three attempted French invasions. The argument was growing in Westminster: "these Irish Ascendancy
men aren't fit to govern. They'll always bully the Catholics.
And the last thing we need, when we're fighting the French, is
trouble on our western flank." Indeed, some thoughtful men
concluded, the system of the two parliaments was inherently
flawed anyway. "The London Parliament will always want to
limit Irish trade, which they see as a threat; and between
Dublin and London, there's always going to be a dispute about
who pays for what." The solution?

Union. Unite England and Ireland. Just as England and
Scotland had been united, the two lands would become a joint
kingdom. A hundred Irish MPs would sit in the London
Parliament and have a vote in governing both lands; thirty-two
Irish peers and bishops would sit in the British House of Lords.

Trade would be unrestricted; Ireland would be better off, as Irishmen and Englishmen joined together to form a stable nation. Wasn't that a better way to proceed?

The Irish did not think so at all. Take away the ancient grandeur of the Dublin Parliament and its magnificent classical building? Anathema. At the start of 1799, they voted it down. But the English government was not to be so easily put off. The proposal was raised again, insistently.

And in the easygoing atmosphere of Georgiana's house, this was soon the main topic of conversation.

She found that her Patriot friends were divided. Grattan's followers eloquently defended the Parliament their leader had created. But some Patriot members, shocked by Hercules and his friends, had lost faith in Dublin and confessed: "We'd probably do better in London."

Nor, for that matter, were the hard men of the Ascendancy all agreed. Some, shaken by the revolt, thought that a united kingdom might indeed bring more safety and order to the island. But Hercules himself was in no doubt. "I've been talking to the Orange lodges up in Ulster," he told her, "and they want none of this union. They think the London men are far too soft on the Catholics. And they're quite right. We must keep the Dublin Parliament."

But even the Protestants of Ulster were by no means agreed.

"Many Ulster Presbyterians are quite in favour of union," Doyle informed her.

"But they rose against the English," she pointed out.

"True, but it didn't work. And they think union would be good for the linen trade." He grinned. "Calvinists like profits, as you know."

"And you," she asked the Dublin merchant, "what do you feel?"

"Oh, I'm quite against it," the old man replied. "If the Parliament moves out of Dublin, it will be terrible for the Dublin tradesmen, and for people like me with houses to let."

But perhaps the most interesting discussion took place at her house at the start of the summer. It was a gathering of old friends, Patriots mainly from the days of old Fortunatus. John MacGowan was there. And one of the Patriots had brought a young lawyer with him. "For I know that you like to meet the coming young men."

The young lawyer was a tall, handsome fellow with a mop of curly brown hair. He came from an old Catholic gentry family in County Kerry. Whether it was normal when one was getting older she didn't know, but she often found that young people were happy to confide in her things that they might have hesitated to say to others. Certainly, young Mr. Daniel O'Connell did not try to hide the fact that he was ambitious.

"I have to make my way in the world, Lady Mountwalsh," he said. "So I have just joined the Freemasons."

"A wise move," she agreed, "especially, if I may say so, for a Catholic."

He nodded when she said this, but at the same time, he sighed.

"To tell you the truth," he confessed, "though my family is Catholic, I've little personal interest in the Catholic religion. You could call me a Deist, I suppose."

He was also frank about his politics.

"I saw the excesses of the French Revolution," he told her, "because I was actually in France at the time. I abhor violence." And he was entirely pragmatic. When one old gentleman, who was an enthusiast for the Irish language, began to wax lyrical upon the subject, O'Connell would have none of it.

"I don't deny the poetry of my ancestral tongue," he said. "I was brought up to speak it. But I must say that I think it tends to hold my fellow countrymen back, and I shouldn't be sorry if it disappeared." The old gentleman was horrified, but O'Connell remarked to Georgiana: "You know, I only said what many ordinary Irish people think."

He wasn't sitting near her at dinner, so they had no further conversation until, with the dessert course, a general discussion broke out upon the question of the union. Several views were expressed. Most of the Patriots were against it on principle. To her surprise, however, John MacGowan, whom everybody knew to be a United Irishman, was prepared to consider it.

"We know we shall never get any satisfaction from the Troika and the Dublin Parliament as things stand," he pointed out. "Even a London Parliament might be better than what we have."

This was immediately countered by a Patriot member.

"For better or worse, there has been a parliament in Ireland for centuries. Take it away, and you'll never get it back," he warned.

"And what," Georgiana asked, looking down the table, "does Mr. O'Connell think?"

She could see that he didn't particularly want to be called upon, but he spoke up nonetheless.

"I don't like the idea of the union, because Ireland is a nation. But of one thing I am certain: whether Ireland forms a union with England or not will scarcely matter as long as the vast majority of Irishmen are treated as inferior citizens because of their ancestral religion." He looked around the company. "Until Catholic disabilities are all removed, until Catholics can enter Parliament and hold office as high as any Protestant, we shall have explosive discontent in Ireland whether the Parliament sits in Dublin or London. It will hardly make a difference."

It was now that a white-haired old Patriot spoke.

"I was one of those who voted with Grattan, so I am not easily persuaded of the benefits of Union. But I was in London recently, and I should tell you this. Cornwallis is entirely of your opinion. Prime Minister Pitt in London is coming round to the same view. They'd like to assure the Catholics and their Patriot allies that, as soon as Ireland is unified with England, the new British Parliament will grant the Catholic Emancipation that you want. The only problem is that they can't say it openly, because if they do, they'll never get the

Protestant majority in the Dublin Parliament to consent to the Union. That's the message, in private, they want to convey."

"Do you mean," said Georgiana, "that the English government has to hoodwink the Irish Protestants?"

"Lady Mountwalsh," the old man said with a smile, "I never used those words at all."

✢

She did not see Daniel O'Connell again for some time, though she heard word that his career was thriving. But the conversation of that evening was often in her mind.

For the old Patriot's words were soon borne out. Nothing official was said, but she heard from friends: hints were being dropped, private assurances given. By the autumn, it was clear that a bill would be brought before the Irish Parliament, around the turn of the year, which would invite that body to vote itself out of existence, and that the Patriots and supporters of Catholic Emancipation had been assured that, soon afterwards, their wishes would be granted. But even if these liberal men could be squared, what about the Ascendancy diehards who formed the majority? How would they be persuaded to give up their local power?

She was rather surprised, therefore, shortly before Christmas, when Hercules casually informed her:

"I've changed my mind. Union's for the best. It's the path of progress, I'm convinced if it."

She wondered why.

✢

The parliamentary debates began in January 1800 and went on for months. Georgiana listened to many of them from the public gallery. There were many fine speeches defending the Irish Parliament, but the most memorable came from Grattan himself, who, though sick at the time, came down to the

Parliament for the late-night debate, dressed in his Volunteer uniform, pale as a ghost, and gave one of the greatest speeches of his life. Hearing such power, logic, and eloquence, Georgiana thought that the Union cause must be lost. Yet as the weeks went by, one by one, those who had opposed it before were rising to speak in favour.

One day she found young Robert Emmet discreetly watching from the gallery, and they chatted briefly. She knew from William's letters that Emmet had been in Paris, too, and he was able to give her news of him. "He speaks excellent French now," he reported. "I shall tell him I saw you upon my return." She asked him what he thought of the prospect of the Catholics getting their Emancipation if the Union came. "I think the English may be somewhat cynical there," he answered. "They must calculate that, in a much larger British Parliament, the number of Irish Catholic members would still be too small a minority to have any effect at all." When she remarked upon the number of members who seemed to be changing their minds about the Union, he grinned. "They've all been bought, Lady Mountwalsh. And for good prices. I think we may be sure of that."

The meeting with Emmet brought her grandson so vividly into her mind. She missed William. She had tried to take an interest in his younger brother, though her cool relations with Hercules did not make it easy. He was a sweet, good-natured boy who loved his brother William. But he was an odd young fellow who lived in a world of his own. He had a great aptitude for mathematics and loved astronomy. His father had even bought him a telescope, and he would occupy himself with it for hours, perfectly contented. She was glad he was happy, but was unable to follow him in these interests.

William's letters came regularly, once a month. She sent him money and was glad to do it. His letters were informative. He had no shortage of Irish company in Paris. There were over a thousand Irishmen in the French capital, he told her, many of them on the run after the revolt. There were United

Irishmen who had left or been exiled; most of the students who had been expelled from Trinity College had graduated to Paris, too. As for the French, Napoleon Bonaparte, the adventurer-general, had now made himself master of France, as consul; and she learned with amusement that the fashionable world of the republic was just as pleasure-loving as it had been under the ancient regime. He said no word about returning to Dublin, though, and she supposed he was glad enough just to be away from his father.

All through the spring and summer, the debates about the Union went on. But when the final votes came, the Union won: Ireland's Parliament voted itself out of existence. And the means by which it was done? Emmet was right.

For if the vote took place in the new century, the process itself belonged, wholeheartedly, to the old. The Parliament, in its final act, brought all the eighteenth-century political arts to a magnificent climax. Jobs, titles, ready money—nobody could remember when they had been promised with such ruthless liberality. Cajoled, flattered, honoured, paid, peers and humble members alike sold their votes.

No wonder Hercules had seen the wisdom of the Union. Not only was his peerage raised in degree, so that instead of being a humble baron, he was now the Earl of Mountwalsh, no less; but he was even chosen as one of the select group of Irish peers with the right to sit in the British House of Lords in London. He was also able to get titles and favours for a number of friends. He even got a knighthood for Arthur Budge, who, he had assured the government, was a loyal fellow who should be encouraged.

It was in this manner that, in the summer of 1800, Ireland and England became united.

⁜

The winter season that followed was a strange one. Georgiana opened her house and people came, but Dublin was half empty. People brought their daughters in to find husbands or enjoy the theatre. But not only was there no Parliament to attend, some of the greatest social and political figures had gone to London. Hercules was so rich that he intended to keep a house in both capitals, but most members of the new Parliament were not so fortunate. Their Dublin houses were standing empty.

The north side of the Liffey was especially hard hit. Across from College Green, the broad artery of Sackville Street had led to a series of terraces and squares favoured by the Parliament men. One November morning, as she was passing through the area in her carriage, Georgiana saw old Doyle standing in front of a handsome town house, directing some workmen. She was never quite sure of his age, but she knew he must be in his eighties. "The spirit of his mother Barbara lives on in him," Fortunatus used to say. "Cousin Barbara never let go of her business until the day she died, nor will he." Telling her coachman to wait, and stepping out, she went to ask the old man what he was doing.

"Making alterations," he growled. "Tenant's gone. Can't find another." He was standing by the open door, and she looked in. The house was typical of its kind. A long hall and staircase; fine decorative plasterwork on the ceiling. Halfway up the stairs, a tall window with a semicircular upper frame graced the return.

"What will you do?" she asked.

"Put a caretaker in the parlour. Let the rest of the house room by room."

"But . . ." she gazed at the noble scale revealed within, "this is a gentleman's house."

"Find me a gentleman."

"What sort of people will rent the rooms?"

"People who pay." He shrugged. "I've three other houses without a tenant, and seven more that will be vacant during the next three years. I'll probably have to do the same to all of them. This is the result of the Union."

"Hercules says that the Union will bring progress," she remarked sadly.

"Not all progress," said the old Irishman wisely, "is for the better."

She looked up at the window over the stair. A grey light was falling slowly through it, onto the empty return. It seemed to presage a new and shabbier world.

But it was not until February that the real bitterness of the Union was tasted. For Georgiana, it came when John MacGowan arrived unexpectedly at her house one afternoon and, with a face more agitated than she had ever seen it before, cried out:

"May England be cursed, Georgiana. We are betrayed."

⁘

You're only a traitor if you're caught. That was how Finn O'Byrne saw it, anyway. There had to be proof. To Deirdre's accusation that he had betrayed the Rathconan men, he would simply point out: "Why would I do such a thing? It makes no sense." As for her claim that he had set the Yeomen on Brigid, he would shake his head and say: "Her grief has affected her brain." Most people, including even Deirdre's own family, were inclined to agree with him.

But she wouldn't give up. She made the air of Rathconan poisonous for him. By the time the Union debates had begun in Parliament, he had decided to leave Rathconan and move into the city. She took some satisfaction in the knowledge that she had driven him out.

Yet the fact was, he considered, that she had done him a favour. He found various kinds of work to keep body and soul together, while he lived in cheap lodgings in the Liberties; but it was after a year in Dublin that he found his niche as a caretaker in one of the houses where Doyle was letting rooms on the north side. Within a few months, he had made himself rather useful to the old man. He kept the house in good order, but he also had an uncanny knack of knowing when a tenant was likely to be late with the rent or, just as important, when they had the money to pay. "You seem to know everyone's business," Doyle said approvingly, and soon he began to give Finn small commissions. He even used him to collect rent from some of his other properties. From these activities, Finn was able to make a modest living; but he also had time to spare, and he wondered how to use it for profit.

The answer was provided by King George III of England.

✢

When John MacGowan had come to Georgiana's house in such distress, he expressed the shock and horror of Catholics all over Ireland. They had been betrayed.

As it happened, the betrayal was not deliberate. When William Pitt had given assurances that something would be done for the Catholics of Ireland, he had honestly believed he could accomplish it. But even the canny Prime Minister had underestimated the forces ranged against him.

Hercules had been especially active. It had not been difficult to convince stolid English gentlemen in the London Parliament that the Catholic menace of 1641 was still alive. "God knows," they would say after listening to him, "he was born and bred there, so he should know." But most effective of all was FitzGibbon, who, once again, got to work upon King George. "I cannot have Catholics in my Parliament," the old king reiterated, "whatever Pitt may think. It's against my coronation oath." And although he was technically incorrect, and Pitt brought all the weight of argument and influence to bear upon him, nothing could break through the barrier of the king's honest, royal obstinacy. Pitt, who was a man of his word, honourably resigned.

But that was little use to the Catholics of Ireland.

"First Cromwell takes all the Catholic land; King William promises Catholic rights, but then we get the Penal Laws instead; now we are betrayed again. You can never trust the English." That was how John MacGowan saw it. That was how United Irishmen all over Ireland saw it, and those in Paris, too. So did Finn O'Byrne. But for him, the betrayal brought an opportunity.

It was not until the autumn of 1801 that he went to see Sir Arthur Budge at his Dublin house. The newly made knight listened to what Finn had to say, then he wrote a letter and told him to take it to Lord Mountwalsh. When Finn presented himself nervously at the house on St. Stephen's Green, he was ushered, after waiting only half an hour, into the bureau of the new Earl of Mountwalsh himself.

Though Finn could not have known it, his timing had been fortuitous. Budge—who didn't much like him, but admitted his usefulness—was about to give up his Dublin house and live entirely at Rathconan, where his old father was now getting too frail to cope alone. So he had passed him on to Hercules for what he was—a small-time informer wanting to be paid—and he had imagined that Hercules would probably pass him on to some minor official at the Castle. But even Finn could discern that, behind the hauteur natural to an aristocrat confronted by such a thing as himself, the earl was actually rather pleased to see him.

The Union was not turning out quite as Hercules had hoped. True, his title was now magnificent and the Catholics had been denied. Both outcomes brought him satisfaction. But life in London had been a disappointment. He had realized, of course, that his political position would be less significant there. He was one of a few Irish peers in a great assembly. But he had not understood that he would suffer a loss of social status. It was subtle: it would only have been apparent to members of his own exalted class—and the upper servants, who lived vicariously through such distinctions. But the fact was that in fashionable London, an Irish peer, even an earl with a seat in the British House of Lords, was not quite the same thing as an English lord. His ancient lineage and nobility were accepted, but his title was not quite, as the English might say, out of the top drawer. Still more important, though his fortune was ample, it was dwarfed by the fortunes of the greater English aristocrats. Without influence, with a second-rate title and a second-class fortune, Hercules found himself for the first time in his life in a position where he couldn't bully people. It distressed him deeply.

While he would rent a house in London, therefore, he had decided to spend a good part of his time in Dublin, where, as he calmly acknowledged, "I am hated, but important."

And this informer Budge had sent him might be rather useful.

Ireland might have the protection of the Union, but that did not mean the island was secure. Nowhere in Europe was safe. To the oppressed of every land, France remained the symbol of Liberty, Equality, Fraternity, and her ruler Napoleon Bonaparte was a hero. Even great artists and musicians, like Beethoven, believed it. In Ireland, too: "The meanest peasant in Connacht believes that Bonaparte will deliver him," Hercules could remark with contempt. The United Irishmen might have lost heart after the rebellion, but if the heroic French appeared on Irish shores, that could change in a moment again. True, there was talk of a truce with the French. Cornwallis was going over to France to see what could be done. But it was unlikely that any peace between the British monarchy and the French republic could last for long. And it was equally unlikely, in Hercules's judgement, that the United Irishmen would behave themselves either. More than a year ago, FitzGibbon had told him: "That wretched little Robert Emmet, that I threw out of Trinity, has been trying to set up a new United leadership here in Dublin. We got wind of it, and if we catch him here again, we'll throw him in jail." A spy on the continent had recently reported that young Emmet was one of a delegation seeking help from Bonaparte.

But not much else was known. Were these plots getting anywhere? What preparations, if any, were now afoot in Ireland?

Nobody in the Castle knew. So if this fellow O'Byrne can infiltrate the United Irishmen and bring me any information,
Hercules considered, he'll perform a useful service, and enhance
my reputation with the government—both worthy causes.

"I pay well," he told O'Byrne, "but I'll only pay for what I
get. You will also report to me, and to me alone."

Finn left delighted by his good fortune.

After he had gone, Hercules remained staring thoughtfully
in front of him. For the running of Finn O'Byrne was not the
only private espionage in which he was nowadays engaged.

It had not been difficult to guess, after young William had
absconded from England, that he must be getting funds from
someone, and the most likely source of funds had been his
grandmother. It had taken patience, but recently he had been
able to persuade his mother to employ a particular footman in
her house in Merrion Square. The fellow knew how to pick
locks, and should therefore be able to open the drawer in her
bureau where he knew she kept her most private correspondence. The man was literate, and his instructions were to tran-
scribe the letters. If, as he guessed, William was sending letters,
he'd like to know what was in them.

He didn't know who his son's associates were, but he suspected they might be fellows like Emmet. Young William had
refused to spy for him when he was at Trinity, which had been
shockingly disloyal. Perhaps now, unwittingly, he could do better.

❖

Yet it was to be another year before anything came from this
source that was really useful.

My dear Grandmother,

Lord Cornwallis's peace still holds, and we see more
English and Irish visitors to Paris than ever. I still continue to
hope that you will come here one day.

Robert Emmet has gone to Amsterdam to join his

brother Tom and his family, and they all think of going to
America. Robert, good fellow that he is, was never happy in
Paris, though with his genius for chemistry and mathematics,
he had made the acquaintance of some of the greatest French
men of science. So as usual, our finest men will go to the new
world, since the old world is not worthy of them.

Will the peace last? Some of the Irish here would be glad
for it to end. For while we were at war, the French government paid to support the United Irishmen in France; and
during the peace, those payments have ended. Some of the
better sort, with no trade to fall back on, are hard-pressed to
put food in their mouths. Worse yet, it is believed that
Bonaparte is quite ready to sell any of the Irish, including
Emmet, to the English in return for some French émigrés.

With each passing month, it becomes clearer that
Napoleon is not a hero but a Tyrant. Even those Irishmen
who still have the strongest hopes of freeing Ireland, and I
include my friend Emmet himself, would sooner have King
George for a master than Bonaparte.

I remain, as always, your loving grandson,
William

Before I seal this letter, I have just received news that
Robert Emmet has left for England, whence he means to
journey to Ireland, I know not upon what cause. But see that
you tell no one else.

Hercules put down the transcript of the letter and smiled.
Finn O'Byrne's monthly reports had been paltry affairs so far,
but perhaps now he could achieve something useful.

Two days later, when Finn O'Byrne appeared, he gave him
a simple order.

"Find Robert Emmet."

By the following April, Finn was getting desperate. His last interview with the earl had been frightening. "If you cannot find anything better than this," Hercules had coolly observed, "I shall conclude that you have joined the conspirators yourself." Finn had broken out in a cold sweat.

"If Emmet's here, he's wearing a cloak of invisibility, your lordship," he'd protested. "There's not a sign of him."

"Find him or suffer the consequences," the aristocrat had replied bleakly.

And the devil of it was, Mountwalsh was right. Several people had whispered to him that Emmet was in Dublin, but nobody knew where. And that wasn't the only problem. From the very start of his attempt to infiltrate the United men—that was eighteen months ago now—he had run into unexpected problems.

The first person he had gone to see had been John MacGowan. He'd remembered his visit to Rathconan with Patrick. If anyone could involve him in the movement again, it would be the Dublin merchant. But he had got nowhere. MacGowan had been straightforward.

"The movement is lying dormant until there's a real chance of success. That much I know. Ulster, Wicklow, and the other regions will only rise if Dublin is secured, and the Dublin men don't want to rise without the French. Who can blame them? The chain of command has also been changed. But that's all I know, because I refuse to take part anymore." When Finn had expressed surprise, he'd explained. "Our rising in '98 failed miserably and cost too many lives. I no longer believe in risings. We can achieve more by patience and peaceful means. Perhaps my children will see justice. Meanwhile, things could be worse. Cornwallis was wise and humane. There are others like him." Seeing that this was not at all what Finn wanted to hear, he added: "You might try the Smith brothers."

When he had told the earl of MacGowan's lack of interest in the cause, Lord Mountwalsh had not been pleased. "A pity," he had declared irritably. "MacGowan is a man who needs to be hanged."

Finn had been hesitant to approach Deirdre's sons, and had tried other avenues first. He soon discovered that MacGowan's reluctance was shared by many of the Dublin tradesmen. Finally, after putting out several feelers, including one to the Smiths, and waited two weeks, he had been visited by a man he did not know, who had invited him to join a small group under his command. But there his progress had halted. Who the other companies might be, to whom his own commander reported, he was never told, nor was there any way of finding out. He was part of an invisible army. And, he soon discovered, this was deliberate. After the failure of the last rebellion, the United Irishmen had learned the value of secrecy. "If you or I are arrested and tortured," his commander told him, "there's almost nothing we can tell them." He grinned. "Next time we fight, it will be like the dead arising from their graves."

And it hadn't got any better. Talking to others, travelling into Wicklow and Kildare, he'd sometimes been able to glean small bits of information; but generally, he'd only been able to tell the contemptuous earl that the United men were biding their time.

So he'd been almost grateful at first for the chance to go after Emmet. At least it was something definite to do.

Old Doctor Emmet had died in December. A family friend was in charge of his affairs, and the house to the south of the city was to be sold. His remaining family had taken lodgings meanwhile. Surely young Robert Emmet might appear at one of these places? Finn had even employed a boy to watch them, but there had been no sign of Emmet.

In late March, however, he had seen a change. His commander had suddenly been more forthcoming. He even looked excited. Something was up. Important men, leaders of the movement, were arriving from France. Were either of the Emmets here now? he ventured. "That is possible," his commander admitted. A few days later, he had made a trip down, himself, to Doctor Emmet's former house.

The house, which was called Casino, was an old structure with eighteenth-century embellishments, sitting in a small park south of Donnybrook, only half an hour's walk south from St. Stephen's Green. It was shuttered and silent. Skirting the house, he found a small window at the back he could force, and moments later he was inside.

The place was empty. Everything had been removed. His footsteps echoed unnervingly. Up on the attic floor where the servants had slept, he found an old bedstead, some bedding, and a couple of ancient blankets, presumably left because they were not worth taking. Had somebody used them? Possibly. He returned downstairs. In the kitchen he found a couple of plates, a cracked pitcher, an empty wine bottle. There were some crumbs on the floor. He couldn't decide how old they were. He went back to the hall. There was only one strange thing about the empty house.

He felt as if he were not alone. He couldn't say why; it was just a sensation. But all the time, as he moved from empty room to empty room, he felt as if some other heart was also beating there, some other person, quite close, yet whom he could not see. He went round once more. Nobody. Nothing. No sounds, no fleeting shadows. Only blankness. He shrugged. His mind must be playing tricks on him. He left, closing the window behind him.

A week later, he nervously made his report to Lord Mountwalsh. "Just a little patience," he begged. "The United men are about to show their faces." But to his surprise, the earl did not seem particularly concerned. Instead, he picked up an oval miniature from his desk and told Finn to look at it. "Can you remember that face?" he asked. The face belonged to a young man. It was broad, strong, and pleasant. "This was done about four years ago," the earl remarked, but the features will not have changed much, I think." Finn nodded. "I believe he is in Dublin. Perhaps with Emmet. Find him."

"I'll try, my lord. But who is it?"

"My son. His name is William. You might start by watching the movements of his grandmother. She lives in Merrion Square."

With this new commission, Finn left, greatly surprised.

My dear Grandmother,

The rumour here is that Bonaparte is preparing for war again. And unofficially, it is said, certain persons close to Bonaparte have approached certain other persons—I could not say who—to know whether a rising might be effected in Ireland.

As you can imagine, this has caused quite a stir among our friends. On the one hand, this might be the opportunity for which they have waited so long; on the other, they are now so anxious that Ireland should not fall under the rule of the French dictator himself, that they are eager to ensure that any rising is under their own control before the French arrive. It is said also that the American ambassador has offered funds from his own pocket to purchase arms.

Meanwhile, I myself think of visiting Italy, so do not be alarmed if a little time passes before you hear from,

Your affectionate grandson,
William

Georgiana gazed at the letter. Almost two months had passed since it arrived, and since then she had received no further letters. It was possible that he had gone to Italy, of course, but she did not think so. It was surely a stratagem to explain the fact that he could not write to her from Paris.

He was probably in Dublin, then. Every day since getting the letter, she had looked out of her window, half hoping to see him walking towards her through Merrion Square. But, of course, she hadn't seen him. And if he was here secretly, he must be with the United men. She trembled to think what danger he was putting himself in.

But the circumstance that had frightened her most of all was something that had happened in her own house. A week after she had locked the letter away, she had taken it out of the locked drawer in her bureau again, and noticed to her astonishment that the letter had been replaced in the drawer the wrong way up. She was quite certain: she had put the letter in there with the writing facing towards her; now it had been reversed. She had tested the drawer after locking it. Someone, therefore, had picked the lock, read the letter, and replaced it. But who had done so, and what did it mean? And how much danger was her grandson in?

⁘

It was strange to be invisible. At first it had seemed exciting, but now William found it lonely.

Robert Emmet was living under an assumed name out at Rathfarnham, a couple of miles farther south. It had been Emmet's idea that William should use Casino. "It's empty," he explained, "and when I was there before, I made some false panels and trapdoors. So if anyone should come there, I can show you how to hide." That was exactly what William had done the day the fellow had come snooping round the house. The hiding place had been effective, but he was sorry that it didn't allow him to get a sight of the intruder's face.

Meanwhile, he had grown a moustache and some bushy side-whiskers of which he was rather proud. On Emmet's advice, he called himself William Casey. "And since nobody outside our Paris group knows a thing about you now," Emmet had pointed out, "you could be very useful." The United leaders, Hamilton, Russell, McCabe, Swiney, were a mixed group, some gentlemen and men of intellect, others artisans, but all idealists. He was the youngest of the men present at the meetings, which were usually held at Rathfarnham. "But we take no account of age," Emmet smiled. Anne Devlin, the girl who acted as housekeeper of the place, was only sixteen, yet they all seemed quite content to trust her with their lives. Men came to see them from all over the island. The men from Wicklow and Ulster promised, "Take Dublin and we'll rise." The men from Kildare said: "We'll help you take it."

But the meetings which most impressed William were the ones with the lesser, local commanders. For this was where Emmet really came into his own. It was extraordinary how persuasive he could be, painting a glowing picture of how things would be as soon as Ireland was free. "Napoleon is looking to us Irishmen," he would tell some humble artisan, "to see whether we have the fight in us. If we want his help, we have to prove ourselves. So where do you stand?" It never seemed to fail.

During May, news came that Napoleon was officially at war with England again. This added urgency to the preparations. By June, a message was sent to Paris to tell Bonaparte that they were almost ready for him.

One evening, they had gone into Dublin to meet some local townsmen. Emmet had been inspiring, but one fellow, who had been especially impressed, had also stared with interest at William, and afterwards had come up to him. Would he also have come from Paris? he asked respectfully. And when William nodded, the fellow remarked: "I could see you were a man of birth and education, Sir. I am Finn O'Byrne, at your service."

"I am William Casey."

Finn nodded. "And would you be living in the city, Sir, might I ask?"

"Outside."

"I am caretaker of a house in the city, Sir, and I have access to others. If ever you should require lodgings, or a place to store anything, I can arrange it and no one need even know you're there. Would you tell Mr. Emmet that as well?"

William said he would, and Finn O'Byrne gave him the address where he could be found. "Would there be anywhere I could find you, Sir?" he asked.

"Through Mr. Emmet," William answered cheerfully, "who can be reached through the usual channels."

"You know where to find me, Sir," Finn repeated, "if ever I can be of service to you."

He seemed a good fellow, thought William.

With Emmet acting as quartermaster, the preparations went forward at speed. There were three secret caches of weapons in the Dublin Liberties. Only a handful of men, which included the Smith brothers, knew where they were. Blacksmiths had made hundreds of pikes. They had flintlocks, pistols, a formidable quantity of gunpowder. William made himself useful acting as a secretary and right-hand man for Emmet. Only one thing was lacking.

"We need money, William," Emmet remarked one day in June. "Can you get us any?"

William had a hundred pounds left. He gave fifty to Emmet. He even thought for a moment of going to his grandmother for funds; but if he did that, he'd break his cover; and besides, even if she'd give him money, he couldn't drag her into the conspiracy in such a way. But thinking about it made him realize with a stab of pain how much he missed his family.

Not that he really missed his parents. He was frankly glad to avoid his father, and his mother, though she loved him, so completely identified with his father's wishes that he never really felt he could talk to her. But Georgiana was another matter. Once or twice, at dusk, he had walked past her house, hoping to catch sight of her at a lighted window. How he'd longed to go up the steps to the door, with its broad fanlight, and make himself known. The second time he had done this, he had been delighted to see the door open and his brother come out. He had watched him walk dreamily along the street, no doubt happily engaged in some mathematical puzzle, and wished so much that he could come up beside him.

William found Emmet more extraordinary every day. Not content with collecting weapons, he was inventing new ones. He had designed a folding pike that could be concealed under a man's greatcoat. The blacksmiths had complained and only made a few, but they worked. As a chemist, he designed grenades and some signal rockets. These last were formidable monsters, with eight-foot poles that would rise hundreds of feet into the sky before discharging different-coloured fireworks that would act as prearranged signals to the troops. Early in July, they tested one, quite effectively, in some fields near Rathfarnham.

William also knew that, at the same time as all these other activities, his friend was conducting a love affair with the daughter of a gentleman whose family house was nearby. William had met Sarah Curran, a dark beauty with a beautiful singing voice, and he counted Emmet a fortunate fellow. His friend was doing so much that it seemed to William that a day of his life must be worth a month of living for most other people.

As July began, however, he could tell that Emmet was concerned. By the middle of the month, he was getting nervous.

"We must act soon, William," the young man confessed. "We're almost out of money, and it can't be long before we're discovered."

"What about the French? We can't go without them," William pointed out.

"Not a word." Emmet paused. He seemed to be considering something, then irritably shook his head. "The time's drawing close," he said suddenly. "I need to be in the city from now on, and you should be, too. Have you a place you can use?"

Remembering the helpful offer from Finn O'Byrne, William had gone to see him the next day. O'Byrne had been delighted. "There's a room you can use in the very house where I live," he assured him. "It'll be no trouble at all."

‡

Finn O'Byrne was in luck. Two weeks ago, when he had reported seeing both Emmet and William, Lord Mountwalsh had been pleased. And now, when he told him about this new arrangement, Lord Mountwalsh even smiled.

"You think the conspiracy is moving towards a final phase?"

"I do, your lordship."

Hercules considered. When O'Byrne had first reported seeing Emmet and William, he had felt duty bound to inform the Castle, at least, about Emmet. But the officials there hadn't been very impressed.

"We know some of the United men have come over from France, but they're small beer. Robert Emmet is very young. He may be here to arrange his family's affairs. Have you anything more specific?"

"No," Hercules had answered regretfully.

But if O'Byrne could place young William under surveillance, William would probably lead him to Emmet, and who knows what else.

"You are to follow my son," he told O'Byrne, "and report to me."

The only thing that puzzled Finn was what this aristocrat meant to do about his son once he had found the conspiracy. Extract the young man to a place of safety, he supposed. Personally, he didn't care, as long as he was paid.

"I will make sure that the young gentleman is not implicated," he said helpfully.

But he didn't know his man.

Hercules gazed at him. When he had first begun this business, he had only wanted information. But that was before he had realized how far his son was involved. But now his view had changed. First the boy had been thrown out of Trinity, then run away to Paris, and now he was planning an insurrection. For a moment, he even allowed himself to show his feelings to this wretched spy.

"He was my son. But he has betrayed his family, his religion, and his country. He has betrayed me. He is no longer my son."

"As your lordship pleases."

"I want him caught in the act, O'Byrne. There must be no uncertainty. The evidence must be irrefutable. I want him arrested. And then I want him hanged."

O'Byrne stared at him.

"You will say nothing to anyone," his lordship continued. "You will keep me fully informed and I shall alert the authorities when appropriate. But if you lead the troops to my son at the right moment, I will give you fifty pounds. Can you accomplish that?"

Fifty pounds was a lot of money.

"Oh yes," said O'Byrne, "I can."

✛

On the evening of July 14, Dublin was startled by a series of bangs and a burst of fireworks over the Liffey. At Dublin Castle, the officer on watch treated the matter calmly.

"It's Bastille Day," he said in a bored voice. "Republican fireworks."

Nonetheless, Dublin city's chief of police, the Town-Major, took a detachment of men down to the quays, where he found a huge bonfire and a crowd, some of whom had discharged shots into the air. He immediately tried to close the festivities down by force. The enraged crowd pelted his men with stones and he was forced to withdraw.

"We must be careful," an official at the Castle remarked afterwards, "before we take these republican displays too seriously. The Town-Major would have done better not to intervene."

✛

On the afternoon of July 15, John MacGowan received an unexpected visit from Georgiana. Her face was pale, and she begged for his help.

"I saw him, John. I saw my grandson. He was in Grafton Street. He turned off and I ran after him, but you know that area. It's a mass of little lanes and alleys. I lost him. But it was William. I know it was." She sighed. "I walked home, then I thought of you. It's not two hours ago."

"Perhaps you were mistaken. The imagination can play tricks."

"John. Help me."

He fell silent.

"What do you think he's doing?" he asked at last.

"He came from Paris. With Emmet probably, and others. You tell me what they're doing."

"I don't know," he answered truthfully. "They came to me, of course, the United men, months ago. But I refused. I no longer believe in risings."

"There's to be a rising?"

"There was talk. That doesn't mean it will happen."

"I lost Patrick. I can't bear to lose this boy as well, John."

"That was a terrible thing," he said quietly. "The boy's father couldn't help?" The expression on her face was enough. "I will ask," he said. "I promise nothing."

He came to her house that evening.

"They are saying nothing." To be exact, Smith the tobacconist had told him: "There is no one of that name involved." And having seen the ambiguity of this statement and asked if he might be under any other name, Smith had asked, "Who wants to know?" His grandmother, he'd said. "Ah, I couldn't say," Smith had replied.

Which told him, of course, that William was there.

MacGowan sat in a wing chair in her parlour. He half-closed one eye and gazed at her thoughtfully with the other, which seemed unnaturally large and all-seeing in the evening light. He felt her distress. It touched his conscience.

"I'm sorry I cannot help," he said. "But wherever he is, he's made his own decisions, and it's clear that he doesn't want to be found."

Having brought Georgiana no comfort, he left.

✢

On Saturday, July 16, the Liberties of Dublin were surprised by a small explosion in a storehouse near St. Patrick's Cathedral. Three men were injured and taken to hospital, where one of them subsequently died. Fortunately, the damage was not great, and the small fires were quickly put out by the men inside, so that when the city firefighters arrived, they were told there was no need for their services.

"You'll only make a bigger mess than there is already," the foreman told them. The little crowd outside watched with interest as the foreman argued with the firemen, who finally left disgruntled. The next day, in the evening, the city police came to look at the premises. They found them deserted, but there were suspicious traces of gunpowder. "Perhaps they were making fireworks," somebody said.

But a report was made.

⁜

The meeting on Sunday morning had been sombre. Emmet's face was pale and drawn.

It had been a close thing, and they all knew it. By dawn that morning, the arms and ammunition had all been transferred to a house on Coal Quay, as the ancient Viking Wood Quay was now called, down on the Liffey. "A couple of night watchmen tried to stop my boys on the way," Smith the tobacconist reported. "They pretended to be drunk, but it was a close thing." He shook his head. "We're going to be found out any day now."

Only a fool would have disagreed. Their time was running out, and they knew it.

It was Russell who spoke now. He was the most experienced of the men of '98, and his voice carried weight.

"We've two options. We can close down the whole operation and disperse. Or we have to start the rising at once. If we don't, we risk losing the element of surprise, or worse, of getting everyone arrested."

"And the French?" asked Emmet.

"Have you any news?" There was no answer. "If we wait for them, we'll all be hanged before they arrive."

There were several murmurs of agreement.

"We're not ready," said Emmet.

"We have a large cache of weapons," another of the old guard, Hamilton, pointed out. "We may never have such a good opportunity again."

"I'll raise the north," promised Russell. "I'll have Ulster marching in three days."

It wasn't clear to William how convinced Emmet was by these arguments, but after some further discussion, it was agreed that the rising should take place as quickly as possible.

"If you want to bring large numbers in from the country, without arousing suspicion," Hamilton reminded them, "Saturday market day is best. You've got all kinds of people coming in anyway, then."

They agreed to go on the twenty-third.

"That gives us five whole days to prepare," Emmet said with a laugh.

❖

If Emmet had any private doubts, you'd never have known. His headquarters and the main arms depot were at the storehouse on Thomas Street, a little beyond the ancient Hospital of St. John that lay in the Liberty to the west of the old city wall. It was a capacious premises with a yard. A narrow street called Marshalsea Lane ran from Thomas Street here, down towards the quays. Here Emmet worked and slept round the clock.

William had never been so excited. It was exhilarating to feel that he was making history. Emmet had a sense of style. A tailor had made green uniforms trimmed with gold and lace. "They are the uniforms of French generals," Emmet explained. "I and the other leaders will wear them. It will remind our men that they are a proper revolutionary army."

There was so much to be made ready: ammunition, supplies, even loaves of bread for the men. It was impossible to keep the depot secret anymore, and numbers of men from the various Dublin brigades were sent on errands there. Soon after William got there on Monday morning, O'Byrne arrived, and he quickly made himself useful, checking all the weapons and noting any deficiencies. "We need more shot, Mr. Emmet," he reported, and William was sent out to buy it. At the end of the day, he accompanied William home, buying him a drink on the way.

Emmet was also busy writing manifestoes. They were long, but powerful. The time had come, he wrote, for Ireland to show the world that she was competent to take her place amongst the nations. Leinster and Ulster would lead; all Ireland would follow; there was no need of foreign assistance. But the rising must be honourably conducted, the manifestoes urged. There must be strict military order, followed by free elections and justice for all. "Get it printed right away, William," he instructed.

Russell, Hamilton, and some of the others went north to raise Ulster. Kildare sent word that they would come in on Saturday with almost two thousand men. Messengers also had to be sent to Wexford and Wicklow.

"Who knows the Wicklow Mountains?" Emmet asked.

"I know them like the back of my hand," O'Byrne volunteered.

"You're the man, then," Emmet told him. And he gave him detailed instructions on the message he should deliver to the commanders there.

"Take care," William said to him, quite affectionately, as he was leaving.

⊹

The Earl of Mountwalsh listened carefully.

"You are sure of all this?"

"I am, my lord." Finn repeated exactly the message he was to deliver. The attack would begin on Saturday night at ten o'clock. A rocket, shooting stars, would be the signal. After collecting arms from the Thomas Street depot, the United men would first take Dublin Castle.

"You are not to deliver the message to Wicklow, but you had better stay out of sight until Saturday," Hercules ordered.

"There's an inn out at Dalkey I could use."

"Good. On Saturday you will return, tell them the message is delivered, and observe the preparations. At one o'clock that day, you will meet me at Strongbow's tomb in Christ Church Cathedral, and I will give you further instructions."

"Your lordship will give me fifty pounds when this is done?"

"When my son is arrested, I will give you a hundred pounds, O'Byrne. Now go."

✢

It was hard for John MacGowan. He was no coward, but he was an older and wiser man than he had been five years ago. And though he wanted the same things as Emmet, he had no belief in a new rising. He found nowadays that he had more belief in people than in causes. And he had patience. If not me, he thought, then my children and grandchildren. In the meantime, as long as England sent over humane men like Cornwallis and the Lord Lieutenant who had now replaced him, life was bearable.

Yet his conscience troubled him.

It was not about the rising, but about friendship. It was Georgiana's face that haunted him. And she was quite right to be afraid. If young William had gone to join Emmet, then he was in great danger. When the conspiracy was discovered, or the rising failed, as it surely would, the authorities would be no more lenient towards him than they had been to Lord Edward Fitzgerald.

He thought he could predict how it would go. The rebels would need to secure Dublin first. A Saturday market day was always the best time for such a thing. But when? He'd no idea. If, as he suspected, the mysterious explosion in the Liberty had anything to do with it, the plans were probably far advanced. Time was not on young William's side, therefore.

Yet what was the boy to him? The son of a man he hated, and who hated him. True, but also the grandson of an old friend. And the cousin of Patrick, a man he had loved.

What could he do anyway? The only way to help the boy would be to talk to him, persuade him to cut and run. And how the devil could he find him? Only by joining the conspirators himself, for long enough to do so—and even then, he probably wouldn't be able to persuade the boy anyway. What would happen then? Would his grandmother come and kidnap him? Actually, he thought with a smile, she probably would.

And if he did such a thing, for her sake, he'd clearly be putting his own life at risk. He'd been lucky not to be arrested in '98. This time, he might not be so lucky. A nice present for his grandchildren—to see their grandfather swinging from a bridge. No, it was young William who'd have to swing. He sighed, and tried to put the matter out of his mind.

He argued with himself this way, every day, for almost a week.

On the evening of Friday, July 22, Smith the tobacconist was surprised to find a visitor waiting for him at his door. It was John MacGowan. He said he wanted to become active again. Smith gazed at him thoughtfully.

"Why have you changed your mind, John? Is this something to do with the Walsh boy you were asking about?"

MacGowan had prepared himself for this.

"In a way, yes. I thought to myself, if he's in it, then why is it that I am not?"

"And if he isn't?"

"If you're not in it," MacGowan grinned, "then I'll stay out, too."

"You'll risk death?"

"I did before. My children are all grown."

Smith nodded thoughtfully. Then he gave MacGowan a long look.

MacGowan knew what he was thinking: Was it possible, the tobacconist must be wondering, that his old comrade had turned into a double agent? Such things had happened. The silence was long. In the end, MacGowan spoke.

"If you don't trust me, it's better I go home. The fear of having a traitor beside you does more harm than any good I could possibly do you." He turned. He was sorry he'd failed, yet also relieved. At least he'd tried; his conscience was clear. He'd gone a dozen paces when he heard Smith's voice behind him.

"Thomas Street. Just past Marshalsea Lane. Tomorrow morning."

❖

By late Saturday morning, the place was crowded and chaotic. Hundreds of men from Kildare had arrived. There were constant demands: "Where are the blunderbusses? We need more ammunition. Who emptied this powder keg?" William was constantly being sent on errands. Several hundred more men came in from Wexford. They had been persuaded to wait down at the storehouse at Coal Quay. Another group of Dublin men was going to congregate at a house in Plunkett Street. Finn O'Byrne had returned to say that the message was delivered, but he couldn't say at what hour the Wicklow men would arrive.

Amidst all the chaos, there was another welcome addition. John MacGowan had appeared early in the morning and been welcomed by several of the men. He was a calm presence, working at William's side.

"It's still set for ten o'clock tonight," Emmet confirmed. "We fire a rocket, then swing down to Coal Quay, collect the Wexford men, and march straight to the Castle."

Finn O'Byrne, who'd been travelling all night, said he was going to rest at his house, but promised to be back later in the day.

⁙

Georgiana was restless. The fact that she had dreamed about William was not surprising. But the sensation that afflicted her now was of a different order. She did not form mental pictures of William. Nor did she feel a sudden panic, like a mother who cannot find her child. The feeling that came to her was not a fear, but a knowledge, quiet but certain, that he was in danger. She had heard people speak of such hidden understandings between people who were close. But she didn't know what she could do about it.

Late in the morning, she ordered her carriage. First she drove to Grafton Street, because that was where she had seen William. Then she went to the house of John MacGowan, to be told that he'd be out all day. After that, to the bafflement of her coachman, who had no idea what she was doing, she drove aimlessly along Dame Street and round by the Castle. She hoped she might receive some sense of where he was, but nothing came. Reluctantly, she went home.

⁙

Lord Mountwalsh was waiting in the shadows, half hidden by a pillar, when Finn O'Byrne reached the tomb of Strongbow. He was wearing a nondescript coat with the collar turned up, and a thin scarf covered the lower part of his face. His boots were hardly polished. The disguise was simple but effective. He might have been any Dublin tradesman.

"Tell me all," he commanded.

Finn gave him a brief account of all that he'd seen. "It will be ten o'clock," he said. "There will be a rocket." And he explained the route that Emmet meant to follow.

"Good. I shall tell the Castle to be ready at ten. Nothing will be done to alert the rebels. We want them to show their hand. I shall remain at my house, but at half past nine, I shall come in a plain carriage to the old Hospital of St. John. Meet me there and we shall walk along Thomas Street together. I think this will be sufficient disguise."

"Yes, my lord. But why do you want to come to Thomas Street?"

"So that you and I may witness Emmet and my son emerging. It might be hard to identify them afterwards, and there must be no question as to their guilt. There must be unimpeachable testimony at their trial." He drew himself up. "I intend to testify myself."

And now there could be no mistaking the terrible Earl of Mountwalsh.

✛

It was during the afternoon that things started to go wrong.

At two o'clock, Emmet went out to a nearby inn with the leaders of the men from Kildare. They were gone a long time. When he returned, Emmet looked pale.

"We may have to do without the Kildare men," he told William quietly. "They aren't satisfied with the preparations." He sighed. "You know, we've had to do everything in such a devil of a hurry. But perhaps some of them will stay."

By late afternoon, though there were still hundreds of men there, the depot was quieter. But the doubts of the Kildare men had affected some of the Dublin commanders, too, and further groups of men were leaving. When Finn O'Byrne reappeared round seven, William explained what had happened. A few minutes later, Emmet called them together.

"With the men here and the Wexford boys, and the other groups who will surely come when the rocket is fired, we still have enough men to surprise the Castle," he announced.

A little before eight o'clock, O'Byrne went out.

"I'm going to see if I can't bring in some more men," he said.

"Be back by ten," said Emmet.

"Take a weapon," said William, and he gave him one of Emmet's folding pikes. "You can hide it under your coat."

"Thank you," said O'Byrne.

⁙

It was two hours since a carriage containing the Lord Lieutenant had rolled out of the gates of Dublin Castle and headed out towards the Liberty.

The Lord Lieutenant had been called in to the Castle that afternoon because of a report that a large insurrection was planned for that night. Both he and the Commander in Chief, General Fox, were sceptical.

"The Earl of Mountwalsh may say what he likes," he had said irritably, "but is there any corroboration? Does he say where these rebels are to be found? How are we to know them? Are we to go out and shoot every drunk on a Saturday night?"

"The signal will be a rocket, at ten o'clock."

General Fox spoke.

"On the last occasion, on Bastille Day, when that fool of a Town-Major stirred up a crowd for no reason, there were rockets."

All the same, the troops in the Castle and out at the nearby barracks were all put on alert. They would certainly be prepared. But by six o'clock, the Lord Lieutenant had had enough.

"Maintain the alert," he'd ordered. "If in doubt deploy, and lock the Castle gates. That's all. Let me know if the revolution starts. I'm going home."

It was one of the pleasant features of his job that it came with a splendid residence set in the magnificent spaces of Phoenix Park. As his carriage and outriders had clattered down from the Liberty and over the Liffey, he reflected upon what his predecessor had told him about the character of the Earl of Mountwalsh.

Lord Cornwallis had not minced his words. "The fellow's a damned nuisance." As usual, Cornwallis was right.

‡

John MacGowan surveyed the scene. Less than two hours to go. How in the world was he to get the boy away?

This rising was going to be a catastrophe: he could feel it in his bones. He realized with a sudden shock that the Smith brothers were not there anymore. Emmet had taken off his coat, which lay on the back of his chair, and put on his green uniform. He looked very splendid in it; but MacGowan suspected that the uniform was serving another purpose also. It was helping Emmet to enter his role, so that there should be no turning back. It might have been a suit of armour.

And what was young William thinking? Had he realized that they were all going to die? At half past eight, he strolled over to William and suggested they should get a breath of air in the yard. Emmet was writing dispatches.

The air outside was warm. There were men resting round the edge of the yard. The rocket, with its eight-foot pole and its long fuse, stood in its heavy trestle launcher, pointing at the sky. Standing beside it, he spoke softly.

"The best men have all left."

"I know," said young William calmly.

"We should save Emmet from himself. The rising will fail, and we shall lose everything."

"The die is cast. He won't turn back. I know him."

"And you?"

"I do not desert my friends." It was said quite straight-forwardly. That was how he chose to live; it would be how he chose to die. MacGowan looked at him with admiration.

"Quite right," he said, and went back inside.

So what the devil was he to do now?

Ten more minutes passed. Emmet was busy at his table,

but MacGowan observed that he looked up nervously from time to time.

MacGowan wandered round the depot. Nobody took much notice of him. He inspected various weapons, but in the end chose a large and heavy pistol, which he stuffed into his belt. He picked up some wadding. In one room there were some ladders and coils of rope. He took a small coil and slung it over his shoulder. He saw a roll of bandage and took that, too.

He had formed a general plan. After that, he would have to improvise. Back in the main room, Emmet and about a hundred men were waiting. He went outside. It was four minutes to nine.

He continued into the street. There were quite a few people about. There were a couple of inns nearby. Dusk was falling now. A lamplighter was making his rounds. A strange, ambiguous time of the day, this borderland between day and night. He took a deep breath, turned, and ran back into the depot.

"Troops! There are troops coming," he cried. "From all sides. They'll surround us. Get out at once."

Emmet leaped up from the table. The men all round the depot were looking at each other. William also stood. He was pale.

"They have us," MacGowan cried.

Now was the moment. The men were faltering. He could see it in their eyes. That was all he needed: the opportunity of a moment's surrender. If Emmet would just say, "It's over boys—run if you can." Then he could get young William away to safety. But Emmet was doing no such thing. Damn his noble spirit.

"Pick up your arms, boys," Emmet was crying. "It's time to fight."

Some of the men were looking uncertain, others sent up a little cheer. Would they follow him?

"Light the rocket," cried Emmet.

"We'll do it," said MacGowan, and grabbing William by the arm, he dragged him into the yard with him. It took only an instant to strike the flint and light a taper. They lit the fuse of the rocket and stood back. After a few moments, the rocket went off with a burst of flame and a roar, climbing high into the sky, hundreds of feet, while they all looked after it as it exploded with a great shower of bright stars. All Dublin must have seen it.

"Come on, boys, let's take the Castle." Emmet's voice. He was leading the men out into the street. How splendid he looked in his green uniform. He was waving a sword in the air and heading along Thomas Street. Presumably, if he encountered troops, he hoped to break through them.

Young William was going to follow him. MacGowan had to think fast.

"Emmet," he called out. "Shall I fetch the Wexford men?"

"Do that," shouted Emmet.

"Can I take William?"

"Yes. William, go with him."

He was at William's side.

"Come, William. Quick, now," cried MacGowan. And they began to hurry down Marshalsea Lane in the direction of the quays.

⁜

Finn O'Byrne had taken his time. He'd decided to stay out of the depot until he met Lord Mountwalsh. If he'd started walking out closer to the hour, it might have looked suspicious.

The fact that many of the Kildare and Dublin men had left didn't concern him. It would just make it easier to see Emmet and William as they came out. It was possible, he supposed, that Emmet would call the whole thing off, but he didn't think that was in Emmet's character.

He had walked along to Christ Church and turned down Winetavern Street to an inn. He might as well drink a Guinness while he waited. The folding pike William had given him was quite heavy, but he could hardly take it out in public, and so he kept it concealed under his coat. He had to confess, the thing was ingenious. And you never knew, it might still come in useful if there was trouble during the evening. Not wanting to draw attention to himself, he sat on a bench in the street, outside the door.

The church bell had just finished striking nine o'clock when he saw the great flash of light in the sky over Thomas Street, and watched the burst of stars as the huge firework exploded in the evening sky.

He stared in horror. Had he mistaken the hour? No. It was nine. The signal had been given an hour early. There was no mistaking it. The rising was starting. And Lord Mountwalsh wasn't even planning to leave his house for half an hour.

He raced up the street. What should he do? Should he wait for Mountwalsh? Might the earl have seen the rocket? Probably not if he was indoors. What the devil should he do?

As he emerged by the cathedral, he saw a hansom cab. He hailed it.

"Whip up your horse," he cried, "and take me to St. Stephen's Green. Fast as you can."

✣

Behind iron railings, a huge rectangular garden ran down the centre of Merrion Square. Georgiana had been pacing there uneasily for over an hour when she saw the rocket rise and explode in a great starburst somewhere in the west behind the Castle.

What did it mean? She left the garden. None of the people on the pavement seemed to have seen the rocket. She walked to the railings of Leinster House and made her way round to St. Stephen's Green. Here she saw several people looking up at the sky; but nobody was doing anything. She wondered if she should walk towards the Castle to see what was going on. It was only a ten-minute walk. Or should she go back and call for her carriage again? She hesitated. The feeling that had been with her all day had become even more insistent now. That rocket was a portent of something terrible. She was sure of it.

She hadn't been there five minutes when she saw the hansom cab come hurtling from the eastern end of the Green and race round to the door of Hercules's house. She saw a figure hurry up the steps and pull the bell furiously. When the door was opened, the figure said something, then hurried back to the waiting cab. Moments later, a figure in a long, slightly shabby greatcoat, and with a hat pulled down over his face, came bounding down the steps and leaped into the cab, which dashed away again with a clatter.

Though he was oddly dressed, she recognized her son at once. She turned, hurried back to Merrion Square, and called for her carriage at once. She was so perturbed that she waited for it outside. While waiting, she was almost certain she heard, in the distance, the sound of a pistol shot.

✢

Lord Mountwalsh glared at him.

"What the devil happened?"

"I don't know, my lord."

"Go to the Castle. I told them ten. I'll have to make sure they know it's begun."

It was only minutes before they reached the Castle gates. It was obvious at once that the garrison had been alerted by the rocket. The main gate was already closed and a detachment of troops was forming up. A brief word with the officer on duty was enough.

"That'll do. On to Thomas Street," cried Hercules.

Finn considered a moment.

"Too late, my lord. They'll have gone down to Coal Quay by now," he said, "to collect the Wexford men. It could be dangerous," he added. But Hercules only gave him a look of contempt.

"To the quays then as fast as you can," he called to the cabby. "All we need," he reminded O'Byrne coldly, "is a clear sight of my son. Nothing else matters now."

⁜

There had been perhaps three hundred men at the Thomas Street depot. A good number had followed Emmet out into Thomas Street. Others looked for the attacking troops, but when they did not see them, retreated back inside.

A short while later, the fellows from Plunkett Street, who'd seen the signal, arrived in haste. The men in the depot quickly supplied them with pikes and arms, and the Plunkett Street party set off after Emmet.

But Robert Emmet's progress towards the Castle had not gone well. His men were nervous and losing heart.

"Come, boys, now is your time for Liberty," he cried, and fired a pistol into the air to encourage them. But as they went along the street, they were hesitating, breaking up into groups, and melting into the alleyways. As they came in sight of the cathedral precincts, Emmet looked round and discovered that he had not twenty men.

There was nothing to be done, and he knew it. To his right lay Francis Street, which led southwards out of the city.

"This way, boys," he said sadly, and started down the road towards the distant Wicklow Mountains.

When the Plunkett Street party came down towards the cathedral only minutes later, they could not find him; and so they, too, broke up into groups and wandered away into the night. It was just as well. The firepower now waiting at the Castle was formidable.

That left only the Wexford men, down by the quay.

⁜

O'Byrne and Lord Mountwalsh had been waiting by an alley

for almost half an hour. The hansom cab was waiting round the corner, not far away.

As soon as they had arrived, they had ascertained that the Wexford men had yet to move, so they had positioned themselves sensibly so that they would see the Thomas Street contingent when they approached. There was even a lamppost nearby, so that they would get a good look at their faces.

But nothing had happened. After a little while, Hercules had begun to be impatient. By now, he was hardly able to stand still. Yet if they moved now, there was always the chance that they'd miss their quarry just as they passed. Finally, one of the Wexford men ran past them up the lane in the direction of the depot. No doubt they, too, wanted to know what was going on. A little while later, he came back and they heard him call:

"They've gone. The depot's empty."

Beside him, Finn heard the earl's muttered curse.

"Come," he hissed, and turned back towards the cab. As they hurried along, Finn could sense the earl trembling with rage in the darkness. "Take me to Thomas Street," he ordered as soon as they reached the cab. "Show me the place."

When they got to the depot, it was just as the Wexford man had said. The mess was remarkable: pikes, swords, even the valuable flintlocks were strewn on the floor. There were pouches of shot, kegs of gunpowder . . . and not a living soul. The last of Emmet's men had fled.

It was frighteningly clear by now that Hercules's rage was rising to the point of danger. He picked up some of Emmet's manifestoes, which were piled on a table, and flung them furiously to the floor. For a terrifying moment, Finn thought he was going to kick a keg of gunpowder. Then he unleashed his fury upon O'Byrne.

"You villain!" he shouted. "You've deliberately led me on a wild-goose chase."

"Would I do such a thing, your lordship? I swear by all the saints . . ."

"Damn your saints," roared the earl. "You Irish rogue, you papist dog! You liar. You think you can double-cross me? Where is Emmet? Where is my son?"

"I do not know," cried Finn in vexation.

"Then I will tell you this." The earl's voice was suddenly cold with fury. "If Emmet and my son are taken and executed, well and good. You, of course, will get nothing. Not a penny. But you will keep your life. But if they escape, then I shall know that you were in league with them." He brought his face close to Finn's. "Remember, O'Byrne, I have seen you here. I know you were one of the rebels, and I shall testify to it." He brought his face even closer, and whispered with deadly intensity: "I will see you hang."

Then he turned on his heel.

"My lord," Finn was at his heel, "we'll take the cab to the Castle. They may be there. You shall see them."

"Damn the cab," cried Hercules unreasonably. "And damn you. I'd rather walk."

"But the fare, my lord," Finn wailed. God knows what the fare would be, with all this time gone. "The fare."

"Pay it yourself," called back his lordship contemptuously.

And in that he made the rich man's mistake, in forgetting the hugeness of a cab fare to the poor. It was a fatal mistake.

For now, as he gazed, speechless, after Lord Mountwalsh, something snapped in Finn O'Byrne. He suddenly realized that he still had the folding pike under his coat. Taking it out, he snapped it open. Hercules heard the sound just before he reached the gate of the yard, and turned—only in time to see O'Byrne rushing at him with the great, gleaming blade of the pike pointing straight at his stomach. He tried, without success, to ward it off as the blade sliced with a ripping sound through his coat, and he felt a huge, fiery pain in his bowels. He sank down on his knees. Finn had his foot against his chest. He was dragging the pike out. Hercules felt another massive pain, heard a sucking sound. Then he saw the terrible, bloody blade of the pike flashing down towards his neck, and felt a blow like a thunderbolt bursting upon him.

Finn stood back. Lord Mountwalsh's body was pumping blood onto the ground. He watched it, quivering. Good. He hoped Emmet and his men had succeeded in breaking into the Castle and done the same to all the cursed Englishmen there.

After all, he might have betrayed Emmet, but at least he liked him.

He looked around. It would be better not to leave the body here. On the other hand, he couldn't drag it out into the street. At one point, he observed, the wall of the yard was only six feet high. He stood on a box and looked over. A small compost heap lay below the other side, at the end of an unkempt piece of waste ground. He went inside, fetched a ladder, and rolled the earl's body onto it. Dragging the ladder and raising the free end onto the wall, he was able then, without too much difficulty, to pull the corpse up a few feet until he had Mountwalsh draped over the wall. With a little lifting and manoeuvring of the ladder, he was able to tip it over so that it fell with a soft thud on the other side. He took off his bloodstained coat and tossed that over, too, along with the pike. Then he wiped the blood off the ladder and replaced it in the house. He found a basin and a pitcher of water in which he washed his hands. He splashed some water on his boots. On the back of a chair in the main room, he saw young Emmet's coat. He didn't suppose Emmet would be needing it now.

When he came back into the yard, he found the cabby waiting there.

"Are you gentlemen done?" the fellow asked.

"Those gentlemen are gone," he replied. "You know who I am?"

"No, Sir."

"I am Robert Emmet, but you never saw me here. Otherwise, you're a dead man."

"All right, Sir. But who'll be paying the fare?"

"Fare? You did it for the cause." He actually gave a fair imitation of Emmet's tones. "Now, go."

"Not without my fare."

"Indeed?" There was a sword lying at his feet. He stooped, picked it up, and rushed at the cabby, who fled into the street. The fellow was so frightened that he didn't even jump onto his coachman's seat, but ran eastwards, towards the city.

It was time to go. Tossing the sword back into the yard, Finn O'Byrne crossed the street. Moments later, he had vanished.

⁜

Georgiana was grim-faced. Her coachman was getting nervous. He still had no idea why his mistress was out like this, but things were getting ugly.

A little while ago, in the streets below Christ Church, they had encountered a large group of men who had stopped the coach and asked, politely enough, if they had seen a young man leading a party of men. "I'm looking for someone, too," she had told them, and described William. But they didn't know him. "Where are you from?" she'd asked. Wexford, they told her, and went on their way. But by now, the streets seemed to be filling with mobs in a very different kind of mood.

"Drive up there," she ordered.

"That'll take us into the Liberty, my lady," the coachman warned. But she made him do it.

The word of the rising had spread like wildfire. Some of the men drinking at the inns still had their weapons with them. Mobs, often half drunk, were forming in the streets, shouting for the rebellion.

Georgiana didn't care. She'd been to the Castle area where the military patrols were out, and she'd been down by the quays. Now she meant to try the Liberties. If there was any chance of catching sight of her grandson, she wasn't giving up. They crossed Francis Street. Several times, knots of men and women slowed their progress and even knocked against the side of the carriage. But when a fellow gave her coachman a thoughtful dig in the ribs with his pike, she knew she couldn't ask him to go on. "Go down to Thomas Street," she said. "It's bigger than these lanes, and we'll go back to Christ Church from there."

But now, as they came out into Thomas Street, they found their way barred. A crowd of several hundred had gathered. And from their shouts and curses it was obvious that they were in a vicious mood. They had just stopped a carriage in the middle of the street. Some of the men were carrying lanterns. By their light, she saw a flash of pikes. The coachman was trying to whip his horses forward, but some of the men had caught them by the bridle. They were forcing one of the carriage doors open, dragging an elderly gentleman out. Then another man, a clergyman by the look of him. She heard screams. They were starting to trample the old man. Then, as if of their own volition, over the heads of the crowd, she saw several pike blades moving towards the spot. She saw one of the blades dip. Then another. The crowd roared. They had just skewered the clergyman.

Her own coachman was trying to back the horses up to turn the carriage, but like a tide, the crowd was running back and flowing round them. There was a hammering on the door.

There was nothing else to do. She pulled down the window and showed her face.

"What is it you want?" she called out.

"A woman. It's a woman," somebody cried out. A man leaped up and poked his head inside. "It's just a woman," he called out. And the crowd slowly parted as her carriage moved through. She tried not to look at where the two men who had been butchered lay. The carriage rolled slowly towards Christ Church.

The assault, when it came, was so sudden that she didn't even have time to be frightened. The man ran out, leaped up to her door, and adroitly swung himself in before she could even scream. The coachman didn't even see it. She gasped and prepared to defend herself. But the intruder threw himself back into the seat.

"Go down Winetavern Street, quickly," said a voice that was familiar. And with a flood of relief, she realized it was John MacGowan.

He did not explain, just quietly gave her directions for the coachman. In moments, they were going westward again, in the area by the quays, then turning up a narrow lane until he asked her to stop by a dark alley.

"Tell the coachman to wait, and whatever you see, don't say a word," he said.

He disappeared into the alley and was gone a little while. At last he reappeared, almost carrying a figure with a bandage round his head. He pushed the figure into the carriage and called up to the coachman: "My nephew. Those rebels set upon him. It'll be safest if you go back along the quays towards College Green."

Once back in the carriage, he leant down to the figure on the floor, who had just let out a groan, and whispered:

"Keep quiet, for the love of God. You're in your grand-mother's carriage now, and it's all over." Then he exchanged a few urgent whispers with Georgiana, who, as they came to College Green, said loudly so that the coachman should hear:

"You'll do no such thing. You'll bring the young man to my house for the night." And she ordered the coachman: "Drive straight home."

In her house, it was easy enough to get the bandaged young man up the candlelit stairs to a bedroom, without any-one having the least idea who he was. There MacGowan remained with him, while Georgiana and the coachman related to the servants how nearly they had all been killed by the rebels who had also assaulted her friend's nephew. When the cook had prepared a bowl of stew and a jug of claret, Georgiana insisted on taking it up to the invalid herself.

᛭

"I had to give him quite a bang on the head with my pistol," MacGowan explained when the three of them were alone. "Then I gagged him and tied him up in the alley, and prayed no one found him before I could get back. I thought I'd have to get a cart from my house when, by God's providence, I recognized your carriage.

"But the rising . . ." William began weakly.

"It's over, William. You could see it was collapsing before Emmet left. There's nothing but some drunks in the street, who have killed several innocent people, and who nearly killed your grandmother. You must rest now. Nobody knows who you are, and that's for the best. We'll decide what to do when we know more in the morning."

❖

It was Georgiana who devised the plan. The following morning, she went to the Castle herself to ask for information. She then declared loudly to the officials there, and to her servants when she got home, that she wasn't staying another day in Dublin if the government couldn't keep better order than that; and she practically ordered MacGowan to accompany her to Mount Walsh, and to bring his nephew with him. By late morning, they were on their way.

They spent the night at Wicklow, where MacGowan made some enquiries. In the morning, capriciously, Lady Mountwalsh decided to board a vessel which was leaving for Bristol that day. MacGowan's nephew went with her as a servant. When they disembarked at Bristol, the young man changed his identity again, between the dock and the inn, so that he now became her grandson William. A week after that, with personal letters to her relations in Philadelphia and letters of credit to several merchant houses, the Honourable William Walsh, who so far as anyone knew hadn't been in Ireland for years, embarked on a ship bound for America.

"As soon as it's certain that no one has given you away, you can return," she told him.

❖

The rising of Robert Emmet was very brief. As a rising, it was an utter failure. The Wexford men, after looking for him half the night, melted away like the rest. Russell, Hamilton, and their friends found the men of Ulster sceptical—with good reason—and Ulster did not rise. The mobs in the Dublin streets were dispersed by troops in the end, with some loss of life, but not before they had killed several innocent people, including the judge and clergyman whose murder Georgiana had witnessed. About a dozen men with pikes were arrested, most of whom were later executed. Some others were transported. But that was all. For weeks the government expected a larger insurrection.

But there was none, and the leadership was gone, and Napoleon looked elsewhere. With only two exceptions, the leaders of the revolt vanished abroad.

Emmet remained. Though racked by a sense of guilt at the useless deaths he had caused, his main reason for continuing to reside near Rathfarnham was the presence of Sarah Curran, the girl he was courting there. He begged her to elope with him to America, and had she agreed, he would have emigrated and become no more than a footnote to history. As it was, more than a month after the rising, he was found and arrested.

The sixteen-year-old girl who had acted as his housekeeper was also thrown in jail. Since she was only the daughter of a farmer, she was interrogated and lightly tortured. The authorities made clear their nicety of feeling, however, when it came to Sarah Curran: as the daughter of a gentleman, she was, of course, only questioned most politely. She was not unpunished, though, for loving Robert Emmet. Her father, a lawyer with liberal ideas, being now desirous of showing his loyalty to the government, threw her out of his house and cut her off entirely.

There was one other casualty. Russell, who had urged that the rising should go ahead, and who had failed to rouse Ulster, returned to Dublin in a futile bid to rescue Emmet from jail, was caught, and was executed. Some of his friends thought he was seeking martyrdom.

✛

But to Georgiana, it was truth which was the greatest casualty. It was not long before the government, reverting to ancient prejudice, declared that the rising had been a strictly Catholic affair. "How they can say it," MacGowan pointed out to her, "when Emmet is a Protestant—as, indeed, is every single one of the leading conspirators—I cannot understand." Even the conservative Roman Church was accused of complicity, since, it was argued, the conspirators must surely have told their priests all about it in the confessional. The spirit of Hercules was still very alive in the Ascendancy.

But the person of Lord Mountwalsh was very dead indeed.

A week went by before a certain smell caused neighbours to seek out the spot where he lay. By then, his disappearance from his household had been well known. Georgiana herself had gone to make the identification. That one of the rebels should have killed such a hated Ascendancy figure was not surprising, but how he came there was a mystery. His servants knew he had left in a hurry. And a military patrol, discovering the depot late on the night of the rising, had reported finding an empty hansom cab waiting at the place. But the cab had vanished later, and the cabby was never heard from. So the thing remained a riddle, and Georgiana herself was not inclined to pursue the matter.

"And the fact is," she would often remark as the years went by, "that it's young Emmet who, after all, has triumphed."

For if Robert Emmet in life had been unfortunate, history had prepared him a place among the heroes. That September, at his trial, he scorned to defend himself; but then, the jury having found him guilty, he claimed the last word by making a speech which all Ireland heard, and which even his accusers admired.

"I was there," Georgiana liked to remind people. "The judge tried to interrupt him, but he had his say. And what a gift he had. I've heard Grattan, and many others, but he would have surpassed them all."

Using the material he had already worked up in his manifesto, but adding to it the passionate inspiration of the final moment, he drew his rising together and launched it into the annals of national legend with his peroration. He asked only, he declared, to depart in silence; his noble motives need not be explained.

> Let them and me repose in obscurity and peace, and my tomb remain uninscribed, until other times, and other men, can do justice to my character; when my country takes her place among the nations of the earth, then, and not till then, let my epitaph be written.

His words would echo, and never cease to echo, in Ireland's mind thereafter.

In March of the following year, young William Walsh, residing in Philadelphia, was greatly surprised to receive a letter from his grandmother telling him firstly that, all enquiries into the rising having ceased without any mention of his name, it was safe for him to return. And secondly, that he should do so at once, since he was already the Earl of Mountwalsh.

FAMINE

⊰ 1828 ⊱

THERE WAS NOBODY like her father. When he picked her up in his great, strong arms and looked at her with his laughing eyes, she knew there was nobody so brave and strong in all of County Clare.

So when her mother said that she was afraid of what Mr. Callan the agent might do to him, Maureen hardly heard. Father could crush little Mr. Callan with one arm, she thought to herself.

Not many people would have cared to take on Eamonn Madden. Though he was the youngest of the four brothers, he was the largest. They were all proud. "On our father's side, there are Maddens with fine estates in many parts of Ireland. On our mother's side, we are the descendants of Brian Boru himself," her father had told her. "Along with all the other O'Briens, of course," he allowed. Down in the rich parklands towards Limerick, a lordly O'Brien owned the huge castle and estate of Dromoland; and there were several other O'Briens among the prominent landowners of Clare. His mother's family might have been only tenant farmers, but they felt themselves, however distantly, to be of the same great descent.

Eamonn was not only large and strong, he could run like a deer. Hurling he loved: he would pluck the ball out of the air and run with it in a single movement that was beautiful to see. "Your father's a wonderful dancer," he mother had also told her.

As a very young man, before he married her mother, Eamonn had a dashing reputation for all sorts of devilment. A dozen years ago, when a landlord a few miles away had threatened to evict a widow from her husband's cottage the very month after his death, a storehouse had been burned and some cattle maimed on his land in the middle of a dark night. A message had been left for the landlord, and the widow had stayed, rent free. Most people believed that Eamonn Madden had led that raid, and it had made him something of a hero in the locality.

Such illicit rough justice had always been part of life in the countryside. Sometimes it might erupt into a local rising, but more often it consisted of isolated incidents. At different times and places, the men who banded together would go by different names, though generally they were known as Ribbonmen, or Whiteboys. But whatever his past, Eamonn Madden did not hold with violence now.

"There are better ways of getting justice than maiming cattle, Maureen," he would tell her. Although she was only nine, both her parents would share their thoughts with her sometimes, because she was the eldest. "Daniel O'Connell has shown us that."

O'Connell, the Liberator, the greatest man in Ireland. If her father was a hero, O'Connell was a god. But it was because of O'Connell that her mother was so worried now.

"For this time," she said, "he's gone too far. And pray to God, child," she said to Maureen, "that he doesn't cost us our house and home, and all that we have."

If Eamonn and his brothers carried themselves with pride, it wasn't just because, like many Irish people, they considered themselves to be the descendants of princes. It was above all because, within living memory, the family had occupied a much larger landholding. Three generations ago, their great-grandfather had been the tenant of a substantial farm, though it actually belonged to a landowner who lived in England. Down the generations, this holding had been subdivided amongst sons, some of whom had left. By the last generation, Eamonn's father had been down to about twenty acres, and now even that had been divided into four. Yet in his own mind, Eamonn felt that he represented, at least, his grandfather's holding, which some of his older neighbours could still remember. As for the land he rented, he privately considered it as his own.

Maureen loved the countryside of County Clare. From the wide waters of the Shannon estuary in the south, to the strange, stony wilderness of the Burren in the north, Clare had a magic all its own. If down in lower Munster, the mountains of Cork and Kerry caused the prevailing south-westerlies to release huge quantities of rain, here in Clare the Atlantic winds swept in unchecked over low hills and bogland, stony fields and water meadows. Sometimes, on windy days, it seemed to Maureen that the little thorn trees and briars dotting their land were so bent by the breeze that they must, at any moment, tear themselves from their roots and fly wildly, like so many witches, towards the island's interior.

Down by the Shannon, the soil was rich. Here in the centre of the county, around the market town of Ennis, the landscape varied, but the soil was relatively poor. Nonetheless, wheat and oats were grown there, barley and flax. And, of course, the potato.

They might have only a few acres, but her family lived quite well. They kept a cow for milking, a number of pigs, some hens, and a dog. There was also a donkey which pulled her father's cart. They grew cabbages, mostly, and potatoes.

Her great-grandfather's sturdy, two-storey farmhouse was still there to be seen; Eamonn's abode was more modest—a long, single-storey cottage with thick, dry-stone walls and a thatched roof. Like everyone else in the region, they had a turf fire, since turf was plentiful and wood fuel almost nonexistent. And if the wind could seep through the dry-stone walls, it hardly signified, for the climate of Clare was mild. There were three children in the family so far: herself, her younger sister Norah, and her little brother William; though another baby was on the way. They had good linen shirts which their mother had made, woollen dresses and stockings, and sound boots for the winter. So they were comfortable enough.

And they ate well—three times a day, usually. If her father had been to the market, then he might bring back a little meat or fish; there was often some cabbage or other green vegetable; and their staple diet, which kept them all well fed and healthy, was the nutritious potato.

The potato: what a blessing it was. "It's manna from heaven," her father always used to say, "America's gift to Ireland."

Her father was an intelligent man. He could read and write, and saw to it that she could, too. He liked to know things; he was always curious. And since she was his eldest child, and his son was still only an infant, he liked to talk to her. She knew, therefore, that the potato had been brought from the New World many generations ago; and when she was a little girl, he had explained its properties to her.

"You see these, Maureen?" He had taken a seed potato, from which little white tubers were sprouting like tiny, curling horns. "Very few roots form their own buds, but the potato does. These tubers contain the nourishment for the new shoots that will grow from them. The shoots will form stems with their own roots and leaves, from which will come the new crop of potatoes. So that's all you need to do: dig up the potatoes, keep some back for seeding, replant the seed potatoes in the spring, and you'll have a fresh crop in the autumn. And as it happens, Ireland has the perfect climate for them. They like our mild, damp weather."

"So do the Indians in America eat the potato wherever they find it, growing in the wild?" she asked him once.

"You would think so. But they do not. Left to themselves, the tubers from the seed potato shoot up towards the surface and catch the light. Then the new potatoes grow near the surface, and they're green and bitter. You wouldn't want to eat them at all. That's why we keep the seed potatoes in a dark place, and pile the earth up over them when they are planted."

Their land lay in stony terrain. But the fields had been cleared and the stones used in dry-stone walls, several feet thick in places. Like his neighbours, Eamonn Madden planted potatoes for an early crop in August, followed by a later crop in October or November. Their nutritional value was unrivalled. With a little butter and milk, a few vegetables or some fish, the potato could produce a race of healthy giants, so long as you ate enough. And the Irish did. When Eamonn Madden was working hard on the land, he'd consume fourteen or fifteen pounds of potato in a day.

Could anything be objected against the potato as a crop?

"It is subject to blight," Eamonn admitted. There had been numerous potato blights, some quite serious, in recent decades. "But against that, you must consider three things," he would add. "The first is that the potato produces far more food per acre than anything else. The second, that the blights are usually local, and soon pass. But the third thing, which is sometimes forgotten, is that potato crop failures are less frequent and less severe than the failures of cereals. There is actually less risk, Maureen, in planting a field of potatoes than there is in sowing a field of wheat or oats."

Her father worked the potato field with his spade, and all the family helped with the harvest. The pigs they kept were partly fed on potato peelings, and provided manure for the fields in turn. Once a year, the family killed a pig for their own consumption, but the rest of the pigs were fattened and sold to market. "That pays the rent," her father told her. This regime left him many months in the year when he could go and work for others. He would also earn money by carting, travelling quite large distances sometimes.

Sometimes, he would take Maureen with him. Once, they went up to the huge, stony wilderness of the Burren. She had been impressed by its bare loveliness, and quite surprised to see sheep grazing there. "You wouldn't think they could find enough nourishment here, would you?" her father remarked. "Yet they do, and the herbs they find amongst the rocks give their meat a particularly fine flavour." They had also visited the mighty cliffs of Moher, and she had gasped at the huge, sheer drop, almost a thousand feet, into the roiling waters of the Atlantic far below. Then, as he held her, he said "Lean forward," and she had leaned out over the cliff and felt the great rush of air as the Atlantic wind struck the cliffs and came racing up, thrillingly supporting her and pushing her back. "There's nothing between us and America from here," he called, "except that churning sea." She didn't know why she found this thought so exciting.

"Shall we ever go there?" she called back. It was a natural question. Most of the farming families she knew seemed to have a relation in America. One of Eamonn's brothers and two of his uncles had gone there with their families. It was the better-off people who went to America. The poor could not afford the fare.

"Why, would you want to leave Clare?" he shouted.

"Never," she cried.

Another time, they went down to the shores of the Shannon and watched the fishermen going out in their little curraghs made of skins.

"The lands along the Shannon here are known as the corcasses," Eamonn said. "The blue corcasses, as we call them, are wonderful soil; but the black carcass is so rich that you can get twenty harvests out of it before you have to manure." He said it with as much pride as if he owned it.

But mostly, he went into the local town of Ennis, taking the cart in early morning and returning at dusk. But whenever he asked her to accompany him there, she tried to find an excuse. She dreaded going into Ennis.

It was not large, but it was a place of some importance. Barges brought goods from the northern inlet of the great Shannon estuary, up the River Fergus to Ennis. It had a cattle market and a courthouse, and you could buy all sorts of things there. Once, she remembered, because it was going cheap, he had bought a load of seaweed there, which had been shipped up from the Shannon estuary. When they got it home, he asked her to help him spread it on the potato field. "It feeds the soil," he told her. "Down by the coast, they use it instead of manure."

But it was the road into Ennis that she hated.

There had been landless folk in Ireland for centuries. In a way, they were part of a natural process. When the lands of a chief were subdivided amongst his sons, they soon took over the lands of the larger tenants, forcing them onto smaller holdings. The tenants, in turn, subdivided their holdings, and so on down the scale to the cottager, with his acre or two, and below him, the landless labourer. Even Cromwell, by kicking out a layer of Irish landlords in favour of English ones, had only added one more to the endless waves of displacement down the generations.

It was this process, during the last century, that the nutritious potato had so rapidly accelerated. Since they could afford to remain on the land and subsist on smaller holdings, Eamonn's father, and his grandfather before that, had married young and produced large families. Eamonn himself had been only twenty when he married, and who knew how many children he might have? Even the poor cottagers with a small patch could survive. As a result, the population of Ireland had hugely grown. It was already over seven million, and still climbing. Ireland was one of the most densely populated countries in Europe. Inevitably, therefore, with so many to feed, the price of food, and of land, was rising. "The landlord can get a higher price for his land, and the richer farmers can pay it.

We are fortunate," Eamonn could tell Maureen, "but some of the poor cottagers can hardly manage their rents." Those who could not were being forced off the land to subsist, as best they could, as labourers. In the slums of London, or the Liberties of Dublin, the sight of the urban poor was common enough. But now, in the countryside of Ireland, a huge new phenomenon could be seen: the slums of the rural poor.

They began about a mile outside Ennis. Some were shacks with roofs, others nothing more than hovels built into the banks of earth. Some families there were able to rent potato patches just for one growing season at a time; others had not even that. They got what work they could; sometimes there was none. It was the same on each of the roads leading into Ennis. As she passed and saw the hapless faces of the men, and the women and children in rags, Maureen would shudder.

"Could that happen to us?" she had once asked her father when she was five.

"Never," he answered boldly.

"Can't we help them?"

"There are too many." He'd smiled sadly. "I am glad that you wish to, however."

It had shocked her to hear the tone of quiet defeat in her father's voice. Until then she had supposed that he could do anything. He knew that, if they went that way together, she would never be quiet unless he gave her some pennies to give to the children as they passed. But, though she never said so, it was the sight of the shantytown that made the little girl shake her head, usually, if he asked her if she wanted to come with him into the town. Last year, however, she had asked a different question. "Can Daniel O'Connell do anything for them?" And at this her father had brightened a little.

"Perhaps." He had nodded. "If anyone can, it would be O'Connell."

So it saddened her that now, for the first time she could remember in her life, her parents should be at odds with one another, and that the cause should be Daniel O'Connell.

She had heard him once. Her father had taken her with him; her mother had refused to go. The great man had come from his home in the mountains of Kerry to address a huge audience that had gathered in a field near Limerick. He was standing on a cart. She and her father were well back in the crowd, but they could see him clearly, for he was an even bigger man than Eamonn, with a broad, cheerful face and a mane of wavy brown hair.

He spoke to them in Irish and English—indeed, like many people in that region, he would go easily from one to the other, sometimes mixing the two together. She did not understand all of what he said, but the crowd did, and they roared approval. What she chiefly remembered, however, was not what he said but the wonderful, musical sound of his voice—sometimes quiet, sometimes rising to a great crescendo. And when he dropped his voice, the entire crowd went as quiet as a mouse, so that you could hear every word. "He has the voice of an angel," her father had remarked. "And the cunning of a devil," he'd added approvingly.

For thirty years now, O'Connell had been a brilliant lawyer who specialized in defending Catholic clients against the Protestant Ascendancy. But if that was the necessary foundation of his career, his genius was for politics. And it was five years ago that he had begun his great political experiment when, with a group of like-minded followers, he had founded the Catholic Association.

There had never been anything like it before. There had been committees of Catholic gentlemen; there had been Patriots who favoured the Catholic cause; there had been Volunteers and local insurrections and revolutionaries. But O'Connell's Catholic Association was none of these. It was a peaceful political movement. But it was a mass movement, open to every Catholic in Ireland who could afford the small minimum subscription of a penny a month. Nothing had ever been seen like this in politics before. Eamonn Madden had joined at once.

The genius of the thing lay in the way it was organised. For when his friends asked him, "However will you administer such an organisation, and who is to collect all the pennies?" O'Connell had cleverly replied: "I shall ask the local priests."

It had worked. In every parish, the priest collected the pennies, kept note of the subscribers, and sent the money on. Why would he not, when the whole purpose of the organisation, in a strictly proper and legal manner, was to get justice for their flock and representation for their faith?

And O'Connell was always careful to show that his followers were law-abiding. At the meeting Maureen had attended with her father, when a detachment of troops had arrived in case of trouble, O'Connell had immediately asked the crowd to give them a cheer.

Of course, it was a great departure for the Church, too. "I'm not sure," Father Casey, their kindly, grey-haired priest, had remarked to Eamonn, "that my predecessor would have done it. He was educated in Rome, you know, and he believed in the old order: 'Obey your governors and know your place.'" But thirty years ago, the government had allowed the Catholic Church to set up a college for training priests at Maynooth, just west of Dublin; and these Irish-trained priests had more modern and nationalist views. "We'll collect the money," they said. And the funds flowing into the Association were huge. The membership was well over a million strong, and the organization taking in an astounding hundred thousand pounds a year.

When she heard her parents argue about O'Connell, Maureen could understand them both. Her mother was small, dark, and practical. She did things quickly. Her big, blue-eyed father was practical, too, but he liked to ponder things, and he would take his time when he thought it was necessary.

"All this money he collects," her mother would object, "what is it for: so that a Catholic may sit in the British House of Parliament?"

"That is the first objective," Eamonn answered. "Do you not find it strange that I, a Catholic, forty-shilling freeholder, have the right to vote—but that I may only vote for a Protestant to represent me?"

The town boroughs were still under the control of rich and powerful gentlemen and their friends; but in the elections to the rural county seats, the ancient forty-shilling property qualification had been eased, so that even a Catholic tenant paying forty shillings a year in rent had the right to vote. For a Protestant, of course. King George III had passed on to his maker now, and his artistic son George IV was on the throne, but he was just as firm as his father had been about having Catholics in Parliament. It was against the coronation oath, he, too, declared.

"What possible good, Eamonn, can such a business do us anyway?" his wife demanded. "A few Catholics in Parliament changes nothing for you and me."

"Not at once, I grant you. But do you not see the principle of the matter? It is the admission that a Catholic is as good as a Protestant."

Maureen knew what he meant, she was sure; but her mother only shrugged.

"And who is to sit in this Parliament now, with all your fine help, if it isn't Daniel O'Connell himself? It's for himself that you're doing this."

"And what better man could there be?" Eamonn asked with a smile.

Maureen knew from the sermons of Father Casey what humiliations were still heaped upon the Catholic Church itself. The British government, for instance, thought it had the right to veto the appointment of any Catholic bishop it did not like. "Think of it," the priest would say. "The Prime Minister tells the Pope himself that the Church may not have the man His Holiness has chosen. Sends His Holiness back to try again, like a naughty schoolboy." Even worse was the long-standing grievance over the tithes. For even now, the Catholics of every parish had to pay to support not their own priest but the Protestant clergyman; and having paid for the Protestant heretic, they, the poorest in part of the community, had to pay a second time if they wanted their own priest not to starve. Beyond these specifics lay the whole panoply of Ascendancy bullying which, whatever concessions the government might allow, still remained unchanged. For weren't almost all the landlords, magistrates, and army officers still Protestant? Just recently, a local landowner called Synge had even compelled his tenants to convert to Protestantism or face eviction. Where were simple Catholics to turn in the face of such power? To the Catholic Association, of course.

"We have an advocate now," Eamonn could say. Instead of burning a bad landlord's barn, the aggrieved could speak to O'Connell, and the great Liberator would speak to the landlord. O'Connell could not right every wrong, but he could make a start.

None of this seemed to matter to her mother, however, in the light of the latest development. For now an election had brought O'Connell to their own doorstep.

It was a strange business. The sitting member for County Clare, a Protestant supporter of the Catholic cause, had been chosen for a government post, and by convention he submitted himself to his electors again before taking it. He was surprised that the Catholic Association should suddenly decide to oppose him—and amazed when the candidate turned out to be Daniel O'Connell himself.

The gauntlet was now thrown down. For the first time, a Catholic was standing for election.

"The beauty of it is this," Eamonn explained to his family with a laugh. "British law does not forbid a Catholic to stand for election. But he cannot take his seat in the British House of Commons unless he takes the Protestant oath—which, of course, he has sworn he will not do. He's using England's own rules to embarrass them. If elected, he leaves them all in an impossible position." It was a clever irony which delighted the Irish mind just as much as it appalled the English.

"And what will you say to Mr. Callan, then, that has been to our door three times looking for you?" she demanded with a look of anger and reproach. "What will you say, Eamonn—that your wife and children are to be put out, to go and beg for bread in Ennis?"

Maureen could not help being frightened when her mother said such things.

"It will not come to that," her father replied.

"And why not? It did in Waterford."

The fact was that, although the forty-shilling men all had the right to vote, it did not mean they could vote as they pleased. Not at all. Not unless they wanted to be evicted. For the landlords expected their tenants to vote as they were told. There could be no doubt about how they voted, either, since the votes were cast in public. Any tenant so rash, so foolish, so disloyal, as to vote against his landlord's wishes was, in effect, declaring himself the enemy of the man whose land he rented. Naturally, therefore, the landlord or his agent would throw him out and seek another, more decent sort of person as tenant in his place. The message was clear and simple: obey or starve.

Not long ago, O'Connell and the Association had run a candidate—a Protestant gentleman, of course, but active in the Catholic cause—against the scion of one of the largest Ascendancy families in the area, who reasonably assumed that the seat was his by right. To the horror of the local landowners, O'Connell and his men had persuaded the tenants, and even their intimate retainers, to abandon their traditional loyalty and vote for the interloper. There had been rage, stupefaction—and evictions. The danger was real, therefore.

"This is not Waterford. This is Clare," said Eamonn.

It was true that in the region, though perhaps a third of the landowners were absentee, most of the gentry were ancient Irish families like the O'Briens, or Old English like the Fitzgeralds who'd been in Ireland for six hundred years—though they had all, Old English and Irish alike, turned Protestant to keep their estates.

"And you think that Mr. Callan cares whether this is Clare or Waterford, or a desert in Asia?" his wife cried. "Or that an O'Brien would hesitate to turn out a tenant any more than an Englishman would?" she added for good measure. For it had to be confessed that there was no evidence that the Irish landowners would be any kinder than their English counterparts.

"And Father Casey: what would you say to him?" asked her father.

At Sunday Mass, the priest had made his view plain when he stood facing them, in front of the altar, and told them: "A vote for O'Connell is a vote for your religion. Be in no doubt, therefore, about what God requires."

"Do you mean, Father," one of his flock had asked him afterwards, "that if my husband votes as Mr. Callan says he must, it would be a mortal sin? Would he be in danger of hellfire?"

The kindly priest had hesitated, but nonetheless declared: "It may be so."

But her mother was not so easily influenced. Maureen had noticed already that, while her mother went regularly to Mass and confession, and insisted that her children learn their catechism, she seemed to keep some part of her mind separate and under her own control.

"Father Casey," she said bleakly, "hasn't a wife and children to support."

As the day of the election drew closer, Maureen asked her father, "What will you do?" And for the first time that she could remember, her big, strong father looked worried and uncertain.

"Truly, my child," he answered, "I do not know."

⁜

Stephen Smith was wearing a green sash with a large medal, and he was happy. What an astounding day. They were making history.

All Ireland was watching. All Britain, too. That was why the Earl of Mountwalsh had turned up, and Stephen was glad that he had; though he wondered who the unsmiling little fellow was that his lordship had brought with him.

You had to like William Mountwalsh. His wife might be silly—very nice, but silly. And perhaps there was something to be smiled at in the way this portly, middle-aged aristocrat was so determined never to miss anything or anybody making news. "I try to know everyone of interest in Ireland," he had cheerfully confessed to Stephen when he first took him up. But then again, Stephen thought, what with the earl's own huge acquaintance, and his brother's scientific friends, he probably did. He'd only to hear of you for an invitation to be issued to his house on St. Stephen's Green; and if he liked you, another to stay a few days down in the magnificence of Mount Walsh, so that he could really pump you. Not that an invitation to Mount Walsh was a thing to turn down. You lived exceedingly well, and the host himself had much to offer. With his large fortune and his seat in the House of Lords, he had a finger in every pie. There wasn't much he couldn't do for you if he chose. And his conversation was excellent. This, after all, was not only the son of the infamous Hercules but the friend of Emmet, a man who'd lived in Paris and America, and who'd publicly insulted the terrifying FitzGibbon when he was still only a youth at Trinity.

But to Stephen Smith, who at twenty was already a cynical and worldly young man, the saving grace of his lordship was that, unlike most aristocrats of that sort, he didn't just drop you as soon as he had satisfied his curiosity. He was your friend for life and he stuck by you. Rare indeed.

So when he saw William waving to him from the steps of the town's best inn, he went across to see him with real pleasure.

"Thought we'd find you here, Stephen," the earl said genially. "Whatever is that sash you're wearing?"

"It bears a medal, too," said Stephen with a grin. "The Order of Liberators. The great man invented it. When I wear it, I think myself very fine."

His lordship shook his head with amusement, then introduced his companion, a serious, quiet man of about twenty-five, who'd been staying at Mount Walsh. Samuel Tidy, he explained, was a Quaker. Stephen was surprised that his lordship would have favoured Tidy with a stay in Wexford. He looked rather dull.

"We set out from Limerick before dawn, Stephen," the earl explained. "Tell us what's going on."

The transformation of Ennis had been remarkable. Perhaps, centuries ago, when there had been a fine Franciscan friary there, or even when the princely descendants of Brian Boru had owned the place, Ennis had been more handsome. But nowadays its burgesses seldom bothered to tidy up its mean and cluttered streets—except twice a year when the justices arrived at the courthouse for the assizes. Today, however, bright banners hung from the windows; the refuse had been swept up; even some of the more unsightly beggars and prostitutes had been rounded up and put in the capacious jailhouse for the duration.

The arrival of O'Connell had been like the progress of a medieval monarch. Although it had been the start of July, it had been pouring rain; but thousands had come out to welcome him as he entered Ennis behind the great blue and gold banner of the county.

"Mind you," Stephen explained, "we'd already prepared the ground. O'Connell's been writing letters to all the leading burgesses. He has a cousin here, too, you know," he added, indicating a substantial house with a balcony some way down the street. "He's staying there. I'll be going back to him shortly."

"We noticed a lot of priests as we came in," Mountwalsh remarked, and Stephen laughed.

"A hundred and fifty, at last count. They've taken over the whole town. Some of them are even stationed at the polling booths to make sure that nobody wavers. It's a crusade. And the discipline is fearful. Ale is permitted, but not a drop of whisky

is to be taken, and God help any good Catholic found in pos-
session of poteen. There are twenty-seven public houses in this
miserable place, my lord, and the priests are watching all of
them. It's a terrible thing to see so many good men sober."

He thought he noticed Tidy wince a little as he said this.

"My grandmother knew O'Connell when he was young,
you know. In those days, she told me, he wasn't nearly such a
Catholic. She said he was a Deist."

"Well, he's certainly a good son of the Church now," said
Stephen. "His whole political career is based upon it. And look
at the results."

"A man may change his views," the Quaker interposed
gently. "No doubt Mr. O'Connell is sincere in his belief."

"I'm not sure," Stephen said honestly, "that any truly political man ever knows what he believes."

At this, Lord Mountwalsh chuckled quietly, but Tidy
looked puzzled.

"You must understand," the earl said to the Quaker, "that
young though he is, Stephen has been educating me about politics for years."

Stephen had been only sixteen when he joined O'Connell,
with nothing but a quick mind to recommend him. Working
his way up from an office boy to an election agent, he had
demonstrated a real flair for the political world. By last year,
he'd impressed enough people for William Mountwalsh to hear
of him and take him up. It seemed that the earl had been
impressed with him; and perhaps he had taken more notice of
Stephen than the young man really deserved when he had discovered that they shared a family connection.

"If you come from Rathconan, would you have known old
Deirdre, the wife of Conall Smith?" the earl had asked him.

"My great-grandmother," Stephen had told him. "I just
remember her, though she must have been a great age when I
was a small child."

"Then you will know the children of my kinsman Patrick
Walsh, that was killed at Vinegar Hill?"

"Indeed, my lord, I know them all."

This had interested his lordship greatly.

"My grandmother Georgiana went up to Rathconan the year before she died," he remembered. "She'd been very close to Patrick, and she wanted to know what had become of his children. She said they were all up there but none wanted to come down. If they had, I think she'd have given them money, you know."

"They wanted nothing to do with Dublin," Stephen had confirmed. "Old Deirdre would have seen to that. They married O'Tooles, O'Byrnes, Brennans, and the like. You couldn't tell them apart now."

"And Brigid," the earl had wanted to know. "Did you ever hear of her?"

"Certainly. She wrote to Deirdre from Australia. She married again. I think she had more children. A dozen years ago, she owned a small hotel in New South Wales. That's all I know."

Such family considerations aside, William Mountwalsh had wanted to know all about Stephen's life and what a young man of his generation hoped for.

"In the long run, the Repeal of the Union and an independent Ireland," Stephen had told him. "But until then, the liberal Whig party in England is our best bet. It was the party of Sheridan, after all. The Whigs are sympathetic to Irish Catholics. As for O'Connell, I believe he can do more for us than any man living."

Stephen had also come to realize that his lordship liked nothing better than to hear the latest political gossip that a young fellow working in the thick of the campaign can always supply. And the juicier the story, the more he liked it.

But what about this Quaker? Stephen did not know much about the Quakers, but he suspected this fellow was far too solemn for his own worldly tastes.

"Have you always been a Quaker, Mr. Tidy?" he politely enquired.

"My father belonged to the established Church, but my mother was a Quaker," Tidy answered. "My father died when I was ten, and as the years passed, I became more drawn to the Friends." Stephen noticed that the slight forward stoop of the small fellow was a permanent feature. With his thin, sandy hair, it gave him an ageless look.

"One of his family was butler to the great Dean Swift, and after that to the Duke of Devonshire, no less. Isn't that right?" said Lord Mountwalsh.

"My father's great-uncle," Tidy acknowledged, and Stephen smiled to himself. Though the earl was remarkable for his lack of snobbery, even in the case of this Quaker, he still liked to know who you were.

"And what do you think of our election?" Stephen asked.

"I had not realized," the Quaker said, "what an effect O'Connell has upon the crowds."

"He's like an Irish prince."

"The O'Connells were princes?"

"No." Stephen smiled. "But they made a small fortune."

"In what business?"

"Smuggling," said Stephen cheerfully.

"Oh." The Quaker looked a little shocked.

"The Catholics trust him," Stephen went on, "because they know that there are no lengths he won't go to for their sake. He proved that as a lawyer. Did you hear the story of how he defended the man accused of murder?"

"I do not think so."

The earl signalled that he knew the story but would be glad to hear it again.

"No one else would help the poor devil. So O'Connell gets up in front of the judge and lets him have it. 'I cannot defend this poor Catholic,' he cries, 'because I know very well that he is condemned to death before this trial even begins. So why waste time? Since your lordship means to hang him anyway, you may as well condemn him now. I'll be no part of it. But this I say to you,' and he gives the judge a terrible look, 'his blood be upon your hands!' And with that, he storms out of the court."

"And what happened?" asked Tidy.

"The judge was so terrified, he let the man off."

"So justice was done after all?"

"Not at all. I asked the great man about it myself. 'I'd no choice,' says he, 'for if it had ever gone to trial, I hadn't a hope. The man was as guilty as sin.'"

William Mountwalsh chuckled appreciatively. Tidy looked grave and said nothing.

"And did he make a good speech here?" the earl asked after a moment's silence.

"Scandalous," said Stephen with a smile. "His opponent Fitzgerald, besides representing the greatest gentry here, is a man of the most liberal principles. His decency is universally admired by Protestant and Catholic alike. So our man gets up and delivers a speech the like of which I never heard. Openly insults him. You'd think Fitzgerald was a Cromwellian in league with every bigot in the Ascendancy. The crowd was roaring. The sheer unfairness of the thing was a work of art." He shook his head admiringly. "He'll have to apologize to Fitzgerald afterwards, of course. But then, he's very good at doing that."

It was all too much for Samuel Tidy.

"Does thy conscience not prick thee?" he cried in reproach. Stephen had heard of the Quaker custom of using the old forms of "thou" and "thee." It was interesting to hear them now. And it had to be admitted that, although every word he had spoken was true, he had half hoped it might provoke a reaction from the solemn dissenter.

"Not," he said firmly, "until after the election."

At this moment, however, a great cry came from farther down the street as the first company of voters came marching into sight.

A county election like this was a lengthy affair. People would be coming in from up to forty miles away, and the polls would be open for five days. Often as not, the landlord himself would be at the head of his tenants in his carriage, while they walked on foot. He'd be leading them as a general leads his troops: expecting a similar obedience, and keeping a sharp eye open to see that he got it. Reaching the polling booths at the courthouse, each man would publicly cast his vote as his landlord directed—if he was wise.

But the sight which greeted their eyes now was without precedent. For marching along the street, with banners flying, came a body of men led not by a landlord but a line of priests. Behind the priests came fifes and a piper. As this procession went by, the people lining the streets cheered. Stephen turned to Mountwalsh.

"Impressed?" he asked, and then excused himself, saying that he had to get back to O'Connell, but promising to return.

⁘

Inside the house, he found a scene of excitement. O'Connell's cousin Charles was at the window of the big upstairs room, watching the men go by. O'Connell himself was surrounded by well-wishers and lieutenants.

"There they go. Another fifty. Brave boys," cried Charles delightedly.

But if everyone else was looking cheerful, the big man himself was surprisingly sombre.

"Brave boys indeed, Charles," he said. "For every one of them is risking eviction, and let's not forget it." He turned to his agent. "From now on, Shiel, your main task is with the landlords. The Orangeists believe that the whole of Catholic Ireland is ready to revolt, and that I'm the only one that can control them and stem the tide. They're wrong, of course, but we can make use of their fear. You must convince them that if they retaliate with evictions, I won't answer for the consequences."

"I'll tell them that any evictions would be against their own interests."

"Make sure they understand."

Charles O'Connell was looking up the street.

"Ah," he said, "here comes a sad crowd."

Stephen joined him at the window. About forty men were walking slowly up the street. They were accompanied by an elderly priest, but at their head marched a small, dark-haired man who looked grim but determined.

"That's Callan the agent," said Charles. "Absentee landlord. Old priest's called Casey. A good man, but I don't know if he can hold them together."

"What's that?" Daniel O'Connell was across the room in a moment. "Open the big window," he commanded, and stepped out onto the balcony. The men below saw him. The people lining the way cheered. O'Connell raised his hand, and the marching men stopped, while the crowd fell silent.

"Are the forty-shilling freeholders slaves?" His voice rolled down from the balcony and filled the street. The men looked up at him, and as he gazed back, his huge figure magically conveyed strength and reassurance. "Are they like Negroes, to be whipped to the slave market?" His eyes searched out each man. "I do not think so."

Callan scowled. The crowd cheered. The men also cheered, but you could tell they were afraid. It was obvious that Callan had threatened them. Voices from the crowd called out: "Come on, boys. Vote for the old religion."

Looking down, Stephen noticed one fellow in particular. A big, handsome, blue-eyed fellow. He had taken his cap off in respect for O'Connell, but he was twisting it in his hands, obviously in some agony of mind.

O'Connell stepped back.

"Poor devils," he remarked. "That little agent's done his work, you can see."

"Threatened them with eviction?" asked Stephen.

"No. More effective than that. Threatened their wives."

But now, just as the men were moving on, Stephen saw them halted again, this time by a priest who, obviously not satisfied with their demeanour, had decided to put some more fire into them. "That's Father Murphy," said Charles O'Connell. "This will be something to hear." And he opened the window again.

Father Murphy was certainly a striking figure. Tall, gaunt, his long white hair falling lankly to his shoulders, his eyes like coals of fire, he glared at the men like a prophet of old and began to harangue them in Irish.

✢

William Mountwalsh was glad he had come to Ennis. He didn't think he'd stay the full five days of the election, but it was a historic occasion, and he'd be able to tell everyone that he was there.

He was amused by young Stephen Smith. Of course, the boy was hard and cynical, and thought life was all a game. But it was William's experience that young men of twenty are either too idealistic or too cynical; time would improve him. As for his new Quaker friend Tidy, he liked him.

Two months ago, he'd had one of the evangelicals down to Mount Walsh. A follower of Wesley. They were spreading quite surprisingly in Ireland, though not as fast as in England, thank God. They meant well, no doubt: they wanted to purify the world. He wasn't sure at his age he wanted the world to be so pure. And it depressed him to hear the Evangelical speak of "subjugating Irish popery to the Faith of Christ." That was what people had done back in the century of Cromwell, and a grim business it had been.

Tidy was entirely different. The Quakers were becoming quite an active community in Dublin and in Cork, so he had thought it time he came to know them better. He had to admit that they puzzled him. Instead of a service, they sat in reverential silence in their meeting houses and got up to speak if the spirit moved them. A strange way to carry on. A Catholic bishop with whom he'd once discussed the Quakers had put it rather well. "I do not for a moment deny that their intentions are well-meaning. What I cannot discover is where their God is to be found."

But a few days with Tidy had impressed the earl enormously. The Quaker did not criticize other churches, and he assured William that his fellow Quakers never tried to convert others away from their faith. He did not sanctify; he did not curse. He merely tried to treat his neighbour in a godly fashion, and his own goodness and sincerity were obvious. Actions, not words seemed to be his daily creed. "You remind me of the Good Samaritan," William had told him, and meant it as a sincere compliment.

Here in Ennis, he could see that Tidy was rather shocked, and he didn't blame him. Indeed, from what he had witnessed so far, he was rather shocked himself. He turned to the Quaker.

"I don't like what I see, Samuel Tidy. Do you?"

"It is not what Quakers believe in."

William nodded and pursed his lips. The trouble was, he thought, he'd seen it all before. He'd seen the French Revolution turn into terror and dictatorship. How quickly the underdog could turn into a tyrant. He'd supported the cause of Catholic emancipation since he was a youth; and God knows, if this peaceful army of O'Connell's was militant, it was understandable. But as he watched the phalanx of priests marching in front of their men, with fifes playing and banners flying, he sensed a triumphalism that disturbed him.

Perhaps it was because he was middle-aged, but the older he got, the more William respected compromise; and from his perspective, these local priests were going further than necessary. Reforms were needed, of course, but there was no need for this bad feeling. For relations between the British government and the Vatican, nowadays, were actually rather cordial. During the years when Napoleon dominated Europe and threatened its Catholic monarchs, Rome had been glad that England stood as the bulwark against him; and after Napoleon's final defeat, when the territories of Europe were reordered at the great Congress of Vienna, a dozen years ago, it had been the British who insisted that the rich Italian Papal States must be given back to the Pope, who had been grateful to Britain ever since. O'Connell and the parish priests had a good case, for instance, when they complained about the tithes; but their outrage about the Prime Minister's veto over bishops was unnecessary. William himself was in a position to know that, behind the scenes, the British government and the Vatican discreetly arranged the top Church appointments together, to everyone's satisfaction.

"I'm with O'Connell on Catholic Emancipation. And since I was never for the Union, I would support its repeal," he remarked to Tidy. "But times change, and one must look for what is practical. This militancy is dangerous."

William usually spent about three months a year in London. He enjoyed sitting in the British House of Lords and keeping up with events in London. And much could be achieved there. Even Grattan thought so, for he'd spent the last fifteen years of his life in the London Parliament. And despite the fear of Catholicism which, William now understood, was ingrained in the English like a race memory, there were many in the British Parliament, especially in the liberal Whig party, who were most anxious to grant the Irish Catholics what they wanted. This very spring, the last legal disabilities had been removed from the Dissenters. It was inevitable that, with time, the Catholics would be similarly treated. Patience was needed.

But what he saw here was war. War of tenant upon landlord, war of Catholic upon Protestant.

"I fear also," Tidy continued, "that this will arouse the worst fears of the Presbyterians and Orangeists."

"How right you are," William concurred. Since he was a boy, the Presbyterians had changed their tune completely. In those days, most Ulster Presbyterians wanted to be free of England and its Church, which made them second-class citizens. But nowadays, with their own rights secured, they were the strongest supporters of the Union. "United with England and Scotland, we are part of a Protestant majority," they judged. "Without England, we become a minority in a sea of Irish papists." And propelled by that fear, their preachers were starting to sound as strident as they had back in the days of Cromwell. When they read of these marching priests and tenants in Clare, it would arouse all their worst fears.

And suddenly, William felt a pang of nostalgia for the days of his youth. He longed for the old Patriots, or the men of '98, like Patrick Walsh or noble young Emmet. They had all shared a common vision—of a free Ireland, where Catholic and Protestant, Presbyterian and Deist, could live together in equality under the law. It might be idealistic, but it was a noble ideal, and he missed it.

Nor was it impractical. For if the new republic of America, with its separation of church and state, could realize such an ideal, then why not here in the Old World, too?

Yet when he considered these men, marching in Ennis—no matter how justified their grievances—Lord Mountwalsh thought he heard not the continuing march of enlightenment, but a heavier, grimmer sound: the slow, sectarian thud of boot on blood, as though, like a returning prophesy, an age-old darkness was closing in again.

꘠

Tidy's thoughts at that moment were following quite a different course. He was glad he had gone to stay with the earl. He had never stayed in a great country house before. He had especially liked the library. He had even liked the earl's wife, whose heart was in the right place, even if she had seemed to him a little foolish. And he was glad that Mountwalsh had brought him to see this election. For this, too, was instructive.

But his thoughts were less on the election than upon what he had seen already in County Clare.

He had never been to the west before. Dublin and Leinster he knew, with their rich farmlands; the busy port of Cork, also.

Ulster he knew, with its farmsteads, its cloth and linen industries. But the rural west of Ireland he did not know.

How was it possible, he asked himself, amidst such magnificent scenery, that the people could be so neglected and so poor? How was it that the burgesses of Ennis could allow the terrible squalour of the shantytowns along the approaches to their town? Were they not ashamed? How could the landlords—not only the absentees, but those there to see, Irishmen of the same blood, if they were Christians—let their neighbours live in such conditions and do nothing about it? How could the poor themselves take so little care that they would have families in the first place, to bring them up in deprivation? Why was there no industry, no enterprise to bring employment? His practical, self-controlled Quaker soul protested against this vast, cruel carelessness.

But now that unpleasant young political man was returning. He had learned as much as he cared to from Stephen Smith. But he took a deep breath and tried to remember that it was not for him to make judgements upon another man.

⁌

Stephen loved the mad business of the election. O'Connell had sent him on an errand, but he had promised to return to Lord Mountwalsh, and as he could only remain with him for a minute or two, he was glad to have something amusing to tell him. The scene he had just witnessed had been quite remarkable. For the harangue Father Murphy had delivered had been mesmerising in its intensity.

"It was all in Irish," he explained. "The O'Connells had to translate, because most of us from Leinster didn't have enough Irish to understand. First, he reminds them of their duty, and they all look suitably solemn, but he isn't sure he has them. Then he reminds them of all the others that are voting as they should, and how accursed they will be by all their fellows if they let them down. That affects them considerably, by the look of it. And then comes the clincher. Did they not know, he cries, wagging his long bony finger at them, that one of the Catholic men voted for the Protestant—and that he was struck down by an apoplexy as soon as he stepped out of the booth? 'Divine retribution will be swift,' he cries. 'You may count upon it. The saints are watching, and taking note!' He was quite terrifying. I was frightened myself."

The earl gave a wry smile. Stephen was chuckling. But Tidy was not amused.

"Do you mean that there was an unfortunate who was struck with an apoplexy, or that there was no such man?" he asked seriously.

"Heavens, man," cried Stephen, "I haven't the least idea. What does it matter?"

"Does it not matter to thee whether a thing is the truth or a lie?" the Quaker asked.

"You haven't the spirit of devilment in you," said Stephen, "or you would understand."

"I hope," answered Tidy quietly, "that I have not."

÷

It was a little while later, walking along the street where the local newspaper, the *Clare Journal*, had its offices, that Stephen caught sight of the big, blue-eyed fellow he had noticed in the band of tenants who'd been harangued by Father Murphy. They'd all voted for O'Connell. He'd checked. Now it remained to be seen whether Callan the agent would evict them, or whether he could be persuaded not to.

The big fellow was standing by a small cart and looking serious. Beside him was a girl, maybe ten or so, pale and with a solemn face. The big man had his arm around her shoulder. Father and daughter, obviously. Was he comforting her, or she him? She must know what he had done.

Pity, he thought, that the girl was so plain.

⊰ 1843 ⊱

It began quietly, in America. A farmer in the New York region, looking out over a field of growing potatoes one day, noticed that something was amiss.

Some of the potato leaves had spots on them. He waited a few days. More of the leaves were spotted now, and the ones he had first noticed had withered. The stems on which they grew seemed to be affected, too. That night, he discussed with his wife whether he should dig them up or lift the entire crop early.

The following morning, when he went out to the field, there was a stench of putrefying matter rising from the ground.

He set to work at once. He dug up everything that looked infected. Many of the potatoes were already rotting; in others, rot had clearly begun. When he had completed this work, he made a large bonfire and burned them all. About half of the crop was still in the ground.

Being a decent man, he went to all his neighbours and then into the local town, to warn of the blight and discover whether others were experiencing similar problems. A number of farmers were reporting the same thing.

Some days later, he saw spotting once again and said to his wife: "Better lift the whole crop. Save what we can." A good many of the potatoes were obviously infected, and these he destroyed, as he had the others. About half the remaining crop, fortunately, appeared to be sound, and these he stored in a pit.

Ten days later, he checked the crop he had saved. He picked out a potato and cut it open with a knife. It was rotten. He tried another. The same. Half the potatoes he had thought were sound were now useless.

✛

Phytophthora infestans: it was a fungal infestation. But where had it come from?

Nobody knew, but the likelihood was that it had come into the United States as an importation. For, desirous of avoiding any degeneracy in the potato stock, the American agriculturalists were in the habit of importing fresh seed potatoes from Peru. Some of the ships also brought guano, the seabird manure used as fertilizer. It seems likely that the fungus spread from the guano to the seed potato on the ship.

Having established itself in New York, the fungus was already starting to spread with astonishing rapidity. It would cross New Jersey and Pennsylvania. By 1845, it would reach the American Midwest.

The trade in seed potato was triangular. From America's eastern seaboard, the seed was exported east to Europe. By the time it was established in the Midwest, the blight would also appear in the Low Countries of Holland and Belgium, and on the south coast of England.

⁘

"You have never read *The Wild Irish Girl*?" Lady Mountwalsh looked at Dudley Doyle with astonishment. She thought everybody had.

Everyone liked Henrietta. She must be fifty, Doyle thought; yet there was still something girlish about the Englishwoman William had chosen as his bride. And the complexion, the peaches-and-cream complexion that had turned heads in every drawing room in London and Dublin—it was still the same. That, and the china-blue eyes that were turned upon him now, and the delectable, plump little breasts. He envied Mountwalsh his marriage bed. The couple had been happy and had raised a healthy family. She might be a little silly, but there was certainly no malice in her. And she was, as he supposed, an enthusiast for all things Irish.

"And you," she said, "with those dark, Celtic good looks."
He smiled. One had to like her.

"You know, Henrietta, in Irish, my name actually means
'dark foreigner.' So I must suppose that my ancestors were
Viking pirates," he explained to her, "rather than Irish heroes."
Vikings who would certainly have married local Irish women,
themselves a mixture of tribes from northern France and, so
the legends said, people from the Spanish peninsula. Since
those ancient days, what other strains would have entered the
blood? Norman, Flemish, Welsh, English, to be sure. Some
more Spanish, probably. His clever, somewhat ruthless mind
enjoyed such analysis. "It's hard to know what Celtic means,
really," he remarked.

But Henrietta knew. It meant the romantic heroine of
Lady Morgan's famous novel, the wild daughter of the "Prince
of Connaught," who wins the heart of the prejudiced
Englishman and teaches him to love the glories of Irish wit and
learning, bravery and generosity. It meant the purity of soul
that came from the timeless Celtic wellsprings. It meant
Hibernia—a land of heroes and mystics, a magical counterpart
to the sterner beauties of Scotland in the novels of Walter
Scott. It had made Ireland quite fashionable. In fact, Doyle had
read the book, though he preferred to tease Henrietta gently by
pretending that he hadn't. And if, to him, it was all nonsense,
the fictional romantic Celt was at least an improvement upon
the traditional view of the Irishman as a bog-dwelling mur-
derer and devious papist—a slander that was still to be found
in the cartoons of *Punch* magazine or the pages of any English
newspaper.

Every time Henrietta went back to London with her husband, she told people about the Ireland she knew. True, he
thought wryly, it was an Ireland that consisted of the big house
on St. Stephen's Green and this great estate in Wexford, with
its rolling pastures and its ornamental gardens. It was a land
where you called upon similar-minded neighbours, enjoyed
their dinner parties, where you were waited upon by their loyal

Irish servants, played cards, went to the club. Since her husband was a decent man and one of the best landlords in Ireland, she had encountered a friendliness from the local Irish tenants and labourers that was entirely genuine. And all this was glossed with a magical Celtic romanticism that coloured the landscape like a charming evening sunset amongst the hills. However, if she induced some members of the English governing class to take a more kindly view of the western island, then so much the better, he supposed.

"This is a most excellent meal," he added with a smile. Gaston, the Mountwalshes' chef, always performed miracles with the produce from the estate whenever he accompanied them into Wexford. Outside, the dusk was gathering. The magical season of Halloween, the old Celtic festival of Samhain, was only days away.

Much as he liked Henrietta, however, it was not her that he had really come to see. He glanced across the table at Stephen Smith. They hadn't spoken much yet, as the fellow had only arrived that afternoon, looking tired. But when William Mountwalsh had invited Doyle to stay, he had told him: "Stephen Smith is a man I think you should know better." And William, he always reckoned, was a fair judge of men. "Though, of course," the peer had added, "I know how hard you are to please."

If his ancestors had always chosen to remain in the merchant class, Dudley Doyle had chosen a slightly different style. To all outward appearances, he looked, dressed, talked, and, to a large extent, thought like a country gentleman. He belonged to the Kildare Street Club, whose members were mostly landowners. But although he owned two farms in Meath, he had always lived in town except in the summer months, when he resided in a seaside villa he had built at Sandymount, in the southern part of Dublin Bay. He had ample funds. The collection of Dublin properties that old Barbara Doyle had passed on to his grandfather was still in his hands. He owned a half share in a thriving wine merchants, and received ground rent from three large pubs. And though he met the country gentry at his club, at the races, or as a guest in their houses, he often preferred the company of the university men. At Trinity College, he had been a precise, classical scholar. But for many years now, he had chosen to occupy his spare time in the private study of political economy. Since being widowed two years ago, he had devoted himself to these studies even more. From time to time, if asked politely, he would even give a lecture upon the subject.

As his eyes took in Stephen Smith, he saw much that he did not like. A trace of carelessness in his dressing. He himself was always fastidious. An intelligent face, certainly, but not a university man. A pity. The earl had said that he was poor, and poverty, Dudley Doyle considered, was always a mistake. Also that he was amusing. But what were his verbal weapons? Were we speaking of a mere gift of utterance, the broad blade of humour, the vagaries of vulgar whimsy, thrown over a company like a gladiator's net? Or were we speaking of something with more politesse, the rapier of repartee, with which he himself was adept, quick, and deadly? It remained to be seen.

"You are an associate of Mr. O'Connell, I understand?" he said to Smith. "Do I take it, therefore, that you are a Whig?"

Since his astonishing election for Clare, fifteen years before, it was hard to imagine how Daniel O'Connell could have played his cards better. The English government had been so shocked by the result that it had promptly removed the right to vote from the forty-shilling freeholders, Catholic and Protestant alike, and raised the qualification so high that only the better sort of farmers—the more responsible element—could vote in future. But they had been forced to give way and let Catholics sit in Parliament. O'Connell, hailed as the Liberator, had gained his main objective. And soon after that, when the liberal Whig party had come to power, O'Connell had seen his chance. Building up a large following of sixty Irish members, he had skilfully managed an alliance with the Whigs that had been fruitful. He charmed the Whig grandees in person; and leading his sixty followers to their aid in close votes, he made them very grateful to him. The Irish Catholics gained. "We'll do all for you that we can," the government promised. A year after young Queen Victoria came to the throne, even the vexed question of tithes was finally resolved. Above all, the long decade of Whig government saw enlightened men sent out to govern Ireland: fine men like the Under Secretary, Thomas Drummond, who came to love the country and who never ceased to remind the Ascendancy landowners: "Property has rights, gentlemen, but it also has responsibilities." A dozen years after his election, O'Connell could say that his compromise with the Whigs had produced real benefits.

Could he have done better? The cause of Repeal—the breaking away from Union with England—had been indefinitely postponed. It couldn't be denied. And some of his younger followers felt that the great Liberator had degenerated into a political deal-maker. "But since the government wasn't going to give us Repeal anyway," he'd remarked to Stephen, "I think I did the right thing."

"I am that noblest of beasts, Sir," Stephen replied to Dudley Doyle with a wry smile. "I am a Catholic Whig."

"For reform, but through Parliament? You are prepared to be patient?"

"I am a political animal. I abhor violence, just as O'Connell does. That is why," he said with a sigh, "I have been his man for twenty years."

"Then what, might I ask, do you intend to do now?" asked Doyle. "After Clontarf?"

Stephen shook his head.

"My life," he answered sadly, "has reached a point of crisis."

It was three years ago that the strategy had started to break down. First Drummond had died, and the Irish had buried him with sorrow. Then the Whig government had fallen and the Tories had come in. What should O'Connell do now? Some of his young followers were certain—Young Ireland, they called themselves, and even had their own journal, *The Nation*. "It's time to fight for Repeal," they declared, "by any and all means, if necessary." The great Liberator wasn't ready to lose the movement he'd built up. He placed himself at their head, and this very year he had launched a campaign of huge rallies across Ireland. O'Connell's monster meetings were beyond anything seen before. Tens of thousands would come to hear the great Liberator speak. All over Leinster, Munster, and Connacht he went: Dublin and Wicklow, Waterford and Wexford, Cork, Sligo, and Mayo; to Ennis, where he had triumphed; even to the ancient royal site of Tara. "We will force the British government," he cried, "to give us justice or our freedom." But Britain's Tory government would not be moved. The monster meetings were to climax with the biggest rally of them all. It was to be held just outside Dublin, on the northern bank of the Liffey estuary, at Clontarf, where, eight centuries before, Ireland's heroic king, Brian Boru, had fought his final battle. The massed ranks of priests, the Repeal men with their banners were all prepared—most of the population of the capital would probably turn up. But the Tory government had had enough.

"Call off your meeting or face jail," it told O'Connell.

It had been the terrible decision. Stephen had been at a meeting with O'Connell and a number of others when the matter was discussed. "We must operate within the law," the Liberator had declared, "or we give up everything we stand for." Stephen himself had agreed. "In politics," he'd reminded everyone, "you can live to fight another day." But not all the great man's followers had agreed, especially the Young Ireland men.

Two weeks ago, O'Connell had called the meeting off. Nobody knew what to do next. Some of the younger men spoke of revolution, which Stephen knew to be useless and mistaken. The movement was in shock. He himself had experienced a huge sense of frustration. And he had been grateful indeed when, shortly afterwards, he had received an invitation from Mountwalsh to come and spend a few days down in Wexford. "It might," his lordship had kindly suggested, "cheer you up."

"A crossroads rather than a crisis, perhaps," Dudley Doyle offered, not unkindly.

"The crossroads, I believe," Stephen said, "is for Ireland rather than myself. For whatever good we have been able to do in these last dozen years is still so little, when you consider the problems that beset our country. The poverty is terrible."

"Take some comfort, Stephen," said William Mountwalsh. "Things here in Leinster are not so bad. And remember," he added, "the war with Napoleon was very good for Ireland, because we sold the English so many provisions. When it ended, we were worried. The beef industry took a terrible knock. Yet look what happened," he went on cheerfully. "Thanks to the new railways in England, we can send live cattle to every part of the market there, which we never could before. There are more people, so the price of grain has held. Our farmers do well. Speaking for myself, I've never done better."

"I accept what you say for Wexford," replied Stephen. "Though I can tell you that up in the mountains of Wicklow, my family and their neighbours live near subsistence. Last time I was up at Rathconan, I found twice the number of folk that I remember as a child, with miserable little potato patches dug right up onto the bare hillside, where nothing but sheep have ever been raised before. Some of the people are quite wretchedly poor."

"That may be," Dudley Doyle countered, "but consider the case of Ulster. The people there have small farms, but they are prosperous. They have the linen industry, and much else besides."

"Ulster I scarcely know," Stephen confessed. "O'Connell never goes there. The Presbyterians have become so strident of late that he'd hardly be welcome." He paused. "But I was thinking of the west above all. Of Clare, Galway, Mayo. The situation there is terrible and getting worse."

"Ah, the west. That is another matter," Mountwalsh acknowledged.

"Isn't it a case of bad landlords?" asked Henrietta. "I mean, if the landlords were like William . . ."

"It would be better," Stephen said politely, "but the problems are too big even for the best landlords to solve. I really don't know what's to be done."

William glanced around the table. There was a fifth person there, who had not yet spoken during the present conversation. He turned to her now.

"And what does Miss Doyle think?"

It was strange that Dudley Doyle's eldest daughter was not married. Both her younger sisters were. She was handsome, and it was known that her father had settled three thousand pounds on her. She was twenty-five, with a calm and pleasant manner; her colouring was good, her brown eyes fine and intelligent. She smiled now.

"I leave those things to the men," she said.

"Oh, so do I," said Henrietta.

Doyle looked at his daughter curiously. Now why, he wondered, would she say that? Stephen also gave her a glance— polite, but just a little weary.

"I fear I disappoint you, Mr. Smith," she said.

"Oh no, not at all," he answered, though of course it was not true.

"The problem really," said William Mountwalsh, "is that there are too many people for this island to support. The government estimates that we are well past eight million now. Farming methods, especially in the west, need much improvement. But it seems that Ireland is living proof of the theories of Malthus: that humans will always breed faster than the food supply increases. That is why we have always had wars down the ages." Having brought the conversation back to life, as a good host should, he turned to Doyle. "You make a study of these things, Dudley. Tell us what is the answer."

Doyle surveyed them all. He did not mind having an audience. He paused for a moment.

"The answer," he said, with a faint smile of satisfaction, "is there is nothing wrong with Ireland at all."

"Nothing wrong?' Stephen looked at him incredulously.

"Nothing," said the economist. "And I am surprised, Mr. Smith, that you, as a Whig—which you say that you are—should think that there is."

"Explain, Dudley," said William with a broad smile, as he settled back in his chair.

"As a Whig," Dudley Doyle addressed Stephen, rather as a lawyer in court addresses a witness before a jury, "you believe in free trade, do you not?"

"I do."

"You do not think that governments should intervene, as the British government was once so fond of doing, to protect inefficient farmers and manufacturers with tariffs or restrictions on trade? You believe in the operation of the free market—that, over time, it is always best?"

"Certainly."

"Then that is what we have. There is now an excess of people in Ireland. Very well. The result is that their labour is cheap. There is therefore an incentive for enterprising manufacturers to employ them."

"That may happen in Ulster, but it does not happen in Clare. And the people go hungry."

"I believe that eventually it will, but no matter. The hunger of the people is not a bad thing. It will drive them to seek work further afield. Do we not see that occurring?"

"Labourers from Clare take their spades and migrate for seasonal work as far as Leinster, or often England," Stephen agreed.

"Excellent. Britain benefits thereby, for the cost of its labour is reduced and the Irishman is fed."

"Many have to leave entirely, though," Stephen said sadly, "forced to emigrate, to England or America."

"Do you know," interposed Mountwalsh, "that over a million people have left this island during my own lifetime? About four hundred thousand in the last decade."

"Splendid," said Doyle, smiling at them both. "The whole world benefits thereby. There are too many people in Ireland? Well and good. America has need of them. A vast, rich continent in need of willing hands. They can do very well there. Indeed, without Ireland, what would America be? We must take a larger view, gentlemen. The temporary misery of the Irish peasant is a blessing in disguise. Do not interfere with the market, therefore. Thanks to the market, the whole world turns."

"But the process is so cruel," Stephen said.

"So is nature."

There was a thoughtful pause.

"Isn't it fascinating to listen to them?" said Henrietta to Caroline Doyle. "I think it's time for the dessert."

⁘

William was delighted when Caroline Doyle asked him to show her the library after dinner. It was he, after all, who'd suggested to Doyle that he should bring her. She admired the collection and found a few of her favourite books. Then she turned to him and smiled.

"Well, Lord Mountwalsh, I know you've asked me here to meet him. So what sort of man is Stephen Smith?"

"I suppose," he answered truthfully, "that I wouldn't have asked you if it were easy to say."

Her father had only agreed to the business because, as he freely confessed to the earl, he didn't know what to do with her. He might have an incisive mind himself, but though he admired his daughter's intelligence, he couldn't really see the point of it in a woman. It was certainly no help in getting married. "I must warn you," he counselled her, "that men don't like too much intelligence in a woman. A man likes a woman with just enough intelligence to appreciate his own. If you wish to be more than that, you would be wise to hide it." But though she agreed to do this—usually—she made a further demand that was just as awkward. "She wants to find a man," he told William, "who she thinks interesting. I told her, 'Interesting men usually give their wives a lot of trouble.' But I'm not sure she believes me."

"Stephen Smith is certainly interesting," the earl continued now.

It was also time he married. He was already thirty-five. A few years more, William considered, and the fellow would become so set in his ways that he'd never tolerate anybody. And it was time that Stephen had a home. He'd been living in lodgings for years.

William Mountwalsh had known other men like Stephen Smith. Men who were so fascinated by the daily business of politics, with its excitement, uncertainties, and nighttime confabulations, not to mention the thrill of feeling you were close to influence and power, that they could spend decades in busy backrooms and corridors, and never realize that life had passed them by. Politics, he knew, was a drug, and Stephen was an addict. He needed to be saved.

William had also observed that these cynical political men were often secret idealists. Stephen Smith did not worship O'Connell; he was too intelligent. But he truly believed that O'Connell was guiding the Irish to a better destiny. Like a prophet of old, the Liberator might not lead his people out of the desert, but he had already taken them part of the way. Sometimes men like Stephen also dreamed of becoming leaders themselves. That was hard for a poor man, though not impossible. Did Stephen have such dreams? Perhaps. William had heard him give a speech once or twice, and he was talented. There was an aura about him. But if the young man had dreams of standing for Parliament, those dreams were probably idealistic. He'd like to be a great figure in a great cause, the earl shrewdly guessed, rather than win just for the sake of winning, as a true politician would. The fellow had one other weakness also, the usual weakness of the poor man: he was proud. "Stephen Smith would rather do anything than have it seem he had been bought or sold," he remarked to the young woman, wondering if she'd understand.

"Does he like women?"

"Yes. When he has time." He paused. "Women like him."

"I expect they do. He has wonderful green eyes."

"Does he? Yes, I suppose he does."

A number of women had been very taken with Stephen. To William's knowledge, he had had affairs with at least two married society ladies, one of which had lasted some years. Whether Stephen's heart had really been engaged, William doubted. Perhaps Smith was a little selfish. Yet if a man with no money likes to move in those circles, what else can he do but have affairs with other men's wives?

Was it his eyes that attracted them? Partly, no doubt. But there was something magical surrounding those dark good looks of his; a fascinating intensity in his manner when he became enthusiastic, and eloquent upon a subject. That, and his occasional depressions, and their knowledge of his vulnerability, were surely the things that had made those aristocratic ladies want to possess him, and to be possessed.

"I feel sure you'll reach your own conclusions," he said. "You should talk to him."

"Have no fear." She smiled. "I shall."

❖

Maureen was in a sunny mood when Mr. Callan came by. She wasn't sure, but she thought he probably liked her. Certainly, in the last two years, he'd always been civil to her and asked after the children. Once, riding by, he had noticed two of the children eyeing a large, shiny apple he was about to eat and had handed it to her, with a half-smile, to give to them.

Today, he had just asked if her father was about, and when she said he was out, Callan had just said, "No matter," and told her he'd pass by later.

The sky was clear that day, and the autumn sun was bright. After so much damp weather all through the summer, the sunny sky made her feel cheerful.

When she considered her life, Maureen felt rather pleased with herself. She knew how much her family needed her. It was two years since her mother had died after giving birth to little Daniel. "Look after him for me," her mother had said to her. As the eldest daughter, she would have expected to help her mother with the children anyway; and, thank God, she had not been married.

Since then, she had taken over the role of mother. There were four children to take care of. The two eldest had left soon after their mother's death. Norah had married and moved with her husband to England. Then William had taken the chance to go with his uncle when Eamonn's remaining brother had left for America. But that had still left the younger ones: Nuala, who was fifteen now; Mary and Caitlin, eight and ten; and little Daniel, who, because of the circumstances of his birth, she thought of almost as her own. And she supposed that, if her father did not marry again, she'd be looking after him for another dozen years or more, until he was old enough to fend for himself in the world. Unless, of course, she married herself, but that was unlikely. She was twenty-four now. And as her mother had warned her years ago: "I'm afraid, Maureen, you're very plain. Though perhaps," she had added, "someone will marry you for your goodness."

She didn't think she was good, but she did try to keep cheerful. No matter how she felt, she tried to be calm at all times and show the little ones a smiling face. It seemed the right thing to do.

And thank God her father was always so strong. She knew it could not have been easy for him without a wife. But he was always even-tempered, and affectionate with the children, and it was clear even to the younger ones that he lived his life according to strong beliefs and principles. He always took the family to Mass. He drank a little ale, but seldom any liquour, and never poteen. She could not imagine him drunk. Both old Father Casey and his successor always told her: "Your father is everything a good Catholic should be."

After his brother and William went, he was the only one of the Maddens left on his father's land. Callan had not taken any action against the tenants who had voted for O'Connell back in '28, and his relationship with her father had been one of guarded politeness ever since. Was Callan even a little afraid of them? There had been some trouble below Ennis last year, some small rioting and looting after a local food shortage, though it hadn't come up here. The Protestant gentry and their agents had all been a bit jumpy, though, while O'Connell's campaign of monster meetings was going on. But he must surely know, she thought, that whatever he might have done in his youth, her father was the most peaceable man in the area. Callan had not been entirely inactive, anyway. As the opportunity arose, he had quietly rationalized the tenancies. A few years ago, the rest of the former Madden holdings had been united again, converted back to cereal crops, and leased to a farmer in the next parish.

But Eamonn Madden always remembered who he was. He'd managed to find money for Norah when she married, so that her husband should be satisfied. He'd had to borrow from a draper in Ennis to pay for William's passage to America, but he'd paid more than half of that back already. As soon as that debt was taken care of, he'd be saving for Nuala's wedding; you could be sure of that. He wouldn't have the family disgraced.

He continued to reverence Daniel O'Connell—little Daniel was named after the great man. He also became an admirer of the Under Secretary Drummond. "That's a good man," he would declare. And he would often quote that statesman's dictum: "Property has rights, but also responsibilities." If he ever heard of a bad action by a landlord, he would sigh and repeat it.

Her father returned early that afternoon. Callan came by about an hour later.

The news he brought was very simple.

"I've had an offer for this land. A higher rent. I came to see if you cared to match it."

"Higher? How much higher?"

"Nearly double what you're paying now. Mind you, I should have raised your rent before, but . . ."

"Double?" Eamonn was dumbfounded. "Impossible. How could anyone afford it?"

"It's the farmer who has the rest of the land here. He won't be living on it, you see. He'll pull down the cottage and turn all the land over to cereals. He'll make a small profit, or he wouldn't have made the offer."

"But this is our land. The Maddens have always lived here."

"Make me an offer." Callan seemed very calm. "But you'll have to come close." Was this a long-delayed revenge for the Clare election? Possibly. But more likely it was just business.

"Property has rights, Mr. Callan," said Eamonn. He indicated his family. "But it also has responsibilities."

"Drummond's dead."

"I'll be needing a little time to think."

"You can have a week," said Callan calmly, and rode away.

For three days, they went over it from every angle, she and her father. Could they find another tenancy? There were none, for they soon discovered the rent Callan was being offered was being asked by other landlords elsewhere. What if she went out to work, if work could be found? Or what if she ran the holding, and he went to England and sent money home? This she was much against. "The children need their father," she told him. Nothing seemed to make sense. But Eamonn could not bring himself to accept it. The thought of losing his land was more than he could bear. On the fourth day, she took matters into her own hands and took their little cart down into Ennis.

✢

They were going to be very happy there. That was what she told the children. And indeed, she had done well.

The long, three-room cottage was one of the better of some six hundred such dwellings in and around Ennis, and by the time the children came there, she had it spotlessly clean. The mud walls were thick and dry, the thatch was good. And she had persuaded the landlord to accept a rent for the cottage of only forty shillings a year. With the livestock all sold for good prices, Eamonn's debt was paid off and there was even some cash on hand. The cash came in handy, also, because when they wanted to rent some conacre ground—mock ground, they called it locally—to raise a potato crop to feed themselves, they found they had to pay cash in advance.

"I never heard of paying in advance before," Eamonn had grumbled; but that was what the agent could get that year.

And now all he had to do was to find work.

In the months that followed, they all came to know the town of Ennis well. The children quite enjoyed being there. The town might be dirty and unkempt, but it was always busy. The little square by the central courthouse was usually full of stalls or hucksters selling all kinds of things. And although nobody ever seemed to want to tidy the place up, improvements were nonetheless visible. A number of public buildings had been added in the last decade. Some of these were rather cheerless, like the new fever hospital. More forbidding, just north of the town, was the dour workhouse for the indigent, which you might have mistaken for a military barracks or a jail. But a rather smart new stone bridge, to celebrate the accession of young Queen Victoria, had improved the route out of the town on one side; and the year they arrived in the town, the whole community, Catholic and Protestant alike, had come to watch the dedication of what, one day, would be a handsome Catholic cathedral to serve the whole area, on a broad site near the newspaper offices.

Other parts of the town were to be avoided. Just across the street began the warren of alleys that led down to the River

Fergus. She had to be very firm with Mary and Caitlin that they must not go down there, for although she had never heard of children coming to any harm, the town's motley collection of prostitutes hung about in the doorways, and there were beggars who, if drunk or angry, had been known to threaten people with shillelaghs. And, of course, there were the meanest of the cabins along the road where they lived themselves, and where the children were in rags. "You must leave them alone," she told the children. What else could she say? There were plenty of streets, dingy but respectable, where they could wander. Or there were the open fields outside the town where they could play.

And it was important that they were known to be respectable. There were about forty families with houses in the surrounding countryside who might be considered local gentry. Most were Protestant, of course, though a few were Catholic. Close to them were the more important merchants with solid houses in the town, the handful of professional men and some others, like Mr. Knox, the owner of the *Clare Journal*, who were entitled to consideration. When she and her father accompanied Nuala to some of these houses when she went to find work as a servant, she was glad to overhear one of the gentlemen tell his wife: "The Maddens? Respectable farming family. Take her on by all means." Nuala found work with a merchant in a very decent house near the offices of the *Clare Journal*, so that she was not even a mile away from her family.

The same reputation helped her father. Some days he would go out to labour on one of the farms of the local gentry. Or he would walk the few miles south, to the little river port where grain was shipped down to the Shannon estuary. They still had some savings, which she guarded carefully. Sometimes, if a week or two went by without Eamonn working, they had to dip into this little hoard. At other times, they were able to replenish it.

And so the new pattern of their lives became established. She kept house, took little Daniel for walks and played with

him. She made Mary and Caitlin do lessons with her so that
they could at least read and write. Once a week, Nuala came
home and shared her wages with them. She was turning into
a pretty young woman, with a slim body and fine blue eyes.
It was obvious that her father was proud of her. She had a
lively sense of humour, too, and made them laugh with stories she had heard about the goings-on in the town. Once,
when she had secretly saved up her wages for a few weeks, she
took the whole family to see a magician who came and performed at the courthouse, which also did service as the town
theatre and concert hall. Mary and Caitlin were thrilled.
Maureen would have liked to hear from Norah in England
and William in America. She wrote to Norah at the only
address she had, but received no reply. No letter had ever
come from William. "He'll write when he has good news to
tell," her father assured her. If the younger children ever
asked, she assured them: "They're both doing well."

The next spring and summer brought more damp weather.
People who had not stored their potatoes carefully enough
found that some of them had rotted in the damp. There was
also a rash of evictions in the county, as agents like Callan
looked for more profitable tenants. Many people complained
they couldn't get any mock ground to grow potatoes. One
landowner, an absentee named Wyndham, donated a hundred
and fifty acres to the community for free plots. "Mind you,"
her father remarked, "he owns thirty-seven thousand acres in
Clare, while he lives comfortably in England, so he can afford
it. On the other hand," he added, "it must be said that he has
helped. Not one of our local gentry has done anything at all."

That autumn, one unpleasant incident occurred. Mr. Callan
came by. He didn't trouble to get down from his horse, but
spoke to Eamonn in front of the cottage. Maureen was at his
side.

"Would you have been visiting your old place?" the agent
enquired. And when Eamonn said that he hadn't: "Can you
prove it?" The farmer who had pulled down their old house

and taken over all the Madden fields had received a visitation. Hands unknown had set fire to a clamp of turf and laid out a grave in the middle of his land, as a warning. Such gestures were not unusual in cases of dispossession, though they seldom resulted in anything. "So I thought of you," Callan said.

"You can think again," replied Eamonn evenly. "But tell me this: are there other people whose land he has now taken over?"

"Yes. Several. He's a good farmer," the agent added cruelly.

"You had better think of them, too. I have not been near the place." He did not add that he preferred not to go up that way because the memory was too painful to him.

"I shall. But you're on my list," Callan replied.

"What worries me," her father confessed to Maureen after the agent had gone, "is that he'll ruin my reputation."

It did not appear that Callan had done so, but such was the steady trickle of similar men into Ennis over the following months, good, able-bodied farmers who could not afford the ever-increasing rents, that it was harder and harder to find work. Most of the time Eamonn managed, but during the following spring and the early summer of 1845, Maureen noticed with some concern that the little stock of money she conserved was gradually dwindling, and seldom, if ever, being replenished.

But she carried on with a cheerful face. Mary and Caitlin seemed to have formed themselves into a team. They were always up to some mischief. She would pretend to be angry, but secretly rejoice in their high spirits. "You're two skinny little urchins, and I'm ashamed of you," she would tell them as they ran off, laughing, to catch a fish in the river or play a prank upon some luckless neighbour. As for little Daniel, he was a sweet-natured fellow, with his father's blue eyes and a mop of light brown hair. She had carefully found him three or four playmates nearby, and she delighted in taking him with her wherever she went. Most people thought she was his mother.

The summer passed uneventfully. In August, they lifted the potatoes on their ground and were able to lay in a good store that would see them through until December. The main crop would be harvested in October, and by the start of September, people were talking of a bumper crop. In the middle of the month, the *Clare Journal* reported a few cases of potato decay. But this might have been camp storage. It was not until the last day of the month that her father returned home, looking concerned. "Some of the farmers coming into Ennis are talking about a blight," he told Maureen, and he went straight out to their ground to check. "They seem to be all right," he said when he came back.

✢

It was mid-October when Caroline Doyle told Stephen that she was going to marry someone else. At first, he couldn't believe it.

"Who is he?"

"A professor. A man of science."

"A scientist? This is a great mistake. Scientists are terribly dull."

"I don't find him so."

"You'd have done better to marry me."

"I don't think so, Stephen. I'm sorry."

He and Caroline had been getting along famously. He had not proposed—it had been too soon for that—but there was an understanding between them. He was sure of it. The trouble, he thought, had been O'Connell.

Although the Liberator had called off the monster meeting at Clontarf, the Tory government had still not been satisfied. "He's gone too far," they said. "This will lead to an insurrection." And they put him in jail. He had stayed there six months, until the British Law Lords had overturned the conviction. During that time, O'Connell had wanted Stephen to attend to all kinds of affairs in London, and Stephen had seen little of Caroline, therefore. He had continued to court her after his return. But he had not been able to see her as often as he would have liked, for there was always political business of one kind or another to take care of.

"I might have loved him," she explained to William Mountwalsh, "and he'd have loved me, I dare say, but only when he had the time."

"You think him lacking in affection?" he asked.

"No," she answered, "but he thinks chiefly of himself." She smiled. "It is childlike, sometimes, which is lovable. But . . . not enough."

The scientist had been a friend of William's brother; he was a gentleman of thirty-five, with a particular interest in astronomy. She had met him on a visit to Parsonstown, the estate of a talented family, which had been ennobled with the title of Rosse. Lord Rosse was a notable astronomer himself.

It was only when he lost her that Stephen realised how much he wanted Caroline. A week after their parting, he wrote a series of poems about her, with more passion than talent. After that, he became rather depressed. It was at the start of December, believing that Stephen needed a change of scene, that the Liberator sent him—upon the pretext that he wanted Stephen to help his cousin edit some political essays—to stay with Charles O'Connell in Ennis.

✛

Stephen had heard there was some trouble with the potato crop. Charles O'Connell, a smaller, darker version of the great man, and always full of information, explained the situation when he arrived.

"The west of Ireland is more affected than other parts. Nearly half the crop has been lost in Clare, and Ennis has been hit the worst. But the trouble strikes unevenly. Even here in County Clare, some places have escaped entirely."

"Is it a blight?"

"Probably. Or too much dampness. Some of the potatoes seemed all right when they came out of the ground, and then went rotten afterwards. Here in Ennis, we think we may need some help from Dublin in the spring." He shrugged. "These things happen in Clare from time to time."

A couple of days later, Stephen heard a somewhat different view when the owner of the *Clare Journal* came to dinner. Mr. Knox was a Protestant Tory and looked like a dour Presbyterian minister. But his family had owned the newspaper for several generations and was well liked in the area.

"The local gentry are useless, and the Lord Lieutenant in Dublin is a complacent ass," Knox announced firmly. "Yesterday, I saw six cartloads of grain on their way to the docks. For export. It shouldn't be allowed. By March at latest, we'll be needing all the food we can lay hands on."

"But what about the farmers?" asked Charles. "They have to sell their grain."

"Of course they do. So give them the price they'd get from the merchants at the dock. And do it now. Otherwise, in the spring, you'll be paying for imported grain, and by then the shortages will be driving all grain prices up even further."

"Some people say there won't be any shortages."

"They are fools."

"What is the nature of this blight?" asked Stephen.

"There is a man called Doctor Evens who has written that it is a fungus," replied Knox. "But truthfully, Mr. Smith, no one knows."

However, as Stephen came from Dublin and had political contacts, the newspaper owner seemed anxious to get his views across to him. The day after the dinner, Stephen and his host worked on the essays together. But the day after that, Knox called for Stephen in his pony and trap, and gave him a tour of the area.

"This shortage is also an opportunity, you know," he told Stephen, as they drove out of Ennis. "Look at these people."

He gestured to the cottages and cabins by the roadside. "Able-bodied men looking for work. What are they going to do when their small stocks of potato are gone? They'll have no money to buy food."

"What's to be done?"

"Employ them. Pay them wages. It's what they want. Make them productive."

"Is there anything for them to do?"

"My dear Sir. You have been here several days and you ask that? There is everything to do. I shall show you." You had to admire Mr. Knox's vigorous mind. "Some of the roadway here, as you can see, has been improved. The new stone bridge we have just crossed is excellent. But we badly need a new road from Ennis to Quin. Let it be built. And there is the River Fergus. At present, all the grain, butter, and livestock sold at Ennis market is taken by barge, at needless extra expense, down to the docks a few miles to the south. The river could perfectly well be made navigable up to Ennis, and new docks be built there, to the great benefit of the town."

"You are full of ideas."

"Not at all, Mr. Smith. These are all existing proposals of years' standing. But they are not acted upon. Did you know that plans are already drawn up for a new courthouse to be built? The old one needs so much repair it would be better to start over again. That's another useful project waiting only to be done. The new Catholic cathedral—the land was given by a Protestant, you know—needs to be completed. That is not a public work, I grant you, but private subscriptions might be raised. My favourite project, however, lies up this way." And after they had driven northwards some distance, he stopped the trap at a bend in the road and gestured to the landscape before them. "There, Sir," he said triumphantly, "what do you think of that?"

As Stephen gazed northwards, he saw nothing but a desolate marshland and swamp. It seemed to stretch for miles. In the December light, it looked bleak and infinitely sad.

"That?"

"The slough of despond, you might think," said Knox. "Yet under it lies Paradise."

"You mean you want to drain it?"

"Precisely. The land under that marsh, Mr. Smith, is very rich. Almost corcass. A huge resource. You could grow enough grain there to feed the whole of Ennis." He sighed. "What I see there, Mr. Smith, is an emblem for Ireland itself: a country of wasted resources."

"Our land is rich," agreed Stephen.

"And our people. The Irishman, Sir, is quick, intelligent, and hardworking. English prejudice has him as slow and lazy, but that is a base calumny. The truth is the opposite. Yet what have we here in Clare? Human resources, as unused as this swamp, and as needlessly miserable."

"I assume you'll use your newspaper, Mr. Knox, to press for these things," remarked Stephen, as they drove back into Ennis later.

"I have written to the Dublin authorities in person, as well as promulgating these views in print, Mr. Smith," Knox replied, "and I shall never give up."

In the days that followed, there was not the least sign of the Dublin authorities taking any action. But despite Knox's concern over the crop as Christmas approached, the winter season in Ennis was not without its amusements. In the middle of the month, the better sort in the town were intrigued by a visit from Mr. Wilson, the famous phrenologist. Setting up in Church Street, he offered, by a careful examination of a person's cranium, to give them an exact and scientific portraiture of their character and abilities, including, perhaps, talents of which they were not even aware. "Since he charges five shillings, which is five or six days' wages for a common labourer," Charles O'Connell remarked, "we shall never know the characters of the poor. But I think you and I should try it, Stephen."

Rather against his will, Stephen was persuaded to sit in Mr. Wilson's contraption while that gentleman, by means of

measuring tapes, callipers, screws, and finger-proddings, examined him and finally pronounced: "Did you know, Sir, that
you have a remarkable bump of benevolence?"

"It must have grown," Stephen said drily, "since I was
younger."

It was about an hour later, walking alone through the
town, that he encountered the young woman. She was waiting
outside the courthouse. Inside, another visitor to Ennis, the
child star Miss Heron, was giving a performance. He hadn't
wanted to go himself, but he knew the house was packed,
including a section in the gallery with cheap seats for the poor.

She was a pale, rather plain young woman; she was holding the hand of a little boy. Idly, as he had nothing better to
do, he paused to ask her what she was doing.

"My sister bought tickets for the performance, Sir," she
answered. "My father and sisters are inside with her. It is a
Christmas treat."

"You did not wish to go in?"

"She had four tickets, Sir. I was happy to wait with my
little brother."

He asked her where she came from, and she briefly told
him their story.

"I am sorry you lost your land," he said.

"There are many like us," she replied. "And we do well
enough, do we not, Daniel?" she said with a sweet smile to the
little boy.

Though she was plain, Stephen thought he liked her. There
was a simpleness and goodness about her.

"I wish you better fortune in the New Year," he said, and
moved on.

Some time later, from the window of Charles O'Connell's
house, he saw the girl and her family walking along the street.
Did the big man, who must be her father, look vaguely familiar? Perhaps. It was hard to be sure, but he had an excellent
memory for faces. He had an idea that he remembered him,
marching to the poll, on that famous day years ago when

Father Murphy had harangued the crowd. Her sisters looked lively enough. But one he noticed especially. A strikingly pretty young thing. He stared. It was really quite remarkable that such a pretty girl could be the sister of one who was so plain.

On Christmas Day, in the afternoon, Charles O'Connell announced: "Before we eat our own dinner, Stephen, I must put in an appearance at the workhouse. Why don't you accompany me and see the place?"

The workhouse. Even the name was enough to frighten you. It was an English institution, the place where, if you were destitute and without work, you went as a haven of last resort. It was run by a Board of Guardians, consisting mostly of local gentlemen. It was a brutal-looking place, just north of the old town, but O'Connell seemed almost proud of it. "It's new," he explained, "and unlike many such places, it's clean."

They passed through a big brick gateway into a large yard. It might have been either a barracks or a prison. On each side were the various wings of the institution.

Perhaps it was just the greyness of the day, but to Stephen, the whole place seemed dreary: dreary doors and dreary windows; dreary brick, dreary mortar; and above, a roof of dark slate, slanting drearily under the blank sky.

"It's run on the strictest English model," Charles told him. "Total segregation. Men, women, and children all kept apart. They separate husbands from wives and mothers from children as soon as they arrive, and send them to different blocks. Give them just enough sustenance to keep them alive, nothing more."

"That is cruel. I wonder why any would stay here."

"That's the idea. The Guardians have ordered it must be kept as unpleasant as possible. Otherwise, since it provides free food and lodging, they'd have half the population of Ennis trying to live here, and never get them out. Or so they believe."

He sighed. "They may not be entirely wrong."

But once a year, on Christmas Day, the rules of the workhouse were relaxed and all the inmates were brought together for a Christmas dinner.

The hall was large. Most of the inmates were men, with rather less women and a sprinkling of children, but they numbered several hundred. They appeared to be somewhat ragged, but clean. They were sitting at long, bare trestle tables. As Stephen watched several members of the Board of Guardians, a clergyman and a priest appeared. The director said a few words of Christmas comfort and ordered a cheer for the queen, which was dutifully supplied. Then a meal of meat, potato, and cabbage was served, comforting proof, perhaps, that here in Ennis food was still in plentiful supply, upon occasion, for even the poorest of the poor.

At the start of the new year, his literary work well completed, Stephen returned to Dublin. His stay in Ennis had been instructive—a change, at least, that had helped distract him from the loss of Caroline. But it had not brought him peace of mind. If anything, the reverse. His life no longer seemed to have the meaning he had supposed it had, and he did not know what to do.

⁜

Stephen was rather surprised, in March, to receive a letter from Mr. Knox. It seemed that once that indefatigable gentleman had you on his list, he did not let you go. And truth to tell, although Stephen's affairs in Dublin kept him very busy, the memory of what he had seen in Ennis had been often in his mind. Having read the letter carefully, he understood exactly why the newspaper owner had written to him. And as he was due to see Lord Mountwalsh that day, he took the letter with him.

The big house on St. Stephen's Green was always a friendly haven, and there was just a small company there, including himself and Dudley Doyle, who had made rather a point of being friendly to him now that his daughter was safely married to someone else.

William Mountwalsh looked amused when he said he had a letter from Mr. Knox. "You know of him, then?" Stephen asked.

"We all know of Mr. Knox," replied the earl with a smile. "But tell us what he has to say."

So Stephen read.

The situation in Ennis is as I predicted, and if anything, worse. The shortages began by February, and with scarcity came a rise in prices. The usual price for a fourteen-pound sack of potatoes in Ennis market is two pence; but now it is five. That is a terrible burden for the poor. Sometimes it has not been possible to obtain potatoes at any price. At the workhouse, they have run out, and are trying to buy in cheap grain, imported from India. Others have tried to eat bad potatoes. In the fever hospital, the patients were fed with bad potatoes, and as a result there has been much sickness of the bowels.

The government has ordered the lords lieutenant of each county to establish relief committees, but progress is far too slow.

Having lost patience, our local magistrates have taken matters into their own hands. Under existing laws, they have the power to provide employment, the cost of which will be half paid for by the government and half financed by a government loan—which, as a community, we shall eventually have to repay. The employment so far consists of some road works and other trivial schemes; though I hope we may later make a start upon some of the projects about which I spoke to you when you were here. But at present I estimate that only one in four of those needing work have employment.

Further to this, we in Ennis have formed a relief committee. Most of the townsmen on it are your own associates—by which I mean that they are O'Connell's men; so most of the local gentry have not cared to join us. I am surely the only Protestant Tory on the committee. Outside Ennis, however, our gentry are trying to provide work and sustenance, and contributions for relief are being solicited. But these efforts form a patchwork and lack proper direction.

Those on the estates of absentees usually fare worse. In one parish, two thousand souls are without any supply of food.

It is remarkable that there have been so few disturbances. This may be partly due to the numbing effect of the weather, for it has been cold and damp; just recently, we have had snow.

It is hard to understand how our government can be so careless of the suffering of its people.

When he had stopped reading, Stephen looked to William Mountwalsh.

"Why is the government so careless? Is Knox exaggerating?"

"Oh no. I'm sure he's telling the truth," replied the earl. "But our friend Knox mistakes for carelessness what is, in fact, a deliberate policy. I spoke to someone at the Castle yesterday. The government is putting off help as long as possible, for a simple reason. It's the only way to get these local people to take any responsibility for their own affairs. Look at Ennis. Knox himself is a great exception, but time and again, the rest of the townsmen and the local gentry there have proved that they never do a damn thing for the place until they're absolutely forced to." He smiled. "I dare say it's human nature. I'm sure I don't do nearly as much as I should, because I don't have to."

"He works very hard," protested Lady Mountwalsh.

"All over Ireland, the landowners want the government to bail them out. And the government isn't going to do it."

"But they can't just let the people starve."

"No. And, in fact, Knox is about to get his wish. The government is going to step in. But the local men will still have to shoulder the burden and take responsibility."

"What form will that take?"

"More or less what Knox wants. A large program of public works. The argument is that it's wrong to give money to those who are able-bodied. It corrupts them and takes away their self-respect. They must be given work for what they get. But he's right about the price of food being too high. There will probably have to be subsidies to keep the prices down."

There was a hissing sound from Dudley Doyle. The economist was shaking his head.

"Take care, gentlemen," he cried. "Take care. You may bring in cheap food, like Indian meal; or you may increase supply sufficiently to bring down prices. But do not subsidise food. It is tempting, but you must not do it. You are subverting the market. That is wrong." He turned to Stephen. "You are a Whig. I count upon you for support."

"I don't know," said Stephen.

✜

The worst moment, Maureen thought, had been on St. Patrick's Day. They had heard about the man killed at noon.

It had happened just outside the town. Nobody seemed to know who had done it, but no one was much surprised. The man was an agent, and he had a reputation for evicting.

It was amazing to Maureen that people could be so cruel. At a time when everyone was suffering, people were still being thrown off the land; but her father seemed to accept it. "With the shortages, the agents can get even higher rents for the land; and the men who rely on potatoes may not be able to pay any rent at all." He sighed. "That's the way of it. If the landlord insists on getting the best return, you can't even blame the agent really, I suppose."

"I can," said Maureen.

So, in all likelihood, had some of the evicted tenants, for the fellow had been left dead by the roadside.

Maureen and her father had been standing in the market by the courthouse when she noticed Callan. He was on his horse, and it looked as if he had just arrived. She noticed that he was very pale. He was staring down at the cobblestones, and his face was working. She wasn't sure, but he seemed to be talking to himself. Then he looked up, and his gaze travelled round the marketplace; he caught sight of them and he stared. She stared back at him and saw, with surprise, that his eyes were full of fear.

He couldn't disguise it. He was afraid. She realised what he must be thinking. Would her father, or someone like him, be leaving him for dead on the road that spring? She knew very well that her father would never do such a thing, but if little Callan was frightened now, so much the better. Let him suffer, too. She did not drop her eyes, but kept on staring boldly. And slowly, seeing her defiance, the fear in his eyes changed to a look of loathing.

Some time later, as they were walking home, the agent came riding up behind them and went past. As he did so, he turned and gave her father a terrible look, which seemed to say: "You want me dead. I'll kill you first."

But the moment she remembered most was back at the house, just before dusk. There was a sharp wind getting up outside, and the children were huddled by the turf fire, but her father had gone into the store at the other end of the cottage. He had a lamp in his hand, and he was surveying the remaining potatoes they had, piled against the wall. As the light caught his broad face, she realised how deep were the lines of stress upon it. Normally, like her, he kept a cheerful countenance in front of the children; but caught for a moment in that pale light, he looked infinitely sad. She put her hand on his arm. He nodded but did not speak. Then he glanced down at her.

"I had hoped to use these," he said quietly. "I didn't tell you, but there's a man I know who has a field. I'm not speaking of mock ground where you've to pay for harvesting a field that's already planted. He'd have let me plant it and harvest it like my own." He gestured to the potatoes in front of them. "These were to be the seed potatoes. But I daren't do it, Maureen, for I can never be sure of keeping the work, and the prices in the market . . . to tell you the truth, it frightens me. So we'll have to eat these and not plant them. You must make them last as long as you can." He shook his head, and then, in a voice in which sadness and bitterness were equally mixed: "And this is Ireland, on Saint Patrick's Day."

The next day, a company of the 66th Regiment hastily arrived in Ennis to reassure the nervous local gentry after the murder.

A few days after that, the snow started.

Compared to many of their neighbours, Eamonn Madden was one of the lucky ones. He had been picked as one of three hundred men to work on the local roads. From England, Colonel Wyndham had sent six hundred pounds for repairing the Ennis streets. "That pays for three hundred men for two months," her father pointed out. Meanwhile, as the snow ended and the weather began to get a little milder, the authorities in Dublin had started to provide some help. Nearly five hundred more labourers were employed on public works, but the progress on Mr. Knox's ambitious projects was continually delayed. And another class of men was also starting to suffer now. "With all this trouble," her father told Maureen, "and people having to dip into their pockets for relief, there's no money spent in Ennis, and the local craftsmen will soon be in as bad a state as ourselves."

In the market, the price of grain was still rising. News came that down on the Shannon estuary, a grain ship had been robbed by hungry local men.

One day, her father went in to work in the morning and returned before noon, looking shaken.

"The wages were lowered. The boys are refusing to work."

"But the wages were ten pence a day. That's only a pittance."

"I know it. And it's to be eight pence now. But the boys will have to give in. I met Mr. Knox himself, and he told me: 'We haven't the money to pay them.'"

Her father proved to be right. The men went back, at eight pence a day. On the first day back, she asked him if there'd been any trouble.

"Not really," he answered, "except for a fine lady passing, who told us she couldn't see why we were making a mess of the street."

The wages were not enough to feed the family, especially with the higher prices of everything; but a few days later, Maureen found some Indian meal that the relief committee had been able to buy in to be sold at cut price. It was poor stuff, she thought, but it kept body and soul together.

And so the town of Ennis staggered from the spring into the summer. The merchants in town did what they could to help; the local gentry, for the most part, did not. Everyone was at a low ebb. But for many in Ennis, hope seemed in sight, for two reasons.

The early potato harvest was in sight. Many people had consumed their seed potatoes during the shortage, but enough had been put in the ground to ensure a decent early harvest. Eamonn had been able to secure a piece of mock ground again that he could harvest. "Just a few more weeks to go," he would encourage his family, "and the worst will be over."

The second cause for hope was political. Since his retreat from Clontarf and his brief time in prison, less had been heard from Daniel O'Connell. There was a rumour that he was unwell. But the Young Ireland men were keeping the cause of Repeal alive, and even if there was no chance of it happening at present, the dream of a free Ireland was still enough to stir the heart. Now, however, a more immediate hope had arisen, of a change of government in England; and late in June it came to pass. The Tories were out; the Whigs were back in. Weren't the Whigs the Liberator's allies? Hadn't they always been sympathetic to Catholic Ireland? The Repealers were delighted. All Catholic Ireland looked for better things. During early July, though the relief funds were almost gone and everyone was hungry, the summer sun seemed to bring promise of hope.

It was on a warm day in the third week of July that Maureen and her father went out to the field where their potatoes were growing. They had been out to inspect them the day before, after the news had begun to spread. Now they gazed in silence.

For the field was an open expanse of blackened leaves. And from it arose a terrible stench that made you want to turn your head away. And all around, the other fields were just the same.

+

He arrived in Ennis on a clear November day. It was entirely thanks to Mountwalsh that he was there.

"Not at all," the kindly earl had assured him when he had proffered his thanks. "They were only too glad to get you, Stephen. Your reputation precedes you, and I reminded them that you were one of the true Catholic Whigs, which I'd say you are. The new government liked that, very much. A sound man, I told them, who dislikes the dangerous tendencies of some of these Young Ireland boys. And an excellent organiser. I've no doubt you'll do very well."

At least it would be a change. For, by the end of that summer, Stephen Smith had had enough. He wanted no more of the world of politics. Not for a while, anyway. Even the return of the Whigs to power had failed to reignite his interest. Had he done anything useful in all these years? he'd asked himself. He hoped so. Was he doing anything useful now? No, he was not. His old master O'Connell was unwell. There was nothing he could really do for him. He disliked the Young Ireland men—William Mountwalsh was perfectly right about that. They meant well, some of them, but they lacked discipline. Some of them even wanted to start an insurrection like Emmet. Futile. And dangerous. They'd go down and take others with them, just as Emmet had done before.

But it had been another letter from Mr. Knox of the *Clare Journal* that had given him the idea. He had been shocked by its contents, and when Knox had described the organisation that was being put in place down there, it had suddenly occurred to him that this might be a chance for him to do something really useful.

So now here he was, as an overseer of the new program of public works that was to save Ennis from starvation. He would be working for Mr. Hennessy, the head overseer for the region, and both would report to a brisk naval officer, known as the Captain, who had charge of the county. He had not wanted to impose upon Charles O'Connell, who had kindly offered him a room in his own house; but Charles had found him lodgings close by.

Hennessy, who saw him his first morning, proved to be a tall, mild, and pleasant man, who quickly outlined the scale of operations. "My own guess," he said, "is that by the end of the year we shall employ fifty thousand men in this county." The new government wanted to control matters strictly. There was a new committee to take over the running of the entire county. It was appointed by the Lord Lieutenant, and although some Catholics served on it, the chairman and most of the members were Protestant gentlemen. Hennessy told Stephen he would be given several projects to manage in Ennis, and also made clear what the rules of operation were to be. "There must be no deviation," he warned. "The new government means to be thorough but firm." Were there any particular problems he should know about? he asked. "Well," Hennessy hesitated, "I think it's fair to say that there's still a bit of catching up to do. Until we got started, there was . . ." he searched for a good word, "a hiatus."

It was that afternoon, when he called upon Mr. Knox at the *Journal*, that Stephen discovered what this meant. Knox, following his usual practice, called for his pony and trap and gave him a quick tour. The difference from his previous visit was astonishing. Where, before, he had seen ragged children and worried faces, he now saw little creatures like skeletons and women with staring eyes.

"These people aren't poor; they're starving."

"Some are, some not. Some died already."

"But how?"

"Very simple. This July and August, the potato harvest failed. When I say failed, I mean that every potato in the market was rotten. I mean that not a single field, not a single garden patch in all of Ennis, produced a single potato that could be eaten. The stink of the rotted fields wafted over the town as if it were an open plague pit. I mean, Smith, that after months of hardship, the people of Ennis failed to produce any food whatsoever of their own. Unfortunately, it was also the time of a change of government. And you know how it is when a government changes. Nothing that was done before can be right."

"And so?"

"Why, they closed down the relief committees, of course. Nothing was done. It remained that way until October. People helped each other not to starve, but especially in the remoter places the old and the sick died off. We reported what we could, but you don't always know at the time. There were many deaths, certainly."

"It will be changed now."

"Will it? How? You will provide public works?"

"On a great scale."

"And will you subsidise food?"

"I understand not."

"Indeed, you will not. For that would distort the market, which, in the eyes of a Whig, is a heinous crime."

Stephen thought of Dudley Doyle.

"I don't deny it," he confessed.

"Then, since the price of food, being so scarce, has now risen to new heights, the wages you pay to these thousands of men will not be sufficient for them to buy food for their families. They will not be idle and starve, Mr. Smith; they will work and starve." He looked at Stephen severely. "I am only a Tory, Sir. You are a Whig, the Irish Catholic's friend. This is your government. Why is your government so foolish?"

"I cannot answer."

"But I can. The Whigs, Sir, have married their devotion to doctrine, to their total ignorance of local conditions. The resulting child will be famine, on a scale we have not yet seen."

"That is not their object. The Whigs are entirely well-meaning."

"Of course they are well-meaning," the newspaper owner cried. "That is the trouble. The present Whig leaders are reformers, they have extended the franchise, they have sought to help the Catholics. They are more than well-meaning: they believe they are righteous. And therefore they will not listen. Therein lies the tragedy." He paused only to draw breath. "What is the greatest crime against humanity, Smith?"

"Deliberate cruelty, I should think."

"And you would be wrong. It is not cruelty, nor evil intent. It is stupidity."

"And why do you tell me this?" asked Stephen.

"In order that you may learn," said Knox. Then he drove him back.

In the days that followed, Stephen was immersed in his work. There seemed to be a new scheme to employ people every few days. Some, like giving Ennis a decent sewer system, were worthwhile. But most were just unnecessary roadwork, whose main effect was to block the road leading into the town. On one occasion, he suggested to Hennessy that a patch of waste ground could be cleared and dug. It belonged to an elderly farmer who had lacked the energy to do it himself. "At least he could grow grain there and increase the food stock," Stephen suggested. But Hennessy had shaken his head and reminded him: "You should know better, Stephen. That's private land. Improving it would be reproductive work, since the grain grown there belongs to the farmer and goes to market. We'd be creating personal profit and interfering with trade. Can't do it. Only public works, my boy, however useless." So the land remained waste.

He'd been there ten days when he witnessed a small incident. He was observing a gang of about fifty men who were cleaning the verges along the road that led down to the docks. The work was proceeding at a snail's pace, but some of the men looked so weak from lack of nourishment that it would have been cruel to push them harder; and since the work was quite pointless, there was no reason to do so anyway.

A cart laden with grain came lumbering down the road in the direction of the docks. The men watched it dully. But then three of them, without a word, detached themselves and went across to it. One of the three was the big fellow Stephen had seen with the plain girl and her sisters the December before. The man, he had since learned, was called Madden. When they reached the cart, Madden spoke to the driver. Stephen couldn't hear what was said, but the big fellow seemed to be quietly reasoning rather than threatening. After a few moments, the driver nodded, the men led the horses round, and the cart began to return from where it had come. The three men, meanwhile, went silently back to their work.

Stephen hesitated. It was obvious that what he had just witnessed was illegal. Should he intervene? He decided to wait and ask Hennessy about it later.

"It happens quite a bit," Hennessy told him. "They won't let grain leave the area. There hasn't been any violence to speak of, but one or two horses have been maimed as a warning. And you can't find anyone in the county that dares to give the farmers a valuation for the horses, so they can't collect any insurance. Technically, it's intimidation, of course. But usually, we just ignore it. You can hardly blame them. That grain leaving for the port might be the last bit of nourishment their children ever see."

Certainly, the men gave him no other trouble. Madden was a dignified figure: a splendid physique, greying now and made gaunt by lack of sustenance. But though it was clear that, amongst the men who worked with him, he had a certain moral ascendancy, he always moved with gentleness. But it seemed that fate had decided that they should come into conflict.

Another week passed before Stephen came face-to-face with the Captain.

The short, peppery naval man whose duty it was to organise some fifty thousand men into work parties across the county was not likely to be popular.

"My job, Mr. Smith," he said, "is to see that those most in need are given work. I won't tolerate troublemakers, and I won't tolerate abuses. Yesterday, I discovered that two of the men on a work detail were farmers with land of their own. One man had fifty acres. But he was a friend of a gentleman on the local committee who thought he'd like to pick up some extra cash in his spare time. Monstrous. I threw him out, and I told the committee man what I thought of him, too. There'll be no fear or favour while I'm over here, is that clear?"

"Yes," said Stephen.

"Good." The Captain was riffling through a sheaf of papers. "You have a man named Madden in one of your details?"

"I do."

"Another fraud. He has a small landholding. Enough to support him. I want him off."

"I believe he lost his holding some time ago."

"Could be. The fools who compiled these sheets aren't much use. Some of the information's out of date. There's a recent report on him anyway from a man named Callan. An agent. Says he's a troublemaker. Possibly violent. Have you seen anything like that?"

"Not exactly."

"Hmm. You hesitated. Throw him out. There are plenty of others who need the work. Now then." He passed to other matters. But when he had finished and Stephen was leaving, he called him back. "Don't forget about Madden, because I shan't." He eyed Stephen sharply. "In that connection, before you go, there's one other thing I'd better explain."

He dismissed Madden the following morning. "You'll be paid for this day, and I'll add two more days' pay," he informed him, "but you're to leave now. I'm sorry."

"I have my family to feed," the big man said. "I ask you to reconsider."

"I'm afraid I can't."

"You are sentencing my children to death."

This was, it seemed to Stephen, a slight exaggeration, but he said nothing. The truth was that he disliked the business very much. Madden turned slowly to leave. It had to be said, he was dignified in his grief.

As Stephen had guessed he would, the Captain himself passed by, in the early afternoon. "Madden gone?" he enquired. Stephen nodded. "Good," the Captain said with a brief nod, and went on his way.

At the end of the day, Stephen took his time going back into Ennis. He walked slowly and thoughtfully. The sequence of events, though inevitable, had disturbed him. The dusk had fallen as he passed some miserable little cabins, then a short stretch of empty roadway, before coming to a wall. As he reached the wall, a figure stepped out.

He started. It was certainly a remarkable apparition. The figure was large, far bigger than he. It was wearing a white dress. Its face was blackened. It stood before him, barring his path.

"You know what this means?" asked the figure.

Of course he knew. Every Irishman knew the traditional warning of the Whiteboys: a man in woman's clothing, with a blackened face, appeared before you; if you ignored the warning, you must expect the consequences.

"Take heed," said the figure. Then it turned away and strode up the road, turning off beside a cottage and vanishing into the dusk.

Stephen continued on his way home.

The next day passed without incident. He briefly considered reporting the matter, but after what the Captain had told him, he decided against it. If the men on the work detail knew he'd been threatened, they gave no sign. The next day was equally uneventful. The day after that, he was not working. And by now, he had decided what to do. It seemed to him that he had two important tasks.

First thing in the morning, he set out on foot, walking briskly northwards to the outskirts of the town. He discovered without difficulty where the cottage he sought was. On reaching it, he found the door and looked in.

"God save all here." He gave the traditional greeting as he entered.

Eamonn Madden looked greatly surprised to see him. He was sitting on a stool, his head bowed, before the small glow of the turf fire. Standing beside him was the plain young woman, his daughter.

"May I sit down?" There was a bench by the fire also. He rested himself upon it.

"We have nothing to offer you, Sir," said the woman.

"I know."

The doorway was open. Further light, of a sort, came from the single window. It had no glass, but across it, in the traditional manner, was stretched a thin sheepskin, which let in some light and kept out the wind. By this dim light, however, he could see that the room, with its earthen floor, was spotlessly clean. On one wall was a cheap print of the Blessed Virgin; on another, a print of Daniel O'Connell. He gazed at the woman. How old was she? In her midtwenties, he supposed, but stress and hunger had made her face haggard. Like her father, however, she had a quiet dignity. "You know who I am?" he asked, and she nodded. "Might I ask your name?"

"I am Maureen Madden," she replied.

"May I know how many others there are in the family? You had a little brother, I remember, when I met you once in the marketplace."

"That is little Daniel, Sir. Then there are my sisters Mary and Caitlin. My other sister, Nuala, works for a family in the town."

"May I see the other children?"

She looked at her father, who said nothing.

"They are resting, Sir, in the other room. They sleep all together, to keep warm."

"They are asleep at this time of the day?"

"It is cold outside. And they have not so much energy." She

went into the next room. Madden glanced at him but said nothing, nor did Stephen say anything to the big man.

When Maureen returned, it was with the three children. They were pale and thin, but what struck him at once was that they moved with a strange slowness. Their eyes seemed slightly unfocussed. Perhaps it was that they had been asleep, but he did not think so. The girls looked at him dully, the little boy with eyes that were large and reproachful.

"How many meals a day have they received?"

"One, Sir. Up until now, while father was working."

"What do you feed them?"

"Whatever I can find. There are no more potatoes. Sometimes there is Indian meal or other grain. Sometimes there are turnips and a little watercress.

"And how do you pass the time with them?"

"I read to them. I teach them also."

"You read and write, then."

"I do, Sir. Little Daniel has all his letters now, do you not, Daniel?" The boy nodded. "He makes them upon the table with his finger. I watch, and I can see if the letters are correct."

"Thank you. If the children wish to rest, I would speak with your father now."

When they were alone, he addressed Eamonn.

"That is all the food you could get with the wages you were paid?"

"It was."

"I see. Your children are wasting."

"A gentleman such as yourself would have no knowledge of people in our condition, I suppose."

"Not so. My family is more like yours than you imagine." And Stephen told him briefly about his family and relations up in Rathconan.

"An labhraionn tu gaeilge?" Madden asked. Do you speak Irish?

"I did as a child. A little. But I have forgotten it now. We speak it less in Leinster."

"And your family. Do they starve also?"

"No." There was considerable hardship up in the Wicklow Mountains, but it was more localised. Little as he liked the Budge family, they had seen to it that the people at Rathconan kept body and soul together. Down in Wexford, where agriculture was mixed, there was little hardship. By the huge Mount Walsh estate, you could be sure, none of the earl's tenants would need to worry. Other parts of the country varied, with the worst conditions in the west. "Now I must ask you a question. Does anyone know that you put on a dress the other night?" Eamonn looked at him evenly from under his heavy eyebrows but said nothing. "I knew it was you," Stephen went on. "Does Maureen know?" Eamonn indicated that she did not. "The other men?"

"They do not."

"I didn't report you. Not out of fear. But I will tell you something you should know. I was half expecting something of the kind. My orders are that if any threat is received, I'm to tell the Captain, and he will close down the entire work detail from which the threat comes. That would have been fifty men out of work. And I've no doubt that he'll do it."

"The man is a devil."

"No, you are wrong. He is quite determined to be fair. He'll fight the local gentry just as fiercely."

"He threw another man out of work because he possessed a cow. Said if he had a cow, he had means of feeding his family. Were the man's seven children to choose between milk and starvation?"

"That is my point. He means well, in fact. But he has not the least understanding of the conditions under which Irish people live. By the way, he says that Callan the agent believes you to be dangerous."

"It's Callan that threw me off my land. I've done nothing to him, but he probably fears that I will. There were threats made against others up there, though not by me."

Maureen came back now. She glanced at Stephen, obviously wondering what his intentions might be. Madden was fortunate in his daughter, Stephen thought. You could not but admire the gentle calmness in her manner as she held that family together. There was a beauty in it.

"I cannot be seen to be threatened, Mr. Madden," he said firmly. "You understand what I mean. But you may report back to work with me tomorrow."

"And the Captain?"

"We shall have to take things day by day."

He bowed his head politely to Maureen and left them.

That afternoon, he set about his second task. This was to compose a letter. It was quite a long letter. It set out clearly what he had seen, including the conduct of the Captain, whom he commended for doing his best within his lights. The conclusion of his letter was forceful.

> I have always believed in the free working of the market, and I still do. But it is also clear to me now that the market does not operate satisfactorily under extreme conditions. And the conditions in Clare now are extreme, and are becoming graver. Because of the high price of food, when it may be had, and our refusal to subsidise it, even those employed are suffering from malnutrition and those out of work will shortly starve.
>
> Unless we feed these people, they will die.

When he had done, he sent it not to the Lord Lieutenant, nor to Dublin Castle. He sent it to the one man who he thought might be able to make something happen. He sent it to kindly William Mountwalsh.

❖

As Christmas approached, the Madden family had good reason to be grateful to Stephen. All over the west, the system of relief was breaking down. In the remoter parts of Clare and Galway, whole parishes were without food. Reports came in of villages starving. Along the street near their cottage, Maureen knew of three old women and an old man who had died of hunger and cold. One day, walking into the town, she saw a body lying frozen outside one of the cottages. By mid-December, there were a dozen poor souls begging in the market. The week before Christmas, it was twice that. If it weren't for the little wage that her father was able to bring, she supposed she might have been begging there herself. She thought with gratitude of Mr. Smith on most days, therefore. She also learned something new about him.

One day, her father came home looking thoughtful.

"I met Mr. Charles O'Connell today. Did you know that Mr. Smith, before he came here, was a close companion of Daniel O'Connell himself for over twenty years? I had no idea of it. He never said a word." He gave a sheepish smile. "When I think of what I . . ." He broke off.

"What, Father?"

"No matter. It gave me a different view of the man, that's all."

Maureen was silent for a moment, looking thoughtful.

"He is very fine," she said with some emotion.

She did not see the curious glance her father gave her.

But even with her father's wages, it was not easy to put food on the table. There was next to nothing in the market now. She was able to buy some Indian meal at a wicked price, some turnips and salt. "They're no better off in the work-house," her father told her. "There's to be no Christmas dinner there. Even the Board of Guardians can't get the food."

On Christmas Eve, Nuala arrived. She, at least, was still being fed, though she told Maureen that the merchant's family were making do with stew on most days now. Maureen noticed that Nuala had a little smile on her face.

"I brought something," she said. And from the folds of her clothes she produced a little hip flask. "I borrowed the flask," she said. "They won't notice."

"What's in it?"

"Brandy." Nuala grinned. "For the man of the house." She gave a sly smile. "I've more." Reaching inside her clothes again, she fumbled for a moment and then drew out, slowly, one, then another, then, with a flourish, a third potato.

"Oh God, Nuala, how did you . . . ?"

"They're only lumpers. Funny, isn't it? The lowest form of potato, Maureen, you wouldn't have looked at once; and now, couldn't I be the Queen of Sheba herself, bringing gifts to Solomon?"

"Yes, but . . ."

"I stole them, of course. Found them down in the cellar. I'm sure nobody knew they were there. They must have been missed, I suppose. They're old, but they aren't spoiled. Well, not entirely."

"But Nuala, if they find out . . ."

"They won't."

"You'd lose your position."

"And what of it?" She laughed. "Then I'll sell my body down by the courthouse."

"Don't even say such a thing."

"So are you going to cook them?"

"Oh God, Nuala. I am." She kissed her sister. "Don't tell Father how you got them. Say you bought them."

Though dusk was falling, their father didn't come home for some reason. And several hours passed without any sign of him. Maureen and Nuala were becoming quite concerned.

"Could he have gone out drinking, do you suppose?" said Nuala. "I see the men coming back from work and spending their wages on drink in the town every day."

"Father? Never." Maureen shook her head. "Please God nothing's happened to him," she whispered, so that the younger ones shouldn't hear.

At last, he came. He was carrying something under his coat. Once safely inside, he pulled it out and put it on the table. It was a hunk of meat.

They looked at it in astonishment.

"Father, however did you . . . ?" Maureen was pale with fear.

"Will you cook that for our Christmas, Maureen?" he said with a tone of satisfaction.

"But where did it come from?"

"It was on a cow when I first saw it. That would be about two hours ago."

"You killed a cow?"

"More than a dozen of us. There's nothing left of the beast now. What couldn't be eaten is buried."

There had been numerous incidents of this kind. Gangs of men would go out into the fields after dark, slaughter a cow, and cut it and strip it on the spot, dividing the meat up and vanishing into the night. But it took Maureen a moment to realise that her father had committed a criminal act.

"You could be transported," she said reproachfully.

"If caught." He took his coat off. "I think I'll rest a while. I'm a little tired." He sighed. "I wish," he confessed, "that I could take a drink."

Nuala smiled.

"You can," she said.

⊹

But if the family ate well that Christmas, the experience was not to be repeated. Local farmers were guarding their livestock with vigilance; there was less food than ever in the market. Halfway through January, Maureen noticed that tufts of Caitlin's hair were falling out. Then, even more strangely, that as if to compensate, a thick down was growing on her upper face so that she began to look like a sad little monkey. Maureen discovered that several other children in the street looked the same way; it was clearly something to do with their lack of nutrition. Once, after she had been discussing the problem quietly with her father—and out of earshot, as she thought, of the other children—she came in to find little Daniel trying to give his morsel of food to his sister. "So that the hair on her face will go back to her head," he said. And overcome with emotion, she put her arm round him and cried, "You dear little boy."

She had to make sure that he ate his food himself after that.

Relief, of a kind, was at hand. But once again, the government was to display its genius for adding insult and injury to every good deed.

"They are going to set up soup kitchens," her father announced one day.

"Then we shall have food?"

"Perhaps." The prospect did not seem to please him. "They will be set up under the Poor Laws. The paupers will be fed." He breathed heavily. "No Madden has ever been called a pauper."

"You are not a pauper, Father. You have work."

"But they're going to close down the public works. Mr. Smith has promised me he'll keep us going as long as he can. They will open two kitchens in Ennis almost at once; the official kitchens will open sometime in February."

"We must feed the children, whatever we are called, Father," she said.

"I know."

But the opening of the kitchens would have one further consequence. For since the Poor Laws placed the cost of providing relief on the local community, the citizens of Ennis were going to have to pay for them. And since it would have been a distortion of the market to subsidise the food, the local people would have to buy in the supplies for the soup kitchens at the present high prices.

Early in February, Nuala appeared at the cottage one morning.

"I've lost my job," she said simply.

"Oh, Nuala, did they find out about what you took at Christmas?"

"Not at all. It wasn't that. But they've to pay so much extra in rates for the new soup kitchens that they told me: 'We can afford you, or the soup kitchens, but not both.'"

"Well, this is your home, and we're glad to have you back," said her father firmly. But after he had gone, Maureen turned to her sister.

"What are we going to do, Nuala?"

"I'll find something," Nuala promised.

Two days later, Eamonn returned after seeing the man from whom he rented the mock ground.

"He can rent me nothing, even if I can pay for it," he told them, "because he can't get any seed potatoes for planting. He's rented all his plots to a farmer, for grain." He made a helpless gesture. "I've asked all round the town, and it's the same everywhere. Blight or no blight, it'll be a miserable potato harvest this year, because so few potatoes will be planted."

All through that month, news came trickling in from other places. If people in Ennis were living in the borderland of starvation, it seemed that more isolated areas had fared even worse. The soup kitchens, if they reached such places, would come too late. Up in the wilder parts of Galway, Sligo, and Mayo, hundreds, thousands of people had died from starvation. Infants and the old were the first to go, but it had gone beyond that. Those who had given up and walked to the towns had stood a chance; people cut off in the wastes, or who had decided to stay in their homes, had gradually weakened until they could do no more. The priests and clergy were doing what they could, but they had no food to give. Nobody had any idea how many had succumbed.

As well as news, there was also a trickle of people coming into Ennis. Maureen found it hard to believe, but people were still regularly being turned off the land.

"You can't even blame the men turning them off, sometimes," her father said. "Some of the tenant farmers have rented out parts of their land, and if they don't get paid, they can't meet their own rent. It's only the landowners who can give relief, and you don't know how much debt some of them may be in themselves." He sighed. "It's like a great wheel, Maureen, rolling over the land and crushing the lives out of all of us."

Two things made their lives a little easier. Nuala was able to find some work. "It's just helping a woman who takes in laundry, but she can let me have a few pence most days," she said. "It's better than nothing." And the soup kitchens began to function in Ennis. When the first one started, seven hundred people turned up that morning. Soon there were several; half the town seemed to be standing in line, and the people running the kitchens couldn't keep track of whom they were feeding. This favoured Maureen. She wasn't supposed to go to the soup kitchen because her father still had employment, but she took the children with her and stood in the line, and the harassed people doling out the grain and meal just put the little measure into her hands without bothering to ask questions. "I feel bad," she told Nuala, "because I'm not supposed to have it, and I'm sure I'm taking food from the mouths of those who have nothing at all. But then I look at Caitlin, with her hair still in patches, and I know I must do it."

"Just feed the children, Maureen," said Nuala. "You have to."

Her father was aware of what she was doing, but they did not discuss it.

It was at the end of the month that the men came to see her father. There were half a dozen of them. She didn't know any of them well, but she recognised them—small tenant farmers from near her old home. They clustered round her father eagerly.

"We need you, Eamonn."

"For what?"

"It's Callan."

It wasn't a surprise. All their farms came under the agent's management, and they were to be dispossessed. Obviously, Callan had either decided or been instructed to have a general clear-out. And the men weren't going to stand for it.

"Something has to be done, Eamonn. A warning has been prepared. And if it is not heeded . . ." They seemed in general agreement. "Justice will have to be done."

"Why come to me? I'm already gone."

"We thought you might want to strike a blow. You're not the only one here in Ennis that Callan has thrown off his land. There are others who'll join us. But they look up to you, Eamonn. You were always the one."

She could see that her father was somewhat pleased by these compliments and this attention. But as she looked at their faces, she saw something else. It was a trap. She could see it clear as day. They wanted to use her father, because he was bolder and braver than they were, and had an old reputation in the area. They'll put you in front of them to do the deed, she wanted to cry out, and when you turn round they'll be gone. She knew she mustn't say it out loud. Not now. It would anger the men and humiliate her father and make him all the more likely to accept. She held her breath.

"Show me the warning," he said quietly.

It was a wretched thing. Callan's name was across the top, and below it was drawn a coffin. Then, not very literate, a warning to leave off his evil ways or consider the fate of other agents. "Remember them," it warned. And it was signed "Captain Starlight," a popular way of ending such missives in the countryside.

Her father considered the document quietly for a minute or two. "Captain Starlight has a fine style," he remarked drily. "But I will improve his message, if you have pen and ink." The man who had composed the message produced these articles from his coat pocket. "Very well," said Eamonn when the man was ready. "There is room for it under the signature. You will write these words of the good Mr. Drummond." And he carefully dictated:

PROPERTY HAS RIGHTS PROPERTY ALSO HAS
RESPONSIBILITIES

When this was duly written, he glanced up at Maureen and gave her a smile. "I'm sorry not to be coming with you, boys.

I've no love for Callan, you may be sure, but I've matters that concern me here. I wish you good luck." And, to her huge relief, he sent them away.

"Do you think they will kill him?" she asked.

He shook his head.

"They haven't the courage." He sighed. "Perhaps I haven't, either. But at least I gave the message a little of the dignity it lacked."

It was one evening in the middle of March that Stephen Smith came to their cottage. He looked tired. Maureen thought it remarkable that he should have gone to such trouble, but for whatever reason, he seemed to feel a personal responsibility for her father.

"I'm sorry," he told Eamonn, "but the work is ending. They wanted to stop us two weeks ago, and I was able to persuade them to continue a little longer. But the Captain told me an hour ago that they can't make an exception for us anymore. There are a few other groups continuing until they finish what they're doing, but it's all over. At least, please God, the soup kitchens should keep people from starving."

"We know you did your best," her father told him, for it was obvious that Smith was distressed.

"What will you do yourself, Mr. Smith?" she dared to ask. "I suppose you'll be leaving Ennis now?" He turned to her. His green eyes, she thought, were quite remarkable.

"I hardly know. I wish to stay—if there is something useful I can do. I've no wish to leave when matters are still so uncertain." After a few more words, and wishing them better days ahead, he left.

The days that followed were difficult for her father. The first few days, he went out trying to find work, but it was a futile quest. There was nothing for anyone. The fourth day, he went to visit the fever hospital, where one of the men he had been working with had been taken after falling sick. He went to see the man again the next day, and the next. But Maureen realised why he had gone. It was not really to see his sick friend.

The following day, he did not go to the hospital. As she was about to go into Ennis, she told him: "They were asking to see you at the soup kitchen yesterday. They're getting stricter. They want to see the whole family, because they're not supposed to give out food to families that have someone working."

"Tomorrow, Maureen," he said vaguely. "Tell them I'm out looking for work."

But she knew very well that he wouldn't come. It was the shame of it: he, a Madden, to be seen in a line begging for food—officially a pauper, the lowest of the low. She knew he'd never go there if he could avoid it. A hospital visit, a useless quest for a job—anything rather than suffer that last humiliation. And the fact—which any woman could see—that everyone else was in the same case, so that it hardly mattered anymore, would not satisfy him at all. So she said nothing and went into the town.

It proved to be a particularly trying day. The soup kitchen was in Mill Street, beside the maze of poor lanes and alleys that led down to the town's riverbank. To call it a soup kitchen was really a misnomer, since the Ennis soup kitchen did not serve soup at all. At present, the only food it had was cheap Indian meal, shipped in from Limerick. Behind a large trestle table, protected by barriers, were two huge vats in which the meal was steeped. How much you got depended on what they had each day. Usually, you might expect a pound of meal; but some days it had been as little as three ounces a head. It could not, therefore, be said that the people were fed, but rather that they were kept just above the point of starvation.

Today, however, tempers were frayed. In the first place, the overseer sent down from Dublin had firm views about preparing the food. All Maureen wanted was some meal that she could cook for the children. But she was told that she could not have it.

"No raw meal," the man cried out. Then he added, so that all might hear: "If you give these people raw meal, half of them'll just sell it, take the money, and go and get drunk on the proceeds." Maureen couldn't think of anyone she knew who would do such a foolish thing, but the man was adamant. This meant that everyone had to wait while batches of meal were cooked. "And once it's cooked," a woman in front of her remarked, "it crumbles so, that you can never get it home without bits of it falling on the road. It's the birds we'll be feeding before our own children."

There were all kinds of people waiting. If they were paupers under the law, Maureen saw several of the town's smaller tradesmen who, with the falling-off in trade, were now almost as destitute as she. The officious fellow from Dublin was equally anxious to make sure that none of this largesse was wasted upon the undeserving.

"Only those whose name is on my list," he called. "All those on my list may come up and take a ticket. When you have a ticket, you must wait in line for your turn. We'll have fairness here," he remarked to someone. "You have to watch these people like a hawk." He started a roll call. When he came to Maureen, he demanded: "Where is your father? It says you have a father. Is he at work?"

"No, Sir," she said.

"Tomorrow, I want to see you all. Father, three sisters, brother. All of you, mind, or you'll get nothing."

Thanks to this cumbersome procedure, she stood there for five hours before finally getting a small portion of cooked meal, which would hardly feed them as it was. She was starting to walk away when she caught sight of Nuala.

She was down one of the alleys, leaning in a doorway. Maureen supposed that this must be where the laundress lived and that Nuala must be taking a rest. She thought she'd ask her when she was coming home and began to walk towards her. As she did so, she saw a man come up the alley from the other direction. Just a poor-looking tradesman. He stopped by Nuala. They spoke together. The two of them disappeared into the doorway. And then she understood, and, like a fool, was so shocked that she dropped the cooked meal, which scattered on the ground, so that she had to gather it together as best she could, and took it back home all spoiled. And when her father saw it he gave a look of vexation and remarked: "Your brother and sisters will be eating dirt and grit with their meal tonight, Maureen. I can't think what made you do such a thing." And she said she was sorry, and she couldn't think either.

Later that night, when she was with Nuala alone, she told her what she'd seen. But Nuala only shrugged.

"I didn't want you to know, Maureen, but there was no work to be had, and my being so young, at least I can get something."

"My God, you're so young, it would be better me than you, Nuala."

"I don't think so, Maureen. I'm quite in demand. Do you realise I've already saved five shillings." She gave a wry smile. "If times were better and I could find a rich man . . ."

"Don't even say such a thing. You must stop, Nuala."

"Stop?" She looked at her elder sister almost angrily. "Don't be a fool, Maureen. With Father earning nothing, how do you think we're going to pay the next rent?" She relented and gave Maureen a kiss. "We all do what we can, Sis. You keep house and I'll sell my body. What does it matter?"

"Don't ever tell Father. It would kill him."

The next morning the whole family, including both her father and Nuala, went to the soup kitchen. Her father was very quiet. He held his body erect, as he always did, but she saw that, instead of looking out with their usual, bold dignity at the world, his eyes were looking down, avoiding the gaze of others. She knew he was inwardly wincing with every pace he took. When they arrived, their names were checked, but, cruelly, the man who took the roll call insisted that they all wait the four hours until they get their ration. With each minute that passed, she knew that her father secretly took another invisible step down the stairway of humiliation in his soul. And with each passing minute, she was silently praying that nobody should come up to her sister, nor say any word that might give away the trade she now followed.

✢

Whatever her fears about her sister, Maureen couldn't help being glad when, shortly after this, Nuala started bringing home items of food: a loaf of bread, a little ham, a cabbage. They pretended to her father that they had managed to buy these things in the town, but Nuala confessed to her: "I have a merchant who likes me. He knows what I need, so he pays me with food for my family." Maureen concluded that there was nothing she could say, since the food was such a boon. The children needed it. Even Caitlin looked a little better.

But the one who seemed to pick up the fastest was little Daniel. Children of six could often be fragile, but thank God, she thought, that her father's only remaining son was such a sturdy little fellow. He seemed to have a remarkable resilience. A short time ago, his blue eyes had looked so large and staring in his sunken face that she had secretly trembled for him; yet now, after some days of better diet, he had already put on a little flesh and gained in energy. When they walked into town together, instead of holding her hand and dragging his feet, he slipped his hand free and even walked ahead.

Further encouragement came one morning when she and Daniel arrived at the soup kitchen to find that there had been a change. Instead of waiting for a daily ticket, they were told to take a ticket for a month. She observed that the line was moving more easily and was told that the meal was being issued fresh now, so that they did not have to wait for it to be cooked. "There's a new supervisor," one of the women told her, but who this might be she did not know until little Daniel suddenly ran across to where Stephen Smith was inspecting a shipment of meal.

"It's Mr. Smith," he cried. "Mr. Smith," he told the bystanders, "is our friend."

Maureen hastened across and apologised for the interruption, but Stephen Smith did not seem to mind at all. He had been asked to supervise the Ennis soup kitchens for the moment, he confirmed. The other man had been removed. He turned his eyes on Daniel.

"Remind me of your name," he said pleasantly.

"Daniel, Sir."

"Ah yes. An excellent name."

"I am named after Daniel O'Connell."

"I know Mr. O'Connell well."

"Does he know that I am named after him?"

Stephen hesitated hardly the fraction of a second, but giving Maureen a smile, he answered.

"Why, to be sure he does. And he is very pleased."

Little Daniel swelled with pride. Maureen silently blessed, and wondered at, the goodness of the man; and when it came to their turn, the people handing out the meal, having observed that this family appeared to be in the favour of the new supervisor, made sure to give her a little more than they would otherwise have done.

⁘

On the second day of April, Eamonn Madden started to feel unwell.

"I've no strength in me today," he said in the morning. He seemed slightly puzzled. It wasn't like him. Normally, he ignored any ailments, as a king might ignore a complaining subject.

Maureen went into Ennis as usual, taking little Daniel with her.

At the end of the day, she noticed that her father was shivering, and he admitted to her that he had a headache. Feeling his brow, she could tell he had a fever. She'd been able to make a little broth, and she gave it to him. The next morning, he was the same; by evening, his brow was burning.

"You'd best keep the children away from me," he told her, and insisted on going into the far room, where they had stored the potatoes once. She made him up a bed with straw and a blanket. "I'll be right enough here," he said.

She talked to Nuala. The doctors in Ennis were all fully occupied with the hospitals, but Nuala found a priest to consult, and he gave her wise advice.

"Whatever you do, don't take him to the fever hospital. That's probably where he got it," he told her. "Keep him away from the children, and pray. I see the fever every day now, and it's getting worse. The people are so weakened through lack of food that they haven't the strength to fight it. There are two forms: the yellow and the black, as they call it. The black is typhus, which is a terrible thing. But most survive it, you know. Is your father a strong man? That is good. Pray for him, then. With luck, after a week, the fever will break."

But it did not. On the fifth day, as she was feeding him, Maureen noticed by the light of the candle that the skin on her father's chest seemed to be mottled. One side of his shirt was open, and when he turned, she saw that there were deep red blotches on his side. She wasn't sure whether he realised, so she said nothing. The next day, the blotches were darker. When the children wanted to go in to see him, she wouldn't let them. She continued to feed him broth.

The next evening, Nuala brought home some milk. "It's good for the fever," she said. "I told my merchant it was for my sisters, to build them up."

"Does he know about Father?"

"Are you mad? He wouldn't touch me if he knew. And then . . ." She made a face. "No more food."

Two days later, the patches on her father were almost black. In the evening, he became delirious, mumbling incoherently. His eyes were open, but Maureen knew he did not see her. Around noon the next day, however, he became lucid again.

"Bring Daniel to me."

She shook her head.

"Just to the door. Only for a moment."

Reluctantly, she complied. Eamonn propped himself up against the wall.

"Daniel, your father has a sickness. I may not see you again. Do you understand?"

The boy stared wide-eyed into the shadowy room but did not know what to say.

"You will be looked after by your sister, and always try to help her," his father went on. "Will you do that for me?" Daniel nodded. "And one day, when you are grown, you will be strong, and never be sick, and then you will be the man of the family, and look after Maureen and your other sisters. Do you promise me that also?"

"Yes," the little boy whispered.

"Good. You are a good boy, Daniel, and I'm very proud of you." He looked to Maureen. "That'll do."

At that moment, Daniel tried to rush to his father, but Maureen managed to catch him just in time.

When they were back in the other room, Daniel turned to her.

"I will look after you, Maureen. I promise I will. Forever and ever."

"I know you will," she said, and kissed him. Then she went back in to help her father. He seemed suddenly very tired.

"I'll speak to the girls together this evening, when Nuala's back," he said.

But by that evening, he was delirious again.

He continued that way for another day. Then he seemed to pass into a kind of stupor. His eyes were open very wide, and his breathing was shallow. Maureen wasn't sure what to do. It was Nuala who brought the priest, who, after giving him the last rites, told them, "I don't think it will be very long now."

Maureen found that he had gone when she went in to him the following morning.

❖

In the month of June in the year 1847, a wonderful thing occurred.

The Irish Famine came to an end.

True, the greater part of the Irish people was close to starvation. The numbers of weakened people dying from disease were rising. So few potatoes had been planted that, even if they escaped blight, they would not be enough to feed the poor folk who relied upon them. More and more of those small tenants and cottagers, besides, were being forced off the land into a condition of helpless destitution. Ireland, that is to say, was a country utterly prostrated.

Yet the Famine came to an end. And how was this wonderful thing accomplished? Why, in the simplest way imaginable. The Famine was legislated out of existence. It had to be. The Whigs were facing a General Election.

And the British public had had enough of the Irish Famine. After all, everyone had done their best. When a voluntary fund to relieve Irish and Scottish distress had been set up that spring, Queen Victoria herself had contributed two thousand pounds, and the donations had soon reached nearly half a million pounds sterling—a huge sum, far surpassing even the value of relief goods sent across the Atlantic in over a hundred ships by the Irish and their sympathisers in America. The government itself had spent millions. By early summer, moreover, the soup kitchens were frequently able to provide a nourishing mixture of maize, rice, and oats, and there was more than enough to go round. The food shortage had been stemmed.

But at great cost. This expenditure of taxpayers' money could not go on indefinitely. Surely by now, reasonable Britons supposed, the Irish should be able to start putting their own house in order. Speeches were made denouncing government waste. Newspapers carried articles about misplaced humanity: one must not, these articles pointed out, be too kind to the Irish, or it would sap their self-reliance.

Faced with such general sentiment, and with an election in prospect, the government decided to do what governments have always done: "If you can't win a war, then you'd better declare a victory."

After all, this year's potatoes appeared to be free of blight, and the Irish grain harvest promised a bumper crop. The fact that the poor Irish had no money to buy any grain was a detail that could be overlooked. The market would take care of such things.

And so an excellent scheme was hit upon. In June that year, a bill was passed in the British Parliament that would reorganise the relief of distress in Ireland entirely. The Poor Law Extension Act was a brilliant instrument. From now on, all those in need of help could apply to the local workhouse, in which they could be either incarcerated or fed. The able-bodied, of course, would not be fed. There were some safeguards, so that this generosity would not be abused. Those who had a vegetable patch for self-support would be turned away. And the men, at least, would be obliged to break stones for, say, ten hours a day, in order to discourage trivial applications for food. But by these means, the costs would fall upon the local Irish authorities, where they belonged. And by this was the stroke of legislative genius, as soon as this was done—by the end of the summer, say—the present costly soup kitchens could be closed down and the suffering English taxpayer be relieved.

The Irish Famine, therefore, had been legislated away. Since it was no longer official, it did not exist. Or if it did, it was a local Irish problem. It was a tribute to the flexibility of the Union.

Thus the British government could face the electorate with a sense of confidence and of duty done.

···

Stephen Smith was most surprised, one day in July, to see Mr. Samuel Tidy standing thoughtfully in the street, watching the soup kitchen. He went over to him at once. And the Quaker was evidently quite as surprised to see him in turn. He listened carefully as Stephen gave him a quick account of how he came to be there, then informed him that he had come to Ennis himself to see what the Quakers might be able to do to help. Since Stephen was to be at the house of Charles O'Connell that evening, he suggested that the Quaker should come, too, since Charles O'Connell would certainly be delighted to welcome him.

He and Daniel O'Connell's cousin had seen a good deal of each other recently. Though he had been well aware that the great man was unwell, Stephen had been shocked when, in May, the Liberator had died trying to make a pilgrimage to Rome. He had naturally called upon Charles O'Connell at once, and they had often dined together since. Charles had been trying to persuade him to resume his political life, but Stephen wasn't sure he wanted to.

The three men dined quietly together. O'Connell apologised for the somewhat simple fare, but though it was not lavish, the meal was perfectly adequate. "It's quite remarkable, really," Charles O'Connell remarked, "how little life for the richer merchants and the local gentry has changed. The gentry are still entertaining in their houses—quietly, I grant you—but you can still dine and play at whist in any of the country houses around. Indeed, it's terrible to say it, but this famine has been a blessing to many of the estates in the county, because it gives the landlords and the larger farmers an excuse to clear out numbers of unwanted tenants. I had one man tell me: 'I've persuaded some of my people to emigrate to America. I'm better off paying their passage and getting the land back.' So there you are, Mr. Tidy. English or Irish, it makes little difference: the richer sort have one set of interests in this matter, and the poor, who are suffering, another. You may say that the situation should never have developed in the first place."

"I certainly would," agreed the Quaker.

"But it has, and there are those who say that there is no way out of our difficulty until we have first gone through this terrible period of readjustment."

"By which," added Stephen with feeling, "they mean starvation. For that is what the British government is now proposing."

"You think the British will deliberately starve the Irish poor?" asked the Quaker.

"Not exactly. But I think that every measure they have introduced has been misconceived. I was helping administer the public works scheme before this. Men were being paid a starvation wage to perform useless tasks, so that they could buy food which wasn't there. It also cost the government a great deal—far more than it would have done to feed people. The entire system broke down, and so they introduced soup kitchens. In some of the more remote areas of Clare, by the way, the soup kitchens took so long to get started that whole villages starved in the meantime. At this moment, starvation has been averted. But in two months, the kitchens will be closed and the workhouses will try to take over."

"This concerns me greatly," Tidy said.

"It should. Do you know how many people we are feeding, at present, in County Clare? A hundred thousand. Do you know how many workhouse places there are in the county? Three thousand. What is to become of the remaining ninety-seven percent? No one can tell me. Here in Ennis," he went on bitterly, "I can feed thirty-five thousand—many of them able-bodied, by the way. The workhouse is being enlarged. Its new capacity will be just over one thousand." He made a gesture of despair with his hands.

The Quaker looked at him with quiet amusement.

"I see you have changed since I first met you, Mr. Smith," he remarked. "You were very much a political man, then."

"Can the Quakers help?" Stephen asked. "It was Quakers, I believe, who first introduced the very idea of soup kitchens."

"We can help," Tidy said, "but we are cautious. There is always the fear, you know, that we would be perceived at trying to proselytise—which, I can assure you, we never do."

"Ah," said Charles O'Connell, "you mean 'soup conversions.'"

Stephen had heard of these: Protestant clergymen or ministers offering food to the starving if they would abandon their Catholic faith.

"I can't say that I've ever seen such a thing myself," he stated. "Does it really happen?"

"It is rare," replied the Quaker. "But I have seen it."

"So what might you do?" Stephen wanted to know.

"We shall probably try to work with the local parishes. Send them supplies—food, clothing, and so forth—and let them make the distributions as they see best. We have facilities down in Limerick. The shipments would come from there."

"I pray to God that you will," Stephen told him. "By the autumn, the scale of the problem will be huge."

They discussed further the various ways in which the Quakers might be able to send aid, and how far it would be possible to reach other parts of Clare. Whatever the Quakers could do, it was certainly not going to combat more than a part of the problem ahead.

After they had talked of this for some time, and knowing their host's interest in the subject, Tidy asked O'Connell about the coming election.

"It'll be a lively business, for sure," he told them. "The borough election comes first, and that's already sewn up. O'Gorman Mahon, that acted as proposer for my cousin back in '28, is standing, and the local tradesmen love him. He's mad as a hatter, actually. God knows what he'll do in London. But his opponent is so crushed already, he's about to withdraw. Then comes the county election. One seat is already spoken for, but the second will be interesting. For we have no less a personage than Sir Lucius O'Brien contesting it." He grinned. "And I'm acting as his agent."

Sir Lucius O'Brien was certainly no ordinary candidate. The most important of all that mighty clan, direct descendant of King Brian Boru himself, and the owner of the huge Dromoland Castle estate down towards Limerick, Sir Lucius

was one of the greatest of the old princes of Ireland remaining
in the west. There was only one problem.

He was a Tory. Unlike his younger brother, who supported
the Young Ireland men, he had concluded that the Union with
England was more to his advantage than otherwise. He supported England, therefore.

"His beliefs, I admit, present a problem," said Charles
O'Connell, "running, as they do, counter to everything that
my cousin Daniel stood for and that the local electors want—
for they want a Repealer, you may be certain, and not a Union
man. But I am nonetheless confident of success."

"How will you do it?" asked Stephen.

"He's a very affable man," said O'Connell. "And he has
never been one to press his beliefs in public—at least not in
any definite way. There is, you could say, a stately ambiguity
about him. And that very ambiguity may help us. Mr. Knox,
you know, despite the fact that he never ceases to campaign
against the government on behalf of the people, dislikes the
idea of Repeal. So the *Clare Journal* will support my man
because Knox believes, correctly as it happens, that he's a Tory.
I have also convinced the local Temperance Society that Sir
Lucius is for them. I can't remember why. The Catholic clergy
are mostly against him, and it will be difficult to fool them.
But we are preparing some speeches that will give the impression that he might be more of a Repealer than you'd have
thought. And because they know that his brother is an avid
Repealer, I'm hoping to leave the idea in our electors' minds
that he might be closer to his brother than supposed. With
luck, they will come to believe that there is no actual reason
why they shouldn't vote for him. Or better yet, they can believe
he's a bit of a Repealer if they want to—which by election day
they will surely wish to do."

"But why," asked the Quaker, "will they want to believe this?"

"Sir Lucius O'Brien is a very rich man. There'll be plenty
of money around. He knows what's expected of him."

"He'll pay them for their votes?"

"I don't know how it is in your parish, Mr. Tidy," said Charles O'Connell genially, "but if you want a man's vote in Ennis, he'll expect to be paid for it. It's the same as in England. And America, too, for all I know," he added.

"I am sorry to hear it," said the Quaker.

"You must consider the effect of the Famine also," O'Connell pointed out. "Our tradesmen have all been badly hit. You can hardly blame them for taking the chance to make a little money if they can. I'm negotiating with the trades body now."

Tidy remained another two days in the area. He and Stephen had another conversation together, and agreed that they would correspond with each other about what might be done for the poor of Ennis after the election.

⁙

There was a monotony about most of Stephen's days, but he didn't mind. The faces at the soup kitchens grew familiar; without even thinking about it, he noticed who had grown sick or disappeared. During those summer months, fever, diarrhoea, dysentery—the bloody flux, as they called it—took their steady toll, especially on the children; he knew what deaths occurred in the hospitals and had some idea of the losses in the town, but who knew how many were dying out in the remoter regions? His only consolation, he supposed, was that if it were not for the soup kitchens, this mortality would be immeasurably higher.

He had been sorry to learn, in April, of the death of Eamonn Madden. Two months later, he saw Maureen looking very downcast. He had learned that it was better not to become too involved with those using the soup kitchens. It made things too difficult. But he went up to her on this occasion and asked what was wrong.

"My sisters Mary and Caitlin both died last week, Sir," she said. "It was the bloody flux." She sighed. "I knew they would."

"You still have your little brother?"

"I do, thanks be to God, little Daniel. And my sister Nuala."

"She works?"

"She has a little occasional work with a laundress, that is all."

He would see her each day, often with the little boy holding her hand; and though they did not know it, they became for him a little symbol of hope that, in all this misery, the good were still surviving and his work was all worthwhile.

✢

The election, when it came, was everything that Charles O'Connell had promised. It was astounding to him, but in the midst of the waiting lines for the soup kitchens and the daily dying all around, the town assumed an almost carnival atmosphere. Cartloads of rowdy men, calling out their support for their candidates, rolled through the streets, ignoring the poor folk they passed entirely. Indeed, the people in the lines seemed to enjoy the distraction of watching and listening to the curious show. The pubs were full of people, for Sir Lucius had given out free drink tokens to all and sundry.

Sir Lucius was a popular candidate. Charles O'Connell had done an excellent job, but he had good material to work with. Not only did Sir Lucius prove to be easy in every company, but to his genuine credit, he had given his own tenants every possible help through the Famine. No one on the vast Dromoland estate had gone hungry, and everyone knew it. The people of Ennis hung green boughs on their houses to welcome him.

His speech, it had to be said, was a masterpiece.

"Was I not born in Ireland?" the aristocrat cried. "Were not my ancestors? Did they not fight for Ireland to be a single kingdom and to be free?"

They did. They did. You had only to look at him to see. For wasn't he the heir of the greatest patriot of them all, who had driven the Vikings back eight hundred years ago? Brian, Son of Kennedy, Brian Boru.

"My roots are in Irish soil. My blood is Irish blood. Where else could my interests lie, if not in Ireland? What land could I possibly love, if not Ireland? For what country could I lay down my life, if not Ireland? Send me to Parliament and I will speak for Ireland."

Stephen noted, with professional appreciation, that he hadn't actually said that he was a Repealer. But you could easily think it.

As for the business of the election, it was no better and no worse, he supposed, than other elections had been in the past or would be in the future. The body of tradesmen were paid two hundred and fifty pounds for their votes, though they had asked for a hundred more. Other individual electors had negotiated various payments for their vote: one cheeky fellow had demanded fifty pounds. Charles O'Connell, as agent, received one hundred and eighteen pounds. "Though I should," he said, "have had more."

I could only wish, thought Stephen, that my poor people in the soup lines had a vote to sell. But some of the poorer townsfolk were able to make a bit when they were employed to kidnap some of the opposition voters and lock them up until the polls closed. One or two of these voters suffered some physical injury, but that was by mistake.

And when it was all over, Sir Lucius O'Brien was triumphantly elected as one of the two members for County Clare, and went to the London Parliament—though whether the good people who elected him would ever hear a word from him on the subject of Repeal was, Stephen considered, highly doubtful.

"Doesn't it make you want to get back into politics, Stephen?" asked Charles O'Connell. "Can't we persuade you?"

"Not really," said Stephen.

✣

Nor, in the weeks that followed, did he think of anything much beyond the immediate task in hand—which was to keep the soup kitchen open for as long as possible.

During the harvest season, there was some casual work in the fields on the larger farms; but many of the smaller tenants, who might have employed a few men for the harvest in normal years, were too pressed for money themselves and were trying to do all the work with family members. The harvest was a good one. But what use was that to the poor, who could not buy food at all? For them, he was sure, to see carts of grain go by must be like standing beside a riverbank when you are dying of thirst and being told you must not drink. It would be small wonder, then, if before long some of those carts would be robbed.

He managed to keep the soup kitchen going until early September. Then it was closed. He had been asked by Charles O'Connell whether he was interested in becoming one of the new relief officers who would be employed by the workhouse under the new arrangements. "It carries quite a good little salary," O'Connell told him. But he had also received a letter from Tidy asking if he would care to go to Limerick to help organise the distribution of food from there. "I think," he told O'Connell, "that I can do more good in Limerick now than I can in Clare." Besides, he had been too long in Ennis. He was getting run-down himself. He needed to get out.

Before he left, he did go to say goodbye to the Madden children. Nuala was not there when he came by their house, but he found Maureen and the little boy.

"It is wonderful how you look after your brother," he said to her. But she only smiled.

"Oh no, Sir, it's Daniel that looks after me." And the little fellow swelled with pride, obviously believing that this was really so.

Stephen hoped, more than he cared to let them see, that they would survive what he feared would be a bitter season ahead.

+

And yet, Maureen reflected, there was truth in it. For more than once now, little Daniel had stolen a cabbage. The farms were well guarded. "But I am small, and they do not see me," he told her proudly. That a Madden should be proud to steal: what had things come to that her little boy should learn such things? But what else could he do to help his sister?

And who knew what other things might be in the child's mind in this new and terrible world they were living in?

When Mary and Caitlin had fallen sick within a day of each other, she had known that they would not live. She couldn't say why. Perhaps it was just that she had seen so many other children die the same way, for the dysentery was so widespread now, and the children's bodies were so weakened that few of them could put up much of a fight against it. She had done her best for them, prayed for Daniel, and hardened her heart. And indeed, she had not suffered so much anguish at their deaths as she should, because something inside her had closed, refusing to accept any more pain. As for Daniel, he had been rather quiet, asking her, wide-eyed, one day: "Are Mary and Caitlin going to die?" In answer to which, she could only tell him: "It's in God's hands." After they had gone, he had said nothing for a day or two; but then, looking thoughtful, he had asked her: "Are they gone to be with God?"

"Yes. Yes they are. And to our father and mother. They are all together with God now."

"Where is God?"

"He is in heaven, Daniel."

He had nodded slowly, as if this explained something.

"I did not think He could be here."

And she knew she should have told him that He was, but she had not the strength just then.

When Mr. Smith came by to say that he was going, she had been very calm and polite. And after he had gone, she had looked after him for a long time, wondering what was to become of them now that the soup kitchens were closing. And as his figure receded along the road, she had felt a terrible sense of loss, and a longing for him to return, or even look back, as if, in him, their hopes themselves were departing.

So she had been startled by Daniel's voice at her side.

"I wish you could marry Mr. Smith, Maureen."

"Oh." She had given a little laugh. "Don't be foolish, Daniel," she said.

⁘

She had not foreseen what Nuala would do.

In the days after the soup kitchens closed, they had waited anxiously to see what would happen. They were able to buy a little food in the market, because Nuala had some small savings. Nobody was sure how the new regime would work. But one day she had noticed that her sister was looking thoughtful.

Since her sister had started her present occupation, Maureen had always had one fear. It was only natural. What if she caught something from one of her men? She knew that girls in the town had suffered this fate, and the hospital would usually refuse to help them. Some girls had committed petty crimes and got themselves caught deliberately, just so they could get sent to jail. Once you were in jail, if they found you had any sort of venereal infection, they put you in the prison sanitarium until you were cured. It was the best way, if you were poor, of getting treatment. Had this happened to Nuala now? Was she thinking of getting herself put in jail? And if so, apart from the shame of it, where would they be then? A day passed, and she was summoning the courage to ask her right out, when Nuala opened the conversation that evening. It wasn't what she'd expected at all.

"We've got to get out of here, Maureen."

"I don't see how."

"If we don't get out, we're all going to die. I know it."

"What are you saying?"

"I can get us all out."

"How?"

"I've a man who'll take me. He says he doesn't mind if you and Daniel come, too."

"But your merchant lives here."

"It's not him. Another fellow. He's going back to Wexford. He says it's not so bad there. At least you could get fed."

"He's going to marry you?"

"I didn't say that. It doesn't matter, Maureen. If he'll just look after me for a while . . ."

"How long have you known him?"

"A few days."

"Oh, Nuala. What would we be getting ourselves into? I can't take little Daniel away on such a promise as that. We'd be better off here."

"No, you wouldn't. You won't be fed. You won't even have a roof over your head. It's the chance we have, Maureen. We have to take it."

"Let me think, Nuala. I'm sure I can't. But let me think at least until the morning."

"I'm leaving in the morning, Maureen. I'm sorry, but I have to. I'm not going to die here."

In the morning, they spoke again, alone.

"I can't, Nuala. Perhaps I haven't the courage, but it doesn't feel right."

"That's what he said you'd say."

"I wish you wouldn't go."

But a hard look had come into Nuala's face.

"Here's ten shillings, Maureen. It'll see you through for a little while. It's all I can spare."

"Shall I get Daniel, for you to say goodbye?"

"No. You can tell him what you want. Goodbye, Maureen." And she was gone.

Later in the morning, Maureen told Daniel with a smile, "Nuala has a job. They will keep her away for a while."

"But we'll see her again?"

"Of course we will."

"Is she in jail?"

"She is not," she cried indignantly.

"That's good," said little Daniel.

In the days that followed, she wondered if she had done the right thing. Without Nuala, there would be no money coming in. That meant that unless she tried to follow the same path as her sister, she wouldn't be able to pay the rent on the cottage for much longer. And in any case, she'd rather conserve what tiny money they had. The place filled her with dread, but she went to the workhouse to find out what help she might get there. Despite the three hundred new places added, there was not space for a single person more inside. She could come again tomorrow, and there might be a little food, they told her; but there was no guarantee.

The next day, there was an argument between two of the relief officers about her status. "She isn't a widow," one pointed out. "And she's able-bodied." The other took a more generous view. "She and the little boy are clearly orphans. They can be fed." But there seemed to be little food available, and there were hundreds more at the gates. They gave her a little meal, but there was no promise as to whether this would be repeated.

"There is a plan to take over the old soup kitchens if we can ever get organised," the more kindly of the two said. "As you see, everything's at sixes and sevens just now."

During the next week, they hardly seemed to get any better.

The day before the next rent was due, she noticed the cabin. It was only thirty yards from her own door. There had been a family in there, but they had gone. It was a hut, really, with a roof made of branches and stalks, caked with mud. But it kept out the rain. Someone had built it there, and if the patch of ground had a landlord, nobody had ever seen him. It was free accommodation.

"We really don't need so much space now, you and I," she told Daniel. "We'd be just as well in here." So the next day, when the agent came by for the rent and declined the opportunity to let them stay where they were without paying for a while, they moved across, easily enough, into their new accommodations.

Then she waited, along with everyone else in Ennis, to see what would happen next. "After all," she remarked to one of her neighbours, "they can't just let everybody starve to death."

It was curious how you could survive, she thought, as the days of September went by. Partly it was a question of listening for news, partly of being lucky. The workhouse system was in a state of shambles. One day there was food at the old soup kitchen in Mill Street, another there wasn't. Some days they were helping people at the workhouse gates, and the next, when hundreds arrived there, they were all turned away. She heard of a shipment of food and clothing from the Quakers arriving at a nearby parish. She went up there and the priest, though he really wanted to feed his own parishioners only, took pity on her and gave her some rice and peas. On another day, early in October, she heard that some men had commandeered a cartload of grain and were passing it out near the new bridge. She left Daniel at the house and ran up there as fast as she could. She came back with five pounds of grain. That kept them alive for more than a week.

The refusal of the workhouse to feed any of the ablebodied men had two results. It encouraged them to go out and rob the grain shipments. That, she thought, was a good thing. But gradually, you could also see many of them, even some of the best, subsiding into a kind of apathy. As October continued and it became colder, it seemed to her that all around her, each day, her neighbours were starting to look a little thinner and weaker. And looking at her own arms one day, and realising how thin they were, she understood that she must look the same to them.

It was halfway through October that Daniel became sick. It wasn't anything serious, fortunately. Something that he had eaten must have disagreed with his stomach, though, and for two days he was prostrated with diarrhoea. She tried to give him liquids and put something in his stomach. It passed, and she thanked God that his constitution was so strong. But it left him pale, and much weaker than before. She wondered what she could do to put a little more colour back into his cheeks.

A kindly neighbour told her what to do. The first time she did it was the hardest. She selected the place with care—you had to, with the farmers watching their fields like hawks. She went out at dusk, so that she had just enough light to see what she was doing. There were three cows by a stone wall. She crept along the ground like a snake, taking her time. When she reached the cows, they glanced at her, but she let them get used to her before she made her move, and she took things very slowly. She had her sharp little knife and a wooden bowl.

All you had to do was to find a good place on the leg and make a tiny cut. If you did it successfully, the cow would hardly feel it. But the blood would come trickling out all right, and you could cup it into a bowl, just like a doctor bleeding a patient.

She held her breath, felt the leg, praying the cow would not suddenly move, and, with a tiny push, made a cut. The cow stirred, but only very slightly. She held the small wooden bowl against the leg. She didn't want more than a trickle, because she didn't want the cow to bleed too much; with luck, the farmer need not notice what had been done. When she had enough, she tied a cloth tightly over the top of the bowl, wiped the cow's leg clean, and crept away.

Back in the cabin, she diluted the blood with water, mixed it with gruel, and, with some difficulty, persuaded Daniel to get it down. "It's good for you, whether you like it or not," she said.

A few days later, she did the same thing again. But this time, she fumbled the cut and the animal bled far too much. On the last day of October, on the eerie and magical eve of Samhain, she went to the field a third time. But as she walked along the path beside the wall, she saw the farmer waiting at the edge of the field. He had a blunderbuss. He was watching her suspiciously, so she gave him a polite good evening and went upon her way. She'd done Daniel some good, she was sure of it. But was it enough?

The month of November was bleak. A cold, raw dampness set in. And now, try though she might, she couldn't get enough food. She had conserved a few shillings of the money Nuala had given her, and she did her best to buy food in the market. At the workhouse, not only were there growing crowds outside the door, but she plainly heard one of the relief officers say to another: "What are we supposed to do, when we have no money?"

By the end of the third week, it was clear to her: Ennis was collapsing. The process was strangely quiet. Nothing was said. Nothing was done. There were no sudden alarms, no shrieks, no cries. Just a cold, dank silence, while the world slowly sank into lethargy, as though life itself had shrunk, along the muddy streets, into a frozen stiffness. She stopped taking Daniel with her into the town now, because she didn't want him to see what she saw. There were families sick and dying all along the way. More than once, she had been obliged to step over corpses in the street. She could not hide it when the family next door became sick. She could only try to keep him away from them.

Then came the rain, followed by a day of icy wind. And then, on the twenty-second, Daniel caught a fever.

She didn't know what it was. It could have been any of a dozen conditions, a random infection. It did not matter. The boy was burning up. She tried to cool his brow and feed him liquid. She stayed by his side. She could feel him burning, hotter and hotter, though she swathed his whole body in a damp blanket now to try to draw the fever. She knew he was strong. That was the most important thing. On the twenty-third, she thought perhaps the fever might break. He was pale now, his eyes staring in a way that she had never seen before.

"You must fight now, Daniel," she said. "You must be a brave boy, and you must fight."

"I am sorry, Maureen," he whispered. "I will try."

Then, the next morning, the rain returned. A miserable, grey rain, falling incessantly, like a dirty shroud, wetting equally the living and the dead. And as the rain fell, she looked into Daniel's eyes and saw what she dreaded, that look she had seen in the eyes of children before, when they have given up.

What could she do? There was nothing she could do. But she could not rest there, she could not just hold his hand while he went—he, the last thing she had to call her own in all the world. So she wrapped him in a shawl she had, and carried him out into the rain, and she ran, as best she could, all the way to the fever hospital, where she showed them the boy at the door and begged them: let us in. But they were full, and besides, they had too much else to do, and they told her: "Go to the workhouse. They may help you there." So once again she set out in the falling rain and stumbled, almost staggered with the weight of him, through the mud until she at last came in sight of that grim, grey bastion. But there were hundreds of people there also, for the doors had been firmly closed, and she could not even get through them.

Though indeed, she discovered, as she pulled back the shawl, she needn't have bothered, since somewhere upon that journey, Daniel had departed.

⁜

On the twenty-fifth of November, Stephen Smith looked out upon the cold, wet streets of Ennis and decided that he would not stay there. He had arrived the evening before and stayed the night at the house of Charles O'Connell. His host had profoundly depressed him.

"At the workhouse now, the guardians are in the ludicrous position of begging the government to give them more relief money, for they are completely without funds. At the same time, they have just had a demand from the government for the repayment of the loan contracted earlier in the year for your working parties and soup kitchens. They won't pay it, of course. But all the same, at such a time, even to be asked . . ."

No, Stephen thought, he would not linger here. His work in Limerick had been worthwhile, but what he could do had been completed. It would be continued, very effectively, by other hands. He was going back to Dublin. In fact, he couldn't wait to be gone. But before he could leave, there were some hours to kill. He might as well go round the place, however depressing. As he started to walk, he found himself wondering what had become of the Maddens.

⁑

As she stood outside the door of the cabin, staring out at the grey nothingness of the sky, and aware only now of the nothingness of her heart, she did not even notice him coming. Only when he stood before her did she realise that he was addressing her. He was asking after her sister, and after Daniel.

"She has left, Sir, but I can't tell where she is. I do not know at all," she answered stupidly.

"And little Daniel."

"He is dead, Sir. Yesterday."

"I am sorry. I am sorry for your trouble." The formula. She bowed her head in nerveless acknowledgement, glanced at his face, which she had seen in her mind's eye so many times before, and stared out at the sky again. Meaningless. "What will you do?" he asked.

"I? Do?" It had not occurred to her. What was there to do? Was there any point? There was no point.

"Will you stay here? Have you a place to go?"

"I have nothing," she said, as though in a daze. "All that I had is gone. I have nothing left at all. But it does not matter."

She was only vaguely aware that he was silent, that he was considering, hesitating.

"You cannot stay here like this," he said at last. "You had better come with me."

"I?" She frowned, not comprehending. "Where?" Would he take her to the workhouse?

"To Dublin," he said.

VICTORIA

EW PEOPLE would have disagreed that, in listing the many pleasant features of Dublin, the canals must be included. Begun late in the previous century, they enclosed the Georgian centre city like two embracing arms. To the north, the Royal Canal swept from the docks beyond the Custom House, up round the Mountjoy estate, and out to the west above Phoenix Park; from there it proceeded across the country, mile after mile, away into the Midlands until at last, over eighty miles away, it joined the huge Shannon river system. By this means, you could nowadays ship goods on barges from one side of Ireland to the other. On the south side of the Liffey, taking its origin from the docks by Ringsend, the Grand Canal, despite its name, was an intimate affair, passing between grassy banks where willow trees grew, in a slow and almost imperceptible curve until, two miles west of St. Stephen's Green, like a man who has enjoyed a delightful rest cure, it decided it must now strike out, boldly, in a straight line, westwards across the fertile Liffey Plain. Along its banks, from wooden lock to wooden lock, a charming suburban towpath ran.

And it was in a neat but capacious brick house, overlooking its grassy banks, that the Tidy family lived. Samuel Tidy and his wife had been married for fifteen years now. They had five children, the youngest of whom was a baby. They were industrious, modestly prosperous, and contented. In their house, as you might expect in a Quaker home, there was an atmosphere of easy quiet that was restful, and healing.

At least, so Maureen Madden found it.

By good fortune, when Stephen Smith had come to them in December of 1847 and said that he was looking for a position for a woman from Clare, they had still one extra bedroom in the house. "I was thinking of asking Lord Mountwalsh," he'd explained, "since between his Dublin and Wexford houses he has such a large establishment. For she certainly can't stay in my lodgings with me. But then I thought I'd mention it to you, too. I have rented a room for her in a house nearby for the present." After a long discussion between themselves, Samuel Tidy and his wife had decided that, for a couple of weeks, they wanted Maureen to remain in her lodging. There had been numerous cases of people coming into Dublin from afflicted areas and bringing disease with them. "We must protect our children first," the Quaker reasonably explained. But after that, they had agreed to take her in. "She can help me with the children," Mrs. Tidy had said. "I'm sure there will be plenty for her to do." Apart from her board, she would also receive a modest salary.

For Maureen, this change in her circumstances had been so unexpected that for several weeks she had gone through her life as if in a dream. The Quaker family lived in a simple manner. They ate with their children, and they decided to treat her as a sort of governess. Indeed, she soon gave evidence that she was able to teach the younger children their letters, and a good deal more besides. "She has excellent self-control," Mrs. Tidy told her husband approvingly. "She's quiet and clean. I'm really very pleased we took her in." And though the winter gave her no chance to lose the paleness that had afflicted her, by the spring

Maureen had put on enough weight to fill out her face and body to their normal condition; she no longer looked gaunt, even if she was still a little subdued.

Early in June, Tidy took a house by the sea for ten days. She returned from this family holiday with some colour in her cheeks and an altogether more healthy air. "I'm so glad she looks better," said Mrs. Tidy. "I'm growing fond of her."

During these months, the family had not seen Stephen Smith. Shortly after his return in December, he had consulted with the Earl of Mountwalsh about what to do with himself, and the earl had responded by employing him on a series of commissions. These had taken him to Wexford, the west, and once to London. Not until late June did he send a note to Tidy to let him know that he was in Dublin and asking if he might call.

Maureen was occupied with the children when he arrived. There was much to talk about meanwhile.

The Famine was having some remarkable effects upon Dublin. The countryside around the capital was one of the least afflicted upon the island. But from farther afield, a stream of people from other parts had been making their way to Dublin in the hope of emigrating, or at least finding shelter. And to a large extent, Dublin had risen to the challenge. Churches and charities, not least the Quakers, of course, had ensured that the arrivals were fed. There was even a large soup kitchen feeding huge numbers in fashionable Merrion Square. Nor had there been any lessening in the numbers arriving. Tidy was glad that Maureen was not in the room—since it might have been painful for her to hear—but he told Stephen now that the wave of evictions in Clare and Mayo had, if anything, increased from the year before.

"The situation you saw in Clare when you left has continued unchanged except that the government has been forced to feed the able-bodied, too. Our best figures are that in Ireland as a whole, at this moment, there are eight hundred thousand on outdoor relief, and nearly half of those are able-bodied. I cannot tell you how many people are at the point of starvation, because nobody knows and nobody wants to know. But it is normal in any western workhouse that there will be fifty, eighty, even a hundred deaths, children mostly, every week."

"And the potato crop?"

"Twice as much is planted this year as last—though that is still less than half the acreage in the days before the blight. We shall have to hope for a good harvest."

"What is remarkable to me is that there are not more people sleeping in the streets here. Where do we put them all?"

"That I can tell you easily. In the big houses that were the glory of Dublin in the old days, before the Act of Union. I walked over to the north side the other day, Stephen," he went on. "Up Sackville Street and round by Mountjoy Square. In street after street, I saw those big terraced houses—which once housed a single family and were afterwards turned into apartments—now turned into tenements. Often, you will now find an entire family occupying a single room. I dare say, at that rate, that we have enough brick and mortar here to shelter most of the population of Ireland. In squalor, of course."

They had just finished this discussion when the younger children, accompanied by Maureen, came into the room.

She was dressed in a simple cotton gown lightly trimmed with lace. Her hair was parted and drawn back, but there was some curl in it, and a slight sheen, from regular brushing, that he had not seen before. He advanced to meet her and smiled.

"Why, Miss Madden, you are looking uncommonly well."

And though she did not mean to, she blushed.

He realised his error at once. A woman such as herself would be entirely unused to compliments. He must be careful not to pay them, except in the most general way, in future.

After some polite enquiries after her health and that of the children, he told them all that he had a piece of news.

"I must ask you to rejoice with me. After entrusting me with some commissions—no doubt to see how I did—Lord Mountwalsh has offered me a position as his business agent.

His former agent is old and was anxious to hand the burden on. I must say, it's uncommonly good of him, and it would be hard to imagine a better employer."

They all congratulated him warmly.

"Where will you reside?" asked Tidy.

"There is an agent's house down at Mount Walsh. But he will require me to make frequent visits to Dublin. His affairs, as you know, are extensive."

"You will promise to visit us when you are here, I hope," said Tidy.

"Indeed I shall," said Stephen, giving them all a smile.

It was not until that night, as they sat in bed together, that Mrs. Tidy remarked softly to her husband: "Did you notice something when Stephen was here?"

"I think so. You are speaking of Maureen?"

"She loves him."

Tidy sighed, but said nothing.

÷

Stephen saw the telescope in August. He was on his way back from County Clare.

If anything confirmed for him the rightness of his decision to abandon politics, it had been the events of the last few weeks. With the Liberator gone, the confusion amongst the Repeal party had only grown worse. The Young Ireland men had found a rallying cry, however. The Famine was the fault of the British, they declared. And that armed revolt was the answer. It was everything his old master had tried to avoid. It was also futile. And, of course, they hadn't the least idea what they were doing. If Emmet's revolt had been a tragedy, this was a farce. Indeed, there hadn't been a revolt. But at the end of July, feeling they must do something, some of the Young Ireland leaders had tried to rouse some villages in Tipperary. The Tipperary men had asked for food but declined to revolt, and a few dozen of the political men had had a brief fight with the local police in a small field. Hearing of it, Stephen had felt saddened.

His visit to Clare had been depressing. Having almost disappeared the previous summer, the potato blight had returned. More than half the crop had been ruined. There would be no letup, therefore: the sad regime of starvation and chronic disease would continue for yet another year. If he had not already been hardened by what he'd seen before, it might have been more than he could bear. Or perhaps—he admitted it frankly to himself—the fact that he'd saved one person, and brought her to Dublin, was enough to ease his conscience now when he saw thousands more who were probably going to die.

But there was also the question of the land. It was not only the poor who were being dispossessed now. The process had gathered a terrible impetus of its own. Cottagers could not pay small farmers. The small farmers could not pay the larger farmers from whom they had sublet; the farmers could not pay the landowners. And many of the landowners, it turned out, were so deep in debt that they were now being forced to sell up. "If this goes on," Lord Mountwalsh had told him, "a large part of the west is going to be for sale."

The question was, what should the Mountwalsh estate be doing about it?

"The government in London wouldn't be sorry to see the western landlords go," the earl had continued. "They believe that most of them are feckless and irresponsible, that they should never have let the countryside get into the condition that gave rise to this Famine, and that they have been shamefully unwilling to help their own people. I can't say, insofar as it goes, that I would disagree."

"The British are equally at fault," Stephen pointed out, "in refusing to recognise that the problem is too big for a local solution."

"Indeed, and history will so judge them. It is truly remarkable to me that, even now, the English can be so utterly ignorant of a country that lies so close to them, and with whom they have so many ties. Anyway, what they are thinking now is that, as soon as the western landlords collapse and sell up, they can solve the problem by turning the place over to honest yeomen farmers, who will look after it better."

"And where will they find them?"

The earl smiled.

"When you think about it, they are saying the same thing now that their ancestors have been saying ever since they first encountered Ireland in the days of the Plantagenets, hundreds of years ago. The Tudors and Stuarts with their plantations were trying to do the same thing. Since the yeoman farmer is the backbone of England—and he is, Stephen—it is only natural that the English should suppose that the yeoman is all that is needed here. And such farmers do exist in Ireland, of course, many of Irish descent. We have them in Wexford. But they won't want to buy land in Clare, and nor will any rich farmers from England. So my belief is that as land in Clare becomes available, it will mostly be bought up by the richer local men. And the question is, should we buy any of it ourselves?"

Stephen had looked hard, talked to Charles O'Connell, and Mr. Knox, and many other local men. After three weeks, he had prepared a report. His conclusions were partly financial and partly political. But at the end of the day, he was sure what he would say: "The Mountwalsh estate and family have built up such a good reputation in Wexford that it would be wiser to reinforce that than risk dissipating it in Clare." Whether this was what the earl wanted to hear or not, he did not know.

He had been ready to leave when he had received a message from the earl, asking him to meet him in Offaly at the estate of a friend where he was staying, near Birr.

The great estate of Parsonstown, the home of the earls of Rosse, was rather what he had expected it would be, a noble place with a fine-looking castle. There was a considerable company there, and he was soon able to have some words with Lord Mountwalsh, who was eager to know his conclusions. He gave him the report but told him at once that he had advised against the investment in Clare.

"I was hoping you would," William said with a smile "I felt I must look at the thing properly, though. I'll read the report carefully, you may be sure."

Their host genially invited him to join the company at dinner, but as he was very tired, he begged to be excused—only to be told that if such was the case, he must spend the following day with them and dine tomorrow evening, before he returned to Dublin.

And he felt much refreshed after breakfast when their host announced to the company:

"For all those who wish, it's time to visit the telescope."

If aristocrats are tempted to be amateurs, this could not be said of the Parsons family. Each generation seemed to produce at least one serious expert in their field. The difference was that they could afford to finance their own research. In the case of their host, the results had been quite awesome.

The great telescope at the seat of the Earls of Rosse was a monster. Sitting majestically in its housing, like a huge cannon pointing at the sky, it weighed four tons. Technically a Newtonian reflector, its polished mirror dish, in which the light of the most distant heavens could be gathered, was six feet across, making it the largest telescope in the world. "They call it," William whispered to him, "the Leviathan."

"The dish is metal—speculum. We actually ground it here on the estate. But in particular, I want to draw your attention to the wrought ironwork on the telescope casing, because it was all done by Mary."

"You realise," William murmured with a smile, "that he means his wife."

"His wife did the ironwork?"

"Yes. She's an accomplished blacksmith. She made the gates to the estate as well."

It gave Stephen an interesting new light upon the aristocracy.

"We've only had this big one up and running for a few years," their host continued, "but it has proved its worth. My contention was always that many of the stars we see are not single entities at all, but clusters of stars themselves, of possibly vast extent." He drew out a paper. "Look at this. It is a meticulous ink drawing of a star that is in fact a nebula. This is what our big dish revealed. You can see, there are hundreds of stars there, and they are arranged in a huge spiral." He passed the paper round.

As Stephen gazed at it with Mountwalsh, he felt a strange sense of wonder and excitement, and William spoke for him, too, when he cried:

"By God, we know nothing of the universe. Nothing! This is truly wonderful."

As they all returned, William Mountwalsh pointed out various other members of the party to him. His own brother was there, with a university colleague; there was a local scholar landowner, a fashionable painter. "And that," William indicated a strong-faced, balding man who walked with a purposeful step, "is the great Professor William Rowan Hamilton, of Dublin. Have you ever heard of quaternions?"

"I have not."

"Well, nor had I. But he's the man who has discovered the formula for them, which to mathematicians is a matter of great significance. They say he's almost the equal of Newton. And he's an Irishman born." He smiled. "What a strange mixture Ireland is, Stephen. On the one hand, we have the tragedy and shame of the Famine, and in other ways, we lead the world."

"I wish," Stephen sighed, "that I'd more of an education."

"You've done well," the earl said, "but I know what you mean." And then he muttered something, which sounded like: "Have a son."

Perhaps he should have thought of it, but Stephen was quite unprepared, as they reached the house again, to find himself face-to-face with Caroline Doyle, or Caroline Barry, as he must call her now. She had just arrived with her husband, who was in another part of the house.

She greeted him pleasantly, and they talked, quite easily, for several minutes.

∻

"And the extraordinary thing was," he told them, "I felt nothing."

It was a week later and he was sitting in their parlour with the two Tidys. Maureen was sitting quietly in a corner. There were very few people with whom Stephen felt he could discuss personal matters, but for some reason, with the Tidy family, he felt secure enough to do so. As for the fact that Maureen was in the room, he didn't suppose it mattered.

"My feelings for her had been tender before, after all; and when she chose another, I suppose I must confess that, after the pain, I may have felt some anger." He smiled. "That was foolish of me. Unpardonable, perhaps. But I think I did."

The meeting with Caroline had really been very agreeable. Before him he had seen a pleasant woman, a little fuller in the figure than before, happy with her husband, the mother of a child. She had been entirely easy in his presence, and the fact that she no longer had any interest in him as a man had probably prevented his experiencing any renewal of his former desire. They had parted the following day as friends. "It is agreeable," he remarked, "that love can turn into friendship."

Mrs. Tidy regarded him with a mild expression. She was a small, neat woman with yellow hair that grew naturally into small curls.

"There is something even better, Stephen," she said. "That is when friendship turns into love."

"Ah, yes," said Stephen. "I'm sure that must be so."

"You are not very knowledgeable in the ways of the heart," said Mrs. Tidy kindly.

"Am I not?"

"No."

It was just before he left that Tidy took him to one side.

"I have a favour to ask," he said. Naturally, Stephen was only too anxious to do anything he could. "It concerns Maureen Madden," the Quaker explained. "When you rescued her, she was entirely alone in the world. And yet she has relations—a brother and two sisters—but where they are now, and whether they are even alive, she does not know. I wonder if you would talk to her, and then make enquiries, to see if anything could be discovered?"

"Certainly," said Stephen. And he agreed to return to interview her the following day.

✛

The year that followed was not easy for the Tidy family. As one of those involved in the provision of relief, Samuel Tidy travelled twice down to Cork and across to Limerick. Each time, he came back more depressed than before. Part of the trouble was the new scourge that arrived on the island in November.

The arrival of cholera was not a surprise. The disease had been pandemic across much of Europe for some time; it was almost inevitable that it would reach Ireland, too, and when it did, it found its way easily into the drains and water supplies of the ports and the market towns where huge numbers of weakened people were seeking shelter. It raged across the country for more than six terrible months, adding to the causes of mortality already so well entrenched.

"We now have a quarter of a million more workhouse places than we had before," Tidy remarked to his wife in the spring. At present, one inmate in eighty dies every week. That is two and a half thousand souls, or a hundred and twenty-five thousand a year. And that's just within the workhouses. In parts of Clare, I've been told, people are dying at four times that rate."

"Is it the workhouses themselves that are hastening the spread of the disease?" asked his wife.

"Possibly. But many of the people who enter the work-houses are dying already. One can hardly even blame the work-house guardians. The system is completely bankrupt, and the government still refuses to give them funds."

One small concession had come in February. The government had sent an extra £50,000 in relief. In England, it had caused a scandal. The *Times* of London had thundered that this extravagant gesture had "almost broken the back of British benevolence."

"I met a poor law official," he told her soon afterwards, "who intends to resign. He showed me the letter he's written. He says that he refuses any longer to be an agent of extermination."

But the worst moment for them both was when, one day, they found Maureen sitting in the kitchen. Upon the table was an English newspaper she had purchased that afternoon. On the page that was open, there was a cartoon. It showed a potato, large, blackened and rotting. But the potato also had a carica-ture Irishman's face, which appeared to be corrupt and suffused with greed. In its putrid roots, the potato held a bag of gold. And under this picture, was the single word ROTTEN.

Maureen had burst into tears.

Conditions on the eastern half of the island were far better than in the prostrated west. Indeed, there were signs of a slow recovery. But the stream of wretched folk still came daily into the capital. And Tidy could see no end to it.

Meanwhile, there was the frustrating business of Stephen.

÷

It did not prove easy to find any information. Stephen went to considerable trouble, but the displacement of people was so large that the chances of tracking a person down, especially a woman, were not good. He had started with Maureen's elder sister, who'd left for England. Since the start of Queen Victoria's reign in 1837, records had been kept of English births, marriages, and deaths. He had employed a clerk to search these. It did not appear that Maureen's sister had featured. She might have died somewhere unrecorded, of course. More likely she was living, unmarried, somewhere in England. He tried advertisements in the more obvious cities: London, Liverpool, Manchester. So far there had been no response. As for her brother, if William and his uncle had disembarked safely in America, they might be easier to find. But with the distances involved, that might take some time. Nuala, also, had vanished without trace. So many nameless people had succumbed already during the Famine that she could easily have died and left no trace. Enquiries in Wexford and Dublin elicited no response. But he kept trying.

And he was glad to help her. He admired her fortitude, and her grace under the circumstances. Each time he came to Dublin, he would come to see the Tidys and, at their request, spend a little time talking to her and telling her about what he was doing. Sometimes, she would politely ask about his own affairs—where he had been and what he had seen. She seemed to take an intelligent interest, though she would apologise for her ignorance.

"You have seen more of life, I dare say, than I," he assured her once.

"Life in the conditions we suffered is not really life, I think," she said.

The Tidys seemed rather proud of the talents they were encouraging in her. On one occasion, when he was offered a slice of rather fine cake, Mrs. Tidy announced: "This, I must tell you, Stephen, was made by Maureen. She has quite a talent in the kitchen. Indeed," she added, "Maureen really runs the whole household better than I do."

Naturally, he complimented her on the cake, which actually seemed excellent. But he was careful not to say too much in case she should blush again.

During the midwinter months, he was not in Dublin much, but at the start of March, the Tidys had a small gathering at their house which he attended, and during this, Mrs. Tidy and Maureen sang together at the piano. Mrs. Tidy had a sweet soprano voice, but Maureen, they had discovered, had a lovely contralto, and it had to be said that, dressed in a long gown that Mrs. Tidy had given her, she showed to advantage. When he applauded warmly and told Maureen that he did not know that she could sing, she replied simply: "I had not sung, Mr. Smith, for a long time. But I assure you we have been practising since Christmas."

Later, he had more conversation with her, and remarked that it must be a joy to use one's talent.

"I agree. You have so many talents, Mr. Smith, do you feel that you are able to use them all?"

"Not so many, I assure you." He thought for a moment. It was true that the agent's job for Lord Mountwalsh called for the use of many talents he possessed. It was both testing and satisfying. He smiled at her. "I think I use most." She was, he thought, a sensible woman.

"I think Maureen has a special kind of beauty, of the spirit as well as of the person," Tidy remarked to him quietly, afterwards.

"Indeed," Stephen said politely.

After he had left, Mr. Tidy remarked to his wife: "I think we made some progress."

"Perhaps. It is hard to tell with him."

"She let him see she liked him, I think."

"I made her."

"But I do not think he knows it. Perhaps she should do more."

"No, Samuel, she cannot. It is up to him now. He must show his interest, or she can do nothing."

In April, he came again. It was a fine day. There were spring flowers along the towpath, and Mrs. Tidy suggested he should take Maureen for a walk along it. As he had been debating whether and how to give her a piece of news he had received, Stephen readily assented. They walked, speaking a little, for about a mile westwards, then turned and slowly retraced their steps. The sun was pleasantly warm.

"You are rather silent today, Mr. Smith," Maureen ventured.

"I am thoughtful. You are right."

"Is there anything you wish to tell me?"

Was there? The report he had received was ambiguous. A young woman, thought to be named Nuala, and similar in description, had been found dead of a fever in a parish in County Cork, not far from the Wexford border. But should he tell her? The thing was so inconclusive. Would it help her to know, or distress her unduly? He had been trying to make up his mind all the way out. He stared at a willow tree.

"It is possible that Nuala may have died," he said at last. "But I cannot be sure."

"Oh." She seemed a little stunned. "I see." How pale she looked. How bitterly disappointed. He shouldn't have told her. "I must thank you for all the trouble you have gone to for me," she said with quiet dignity. "Is there any further information you can give me?"

He told her all he knew.

After they had walked on in silence for a little way, she began to weep, and so, not knowing what to do, he put his arm around her.

"I am so sorry," she said, "so sorry."

Yet two days later, when he called again before returning to Wexford, she surprised him with her powers of recovery. Not only was she self-possessed, but he saw that she had been reading the newspaper, and upon making some enquiries as to her views on the political situation, found her to be surprisingly well-informed. Not only that, but she made some shrewd and quite cynical observations upon political events, which interested him, truth to tell, far more than her cake or even her singing had ever done. Her face, he reflected, might be somewhat plain, but it had an intelligence that was quite pleasing.

He did not see her for another month. But in May he returned, and this time, he had news.

"We have found your brother William," he reported. There is no doubt about the matter. He is living in Boston. It seems that he had attempted to make contact with you, but had failed to find you and supposed you must be either dead or have moved away. I have his address, and also that of your uncle. Their circumstances are not especially prosperous, but they are employed and in good health." He smiled. "You are not alone in the world, then."

She thanked him deeply, and that evening, he joined the whole family to eat, and rejoice at this happy turn of events.

⁂

For Samuel Tidy, the month of June was very difficult. For it was then that the Quaker community, having won the admiration of all parties for its dedication to the welfare of Famine-stricken Ireland, finally announced that it had had enough. The Quaker relief work was ending. Was it the right thing to do? Samuel himself wasn't sure.

"One thing is quite certain," he told his family. "Neither the Quakers nor anyone else have the resources to feed the starving and help the sick. Only the government can do it. The problem is too huge for anything else." And there was another factor to consider. "So long as the government can persuade itself that the problems are being solved by others, I fear it will continue to do nothing. The Quakers cannot continue forever as an excuse for government neglect." While the argument was perfectly sound, he felt uncomfortable with it, and for several days his family found him to be quite short with them.

At the end of the month, his wife gave him a further piece of news.

"Maureen wants to go to America. She wants to be with her brother."

"Will anything change her mind, do you think?"

"Who knows? You can hardly blame her. He's the only family she has. And there is no other reason for her to stay."

"Has she written to her brother?"

"She means to go and seek him out instead."

"When will she go?"

"When she has the money. She has saved every penny we have given her. She hasn't enough yet, but soon . . ."

"Perhaps the fact she is going will cause Stephen . . ." He left the sentence unfinished.

"Perhaps."

He saw Stephen two weeks later, in Dublin, and informed him of this development.

"We shall miss her when she does go, I must say," Tidy said.

Stephen looked thoughtful.

"Yes," he replied. "Yes. I shall miss her, too."

"You'll wish to see her, no doubt, before she leaves."

"Oh, I will." Stephen frowned. "Certainly."

A week passed.

Then news came of a very different kind.

⌗

When Queen Victoria of England had come to the throne a dozen years ago, she had only been a girl of just eighteen. She was a young woman of thirty now, married to her German cousin, Prince Albert, and with a young family.

They were a charming young couple. Some, it was true, found Albert rather serious. He drank little, disliked bad language, and had a passionate belief in man's capacity to improve himself and the world. But he and his wife seemed to be utterly devoted to each other, and anxious to do right in every way. Nobody doubted their good intentions. All in all, therefore, they were well liked.

So it had seemed a good idea to the British cabinet, in the summer of 1849, that the royal couple should make a visit to Ireland.

"It will spread good feeling. Improve relations," they judged. "It will show that this wretched Famine is—to all intents and purposes—over."

Based upon this remarkable assertion, the visit was to take place in August.

⊹

Stephen had given the matter a great deal of thought. He was quite surprised himself by how much the thought of Maureen's leaving affected him. He supposed, because she was the one person he had been able to save from those terrible days in Ennis, when his own life, too, was in such a state of flux, that she had come to mean more in his imagination, and his heart, than she should. At a time when the continuing crisis in Ireland and the large volume of business he was transacting for the earl were keeping him as busy as he had ever been in his political life, her presence with the Tidy family had come to seem like a fact, a constant in his life. He wished she were not going. And he felt an urge to do something for her.

On a sunny morning in early July, therefore, he presented himself at the Tidy house and asked if he might have a private conference with her. She sat in the parlour.

"I could not let you contemplate leaving for America, Miss Madden," his words, for some reason, sounded oddly stiff, "without some token of my respect and warm feeling towards you." She was looking at him with an expression of uncertainty. "Indeed, I feel," he continued, "after all we have seen together, and the time in Dublin which has followed, that we have become true friends. I hope I may say so."

"I feel so, too, Mr. Smith," she said quietly.

"And so I hope that you will accept this from me, as a dear friend, who wishes you well and who will ever keep you in his thoughts." And he handed her an envelope. "You will find in there all that you will require for your voyage to America. For a cabin on a good ship. And something else besides, to ensure you have lodgings there. I beg you to accept this from one who would wish, most truly, to be your friend." He smiled. "Even a brother."

She was pale as a ghost. He supposed it was to be expected. She bowed her head.

"You have always been my benefactor," she said softly.

"It is my honour, Miss Madden, to be of assistance."

Still she could not look up.

"You saved my life, Mr. Smith. I shall remember it as long as I live. Forgive me if I express my feelings as they should properly be expressed, when I have collected myself." She rose.

"Of course."

She left the room.

He spoke to Mrs. Tidy before he left.

"She was moved, I think," he said.

"You gave her the fare to America? So that she could leave?"

"I did." He felt a glow of emotion at what he'd done, for it was no small sum of money, and he had given up a couple of months of his salary to do it.

Mrs. Tidy sighed. But she said nothing.

✢

It was a splendid August day when the royal yacht came in sight. It was not a large vessel, but decidedly handsome, sides painted black and gold, with a tall funnel, and the royal ensign gallantly flying from its masthead in the breeze. Everyone was excited as they saw it appear round the southern point of Dublin Bay.

Queen Victoria and her Consort might well have felt pleasure as they enjoyed that sunlit day. Wisely, their government had not thought it right that they should see the western part of the island, where, it had to be said, their subjects were not yet quite in a fit state to receive them as, doubtless, they would have wished. They had begun their visit in Cork, therefore, where the merchant community had made sure they received a splendid welcome. "Such kind, such loyal people," the young queen had innocently remarked. Today, they would visit Dublin, and thence to Belfast.

And what a charming prospect the royal couple must have enjoyed as they approached. Having come up from the south, past the lovely, volcanic mountains that graced the Wicklow coastline, and steamed past the high southern point, and Dalkey Island, the whole expanse of the bay would have suddenly opened up before them. By the shore, starting a few miles down the coast at Bray, they would have noticed another, man-made feature. For every few miles along this part of the coast there was now a small, grey-stone, round tower with gunrests and parapet, standing plump and stately by the shore. Martello towers, they were called, and they had been built there as a defence against invasion by Napoleon the generation before. They continued round the bay, past Howth, up to Malahide, and beyond. There was one at Dalkey, and another, only half a mile farther, at a charming little sandy cove beyond.

The harbour towards which the royal yacht was heading was not the great port of Dublin in the centre of the bay, but a smaller and altogether more elegant place, half mail boat terminal, half resort, that lay just a short way farther into the bay from Dalkey. Dun Laoghaire, this hamlet had once been called—but even though the English had learned that this barbarous-looking Irish name was simply pronounced Dunleery, they had decided to simplify matters and rename it Kingstown.

Apart from the mail packet, there had not been much activity there until the building of a jolly little steam train line out to Dalkey, fifteen years ago, had made the place easily accessible. And now, as well as the broad quay, a big church, and some gentlemen's villas, and pleasant stucco terraces overlooking the sea were starting to give the place a new air of gentility.

Along the quay today, a long temporary pavilion, with a blue and white striped canvas top, stretched out in gracious welcome. Above it, and on every available flagpole, St. George's flags flapped their bright red crosses in the sky. There was a red-coated guard of honour all smartly drawn up, and a brass band playing a patriotic melody to the awaiting crowds.

Just behind the official reception committee stood a company of aristocrats and gentlemen. And amongst these were Lord and Lady Mountwalsh, who, with typical generosity, had told Stephen to accompany them so that he should get a good view of the proceedings.

The Mountwalshes were greatly surprised, therefore, just as the royal yacht had rounded the point, to see the respectable but flustered figure of Samuel Tidy pushing his way through the crowd towards them.

"Stephen. Stephen Smith," he called. "You must come at once."

✢

As Tidy drove his pony and trap briskly along, he explained. He had written to Stephen at Mount Walsh, but the letter had missed Stephen, since he had left for Kildare, where he had been a week before getting to Dublin two days before.

"If you hadn't sent me a note yesterday to say you were in Dublin, and coming down here with Lord Mountwalsh, I shouldn't have known how to find you," the Quaker explained. "I hope Lord Mountwalsh will forgive my intrusion."

The two Mountwalshes had behaved with typical grace. "Oh, Stephen, you'll miss the queen," Lady Mountwalsh had cried, and given him a pitying look. "If he has to go, he has to go," said William. "But you'd better go quickly, Stephen, because you can't walk out on a monarch, you know. It's not allowed."

So now they rattled along from Kingstown up to Ballsbridge, over the Grand Canal and up to the Liffey, towards the docks where the steamer to Liverpool was due to leave.

There were several ways to reach America, but the most favoured was to cross to England, and there take the ship to New York or Boston. "I secured Maureen an excellent berth," Tidy explained, "on a first-rate ship from Liverpool. She'll travel in comfort, insofar as anyone can. And she has money left over when she arrives." The fact that he and his wife had augmented her savings still further was not something he needed to say. "But I knew you would not wish to let her depart without a word of farewell."

"No. Of course," said Stephen.

It was not until they were at the Liffey that Samuel Tidy said what was really in his mind. It came out quite suddenly.

"I must speak plainly with thee, Stephen Smith," he said, as they passed Trinity College. "This day decides whether you are a wise man or a great fool."

"How so?"

"Have you not understood that Maureen Madden loves you?"

"Loves me? She likes me, I think. She is grateful, I know."

"You do not realise, then, that you are loved? You have not seen what should be obvious to any man with half an eye, that for the last year at least, and perhaps much longer, she has suffered all the pain of a passion unrequited?"

"No. What makes you suppose this is so?"

"It has been plain enough to myself and Mrs. Tidy since the spring of last year. And two weeks ago, to my wife, upon some gentle questioning, she confessed the same. So there is the matter. I put it plainly before you. Have you any tender feelings towards her?"

"Yes. I think so."

"Would you consider making her your wife?"

"My wife?"

"You have a good position now. You are not ambitious for fortune. You have known what it is to suffer and to be grateful for life. Why have you never considered her? We cannot understand it. For there is no better thing in all the world—I speak from experience—than to have at one's side a woman who is loving and tender."

"This comes a little suddenly, Tidy. She has never said anything."

"Of course she has not. How could she? And you have done nothing yourself to encourage her. Quite the reverse. So I ask you plainly—is it really your wish that the woman who secretly loves you should now sail to America and never see you again?"

"I should have to consider the matter."

"The ship sails in less than an hour," said Tidy bluntly, and then said no more. He did not often speak so much, and he never meddled in the affairs of others; but his conscience had told him that he should take matters into his own hands, even at this late date, and he was glad that he had.

They had already crossed the Liffey. They were bowling towards the place where the cross-channel steamers left for Liverpool.

As they drew near, it was a dreary picture that met their eyes. There was the usual mess of barrels and crates, bustling porters and carters, loitering passengers and sailors on the quay where the ships were tied up. But there was also another, sadder, sight.

For the traffic in humans between Ireland and England was not a simple one. The majority of those at the dock were those who were leaving. The more fortunate would take ship to America, either in the relative comfort purchased to Maureen Madden, or in miserable steerage accommodation which might, or might not, prove healthy and safe enough during the long voyage. The less fortunate, not having the wherewithal to go to America, would sail no farther than Liverpool, and drift into the poorer parts of that huge port or one of the other industrial cities of England, where they might hope to find manual labour.

But there was another class nowadays, and it was a large one. For the Famine had produced a great army of the starving and the sick. And these wretched folk, having managed to make the crossing to Liverpool, had not remained there. For when the English authorities had looked at them and seen what they were—men and women too weak to work, and carrying disease—they had told the shipmasters: "Take them back. We cannot admit them here." And so back they would come, to their native land, and stand on the dock, helplessly, having neither place to rest, nor chance of escape. It happened every day.

There were about two hundred of these folk at the dockside now.

Ignoring them, Tidy pulled up near the steamer but behind a pile of crates, so that they should not be seen. He glanced at Stephen.

Stephen sat where he was. He did not speak. He did not move. He sat there for several minutes.

Then he started to move. Tidy looked at him.

"What will you do?"

"I shall fetch her."

Tidy put out his hand and took Stephen by the arm.

"You are sure? For her sake, you cannot change your mind. She has suffered enough."

"I am sure." Stephen smiled. "Truly, I am sure."

"I shall come with thee," said the Quaker.

So they went up the gangplank onto the little steamer, and on the deck they found Maureen, who had been looking out across the Liffey and had not seen them coming. And having not much time, Stephen went up to her and, after a few words expressing the tenderness of his feelings for her and the realization that he could not allow her to depart forever without acquainting her of those feelings, asked her gently if she would be his wife. And she stared at him, almost blankly at first, not knowing whether she had comprehended. So he said it again. And still she stared, very pale, almost numb. And Tidy smiled and said: "It's all right." But still she said nothing.

What could she say? For a time, in the comfortable Tidy house, she had felt a sense of healing and of warmth. She had felt ready to live again, and she had even dared to hope. But that had been weeks ago. Since then, something had quietly died within her again.

Then Stephen said that he was sorry that he should have asked her at such a moment when she would wish to have time to consider. And perhaps she might like to consider the matter on her way to Liverpool, and, if it was possible, give him her answer before the ship sailed to America; and that he would gladly await her decision in Liverpool.

Maureen said, very quietly, "I do not know," as if in a daze. But she did not mean that she did not know if she loved him, or whether she desired to marry him. She meant that she did not know if he truly wished it, or even, if he did, whether she—after so much time and so much pain—a woman of thirty now, who had never been kissed and lost all that she'd loved, could make him a wife.

Somewhere on the ship, a bell was rung and a voice cried out that those not sailing should soon disembark.

Then Tidy placed his arm around her and said to her:

"Come. You have nothing to lose."

Had she not? She could not tell.

"Come, Maureen, it will be all right."

So, her heart beginning to tremble suddenly so that, unable to help it, she started to shake, and held between the two of them, she let Stephen and Tidy lead her down the gang-plank and off the ship.

RISING

I T BEGAN, though he, Fintan, could not have foreseen the consequences, in the high, secret places in the Wicklow Mountains where the little streams gather and run down, like the River Liffey itself, into the wider world.

He did not know—as fathers often do not know—what influence he had upon the boy. But then, with his feelings for the place and the memories he had, how could he not pass them on?

He was a long-legged man, with a dark, hanging moustache and thinning hair that rose in brave spiralling curls from his head. He loved to put the boy on his shoulders and stride up into the mountains. And always he'd be telling him things. He couldn't help it. A year ago he'd taken Willy to Glendalough. God knows what the boy had understood. He'd only been six. "In my grandfather's day," Fintan had told him, "this was a strange sort of a place, all grown over, with a pagan reputation. 'There were junketings at Glendalough on mid-summer nights that cannot be spoken of,' he used to say. Until the priests put a stop to it, you know." Willy noted a certain wistfulness in his father's voice, even though its significance was unknown to him. Fintan had shown Willy the two lakes and the hermitage of St. Kevin and the monastery buildings with their round tower. "When I was young," he explained, "it was Sir William Wilde, the eminent surgeon from Dublin, that used to bring parties of people up here. But there was nothing of the pagan about him. He was all for uncovering the ruins and restoring the place. A distinguished old gentleman. He had a long white beard. And it's his son Oscar, the writer, that's made such a name for himself in London now with his plays." For if Fintan O'Byrne was not an educated man, he was a great reader of newspapers, and it was often surprising what he knew.

His grandmother was one of the numerous descendants of Patrick Walsh and Brigid, so he was aware that the blood of Walsh and Smith, as well as O'Byrne, ran in his veins. He was especially proud of being an O'Byrne however, for two reasons. The first was that, by tradition, he took it as a given that the estate of Rathconan, by rights, belonged to his family.

The second concerned his great-grandfather, Finn O'Byrne. For about a dozen years after Emmet's rebellion, Finn had returned to Rathconan with his family. It had been known that he'd had some part in Emmet's noble undertaking, but in the safety of his old age, when Finn had let people know that it was he who had killed the infamous Lord Mountwalsh, he had naturally become something of a local celebrity. Fintan himself had always been a law-abiding man, but he was certainly proud that his ancestors should include such a noble and heroic revolutionary as Finn O'Byrne.

But if he brought up his family to be proud of the area to which they belonged, and their place in it, there was one figure he insisted that they revere.

"Haven't I stood beside him in a mountain stream, just the two of us, like ancient Irishmen, panning for gold, to make a ring for Katherine O'Shea?" he would cry with pained emotion.

Parnell. Parnell the patriot. Parnell the leader, whose beloved home of Avondale lay only a few miles down beyond Glendalough.

And what was the word the boy would hear again and again—and with good reason—whenever that blessed name was said? "Betrayed, boy. Betrayed by his own. Betrayed by the priests as well, it has to be said. Betrayed."

"What else could the priests do," his mother would protest, "with him a known adulterer? They could hardly condone it." His mother's role was to ensure that religion was respected in the house. Willy understood. "It was the British that betrayed him. Murderers that they are."

Her own mother had lost all her family in the Famine before she came to County Wicklow. And she had brought up her daughter to know that it was the English policy of deliberate murder that had done it.

But it was a single day, in October, that Willy would remember best.

✢

"Come, Willy," said his father, "we'll go up to the big house and see Mrs. Budge." He smiled. "She won't eat you."

Willy was not so sure.

The return of Rose Budge to Rathconan that summer had been the subject of much curiosity. Though her father had left her the estate some years before, she hadn't been seen there for almost twenty years. Her husband, Colonel Browne, was scarcely remembered at all, though Willy had heard his father describe him once. "A great gentleman he was. And a hunting man. There wasn't a fence he wouldn't take. And a scholar too, I believe."

This last was true. It was really a tragedy that the Colonel and Rose had never had any children, for the Colonel was not only a fair mathematician, but an excellent linguist who had studied the cultures of India, to which his military service had taken him. Rose had never been brought up to be anything but the wife of an Irish landowner or military man; but having no children, she had perforce to join in her husband's interests or find herself rather lonely. And Colonel Browne, being a kindly man, shared as much with her as he could, without over-taxing her intelligence. As a result, her imagination had become like some large store room in an oriental bazaar, containing a random selection of exotic objects. And it was with all these memories of oriental customs, and huge Indian skies that, upon the untimely death of the Colonel earlier that year, she had returned—middle-aged, but still the same strong, rangy figure she had been in her youth—to take up residence, as the last of the Budges, at her ancestral home.

Willy and his father were shown into the library.

Though it had two windows and a fireplace, it was not a large room, and had never contained more than a modicum of books; but it had to be said that to enter it now was to be impressed.

For a start, the room was stiflingly hot. Though it was a warm October day outside, the windows were all tightly closed, and the fire was well stoked. The curtains had been almost drawn together, so that each window now appeared as a bright slit, through which the sunlight came like a knife. She must have taken a meal in there, for Willy's senses were affronted by the spicy, sweet, unfamiliar smell of curry, which permeated the air and made him feel slightly dizzy. On one wall there now hung a picture of an Indian temple under an orange sky which, it seemed, must also have smelled of curry. And in front of some empty bookshelves, in a black frame, there was a sepia photograph of an oriental wall carving of such startling eroticism that, if there was any chance the boy might have understood it, his father would have been obliged to cover his eyes. But it was not at the photograph, but at the figure of Mrs. Budge, that Willy was staring in alarm.

She was sitting upright in a wooden-backed chair, wearing a long, dark red gown and a turban.

Why she had started to wear this strange headgear was known only to herself. She had made it one afternoon in September, put it on her head, looked in the glass and, presumably, liked what she saw: for she had been wearing it ever since.

"Good afternoon, Mrs. Budge," said Fintan.

There had been some uncertainty, when she first arrived back, as to what she should be called. As the Colonel's widow, she was, of course, Mrs. Browne. But when the oldest member of the household, Mrs. Brennan, who had been cook to her father, tentatively called her by that name, the lady of the house had looked thoughtful and remarked, "I was always Rose Budge, when I was here before." And when, as an experiment, the cook called her "Mrs. Budge" the next time, she received a nod which seemed to indicate approval. So it was always "Mrs. Budge" now, which served as a gentle reminder that the family were still the masters of Rathconan.

And did she mean to keep the place? It seemed so. For when Mrs. Brennan enquired, "Will you be staying here a while, do you think, Mrs. Budge?" she had received the firmest of replies.

"Where else would I stay but at Rathconan, where my family has been for two hundred and fifty years?"

She looked at her tenant now, and asked him politely enough what he wanted.

"It's about my land, Mrs. Budge," he said. "We've been tenants on it as long as the Budge family has been here."

"And you've more now, I think, than was ever the case before," she remarked with a nod.

If the Famine had taken lives—and over a million had died—it was the larger process the blight had set in motion that had really changed the face of Ireland—eviction. In the years of the Famine and those that followed, the evictions had continued at a staggering pace. In the west of course, but in most parts of Ireland also, not tens but hundreds of thousands of families had been pushed out of their small, subdivided, and unprofitable holdings. Clusters of cottages, each with an acre or two, had been pulled down and put under plough or returned to pasture. In some areas, entire populations had receded, like an ebbing tide, from the land. Sometimes, large landholdings were left untenanted, or let to shrewd-eyed graziers. Often, the more successful tenants gained larger farms. An individual tenant was far more likely to be farming fifteen, thirty, or more acres, nowadays. And the new generation had learned a terrible lesson: the farm would not be subdivided now; it would pass on intact, to a son who, like as not had married later than his father had, and whose brothers would have to go out and make their own way in the world.

In a way, it might almost be said that the English, who had always dreamed of populating Ireland with sturdy yeoman farmers, had got their wish—except for two differences: these family holdings were not English Protestant, but Irish Catholic farms; and with the memory of the Famine always hanging like a great cloud of anguish over the land, the farmers desired only to secure their hold upon their farms and, as soon as God granted, to see the usurping English landlords depart from them, never to return.

The case of Fintan O'Byrne was of this kind. The clearances at Rathconan had not been wholesale like those in the west, but Mrs. Budge's father had cleared out the subdivided holdings, and Fintan's father had been one of the beneficiaries. The potato fields that had extended up the ancient hillside had been returned to grazing pasture now—though you could see their outlines clearly—and Fintan was tenant of dozens of acres, where his relations before the Famine had survived on little patches. In short, Rathconan had returned to something more like its traditional state, when Fintan's ancestors had grazed their cattle upon the mountain slopes. And if Fintan had his way, the ownership of the land would soon return to him as well.

"It's my security I have in mind," he said.

"You're a good tenant, I know," she answered. "And there are no Captain Boycotts here."

It was forty years since the Tenants League had started to agitate for tenants' rights in Ireland. Great men had taken the tenants' side. In England, Gladstone, the powerful leader of the Liberal party, successors to the Whigs, had designed new laws to give them some protection. Most important of all, Parnell had been their champion. But progress had been slow. When, fifteen years ago, a new potato blight had started another wave of evictions—not without some violence—Parnell had given his famous order. Do not speak, he told the Irish, to any man who evicts his tenants; have no dealings with them, let them be isolated. "Shun them," he commanded, "like a leper of old." Captain Boycott, an agent responsible for numerous evictions, had been especially singled out. Since then, tenants had gained some further protections, but still not enough.

"I was wishing to purchase the land I rent from you."

"To buy it?"

"The Act allows . . ."

She gave him a stony look.

"I know about the Act."

It was a tribute to the effectiveness of Parnell in the London Parliament that not only the Liberals, but even the Tory party had now taken up the case of the Irish tenant. The government now wanted to encourage the tenant to buy his own land; and the latest legislation even offered a government loan to help him do so. If in his heart Fintan resented having to pay anything to recover land that, in his view, had been taken from him in the first place, he wouldn't deny that the terms offered were quite attractive. "Four percent over forty-nine years. Over time that will be less than the rent I'd be paying," he had calculated. Nor could Mrs. Budge have been surprised that he made the request. All over Ireland, during recent years, land had been changing hands from Protestant landlord to Catholic tenant at a remarkable rate. More than twenty-five thousand tenants had already taken up the government loans.

"I suppose," she continued quietly, "it's Home Rule you'll be wanting next."

He was silent. He wouldn't deny it.

Willy looked at the strange lady in her turban, and tried to work out how it was that the open mountain acres he knew and loved so well could depend upon the will of this being from another world in her frightening, spice-laden cocoon. The colour of her eyes was blue. That much seemed familiar. Her hair, and her face itself, it seemed to him, were drawn back and up into the tight recesses of that turban. Her features carried no expression that he could recognise.

"I will consider the matter, Fintan, and we shall speak in a few days," she said finally.

Once outside, relieved to be in the fresh air, Willy turned to his father.

"Shall we own our land again?" he asked.

"Perhaps." His father sighed. "But God knows what passes in that woman's mind."

✢

After they had gone, Rose Budge sat very still in her chair, thinking. She did not know why Fintan had brought the boy with him, to have the child standing there staring at her with eyes like saucers. Well, what of it? She must concentrate upon the matter in hand. She stared at the bright, intrusive slit of sunlight—the sunbeams, like so many thieves, softly stealing into the warm comfort of her home.

So it had come to this. She did not blame Fintan O'Byrne. It was not he, but the man whom, no doubt, he worshipped, that was the cause of all this. Damned Parnell.

Though they were neighbours and belonged to the same Protestant landowner class, the Budges had never cared for Parnell. "He has an American mother," her father had always said. "That's probably what's the matter with him." She herself had been abroad during his parliamentary career, but she had been kept well-informed.

And scandalised. How could it be that Parnell, a Protestant

landowner like herself, should so entirely have assumed the mantle of Daniel O'Connell? For that was what Parnell had done when, a dozen years ago he had burst, like a meteor, over the parliamentary sky. True, he could not be the champion of the Catholic Church. But he was the champion of the Catholic tenant and he had a formidable organisation. Moreover, he had taken O'Connell's tactics to new heights, several times holding the balance of power in the British House of Commons and ruthlessly compelling both parties to legislate for the good of Ireland.

And if Daniel O'Connell had hoped for the eventual Repeal of the Union with England, Parnell had been more blunt. He demanded Home Rule, loudly and firmly; he had even pushed Gladstone to introduce a Home Rule Bill into Parliament. Personally, she had thought the whole thing folly. Even if the Ascendancy families like her own could be cowed or cheated into submission, there were others in Ireland made of sterner stuff. If the London men supposed that the Presbyterians up in Ulster would stand to be ruled by Catholics, they'd have a rude awakening. Lord Randolph Churchill had been correct when he had warned them: "Ulster will fight. And Ulster will be right." Thank God Gladstone's foolish measure had been smashed by conservative opposition. But that hadn't quietened Parnell. In no time he'd had the Tory government doing everything it could, short of granting independence, to keep the Irish contented. Including this wretched business now of giving Fintan O'Byrne money to buy her out.

"Traitor." She said the word out loud to the listening room. A man who betrayed his class. Worse: because of him, the whole British Parliament was turning against their own kith and kin, the Irish Ascendancy. To pay the Catholics to buy us out of our homes, where we've been for centuries, and leave us to retire like servants pensioned off—to what? An apartment in Dublin or a suburban villa in England—we who were lords of the wide lands of Ireland? "Traitor." She said it again, to the fire.

At least, people said, he was a parliamentary man. There were others in Ireland who'd use other means entirely, murder even, to reach their ends. But weren't some of those devils followers of Parnell, too? Some years ago, in Phoenix Park, the Chief Secretary, poor Lord Frederick Cavendish, had been murdered by extremists. At the time, she'd read that Parnell was behind it. Everybody nowadays told her no, it was all a forgery, he'd nothing to do with it. That might be the case. She couldn't say. But he was a villain even so.

He'd been punished, anyway. She wasn't sorry. She'd heard that he'd been living with a woman not his wife, but the estranged wife of another. Mrs. O'Shea, they said, was a nice woman, and her husband had no interest in her. And certainly, those being the circumstances and after all those years, for O'Shea to have divorced her and named Parnell was quite uncalled for. It wasn't what a gentleman would do at all. And it had destroyed the man. The English wouldn't stand for it. Nor would the Catholic Church in Ireland, which had never been so pleased at his being a Protestant in the first place. They'd driven him out of politics. He was destroyed.

It was a poor end, certainly. But she wasn't sorry.

The question now was, what to do with the mess Parnell had created on her own doorstep? What should she do about Fintan O'Byrne?

The next morning, she went down to Wicklow. For this expedition, she did not wear her turban, but a felt flower-pot hat. In Wicklow, she went straight to the offices of her solicitor, Mr. Quinlan Smith. After listening to her carefully, he nodded and asked her a single question.

"Do you want to sell this farm to Fintan O'Byrne?"

"Certainly not."

"Might I ask why?"

"Because," she answered truthfully, "it is mine and my family's, and I didn't come half-way round the world just to give it all away."

"You feel you belong here."

"Of course I belong here. Where else would I belong?"

"I understand." He nodded thoughtfully. "Though you might be surprised at how many people, with families just as old, are selling up now." He paused. "I need hardly tell you that there's no reason for you to sell if you do not wish to."

"Good."

The interview could have ended there, but she did not move. He gave her a moment or two, and then gently probed.

"You still feel concern, perhaps."

"Perhaps."

"You are concerned that your refusal might cause bad feeling?"

"I'm not afraid of him, if that's what you mean."

"The thought never occurred to me," he answered gently.

"I haven't been there for so many years," she said, a little sadly. "Half the people I used to know are dead. I'm living among strangers, in my own home. But I have to live with them, you see."

"Indeed."

"If my husband were here, it would be different. It's a funny feeling: I hardly know Fintan O'Byrne. I remember him as a boy, but I scarcely know what sort of man he is."

"He has no bad reputation. If he did, I should certainly know." He considered. "Things have changed in the years of your absence, of course. And I think they will change more. But I am quite sure that, within a little time, you will come to feel yourself as much at home with the people at Rathconan as ever you did before. They are still the same sort of people. Do you wish me to speak to O'Byrne?"

"I think I'd better do it myself."

"I agree. I shall be in the vicinity of Rathconan, as it happens, next week. Perhaps I might call in at that time."

She indicated with a nod that this would be gratefully received.

"I should recommend, if I may, that you might care to visit Wicklow from time to time, and Dublin also. There is always plenty to do, and it is an admirable way of keeping in touch with public opinion in these changing times." He smiled. "Speaking of which, have you heard the latest news? I was just given word of it this morning?"

She shook her head.

"Parnell has died. He'd been sick for some time, as you may know. He died in England, in Brighton, down by the sea. I understand that his wife, that was Mrs. O'Shea, was at his side." He sighed. "He was only forty-five, you know."

It was still light when she got back to Rathconan. She sent for Fintan at once. He came, accompanied by the boy. She couldn't imagine why the child was there again.

"I'm sorry, Fintan," she told him, "but I can't let you have that land. Not at present, anyway."

"I'm sorry to hear that, Mrs. Budge."

"Well, there it is." She nodded, to indicate that she had nothing more to say. Then, as he turned to go, she thought of something. "By the way, I heard in Wicklow today: Parnell is dead."

"Dead?" He winced as if he had been struck, then bowed his head and left, without any further word.

She watched him. She did not think to look at the boy.

✛

Willy had watched everything carefully. He had seen his father denied his land. Also, it seemed to him, the casual way Mrs. Budge threw the death of Parnell in his face was a deliberate insult to hurt and humiliate him. On the way home, he realised that his father was so close to tears that he did not dare speak to him.

The next day, he heard his father say gloomily to his mother:

"We'll never get our land back until that woman's dead."

Two weeks later, his father told him:

"You're to go down to your aunt's in Dublin, Willy. You're to go to school down there."

"But I want to stay at home," he cried.

"It's for the best. I want you to have an education, Willy. You'll do very well, I know. And you'll be up here all the holidays."

He could not tell why, but he was sure that his father's interview with Mrs. Budge and his own exile from his home were in some way related.

⊰ 1903 ⊱

Sheridan Smith looked out of his capacious window at the mist and wondered if they'd all find their way to the house. He supposed they would. It was easy enough: straight down Baggot Street from St. Stephen's Green, over the canal, continue a furlong, and turn right. A fool could do it. And besides, the mist was lifting. An hour ago you couldn't even see the house across the street.

He did not care to admit it, but he was enough of a snob to be a little anxious. For the Count was coming. And the Count had never been to his house before.

Wellington Road was a very pleasant place. Broad, lined with little trees, its handsome terraces set well back behind long lawns and gravel paths, it had almost the atmosphere of a leafy Parisian boulevard. It was part of the well-managed Pembroke family estate, which included the former villages of Ballsbridge and Donnybrook. Together with Ranelagh and Rathmines to the west, they formed a collection of genteel suburbs south of the Grand Canal, but all within a mile or so of St. Stephen's Green, where lawyers, civil servants, financial and professional men, with perhaps more Protestants than Catholics, could escape both the old city's municipal taxes, and the poor folk who infested its tenements and streets.

Sheridan Smith and his family liked to have company at

Sunday lunch, and the company was usually good. Sheridan's position as a newspaper editor would in any case allow him a wide circle of acquaintance, but he made a point of cultivating friendships in every quarter. It was something the Smith family had learned from the Mountwalshes.

There was no question, the family of Stephen Smith and Maureen Madden had done remarkably well. They had had three children: Mary, followed at intervals by the two boys, Sheridan and Quinlan. Stephen had remained as agent to the family for the rest of his working life, and no doubt the frequent contact with that aristocratic family had been a useful influence on his children. Sheridan was a man of some position in Dublin. His brother Quinlan Smith, down in Wicklow, was the same way on a smaller stage. And since his own temperament inclined towards the theatre and the arts, as well as politics, Sheridan Smith's range was broad indeed. "I can open every door in Dublin," he liked to say to himself—not out loud, of course; but he was glad if people knew it.

Sheridan had married quite well—his wife belonged to the branch of the MacGowans with the most money—and they lived, if not in one of the largest, still in a very comfortable house on the northern side of the street; for all the houses in Wellington Road were good.

Sheridan quickly went over the company he was expecting. His mother first: widowed for nearly twenty years now, Maureen Smith was still an upright, active woman, with a sharp mind. Then Father Brendan MacGowan, a cousin of his wife's, who was bringing a young man he wanted him to do something for. Sheridan had asked young Gogarty, too. That was a lively fellow who'd go far. A gentleman also. He'd put up a good show. And then the Count and Countess: "The aristocratic side of my family," as he'd said to his wife with a smile.

It must have been a shock to the Mountwalsh family when the old earl's youngest grandson had fallen in love with Stephen Smith's daughter, Mary. But they had been very gracious about it; and the marriage had taken place. Sheridan had

still been only a boy at the time. Mary's daughter Louisa and
he had always been rather friendly. And Louisa had made
things even more interesting, it seemed to him, when she had
married a most elegant older man, Count Birne. Louisa and
the Count now divided their time between County Meath,
where they had bought an estate, and Paris. In Dublin for a few
days now, they had promised to come to the Sunday meal and
would be bringing their little daughter.

Should he have striven for a more distinguished company?
Of course not, he told himself. This was a family occasion. This
was solid, middle-class Dublin, and none the worse for it. He
was conscious also that, although the old landed aristocracy carried huge prestige, it was actually his own sort—more so with
every year that went by—who were determining the course of
affairs in Ireland. If the Count ever had any desire to take part
in the public affairs of Ireland—though, it had to be said, not a
hint of such a notion had ever been apparent—he'd probably be
quite glad, Sheridan told himself, to be related to me.

And now, faintly through the mist, he heard the ring of a
bell, and a little toot from a horn, and, in brisk style, his first
guest, half an hour early, came rapidly along the street on a
bicycle.

÷

Willy O'Byrne walked briskly. He had been on a small errand.
But it wouldn't do to miss Father Brendan MacGowan and,
perhaps, his destiny. "Don't be late," the priest, who knew him
well, had said, "for I shan't wait for you."

Montgomery Street. It ran at a sleazy slant only a hundred
yards behind the sleek Palladian presence of the Custom House
on the Liffey's northern bank. Sublime Georgian Dublin stared
graciously over the water towards Trinity, while at its backside,
like a genial sewer, ran the city's other life. Monto—street of
whores, street of his sin and shame. Necessary street. Quiet,
almost empty for once, on a Sunday morning. He passed down

THE REBELS OF IRELAND

it, ducked along Abbey Street, and out into the broad grandeur of Sackville Street, that marched grandly northwards from the river like a military parade. Respectable again. He proceeded south. Across the Liffey. He could have done it blindfolded.

City under a white mist. It was as if all the waters from mountain and stream had met the exhalations of last night's humanity—its drunkenness and its dreams, its whispers and its breathings—and that the two had coalesced, *e pluribus unum*, dissolving into this dank mist over the Liffey that hung by the bridges as if reluctant to leave Dublin and be gone, into the open sea.

It clung to him in dingy droplets, enveloped him. You could not escape it.

He hurried past the entrance to Trinity College. No point in glancing through its portals, since he wouldn't be going there. Then, keeping its wall on his left, he walked eastwards with the shops on his right, past Dawson Street until, soon afterwards, he saw the shuttered bookshop where he was to meet him.

Willy tapped on the shutters, as instructed. A moment or two later, a door beside him opened, and the priest came out. Crinkly grey hair, a little stout, friendly, purposeful: Father Brendan MacGowan closed the door behind him with a sharp bang, extracted a small silver watch from a pocket, glanced at it, and smiled.

"You're on time," he said, surprised. He gave a nod at the tightly closed green shutters behind him. "My brother's bookshop," he said. "Do you know my brother?"

He knew all about him. MacGowan's bookshop was a world of its own, over which the priest's younger brother presided in a silent manner. If you dared to touch any of the books, it was said, he had a nasty way of half-closing one eye and staring at you with the other, so that people called him the Cyclops. Willy had heard that if he liked you, he was pleasant enough.

"I don't," he said.

The priest was already sailing along at a good clip.

"There are three of us, you know," he remarked. "My elder brother has the farm. My father bought it. Up in County Meath." He waved, vaguely, in the direction of Tara. "I became the priest, and my younger brother has the shop. Your aunt and uncle are both well, I hope?"

His uncle, who had married his father's sister, had a job with the Guinness Brewery. You couldn't do better than that. Set for life, once you got in there. Good pay. Always looked after. The great brewery buildings and their associated smells rose like some huge, incense-laden temple, as if the city had a third, nondenominational cathedral out west of the Castle towards Kilmainham barracks. Generations of a family would work in there, secure in the knowledge that the holy black liquid they produced was the healthy life-blood of the people. Had his father hoped that his uncle, having only daughters but no living son, might find a place for him there, from which, perhaps, he might even rise into a position of minor authority? Had his father hinted something of the kind to his uncle, that day, when he had come into the city and, with his uncle, taken him, Willy, out to the pub as a father should, for the formal initiation into manhood—the taking of a tankard of the same liquid? Willy didn't know, but no such suggestion had ever been proffered; and he was secretly glad of it, for although he hadn't the slightest objection to the brewery, it would have been awkward to have to refuse such a gift.

"Yes, Father."

They were well. They were very well. They were snugly well. They breathed the thick mist of Dublin and were sustained by it.

"And your cousins? They've three daughters I believe."

"Yes, Father." Thriving. If a man's best hope was the Guinness Brewery, a woman's was just half a mile south of the Castle, close to St. Patrick's Cathedral. For here a sister temple arose: The Jacobs Biscuit Factory.

If the Quakers had long been making a quiet contribution to the commerce, and the welfare, of Ireland, some of them

had now been raised, by their diligence, into a veritable patri-
archate: Jacobs, Newsoms, Bewleys, they controlled great
wealth. Jacobs Cream Crackers and the brightly coloured
Jacobs Biscuit tins were known over much of the globe. And in
the usual Quaker fashion, the Jacobs were good employers,
with about fourteen hundred men and women working in
Dublin, and more brought in for the Christmas rush. The
women were paid less than the men, of course. The men would
have been outraged otherwise. But two of his aunt's three
daughters were earning quite well, with piecework, in the
bakehouse.

"Here we go," said Father MacGowan, as they turned up
Kildare Street. On the corner, its dark redbrick portals and
cavernous marble halls rising like a rampant oriental palace,
stood the Kildare Street Club, bastion of social might. Could
Father MacGowan enter those portals? Willy wondered.
Probably not. He, for certain, would never set foot in the place
unless in some menial capacity. For all he knew, there might be
a maze underneath it, and a minotaur.

Then came the National Library, and Leinster House, and
the National Museum. He could enter there, at least. They
came out at the top of the street and into St. Stephen's Green.
"Ah," said Father MacGowan, "the Shelburne Hotel. That is
the place where you meet the best people." And then, by a
train of thought that was not quite apparent to Willy: "You
have never thought of entering the priesthood, I suppose?"

He had not been to the best of schools, the Jesuit schools;
but, albeit often at the end of a strap, the Christian Brothers
had taught him thoroughly. He was deemed to be intelligent.
Possible material for the priesthood, therefore. Another kind of
security was being offered, better than the brewery perhaps.
There was a prestige in being a priest, too. Your family was
proud of you. Not to mention the enhancement of your soul.

"I suppose I should like to marry some day," he answered.

"Well," said Father MacGowan, "we shall have an excellent
meal, I am sure, with Sheridan Smith."

✠

Oliver St. John Gogarty was something of a young hero. Scholar, poet, athlete: Mahaffy at Trinity College said he was the best pupil he'd ever had. And he had taught Oscar Wilde, too—though of course, since the trial and disgrace, Wilde's name was not one to be mentioned, under any circumstances, in Dublin now. Gogarty had won the poetry prize three times, an astounding feat, favoured Greek metre over predictable English pentameters, and was an accomplished practical joker as well. With his smoky blue eyes and his thick brown hair flecked with fair highlights, he resembled, if not a Greek god, at least a Hibernian hero.

"I tried to bring my friend Joyce," he had remarked pleasantly to his host when he had parked his bicycle, "but he wouldn't come."

Sheridan Smith wasn't entirely sorry. He didn't know Joyce, but he was well aware that Gogarty, who was a generous fellow, swore by the young man's genius, and promoted his reputation at every opportunity. Not, he felt sure, that young Joyce could possibly be in the same league as Gogarty himself. Besides, Gogarty was a gentleman and poor Joyce, he'd heard, was not. He thought of Joyce and the Count and was glad of the young man's absence.

"Father MacGowan's bringing a poor young student with him," he told Gogarty. "If I'm occupied, would you be nice to him?"

✠

When Willy Byrne approached the house, he felt some trepidation. It had been kind of Father MacGowan, who'd only come to know him because he came to give classes occasionally at the school, to have taken an interest in him. Apart from the priest, and the very limited resources of his own family, he had no one to sponsor him in the world. As he entered Wellington

Road and saw the big, bland terraces staring down at him mistily, he realised suddenly that he had never been inside such a house before. Though the priest hadn't said so directly, it was obvious that he hoped their host might do something for Willy. But what if he made a bad impression? Would that make the priest lose interest in him? What should he say?

"Just observe," Father MacGowan said,. as if reading his thoughts. "Answer politely when spoken to. You'll do very well. I wouldn't have brought you here otherwise. Well, here we are."

Three minutes later, rather pale, he was silently observing for dear life. He'd never been faced with a Count before.

You could see that Count Birne was not entirely well. He was tall and he was thin; he was wearing one of the new, double-breasted jackets, and trousers with turn-ups—a fashionable elegance hardly· seen yet, even in the Kildare Street Club, of which he was a member. His black hair, streaked with grey, was parted near the crown of his noble head. He wore a moustache, parted neatly in the middle and brushed along the lip. His nose was somewhat larger than one might have expected from such an exquisitely manicured figure. In his right hand, between his second and third fingers, he languidly held a Turkish cigarette. His eyes, brown and melancholic, gazed down with soft good manners at whomever he was talking to—which in this case was young Gogarty, who seemed to take such a personage entirely in his stride. In answer to Gogarty's question, as to the provenance of his title, he answered quietly:

"I am a Count of the Holy Roman Empire."

You could tell he was not well from the way, very discreetly, he leant against the ebony walking stick he held, at a slight angle to the back of his thigh, in his left hand. From his answer, however, Willy derived one piece of comfort. At least this daunting person was a Catholic.

His own companion was old Mrs. Maureen Smith, who asked him about himself, and was easy to talk to. By and by, while Father MacGowan spoke to the Count, Gogarty came over and chatted in a friendly way. Willy learned that he planned to become a doctor. Gogarty was only a little older than he was, but Willy could see at once how great the young man's advantages were compared to his own. He'd never met someone of that age who had such social ease and graces. Various children appeared. The countess had disappeared upstairs with her own daughter who, it seemed, had chosen her arrival at the house as a moment to be sick. The countess came down in due course, without her daughter. She was elegant, but entirely friendly. Then they all sat down to eat.

The Sunday family meal at Sheridan Smith's was a very relaxed affair. The children ate with the grown-ups, but at a certain point were excused. Only then did the conversation become more interesting.

And to his surprise, Willy quickly discovered that, rather than be questioned about his own exalted life, the Count was anxious to know the opinion of the company on a number of matters. "I have not spent enough time in Ireland during the last few years," he explained, "and each time I return, I become more confused." He smiled. "Some years ago, we heard much of Home Rule. For ten years now, we have heard less. But now I see that Mr. Redmond, who occupies the place that Parnell had, leads no less that eighty MPs in the British Parliament, and hopes for Home Rule once again.

"We used to hear of extremists, too, who were ready to use violence to turn the British out. What has happened to them? Have they disappeared? Meanwhile, the British government seems to do all it can to destroy the old Protestant interest. So what does it mean? Is the ghost of Parnell to rise from the grave? Are we supposed to be British or Irish, Protestant or Catholic?" He looked round the table. "Father MacGowan, tell me, where does the Church—my Church—stand?"

"I shall tell you exactly," said the priest with a smile.

"Which means, since he has a Jesuitical streak," said Sheridan Smith with a smile, "that he won't tell you at all."

The priest blandly ignored him.

"Many of the priests, and even some of the bishops, remembering the heady days of Daniel O'Connell, have been somewhat inclined to support the movements for Home Rule."

"Though they destroyed Parnell," his host reminded him.

"They could not ignore his adultery," Father MacGowan said reasonably. "Not once it became so public." He took a sip of wine. "But that is not the point. What really mattered, and what matters still, is that the view—I should say the indomitable personality—of Cardinal Cullen prevailed. He condemned the extremists, of course. That need not be discussed. But he refused to allow the Irish Church to become involved in politics whatsoever, on either side. Remember, when the British government offered to subsidise the Catholic Church along with the Church of Ireland and the Presbyterians, he would not take their money. And when you look at the spate of Catholic church building in the last three decades, we seem to have done very well without it. The Church will not stoop, therefore. If we are to keep our authority, we must be above such things. The fact that he spent so many years in Rome no doubt helped to give him a larger view than many of the local priests. And in the long run he will be proved right. Then the Church will take its proper place, as the higher authority, when Ireland becomes independent, which she will."

"You think it will?"

"Without a doubt. Redmond and his IPP have eighty seats. They will press the government until the British are sick of them. And sooner or later, just as happened with Parnell before, some future election will leave them with the balance of power. Home Rule will be the price. It may take time. We must be patient. But it will come."

"I see," the Count remarked with a gentle smile, "that you have not entirely abandoned politics yourself. But tell me, Sheridan, is that your view, too?"

"It is not. And I will make a quite different prediction." Their host considered. "Firstly, there is a weakness in your political case, Father. Redmond may hold the balance of power in the House of Commons and get a bill passed. That has happened before, with Gladstone's Home Rule Bill. It's the British House of Lords who will throw the measure out, and I suspect they will do so until Doomsday." He glanced round them all. "But it does not matter anyway. Because the present British policy towards Ireland is going to work."

A few years ago, when the British took local government out of the hands of the Protestant gentry and effectively gave it to local, mostly Catholic men—merchants, tradesmen, solicitors—the landowners had effectively lost their power, he reminded them. This August, a new and improved Land Act had just been passed.

"And have you looked carefully at its terms? They are quite extraordinary. Effectively, the British government is buying out the Ascendancy. Ten years from now, the Protestant Ascendancy will be over. Completely. Ireland will be a land of Catholic farmers.

"I suppose that Redmond and his men will still try for Home Rule. But if they can't get it, I doubt very much whether many people in Ireland are going to care enough to make a fuss."

Sheridan Smith had done. He looked quite pleased with himself. The Count nodded thoughtfully. His eyes travelled round the table. They stopped at Willy.

"And what, I wonder, does this young man think?" he asked kindly.

Willy felt himself go pale.

They were all watching him. What was he supposed to say? Was he going to offend somebody and ruin his chances here? He glanced about. Gogarty was watching him, curious. Damn it. No doubt he'd have something clever to say. He looked at Father MacGowan and the priest smiled at him, encouragingly. Encouraging him to do what, for God's sake? He took a deep breath.

"My father is a tenant. All he wants is to buy his land." He paused. Everybody was nodding. That was all right, then. He could shut up. But even as he relaxed, the image of his father and Mrs. Budge came into his mind. Then he thought of his mother, and of her anger, too. He'd told them the truth—but not the whole truth. Did Father MacGowan know that? Was he, as he might have been in the confessional, waiting for something more, wanting the good stuff? As if sensing his hesitation, nobody had spoken yet. He looked down at the table, and then—fool, no doubt, that he was—he let his conscience lead him. "But the truth is that neither he nor my mother will really be happy until every Protestant Englishman is out of Ireland, and Ireland is free."

Ah. It was said. A tiny intake of breath seemed to pass round the table. Had he just destroyed himself? Certainly he'd just contradicted, and probably annoyed, the newspaperman who might, perhaps, have given him a job. He had failed before he had even started. He was doomed.

The Count, knowing nothing of such mundane matters, seemed pleased. Gogarty, understanding better, cheerfully leaped in.

"He's absolutely right, of course," he cried. "I'd have said the same thing. But do you know what I fear most, when we have our independence?"

"I don't," said Sheridan Smith with a smile, appreciating what was done, "but I know you're going to tell us."

"That terrible Lady Gregory," said Gogarty with feeling.

People laughed. "Unfair," said Sheridan Smith. "Cruel, Gogarty." But Willy did not laugh. He knew that Gogarty spoke half in jest, yet still the jest affronted him.

Lady Gregory, the widowed Galway landowner who, all alone, had set herself to learn the Irish language.

She was not alone. There was quite a movement, nowadays, to celebrate the rich Celtic heritage of Ireland. The image—the magnificence of the old illuminated books, the Celtic crosses and artefacts with their echoing designs—that was easy to admire. But the word: that was harder. The Irish language was not an easy thing to learn, unless you had it from birth. It had been prevalent in the west, but the great exodus and dislocation of the Famine had reduced the Gaelic tongue to the corners of Connacht and the wilder places nowadays. Many had thought that the language might be lost.

Yet dedicated men had rescued it. Yeats, the poet, had caught its inspiration and mined its lore. Hyde, a Protestant son of the manse with a German wife, had founded the Gaelic League—Conradh na Gaeilge, to save the old language from extinction, and now it was promoted widely. He'd even scandalised Trinity College when he'd announced his mission "to de-Anglicise the Irish Nation."

Yet it was Lady Gregory, only a woman, and outside the charmed circle, who'd performed, it seemed to Willy, the most important task of all. Delving not only into the spoken language, but into the often obscure and complex forms to be found in medieval manuscripts, she had collected all manner of ancient texts and from them culled ancient Irish tales that had first been written down, quite likely, not long after the time of Saint Patrick. Then she had translated them into English. The first collection, concerning the great warrior Cuchulainn, had been published a year ago. He had been lent it by a friend, and read it avidly. Another collection was due shortly.

"She has given us back our ancient heroes," he said quietly.

"I don't deny that," said Gogarty. He smiled slyly. "Have you noticed, by the way, that the greatest enthusiasts for the Irish language all seem to have English names: Yeats, Gregory, Hyde? But I will tell you my objections to Lady Gregory, for I have two.

"The first objection is to her idiom. She says it is the idiom of the local people of Kiltartan. It may be so. But when you take the syntax of Irish and translate it directly into English, the effect is unnatural. I do not say: 'There would be great grief on me indeed' if some disaster occurred. Nor can I feel much for a hero who declares: 'It is not trusting to a woman's protection I am in this work I have in my hands.' It is stilted. Page after page, it becomes cloying. I have the right to make this complaint, for my own name, Gogarty, is certainly Celtic. And I do not want my ancestors to be Kiltartanised. Now Yeats, who is quite as well versed in ancient Irish as Lady Gregory, never plays such games. He writes in modern English. But he is a great poet."

Willy was silent. He did not know what to say to this. But Father MacGowan had the authority.

"Fair, up to a point," he said. "But I take note from your own excellent verses, Gogarty, that you abhor the usual, dull pentameters of English as spoken by the English. The English spoken by Irish people has a special richness, and a rhythmic beauty that have yet to find a champion. Nonetheless, Lady Gregory, whatever her limitations, has performed a remarkable service to Ireland, and is to be applauded, not mocked."

"I accept what you say. Hear my second objection, then. I fear this Gaelic revival, that she is part of, because it is not Ireland." He waited a moment, for effect.

Willy frowned. The Gaelic revival went far beyond things literary. For most people, indeed, it meant the promotion of Gaelic sports, like the ancient and noble game of hurling. The Gaelic Athletic Association had attracted a large following in the last twenty years.

"You dislike the GAA?" he asked.

"Not as such. But why is that, if a member of the GAA is seen, even once, playing a game like cricket, he is expelled?"

"You must allow some natural reaction against the domination of England," said Father MacGowan.

"I am Irish," replied Gogarty. "I couldn't be more so. But I do not care to be so circumscribed. What is it to be Irish anyway? Is it to be Celtic, whatever that is? I should think half the blood of the Irish was Viking anyway, before the English came. Do you know that one in six Irish names is Norman? But what really concerns me is the desire, in turning away from England, to look inward into this small island, instead of outward. Through all our history, we have been involved with wider shores, with the great culture, the religion, and the trade of Catholic Europe. I fear that this Gaelic fixation demands that, as an Irishman, I become something less than an Irishman is."

And now a most remarkable thing occurred. The Count rapped his hand on the table.

"Ah," he cried. "Aha!" Even Sheridan Smith started in surprise. Nobody knew the high-born personage could become so animated. "That is right, young man. Do not forget us, the Wild Geese, the great Irish community of Europe."

Willy gazed at him. He'd always heard of the Wild Geese, those gallant men who had flown away out of Ireland two centuries ago, rather than live under English rule. But he had never thought to see one. So this strange, aristocratic figure was a Wild Goose. Somehow, it wasn't what he'd expected.

The Count, however was waxing eloquent by now.

"There's not a Catholic country, not a city where you won't find us. Military men and counsellors, priests and lawyers, merchants and traders, too, no doubt, but always men of honour, held in respect. And we never forget. We are still Irishmen. You will find us at the Irish colleges in the capitals. It was émigrés who founded the Irish Franciscan College of Prague, you know. And, if I may say it, no nation has garnered greater honours. Numerous Irishmen have worn the Order of the Golden Fleece—that which there is no higher. Two hundred knights of the Spanish Order of Santiago. As for titles . . ." His eyes assumed an almost dreamy, mystical expression: "Burkes and Butlers, Leslies and Taafes, Kavanaghs, Walshes—the Counts von Wallis, you know, are the Walshes of Carrickmines. There are so many. As for my own family, there are numerous barons Byrne. We ourselves, the counts Birne, as we spell it now, were O'Byrnes originally, before we left."

"And which of the many O'Byrnes would that be?" asked Father MacGowan.

"We had quite modest lands," the Count replied. "You probably won't know of the place. It is called Rathconan, up in the Wicklow Mountains. A family called Budge has it now," he remarked with an aristocratic shrug. "I know nothing about them."

O'Byrne of Rathconan? Willy stared in amazement. It had never occurred to him to connect this fastidious nobleman with his home. And then another realisation hit him. Damn it. And we thought that the place was ours.

So awesome and exotic was this aristocratic catalogue that, even here in the not-to-be-sneezed-at surroundings of Wellington Road, it reduced the table to silence.

Until, Willy could have sworn, there emanated from old Mrs. Smith, who so far hadn't said a word, a distinct sniff. But now that she did speak, she spoke quietly.

"It's strange to me," she said, "that no one has mentioned the most important place of all. For there are two Irelands, not one." She was an old lady, in comfortable circumstances, but it seemed to Willy that under her pale old face, there was something calm, yet strangely cold, and absolute. "If my husband, God rest his soul, had not saved me, most of you wouldn't be here. I'd have died in the Famine in Clare, along with the rest of my family." She looked at Willy. "Do you know how many left Ireland for America in the decade of the Famine?" She did not wait for a reply. "Three quarters of a million. And in the ten years after? Another million. And a constant stream since then, year after year. There are two Irelands: Ireland in Ireland, and Ireland in America. And America remembers the Famine." She glanced at Sheridan. "Your cousin Martin Madden in Boston collects money for Ireland. Did you know that?"

"I didn't actually."

"My brother William's son. He is quite prosperous now, I believe. He collects money. And it will be collected and given as long as there are people in Ireland who want to be free of England. The English may try to kill the Irish in Ireland with kindness, but they will never appease the Irish in America."

"Or those in Australia," added Father MacGowan, softly, "but they are too far away."

"To whom does Martin Madden give money, might I ask?" said Sheridan Smith.

"To those who need it," his mother answered, with a grim finality.

"Oh." He looked embarrassed.

The Count glanced at the old lady curiously.

"I'd better go and see to my daughter," said the Countess.

"We're all done, I think," said Sheridan's wife.

"Perhaps," said Father MacGowan, "I'll stretch my legs. Gogarty, have you a moment?" He gave Sheridan Smith a meaningful look as he and Gogarty went out, and indicated Willy.

"Oh yes," said the newspaperman, glad to change the subject. And a moment later he drew Willy aside.

He didn't need to know much about him, he told the young man, to set him at ease. A recommendation from Father MacGowan was quite enough. Did he know what he wanted to do with his life? Well, nor had he at that age. "How can you possibly tell," he asked obligingly, "until you've tried a thing or two?" There were some small jobs at the newspaper where a young fellow could get a look at things, so to speak. Not much pay, of course. Could he continue to live with his uncle and aunt? Good. Hmm. He'd never sold anything of course. "But you might find a talent for it. I've a good man who sells advertising space for the paper. To tradesmen, mostly, and that sort of thing. Advertising is very important to a newspaper, you know. You might go round with him for a bit. Learn the ropes." There would be other things to do about the place, as well. Would that suit him?

Indeed it would.

"Splendid then. Come into the office tomorrow morning. Oh." The newspaper man's eyes were suddenly riveted on the doorway. He stared. So did Willy.

The little girl who had just come in with the Countess must have been five or six. She was pale and slim; she had a cascade of raven hair. And a pair of green eyes, emerald green, that seemed to generate a light of their own. Willy had never seen any eyes like them.

"She's better," said the Countess.

"I'm hungry," said the child. "Hello Great Granny." She ran over and kissed the old lady.

"I'm your Great Uncle Sheridan," said Sheridan. "You were tiny when I last saw you. Do you remember me?"

"No," said the child. Then she gave him a brilliant smile. "But I shall now." She turned to Willy. "Who are you?"

"I'm just Willy," said Willy.

"How do you do, Just Willy. My name is Caitlin. That's because I'm Irish."

"Just Caitlin?"

"Oh." She laughed. "I see. I am Countess Caitlin Birne."

"I am Willy O'Byrne."

"Really?" She glanced at her father for guidance. "Are we related?"

Sheridan Smith intervened smoothly.

"Father MacGowan is outside, he's just sent in word that you should accompany him back. Come, I'll take you to the door." At the door, however, he detained Willy for a minute. "Going round Dublin, of course, you'll meet all kinds of people. Some are better to know than others. You can always ask me, if you wish."

"Thank you," said Willy.

Sheridan Smith nodded.

"One small word of advice, perhaps. Not to be shared, you understand? Not even with Father MacGowan." He paused, while Willy listened respectfully. "Do you know his brother? He keeps a bookshop."

"Only by sight."

"Good. Well, take my advice. Avoid him."

✢

As he walked back through the mist which, with the hint of

coolness developing in the autumn afternoon, seemed ready to close in upon them again, Willy was lost in thought. So many sensations, so many discoveries in a short space of time: his mind was still trying to take them in. Then the strange shock of meeting the most beautiful child he'd ever seen; and the unexpected warning: he hardly knew what to make of it all.

And how curious that the old lady should be a Madden from Clare. His grandmother, he knew, had been a Nuala Madden from that region. But he'd seen a photograph of her, and she looked nothing like the old lady he'd just met. Well, Madden was a common name in Connacht. He was no more likely to be related to the old lady than he was to the Count.

Yet still, in the misty afternoon, he could not escape a sense that the whole world were covered by some hidden skein of relationships, under the ground perhaps, or above the mist, like flocks of birds, eternally migrating back and forth.

"What are you thinking?" asked the priest.

"I was thinking, Father," he replied truthfully, "of the strange interrelatedness of things."

"Ah. Indeed. It is one of the ways, you know, by which we may discern God's Providence."

"Yes," said Willy. "I suppose so."

"And the further proof," the priest added cheerfully, "is that you have a job."

❖

The months that followed were exciting ones for Willy. He did as he was told, toured the city looking for advertisers, and made himself useful to Sheridan Smith, who after a few months pronounced himself satisfied. He was even given a small increase in wages. His aunt and uncle were glad to receive his rent.

Sheridan Smith also kept an eye out for him in other ways. "Here's a book I reviewed. I don't want it myself. Give it to someone if you don't want to read it," he'd say casually. But he noticed that his employer always chose well for him. He obtained the next volume of Lady Gregory's work in this manner and, Kiltartan English or not, immersed himself joyfully in the stories of the Children of Lir, Diarmait and Grania, the Fianna, and many others. And when the good lady and the poet Yeats opened their new Abbey Theatre, he would push a ticket at Willy and remark, "They send us these complimentary tickets sometimes. Go along if you want to."

Several times during the summer, he had been up to see his family; and during these visits, he had had some long conversations with his father. Mrs. Budge was up at Rathconan in the summer, but often in the winter months now, she would go into Dublin, where she had taken a small house at Rathmines. From there, she would make sorties into the city centre. "She has even more opportunity to be insane in Dublin than she does here," his father remarked bitterly. His father avoided her as much as he could nowadays. But nonetheless, there was something he wanted from her; and after much discussion, it was he who finally suggested: "Go and talk to her in Dublin if you like, then, Willy. You may do better than I can."

It was not until late the following year, however, that Willy finally ventured out to see Mrs. Budge at Rathmines. Her house was modest—two-storey over basement, with a small garden in front made lightless by some large evergreen bushes. He went up to the front door and was ushered in by a maid that he didn't know. She must have been hired in Dublin. She asked him to sit on a chair in the narrow hall.

He wondered whether Mrs. Budge would be the same in Dublin as she was up at Rathconan. There she had developed a reputation for increasing eccentricity. "She knows what's going on, mind you," his father had told him. "If a cow's not milking well, she'll know it before you do, and God help you if anything's mislaid." But the turban seemed to have permanently attached itself to her head now, and she had taken to reading strange books that were reputed to be occult.

Once, about a year after she had arrived, she had gone to the nearest Church of Ireland church. Normally, the Protestant clergymen were only too grateful for any extra congregation they could get. Gladstone had disestablished the Church some time ago now, so they lacked the official backing they had enjoyed before. The number of Protestant landowners was falling, and nobody, in Rathconan at least, had ever heard of anyone being converted by a clergyman to join that church. He may therefore have looked up hopefully at the sight of Mrs. Budge, even with her turban on, sitting in his church one morning. Her conduct was not encouraging, however. She had sat, and she had continued to sit. Her face was neither approving nor disapproving. She might have been a dispassionate observer from a far-off land. Somewhat to his relief, he had not seen her since. Mrs. Budge's Dublin residence had a front parlour, or drawing room, which connected to a dining room that faced the garden at the back. When he was ushered into the front room, Willy noticed at once that the curtains were half drawn, so that the space was shadowy. There was a fire burning in the grate, and a lamp beside her wing chair provided the light by which, evidently, she had been reading the newspaper. On one wall there was a picture, of the early nineteenth century, depicting a view of Rathconan. On another, a sporting print and, not far from it, the sepia photograph of an erotic Indian wall carving that he remembered seeing in the big house. Did she take it with her, he wondered, like a talisman? On a low table were some theatre programmes. It seemed that she went to musicals, as most people in Dublin did. But beside one of these he saw a pamphlet on which, he was almost sure, he could make out the words "Theosophical Society." If she entertained in here, it was obviously her personal den. Perhaps her visitors were part of a coterie of some kind. His father swore she had séances. It might well be so.

She was wearing a turban, this one made of a cloth with a brownish paisley design. She had an Indian shawl round her shoulders. She had not changed much down the years, except that her face was worn a little looser now.

"You are quite a young man, Willy," she said.

He glanced at a chair and she indicated that he should sit in it. He did not feel intimidated. His time out in the commercial world of Dublin had given him a certain confidence, and, as he had reminded himself, this was business after all. He had also developed a fairly pleasing manner. Very politely, but clearly, he explained the matter in hand. "I have come, Mrs. Budge," he said, "on behalf of my father."

The terms offered by the new Wyndham land legislation were really quite extraordinary. The price to be paid for land was twenty-eight times the annual rent. A landowner accepting this money, in a single, immediate payment from the government, would almost certainly be able to invest the proceeds at a higher return. The tenant was not required to make any down payment at all. And the government asked only a three percent mortgage rate, payable over sixty-eight years. Quite apart from the fact that even a modest rate of inflation would reduce these payments to trivial sums, the effect would almost certainly be a sharp reduction in the tenant's outgoings. To all intents and purposes, the government was using some of the wealth it had acquired from its empire to buy out the Ascendancy and return its lands to Irish hands. It was hardly surprising then, that the numbers taking up the offer exceeded anything seen before by a factor of about twelve times. The prediction of Sheridan Smith looked likely to be born out: some people were guessing that a third or more of the entire island might change hands.

Carefully, and very politely, Willy outlined the legislation. He explained that the terms were so remarkable that both his father, and doubtless she herself, could hardly wish to pass them up. He stressed, albeit untruthfully, the affection his father had for the Budge estate, and how he desired to live in harmony with them. Nothing would change, except that all the parties would be better off. He did it respectfully and very nicely. She listened to him carefully. When he had done, she was silent for some time. Then she half smiled.

"Do you believe, Willy," she asked, "in the transmigration of souls?"

He stared at her, hardly comprehending at first.

"I'd have to ask Father MacGowan," he managed at last. "But I don't think so."

"You should study it," she cried. "It is a most interesting subject. I was wondering what you might have been before this life. I myself . . ." She did not divulge what it was that she had been. Probably something too exotic for humble ears to hear. "We are all," she glanced towards the sepia photograph on the wall, "more than we imagine. Here in Dublin, many people are taking an interest in Theosophy, you know. Mr. Yeats himself has been a student of the subject. We are all connected, you see. These things only become clear as we achieve spiritual enlightenment. Buddhism, Hinduism, even Christianity: they are all related. That is the path to the future, I do believe. We think too much of material things."

Were her own thoughts connected? It was hard to tell. But he recognised her well enough, as a general type. Clearly she had decided to become a Dublin eccentric. There were quite a number of them. He supposed such people existed in other places, too, but Dublin, with its special leisurely pace, seemed to encourage their growth.

If you had nothing else to do, perhaps if you were a little short of money—and who was not?—then to be an eccentric was an easy passport through the rest of your life. You could get away with anything.

Then, suddenly, he saw through her. She had nothing else to cling on to, of course. He understood that. Her land up at Rathconan was what she was. She would never give it up. This talk of spiritual things was nothing but a tatty old screen to hide her real intentions.

"And my father's land?" he asked.

"I'll have to think about that, Willy. But we're all very well as we are. Tell your father that. These things are quite temporal," she cried, as if that signified something.

He bowed his head. The maid showed him out.

The old woman thinks she's fobbed me off, he considered to himself. But she hasn't. For now, this is war.

✢

He was walking along from Trinity towards Merrion Square the following day, wondering how to write to his father, and what account of the meeting he could give him, when he noticed that the green door of MacGowan's bookshop was open. He did not think that he had ever seen it open before. By its very nature, it seemed to him, it should be closed. And simply because of this unusual circumstance, he decided to go in. Why not, after all? Sheridan Smith might have told him to avoid the owner, but that wasn't, surely, a prohibition against even looking at the books there. Besides, he was curious to see whether he would still find MacGowan as daunting as he had when he was younger. He entered.

MacGowan was sitting at a table at the back. He was examining a volume, evidently trying to decide how to price it. He was smoking a cigarette that was hardly more than a stub. Willy noticed how stained the bookseller's fingers were with nicotine. He went to a bookshelf. In front of him was a book of sermons by some eighteenth-century divine. He took it out and pretended to look at it.

Sure enough, the single eye was upon him. He held the book in his hand. The single eye remained fixed. But he was not afraid. He felt rather proud of himself.

"Are you interested in that book?" said MacGowan.

"No."

Willy moved along the shelf. A book on South American plants, with line illustrations. He looked at the pictures. Quite fine, in their way.

"I'm surprised," said MacGowan, "given that you've no interest in books, that you aren't playing a sport. Have you joined the GAA?"

"I haven't."

"Do you speak the language?" Irish. Gaelic. The language of honour.

"A little. My mother does."

"You should join the GAA. Though I suppose you get enough exercise," he remarked, "running errands for Sheridan Smith." He saw Willy start with surprise. "I know who you are. My brother has told me about you."

"Father MacGowan's been very good to me."

"No doubt. He is a kindly man." He took a drag on the remains of his cigarette. "But mistaken." He continued, almost miraculously it seemed to Willy, to find combustible weed in the ragged paper leavings between his fingers, drew upon the stub twice more, then, indifferently, let it drop into a small, stone ashtray, pressing the last life out of the little glow, somewhat cruelly, with his thumbnail. He glanced up, as if to check whether Willy was still there. "A good man, certainly. It's a pity," he added regretfully, "that he's a priest."

Willy looked at him in great astonishment.

"I assumed all his family would be proud . . ."

"My mother was. My father, too." He glanced down at the book on the desk, wrote "Ten shillings" in pencil inside the cover, and closed it. "Personally, I've no great use for priests. It was the priests that destroyed Parnell."

"A special case."

"The men of '98 knew how to keep the priests in their place. Emmet, too."

Willy nodded. There were plenty of men in Dublin with similar opinions. He had not felt impelled to join any political cause himself, but you had only to go into any Dublin pub to hear strong opinions voiced. A few were extremist— out and out socialists. Then there was the Irish Republican Brotherhood, the Fenians—ultimate heirs of the French Revolution and of Young Ireland, it might be said—but secretive, shadowy. Most of them had little patience with Church interference. Then there was Redmond's Irish

Parliamentary Party, of course, dedicated to Home Rule by more patient, parliamentary means. But you could seldom be sure where people really stood. The GAA was officially dedicated to sport, but it was quasi-political really. There were Fenians in the GAA all right. Evidently the priest's brother belonged somewhere along this spectrum—towards the radical end of it, perhaps, if it put him so at variance with his Father MacGowan.

Deciding that some response was required, but that he'd better leave Father MacGowan and the Church out of it, he remarked:

"I'd be glad to see the English out of Ireland." He thought of Mrs. Budge. "But I sometimes wonder if it will ever happen."

The bookseller stood up. He was somewhat corpulent. But the surprising deftness of his gait suggested he could move very fast if he wanted to.

"I sell newspapers here, as well as books," he remarked. "Old issues." He pulled down a broadsheet from a shelf. "This is the first issue of *The United Irishman*. Arthur Griffith produced it for the centenary of 1798." He nodded. "A remarkable thing to have done." He showed it to Willy. "You should read it," he said. He turned and stared towards the open door. Apart from the two of them, the shop was quite empty.

"The trouble with Sheridan Smith," he said, "is that he and his like—not to mention the Catholic farmers who don't want to be bothered with anything but their land—will give away Ireland's birthright. Our nationhood. In another twenty years we shall all be living as West Britons, which is exactly what the English want. The only way to stop that is to drive them out: when the time is right, when we are ready for it. That may come through Parliament. Or more radical means. Fenian perhaps. With the help of Clan na Gael in America, of course." He smiled. "America is where the money comes from. I lived there once, you know. Many years ago."

"When I was a child," said Willy, "the Clan na Gael sent men over to plant bombs in England. It did no good at all, and most of them were caught."

"I know." MacGowan sighed. "Twenty years in jail, some of them got. A particular friend of mine . . ." He stopped himself. "They've learned since." He paused for a few moments. "Well." He returned the newspaper to its shelf. "Do you know what the Church said about the Fenians. Bishop Moriarty, it was. He and Cullen were thick as thieves. 'Eternity is not long enough,' he said, 'nor hell hot enough to punish them for their sins.' There, you can think about that," he concluded. "But don't tell my brother."

"No," said Willy, "I won't."

"Come again," said MacGowan. "You should read that newspaper. I have postcards, also, from France."

As Willy continued on his way, he thought of Sheridan Smith's injunction. He had not deliberately disobeyed it. He couldn't have foreseen that the man would talk to him. In any case, the encounter had taken place, and there was no harm done.

⊰ **1909** ⊱

She had been waiting for this visit today with great eagerness. He was delighted to see her so happy.

The brief December afternoon was already drawing in as Sheridan Smith and Caitlin walked across the Liffey. She was still only eleven, but today she had put up her long dark hair, like an adult, and linked her arm in his. He felt so proud. And he smiled to himself with amusement. Instead of foster-father and daughter, they were walking like a pair of lovers.

Her long legs had a wonderful, swinging motion. Part countess, three parts a mountain child: her mind also, he knew, moved with the same, grand freedom.

It was two years since her father had died. Both she and her mother had wished to remain in Ireland; so, while they kept the estate in the country, they had bought a house in Fitzwilliam Square. And as Sheridan was only ten years older than Caitlin's mother, it had happened quite naturally that he had taken on the role of unofficial foster-father. Although technically he was the child's great uncle, she simply called him Uncle Sherry.

The loss of her father had also had another effect upon the child. It had brought her into more contact with old Maureen.

Sheridan had to admire his old mother. She was fortunate, of course, that she had kept her strength and health to such a great age. Perhaps the hardships of her youth during the Famine had toughened her, or perhaps she had been unusually hardy before. Her sight was still good, her hearing almost as acute, and she insisted on walking upstairs. When the Count had died, it had been natural, he supposed, that the girl should have taken special pleasure in the company of the old woman who represented such long life and family continuity. A chance remark had brought the two of them even closer together.

"It's a pity," the old lady had said one day, "that you don't speak the language of your ancestors—on your father's side as well as mine, of course. They tell me the speaking of Irish has become quite the fashion nowadays."

Indeed the combined efforts of Yeats and his friends, the GAA, and the Gaelic League had been so successful that the University of Ireland was even making Irish a compulsory subject for matriculation.

"I think I should like to learn," Caitlin had answered. "Will you teach me?" Ever since, on three afternoons a week, the old lady and the child had sat together for an hour at tea time; and old Maureen had taught Caitlin to speak Gaelic. She was becoming quite proficient.

Their conversations had also made the girl more curious about history. Her great-grandmother would tell Caitlin all about her early life, the Famine, and her escape to Dublin. She spoke of her relations in America and of her bitter feelings towards England. "Your own O'Byrne ancestors were driven out of Ireland, Caitlin, remember," she would point out. "The Wild Geese, they were. And look what they made of their lives. Titles and estates they fought for and earned, and good luck to them. The Maddens in America have prospered, too, thank God. It's only the English who have chosen to despise the Irish. Wherever else they have gone in the world, they have risen to the top."

Recently, Sheridan had been rather pleased when Caitlin had asked him some intelligent questions about the political situation. Was there really hope, she wanted to know, that Ireland would gain its freedom, at last, from England?

"As a matter of fact," he told her, "things have just taken an interesting turn." And he explained why.

The turn of events had originated in a dispute that had nothing to do, directly, with Ireland. This year of 1909, a change of great significance had taken place in the London Parliament. Up to now, the House of Lords, traditionally filled with conservative-minded hereditary peers, had always been able to block legislation. Finding its budget blocked in this way, the present Liberal government, with the aid of Redmond's Irish MPs, had just forced through a constitutional change. From now on, the Lords would no longer be able to block legislation, but only delay it. As the price of their help, the Irish party had extracted a promise that a new Home Rule Bill would be prepared and introduced. "In the past," Sheridan explained to Caitlin, "Home Rule Bills, giving Ireland her freedom, have been passed by the British House of Commons. The reason why Ireland isn't free already is that those Bills have always been blocked in the Lords. But when the next Home Rule Bill passes the Commons, the Lords won't be able to stop it any more. Those who want Ireland to be separate will get what they want, without any bloodshed. It's only a question of time, now. Within the next few years, I'd say."

"That is good, isn't it, Uncle Sherry?"

"What do you think?"

"I think it is good," she said.

Today's visit was the result of a promise he'd made two weeks ago. He was taking her to a rehearsal at the Abbey Theatre.

It was new, this fascination of Caitlin's with the theatre. She and her mother had liked to go to the usual Dublin round of pantomime and music hall. This somewhat precocious interest in drama, however, could also be attributed to the influence of old Maureen.

The old lady's interest in the Abbey Theatre had come about quite unexpectedly.

It had been back in January 1907 that Yeats and Lady Gregory had staged the production of a play by J. M. Synge that had caused a great stir. *The Playboy of the Western World*, with its haunting language and anarchic themes was unlike anything the Dublin audience had ever witnessed before. And they didn't like it. "This is not Ireland," they protested. "People do not speak like that," they said of the language. As for the play's strange action: "It's the raving of a diseased imagination." By the end of the performance there had almost been a riot. "I have heard such speech on the west coast," the playwright answered, "and even amongst Dublin folk too." So great was the public stir that Maureen had insisted Sheridan take her to see the play. "I come from the west," she declared, "so I shall judge for myself." There was so much noise from the audience, who by now had come to howl the play down, that it had not been easy to hear all of the play, but Maureen had announced that she liked it. More important, it seemed that she approved of the theatre's efforts to promote Irish drama, and to his surprise, in her ninetieth year, she had suddenly started going to the theatre. She went almost every month. Earlier this year, she had decided that Caitlin should accompany her. Caitlin's mother had been afraid that the girl might be bored. But not a bit of it. Quite the reverse, in fact. She'd recently announced that she wanted to go on the stage herself. "My dear Sherry," her mother had complained, "my daughter's completely stage-struck. What am I to do?"

"Nothing," he told her with a smile. It was hardly so unusual for an eleven-year-old girl to be stage-struck. So when he had used his contacts at the Abbey to arrange for a private visit backstage during a rehearsal, Caitlin's excitement had been great indeed.

They had crossed the Liffey. Ahead stretched the broad expanse of Sackville Street. On the left, the square mass of the General Post Office with its big six-column portico, looked like a barracks; in front of it, in the centre of the thoroughfare, Nelson's high pillar gave the place an imperial air. Older than its tall sister in London's Trafalgar Square, the pillar to England's great naval commander had always rather pleased Sheridan. If you were going to have such an object in the middle of the street, it seemed to him, it should serve some useful purpose. You could mount the interior staircase in the pillar and emerge onto the platform near the top, from which there were splendid views of the city. They were just approaching the pillar when they saw Father Brendan MacGowan.

He greeted them warmly. Yes, they were well. Had they noticed the sharp wind from the east? They would feel it in their faces as they went into Abbey Street. He was going upon his rounds. He parted from them cheerfully and, with the wind behind him, went westwards, under full sail. They, meanwhile, turned into Abbey Street and approached the theatre.

"You've just missed Mr. Yeats," the doorman told them. But Yeats could be seen almost any day in Dublin. You had only to go to St. Stephen's Green to catch sight of his tall figure, his lock of dark hair falling down his brow, as he drifted round the railings, in a state of abstraction, like an angel on a cloud.

Once inside, Sheridan's task was easy. Having delivered Caitlin into the hands of one of the company, he could walk about or sit in one of the empty seats while they showed her round backstage. The dressing rooms, the grease paint, the scenery with pulleys, the store where the props were kept—the everyday business of the theatre would seem like magic to her, no doubt. The stage manager appeared. There was a scene to rehearse. He could not see Caitlin, but knew that she would be standing there in the wings, watching every move, listening to every word. And for him, too, so long accustomed to such things, there was still the special feeling of a theatrical space, which, for those who love the theatre, partakes, even more than a religious space, of the eternal. He sat in the empty stalls and closed his eyes.

It was an hour and a half before she appeared. Her eyes were glowing. Sheridan smiled. Obviously the visit had been a success. A stage hand was accompanying her. He was smiling. "She enjoyed herself," he told Sheridan. "We liked having her," he added, in a way that suggested he felt Caitlin belonged there. Just then, from somewhere above, a door opened with a slight creak and then banged shut. The stage hand glanced up, then, with a parting smile to them both, went back behind the scenes. Sheridan and Caitlin started to move towards the exit. But they had just reached the hallway that led towards the stage door, when a commanding woman in a fur coat and a large, wide-brimmed felt hat swept down upon them.

"Stop," she cried. "I wish to look at you." She gave a nod. "Sheridan."

"I thought," he said, "that you were in Paris."

"I am in Dublin for two days. Nobody knows I am here." She gazed at Caitlin. "And who," she demanded, "is this simply wonderful child?"

"Countess Caitlin Birne," he said quietly. "This," he said to the girl, "is Miss Gonne." Then he drew back slightly, since he knew very well there was nothing to be done now, until the lady had finished.

"My dear child," said the lady. "You have the most remarkable eyes. I take it you are going on the stage."

How was it, Sheridan wondered, not for the first time, that Maud Gonne had achieved her curious position? Born in England, the daughter of an officer in the British army, she had reinvented herself entirely. Her father having left her with independent means, she lived in Paris, mostly. For years she'd been the mistress of a French journalist who'd given her two children. But none of that had stopped Yeats wanting to marry her or casting her in a play as an Irish heroine. Instead of Yeats, she'd since married an Irish patriot; but the marriage hadn't lasted long. She ran a French Irish newspaper, these days, and made occasional visits to Dublin. But whenever she arrived, it seemed to Sheridan, she came in like a cavalry charge.

The fact that Caitlin was a countess, he knew very well, would intrigue her at once. With her large, staring eyes and her powerful chin, Maud Gonne was the very picture of a wilful society lady. This seemed to be a type that attracted Yeats, he mused. Questioning Caitlin now, it did not take her long to find out all she wanted. And she was enchanted.

"This is wonderful," she declared. "Quite wonderful. A true Irish noblewoman, returned to her country. And she speaks the language of her ancestors as well. My dear child, you must join us. *Inghinidhe na hEireann* was made for you. It is your home."

Inghinidhe na hEireann: the Daughters of Erin. It was Maud Gonne herself who had founded the movement when the nationalist groups wouldn't have her because she was a woman. It was dedicated to combatting the malign influence of England upon Irish culture, and it went a good deal further than that. Not only did the Daughters of Erin give Irish language classes to the children of the poor, but they told Irish girls not to go out with English soldiers, and distributed leaflets warning them of the dangers of having illegitimate babies. To join, you had to be of Irish birth. "It is curious," Sheridan had once observed, "that Maud Gonne dedicates her life to combating so many things she represents herself." Some of the leading members had even taken new, Irish names by which they were known within the organisation. Maud Gonne herself was known as Maeve.

"Here." She reached into the pocket of her fur coat and

drew something out. It was a little circular brooch in the shape of an ancient Irish torc. "This is the badge the Daughters of Erin wear. It's yours. A present. You shall wear it when you are older." She smiled, but her eyes were looking deep into Caitlin's. "You have not only a great role to play on the stage, my child. And with your hair and your eyes, you will create a sensation. But you have a great role ahead of you in the life of your country." She paused, then gave her another tremendous stare. "Never forget that, Caitlin. It is what you were born to. It is your destiny."

With that, she swept out, with Caitlin gazing, fascinated, after her. And Sheridan was left wondering whether, perhaps, this visit to the Abbey Theatre might have done more than he had intended.

+

As he grew older, Father Brendan MacGowan did not curtail his many kindly visits around the city. But he became a better navigator. As he came westwards along Mary Street, therefore, he kept his plump back turned at a slight angle to the east wind, so that it should gently propel him along without pushing him off balance. He was moving along nicely at a couple of knots or more when he caught sight of Willy O'Byrne coming towards him. Willy was accompanied by a young woman. At the sight of the young man, the priest frowned.

He wasn't sure what he felt about Willy. He'd been glad, of course, to have started him upon his way. And Sheridan Smith seemed perfectly happy with him. Young Willy had his own territory now; he brought in advertising rather successfully. People seemed to like him. He'd got his own lodgings nowadays, up near Mountjoy Square, Father Brendan had heard. No harm in all that. Nor did the priest mind that Willy spent so much time in the bookshop of his anticlerical brother. Willy probably didn't know that he knew all about these activities. He hoped it hadn't turned the young man against his faith, but in his own experience, even when people did turn away from the Church, it only took some small crisis in their lives, often as not, to bring them back.

No, his objection to Willy was altogether more practical and down to earth. It seemed to the kindly priest that he detected signs that Willy was becoming callous.

It had been a single event that had put him on his guard: a story that he had heard from another source. Not long after Willy had moved to his own lodgings, his uncle had died. There had been friction between them while he was still living in his uncle's house, it seemed. Willy had said some things, of a political nature, that his uncle did not like. It may have been this disagreement which encouraged Willy to leave. But there had not been a major split in the family, as far as Father Brendan was aware. Yet when his uncle had died, Willy had not bothered to go to the wake or the funeral. He had not gone to see the family at all. And by all accounts, his aunt had been very hurt.

Some weeks afterwards, meeting Willy one day, he had tackled him about it. Surely, he had suggested, it had not been a very kind thing to do. Willy had not been annoyed, but had appeared puzzled.

"I never really liked him," he said.

"That may be. But should you not have considered the feelings of your aunt and your cousins?"

"The girls didn't mind. I couldn't see the point of being dishonest, I suppose." He had shrugged. "He wasn't a very nice man."

"That is not for you to judge. Can you not see that your action was cruel?"

It had seemed to Father Brendan that, if he did see, and it was inconceivable that he did not, Willy did not greatly care.

He was glad to observe that the young woman accompanying Willy now was one of his aunt's three daughters. Perhaps the young man was making amends. In answer to his greeting, and his general enquiry as to what they were doing that afternoon, Willy informed him that he had just taken his cousin to see the moving pictures at the little theatre that had recently opened for the purpose.

"It's called the Volta, Father, just behind us. Have you been in there?"

"I haven't," the priest said. "Was it well attended?"

"Only a few people, besides ourselves. I tried to sell Joyce some advertising, but he couldn't afford it. The business isn't prospering, I'm afraid."

Father Brendan had heard about the venture. Joyce: Gogarty's protégé. Whatever Oliver St. John Gogarty liked to say, from all the priest had heard, young Joyce had not turned out too well at all. For a start, he'd run off with a servant girl and never married her, so far as he had heard. That was both an immoral and a foolish thing to do. He might have tried for a profession of some kind, perhaps, or at least sought regular employment; but he hadn't the application of Gogarty, who was already well on the way to becoming a surgeon of repute. But Joyce wasn't solid enough. He'd never make his mark. Father Brendan corrected himself. One mustn't judge, of course. God's grace might be bestowed in unseen ways. The fellow had gone off to the continent anyway; been living in Trieste, for reasons unknown. And now he'd come back to Dublin to open a movie theatre in Mary Street. Backed by some investors from Trieste, apparently. Though what the men from Trieste would know about the appetite of Dubliners for moving pictures, the priest couldn't guess. He'd noticed the young man's tall, slim figure lounging by the entrance of the place, looking disconsolate, but had not chosen to speak with him.

"They say it's catching on everywhere," Willy said. "But not in Dublin. Not yet, anyway. I think Joyce is too early with it myself."

"No doubt," said Father MacGowan. "Well, I've a lady to see in the Rotunda Hospital, so I must be going along."

✢

"He thinks me cruel," said Willy, after the priest had gone.

"You are not always kind," his cousin Rita replied.

Willy shrugged.

"Besides," said Rita, "you did not answer the question I asked you before Father MacGowan came along. I don't believe," she added, "that you care."

Willy considered. He didn't care, in fact. But he would not say that to Rita. She was the one member of her family with whom he had always got on rather well. And he could see her point.

Why was it, she had asked, that working at Jacobs Biscuit factory, the older men could earn over a pound a week, while she earned less than a third of that? They have families to support, he had answered. It had always been so. Nobody had ever complained before. "We are complaining now," she had said. Some of the young men—who did better than the women, of course, but still got far less than their seniors for the same work—had been complaining, too. "There's a union now, at least," Rita had pointed out.

An Irish trade union had been set up recently by James Larkin. The membership was growing rapidly. But whether they would do much for women remained to be seen. "They say that the union favours equality for women. But I should guess," Willy told her truthfully, "that most of the union men won't be anxious to see women paid the same, any more than the employers would be. You'd need a women's union for that."

"There isn't one."

"I know." He considered. "Are you just complaining, or do you want to do something about these things yourself?"

"I might."

"It's dangerous." Employers usually dismissed trouble-makers. He waited for her to respond, but as she didn't, he went on. "You know, there are women on the executive of Sinn Fein."

It had been Arthur Griffith, after starting *The United Irishman* newspaper, who had started the Sinn Fein movement. "Ourselves Alone" the name meant, and his idea was to boycott English goods wherever it was possible to produce the same in Ireland. "We need economic self-sufficiency," his supporters declared, "to show Ireland how to stand up for herself as a free and independent nation." Since then, Sinn Fein had grown into an amalgam of groups dedicated to a general, but nonviolent resistance to England's rule.

"You're in Sinn Fein, aren't you?"

He nodded.

"What made you join?"

"Many reasons. I suppose it was MacGowan the bookseller—he's Father MacGowan's brother, you know—who encouraged me in that direction. It was natural, really. I wanted the English out of Ireland."

"Well, I might consider it." She nodded. "Do they also want votes for women?"

"You're turning into a suffragist as well? I didn't know you were such a radical."

"I never was. But when I started thinking about the wages, then I wondered why women shouldn't vote, as well. The movement is well-developed in England."

"Leave it alone, Rita. For the present."

"Why?"

"Two reasons. Firstly, it's better to do one thing at a time. Secondly, we don't want votes for women in Ireland yet."

"Why not?"

"Because we don't want them coming from the British. That's something that should come from Ireland."

She considered this.

"I'm not sure you really care about for votes for women, Willy," she said after a while.

"So you say."

"But I'll think about Sinn Fein, all the same. Thank you for taking me to the movies."

"Did you enjoy it?"

"Not much. But it was interesting."

"Well, at least you've seen them while they're here. I don't think Joyce can keep the Volta going much longer. I'll walk you home."

"Will you come in when we get there?"

"No."

⁜

It was getting late when Father Brendan MacGowan set out from the Rotunda Hospital. His visit had been a success. But as he considered what course to set, he frowned. His best way would be along Parnell Street. It was a busy street. It ran across this part of the city, cutting at an angle, from north-east to south-west across the top of Sackville Street where it met the Rotunda. It was, for Father MacGowan, rather a convenient street. Yet for the last two years, Parnell Street had no longer found favour with the priest, and he had tended to avoid it. He had done so ever since Tom Clarke had opened a tobacconist's shop there.

Father MacGowan didn't like Tom Clarke.

His brother the bookseller had known Clarke, been quite friendly with him, even, years ago in America. That was before Tom Clarke went over to plant bombs in England and got himself thrown in jail. He'd come back to Ireland now.

The long years in an English jail had transformed him physically. Gaunt, with thinning hair, he looked twenty years older than he was. Deceptive. It made him all the more dangerous. Behind his metal-rimmed spectacles there was a cold passion and intensity that the priest did not like at all. The bookseller didn't care for Clarke, either. Their friendship had ended. And his tobacconist's shop had become a meeting place for the Fenians. The IRB: the Irish Republican Brotherhood. God knows what those fellows were plotting. You never knew because they were so secretive you didn't even know who they were. You could probably identify quite a few of them if you watched to see who was hanging around with Tom Clarke in his shop. But Father MacGowan didn't care to know; and he preferred not to pass by the tobacconist's at all. He normally set a different course.

But this evening the wind had veered, and his quickest journey would take him past that dangerous and infernal establishment. And so, like a sailor strapped to the mast to protect himself from the sirens, he prepared to slip past as quick as he could. He drew close, sailed by, and glanced in, just for an instant. The store was small but brightly lit. In the window, also brightly illuminated, was a cardboard figure of a Round Tower, advertising Banba Irish Tobacco. Through the glass of the door, he could see several figures standing in the narrow space in front of the counter, behind which Clarke presided. And as he looked, Father MacGowan uttered a groan.

One of the men standing there was a figure he had seen only a couple of hours before. It was Willy O'Byrne.

⊨ 1916 ⊨

It was only when young Ian Law had confronted him in his office on a January day in 1912, that Sheridan Smith began to realise that he, and many others, had made one, horrible mistake.

When the young man had turned up at the offices, the man at the door had wanted to throw him out.

"You can't just come in here and speak to Mr. Smith, you know," he told him. "Does he know you? Have you an appointment?" If Sheridan hadn't happened to be passing down the hall at that moment and, witnessing the scene, been struck by the look of moral outrage upon the young man's face, no doubt Mr. Ian Law would have been summarily ejected. As it was, he brought him into his office and asked him courteously what was the matter.

The young man appeared to belong to the superior artisan class. He was a shipyard worker in Belfast. He had been visiting Dublin, where he had never been before, and had read the latest issue of the newspaper. In it he had read an editorial, a measured and reasonable piece in Sheridan's opinion, on the prospects for Home Rule. And he was outraged. He did not mean to be discourteous to Sheridan, evidently. But he seemed astounded that Sheridan and his newspaper could even consider that Home Rule was a possibility.

"How can your newspaper suggest," he demanded, "that we should give up every loyalty that we have? Am I to turn my face away from my King and from my God?" He said the words with such certainty and such pride that Sheridan was quite taken aback. "We remember the Battle of the Boyne," the young man continued. "We remember Derry. Our ancestors fought and died for freedom. Yet your newspaper tells me to submit myself to popery? Never. I will never do such a thing. I don't know anyone who would."

He was an honest young man. Sheridan could see that at once. No doubt he came from a hard-working Presbyterian family. His outrage was certainly real.

"I don't think that Irish Home Rule would affect the practice of your religion," Sheridan pointed out. But young Mr. Law only looked at him with disgust.

"Home Rule is Rome rule," he said bluntly. "We'll fight, I can promise you." Having received no satisfaction, he left soon afterwards.

And as he pondered the conversation afterwards, it occurred to Sheridan that, though he couldn't of course agree with the young man's view of the world, Law had nonetheless administered a corrective to a long-held view of matters in Dublin.

The truth was, it seemed to Sheridan, that none of those who had wanted independence for Ireland had thought about

Ulster very much. Daniel O'Connell had always cheerfully admitted that he scarcely knew the province. Even Parnell, Protestant though he was, had never had much interest in the northern province. After that, it was so fixed in everyone's minds that the Protestants were the oppressors in Ireland, and that once the English were gone, the island would be free, and nobody had troubled much about the fact that up in Ulster, the situation was entirely different.

After all, he thought, what was the Protestant Church in most of Ireland? The Ascendancy's Church of Ireland. Poorly attended, with little enthusiasm, its churches slowly crumbling for lack of funds and interest, the Church of Ireland was a social institution, for the most part, serving a small, slowly degenerating minority of Cromwellian settlers and ancient landowners. Take away the Ascendancy, and the Protestants become a tiny, toothless minority which can safely be left alone.

But up in Ulster, you had a whole country where, though Catholics were numerous, Protestants were in a majority. And they were not just the gentry. Small farmers, shopkeepers, the large and skilled workforce, were mostly Protestant. Not only that, the Presbyterians who constituted the largest element were passionate about their faith. If, in Ireland's other three provinces, the Protestant ruling class had some secret fears or moral qualms about their legitimacy, nowadays, the Ulster Presbyterians had no such doubts at all. God had placed them there to build His kingdom. They were sure of it.

Yet even then, Sheridan had been shocked by the strength of the response. For when they saw that the independence legislation might actually go through the parliamentary system now, it was not only the Protestants of Ulster who were up in arms. Like their Scottish ancestors from three centuries before, they came together to pledge a Solemn League and Covenant. Led by Carson, an eloquent Unionist lawyer, and Craig, a Belfast millionaire, by the next year, they had formed a huge force of volunteers. The Ulster Volunteer Force had only wooden rifles, but they mounted impressive parades. Equally alarming, the leader of the British Tory party, himself of Ulster Protestant descent, not only supported them, but even hinted at the necessity of armed resistance. At the great military encampment of the Curragh, out in County Kildare, the officers of the British army let it be known that, if asked to enforce Irish independence upon the loyal Ulstermen, they would refuse to obey orders.

"To be frank with you," an English journalist visiting the paper told him, "the British people feel a strong sympathy with the Ulster Protestants for two reasons. Firstly, we in England have never lost our deep-rooted fear of Catholicism. Few Englishmen would tolerate the thought of being dominated by Catholics, and we can't see why the Protestants of Ulster should have to go that way either. But we also think that the Ulster Scots are people like us. They have industry and commerce, they have shipyards now, and linen manufacture. They're hard-working and industrial. Whereas the Irish are seen as another sort of people entirely—rural, lazy, disorganised. We actually believe them to be of a different race from the men in the north."

"Did you know that originally, it was men from Ireland who went over and settled Scotland? The very name, 'Scot,' in ancient times meant a person from Ireland. The Scots are actually Irish, you might say."

"The English, I can assure you, are not aware of that. And you can't deny that the Protestants up in Ulster are very different."

That he could not deny. By the spring of 1914, the Ulster Volunteers were shipping in quantities of arms.

Meanwhile, it seemed that the Protestants in the north were to be met with an equal response. An Irish Volunteer Force was being formed in answer. Soon, news came that they were getting arms shipped in as well. Was the country drifting towards some sort of Civil War? Sheridan did not know what might have happened had it not been for the intervention, just then, of a wider conflict that overshadowed everything else.

Down in Sarajevo, an Austrian archduke was assassinated, and suddenly the whole of Europe found itself at war.

It was a curious feature of the Great War that for many of those who loved Ireland, it came as a relief. The British government, anxious that nothing should distract from the war effort, promised that there should be independence for the island, to be deferred until the war was over. "Since nobody thinks the war can last more than a few months, nobody minds waiting," Sheridan pointed out. As for Ulster, it was agreed that some special arrangement would have to be made. What form that might take remained to be seen. But at least the threat of internal conflict had been shelved. Indeed, Redmond encouraged all those who had flocked to join the Irish Volunteers: "The British have promised us our freedom. Let us help them with their war effort, that our freedom may come all the sooner." Tens of thousands of Irishmen, Protestants and Catholics alike, were joining the volunteer British army. "I find it heart-warming to see such friendship," Sheridan Smith declared. The great conflict, therefore, brought him a certain lightening of the heart.

And in his own life, also, he entered a period of unexpected happiness. The cause was Caitlin.

Her interest in the stage, fortunately, had not developed into an obsession. If anything, it had aided in her schoolwork. Certainly the Dominican nuns in Eccles Street, where she went to school, were delighted with her. By the time she was sixteen, she had announced that when she finished school, she wanted to go to St. Mary's University to study modern languages. At the same time, she was developing not only into a beautiful young woman but into a thoughtful one as well. Late in 1914, after a short illness, old Maureen Smith had peacefully died, and Caitlin had helped to nurse her at the end. By the time she was seventeen, when her mother made a visit to England for a month, she had felt quite confident that she could leave Caitlin in charge of the house in Fitzwilliam Square. The servants were there to take care of her, of course, and Sheridan had looked in every day. "But the truth is," her mother said, "she could do perfectly well without us."

She had also joined the Daughters of Erin. Sheridan was not sure what he felt about this. When he questioned her about it, however, she had just laughed. "I teach Irish to illiterate children—which really means that I tell them stories," she told him. No doubt this was true. But Sheridan had heard that some of the women in the organisation were involved in other activities that were more disturbing.

The labour movement had been growing rapidly in the last few years. The union had a big headquarters called Liberty Hall down on the quays nowadays; a women's union had been started as well. And the movement had a new leader, too—a socialist firebrand called James Connolly. In 1913 Connolly had led a huge strike for improved conditions that had closed all sorts of businesses for weeks. Even staid old Jacobs Biscuits had been hit. Some of the Daughters of Erin had taken part in the strikes. They were getting involved with Sinn Fein and some other dubious organisations. "You take care who you become friendly with," he had advised her. But she was a sensible girl; so he wasn't seriously worried. Meanwhile, he had had the joy of watching a marvellous child blossom, before his eyes, into a talented young woman. Even when her mother was there, he saw her every week. He delighted in her company.

It was in the summer of 1915 that he had taken Caitlin and her mother up into the Wicklow Mountains. Their purpose had been twofold: to visit the lovely old site of Glendalough and to see Rathconan. Rather surprisingly, the Count had never cared to go up to look at his ancestral estate when he was alive, and as a result, neither Caitlin nor her mother had ever been there. Caitlin, especially, had been eager to go. The visit to the old monastery and its two lakes had been a great success. But when they had come to Rathconan, Caitlin had been enraptured. Its eccentric owner had been in residence at the time, turban and all. Sheridan hadn't been too sure what sort of reception they'd get; but learning who they were, old

Mrs. Budge had been quite happy to show them the place, without even giving them a lecture on the transmigration of souls. But when, at the end, Caitlin had exclaimed: "Oh, how I should like to live here," the old lady had responded rather sharply: "The Budges will be staying at Rathconan long after I've gone; so there'll be no place for you. None at all." And then, rather disconcertingly: "I shall be staying here, too," she'd added. "I'm going to be a hawk, you know. I shall fly over the hills and eat mice."

Sheridan had always heard that Rose Budge was the last of the family. But meeting his brother a few weeks later, he had asked about it, and Quinlan had informed him: "I had supposed so, too. But it turns out that the grandfather had a younger brother who went to England many years ago. The old lady has a second cousin, a Budge, who has a son. They've never met, and the son doesn't even know it, but she's left him Rathconan." He'd shaken his head. "She's full of surprises."

"Did you know that she is going to return in her next life as a hawk?"

"Ah, now that," said his brother, "doesn't surprise me in the least."

The rest of that year had passed quietly. The war had dragged on—into what, to Sheridan, seemed like a terrible, bloody stalemate. But in Ireland, things seemed quiet enough. There were rumours of trouble, from time to time. Personally he tended to discount them. Caitlin's mother developed a bronchial condition over the New Year. Her doctor told her that she should go to a warmer climate for some weeks. The south of France was suggested. In March, therefore, she had departed, leaving Caitlin once again in the house in Fitzwilliam Square, under the general eye of Sheridan.

It was in the third week of April that Sheridan discovered Caitlin had been deceiving him.

He had been with her in the house at tea time. She had finished her schooling just before Christmas, and she was intending to begin at the university the following autumn. It had been suggested to her that she should travel, in the mean-time, but she had insisted that she wished to remain in Dublin, and since she had involved herself with the theatre, this was understandable. At six o'clock in the evening, he had left her to walk home to Wellington Road. He had crossed the canal, and gone a little way when he realised that he had left his umbrella at the house, and so retraced his steps to Fitzwilliam Square. He had seen her from a hundred yards off, just as she was getting onto a bicycle in front of her house. She seemed to be in a hurry. He might have supposed that she was going to the theatre; but even in the dusk, he could see that she was not dressed for the theatre at all. She was wearing a green tweed uniform.

The uniform of Cumann na mBan.

The Irishwomen's Council: that was what the words meant. But what did they signify? The thing hadn't existed two years yet. It was another of the creations of Maud Gonne and her friends; but whatever you thought of Maud Gonne, you couldn't deny her genius for organisation. Cumann na mBan were certainly nationalist. But what did they actually do? Some people said that they practised nursing. Others that they were mixed in with far more sinister groups. She certainly should have told him about any such activity. He knew very well that her mother wouldn't approve. He would have to take steps. He almost hailed her on the spot, but then thought better of it. Whatever she was up to, she couldn't come to great harm at the moment. Why risk a confrontation with her now? He thought quickly. It was Easter week. There was to be a family gathering at his house on Easter Monday. Either then, or soon after, he would sit down with her and have a quiet talk. Moments later, he was retracing his steps home.

Easter week passed quietly. He saw Caitlin briefly on Easter Saturday. Sunday was spent quietly at home. On Monday, they prepared to receive their guests in the afternoon. It was a little before one o'clock that a neighbour came to their house with the news.

"Something's going on in the city. They say it's a rising. A soldier's been killed."

"A rising? Why-ever would anyone want to start a rising now?" It made no sense. Soon afterwards, further news came. They've occupied the General Post Office in Sackville Street. They've proclaimed a republic."

"This is madness."

But soon the word was everywhere. There was a rising. Something big.

"I'd best go over and collect Caitlin," he said. "Make sure she's safe. It's not far to Fitzwilliam Square."

But when he got there, he found no sign of her. Nor did she appear at all that day, or the next.

✢

She hadn't even been sure she liked Willy O'Byrne at first. It was his cousin Rita who'd introduced them.

She'd met Rita at a meeting of the Daughters of Erin, and some other groups. Maud Gonne might be a society lady, but Caitlin liked the fact that her organisation contained all kinds of people, and that once you were in it, all questions of class seemed to disappear. Rita had worked at the Jacobs Biscuit Factory until the great strike of 1913. After that, they had refused to take her back. By the time Caitlin met her, she was an organiser for the women's union and a member of the Irish Citizens Army. She was often at the big union headquarters of Liberty Hall, on the northern quay near the Custom House. "You can easily look in there on your way to the Abbey Theatre," she said with a laugh.

Despite its name, the ICA was a union group. Connolly had started it at the time of the strike, to defend striking workers from vigilantes hired by the employers; but it was a trained force nowadays, open equally to men and women. Rita had intrigued Caitlin; she was a small woman, with reddish hair, and inclined to plumpness. Caitlin instinctively liked her, and they had agreed to meet a week later. And on that occasion, Rita had turned up with her cousin Willy O'Byrne.

Looking back, Caitlin remembered that it wasn't Willy's dark good looks, or even his occasional intensity that had impressed her. It was his calmness and the quiet logic of his thoughts. They had spoken about the women's movement, and the union, but when they came to discuss the war that had recently started, Willy had been quietly uncompromising.

"Ireland, with the best of intentions, has made a huge mistake," he said. "By Ireland, I mean Redmond and the majority of the Volunteers."

When, in answer to the threat from the Ulster Protestants in 1914, the Irish Volunteers had been started, the response had been quite astonishing. In no time at all, there were over a hundred and fifty thousand men. Few of them had arms, of course, but they were ready to drill, and train, and make a fine show of themselves, just as their Patriot namesakes had a century and a half before. Indeed, so large were the numbers that the organisation seemed almost to overshadow the Parliament men. Nominally, at least, as leader of the parliamentary party, Redmond was at their head. When Britain had promised Ireland her freedom and asked for help against the Germans meanwhile, and Redmond had told the Volunteers that they should oblige, about a hundred and seventy thousand Volunteers had gone along with him. But a smaller group, about ten thousand strong, had refused. The Irish Volunteers, they'd called themselves, and clearly Willy O'Byrne was on their side.

"It's not that I don't understand Redmond," he had quietly told her. "I don't even blame the thousands of poor Catholic boys who've gone to fight in the British army. It's just employment, for them, and Redmond's promised them that if they do it, Ireland will be free. But the whole business is a huge fraud, that's all."

"You don't think that the British will live up to the bargain?"

"I don't. The Ulster Protestants won't let them; and the British like the Ulster Protestants and despise the Irish Catholics anyway. The best we can hope for is a divided Ireland, which is no solution anyway. Redmond doesn't want to see that, of course. Because if he can't achieve anything useful, where does that leave him?" He shrugged. "At some point you have to face reality. There's going to be a fight. It can't be avoided."

There was something almost cold about him, she thought. Cold but compelling.

"The worst of it is," he went on, "that by supporting the British in their war, we play into their hands. Our own Volunteers are obligingly getting themselves killed in a British war fighting the Germans. At the very moment when, because of the war, it would be the easiest time to kick the British out."

"Perhaps the British will feel differently about us by the time the war is over."

"Hmm. Have you considered another possibility? What if the Germans win? We might be better off having them for friends."

She looked at him thoughtfully. Yes, she decided, his mind is very hard. He read her thoughts.

"It's better to face a harsh reality than delude oneself," he remarked. "Besides, it's you women who are the practical ones. It's you who have formed Cumann na mBan to aid the nationalist cause. And when you did, not a single one of the branches voted to go with Redmond. You all supported the Irish Volunteers. So I leave myself in the hands of the women."

Rita grinned.

"He's good, isn't he?"

He's in the IRB, thought Caitlin.

The Irish Republican Brotherhood were just as secretive as ever. There was no doubt but that they'd be in the Irish Volunteers, for instance; but you wouldn't know for certain who they were. She decided to challenge him.

"Are you in the IRB?"

He stared at her, evenly.

"Why would you ask?"

"Are you?"

"They never say, I've heard. So it would be pointless asking."

"I'll tell you this," Rita said with a laugh. "They won't have any women in the IRB, will they, Willy? He never tells me anything, you know."

Willy shrugged.

"I can't tell what I don't know," he said. Then he smiled at Caitlin. His smile was charming. "I've met you before, by the way. You were a Countess then."

Rita looked at Caitlin, surprised. Rita shook her head. When she had joined the Daughters of Erin, she had stopped using her title. There were enough countesses about already, she had decided. One of these was the leader of Cumann ne mBan, the Countess Markievicz, a flamboyant Anglo-Irish aristocrat who'd married a penniless Polish count, and who liked to wear uniforms and carry a revolver. The other was Countess Plunkett, whose husband, heir to a rich Dublin builder, had been made a Papal Count for his generous donations to the Church. The Plunketts and their children were prominent supporters of the various nationalist movements. Two countesses were enough, Caitlin had thought. She went by the name of Caitlin Byrne.

Willy reminded her of the occasion when he had met her at her uncle Sheridan Smith's house. "You were five or six, I think. You were sick."

"I'm afraid I don't remember you," she confessed.

"No. But I remembered you. By the way," he added, "I work for Sheridan Smith. But I never discuss my politics with him."

"Then nor will I," she promised him.

She hadn't seen him for some weeks after that.

She had first put on the uniform of Cumann na mBan in May 1915. She was seventeen. The uniform was not issued. Many of the women made their own. Green tweed was prescribed: a long military jacket with big flap pockets, a long skirt, white shirt, green cloth tie. And the all-important pin brooch—the initials "C na mB" in gold, with a rifle through them.

She had kept it hidden from her mother in a suitcase, and worn a long mackintosh over it when she went out to the meeting.

The purpose of Cumann na mBan was auxiliary. They trained together in first aid and signalling. Many of the women learned to shoot a rifle also; and it was at target practice one day that she saw Willy O'Byrne again. He had come by to watch. As it happened, she had discovered that when it came to shooting a rifle, she was a natural marksman. "Annie Oakley," the other girls called her. She found him standing behind her as she finished.

"Impressive."

"Thank you."

He gave her a look that was appreciative.

"The uniform suits you." He thought for a moment. "Ever used a pistol?"

"No."

"Try this." He pulled out a pistol and gave it to her. It felt surprisingly heavy in her hand. "Here." He took her arm and held it in position. "I'll show you."

It took her a little time to master the technique, but after a few days of practice, she became quite proficient.

He had encountered her several times in the weeks after that. He would just stop by the house where they met; or if she had gone down to see Rita at Liberty Hall, down on the quay, she might find him there. He would speak to her in a friendly way, just for a few minutes usually; then he'd be gone. One day at the end of August, meeting her at Liberty Hall, he produced a sheet of paper and pressed it into her hand. "I had it printed," he told her. It was a funeral oration for an old Fenian. It had been given by Patrick Pearse, one of the most inspired of the Irish language enthusiasts, who had done much to further the cause of Irish education. She could see why Willy O'Byrne had gone to such trouble to have it copied down and printed: the oration was magnificent. Many of its phrases struck her. He invoked the memory of Wolfe Tone. His words had the inspiration of another Emmet. "Life springs from death," he urged, "and from the graves of Patriot men and women spring living nations." But it was his final peroration that was the most memorable of all. The British thought they had pacified or intimidated the Irish. How wrong they were. "The fools! the fools! the fools!—they have left us our Fenian dead, and while Ireland holds these graves, Ireland unfree shall never be at peace."

As he urged her to read it, she noticed a look in his eye that she had not seen before, and realised that, after all, he was capable of being moved.

Several times after that, during the autumn months, she was able to have quite lengthy conversations with him. Once, he even told her about his childhood at Rathconan, and how his father had tried unsuccessfully to buy his tenancy from old Mrs. Budge. She told him about her own encounter with the lady. He was curious to learn that she would return in another life as a bird of prey. Perhaps it was this link with his childhood that quite often made him come and talk to her if he saw her in a crowded room.

It was a little before Christmas that he turned up at a meeting and afterwards beckoned her to one side.

"I have something for you." He smiled. "A Christmas present." He took out a carefully wrapped rectangular package and handed it to her. It was quite heavy. "Better open it when you get home. Don't let anyone see you." Then he turned away.

In her room at home, when she had locked the door, she opened the box. She had already guessed. It was a pistol: a Webley, long-barrelled, deadly. And ammunition. She wondered what she could give him in return.

The next day, to her surprise, her mother had found her knitting.

"I thought you hated knitting," she remarked.

"Just something that I promised to do for a friend," she

remarked. Two days later, it was done. Not a terribly good production, perhaps, but adequate. She saw him at Liberty Hall on Christmas Eve. "Here's your present," she told him, with a smile. "Better not unwrap it here though."

Early in the New Year, however, she was delighted to see him wearing the scarf she had knitted. It was green. It looked very well on him, she thought.

By now, it seemed to Caitlin, the Irish Volunteers were highly organised and well trained. They had branches all over the country. Their leader, a man named Mac Neill, kept them in excellent order. There was always the risk that the British authorities would clamp down on them; but so far they had obviously thought it wiser to do nothing. The people of Dublin were quite used to seeing their orderly parades. As for the women in Cumann na mBan, some were quite open, others preferred not to advertise their connection with the movement. She herself had never mentioned it to her mother or Sheridan. On the pretext of going to an art lecture, she would often slip out in uniform. But she usually wore something over it. The servants knew, but said nothing.

One thing did strike her, however. Once, walking back from a meeting, pushing her bicycle while Willy O'Byrne walked beside her, they had been speaking of the considerable forces at the government's command. The British still had twenty thousand regular troops in barracks. In addition, there was the Royal Irish Constabulary. And ironically, there were also a considerable number of Redmond's Volunteers, who were supposed to be helping the British for the war's duration. When you thought of all these numbers that the British could arm, her question seemed obvious.

"If ever the time should come when there is actually a rising," she said, "our Irish Volunteers are going to need a lot more arms than they've got now. How will they be supplied? I shouldn't think another run like the *Asgard* would do it."

Back in 1914, when in answer to the Ulster arms shipments, the Volunteers had needed their own arms, the rich author Erskine Childers had let his sailing ketch, the *Asgard,* be used to run arms in by the Ben of Howth. The incident had been famous; but for a proper rising, something on a far larger scale would be needed. She thought of what old Maureen had told her about the Maddens in America. "Would the Americans finance such a thing?" she asked.

"Perhaps. Or even the Germans, I suppose," he said with a shrug. She glanced at him, but did not ask further. She had the distinct impression, however, that he knew more than he'd said.

In April she noticed a change in him. She met him and Rita one evening, and though he talked as usual, he seemed abstracted. Easter week approached. On Palm Sunday, she saw Rita, and again on Wednesday. On the second occasion, Rita confided in her, "Something's coming up. I don't know what, but in the ICA, we've been told there will be manoeuvres on Easter weekend. She gave Caitlin a meaningful look. Important manoeuvres." On Thursday morning, Caitlin chanced to see Willy in the street. They only exchanged a few words, but she thought there was an air of suppressed excitement about him.

She was surprised to see him coming from the quays across College Green that evening. He was walking slowly, his head bowed, and he appeared to be muttering to himself. She had actually been attending an art class, and as he started to walk eastwards along the wall of Trinity, she rode her bicycle by him. He was not aware of her, and glancing back, she hesitated to interrupt him. Yet he looked so troubled that, fifty yards farther on, she put on her brakes and, resting her foot on the side of the road, waited for him to draw up.

"Are you all right?"

He glanced at her, still frowning. She was afraid that she had trespassed upon his private thoughts.

"No." He gave her a nod that indicated she should remain in his company. He wasn't wearing her scarf today, she noticed. She dismounted completely and began to walk beside him. The street was almost empty. They went in silence for a hundred yards. "I know you don't talk," he said finally.

"I should know that."

"It'll be out anyway, soon enough now." He shook his head. "You remember you asked about arms?"

"Yes."

"They came today. Actually, this man Sir Roger Casement has been negotiating for us in Germany for more than a year. Strange isn't it, an English public servant, knighted, yet sympathetic to Ireland as well? We asked for troops. They wouldn't give them. But twenty thousand rifles and a million rounds of ammunition were to be landed with Casement in Kerry today. They came, too. But something went wrong. The ship was intercepted. Casement's arrested."

"I heard something might happen this weekend."

"Perhaps it will. Say nothing of what I've told you. But keep going down to Liberty Hall. If there's more to hear, you'll hear it there. Don't be seen with me now. Good night."

⊹

The next three days had been strange indeed. Half the time, nobody seemed to know what was going on. But gradually she began to understand. The rising had been planned. The IRB was behind it. They'd even sent out orders to the Irish Volunteers, all over the country, to rise on Easter Sunday. They hadn't even told Mac Neill, who was supposed to be in charge. With the arms from Casement lost, Mac Neill countermanded the order. But Tom Clarke, the deadly tobacconist, and Pearse and the other IRB men wanted to go ahead anyway. They started sending Cumann na mBan girls off with new orders for a rising on Monday instead. Each time Caitlin arrived at Liberty Hall, she found more confusion than she had before. But on Sunday, Willy was there.

"Be here tomorrow morning," he told her firmly. "There'll be plenty for you to do."

✢

That proved to be an understatement. The Easter Rising was a strange business, but it was certainly a week to be remembered. For a start, there was the question of numbers.

It was clear to her from the moment she arrived at Liberty Hall that the order and counter-order of the weekend had taken a heavy toll. Most of the Volunteers, especially outside Dublin, had believed that the rising was cancelled. Only about fourteen hundred of the Irish Volunteers were at the quay, together with about another two hundred of the trade union ICA. She saw Rita among them. It seemed that the leaders had a plan, though. It was interesting to see how several of the men directing affairs now were obviously members of the secretive IRB. The poetic Pearse and the gaunt tobacconist Tom Clarke were among them. James Connolly of the union was taking a leading role, also. Though not one of the leaders, she could see from the way that he bustled about that Willy O'Byrne had their confidence.

Despite their modest numbers, the plan was to take control of a number of strategic points in the city. The General Post Office on Sackville Street, opposite Nelson's pillar, would be the headquarters. Then there would be garrisons in the Four Courts a short way upstream, the Castle and City Hall, Jacobs Biscuit Factory to the south; another industrial building, Boland's Mills, in the southeast, by the Grand Canal docks; and several other places. People were being chosen for each location.

Just for a moment, she asked herself what she was doing there. The enterprise seemed hasty and almost sure to fail. Even now, she guessed that the British forces in Dublin probably outnumbered theirs by three to one. But as she caught sight of Rita's excited face, and the faces of other young women she knew, she chided herself. If they are ready to fight for Ireland, then so should I be, she thought. She wondered where she should be posted. Somebody pointed to her and said that as she was such a good marksman, she ought to be a sniper. There was some hesitation. Then Willy appeared. She saw him converse briefly with some of the leading men, pointing to her. Then he came over.

"Did you come here on your bicycle?"

"I did. Why?"

"Go home quickly." Her face must have registered dismay, because he laughed. "Don't worry, I'll give you every chance to get killed. But I want you to come back here dressed as if you were going to an art lecture, or to the Abbey. You may be more use like that. I need you to look like," he grinned, "a young countess."

"I'm not giving up my Webley."

"Hide it somewhere, that's all."

She was back in half an hour. When he saw her, Willy nodded approval. When she asked him what he wanted her to do, he just said: "You'll see."

The detachments started marching out at eleven o'clock. She watched them go down the street. As it was the Easter holiday, there were quite a few people strolling about. They'd seen the Volunteers march about before, so they evidently supposed this was some sort of Easter parade. Nobody took more than the most cursory notice.

An hour later, to the public's great astonishment, Pearse the orator came out in front of the General Post Office and proclaimed an Irish Republic.

❖

A week to be remembered. It was not long before she understood the reason why Willy had asked her to change her clothes. Within a day, there were cordons and barricades all over the centre of the city. The GPO and the Four Courts particularly were under heavy fire. There were snipers on the rooftops. More and more British troops were coming into the city to cordon off the whole centre. Later in the week, a gunboat came up the Liffey and started pounding the rebel positions. And the most useful task she could perform was to carry messages, without incurring suspicion.

If she had any talent for acting, she realised, now was the time to use it. She did rather well. To her surprise, she found that she could get in and out of the GPO. The women were running both a kitchen and a field hospital there. By taking a careful route, she could get to the Four Courts. Though it got harder as the days went by, she was able to cross the Liffey and get to St. Stephen's Green, where the women had another field hospital set up, to City Hall and points beyond. She was proud to find that in most of the garrisons, the women were soon relieving the men as snipers. When she was sent down to the Jacobs factory, she found Rita in high good humour. "They threw me out, so I've occupied them," she announced. "And before we leave, we'll eat all their biscuits!" Only at Boland's Mills did she find that there were no women. The commander there was a tall, bony-faced Irish American in his early thirties with a strange Spanish name: de Valera. He told her frankly, "I won't have women under my command."

"You think we'll run away?" Caitlin demanded.

"Not at all." He laughed. "The women are too brave. They take so many risks I can't control them." He wrote a message on a scrap of paper and asked her to take it to the GPO. "What will you do with the message if the soldiers take you?" he asked.

"Eat it," she answered simply.

But the soldiers never did take her. The snipers nearly shot her a score of times. Indeed, since the Dubliners could never resist the urge to have a peek to see what was going on, she saw many of them hit by snipers or stray bullets. But she became adept at knowing where the dangerous corners and crossings were. Her genius lay in her ability to bicycle up to a group of English soldiers and ask for their help in getting through. She always had an excuse. She had to see her art professor, go to the theatre to collect a play script, visit her great aunt. Once she carefully loosened her bicycle chain and begged the soldiers to help her get it back on. Sometimes, of course, they refused to let her through, and she had to find a detour to come at her objective some other way. But often as not, they took the pretty, well-spoken girl with the expensive clothes and the flashing green eyes for a harmless young aristocrat, and let her pass with a warning that she'd better take care.

Nor were the soldiers so foolish to do so. After all, the Volunteers were barricaded in their occupied buildings. Some of their women were insisting they were nurses, when they weren't sniping from the windows; but they were nearly all in uniform of one sort or another. And above all, most of the people of Dublin had not only been taken by surprise by the rising, they wanted nothing to do with it.

Caitlin heard their comments frequently. What was the point of all this fuss, it was asked, when independence had already been promised? Shopkeepers and businessmen were not pleased at the damage done to the city, especially after the gunboat started pounding the rebel positions. "Sackville Street," a grocer complained to her, "is being turned into a ruin. And who will pay for all this? We shall. You can be sure of it." More than once, going through the Liberties in the latter part of the week, she heard furious complaints from Catholic mothers, because the disruption had delayed the pay packets they got from their sons in the British army.

Yet somehow this lack of sympathy made Caitlin admire the rising even more. The gesture, the bravery—and who knew, if Willy was right, the necessity of it—were to be admired. The people in the buildings, surrounded by ever more British troops, were her countrymen and her friends. She wished she could talk to Willy O'Byrne about it. But she hadn't seen him since Monday. She believed he had gone to the Four Courts.

On Monday night, she had slept at the GPO. On Tuesday night, she had returned to sleep at her home, and found an urgent note from Sheridan Smith demanding to know where she was. At dawn the next day, she dropped a reply through his letter box telling him that she was well and busy with her studies, and that she'd come to see him in a few days. He mightn't believe it, but at least she'd replied, and he'd know she was alive. She spent the next night at the biscuit factory with Rita. By Thursday, it was becoming clear that the GPO couldn't hold out much longer. Some of the women there were sent to their homes. On Friday morning, much of the area was in flames, and a fire broke out in the building.

For Caitlin, the rising ended at noon on Friday. She had been up all the night before and gone home to rest. Entering the house in Fitzwilliam Square, she had experienced a sense that something was amiss. The maid had given her a strange look. Then, turning, she had realised that Sheridan Smith was standing between her and the door. He was looking very grave.

"You will not be going out again," he said quietly. "If necessary, Caitlin, I will prevent you."

She said nothing, but started up the stairs to her room. The door was open. On the floor, she saw the suitcase into which she had thrust her green uniform on Monday. The case was empty now.

"I have burned it," Sheridan said. "Your mother, by the way, is on her way home."

Still she made no reply. There wasn't much point. She had to sleep anyway. She made to close the door, but Sheridan shook his head. "I shall keep you in my sight," he said, not unkindly. She sat down on the bed, and then smiled to herself.

"You must give me a moment's privacy Uncle Sherry," she said.

She needed to hide her revolver.

‡

By the time she awoke, it was clear that there was nothing left for her to do. The GPO could no longer be held. Its gallant defenders, including Pearse, had to abandon it. By Sunday, the last of the Volunteer garrisons had surrendered.

It was on Sunday morning that the soldiers came to Fitzwilliam Square. They went from door to door. They announced that they were checking every house for "Sinn Feiners." Caitlin had already noticed this confusion on the part of the British troops, and even the British newspapers. Perhaps, hearing the IRB men referred to as Fenians—which derived from the army of Irish legend—they supposed this to be the same as Griffith's nonviolent nationalist movement, Sinn Fein, which hadn't joined the rising at all. It was typical, she thought, that the British authorities should even have misunderstood who their enemy was.

Sheridan Smith, anticipating a visitation of this kind, had decided it was better for them both to remain in the house; and she had to admit, he handled the situation very well. His own well-known respectability was a help, no doubt. There were no "Sinn Feiners" in the house, he assured them, only his great niece, a student, and he himself, who was staying in the house until the girl's mother returned from abroad. He encouraged them to search thoroughly, all the same. They only had the most cursory glance around and politely left. They did not find her Webley.

Meanwhile, the tough British General, Maxwell, who had been sent to sort the place out, was moving swiftly to court-martial the leaders of the rising. By midweek, Sheridan told her: "I believe about a hundred and eighty men are selected, and one woman, Countess Markievicz." The trials went swiftly. The next day, he came to the house looking grim.

"I have sad news. Did you know an employee of mine, Willy O'Byrne? I had guessed he was mixed up in this when he didn't appear, but it seems he must have been further in than I thought. Anyway, he was one of those court-martialled today." He shook his head sadly. "I'm afraid he's to be shot."

✢

The fools! The fools! She might have echoed it then. But it was during the coming months that she really came to think it.

One couldn't say that, by the standards of the day, the British had been harsh. Indeed, they had probably been kinder than any other country would have been. But they had not been clever.

Before the garrisons surrendered, several of them made the women leave. Most of these, after being questioned by the British officers they encountered, were told to go home. The truth was, the British hardly knew what to do with them. Seventy-nine women were arrested. Seventy-three of these, also, were soon released. Caitlin was glad to hear that Rita was one of those set free. A handful were held in Kilmainham, then sent to the Mountjoy prison, then deported to serve time in England. Only Countess Markievicz, who had made such play with her revolver and encouraged others to do the same, was sentenced to be shot.

Nearly three and a half thousand men were taken. Almost fifteen hundred were released. The rest were interned in England, except for the hundred and eighty-six selected for court-martial. Of these, eighty-eight, including de Valera, were sentenced to the firing squad.

And most of the sentences were not carried out. The Countess was interned, because she was a woman. De Valera got off, perhaps because he was deemed an American citizen. All but fifteen of the sentences were also commuted to life sentences—including, Caitlin was delighted to discover, that of Willy O'Byrne. Under amnesty, most of these were also to be freed within a year or so.

But the fifteen men shot served their cause better than they could have imagined. Pearse, the poetic soul, greatly loved. He'd led the men into the GPO and proclaimed a republic. He had to know he'd be shot. But his little brother? Singled out, so far as anyone could see, just for being a brother. Joseph Plunkett, dying of sickness anyway, married his sweetheart hours before the firing squad, and became a figure of romance.

James Connolly, the union man: he'd been so badly wounded already that they tied him to a chair to shoot him. For ten days these executions went on, and by the end, few though they were, nobody saw any justice in it.

And public sentiment began to turn. When one of the heroes of the rising went on a hunger strike the next year, the prison men managed to kill him during force feeding. It was not meant to happen. But it did.

By late 1917, the moderates of the Sinn Fein organisation, whom the British mistook for the Fenians, and the more militant nationalists came together to form a political party, and chose de Valera to be their leader. "We want an Irish Republic," they frankly declared, "and we'll contest seats in local and parliamentary elections." The next year, the British government arrested all its leaders.

And then, locked in its desperate struggle with Germany, and hungry for troops, instead of thanking Ireland for her many volunteers, the British government suddenly threatened the Irish with conscription. "You see," Willy O'Byrne and others like him could say, "the British make agreements, but they cannot be trusted."

The fools: even Sheridan Smith said it now. "If the British wanted to prove that the men of the rising were right," he remarked, "they could hardly have set about it better." As the Great War reached its end in 1918, a General Election was called. Redmond's old party had only six seats. The Unionists, meaning Protestant Ulster really, had twenty-six. The new Sinn Fein amalgam had seventy-three. "The world has changed," Sheridan Smith concluded. "Changed utterly."

But it had changed even more than people had expected. For having been elected, all the Irish Members of Parliament, with the exception of the Unionist and Redmond's handful of men, did what they thought was the only logical thing to do for men with their beliefs. Not only did they refuse to take their seats in the British Parliament at Westminster, they went one better than that. They set up their own Assembly of

Ireland, the Dail Eireann, in Dublin. "We are the true government of Ireland now, they said." By the spring, they had constituted ministries headed by Griffith, Countess Markievicz, Count Plunkett, Mac Neill, of the former Volunteers, Collins, a vigorous young IRB man, and others. De Valera was President. "We are a republic," they said. "We refuse to recognise English rule any longer." And so, in the spring of 1919, Ireland was in the strange state of having a British government, with rules, regulations, and administrators at Dublin Castle, and a second, shadow state, far more popular, claiming legitimacy even if it lacked the power to impose itself. The moral and political victory, as far as the Sinn Fein members were concerned, was already theirs. It was up to England to recognise the fact. Nobody quite knew what to do.

⁘

It had changed for Caitlin, too, in an unexpected way. When her mother had returned to Dublin after the rising in 1916, she had seemed quite content to stay there. Whether, in the event, she would have done better to spend her winters in France, one could never know for certain. But when a huge influenza epidemic spread across Europe just after the ending of the Great War, she succumbed to it. In the spring of 1919, Countess Caitlin Birne suddenly found herself twenty years old, soon to be twenty-one, and a rich young woman. She resolved, very sensibly, to do nothing at all and complete her studies.

She had not seen Willy O'Byrne for a long time. She was quite surprised, in the summer, to receive a message that he would like to call for her one Saturday and take her out for the day.

She knew a little of his activities. After he had returned from jail, she had not seen him, but Sheridan Smith had told her: "He no longer works for me. He has gone into partnership with Father MacGowan's brother, that runs the bookshop." He paused. "Part of his business, I believe, is to go to America to collect funds for political purposes. "And he gave her a wry smile. "He gets some of his funds, I believe, from the hands of my own Madden relations."

Willy turned up in a car. He was quite unchanged, but he looked well, she thought, and happy. "I thought," he announced, "that I'd drive up to Rathconan, if you'd like to come."

It was a beautiful day. The road up into the Wicklow Mountains was narrow. Stone walls sometimes shut out the view. At other times she could see huge sweeps down towards the sea. He seemed delighted to be going up to his childhood home.

"The old lady's not there. I already checked," he said with a smile. "But there's someone else I'd like you to meet."

"Your mother?"

"No, she died I'm afraid. But my father is still living." He seemed to find this thought amusing for some reason.

She was pleased to find, when they got to the long, white-walled cottage where the old man lived, that old Fintan O'Byrne was a tall, fine-looking man, with sparse grey hair and a long white moustache. He welcomed her to his cottage courteously, told her that his son had spoken of her, and offered them both a simple meal. Bacon, black pudding, potato. "I live very simply," he said with a smile, "but I hope to live a good while yet. I think," he added, "that the air up here must be good. People live a long time. And perhaps if you belong to a place, that helps, too. Or so I believe."

"My father believes that Rathconan should be his," Willy said with a smile. "He will never rest in his grave until that mad old woman has given him his own land, at least. But you know, Father," he said almost gleefully, "the estate was never ours at all. The rightful heir is this young lady sitting in front of you now." He turned to Caitlin with a grin. "I have been longing for the day when the two claimants could see each other face-to-face, Caitlin. Now you'll have to fight it out!"

But his father only smiled at her benignly.

"I can see you're an O'Byrne," he said. "No doubt of that. As to whether your branch should have had this place, or mine, that is a question too long ago to think of. Certainly it was your ancestors who were chieftains here, when mine were not. But you know," he turned to Willy, "I've a piece of news for you, and for this young lady, as regards the estate. There is an heir. A Budge." He said the name with mild disgust. "A cousin forgotten by all of us, but remembered by the old lady, it seems. He's to have it after her, if he wants it. And I dare say he will."

"I didn't know," said Willy. "What is he called?"

"His name is Victor Budge. He lives in England. He has been in correspondence with her. He has done some military service, but I understand he works for a brewery now. I do not know in what capacity. My impression," Fintan O'Byrne added with faint irony, "is that he is not always employed."

He took them all round the place, and walked them a little way up the hillside, to where there was a magnificent view. Pointing along the slope, he indicated to Caitlin the area where you could still see the outline of the fields that had been planted with potatoes before the Famine. The more time she spent with him the more she liked him. When it was time for them to leave, she parted from him with real regret.

Was it possible that Willy had some other motive in introducing her to his father? she wondered. If so, he gave no sign of it.

For on their return journey, he seemed to want to talk about a very different subject.

"You know," he said, "that there is going to be another fight." Indeed, small skirmishes between the British government forces, and the Irish Republican Army, as the Irish Volunteers now called themselves, had started months ago. "Unless the British and the Ulster Protestants are ready to concede something that de Valera and the Sinn Fein men in the Dail can accept, then there's no alternative. And when that comes"—he glanced at her—"the women were very important in the rising, you know. They'll be even more important in the future. You could have an important role."

"I was just a courier."

"A brilliant one. You have remarkable talents. And of course," he smiled, "you can pick off any man at a hundred yards."

"I'm not sure I want to," she said. "I support the cause but . . ." She hardly knew why it was—not cowardice, she was fairly sure—but she didn't want to join the armed struggle any more. "I will consider it," she promised him. "If I want to do anything, I'll let you know."

"As you wish." He gave her a nod which seemed to imply that he respected her decision. "You know your own mind. That's for certain."

He drove her back to Fitzwilliam Square and left her at her house. When she thanked him for the day, he seemed quite pleased. But perhaps she was a little disappointed that she never heard from him again. Not for more than a year.

✢

He was right, of course. The fight couldn't be avoided, because neither side could give what the other wanted. It was a grim little business at first, especially because the skirmishes tended to be between the IRA and their fellow Irishmen in the government constabulary. The pace was heated up by the young IRB man, Michael Collins, who with his daring raids and lightning strikes was making quite a name for himself. But it was very partial warfare, all the same. The British government finally struck a deal with the Ulster Protestants, giving them a separate parliament of their own up in the northern counties. But that meant that the Catholics of Ulster were once again trapped under the dominance of a Protestant caste, as they had been in the seventeenth and eighteenth centuries. Soon there were riots up in Ulster.

But for the rest of Ireland, there was to be one more hateful invasion. In began in January 1920.

"If they had to send help," Sheridan Smith complained, "could they not have found men better than these?"

The Black and Tans. Ex-soldiers and sailors, mostly, quickly recruited. Mercenaries really, to fight the Irish guerrilla tactics of Collins's IRA. When they joined, or arrived in Ireland, they were given standard issue army trousers, which were khaki, and green police uniform jackets. This ugly mixture of khaki and green soon earned them their descriptive nickname: Black and Tans. By the latter part of the year, there were ten thousand of them in Ireland. And their game was very simple: strike and retaliate. Shoot first and ask questions afterwards. Suspicion is proof, especially if the suspect is dead. In many ways, they ignored law and justice entirely. When Collins and a hit squad caught and killed a group if British intelligence officers one Sunday morning in November, the Black and Tans didn't bother to go looking for Collins. They just went round to the big football game in Dublin's Croke Park and opened fire on the crowd. Twelve innocent spectators were killed in that affair.

If they were meant to frighten, they did. If they were intended to impress, they did not, for they were despised. But if they had your identity as a "Sinn Feiner," they were after you like a pack of wild dogs.

⁜

It was five days after the Croke Park incident that early one afternoon, Caitlin heard a knocking at the front door of he house. As she happened to be in the hall, she opened the door herself, and was rather surprised when Willy O'Byrne stepped into the hall, closed the door quickly behind him, and said:

"Would you like to save my life?"

"If you tell me why."

"I've not much time. I got one of the Croke Park Black and Tans. His best friend is after me. I was trying to kill him as well, but he has reinforcements. I gave them the slip only a moment ago, in the lane. But they'll go house to house I'm sure. They know me, unfortunately."

"By name?"

"And by face." He glanced out of the window. "Better get out of sight. Unless you want me to go out and face them."

"This way." She indicated the drawing room, which was at the back of the house and gave onto the garden.

"The irony is, you'll never guess the name of the man that's after me. God I should have shot him first, before the other one."

"Tell me."

"Victor Budge. The old woman's heir. Out-of-work army man. He's a devil. I'll see him dead yet."

The knocker on the front door sounded. Caitlin had to think fast. "If you go out through the garden, there's a lane at the back. But . . ."

"Exactly. They'll have a man waiting there."

She looked at the window that gave out onto the back. It had long, heavy curtains that fell to the floor and, in the best manner, swept the carpet like a long train on a dress. It was so obvious, it would do.

"Get behind it and don't move," she said. She would have to think very fast indeed.

A moment later, the maid announced that some soldiers wanted to come in. Caitlin sat down on an upright chair near the centre of the room.

"Show them in."

"There were half a dozen of them. The officer was a big man with a brutal face. She smiled at him.

"We are searching for a fugitive. Has anyone come into this house?"

"Only yourselves. But what sort of fugitive is it? Am I in danger?"

The idea that she might be in danger did not seem to interest them.

"Dark-haired man." The officer was looking round the room.

"I am Countess Caitlin Birne. And you, Sir?"

"Beg pardon. Captain Budge."

"Budge?" Her face lit up as if she'd hoped to meet him all her life. "You are not connected with Mrs. Budge of Rathconan? But you must be."

"She is a kinswoman." His manner altered, softened a little.

"I cannot help you with any fugitive, Captain Budge, but I do hope you will stop and take a little tea with me." She looked at his men. "I know the Captain's family," she explained, unnecessarily, with a beaming smile. "Do sit down. I will call for tea."

"Really can't," said Budge.

"Your aunt is one of our greatest characters. You know, of course, that she says she's coming back to Rathconan in her next life, as a bird? Don't you think it wonderful?" Budge looked awkward. "They say she has worn the same turban and never taken it off in thirty years," she rattled on happily. "You have seen her drawings of the naked Indian dancers, of course."

By now Budge was growing red. His men were looking as if they'd be glad to hear more.

"Do you also, Captain, believe in the transmigration of souls?" she ventured.

"Certainly not. Church of England. Eccentric old lady. Must go."

"I do wish," she said wistfully, "that you'd stay."

But the little group of Black and Tans were already being led out of the room. After the front door had closed behind them, there was a long pause. Then Willy's voice came from behind the curtain.

"If I'd laughed, that would have been the end of me."

"I suppose," she said, "you'd better stay here for a bit."

✣

It was that evening after they had dined together, and they were sitting alone in the drawing room, with the curtains carefully drawn, when she found herself looking at him thoughtfully. He was a handsome man. He was capable of warmth, but never, she felt sure, as much as his old father was. Well, she thought, he has proved right about most things, all the same. If that makes him cold, it is his destiny.

He was looking at her.

"Have you ever had a lover?" he asked.

"No." She paused. "I assume there have been many women in your life."

"A few. Of course." He nodded, then smiled. "Do you think it's time?"

"Yes," she said, "I think it is."

It was certainly time. For him, God knows, she thought, as for any other. He stayed in hiding in her house for ten days.

᛭

If the affair was not continued, she was not greatly hurt. She had known, she supposed, that it would not be. He had made another journey to America. And after that he was away again.

And she was glad that she had taken no further part in the fighting, for the painful choices that followed would have been impossible for her. When, a year later, the Sinn Fein negotiators, including ruthless Collins himself, had signed a treaty with Britain to bring the conflict to an end, it had been an imperfect thing. Ireland was to become a Free State, a dominion of the British Empire like Canada. Six of the northern counties were to be grouped together in a safe haven for Protestants and an oppression for the Catholics still living there. Even the border was unclear. She could see why de Valera refused to go along with it.

But she herself, like the majority of Irish people, could live with even an imperfect treaty, perhaps not forever, but for a generation. And when de Valera and his followers started a second conflict, at war with their own colleagues now, she found herself asking not why, but when—when will it ever end? The Civil War was full of anomalies. Collins, the IRB firebrand, was now defending the compromise treaty, quite ruthlessly, against a new republican army known as the Irregulars. Old comrades in arms were killing each other. Collins himself was assassinated before it was over. Strangely, most of the women she had trained with in Cumann na mBan, had chosen to go with de Valera. Even kindly, funny Rita had done so. Caitlin could not have gone that way herself. And when, in 1923, the conflict had finally wound down, she had been relieved only that the Irish Free State, however imperfect, could now live in peace.

⊹

Only once was she called into action. Late in July, in 1922, she received an unexpected letter. It was delivered by hand by a boy on a bicycle who would not stay.

When she had read the letter, she did not hesitate. She went to the bank and made a withdrawal. She packed a number of items carefully, including one or two that she might need herself. She owned a car, nowadays, which she liked to drive herself. She carefully put everything in it, told the housekeeper that she might be away for a few days, and drove southwards towards the western side of the Wicklow Mountains.

She found the farmhouse quite easily. It was near the village of Blessington.

He was remarkably little changed. It was obvious that he had suffered a good deal, and having examined his leg, she told him: "It's not a break, but it's a very bad sprain. You'll have to rest it if you want to walk."

"It's good of you to come," Willy said. "I knew you would."

"What happened?" she asked.

The story was not a long one. She hadn't been entirely surprised when she'd heard that Willy O'Byrne had joined the anti-Treaty republican forces in the Civil War. And things were going badly with them. He'd gone out to rendezvous with republican forces gathering from several parts of the island at Blessington. They had been badly mauled by the Provisional Government men and had to fall back. From Blessington, they had had to disperse. But he couldn't walk, and as he'd quarrelled with the leader of the men who'd gone up into the hills, he'd thought it best to wait down there alone. "It's over for me, I think," he told her. "The struggle isn't worth it any more." But he couldn't just wait for the Provisional government men to find him. The Civil War was proving a far bloodier business than the old conflict with the British had been. "If they find me, I'm a dead man," he told her calmly.

"I can hide you in Dublin if you want," she said.

"No. It's Rathconan I'd like to get to," he replied. "I think my father could look after me. If not . . ."

"I brought you two hundred pounds," she said. "That would take you to France, if you need."

"My only worry," he said, "is those fellows who went up into the mountains ahead of me. They were an undisciplined rabble, and they had no love for me."

"I'll drive you up there," she reassured him, "and I brought the Webley."

It was a small, winding road. Now and then, looking back, one could see the huge panorama of the Liffey Plain spreading out all the way to Kildare. Willy sat in the front with her. He seemed more interested in looking ahead. Once passing a cattle man, he asked if a party of troops from Blessington had come up that way the day before. Yes, the man said, but they'd taken the road southwards. They hadn't gone across the mountain road towards Rathconan. This seemed to please Willy considerably. "We shall be there soon," he remarked. "You'll see my father again." Going over the top of the mountain pass and starting to descend again, the little road was hardly more than a track. And as at last they came towards Rathconan, a little group of children by the roadside turned to stare, and ran to spread the news; for a motor car was a rarity indeed up there.

As they approached, she smiled as she caught sight of the long, lovely vista down towards the Irish Sea. The car backfired with a loud bang as they passed the gates of the big house. She laughed. If old Rosa Budge was there, she'd probably think it was a message from the spirit world.

Fintan O"Byrne's cottage seemed to be deserted. She looked inside. No sign of him.

"Do you want me to help you in?" she called.

"No. I'll sit here in the sun," Willy said. "I'll stay where I am. If you walk down the lane to the Brennans, they'll probably know where he is."

"You'll be all right?"

"Why wouldn't I be, at my father's house at Rathconan?"

"I'll be back," she said.

⁌

The feel of the afternoon sun on his face was really very pleasant. It seemed to Willy that when the business of war was over, he could do worse than return up here. He might find a wife. It was time he married. What should she be like? Like Caitlin, perhaps, but not like Caitlin. Money was a terrible thing, when you came down to it. The ten days he'd spent in her fine house on Fitzwilliam Square had taught him that. Comfortable, splendid even. But suffocating. By the end of it, he could scarcely breathe. He hadn't told her that, though. No point. Apart from that, he'd loved her. Should he ever tell her so? he wondered. He closed his eyes.

Had he not been up in the safety of Rathconan, he'd have heard the steps when they were farther off. As it was, they were only ten feet away when he heard the soft tread on the turf. Even so, he didn't open his eyes. He tried to decide who they belonged to. Not Caitlin. A little too heavy. His father? Possibly. One of the Brennans? Could be. He smiled and waited.

"Asleep?"

He opened his eyes. The thickset face was smiling. The eyes hard. The twin barrels of the shotgun a foot from his nose.

"Heard a car backfire. Thought I'd take a look. Never know who may be paying you a visit, these days."

Victor Budge. He'd forgotten him. Supposed he'd gone back to England. Willy was quite sure that he'd have heard if old Rose Budge had died and Victor had come into his own. Mind you, with all the fighting and the travelling of the last few months, he'd been sadly out of touch with his father.

"Is old Mrs Budge . . . ?"

"Alive and well. Still waiting to turn into a hawk." He seemed to find this funny. But the gun didn't move. "We have an arrangement. I take care of the estate now. I've been up here two months. I wondered if I might see you here some day."

"Aren't you afraid? A man like yourself mightn't be liked too well up here, I should say."

"I'll take my chances. We have a score to settle. You killed a friend of mine, remember?"

"Perhaps. A long time ago."

"I don't think so."

Caitlin had told him she'd brought her pistol. He wondered where it was. He didn't think she'd be carrying it with her. Under the seat perhaps? He could try to dive for it, but he'd have to be right. First time. Even if his leg let him move like that. He couldn't think where else to try. On the other hand, to duck like that: afterwards it would look as if he'd been too much of a coward to face his death.

He might make a grab for the barrel of Budge's gun. Foolish thought. Budge knew what he was doing. He'd just die looking like an idiot. So he leaned back.

"You would shoot a man in cold blood?"

"I'll shoot you like a dog."

"How will you explain it?"

"Doubt that I'll need to. Times like these."

"Ireland's curse upon you, then."

✛

Caitlin heard the bang when she was standing outside the Brennans' cottage. She ran. She raced up the track towards the car, in time to see that Willy had been pulled onto the ground. A man was walking away. He was carrying a shotgun. She looked down at Willy's face. It wasn't there, just a great red mess of flesh and shot.

She reached under the car seat, and called out. She man turned. She recognised him. Victor Budge. The Black and Tan who'd come looking for Willy. He recognised her, too. The girl who'd known old Rosa. He frowned as he worked it all out.

"You killed him," she called.

"What of that?"

The single shot caught him exactly between the eyes. She hadn't lost her skill. She stared at Budge for a moment, nodded to herself, and put her Webley on Willy's right hand, curling his fingers round it.

She heard voices. She stepped back. Several people were arriving. One of them, she saw at once, was old Fintan O'Byrne.

At first, seeing the bloody mess of the face on the ground, he did not understand. Then, as she came towards him and took his arm, he did. He bowed his head and sank to his knees.

He had been kneeling by Willy for a minute or two when he looked up at her.

"They shot each other?'

"They must have," she said.

"I thought the two shots were some time apart."

"They can't have been."

He paused to look at her a long while.

"No. I must have been mistaken."

He got up stiffly to his feet, walked over to Victor Budge, noted the hole neatly between the eyes, and nodded. As he passed by her again, he touched her arm, and quietly murmured, "Thank you."

✛

Some years later, when Mrs. Rosa Budge passed to her next life, the Rathconan estate was sold. Sometimes new owners of such estates would find the local people a little shy with them. They have learned, after all, to guard against strangers coming to dwell upon their land. It is a lesson learned down many centuries. But the new owner of Rathconan, with her flashing green eyes and her husband and children was always welcome from the first. After all, Caitlin belonged there.

Also by

EDWARD RUTHERFURD

ThE PRINCES OF IRELAND

The first novel in the Dublin Saga

Brilliantly weaving impeccable historical research with stirring storytelling, Edward Rutherfurd explores our shared Celtic roots in a magnificent epic of Ireland spanning eleven centuries. While vividly conveying the passions and struggles that shaped particularly the character of Dublin, Rutherfurd portrays the major events in Irish history.

Through the interlocking stories of a memorable case of characters—druids and chieftains, monks and smugglers, noblewomen and farmwives, labourers and orphans, rebels and cowards—Rutherfurd captures the essence of a place and its people in a thrilling tale steeped in the tragedy and glory that are Ireland.

SEAL BOOKS / ISBN: 978-0-7704-2907-2